ELIJAH KINCH SPECTOR

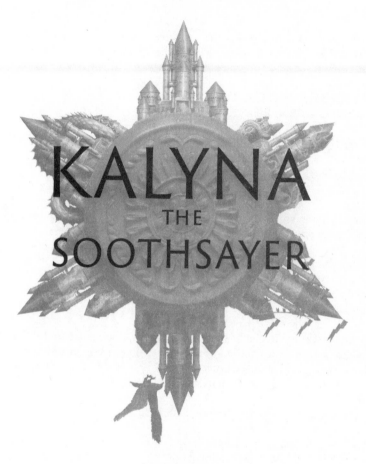

KALYNA
THE
SOOTHSAYER

EREWHON

KALYNA THE SOOTHSAYER
Copyright © 2022 by Elijah Kinch Spector

First published in North America by Erewhon Books, LLC in 2022

Edited by Sarah T. Guan

Erewhon Books
2 W. 29th Street, Suite 3S
New York, NY 10001
www.erewhonbooks.com

Erewhon books are available at special discounts when purchased in bulk for premiums and sales promotions as well as for fund-raising or educational use. Special editions or book excerpts can also be created to specification. For details, send an email to specialmarkets@workman.com.

Library of Congress Control Number: 2022932280

ISBN 978-1-64566-038-5 (hardcover)
ISBN 978-1-64566-039-2 (ebook)

Cover design by Sasha Vinogradova
Interior design by Cassandra Farrin and Leah Marsh
Author photograph by Walter Wlodarczyk

Excerpt from *F for Fake* on p. 5 courtesy the Orson Welles Estate. All Rights Reserved.

Printed in the United States of America

First US Edition: August 2022
10 9 8 7 6 5 4 3 2 1

For Brittany Marie, who told me to stop working on an irretrievably broken novel and start on this one instead.

But everything must finally fall in war, or wear away into the ultimate and universal ash. The triumphs and the frauds, the treasures and the fakes.

—Orson Welles, *F for Fake*

Some of the People Who Made My Life Harder

My Family

ALJOSA VÜSALAVICH: My father, the greatest soothsayer I have ever known. (His second name means "son of Vüsala" in Masovskani, because he was born in Masovska.)

VÜSALA MILDOQIZ: My grandmother, the worst person I have ever known. (Her second name means "daughter of Mildo" in Cöllüknit, because she was born in Quruscan.)

Those Who Have Their Own Armies

KING GERHOLD VIII: King of Rotfelsen. Quite blank in face and mind. His army: the Reds.

QUEEN BIRUTÉ: Wife of King Gerhold. Originally from Skydašiai. Her army: those amongst the Reds who obey only her.

PRINCE FRIEDHELM: Younger brother to King Gerhold. Seems to be a thoughtless, sybaritic prince; is both *more* than that and *exactly* that. His army: the Yellows.

HIGH GENERAL FRANZ DREHER: The somewhat avuncular defender of Rotfelsen. His army: the Greens, who actually fight wars and guard the borders.

COURT PHILOSOPHER OTTO VOROSKNECHT: A dangerous fool who talks a lot. His army: the Purples.

Those I Met in Masovska

EIGHT-TOED GUSTAW FROM DOWN VALLEY WAY: The name tells all you need to know.

RAMUNAS: A flamboyant legal advocate and informant, who likes to send messages by terrifying bird.

KLEMENS GUSTAVUS: A very important little rich boy. Heir to a number of changing banks.

BOZENA GUSTAVUS: His slightly smarter sister, whom I heard of in Masovska.

LENZ FELSKNECHT: Best forgotten.

THOSE I MET IN ROTFELSEN

TURAL: The Master of Fruit, and my neighbor. Eccentric, but nice.

JÖRDIS JAGLOBEN: Chief Ethicist, and my neighbor. Perhaps also nice?

VONDEL: Tenth Butler to High General Dreher. A real stickler for etiquette and tradition, but not in an overbearing way.

GUNTHER: The tall barkeep at the Inn of Ottilie's Rock. Beautiful smile; supplier of starka.

AUE: A talented doctor who looks after royalty and nobility.

GABOR: Very chipper for a man who lives in a cave.

MARTIN-FREDERICK REINHOLD-BOSCH: A young swordsman employed by the High General. Within spitting distance of the throne. Arrogant, but pretty.

"DUGMUSH": A tall and frightening soldier in the service of Prince Friedhelm. I had trouble remembering her name.

BEHRENS: A sharpshooter in the service of Prince Friedhelm. Quite friendly, when he isn't looking down the barrel of his harquebus.

ALBAN: A brute in the service of Court Philosopher Vorosknecht.

SELVOSCH: The Lord High Quarrymaster. Unpleasant.

EDELTRAUD VON EDELTRAUD: Mistress of the Rotfelsen Coin. A powerful and nervous noblewoman.

ANDELKA: An emissary from Rituo, one of the countries that make up the Bandit States. Acts as though she is very important.

OLAF: A lucky drifter.

CHASIKU: A threat.

KALYNA
THE
SOOTHSAYER

PART ONE

MY MOTHER

"You killed your mother twice over, you know," said Grandmother.

She pinched my cheek ironically and chewed on her gnarled, old pipe stem. Grandmother seemed to get more from rolling it around between her white teeth than from the scant smoke that leaked out.

I sat still in the dirt at her feet and rubbed my cheek where her thumbnail had left a deliberate indent.

"You killed her first, of course, with your birth: when you selfishly tore your way out, making your poor mother bleed so, so much." Grandmother removed the long wooden pipe and curled her papery lips to luxuriously exhale a small amount of smoke.

I nodded slowly. I meant to show I was listening, but it looked like I agreed.

"And you killed her *again* two days later, when she, weakened and bloodless as she was, learned from your father's visions that you would never possess the Gift."

I nodded again from where I sat, looking up at Grandmother as she noisily replaced the pipe between her teeth. Her hard face, the small tattoo above her left eyebrow, peeking out from her scarf, and her thin old nostrils, full of char.

"Maybe," I hazarded, in a squeak, "maybe she only died from the bleeding? Maybe . . . maybe I only killed Mama once?"

Grandmother looked down at me, then closed her eyes as though she need see nothing else ever again.

"Finally," Grandmother sighed, "she admits it."

As she sat back in her red velvet chair, unmoving, I wondered if Grandmother had died. If she had savored a last bitter happiness after I admitted the evil I'd done in this world and then, pleased with herself, expired.

If only.

Had I the Gift, I might have known better. I might have known that as I passed through the years, I would do so with Grandmother always at my back—remaining stubbornly, infuriatingly, alive and lucid.

Two of those decades later, I was twenty-seven and still sitting in the dirt at the foot of her chair, from which the velvet was all gone. Grandmother was unchanged since the day she told me I twice murdered my mother, except that her pipe was empty and unlit: she couldn't smoke anymore, said it made her cough too much, so she spent her days chewing the cold pipe stem and spitting.

Grandmother was my father's mother, and she cared for him above all else. Nothing ever seemed good enough for her son, and so we couldn't understand how she had come to genuinely love and miss her daughter-in-law. But she did, fiercely.

It was to Papa that Grandmother had passed the Gift, and through him that it was meant to go to me. The Gift had been in our family for generation upon generation, through thousands of years; farther back than even Loashti nobles traced their lineages, let alone poor nomads like us. The Gift cared not for gender, legitimacy, national boundaries, nor family name, and was all that delineated our family down through the ages.

Until me.

AUTUMN FURS

At the end of autumn in that, my twenty-seventh year, our horse died. The following day, I untied the furs that had been stored neatly at the peaks of our tents. The soft remains of long-dead polecats, wolves, and marmots tumbled down, thick and stale, smelling like the previous winter in the kingdom of Quruscan: all cold mutton and maple and mildew. We had spent this autumn, which was now ending, on a grassy hill in the Great Field, north of the town of Gniezto, in the kingdom of Masovska.

Our goal was to keep from starving to death during the onrushing winter, just like it was every autumn. But now we were stranded with no horse, serving our few customers and building up meager winter supplies, which would mean nothing if we froze in our tents. I tried not to think of all the ways we could die before spring, nor of how we would ever afford a new horse. For now, I could only roll down the furs to keep out the cold winds.

These winds had cut through the Great Field all autumn, and would only worsen in winter, as I remembered from previous years we had spent here. At least when the snows came, we could winter among the tents crowding the Ruinous Temple. Perhaps it would have been better to go broke buying Papa a room in an inn, with four walls and a roof, but our family's way has always been to move. Walls are traps.

In my time, we moved from place to place at a greater speed than even my ancestors had. We did so to escape reprisals, you see: sometimes long before my ruses were discovered, and sometimes fleeing angry mobs. I was, after all, lacking the Gift, and therefore an inveterate liar.

THE GIFT

The Gift is that of prophecy and soothsaying. Anyone possessing it can see the future, with limitations: the most important being that the better known a subject is to the bearer of the Gift, the less can be seen. Such a future is, to put it simply, blocked by the clarity of the present. This is why Papa and Grandmother couldn't see my future, nor their own, nor each other's, and why no one saw my mother's death coming. This is also why a fortuneteller must make her living telling the futures of strangers, rather than making herself very rich by knowing whom to befriend, whom to kill, or where to open a changing bank. The moment any threads threaten to involve the soothsayer, she is less likely to see their ends.

This limitation can be stretched and twisted when the bearer of the Gift is near death. Papa almost died of sickness and starvation when he was looking after my mother in her final days, and it was in a fit of near-death, when his spirit was not so close to us, that he gained the distance to see that the Gift would never be mine. Knowing this, of course, killed my mother. Finally. Again.

These capricious workings of the Gift are another reason I prayed for Grandmother to finally die, as was her due. Perhaps on her deathbed she could tell us if there was any chance of the Gift skipping a generation, of my child not being hollow like its mother. However, by the time I hit my mid-twenties, she seemed to have decided the line ended with my father. Perhaps, in her old age, she once came closer to death than she ever let on, foresaw my failure, and then clawed her way back to life to continue tormenting me?

I often wonder whether the Gift is in me somewhere, and instead of being broken, I am simply too stupid to access it.

THE GREAT FIELD

Masovska's Great Field was not very great. It was less than a mile wide, and only a few miles long. In Quruscan's minor steppes, for comparison, the grass could stretch in every direction until you got lost and spun in circles and felt as though you were drowning on a dry sunny day. I have heard that the major steppes drove travelers insane, and had oak-high grasses riddled with the corpses of birds in sizes never seen by polite civilization. The birds had, supposedly, lost their minds and their way as surely as any human traveler.

The so-called Great Field, however, was just a patch of shrubs and hills, with a sad old ruin in the middle. This Ruinous Temple had been constructed long before recorded history, from that supposedly unbreakable stone of the Ancients, before it was, somehow, torn apart. The prevailing theory was that the Ancients built the place to enact the hubristic, and *ruinous*, act of speaking the gods' names out loud, thus dooming themselves. (No one ever seemed to ask how many names they got through before disaster struck.) Whatever its origin, from the Ruinous Temple you could see, and hear, the forests at the

Field's borders. I suppose the Field was considered "Great" because most of Masovska was forest: the kind where trees grow so tightly into one another that there's no room for air or light, yet somehow giant boar and packs of wolves can slip between. The Great Field may well have been Masovska's only field that was not human-made.

But, I suppose, to those who had seen no better, the Field could be "Great," and in those days, it bustled with commerce right up to the edge of winter. Due to a local ordinance about A Certain Sort of Business, one could always find merchants, hucksters, prostitutes, mystics, messiahs, revolutionaries, and others who didn't fit Masovska's mores camping out in those shrubs and hills outside of Gniezto. The most lucrative ones formed a marketplace in the Ruinous Temple, which led to fistfights and sales wars, until winter chased away those who could afford to run.

We untrustworthy parties banished to the Great Field maintained cold cordiality with one another: businesslike, but never trusting. I have heard of fanciful thieves' guilds—secret criminal societies buttressed by codes and mutual respect—that may or may not have existed outside of stories, but the trick of the Great Field was that everyone there felt themselves to be more legitimate than the rest. Surely one was dishonest, but he was not *sacrilegious*; while another was sacrilegious, but not *foreign*; and the foreigner could at least be sure that she was not *unladylike*; and the unladylike knew that she was not some disloyal *dissident*; and so forth. This way of looking at one's neighbors was not conducive to respect or professional courtesy.

When winter arrived, most residents fled to more sturdy surroundings in towns and villages, where they continued to bicker, but those like us who could not afford traditional lodgings would crowd uneasily beneath huge canvases, heavy with snow, in the Ruinous Temple. I had pleasant memories of this arrangement from childhood, back when new smells, new voices, and excessive cold made things exciting. Papa told stories back then, and made it an adventure, but later I saw how close we came to having our food, clothes, and furs stolen. Not that a stable community has ever been quick to shelter my family either: few care for the survival prospects of an invalid huckster, his diminished shadow of a daughter, and his rancorous mother.

It lay upon me to keep Papa (and, I suppose, Grandmother) from starving in winter, and this year I was doing a terrible job. We did not have enough salted meat or kasha for half the season, and we could not even eat our poor horse. Yellow blight had sent the poor beast off to canter unsteadily across the sky with his twenty-legged horse god, and his meat was quite poisonous (although his hide would serve to patch up our tents). So, on the morning that I set the tent-furs, I saw a horrid bird landing on our hill, and hoped that it carried good news.

A LAMMERGEIER

The bird was a huge, red-eyed lammergeier, with black and white streaked wings longer than I was tall, and a body the bronze of sunset. It carried a message from Ramunas, for whom a gray messenger pigeon would have been passé.

The curled parchment tied to the beast read: "GNIEZTO SQUARE, TOMORROW MORNING. FOR EIGHT-TOES. —RAMUNAS." As though such a message could have come from anyone else. For tasks like this he had bought this terrifying bird, had it trained, barely, by handler-mages, and forced me to disengage the parchment from its gnarled, angry claws. I think the thing sneered at me as it flew away.

Ramunas was an ostentatious informant who often helped me form my false prophecies: he seemed to know everything that went on in the town of Gniezto, and the greater Gniezto Oblast that surrounded it. I had met him early during this stay in the Great Field, and his information had more than once paid for itself. Whether or not I liked him, he was effective and cheap, and always seemed to know a little more than anyone else I could afford. How such a flamboyant and theatrical man learned so many secrets was still beyond me. I had told him that even a prophet needed a bit of help and context for her visions, at times— which, in my father's day, had been true—and Ramunas either believed me or did not care about my legitimacy.

What Ramunas had to tell me about a customer I knew as Eight-Toed Gustaw from Down Valley Way, or why it needed to be said in Gniezto proper, I did not know. But a promise of decent information, even for a price, was welcome. All good news was holy, just then.

Once I was sure the flying beast was gone, I checked in on Papa and assured him that, yes, there actually *had* been a great bronze bird. I held his shaking, sweaty hand and kissed his red-brown brow until he went back to sleep.

EIGHT-TOED GUSTAW FROM
DOWN VALLEY WAY

When he had been able, Papa had taught me how to get by as a soothsayer on observation and generalities, which even those with the Gift must employ. I can often tell a man he will throw out his back if I see how he carries his goods, or tell a pretty young woman she has an admirer because of course she does. One with no skill, like myself, can do decent business with finesse: telling customers what is apparent, what they want to hear, and what is deeply vague. The rest is made up through theatricality, distraction, and research, such as that which comes by lammergeier.

Which brings us to Eight-Toed Gustaw from Down Valley Way. Gustaw was the best sort of customer: a returning one. Fourteen years previous, our travels had brought us to the Great Field. Back then, Papa had still been the soothsayer, even as his health failed and his mind hiccoughed, and Eight-Toed Gustaw from Down Valley Way had possessed a shorter name.

On a summer day in that year, Gustaw and his stupid friends drank at the Ruinous Temple market and stumbled about the Great Field, laughing and fighting and sweating as men in their early twenties do when they're drunker on blazing sunlight than ale. Sallow Gniezto residents lose their minds when they are not shaded by trees. At our tents, Gustaw's stupid friends dared him into a session with the spooky, exotic, legless soothsayer. I curtsied carefully and pivoted to usher Gustaw inside to see my father. His stupid friends leered at me and retched shredded goat meat onto the green grass.

Papa could barely do his job by the time I was thirteen. He was no longer the unflappable, endlessly confident prophet of my early years, who could recite perfect mixtures of truth and lie while running about on his hands faster than most men did on their legs. No, that day, seated on his great pillow, his hands shook, knocking over candles and ruining the mystique, and he often forgot the very real futures the Gift showed him. He did manage to blurt out that if Gustaw wasn't careful, his left foot would be injured. Gustaw laughed his way outside, where his stupid friends burned their pale skins in the sun and suggested that the legless man only wanted to put a scare in him.

Based on the name Eight-Toed Gustaw from Down Valley Way,

I'm sure you can guess what followed. Gustaw and his stupid friends got into a drunken altercation that night with a man who was not drunk, and who was armed. A cross-guarded sabre took off Gustaw's big toe and the one next, along with a triangular section of his foot.

Eight-Toed Gustaw from Down Valley Way came to us again eight years later, when I had taken over from my father and we once more spent a season in the Great Field. That year, I (somehow) foretold Gustaw's yet-unborn third daughter in enough detail to be convincing.

Now, in this waning autumn when I was twenty-seven, Eight-Toed Gustaw from Down Valley Way visited us once more. He had come to respect and fear the Gift, and was well-liked enough in his community that some others did too. What's more, Gustaw possessed some sort of affection for us: perhaps as a nostalgic vision of the end of mindless youth, and the beginning of slightly less mindless adulthood. I believe he still had the same friends, but they may have become less stupid.

He paid me in copper coins for a pleasant chat laced with vagaries and wish fulfillment. It was all so simple that I got none of the thrill of a well-executed deception, until he asked if there was any money coming his way. Here I found the seeds of a greater piece of fraud, and asked him to return soon if he wanted to learn more. I did not ask *him* why he expected to become richer.

Instead, I asked Ramunas. And a week later, I received his lammergeier.

FATHER AND THE GIFT

It was not long after Gustaw's severing, when I was thirteen, that Papa became too sick and distraught to work. I became his broken replacement. Sometimes luck would bring him a prophecy I could use, but I never counted on that.

You may wonder why my father could not do the soothsaying himself, as he was still possessed of the Gift. Why, instead, a broken failure like me? The short answer is tradition. In the extended history of our family, the next one with the Gift has always taken over upon turning twenty, no matter gender, station, or parentage. (We are like royalty and nobility, in that we actually track our ages very carefully.) At this time, the parent was meant to sit back and enjoy the fruits of their labors, advising future generations while no longer being expected to laboriously pick through their own fevered visions.

The long answer is that Papa's mind was troubled. When my mother was dying, he took terrible care of himself and became afflicted with both freezerot and redspit: these and grief addled him. His Gift was there, stronger than ever, but he lost tact, showmanship, restraint. If one asked my father about their future, they would hear *everything he could see*, with no preamble, no teasing, no vagaries, no withholding.

Imagine asking a soothsayer if this year's harvest will be good and being told that it will be passable, and also your wife will be taken from you by a noble in a year, your son will die of consumption in two and a half, and you will follow only four months later when you hang yourself, unsuccessfully at first try, from that rotted beam in your home, which you chose because deep down you did not have the courage to end it all.

Now imagine that the string of deaths told to you includes your neighbor, a stranger, and a woman not yet born. His visions were scattered: he might see one innocuous moment from ten years in a customer's future, or get snatches of tomorrow for everyone within three miles. Papa was done with the business long before I turned twenty.

Grandmother also had the Gift, but refused to help. Even if it meant we starved. She would watch me, angry at how bad a job I did, but offer nothing beyond her "encouragement."

"You're the soothsayer now, aren't you?" she said when I was fifteen. "Aren't you supposed to be getting us fed? Do whatever it takes: you could hardly debase our line further than you already have." She spat. "And when you *fail* and my sweet Aljosa *dies*, he will be better off, while you will deserve whatever comes to you."

On Food

After receiving the lammergeier, I worked until the evening. I had a few customers, who only required a little knowledge of human nature and a lot of leading questions, while I distracted them with smoke and trinkets. I smiled at each one as though they were the only person in the world, and when they believed me, I drank it in.

Besides that, I cleaned, packed, counted, and worried. A few townsfolk wandered past our hill in search of whatever sort of business they were looking for, but it was a quiet day in a quiet time of year. When the sky was red and the sun had disappeared behind the forest, I circled behind the large tent toward the fire pit, to make a weak stew over a weak flame.

My family of three traveled with two tents: one for plying the trade and one for Papa and me to sleep in. Grandmother stayed in the cart, where she could benefit from wooden barriers on all sides but the roof. A canvas on a stick was set up in the cart to keep me from seeing her angry gaze, and it was becoming too cold for her to place her skeleton of a chair outside. I wondered what would happen if the cart were to just roll down the hill and crash at its base while Grandmother lay inside.

She would survive on spite, I'm sure, and we would no longer have a horse *or* a cart.

The fire pit sat between the tents and the carriage, exactly where I had cracked half my fingernails and purpled my toe digging it months earlier. It was sheltered there, but with the cold winds picking up, I would have had to put my feet directly in the burning coals to keep warm. At least the fire lit, this time.

In my life at this point, food held no joy for me. I had wisps of memories from early childhood in which Papa, walking over to the fire on his hands and putting on the brave face of an adult, had cooked for Grandmother and me with something approaching relish. I remembered looking forward to the sounds of frying, and of onions and turnips shifting noisily about a pan. I even remembered that I liked their smells and tastes, but had no recollection of *how* they had actually smelled and tasted. Just that I had liked them.

Barring those phantom happinesses, meals had only ever been sustenance to me. I bought the cheapest and most filling foods—beans, potatoes, sometimes the intestines of a scrawny pig or goat that had been sold cheap—chopped them and boiled them into a sad stew every night. Grandmother always said that spices were decadent.

I would then bring a piping hot bowl of mushy stew to Grandmother. That evening, she was bundled in the back of the cart, leaning against her old, stripped frame of a chair, which lay on its side. Two eyes and a dead pipe stuck out from between blankets. She spat on the floor of the cart and cursed me for a failure, and my food as well. Had I brought her a perfectly poached egg of cassowary, imported from Loashti reaches, she would have done the same. And called me "soft" besides. So I knelt in the cart, let her think it was in obeisance, handed her the bowl, and hoped she burned her tongue.

"What, freak?" she snapped.

I had said nothing, but she saw through me. I shook my head and muttered, backing out of the cart and leaving her to her useless rage.

A few moments later, I heard her yelp at burning her tongue. I smiled broadly at my tawdry, pathetic revenge and sat back by the fire. In a few hours, Papa would wake in the middle of the night, and I would have his soft and lumpy stew ready for him.

I stared at the empty, cold kettle leaning against a rock on the far side of the fire pit. My throat parched in that moment, as though it had waited for me to notice it. We were almost out of tea, and could use more root vegetables besides. I had in total thirty-six Masovskan copper coins, officially called "little grivnas," and ten of those would go to Ramunas in two days. Gustaw would have to pay me more if we were to survive the winter. A lot more.

MY FATHER

I was in the large tent sweeping the rug when I heard Papa snort and moan through the canvas; he had woken up. The broom clattered against the dais behind me as I ducked outside.

I did not throw on a shawl, and just the twenty steps from the large tent around and back to the smaller one chilled me. I was shivering when I rolled down the leather door-flap behind me and saw my father.

Right by the door was the tall pile of furs, blankets, and pillows that made Papa's bed, which lifted his prone body up high enough that when I sat on my own bedroll, I could look him straight in the eye. Having no legs, Papa and his bed didn't take up much ground, and so I slept on a small cushion flush against the ratty, old bearskin rug. I wonder what great warrior far off in our lineage must have killed that striped Quru bear—my family tend not to be that type.

"Welcome, stranger," Papa coughed out as I approached him, smoothing his gray beard, "to the tent of Aljosa the Prophet! In this humble place I will untangle the strands of fate that— Oh! It's you, Kalynishka!"

He laughed at his little joke, the same little joke he made every night.

I sat on my bedroll and took his hand. It felt like a clammy little sun, radiating heat even as his teeth chattered. Papa's drawn face rolled toward me, and just as quickly as he had smiled at his joke, the corners of his mouth fell.

"Oh, Kalynishka, I'm not well."

"I know, Papa. I know."

From the cart next door, Grandmother coughed herself awake. Her throat was a desiccated wasteland, but the cough was still exaggerated. She didn't like me, but she didn't like being left out either. Good. I ignored her.

I cared for my father as I did every night. Did he want some tea? He did not, but I brought him what I had brewed for myself and made him drink it. Would he eat? Just a bite, Kalynishka, just a bite, but he emptied the bowl. Once he was as sated as he was going to be, Papa settled back into his bedding and passed gas. I drew the furs covering his torso up to his neck, tightened his fur hat, and braced myself for what was always next: the Gift would come for him.

When Papa was comfortable and relatively awake, he began ranting about sundry futures, most of people he would never meet. It always pained him, and was almost never helpful. Often he would only see red and brown and green, maybe a tree, a button, or a stepping boot heel. Now and then he would see actual events, like an old woman dying or a boy touching himself. He was never sure what he was seeing; each vision was a question, a melting mist. He had no control over the Gift, and any attempt to concentrate on what he saw, or to see anything specific, ended in frustration.

That night, I held his hand particularly tightly and hoped beyond hope he would see something relating to Eight-Toed Gustaw from Down Valley Way's inheritance. I did not ask anything of him: Papa liked very much to feel useful, but not half so much as he hated to feel useless.

For a good half hour, Papa twisted and held my hand and muttered vagaries.

"A clove of garlic, Kalynishka, rotted. There is a bird. A string? Thousands of them, in all colors! Fluttering in the wind—and that wind is so strong, Kalynishka, so strong. Stone walls and lanterns, and blood and corn. Blood *on* corn. A great eye and a limping mustache. Sand? Where in the world could there be so much sand, Dilara?"

Dilara was a Quru name, my mother's.

I daubed his brow and leaned in to listen closer. I did this every night, even though he always looked past me and never noticed. Papa was plagued by things only he could see, and since he was beneath the notice of most people, it seemed only right that someone be there to hear him. Even so, his colors and objects became chatter to me, and I listened only for knowledge of Gustaw's future. Or my own.

". . . Kalyna."

Papa was looking at me unwaveringly. I met his gaze, and he stared directly into my eyes.

"I . . . Yes, Papa?"

"Kalyna," he repeated. "Listen." His voice was firm. The set of his jaw showed a conviction I hardly remembered in him.

I nodded. His face didn't move, but his gaze was far away again. A tear formed in his right eye.

"This country," he began, "this country will collapse in chaos and war, Kalyna."

I exhaled. It was nothing about Gustaw or myself. I daubed his brow again and then leaned in to hug him. "Of course it will, Papa," I said into his ear. "They all do. Countries and borders are fluid, and they are moved by war. Now try to relax."

"No!" He tore himself backward out of my grip, which he had never done before. His whole face full of . . . not terror, but deep sadness.

"No," Papa repeated quietly, understanding that he had been too loud. "No, no, Kalynishka, some endings are worse than others." He shook his head. "This one will be very bad," he said as though he were appraising a rotted apple.

I wondered if perhaps we could use this information. Prophetic books of future history sell wonderfully, if convincing.

"No weak skirmishes and redrawing of borders," he continued. "War will pour in like a deluge, change will come to mountains, valleys, and steppes with fire and sword. Not just Masovska, but the whole Tetrarchia. Survivors will not live the same lives beneath different flags, they will be ruined and enslaved, or strung out beneath the sun with their entrails stretched across the landscape, and their children thrown among Rotfelsen's shattered remains. Do you see? When our country ends, it will end terribly."

I sat back to look at him better. It was entirely dark outside, and I kept only the smallest lamp in the tent with him. Grandmother coughed quietly from the cart; she was probably back to sleep.

"But when will this all happen, Papa? This terror and entrailstretching?" I asked. "Fifty years from now? Five hundred? In a time so different that you can barely recognize—"

"Three months." He blinked.

"Oh," I said.

ŞEBEK IN A CLOUD

"Let me tell you a story, little monster," said Grandmother.

I chopped wood harder and louder.

It was the morning after my father's prophecy. Our corner of the Field was quiet, and it was the kind of sunny, calm, cold day that I suppose one is meant to languidly enjoy by an outdoor fire. Perhaps with friends. I was by the cold fire pit, trying very hard to *not* see the Great Field as the part of Masovska best suited to mass graves for the nameless. To not imagine farmers penned into the Ruinous Temple and slaughtered. But slaughtered by whom? Where would this destruction come from? How literal were words like "deluge," "fire," and "shattered" in Papa's mouth? How could this be our *future*, when for years, Papa had seen the lives of others stretch into the oncoming decades? I tried to distract myself with anger at Grandmother and succeeded marvelously.

She sat on the lip of the cart and began to tell me about when she and my father had stayed in a village called Şebek, long before I was born. This was the story she *always* told when she wanted to yell at me about duty.

"Şebek," she explained every time, "is a series of baskets that hangs between two mountainous outcroppings, themselves atop a higher mountain. You could say the town is at the crotch of the peaks. Şebek floats in the clouds, all baskets and nets and wooden platforms. It was well hidden, and we were on the run. You scowl at one idiot child and suddenly you are to blame for it dropping dead? Honestly. Not my fault the parents didn't pay me to see whether their brat would get a bog-plague."

From here she went on, as always, about how she had coddled Papa in his youth. "*If* ever I had a flaw," she said, "it is that I love too much." As such, she had not yet let him take over the business when they were in Şebek, despite Papa being "twenty-two, full of the Gift, and flush with showmanship."

I mouthed the words along with her under my breath when my back was turned, making angry faces she would never see.

The long and the short of this oft-told story was that while they were there, Şebek was attacked—whether by the town's enemies or my family's, she never knew. Either way, nequş birds were released into the village: little flightless, scuttling creatures that eat nothing but oily plants, giving their feathers a gloss that can be easily lit on fire. They ran about, leaking flame and causing havoc. Papa found his mother and led her down the mountain, running on his hands and quietly scouting ahead to see whether the way was clear. During that perilous escape, he repeatedly avoided mobs that were drawn, I'm sure, by Grandmother's refusal to keep her voice down.

Once they were both safe, Grandmother realized Papa was truly an adult, saw the error of her ways, and the family business passed to him.

"And *he*," she finished, as always, "went on to do his duty as a soothsayer! Unlike the twisted doll that he spawned."

I kept chopping.

"Perhaps you should give up soothsaying entirely," she said. "The Gift is dead. You killed it with your sloth, just as you killed your mother. Why pretend to be what you are not? Let my son and I die in peace—by which I mean on the road—knowing that we did everything we could to continue our illustrious line. Until you destroyed it."

I laughed to myself at the very idea. Nothing would make her more angry than if I stopped being a "soothsayer."

"Did you say something, freak?"

"A splinter was in my mouth."

"Just so."

In the light of day, the previous night's prophecy seemed a dream. But it had looked real enough to my father, realer indeed than my presence, his existence, or anything of the last two decades. I would have been stupid to ignore him. When things fall apart, women, foreigners, cheats, and mystics are always dragged out, humiliated, ruined, and slaughtered first. I was all four of these. We had to escape the Tetrarchia's doom.

Once I was done chopping wood, it was time to go to meet Ramunas in Gniezto. I wore an orange dress of tightly wound, thornproof wool, and wrapped two shawls about my holed sheepskin coat, packed a satchel with copper coins and incense, and slipped my sickle into my belt.

SICKLE

A sickle as a weapon is an awkward thing, but I like it. With its short handle, it's small enough to be hidden in skirts, with a wickedly curved blade that can discourage troublemakers without the pinpoint accuracy of a stiletto. And if one poses as a farmer's daughter, it needn't even be hidden.

Those of my lineage are no hussars, but I have learned to defend myself. When one travels up and down these beautiful kingdoms of bandits, pimps, and con artists (like myself) accompanied only by an ancient grandmother and a delirious father; when one is a relatively young, unmarried woman who is not forever wreathed by threatening relatives; when one looks "foreign," and practices a trade that regularly incites anger, one must absolutely be able to open a forehead or hack off a hand here and there.

There are, in fact, stained and cracking combat treatises for the sickle, illustrated with paper-flat men in the rounded and buttressed clothing of centuries ago, holding stances and demonstrating cuts. Such documents for sword, spear, harquebus, and other actual weapons were only legally owned by nobles, but those for sickle, pitchfork, or pliers (terrifying) were intended for peasants. I believe they hearkened back to the constant border wars in the time before the Tetrarchia's formation, when peasants were conscripted into battle and never outfitted; when it was useful to roil up the peasants against the "foreign" nobility.

By my own time, centuries later, our nobility had learned they had more in common with each other than with their local peasantry. I bought my sickle treatise in a Hidden Market on the Masovska-Skydašiai border when I was a teenager, plucked from amongst a stack of nationalist, separatist, and otherwise dissident literature. It was, by then, quite as illegal as a real weapon treatise: nobody wants farmers to know how to murder—or, even worse, *parry*—with their implements.

Unfortunately, knowing the enormity of what was coming for the Tetrarchia made my small piece of sharp, curved metal much less comforting. Perhaps our nation's destruction would come from the commoners rising up and turning their pliers upon the nobles? A nice thought, but I doubted it would make me any less likely to die in such a war.

RAMUNAS

It felt incredibly dangerous to go into Gniezto's very seat of power, but I had little choice. Besides, wouldn't we all die in three months? Or perhaps I could make enough from Gustaw to escape, and only *everyone around me* would die. Lovely.

I met Ramunas, my informant, in Gniezto proper: at the government square, between the squat green municipal building and the squat tan guardhouse. He was wearing the brown robe and ceremonial gorget of an advocate, but the robe was held together by glistening horn clasps and splashed at the arms and collar with stitched blue flowers in groups of three. When he moved, his robe shifted to show off its lining, and spiderwebs of gold lacing appeared in small bursts about his legs. Ramunas was from Skydašiai, Masovska's warmer neighbor to the north, but he always wore some version of local garb, in colors of an intensity one would never find on an actual Masovskan. Skydašian clothing tended toward brighter dyes than Masovskan, but Ramunas would have been excessive in his homeland as well—he was just that type.

He offered me his arm, which made me uncomfortable because I had seldom before walked arm-in-arm, publicly, with anyone who wasn't Grandmother. But he gave me a nudge, and I hooked my arm into his, finding that the sensation was not unpleasant.

"Not ashamed to be seen in town with a Ruinous Temple prophet?" I asked.

"There is a mania for the theatre of law in Gniezto, you know," he replied. "It is why I came here. And, as a respected advocate, if I meet with any shady characters on the side"—he nodded at me—"why, they must simply be part of a case."

"Why sell me information at all?" I asked. "Surely, my ten little grivnas aren't much to a *respected advocate*." I had long since stopped attempting to charm Ramunas; he reacted better to bluntness.

He made a face at my tone, but answered my question. "While I don't mind a little more spending money, it's mostly because the information I feed you helps the Gniezto locals you relay it to. A way for me to assist my neighbors when going to court isn't viable." He shrugged. "And today, Kalyna Aljosanovna"—he flourished a hand out of its sleeve and pressed it to his chest—"is on the house."

I shook my head at him, but was also relieved to hold onto my ten copper coins. Arm-in-arm, we began to take a sort of stroll around the square.

Ramunas often confused me, but he had been right about Rot-felsenisch nobles buying up beet-growing lands two months ago, and about Olga Child-Skinner after that. With his help, I *had* in fact been able to help a few people, even save a life, and get paid a bit besides. As informants went, Ramunas had done right by me. So far. I suppose it saddened me to imagine him slaughtered.

"So, what's this about my customer?" I asked in his native language of Skydašiavos.

"Well, Kalyna Aljosanovna, your Eight-Toed Gustaw from Down Valley Way has an uncle," he replied in the same. "A good uncle to have."

"Good how?"

"He is rich, and he is dead."

I leaned closer. "And will his money fall to Gustaw?"

"Shouldn't a prophet already know this?"

I glared at him.

"Yes! Yes, it will!" He threw up his free hand and laughed. "Maybe."

We turned a corner and began another circuit of the square, passing a statue of a male figure with one leg bent and the arm up, hips jutting. It was a figure in the unbreakable Ancients' stone: a beatific god swiped from the Ruinous Temple. At least, it was assumed he was a god—assumed that each of the Ancients' statues of impossibly supple humans corresponded to deities in our own "pan-theon," which was but a lumpy and incomplete rabble. The gods of the Tetrarchia existed in shapes we sometimes could not depict, going by names only the priests of their orders could say; they were cobbled together from hundreds of long-subsumed peoples, all of whom came to these lands long after the Ancients spoke themselves into oblivion.

I, like everyone, had my favorite gods, whom I hoped would look after me, and whom I will absolutely not vex by writing their names here. The goddess of travelers is, naturally, near to my heart; I have always prayed to the trickster god, but that is not devotion so much as compulsion; and for some reason I have always had a deep love for R——, the local goddess of Keçepel Mountain.

As for the "god" whose statue had been taken from the Ruinous Temple, a dove was perched on his phallus, and his blue-veined buttocks looked to me like they were cold. Behind him was another statue in the same pose: a great local judge, whose jowls were perfectly carved into a workmanlike granite. Unlike the old god before him, the judge's stone would break beneath cannonballs. Also, he was clothed.

"Gustaw's uncle," Ramunas continued, "is also a Gustaw. Gustaw Close-Hand, he's called."

"'Close-Hand.' Not a good sign for his inheritance."

"It is for your farmer friend. You see, Kalyna Aljosanovna, there's a great distance of land between these two Gustaws: they may have met once, or never at all. The family on *this* side of the western forest"—he jabbed down toward the muddy ground—"are meager farmers, and on *that side*"—he pointed in the general direction of the western sky—"are very rich."

"So has . . . that family"—I pointed at the sky—"decided to favor this one?"

"Not exactly. Gustaw Close-Hand is why that arm of the family is rich. He made his fortune in the fish market—beginning as a simple fisherman at a nearby lake, and ending up as the mogul of the Tetrarchia's largest changing bank. Your Gustaw," he said, "is probably hoping for the funeral gift."

"The what?"

"You aren't from Masovska, are you?"

"I was born here," I said. It was the truth.

"Really?"

It was easy to see why he doubted me. Coming from about the center, north-to-south-wise, of Skydašiai, Ramunas was light brown, with curly hair, neither of which were considered to be Masovskan. I shared some of his features, and others besides. My family, over the centuries, had come from everywhere, and so I looked foreign everywhere.

"Yes, really," I said. "But do go on."

"Well, the funeral gift is important here in my adopted home. You see, if the deceased is the last of his or her generation in the family, ten percent of their belongings are split between all extended family who are not properly in the will. That is the funeral gift. It isn't law, but tradition."

"Ah. Not the sort of tradition I would expect a man called 'Close-Hand' to go in for."

"True enough, Kalyna Aljosanovna. He did something worse."

He paused for effect. I groaned at him.

"Gustaw Close-Hand," Ramunas continued, "had three children: Bernard, Bozena, and Klemens, whose family name became Gustavus, as a way to separate themselves from the rest, who are identified by 'Eight-Toed' or 'Fish-Eye,' or, well, 'Close-Hand.'"

I nodded.

"Old Close-Hand raised his children as rich and spoiled as could be, but it seems near the end of his life, the old mendicant had a crisis of conscience: most likely, this was after Klemens killed a vagrant for fun and was never charged. Allegedly. The patriarch decided that his children needed to earn their fortunes, just as he had; that this was the true path to redemption."

"Isn't redemption for murder meant to be found in prison?"

Ramunas smiled. "The rich are not like us. So, in order to keep his spawn from staying spoiled, Close-Hand chopped up the inheritance—the whole thing, no measly ten percent—between all relatives of the next generation. His children, his nephews and so on: they all get the same amount. Just enough to coax future ventures into being." He clicked his tongue. "Of course, his children still get his banks and other businesses, so they won't exactly be destitute."

"Then Gustaw, *my* Gustaw, doesn't have much coming to him."

"Ah-ha!" laughed Ramunas. "But you see, a pittance to the Gustavus children is a great deal to our eight-toed friend."

"How m—"

"Fifty grivnas."

In Masovska, a grivna was a gold coin. Hence, silver coins were "lesser grivnas," and the coppers that I had on me were "little grivnas." I had only ever owned one solitary gold coin of any sort at a time. And not often. I breathed a huge sigh of relief and actually did allow myself to smile. Perhaps grin. I was saved.

"Well," I said, "that sounds grand. Why did I need to be here for you tell me all that?"

Ramunas bowed and flourished toward the courthouse. "Come on in and I'll show you."

ADVOCATES

We walked quietly, still arm-in-arm, into the courthouse from the government square. A bored guard in a mud-spattered tunic and helmet, whose cross-shaped sword hilt did not look like it was attached to anything, watched us enter the squat courthouse without bothering to crane his neck. The vestibule was a wide, low room in chestnut with a straw floor, and there was a small crowd milling about there, waiting to be allowed into the gallery.

In the crowd, I counted seventeen elderly locals who chatted while waiting for a warm place to sit, away from their homes and demanding families. They leaned against long-grubby paintings of kings, officials, local martyrs, and forest landscapes. There were nine or ten children, of ages ranging perhaps from three to fifteen, spitting and running about the room on their own or in packs, but never with adults. There were also two drunks. The vestibule was filled with those who had no work to do in the morning.

Ramunas assured me this was a normal crowd for a day on which no major decisions would be brought to the courthouse. I marveled at how boring Gniezto must be if an exciting day at municipal court was all that was available for those who were not in the Great Field.

However, somewhere on our way to the other end of the vestibule, where a harried official awaited us, I noticed that these elders and children and drunks looked genuinely interested in being there. Excited, even, to spend their day listening to advocates outline arguments and quote minutiae. A lone little child, blowing snot bubbles and wandering between the old-timers' legs, asked another child, excitedly, if Przemysław, the famous advocate, would be arguing today.

Ramunas had not lied about Gniezto's fascination with the "theatre of law." What a terrifying people.

The official at the entrance to the gallery wore a long gray robe with thick black clasps across the chest and gray fur at the shoulders. He was shivering anyway, probably because the vestibule floor was mud and straw, and his leather boots were coming apart at every seam. He sighed unheard imprecations at a group of teenaged boys fist-fighting in that way that's never clearly a practice game or a real grievance, until he saw us.

The official's gray little face lit up when he saw Ramunas. He grabbed my informer's bejeweled hand, which was a most affectionate greeting in Masovska, and gushed about how happy he was to see him in today. I may as well have not existed to this official, which was fine with me.

The muddy ground, the gray official, the sad drunks excited for a chance to see advocates bicker over property rights: it occurred to me that a fop like Ramunas probably brightened these people's days with his over-practiced grace and garish colors. He illuminated this cold land of wolves and treatises.

We were gestured into the court itself, which thankfully had a real floor of creaking pine. It was a wide, low room filled with pews that may have been torn from a small temple. By the entrance, there was a row of wolves carved from wood painted brown and gray, each baring its fangs and raising its bristles in anger. Those bristles were horsehair and the wolves were boot scrapers, of which I made use.

Far from us, in the front of the room, was a small barrier separating the pews from a raised dais. The dais was marble that must have been shipped westward from Rotfelsen, and was the only part of the room not made of wood. It may well have been the only thing in Gniezto proper made of stone that wasn't a statue. Atop the dais was a small pot of red clay.

Advocates and whoever else were involved in the day's cases were bustling about, rustling papers and muttering to each other, or actively *not* muttering to each other. The pews were mostly empty, waiting for the elderly derelicts and violent youths gathered outside.

We sat toward the front of the courtroom, alone, on an uncomfortable pew. Everyone near the dais greeted Ramunas with smiles or conversation. One or two of them greeted me as well; I coughed and nodded, then sat in silence as Ramunas chattered until the doors were finally opened for the Masovskan rabble.

Once the coughing, laughing, and running had subsided, the pews were a good two-thirds full. A boy who had been half-trampled by older girls was trying very hard to stop crying. The judge entered in front of us, carrying a ceremonial hammer, and walked slowly toward the dais. A grouse drummed at the window frame—which was large, with no bars or glass.

Ramunas assured me that on the occasion of a very important or sensational case, the aisles would be full of spectators stepping on each other, cursing, and fighting up until the moment the proceedings commenced, while yet more people nearly fell in through the windows. He kindly elaborated the sorts of cases to draw crowds: a ghastly murder, a great swindle, a charlatan unmasked. This last one made me quiet.

The commencement was signaled when the judge smashed the red ceramic pot atop the dais with his hammer. It was to represent, Ramunas whispered to me, that any decisions following its destruction would be just as irreversible. The pot had looked utilitarian and rustic in life, but its shards showed a vessel too thin, delicate, and easily broken to have ever been used for carrying anything. The clattering of ceramic shards with the judge's ornate silver hammer shut up every mouth in the room.

The judge himself was a round man in a pink powdered wig. I don't know if it was meant to be pink, or if its red had faded. The wig's ends stood straight up, looking as though his brain was frozen in the process of blowing out the top of his head. I would have laughed if I hadn't noticed that the teenager next to me with the at-least-twice-broken nose, who had shoved an old man down in order to sit in the front, was silent with admiration.

The judge presided over five disputes before Ramunas jabbed my ribs to make sure I was paying attention. Those first five were divorces, land rights, and some things I didn't understand. Investments? The room was riveted. Sometimes they cheered, but never for the accused or accusing, always for the advocates. I tried to pay attention, but the encroaching possibility of freezing to death before I could starve, or starving before my entrails could be spread throughout Masovska, or even successfully escaping while the victors in these cases stayed to die, didn't make it easy for me to care about such things.

With my ribs aching from Ramunas' elbow, I trained my eyes on a man the judge was now addressing for this sixth case, which Ramunas so wanted me to see.

"Name," demanded the judge. If he could have sneaked a rolled R into the word "name," he would have.

"Klemens Gustavus," sighed the man on the stand.

I didn't need Ramunas to jab me anymore: this was the youngest son of Gustaw Close-Hand. Klemens sat straight, with his hands on his knees—proper—and looked the judge directly in the eyes. There was nothing to criticize about his manner, his words, nor even his tone, and yet there was *something* wholly disrespectful and indignant in him that I couldn't define. It was as if showing respect, not for a judge, but just for the time and existence of other humans, was an act that he was putting on, and he wanted us to commend his performance.

It didn't surprise me that this was the Gustavus child who had once, supposedly, committed murder and gotten away with it.

THE GREATER EASTERN TETRARCHIA

The judge swore Klemens Gustavus in the same way he swore in everyone that day: four times, once in each major language of the Tetrarchia.

The Tetrarchia—if you, whoever you are, are reading this hundreds of years removed from me and have no history—was a tetrarchy, a country made up of four separately ruled parts, as its name implies. So, all of its most important administrative and legal duties were executed in four languages. Before our Tetrarchia was born, the very idea of a tetrarchy, or any differently numbered combination, was only a theoretical exercise: argued for or against in rhetorical treatises, but never put into practice.

Soon enough, I would come to learn *far more* about the politics of my country than I had ever wanted. Nonetheless, let me explain what I, as a laywoman, already knew by the time Ramunas took me into that little Masovskan courthouse. By then, I had been all over, and beyond, the Tetrarchia, which I was now planning to escape.

As I told my father, kingdoms and borders are always fluid, no matter what a king and his advisors would have you believe. As I understood it, our great country was once a mass of city-states that warred with, absorbed, and wiped out one another. Each had its own language and culture and ways and exports, and even within a city or town, there were varied traditions and peoples. Over time, these coalesced painfully into seven to ten kingdoms, which eventually boiled down and reduced to four, wedged tremblingly between mighty Loasht to the north and the whirlwind Bandit States to the south.

These four kingdoms—cold and superstitious Masovska; jagged and paranoid Rotfelsen; precarious and discrete Quruscan; fertile and motley Skydašiai—leaned against each other for a few hundred years, skirmishing, trading, and taking each other's measure, until a surprising decision was reached.

The official version was that the four kings recognized the spark of divine rule in each other and, instead of risking further war, banded together. This began the Tetrarchic Experiment, in which one gigantic country was ruled by a council of four monarchs.

The version I heard in taverns across the breadth of the Tetrarchia was that the merchant guilds got sick of having their goods raided in every half-war between kingdoms. So, they banded with a group of young knights who were desperate to prove themselves in greater battles, and forced the kings into a corner: genuine compromise or all-out, four-way war. This began the Tetrarchic Experiment, in which one gigantic country was ruled by a council of four monarchs.

Certainly, unification in the face of the Bandit States' constant war, and Loasht's looming, antique power, didn't hurt.

The Tetrarchia was always a country too large for itself. It had no natural or cultural reason to be one nation, besides a strange quirk of mercantile history. The Tetrarchia's four monarchs, complacent in their safety, only met once a year (at the Council of Barbarians), and could hardly stand one another. Masovska felt that its bitter cold kept its people strong, and that everyone else would collapse without wood imported from its vast forests. Rotfelsen believed similarly about its exported stone, and viewed the rest of the nation with stewing, insular disdain. Quruscan deemed itself unconcerned with anyone unable to survive its mountains and steppes, and it was felt that they alone protected the Tetrarchia from Loasht. Skydašiai was *also* the Tetrarchia's "only" protector from Loasht, and provided most of the nation's produce besides.

Outside of the most sweeping laws, nothing was consistent from one kingdom to the next: not culture, legality, manners, or how regions within each kingdom were defined. The very idea of unity within the Tetrarchia was laughable: we were held together by momentum and fear. Fear of the Bandit States, fear of Loasht, and fear of our own internecine squabbles bubbling up once more.

Each kingdom had its own official administrative language, which was used, unsuccessfully, to grind out the dozens of other languages that still existed within its borders. Swearing in and sentencing were given in all four official languages: Masovskani, Cöllüknit, Skydašiavos, and Rotfelsenisch, as were royal decrees, customs forms, money-changing, and pronouncements made before executions. All of the *other* languages became half-remembered dialects, mournful prayers, separatist rallying points, and the like.

The country's full name was The Immovable Confluence of Four also Being the Greater Eastern Tetrarchia of Dirt, Rain, Stone, and Wood Watched Over by the Divine Four Kings of All Known Time, but I had only heard this said out loud once or twice in my life. I had been to its every corner, and spoke all four of its official languages (among others), but, like most citizens, I knew our kingdom as the Greater Eastern Tetrarchia, or simply the Tetrarchia.

KLEMENS

Once Klemens Gustavus had repeated "on my soul" in four different languages, some of which he may not have understood, he leaned back ever so slightly. An inch, maybe. It gave the same impression as if he had thrown his leg up over the barrier, loosened his shirt front to scratch his chest hair, and burped. It amazed me how much contempt he could convey while giving no real offense.

Klemens was a medium-sized man with hair that may not have been black, but looked that way when it was greased down to both sides of his head. I could smell the fishgrease he used from where I was sitting, as well as the lavender with which he tried to stifle it. He had the thick mustache of a grown man grafted over a youth's beard: all spots and neck patches and tufts beneath the eyes. He wore a long coat accented with fur that had been dyed a bright, unnatural blue. The coat itself had heavy clasps, a large collar, and a lined hood, as if to suggest he had trudged all the way through the forest to Gniezto on foot, and was ready to leave the same way at any time.

I had by now learned that it was normal for anyone on the stand to have their advocate hovering just behind them, ready to pounce on any untoward recriminations. Klemens' advocate, a reedy little man who gulped constantly, looked like he had never pounced in his life. He blinked and drummed his fingers on the back of his client's chair and gulped some more. He was there to dutifully find cause for whatever Klemens wanted—even I could tell that. And if it was obvious to me, this litigation-happy Gniezto rabble must have been picking up on all sorts of signs and symbols about the power the magnate's son wielded.

I glared at Klemens hard, squinted, and prayed that if the gods had seen fit to delay my Gift, they would give it to me in this moment. I wanted to see what would come to the rich brat, just to feel a bit of power. But then, I knew what was coming to everyone here, didn't I?

"Klemens Gustavus," boomed the judge, "do you know why you sit before me today?"

"No," Klemens lied.

The judge sighed and looked at the reedy advocate. "Counsel, your client . . . ?"

"My . . . my client," sputtered the advocate, "would very much like to be fully apprised of whatever it is that—"

"Fine. Fine," sighed the judge. He pushed up the pink wig to scratch his hair, which was gray-brown. "Klemens Gustavus, you are here today as a representative of your family in the matter of your father, Gustaw Close-Hand's—"

"Gustaw Gustavus," corrected Klemens. He interrupted as though this had been a natural break in the judge's speech.

The judge chewed so far down on his lower lip that I heard his teeth scrape at beard stubble.

"Gustaw *Close-Hand*," the judge continued, "never took that name."

At this point, I gathered that Klemens was not accused of anything, as there was no other advocate involved, and so the judge had to bear the brunt of him. I spared a quick look behind me to see that the crowd had grown bored at the lack of sparring advocates. One child began punching her neighbor.

"You are here," the judge tried again, "as a representative of your direct family, the progeny of Gustaw *Close-Hand*."

The judge glared at Klemens, who kept silent but put his nose in the air.

"This is in regard," the judge continued, "to your late father's bequest."

Klemens nodded. Slightly.

"It seems that your father's will, which was read at an inquest in your home of Rybochyksta, named certain beneficiaries in the greater Gniezto Oblast, is that correct?"

"Must I answer a judge's questions as though he is an advocate?" Klemens bent his neck back to pose this question to his own advocate, but his eyes never left the judge.

The reedy man behind him gulped loudly, and a ceremonial silver gorget with an engraved skull upon it bounced up and down along his neck. "Well, sir, yes, sir. That is, if you do not, he will call up an advocate to ask the same questions for him. Then you will have to answer."

Klemens pondered this. He seemed to be working over in his mind how much theatricality made him look in control, and how much would be too much. Ramunas put his hands on the pew and strained, almost standing up. His eyes were wide. He was waiting for the judge to call for a volunteer. I found myself admiring something in him.

Klemens looked around slowly to gauge the reaction of the crowd. He seemed to notice Ramunas' eagerness, and frowned.

Klemens sighed. "Yes, there are beneficiaries of the will in this general area."

Ramunas also sighed. The bench creaked and settled.

"Well, this hearing has been called," said the judge, "because your family never informed local beneficiaries, nor the local government"— at this, the judge indicated himself with a flourish—"that this was the case. It was only by luck that we learned of it here in Gniezto."

Klemens smiled a little too wide for my taste and leaned toward the judge. "Luck indeed. I wonder who tattled, eh?" he asked in a stage whisper.

The judge cleared his throat pointedly. I glanced at Ramunas, and wondered if he had been the "tattler." He betrayed nothing.

Well, likely enough, Masovska would collapse in fire and pain before Ramunas' nosiness got him killed. One could only hope.

"Why were no beneficiaries informed?" asked the judge.

"We rather felt it was a beneficiary's responsibility to dig out his own gold."

"Any beneficiaries are your own family!"

Klemens shrugged.

The judge sighed and rubbed his forehead. He did not seem to notice his wig shifting back. "Klemens Gustavus, this court will send couriers to all local beneficiaries. Your family is hereby required to reimburse the payment of these couriers, is that understood?"

Klemens narrowed his eyes. "Is that enforceable?" His advocate cleared his throat and began some half words.

"It is not," replied the judge, "but it will be cheaper than the lawsuit that will ensue if you refuse."

A child just behind me cheered prematurely, and then let the cheer die out halfway as he realized he was too young to know which parts he was meant to care about.

"I accept." Klemens smiled in a way that suggested he was not acquiescing at all. "Besides, I'm going for a little jaunt tomorrow, and haven't the time for a lot of legal nonsense."

The judge grumbled.

Klemens Gustavus stood and gathered up his coat in preparation to leave. After taking a step away, he stopped and turned around as though he had just thought of something. I rolled my eyes.

"A small question, Honored One."

"Yes?" said the judge through his teeth.

"Seeing as my family is *paying* for these couriers, it seems only right my sister Bozena be allowed to review and approve their schedules, routes, and expenses. To confirm that they do not travel all roundabout to the nicest taverns, you know."

The judge waved him away telling him that yes, that would be fine. Ramunas nudged me hard in the gut to make sure I didn't miss the significance.

I had not. Klemens Gustavus certainly planned to have those couriers murdered before they reached his extended family. I put my head in my hands and groaned at what I would have to do next. It seemed that before I could freeze to death, before I could be murdered in a great war, I would die along the road Down Valley Way.

TWO NIGHTS FROM NOW

A few days later, Eight-Toed Gustaw from Down Valley Way came trudging up our hill. I had been practicing a stance from my sickle treatise, with the blade by the left side of my face, ready to strike down or across, as needed, while Grandmother screamed that I was handling Papa's freezerot all wrong. She preferred to believe that old illnesses still lingered on inside him, rather than accepting that his mind was troubled.

When Gustaw got to the top of our hill, Grandmother swallowed her next insult and was quiet. Gustaw rubbed his bald head, and then shook my hand enthusiastically with his great, calloused mitt.

"Kalyna Aljosanovna"—he smiled down at me—"you have gotten big. Did I tell you this last time I stopped by?"

"So have you. And you did not."

Gustaw laughed. His breath smelled of beer: a faint whiff of dark stout to get him through a cold day, not the reek of watery summer ale from his youth. I ushered him into the large tent in front, with its pointed top that dripped lace and fringe, holding up the curtain of shimmering glass beads for him.

"Thank you," he grunted.

"Of course. You are now in the presence of a prophet," I said as though we were joking together: Gustaw had heard such greetings many times.

The large tent was not for sleeping: it was too nice. At its center was our small dais, made of various and variously shaped cheap woods that had been stuck together, and painted to look, in dim light, like mahogany. A heavy Quru rug crushed the grass, and atop it were large pillows: the most comfortable things we owned. I sat on one pillow and Gustaw fell into the other, across the dais from me.

Inside the dais were cards, crystals, chicken feathers, and everything else I used to stall and distract. But today I only used my bright purple dress—advertisement and distraction in one—and lit the swan-shaped incense holder. I breathed in the smoke and felt a rare moment of ease. Gustaw needed a real prophecy from me, and I suppose I had one. If it didn't come true, I would not live to see his disappointment.

Ramunas had gotten his hands on the couriers' schedules, which I *would* have to pay him back for, and so I had formed a plan. The plan was not good, or smart, or likely, but it was all I had. With great, impossible, godly luck, and money, we would escape the Tetrarchia right away, before the snows stopped us, before its collapse, spending everything and ruining ourselves in the process, while poor Gustaw would barely get a chance to spend his new fortune. There was something to look forward to.

"I have been thinking, madam," began Eight-Toed Gustaw from Down Valley Way, "about when you said I would ride in a carriage someday?"

"And you will," I said, leaning forward, chin on my hands and elbows on the dais. I prayed for the pasted wood to hold.

"When?"

"Gustaw," I smiled, "if I knew everything, I would tell you everything, but that is not how it works." I tapped my temple. "You know how it is: the demigods rule the future, and nothing else, so they are jealous of it. If I take too much of it . . ." I reached out in a grabbing motion and trailed off, letting him take this only as literally as he wished to.

"You only rent, eh?" he asked, smiling.

I nodded. "Just so."

He nodded back and grinned. He believed me, but also wanted to feel savvy to the game we were playing.

"We have known each other forever, so I will not spout a lot of nonsense," I lied. "A great change is coming in your life."

"Good change, I hope."

I straightened, went from chummy to mysterious. He had leaned in to meet my low gaze, and so I was now looking down at him.

"Yes, very," I said.

"Are . . . are you sure?"

"Has my family ever steered you wrong?" Imperious, now.

"No."

I smiled and nodded.

"Two nights from now," I moaned from somewhere deep in my abdomen, eyes closed, lips trembling, "when your animals show great unrest in the darkest time, if you begin to make ten circuits 'round your home, your fortune will come on horseback."

"My fortune?" Gustaw replied.

"Yes."

"A *monetary* fortune?"

"Yes."

"How much?"

"Enough that I hope you will not forget a lowly beggar prophet."

"Oh! Of course not!"

Then there was a long pause as Eight-Toed Gustaw from Down Valley Way considered my prophecy. Eventually, I shifted forward on my pillow and opened one eye to see what he was doing.

Gustaw's massive hand stroked his massive chin, and he looked at me intently with large brown eyes. He reached down and scratched his left ankle, probably because he couldn't reach through the boot to his truncated foot.

"'Ten circuits 'round my home,' you say?"

I nodded slowly.

"Now what exactly is a home, according to the knowledge of the Ancients and demigods? Am I to go ten times 'round my shack, madam? Or the gates of my farm? Or the farthest borders of my lands?"

I opened my eyes the rest of the way and lit a new pyre of incense, more for the smoke than the smell. Better he not see me clearly. Even through my worries, I felt a tingle of the thrill that comes with successful trickery.

"Your farm, Gustaw. Circle your farm."

Circuits around the farm would, I hoped, take him long enough for me to enact my prophecy. The unrest of the animals was a way to make him wait a good while. At some point in the night, either the courier or the fighting would rouse them, or he would simply convince himself he heard his animals squealing.

Gustaw sighed and nodded and checked again, just to be sure, that if he followed these instructions his fortune would be made. I reminded him that the fates are fickle, but it would not be the first time my family accurately beheld his future. I then felt a jabbing pang of guilt because, from Papa's prophecy, I almost certainly knew what Gustaw's short future held.

If I succeeded and he got his money, I thought to myself, then perhaps I could tell him about what was coming, and we could escape together. Being piled into a carriage with Gustaw and his family did not seem like the worst way to leave the Tetrarchia. At least we would have company, and money, in our desolation.

Gustaw sucked his lip and nodded, glanced at his foot, grunted up off the ground, assured me he would go 'round ten times, and limped off. I slumped against the side of the tent, exhaling loudly at the effort of being charming and aloof, conspiratorial and unknowable, all at once. The tent shook slightly.

I felt bad asking him to do so much walking: he did, after all, have only eight toes. But even where fate is concerned, a human must feel they are doing something.

FREE WILL

Now, you might think that Eight-Toed Gustaw from Down Valley Way would wonder why it was he had to do *anything* in order to make the future arrive. After all, is the future not inevitable? Well, you would be very wrong.

After all, if a drunken man had listened to my father fourteen years earlier, he would be called Stupid Drunk Gustaw from Down Valley Way. A prophecy that comes through the Gift is not immutable, but it is the most likely outcome, although the how and the why are not always clear.

For example, imagine a man coming to my father back when he was at the peak of his powers, in the prime of his life, with a brown beard and a booming voice, our large tent perfectly outfitted. Imagine, as I say, that a man comes to him with general inquiries: no particular aim or hope, just curious about the future. My father smiles, closes his eyes, and sees that on the following day, this man will fall and crack open his skull, dying. He tells the man this, but does not see where, when, or exactly how.

This unlucky man may spend the next day walking carefully, eyes on the ground, searching every pothole and pebble, and in doing so, not see the cart that barrels into him, knocking him over and killing him exactly as foretold. How *ironic*, you may think. On the other hand, it's entirely possible he'll spend the next day walking carefully, always watching where he is going, and in so doing avoid what my father saw, going on to live for thirty more years of fulfillment and happiness.

And yet, my father had often seen thirty or forty years into happy futures spent in the Tetrarchia: spent right where we now know there would be war, slaughter, and possibly natural disasters, depending on how literal my father had been. Deluge or no, something in our country had changed recently, some new wrinkle to old problems, most like, that made disaster the most likely future by an impossibly high margin.

If everything my forebears saw in their visions was ironclad, they would never have made enough to live on. Giving someone *exactly* what they wanted was the domain of those sorcerers who enacted spells through complex ritual and elaborate set design, while still managing to fail most of the time. Our customers simply wanted to know how to find fortune and avoid catastrophe, or they wanted to be reassured that the future was exactly what they wanted.

Knowing a possible future gave one, at least, the chance to act. This was why it was good to give Eight-Toed Gustaw from Down Valley Way some extra work.

This was also why we had to escape. There was no way I knew of to make the entire Tetrarchia avoid its end in three months. I could mourn it later, with the other refugees.

Saving Gustaw's Money

A small dirt road, barely wide enough for two horses abreast, wound down through the impossibly thick Masovskan forest into a little valley, toward the farm of Eight-Toed Gustaw from Down Valley Way. I was not walking on it.

Instead, I was stumbling through the underbrush on the right side of the road, leaving at least one layer of trees between myself and anyone who came down in the open air. It was late at night, and I hadn't seen a single worthless soul since leaving the Great Field, but I was best hidden nonetheless. The moon was just bright enough to illuminate the road, while only penetrating the forest enough to show what was directly in front of me.

I drummed the handle of my sickle idly. Stuck in my belt, the point rasped quietly against my plain, rough leather trousers. I became bored, and so began to reflect on whether moving and fighting was actually easier to do in so-called men's clothes, like trousers, or whether growing up in the Tetrarchia had simply convinced me that it was so. Though the rules changed (maddeningly) from kingdom to kingdom and town to town, violence in my home country was generally considered to be masculine, and so if a woman involved herself in it, she was expected to look the part. It was all rather silly when I thought about it too much, especially considering how differently the *supposed* divide between men and women was often viewed outside of the Tetrarchia's kingdoms.

It was about then that a twig snapped under my boot, and I cursed myself for a fool because I had not been paying attention. I hoped it hadn't mattered this time, as there were owls, crickets, and creatures I preferred not to think about making noise all about me. I had heard nothing of a human being, but even so I went slower and quieter downhill through the rocks and bushes.

A courier was on the way to Eight-Toed Gustaw from Down Valley Way tonight, and I was sure that Klemens Gustavus had planned an ambush. One could pay the court's required fees and afford mercenaries to lie in wait while hardly denting fifty grivnas.

I assumed that Klemens and his siblings had similar ambushes ready wherever their distant relatives stood to gain fifty grivnas. No matter how convenient it might be for *every single courier* to have their throat slit on the road, there would be, Ramunas told me, no real evidence that could be brought against rich, important defendants who ran a major bank. It was a shame I couldn't help these other unfortunate cousins, but I had to harden myself to that sort of feeling. War, disaster, or whatever was coming would swallow them all up soon enough.

I crested a small ridge, and through the trees saw the bottom of the little valley far below. It was all a dark mass, with no individual tree and no piece of road making itself known, all surrounding one little lit-up spot in the center. Gustaw's farmhouse was no larger than my thumb from this distance, but there were lanterns lit outside, showing me its round-topped, squat little shape.

Seeing a warm, safe home nestled in the middle of that forested valley made me realize how cold I was, and I pulled my shawl tighter around my shoulders. I wondered if a tiny Gustaw was trudging around his farm in circles yet.

I heard a lone horse clopping somewhere far away uphill, behind me. I arced toward the road to avoid a particularly thick clump of trees and allowed myself a deep sigh. If it was only one horse, then it was probably the courier bringing Gustaw news of his payday. Perhaps, I thought, the Gustavus brat was going to leave the poor wretch alone after all. Then I nearly tripped over the first mercenary.

He had been crouched by the road, looking intently up it toward the far-off sound, and had never thought to glance into the trees. He was in a bush, bracing himself against the ground with one hand, and I honestly didn't see him until I had crushed the fingers of that hand beneath my heel. He did not cry out.

I, idiot that I am, mumbled, "Pardon!" before I could stop myself.

Instead of a pardon, I received a dagger in my left arm.

I reeled back and fought very hard to use my right hand for drawing my sickle, rather than for pressing the wound on my left arm. I lifted the sickle to the left side of my head. I knew the mercenary didn't need to yell for his cronies to hear us, and sure enough, I heard shuffling through the underbrush come toward us.

The mercenary was still crouching, dagger out, with the moon behind him. I saw the outline of a carefully curled mustache. He was certainly not some starving forest-dweller. Others were crashing closer through the bushes, and I saw one more run across the road from the other side. They said nothing, but did not hide their footsteps. I had to finish with the man in front of me quickly, and I hoped he was distracted enough by his pain to fall for something simple.

I feinted and pivoted back when he stabbed up at me. Then I cut his knife hand clean off. It flew away into the forest, blade glistening with it. He made a gulping noise and bent over forward. I kicked him in the face to keep him out of my way.

At least two were almost upon me from behind, and there was another who had crossed the road somewhere in front of me. I dashed deeper into the forest, away from the road, slipping behind two huge trees grown together. I dropped to the ground and bit my lip. One mercenary tromped toward me, but I couldn't see him in that thick forest until his boot landed a hand-span from my face. I whipped the sickle blade around and sliced open his boot, as well as his tendon.

I never saw this one's face, but he was not as stoic as his comrade. He fell close enough to lie screaming in my ear. The horse was coming closer now, and it seemed to have sped up.

Now that no one was surprised, and the others knew where I was, I needed to get out of the forest and onto the road. I didn't want the courier to see me, but I very much *did* want to see whoever was coming for me next.

You don't realize how instrumental your arms are in keeping balance until you have to leap to your feet with a weapon in one hand and a wound bleeding down into the other. I flopped up awkwardly, inadvertently kicking the screaming man in the process, and sprinted out toward the road.

I dashed through the trees as well as I could. Somewhere in that dark forest, I actually bumped right into another man, the same way one would in a crowded marketplace. He grunted and reeled, and I heard a blade cut air behind me. If my hair had not been tied up tight, I would have lost some.

I burst out of the bushes into the road, which the moon was turning a brilliant silver just below the ridge. The horse could not have been far now; its hooves drummed down toward us.

Two men came out of the forest after me. They were absolutely not desperate highwaymen: freshly shaved, with pristine fur caps and gold chains that clanked against their cloaks. They also both had sabres out. I felt myself hyperventilate. I put the sickle up by my head, and lifted my aching left arm to grab hold of my shawl.

One was a half-step in front of the other. I dashed right of him, putting him between myself and his comrade, and threw my shawl into his face. I stepped in and cut him down, across the head and neck. I felt him yield, and the cream-colored shawl stippled with red as he fell.

The remaining mercenary leaped over the fallen body toward me, and I backed away. He was all that was left of the Gustavus' thugs, and I began to feel truly confident. I thought I could really do this; perhaps there were things in this world I was good at.

He disappeared as I fell over backward. I yelled, "Cock!" as my head hit the packed earth. The mercenaries had stretched a tripwire across the road for the courier's horse, and I stumbled right over it.

My ears were ringing as this remaining mercenary appeared above me. I don't know if he was a large man or just looked that way when I was on my back. He raised his sword, and suddenly disappeared.

I blinked and shook the noise out of my head as I sat up. The mercenary was sprawled on the ground in a puddle of blood, unmoving. As my ears began to work again, I made out the last echoes of a gunshot I hadn't initially heard.

I looked around for the source of the shot before realizing the courier's horse was nearly upon me, galloping down. I fumbled with the tripwire, hacking at it with my sickle.

I saw the heads of horse and rider bob up above the ridge. Even in the middle of the night I could see the horse was wide-eyed and frothing. My bloody left hand joined my right on the sickle's handle. My left arm felt like it would wither and fall off.

The horse's full body appeared. The tripwire severed and snapped away from me. I fell over backward and rolled clumsily into the bushes as the horse tore past and headed down the road towards Gustaw's farm. I lay there and watched it, deciding that, when Gustaw came to pay me, I would tell him everything Papa had seen. That we *would* escape this doomed country together, northward into Loasht itself.

I never saw if the courier was tall or short, scared or composed. They never knew I had been the guardian of that night's journey. The horse turned that last mercenary's skull to jelly.

Killers

There were two dead mercenaries in the road, one of whom I had killed. At that point in my life, when I defended myself, I gave out flesh wounds or cut pieces off of people. I had only ended a human life once before, when I was still mostly a child. That first time, I had felt nothing but relief at my safety.

This time, I lay in the forest and waited for the knowledge that this had been a human being, born of human parents, to draw a reaction from me. Nothing came. It felt no different than wounding someone. I decided I did not have the room in my life to agonize over men who had been trying to kill me.

But who had killed the second mercenary?

There were still two injured, but alive, mercenaries somewhere in the forest. How injured were they? I could not remember. Were they near me now? Would they come for me soon?

For one unreasoning moment, I intended to get up, traipse into the road, and take my shawl back from the man I'd killed, looting his pockets in the process. I shook that thought out of my head: whatever hidden harquebus had killed the other one could surely have been reloaded by now. There was no reason to think this shooter wanted to be my savior. The Gustavuses must have had many enemies.

I heard shifting and cracking move through the forest, louder and more deliberate than the mercenaries had been earlier. I sat up quietly as I could, wincing in pain when I pushed myself up with my hurt arm—I had entirely forgotten about it. At least two pairs of boots crunched uncaringly through the underbrush. I sat awkwardly and gripped my sickle. Could it have been the first two mercenaries coming for revenge? I hoped they would be too badly injured to bother. But then, I was injured too.

"Wait—!" croaked a voice in Masovskani. Then there was another shot, so close it deafened me. I turned toward it and saw, between the trees, a dark yellow smudge.

I caught another such smudge in my peripheral vision, moving in time with the sound of boots in the forest. I turned to look and heard another sound, like an animal scrambling through the dirt. The yellow smudge lifted an arm and a lantern shined out ahead of it, illuminating a man who was desperately trying to crawl away on his elbows. One hand was broken, the other a stump.

A final shot, and this time I saw the report light up its section of the forest even brighter, for just a moment. I almost fell over backward.

I sat perfectly still. Scrambling on injured limbs clearly did not arouse the sympathy of these mysterious yellow smudges. I heard them speak to each other in guttural, halting Rotfelsenisch, too quiet for me to make it out. My heart seized up so wildly in that moment that I still wonder if I died then, and the rest of the story I will tell you has simply been a terrible afterlife.

The lantern went out and I was in pitch blackness. I heard more boots, more crunching branches, more Rotfelsenisch, and I prayed that it was as dark where I was as it looked to me.

Something nudged my back. I turned, and it was a man in a yellow soldier's uniform, holding a long-barreled harquebus. Another was walking up behind him.

"Kalyna Aljosanovna?" said the first one.

I nodded numbly.

"Come with us, please and thank you," he said, in Rotfelsenisch.

CONSCRIPTION

I was relatively sure I had seen a soldier in yellow before, the last time I was in the suspicious little kingdom of Rotfelsen, but what that meant escaped me. That kingdom of our Tetrarchia was a confusing mess of parti-colored armies, as though someone had covered it in confetti, and then given that confetti swords. The last time I had been there, I remembered seeing Rotfelsenisch soldiers in green, mostly, and some in yellow. There had been other colored uniforms, but I could not place them in that moment.

These three yellow soldiers, all men and all harquebusiers, led me back up the road for a good mile. They surrounded me but, surprisingly enough, did not jab me with weapons or tell me I was scum. This did not convince me I wasn't on my way to death. They were almost chatty, but told me little useful. The moonlit road was a very different experience on the way back.

"We had to come awfully far out here to find you," chirped one. "Were you trying to escape those brigands?"

I grunted.

At about a mile, we came across a great road that sprouted off from ours, and it was indicated, politely, that I should sit on a large stone at its entrance.

"You must be tired," said the lead, who had done most of the talking.

I almost pointed out that of course I was, I only did all the fighting, while they came in afterward to execute the survivors. But thought better of it and sat.

One of them ran off down this other road, which, despite its large width, twisted off into the forest, and another knelt next to me, to poultice and bandage my bleeding arm. He told me that I could see a flesh-alchemist tomorrow, and then it would be just fine. I did not thank him. In some "civilized" places, the condemned must be healthy before execution, for some reason I do not fathom.

I wondered idly if I should have let the arm gangrene and fall off. Then I would have a soothsayer gimmick. If only I didn't also need it to cook, clean, chop wood, guide our cart, tuck in Papa, defend myself, unpack tents, pack tents, and someday get up the nerve to slap the bile out of Grandmother. If I survived the winter. If I survived this night.

I sighed. I had been terrified for hours, and was simply too exhausted to work up any more terror. If they killed me, they killed me.

I wondered if the courier had made it to Gustaw yet. Was he cavorting through his home, hugging his wife, crying? I hoped so. He deserved that, at least, even if he wouldn't have time to spend it. Even if there were ants in this forest that would probably outlive the very society that made his money viable.

I was tired and, I admit, a little loopy, so when I heard a rumbling, I assumed, first, that it was in my head. Then I wondered if Papa had been off by three months, and the armies were coming now.

"Fine," I said, "let them come."

The soldier finished his bandaging and gave me a perplexed look. I shrugged it off. He could think what he wanted, but the rumbling was getting louder.

I looked down the road, over the soldier's head. The rumbling got even harder to ignore, and a bright light shone out from between the trees. Then I saw, rolling around a bend in the road, the largest carriage I had ever seen.

It was the size of a small hut, had eight wheels in total, and was dragged by ten horses, each much larger than our dearly departed, rock-kneed old horse. Its body was wood, like any other carriage, but its sides were reinforced with iron layered in sheets like an old suit of armor, complete with overly intricate swirls and spikes. The top formed into a silver and red turret that I soon realized was not an ornament. The carriage actually had a small, pointed second story. I could see all of this thanks to great lanterns that hung from its corners: it seemed to travel in a halo. I wondered if it was here to take me to join my ancestors.

Two soldiers, also in yellow, sat in front, one guiding the horses while the other hoisted a harquebus on his shoulder. I would soon learn that the three who walked me here had their own perches, at a small railing on the carriage's roof, and atop an outcropping at the back, respectively.

The carriage ground to a halt just in front of me. I stood up, bewildered, as a door on its side creaked open, revealing an interior of dark green velvet with deep purple trimmings.

A man who was not wearing a uniform stepped out with a slight limp.

"Kalyna Aljosanovna the soothsayer," he said, "for the good of the Greater Eastern Tetrarchia, and its Divine Four Kings, in the name of His Most Serene Majesty One-of-Four Gerhold VIII"—he winked, as though it were a joke between us that he was using such formal language—"I hereby requisition the use of your Gift."

This man's clothing, pinkish skin, and the stop-and-start rhythm of his language made it clear enough to anyone that he was from Rotfelsen, the kingdom in the southeastern corner of our Tetrarchia. At his side he wore a long, thin rapier with an ornate, enclosed hilt, unlike the Masovskan cross-guarded sabre. He also wore a yellow silk doublet with leather riding trousers and only a blue half-cape on top, with no robe to keep warm. He knew he would not have to stand outside in the chilling local winds for long.

My pain and exhaustion disappeared in the face of pure, numb confusion.

"I . . . I'm sorry?" I managed to say.

He walked up to me, favoring his left leg, and stopped at the perfect distance to be in control of the space I occupied without being invasive. The lantern light flickered on the right side of his face. His jaw was set, but not too hard, his face angular and serious without being stern, neither enjoying nor abhorring his duty. His dark brown hair was gray-streaked and worn long, but messy and nearly vertical, as though he had just woken up from his carriage bench, and his mustache was heavy without support from a goatee, which went against Rotfelsen noble style. He was dressed well, I gathered, because he was some sort of officer or official, but it was also clear that he came from peasant origins.

He pulled a parchment from his belt, its rustling louder to me than the harquebus shots.

"My name is Lenz Felsknecht, and I have here an order signed by the hand of His Most Serene Majesty's younger brother, Dutiful Prince Friedhelm, Landgrave of the Two Great Caves and the Spire, that calls for the requisition of—"

"You can't 'requisition' my Gift," I said. I felt I had taken a bit of his measure, and the melting of pain and exhaustion had allowed me to return to myself. "It's part of me, do you understand? Attached. In here." I pointed to my temple, perhaps condescendingly.

"Just so. But as I doubt bringing only your *head* will do, you must come with me."

He opened the parchment and showed it to me. I had seen a royal seal once or twice before, although never on orders concerning me. It certainly looked legitimate. So did the harquebusiers. He laid his other hand, in a thick glove, on my shoulder.

"Step into the carriage, Kalyna Aljosanovna," he said. "We've kept a close eye on you, and we know the great prophetic strength of your Gift, of which . . ."

Was this sarcasm? Did he know?

". . . the Prince has need. Think of him as a customer. One who will pay well, but whom you cannot turn down."

In that moment, I think I could have gutted him with my sickle and run off through the dark woods before the harquebusiers took decent aim. It occurred to me, but did not seem worth the immediate effort. Had I a better idea of what was coming, I would have tried.

PART TWO

FORCED LUXURY

I would have enjoyed traveling in that carriage, with its plush seats and its safety, if not for the company, the destination, and having been kidnapped.

The monstrous vehicle's interior, not including the unnecessary turret on top, was larger than my family's two tents put together. Lenz and I began by sitting diagonally at opposite ends, on separate seats against the front and back walls, respectively, and there were two more rows of seats that ran through the center, separating us. It was almost too much space for me. It made me feel uncomfortable; adrift. This monstrosity could have sat twelve spoiled nobles in relative comfort. Soldiers sitting on the floor could likely have numbered twenty, provided most of the filigrees and luxuries were removed to make room for them.

Yet none of the harquebusiers were inside with us. They sat on little platforms with guardrails, and took shifts sleeping in an enclosed area about the size of my bedroll, which bulged out from the back of the carriage. There was no door between their sleeping chamber and where we sat—this carriage was also built to be a prison, if necessary.

So, Lenz and I had the inside of this rolling cathedral to ourselves, and I sat as far from him as possible. The benches were backed with silk cushions, and the carriage interior was all rich woods and velvets, with gold-plate in the shape of grape leaves everywhere—as though anyone in Rotfelsen's dank caves had even seen a grape that wasn't first stomped and turned into wine beneath a Skydašian sky. Overall, this carriage was more expensively designed than any building I'd ever been inside; and perhaps more sturdily built (excluding dungeons).

As the soldier patching me up had promised, we did indeed stop to find a good flesh-alchemist, who cheerily got on board and spent a good hour mending my arm as we rolled along. I had been injured many times in my life, but only rarely been willing (or able) to pay for flesh-alchemy. It was still quite impressive, to me, to see how his gritty little salve, still warm to the touch, closed up my wound before my very eyes, although Lenz seemed quite disinterested.

Of this relatively new art, Grandmother had always said, "Bandages and bed rest were good enough for our ancestors, and they're good enough for you!" Never thinking, of course, of all the necessities and luxuries she enjoyed that many of her ancestors had not: tobacco from the Bandit States, Loashti gunpowder for a soothsayer to make a stunning entrance, the velvet she'd torn out of her chair. Flesh-alchemy had simply been unlucky enough to come about during Grandmother's adulthood, and was therefore a decadent luxury. (Unlike *tobacco*.)

She also did not bother to think of how her own grandfather, Huso, had escaped a mob only to bleed to death of a wound that could have been easily fixed by flesh-alchemy. But, of course, this new medicine was no help for internal bleeding, and so would have done nothing for my mother when I killed her.

The flesh-alchemist was a pleasant little man in a fur coat whose normal rate was a *ludicrous* (to me) ten gold grivnas. He was given another ten for his silence, and five more besides to pay his way back home from the nearest inn—a trip that would cost, at most, a few silver grivnas. Lenz had just handed out half of Eight-Toed Gustaw from Down Valley Way's fortune on fixing my arm. I stared up at my kidnapper, who was standing by the door, as the carriage lurched back to life.

"Why," I asked, "could the Dutiful Prince Friedhelm, Landgrave of the Two Great Caves and the Spire, not come to my tent like a decent person?" I looked down at my arm, flexing it lightly and feeling the newly knitted flesh tingle.

"Gniezto is farther than our good Prince can travel just now," said Lenz. "It's a well-kept secret that Prince Friedhelm is one of the hardest working people in Rotfelsen."

"Is he in Masovska at all?"

"No."

"You . . ." Lenz may have heard me grind my teeth. "You are taking me all the way to Rotfelsen, aren't you?"

"Did you think the Landgrave of the Two Great Caves and the Spire was just over the next Masovskan hill?"

"I dared to hope."

At least Lenz did not laugh at me. He braced his hand against the wall of the carriage, but did not move to sit down.

"Surely you know," he said, "that most Rots don't like to leave their land."

"'Land' is generous," I sneered. "Their rock, you mean. But of course, who would ever want to leave such a *charming* place?"

"Personally, I quite enjoy travel."

I was feeling very Masovskan just then, and almost told him just where in his Prince he could travel. But I held it in.

"*Sir,*" I said instead, "I have customers, one of whom owes me a payment, and an invalid father besides. I cannot simply disappear from Gniezto without a trace."

I did not tell him I also had an informant to pay off and a societal (or natural?) collapse to avoid.

"It seems *someone* in Gniezto didn't want you around anymore," he said. "Some well-off type dislike his fortune, perhaps? We took care of his goons for you, and the Prince will pay you more than any other customers could."

I groaned theatrically. Even if this Lenz were to give me five hundred Masovskan grivnas, I had done *so much* for a fragment of Gustaw's fifty.

"And," he continued, "your father and grandmother will be spirited to your side. I have a suite, complete with servants and four sturdy walls, prepared for them."

I admit that the thought of Papa being comfortable and safe for the winter would have been tempting, if we didn't need to escape the Tetrarchia entirely. If I ignored the imminent collapse of our country, then my jailer was promising to do more for Papa than his own daughter ever had. Provided Lenz was telling the truth.

"Just a little way from here," he said, "is another carriage of ours, which I will send back for your family, and your things, and bring them after us. At a less strenuous pace than you and I are traveling. The soldiers within will collect your father and grandmother, as well as your possessions."

"No soldiers!" I hadn't meant to yell, but I did. A harquebusier on the roof knocked against the hard metal door to make sure Lenz was alright.

"All's well!" Lenz yelled upward. He walked back to his side of the carriage and sat.

"No soldiers," I repeated, quieter. I stood up and paced the carriage to do something with my energy. My hands were shaking, and I stopped myself just before pulling at my own hair many times. "Everywhere we go, we are hunted, arrested, blamed, burned. If a woman has a miscarriage, I must have looked at her; if vengeful spirits have been causing trouble, my father drew them with his madness. More often than it's an unruly mob coming for us, it is *soldiers*."

I threw my arms up and turned away from him. The carriage bounced and I stumbled, which didn't look very threatening. I turned back to face him, glaring.

"If Grandmother sees soldiers coming for her," I said, "she'll do whatever she can to get my father and herself killed, rather than captured. She will be surprisingly good at it."

"And so I should . . . what?" Lenz was listening, but seemed unbothered.

"Put some of your soldiers in servant's livery, and have them say I'm . . . I'm working for the Prince of my own free will, which is but half a lie."

"Hmm." Lenz scratched his head. "That's a lot of trouble."

"I can also be a lot of trouble."

"I'm sure you can. I'll see what I can do."

Would he? Or was he was only humoring me while he left them to starve? Or freeze? I had only his word to go on.

I walked back and fell into my seat. "Well . . ." I laughed to myself. "Maybe it would be all right if Grandmother was . . . misplaced along the way."

"Don't say that unless you mean it."

I looked back at Lenz, and he seemed serious—more so than when conveying the Prince's orders. Who *was* this man?

"If you mean it," he continued, "it's done."

I may have considered his offer.

But finally, I said, "Forget it."

"Forgotten."

The carriage rumbled through the Masovskan forest, and I glanced at the sun beginning to rise above the trees. Lenz stood up and opened a compartment. In it was a large and ornate gleaming silver samovar, which rattled softly with the carriage's movement.

"You don't smell good enough to be a spoiled noble," I said.

"Just a soldier, Kalyna Aljosanovna." He pointed with his thumb to his yellow doublet. "The luxury is for you." Then he poured two cups of tea.

"When a powerful man abducts a woman, the luxury is never for her. You are showing me your power."

"I am showing you the Prince's power."

"Hmm. I wonder what he really wants from me."

"What do you think?" he asked as he watered down the tea.

"Perhaps the Prince has a *social disease* and rubbing the ashes of a prophet on his balls will cure it."

"That's ridiculous," he said, walking over to me. Then he smiled. "The Prince is nowhere near as lecherous as his reputation. Hardly anyone could be."

I shrugged and grimaced. "I've never heard of your blasted Prince, or his *reputation*. I'm just assuming."

"I promise you, Kalyna," he said as he handed me a teacup, "his only interest is in your Gift."

"What does he want from my Gift? To supplant his brother, I suppose?" I sniffed at the tea.

Lenz then proceeded to tell me what it was the Prince wanted. He did so in every human being's favorite way to communicate: through a story about oneself.

LENZ'S STORY

When I first came to the Dutiful Prince Friedhelm's apartments in the Sunset Palace, Kalyna, I was dressed to be murdered.

My full formal uniform—green, at the time—was stiff with disuse and completed by a great empty space on the chest for the medals I did not have. My hair and mustaches I had combed, curled, twisted, and slicked so heavily that I could not tell my own sweat from running pig fat. With all that and my limp, I was a sight to behold.

The Prince's guards—yellow, they wear, as I do now—took my sword but allowed me to wander his apartments unaccompanied. I assumed this was permitted because I would not leave those apartments alive, and I decided that if I was to become a corpse, I would see absolutely every room first. Have some new sights to mull over while I waited in the void for the spirits of my ancestors to come find me.

Prince Friedhelm's apartments, with which you will soon be familiar, are a dizzying array of sitting rooms, library-studies, bedrooms of sundry themes, and a complex of baths. You can tell one sort of room from another by the variety of couch that it has. (They *all* have couches.) Some are sectional and curved for lounging groups, some are straight and comfortable with an end table on which to set paperwork when the eyes get tired. One couch is velvet, and its armrests are gold-plated nudes bent at ninety degrees.

Thus I lingered before entering the audience chamber. I saw every book, wall, and device in those apartments, in order to delay my death a little longer. I see you are disappointed I did not meet it. A guard in yellow eventually indicated that I should really get going, and he did so unkindly, as the Yellows and the Greens have never been close. Rotfelsen has four separate armies, you see, each of which supposedly serve the kingdom, and through it our greater Tetrarchia, in their own way. None of them like one another.

Now, this was only last spring. At the time, I was a minor officer, unnoticeable by my own design, in High General Dreher's army. In other words, I was a Green. The way I looked at it, I'd made a deal with my superiors: I took a bullet in my left leg for Rotfelsen during a skirmish in my youth, and now I would fill out acquisitions forms for grain and saltfish and carry no ambitions, so long as they sent me limping into no more battles. Raids from the Bandit States would be curbed well enough without my sword: I was happily beneath anyone's interest.

Oh yes, I was also stealing privileged information. Constantly. Not for any purpose, mind you, but it's amazing how many matters of grave importance will be written right into the blandest paperwork with no thought as to whose eyes may run over them. I had in my home books upon books I'd written with my own hand, filled with secrets about the army, the nobility, the royal family, our neighbors, and anything else. I had no use for any of this, but it seemed such a waste not to collect what was right in front of me every day. I was driven chiefly by curiosity, incredulity at so much being available to me, and deep boredom. Of course, I knew it was dangerous, and perhaps a part of me wanted the excitement.

So I thought I knew why the Prince had called me from my windowless office, up to his towering and very windowed one. I was to disappear, or go out those windows and bounce on the red stone, after he figured out what my shadowy, and entirely fictional, masters wanted with my secret history, and how much I had told them. I fancied I had been taken for a Loashti spy.

I paced the Prince's audience chamber and pretended not to notice the secret door in his bookshelf. A room has never had a secret passage that did not also have a secret peephole, so I behaved myself. There was a very sharp letter opener on his desk, and I wondered if he expected me to pick it up and hide it.

Soon enough, the Prince came out of his bookshelf and looked me over. He's a short man who bears the features of the inbred, a strange jaw and nose, but is also the rare royal who would attract admirers even as a tailor or blacksmith. But you'll meet him soon enough.

He greeted me warmly and asked if I'd drifted back toward his desk because I recognized what he was reading. I lied and said that I had. The open book on his desk was in my handwriting: a volume on his older brother, King Gerhold VIII, open to a page on our monarch's childlessness.

"'Many in the court'"—the Prince quoted a passage of mine from memory—"'whisper that the King has specific predilections that keep him from fathering children. Such as an interest in men, or . . .' Well, you know. 'And,'" the Prince continued, in my voice, "'that such desires could also explain his periodic disappearances to his hunting lodge down in the southern caves. But this seems unlikely, as to marry and create royal offspring is a duty beyond something so simple as personal tastes. More likely, the King or the Queen simply cannot have children.'"

The Prince then asked me from whom these speculations had come, and I told him they were my own.

The Prince told me it was treason to even suggest that the King's issue was anything but potent. It was also treason to suggest the King may have preferred men, as such things are frowned upon in Rotfelsen, past a certain age. Although the Prince was quick to point out that this would not have been a great hindrance.

"I assure you," I remember he said, "to ensure his legacy, a King can grit his teeth and bear anything."

I told him that was exactly what I had been trying to say in my book.

"Lenz Felsknecht, Acquisitions Officer in the High General's army," he said to me, "why do you suspect you're here? Assuming it's not to have you thrown from my window, which it may well be."

I told him I was sure I didn't know.

Now, I'll always remember this next thing he said perfectly: "These books of yours are better curated and organized than any records I have seen."

I thanked him for the compliment, of course, and then told our Dutiful Prince Friedhelm, "You want my help in intriguing against your brother."

The Prince laughed and asked me why in the world he would ever want that.

"If," the Prince told me, "my brother dies, or is exiled, while childless, I am King. If my brother survives every plot against his life, and manages to somehow produce an heir, what do I receive?"

"Nothing?"

"Nothing. Except a lifetime of riches and parties and pleasures with no consequences. I love my brother no more than an evil prince from an old story does his, but the last thing I want is his death before I have a niece or nephew."

In all my prying, I had not suspected our Prince was so motivated.

"But the plots in our wretched kingdom grow faster than the divided King's Guard can prune them. No matter how hard I have tried, I am not so blind to politics as to miss how suspicious centuries living in *this place* have made us. I feel that in every little hollow there is sedition breeding—that our people get strange ideas when they live away from the sun for so long. So, your job will be to serve me, as one of my Yellows, in keeping my brother safe from the shadows to ensure my indolence. I can't use anyone known to the court."

I bowed and accepted this new position immediately, to preserve my life.

"Keep my brother alive, Lenz, at least until he can have children *somehow*. Keep this festering boil of a kingdom from bursting until I've died happy in my wine and my lovers."

DON'T BRING ME NEAR THE KING

I sat quietly through his story, holding a cup of untouched tea in a sad attempt at repose. We were still somewhere in Masovska's thick forest, and it was only midmorning. The tea smelled strangely intense, almost like smoked meat.

"Well," I said, "now I know what the Prince wants, but nothing about *my* involvement."

"Oh, that." Lenz laughed. "The Prince thought a prophet might be useful. For anticipating plots."

"You could have just said, 'We're spies!' and skipped the story."

"I wanted you to understand my position in all this."

"I do not care to."

Lenz shrugged and sat back, scratching his messy hair. The carriage crashed over a bump in the road.

"So," I said, putting down my untouched tea, "the Prince wants me to read the King's future and point out a couple of dignitaries who are eyeing the throne for their masters, for a hefty fee."

"Essentially. We will be there just in time for the Winter Ball."

"What's that?" I asked.

"The Splendid Royal Ball of the Entering into the Winter Months, Wreathed by Snow and Ice, although likely none will have formed yet. It's a party with hundreds of guests, some of whom may have harmful plans."

"Perfect, I can see all the dignitaries and third-tier royal bastards in one place." I clapped my free hand against my thigh, with finality. "A good night's work!"

It would be a crowning achievement of lying for me, the monumental fraud, to successfully prophesize for a king, a prince, and a spy. So satisfying would be the success, and so easily could I afford to get Papa out of the Tetrarchia on a Prince's money. I would escape the Tetrarchia in time *and* be proud of my greatest deception. Perhaps that would comfort me through the long hours of contemplating my homeland's death from afar.

But Lenz looked very sorry about what he was about to say. "No. You are conscripted to join me as a spy for . . . quite some time. The ball's a good start, but we will need regular reads on the court."

"How long?"

"Well, your father and grandmother will have a nice warm place to stay for the winter. For the next few winters."

"The next—!" I gulped back the rest.

"Kalyna Aljosanovna, you will know too much for us to just let you go."

"Then don't tell me your secrets! I don't care to know them. And I could not begin to care about royalty."

"You're a soothsayer."

"Then *don't bring me near the King!*" I cried. "That way I will know nothing!"

"You may well never see the King," said Lenz, "but you'll tell us about many important people."

My head spun. How long could an imposter possibly survive at any court, much less the insular and cagey Rotfelsenisch court? What's more, were I whispering false prophecies into a Prince's ear, couldn't my incompetence then be *directly* responsible for the Tetrarchia's collapse?

This last was actually a strangely comforting thought.

But what was not comforting was the image of Papa waking up alone and confused in his tent. What was certainly not comforting was the fact that this job for a sybaritic prince was not going to be the greatest con of my career, but a death sentence. Even without the looming end of the Tetrarchia, there was no freedom on the horizon.

Every failed prophecy would be a chance to be discovered and executed, and every successful one would keep me there for when Rotfelsen crumbled to red dust beneath Papa's prophesized destruction. I would have to reform my escape plans, as leaving the Tetrarchia from Rotfelsen was entirely different than from Masovska. Rotfelsen's very structure was that of a fortress—it was the hardest kingdom to escape, as I knew from past experience. Could we make it south into the Bandit States while they picked at the edges of the Tetrarchia's despair? I was doomed.

I watched the Masovskan trees speed by through the window's bars and thought about them being leveled for siege engines. Even then, as winter encroached, most were still green and vibrant. As I stared out, Lenz spoke about paying off my Gniezto debts, about making sure to collect my fee from Eight-Toed Gustaw from Down Valley Way, and all other manner of things to show how much he knew about me. At least he did not seem to understand my relationship to Ramunas.

"How long did it take you to get to Gniezto?" I finally asked.

"A week, at full speed."

"A week? I'll be trapped in here with you for a week?"

Gods, a *whole week*. I would arrive in Rotfelsen's capital, Turmenbach, with maybe two and a half months until the Tetrarchia was supposed to collapse around me.

"Yes," said Lenz, "we will be stuck with each other for a week, before we are stuck with each other for years."

I sat still, staring at him for a good minute or two, and then realized that I was very tired. I said as much.

"You can sleep in the turret," he said.

"'Can,' so I have privacy? Or '*will*,' so I am farther from the doors?"

"Yes to both. Although the doors are steel, and locked, with harquebusiers watching the road fly by at impossible speeds."

I sighed. I was beginning to have trouble keeping my eyes open.

"Will my father catch up with us along the way?" I asked.

"Oh my, no. We will change horses, but otherwise it's straight on through half of Masovska and into Rotfelsen. No stops. Your elderly family will be stopping for rest, so that they are not constantly jostled."

I had not gotten to say goodbye. Papa would be so scared and confused when Lenz's people came for him, however they were dressed. If Lenz wasn't lying and they did so at all. Papa might simply sit in the tent waiting for me until he froze or starved. Or perhaps Lenz's soldiers had slit his throat and been done with it. I had no reason to think I would see Papa ever again.

I was now tired enough to realize that the carriage could have been crashing off Rotfelsen's red cliffs and I would have fallen asleep in the middle of it. I did not even have the energy to continue worrying about Papa.

Tomorrow. Tomorrow there would be much worrying.

I stood up and stumbled to the little ladder. I remember from later in the trip that where each of the ladder's rails punched through the sides to anchor itself, there was a bronze face staring out the other end, as if to guard anyone ascending it. All human faces, and each one different.

I certainly didn't notice this on that first evening, however. I have a vague memory of being halfway up the ladder, and the next thing I remember is waking up in the turret the following day. I was wrapped in five blankets as I pulled open the curtains to see the harquebusier on the roof. He smiled and waved at me.

BOHDAN'S BOTANICALS

That next morning, I was presented with a few sets of clean clothes and a bright sky above the Masovskan woods that did not look like they could ever become a battlefield, or be even the least bit affected by human concerns. I changed, awkwardly, from trousers back into a dress inside the little turret, kicking its sides a lot in the process and feeling the new alchemy-crafted skin on my arm stretch strangely. Thus, I stopped looking like some midnight cutthroat, and was once again a soothsayer. The dress was a deep ochre with blue-green embroidered accents—the sort of colorful clothing I preferred, but better made than anything I owned. Pity it was tight in the shoulders.

I climbed down the ladder and was provided a warm meal of roasted beets and turnips scrambled with egg and thin slices of ham, alongside a mug of warm cider. The food and drink had waited for me on a little table rooted to the floor, the surface of which was on some sort of hinge that kept it always upright and still, no matter how the carriage bumped and rolled beneath us. I cannot pretend I understand how that worked.

Part of my family's excuse for meager meals had always been that we were constantly traveling, and yet here was travel desperate to seem like decadent, stationary life. I have known nomadic peoples who traveled with a collection of huge tents, each with thick rugs and wooden furniture, serving a feast of pickles and preserves, but they never acted as though they were *not* traveling. This thing was pretending to be a house as it bumped along the road. But I supposed the Rotfelsenisch mind always craved *enclosure*.

"Is a cook sweating into a fire in that closet?" I asked with my mouth full, spitting bits of ham. I pointed with my spoon to a small closet at the rear of the carriage, which could not have fit more than three jackets and some boots.

"We changed horses at an inn ten minutes before you woke; this was cooked there." Lenz was picking at a plate of the same, and still did me the courtesy of sitting at the far side of the carriage. He seemed annoyed at having to speak up.

"Ah."

"We have alchemically warmed pots stored below us"—he stomped on the floor—"filled with that cider, soups, stews, and we have the samovar as well, but I assure you that's the limit."

"Oh yes, quite limited," I grunted as I crammed the rest of the ham and the last round of turnip into my mouth. The food and cider were both delicately spiced with flavors I did not yet recognize, but the child at the bottom of my consciousness stirred with memories of Papa crushing small leaves in his palm and sprinkling them over a pan.

I thought about allowing Lenz to sit closer, so that we could chat and I could try to wheedle useful things out of him, until I remembered I was being kidnapped in a carriage dripping with soldiers. Suddenly I did not have the energy for such subterfuge. Later. We had a *week*, after all.

"There's a library in here, you know," said Lenz.

"Naturally!" I said.

He indicated a handle on the floor. I knelt, grabbed it, and yanked up as hard as I could, only for the bookshelf to slide up so easily that I fell on my rear. Lenz was good enough to pretend he had seen nothing. The bookshelf came right up out of the floor to my waist: a square column with books on all four sides.

"About half of them are my own volumes," said Lenz. "Just a few slices of my history that are pertinent to those we'll see at the Winter Ball."

I looked up at him: smiling and relaxed, the way someone with power over one's life can afford to be. I wanted to jump up and throttle him. I was sure I could at least kill Lenz before the soldiers got to me.

Sitting on the floor, I gritted my teeth, grabbed a book, and began reading Lenz's extensive secret history of Rotfelsenisch politics—the work that had gotten him in trouble, and also hired. This would, I hoped, give me somewhere to begin when I was trapped in Rotfelsen, producing futures for the Prince. Lenz didn't wonder why I needed to read them because he understood how the Gift worked, and so knew the importance of context.

Context, however, I did not achieve, at least not yet. I began eagerly, for here was a chance to better formulate my "prophecies." But with no points of reference for the major figures, scandals, and battles, it read as a jumble of guttural monikers and meaningless observations.

Reading about the royal family and all attendant nobles was useless— I had no faces to put to names. How was I to know Frederick from Johann-Frederick from Frederick-Johann in a pinch, when all were names on paper, and all heirs to the Dukedom of the Blue Fields, of which I had never heard? The current, ailing Duke was Hans-Robler XII, not to be confused with Robler-Hans IV, Viscount of the Web Tunnels, who had been mentioned twenty pages earlier as a minor leader of the South Cave Separatists, who had attempted to split off from Rotfelsen entirely.

Every person, place, political idea, or event I did not know had to be further researched, and within its definition—if one was even provided—I would find more I did not know. The words all made sense on their own, but together it was a jumble of strangers doing things to each other that I did not understand.

I gave up and slammed one of Lenz's volumes shut in frustration. These idiots would all be dead soon anyway. He sighed and told me that if I wanted something else to pass the time, there were other works, which he had not written.

I had initially learned to read all my languages through unfulfilled contracts, vicious edicts, and wanted posters. (In my teen years, one such poster, covered in the globes and loops of Skydašiavos, claimed that my presence had "soured almond milk and twisted the beanstalks of unmarried young men like sourdough pretzels.") But the only time before my trip with Lenz that I had *enjoyed* reading had been in my fifteenth year, when Papa caught a pneumonia so bad that we spent a week with a doctor. I hemorrhaged silver that week but refused to leave his side, and so spent his sleeping hours reading medical texts. It helped me learn where to cut people.

So, now that I had nothing to do, I would try to learn more. I looked at what else Lenz had in his little library: *The Fundamentals of Historical Ethics as Told Through the Failures of the Pre-Tetrarchic Eras*, *The Cleaving Battle of Selju Cliffs*, *Half-Fabulous Creatures of Misted Places*, *Loashti Diplomacy*, *Goëmann's Honey Conspiracy*, *The Skydašian Tower of Nine-Toed Feet*, and on and on and on. There were some whose titles were in archaic forms of Rotfelsenisch beyond my understanding.

I chose *Bohdan's Botanicals*, second edition, because I hoped to learn how to poison my captor. The title *Bohdan's Botanicals* was alliterative in Rotfelsenisch, but not in the original Masovskani from which it had been translated. The words of each page's descriptions wrapped themselves about a desiccated flower, leaf, or stem pressed onto the page. It must have been a terribly expensive book to produce. Many times, the guide's informative prose broke down amidst invective against "the Skydašian bandit-naturalist Adomas."

I searched and searched that book for a harmful flower to crumble into Lenz's tea. Unfortunately, every hallucinatory candleflower, itchy dogwhisker, and purple poison rotprick was divested of its poisonous innards before pressing. The prose excitedly promised this on every page. I wonder if the first edition had caused poor Bohdan a lawsuit. I hope he stayed out of Gniezto.

THE COUNCIL OF BARBARIANS

By the third day of our trip, Lenz had formed strong opinions about how little preparatory reading I'd done. So he told me why the Winter Ball was so very important, hoping that this would convince me to pick up his histories again. I had not only avoided them because they were mystifying: reading those books began to feel like a capitulation to the desires of my jailer. I knew that if I was to survive this Winter Ball, I would need to learn something ahead of time, but I continued to tell myself I would get to it *later* in our trip.

The Winter Ball this year was when the King would begin to entertain delegations from the other three kingdoms of the Tetrarchia, as well as his own, in early preparation for the Council of Barbarians. The Council's existence was a fact of life in the Tetrarchia, but I must remember that someone reading this may well be from anywhere else, so I will explain.

Every year at the dawn of spring, provided there were no succession crises in process, the monarchs of the four Tetrarchic states—Rotfelsen, Masovska, Quruscan, Skydašiai—would meet in one of their capitals to discuss the running of our lumbering, unwieldy monster of a country. This was officially known as The Divine Monarchic Council of Pure Blessed Blood for the Furtherance of the Greater Eastern Tetrarchia as a Bulwark to its Devious Neighbors and a Net Spread to Catch the Dropped Blessings of Its Gods.

"Council of Barbarians" started as a tongue-in-cheek title, used behind closed doors by drunken clerks and ministers. It came out of the fact that, at the Tetrarchia's advent, each of its states officially saw its neighbors as, well, barbarians. So when all those retainers and delegates and clerks and ministers drank together, they were tickled to find that they all used different words for the same thing. Well, tickled when they were not fighting. Naturally, each Tetrarchic state *still* sees its neighbors as barbarians, but not as a matter of policy, and the names are subtler.

In those shaky days of the first councils, the kings and ministers who took part were so quick to threaten abdication or war, so eager to stab one another in the back (literally, I mean), that they were, by any metric, barbarous. But the name "Council of Barbarians," which had originally been whispered (and drunkenly shouted) in secret, began to wriggle its way toward acceptance. By a hundred years into the Tetrarchic Experiment, it was being inscribed on everything but the most official papers, and being said everywhere but the Opening Invocation. By this time, the proceedings had become less violent than pettily bureaucratic, and even the monarchs enjoyed the short and playful name.

So, once a year, as winter faded and spring crept in, the Council of Barbarians would meet in a capital—Skydašiai, Masovska, Quruscan, Rotfelsen, Skydašiai, and so forth, in that order—to discuss matters of state. About infighting and drunken clerks, I have a working knowledge, but if you wish to learn statecraft, you will have to look elsewhere.

I doubt it will surprise you to know that the Council of Barbarians was scheduled to meet in Rotfelsen just *three months* from the day my father had his vision. Specifically, his *very* clear vision of the Tetrarchia's end, which he had then said would happen in "three months."

FÁNTUTAZH LAKE

Soon enough, the forest we were passing through was thicker even than the one Down Valley Way. The rumbling of our metal terror scared the wolves, tree cats, and hoopoes away, so all I saw through the bars of my window was a wall of trees and occasional beams of sunlight.

When a sad, desperate group of bandits, or separatists, or loyalists, or whatever they were emerged from the trees to waylay our carriage, the harquebusiers handled them so swiftly that Lenz did not even look up. I watched their starved bodies disappear behind us, and wondered what fickle gods had put me in this monstrous, armored luxury carriage, rather than out there with them.

But then, perhaps they were lucky. I still did not know what exactly was coming, but perhaps being shot quickly in a forest was better than whatever I would have to deal with. Better than the terror of collapse, the uncertainty of invasion, the bleak drudgery of prison camps, the pain of forced marches. After all, *they* had died knowing the Tetrarchia was a thing that existed, and would continue to exist—for all the comfort this thought may have brought them.

"Isn't it nice to have soldiers to do the fighting?" asked Lenz, a bit after the encounter. "This is how it will be, from now on, Kalyna: I'll read the past, and you the future, while we sit comfortably far from the dangers we see."

Remembering, just now, that Lenz said this has caused me to suffer a fit of laughter.

There were, of course, breaks in that Masovskan forest, and near the halfway point of our journey, we passed Fántutazh Lake. At the inn by its shore, I received a cask of piping hot fish stew, the taste of which I wish I remembered better. Trees don't grow a mile from the lake in all directions, although no one knows quite why. There is a theory that the Ancients over-planted and mined the land until it was near barren. I read this as a quick background note in Lenz's exhaustive history, which I was now attempting to tackle by starting on the strangest tangents I could find.

Fántutazh Lake itself is immense, and shaped like a horseshoe. I knew, from a previous visit, that the city hall sat in its interior bend, where water protected it on three sides. That is the one place in Fántutazh where trees grow on land. There are also the sinuous, flexible trees that grow right up from the water and dot the lake.

When I was younger, a boy showed me how young lakefolk swam out to those lake trees, perched in them, and caught, with darts and nets, those fish that eat only the moss that grows at the base of such trees. The boy told me that when one became too heavy to sit in a lake tree without it bending down to the water, leaves skimming the surface, then one was considered a full adult, ready to hunt other sorts of fish. Larger and more robust fish, but less tender. Such adulthood comes late there, but when it does, they grow quite stout indeed. He was not yet stout, and had the most lithe legs I had ever seen, like a statue from the Ruinous Temple. I would have stayed up in the tree with him more often, had my father's wails not carried easily across the surface of the lake. I was so embarrassed by his pain, back then.

As I passed the lake in my carriage-prison, an adult with no time for lithe legs and treetop whispers, I wondered if the boy was still somewhere on Fántutazh Lake, too heavy for the trees now, floating in a boat past fluffy, paddling grebes with minnows in their beaks. Or perhaps he was in one of those huts, each one wafting lazy notes from stringed instruments, with a similarly stout wife, raising children who scrambled out into the trees.

BORDER LANGUAGES

Crossing any border that isn't an ocean is incremental, even when entering a place as singular and fortressed as Rotfelsen. Populations always change like the layers in a Quru cake, where each is a different flavor, but the syrups seep into one another: the orange syrup inflects both the berry and the lychee layers, while the orange layer itself tastes faintly of tangy berries and sweet lychee. (This comparison did not occur to me at the time, as I had yet only eaten Quru cake of the stale, week-old variety.)

Populations especially melted into one another in a place like the Tetrarchia, where we were all, technically, one happy family and country. The borders between our four kingdoms were wide open even to the most wretched and despised citizen, although it seemed an almost yearly occurrence for some monarch or dignitary—usually a Rotfelsenisch one—to suggest reversing this.

Closing the borders had never yet been managed: the desire of one kingdom or ethnic group to seal themselves off from the outside world, to bask in their sameness, seemed unable to survive the needs of capital. Merchants liked being able to travel from kingdom to kingdom, and they would not allow too much paperwork or nationalism to get in their way. It seemed that the Tetrarchic Experiment was simply too big to be pushed backward into the realm of ideas, at least by anything less than war and destruction. Utter destruction. Which I expected very soon, at the exact time of the Council of Barbarians.

The last Masovskan inn where Lenz and I changed horses and got fresh food was little different than the first one in Rotfelsen would be. Both Masovskani and Rotfelsenisch could be heard lilting and tumbling, respectively, in through the carriage's barred windows, in a variety of border dialects. When the matron of the inn counted out Lenz's change in little grivnas, her numbering was in another language entirely. It is always in numbers, at outposts, that the last breaths of a language hang in the air.

We did not see Rotfelsen's characteristic red cliffs looming up above us, as I had in past trips to that kingdom, because the forest was simply too thick. Soon our carriage entered a wide tunnel, the mouth of which was hidden by trees, bushes, and guards. Inside the tunnel it was too dark to see the color of the stone, except for a halo around the odd wall-socketed lantern, and we began moving upward. Only one place in the world that I knew of had roads through solid rock.

An hour after entering a tunnel in the thick forests of Masovska, we emerged high on the elevated cliff roads of Rotfelsen, beneath the wide sky, without a tree in sight. Lenz sipped tea and watched huge plateaus of red stone appear out his window, sighing with the wistfulness that comes from returning home. A sensation I have never felt.

I looked up from a volume of Lenz's secret history and decided to say *something*, in order to break his reverie and steal at least a little happiness from him.

"And what does King Lubomir XIII of Masovska think about a guarded Rotfelsenisch tunnel road in his forest?" I asked.

"I expect," he answered, "he thinks about it as intently as you think about the blood moving through your veins."

"Well"—I stretched my arm—"I've been thinking about *that* much more lately, as this injury closes up. The new skin still feels slightly off."

"It will feel normal soon enough. And you're welcome."

"I'm sure it would have healed eventually without flesh-alchemy."

"I meant," he said, finally looking at me, "for saving you from getting killed in Masovska."

I supposed he had. But we were all doomed anyway, so I didn't let it endear him to me.

"Masovskans," he continued, "aren't fond of outsiders."

I laughed unhappily. "That is audacious, coming from a Rot. I have not yet found a people that *is* fond of outsiders, although your kingdom may be the worst." I sipped my own tea, and made my own show of looking out the window. "Anyway, I am Masovskan."

"How do you mean?" He did not ask it like a cagey spy, more like a student fascinated by his subject.

I smiled because here was proof he did not know everything about me. "Well, I was born in Masovska and my name is Masovskan. What more do you need?"

"You don't look it."

"Of course not."

"You look . . ."

"Foreign?" I looked back at him. Training my gaze directly on his. "That is as much my birthright as the Gift. My family are wanderers by necessity, and we have been everywhere. In my family, each child's name is appropriate to the land of its birth. How else to name ourselves? It has always been so, since even the families who rule the Tetrarchia were nobodies squabbling over long-forgotten city-states. Long before that, even. By purest coincidence, my father was also Masovska-born, hence Aljosa."

"Your grandmother must have been born somewhere in Quruscan. Vüsala, yes?"

So much for reveling in Lenz's ignorance. Grandmother liked strangers even less than she liked me; how had he learned her name? But then, I was no stranger to paying informants. Lenz may have even learned about me from Ramunas, although I preferred to think better of the Skydašian advocate than that.

"So then you aren't really . . ."

"I am as Masovskan as I am anything. And I am *everything*."

"Is that so?"

"My nose is too hooked for Rotfelsen, my eyes too narrow for Masovska, my hair too curly for Quruscan, with a bronzy redness only seen in our Loashti neighbors, and my skin too dark for roughly half of Skydašiai. I have got something from everywhere and I am exotic to all. It is useful for business, and also for being dragged out by a mob to be throttled. Throttled first, if I'm lucky."

"Well, that won't happen here."

"I have heaved my father onto my back and fled your fine land before."

"Isn't it your land, too?"

"Of course. The whole Tetrarchia is my people, and I am also a foreigner here."

"Sounds inconvenient."

"Yes. Especially when it gets me kidnapped and forced to read dry histories."

"'Dry'?" he cried, with mock insult, which I suspect was covering up real insult.

"Is there anyone," I said, holding up the book, "in this volume that you, or the Prince, think I should particularly keep an eye out for?"

"I don't want to prejudice you. Have your context, and we'll see what you . . . *see* when you're in the palace."

I decided to smile at him in answer. Not a big smile, just enough to let him think I was being a good student. Then I went back to reading about the many suitors of someone named Edeltraud von Edeltraud.

Soon after, we rolled up to that first Rotfelsenisch inn, which *was* just like the last Masovskan one, except that it sat atop a high cliff of red rock. Next to it was a little outpost changing bank (owned, I learned later, by the Gustavus siblings) where we traded in Masovskan grivnas for Rotfelsenisch gold marks stamped with the smooth, expressionless face of Rotfelsen's King Gerhold VIII. I was well and truly trapped now.

ROTFELSENISCH GEOGRAPHY

In the last days of our trip, the carriage dipped in and out of tunnels in the rock many times, sometimes for intervals of only a few minutes.

The kingdom of Rotfelsen was contained almost entirely within and upon its great red cliffs. It was, mostly, one huge piece of red rock, as though the gods had made an island for the guttural, pink people but mistakenly dropped it onto a continent instead of in the sea. There was no sign of impact in the surrounding dirt, but jutting up out of the ground was a bulging, many-sided, multispired rock of tiered cliffs the size of a small kingdom. A rock that *was* a small kingdom, with a verticality that made it larger and more populous than its length from end to end would suggest. Some towns were entirely enclosed, while others were entirely on the surface. Most, and major cities particularly, were both. There were a few small tracts of dirt (primarily farmland) beyond the rock that were claimed by the kingdom's borders, and most Rots acted as though the people living *there* were the strange ones.

No one in Rotfelsen seemed to find their way of living odd: the feeling in the rest of the Tetrarchia was that the Rots must spend all their time, every day, telling each other it was all perfectly normal. (At least I have the humility to know that my upbringing was abnormal.) Rotfelsen was still very much part of the Tetrarchia, taking part in trade, and even immigration, throughout the larger country, but it also felt the most apart from the rest of us. And, for the Tetrarchia, that was saying something.

Of course, the Rots also lived in a giant fortress, which may have helped create and sustain the kingdom's insular nature. Conquering a mass of rock webbed with towns and tunnels is hard work, even if those towns and tunnels could also become furnaces. In fact, a number of entirely enclosed Rotfelsenisch towns had cave walls still blackened by fires from Skydašiai's most earnest attempt at conquest in the days before the Tetrarchia. Such scorch marks were often preserved intentionally as proof that invasions had failed, and as reminders to distrust Skydašians.

However, these days such threats supposedly came from the Bandit States to the south: always a popular topic of conversation because they were scary, but not *as* scary as Loasht. This insulting name represented a group of small nations that shared some linguistic and cultural forebears, but were otherwise unrelated. Some people from some of these states had histories of raiding Rotfelsen and Masovska, and of attacking trade convoys, and so the name Bandit States was born. Where their governments ended and local criminals began was often blurred from the Tetrarchic point of view, as was the role of our own history of attacks upon them.

Conventional wisdom told us that Bandit States' raids never got into Rotfelsen's actual rock anymore, thanks to the kingdom's courageous and powerful High General. Certainly, sometimes they would maraud at the southern border, pillaging those Rotfelsenisch farms and villages unfortunate to exist on normal land outside the rock. In those cases, the High General's army would sweep out and burn some of *their* villages as a matter of course, but they never stayed to protect their people on those dirt outposts. (And whether they would even burn the villages of the "correct" Bandit State is up for debate.)

The singular variety of stone making up the kingdom, which was red but not porous or volcanic, had been named, simply enough, rotrock. Would this great stone shatter in the spring, or had Papa's talk of "shattered remains" been metaphor? Since it was to happen at the same time as the Council, I leaned toward the cause being war or political unrest, but in that case, how would the entire kingdom of Rotfelsen simply . . . break?

The villages within the rock had gardens of cave plants that I could not see very well, often surrounding whole lively town squares that seemed to exist only within the light of torches. I would catch flickers of people living their lives, arguing, laughing, buying groceries, completely within some great cave strewn with stalactites. Then, every time we rolled out onto the surface, in the open, I saw green patches, some nearby and some on sections of rotrock thousands of feet below us. There were, of course, no great farms nor fields on the rock, but Rotfelsen was full of imported fruits and vegetables that could be grown in pots of imported dirt. There were also great numbers of ornamental gardens, full of flowers and ginkgoes and other plants that could only exist there through trade with the outside world.

The strange feeling of traveling through Rotfelsen is that of being within subterranean caverns while knowing yourself to be far above the *actual* ground. The tunnels through which we passed varied as much as any roads do. Some were wide, some barely big enough for the monstrous carriage (at one time, a poor merchant had to back up for a good hour to the far end of the tunnel so we could pass: the harquebusiers were apologetic, but firm), some were public and some private. Most were natural tunnels, caves, and cracks, expanded to a width appropriate for carriages, while others had been carved out entirely by exhausted human beings. In every tunnel, lamps were hung and still burned, making iron and copper deposits, which were sometimes in the process of being mined, glimmer on the walls like lines of saliva. Rotfelsen's wealth was in its stones and metals.

From past trips, when I was not escorted along the King's own routes, I remembered many dark, disrepaired tunnels that threatened to fall in at every moment. My family sometimes lived in them for weeks, in total darkness, to avoid being murdered. We did not work in Rotfelsen often once I took over the business—how do you con a person whose thinking you cannot understand?

A MILLION LITTLE FEET

On our last day of travel, the Great Field felt very far away indeed. We passed through our final tunnel, which had so many torches as to feel like a Skydašian midday, and which would deposit us at Rotfelsen's palace grounds, above the capital city of Turmenbach. I had never been to that city before, and wondered whether its people resented the royals above them—whether the secret tunnels we traveled existed in order to avoid seeing the lower classes at all.

Then I wondered how I would ever escape this place. Perhaps by jumping off the edge of the kingdom.

"I understand Turmenbach is quite big," I said. "There must be fortunetellers and mystics here. Why didn't you kidnap any of *them*?"

"We looked into it. They were all frauds."

"How did you know?"

"They didn't recognize the Prince after a little spirit gum, and had . . . unfitting futures for him."

I cocked my head to the side and looked at him. I forced a hint of smile, both to disarm, and to hide a dull fear in my gut of such tricks being played on me.

"But I was spared this indignity?" I asked. "Or are *you* actually the Prince? I have never seen the Prince of Rotfelsen before, so I don't know how I'd be expected to—"

He laughed. "No, Kalyna, I am not the Prince. Unlike our local frauds, you already had a reputation."

I thought of Eight-Toed Gustaw from Down Valley Way telling his friends about my family. I hoped he was living it up, maybe in a quick, sporty little carriage, wearing a ring on every finger.

"And," Lenz continued, "unlike them, you don't promise *everything*. Futures, pasts, demons from the hells, control over unborn grandchildren, communion with gods, conversation with ancestors, and so forth."

I laughed. "Your Rotfelsenisch frauds sound very presumptuous. And your people sound deeply gullible."

I went back to trying to read one of Lenz's books, while wondering what tricks he or his Prince might have in store for me. Outside, travelers were yelling as they passed one another. In that echoing tunnel, I couldn't tell which yells were friendly and which were threatening. I tried to imagine life when *every* yell, every raised voice, is echoed and echoed and echoed. It sounded like a nightmare.

After a bit, Lenz stood up and hunched over near my window.

"Kalyna," he said, "I want to show you something that isn't in any of the books here."

"Is it more rock?"

"Well, yes. The walls of this tunnel are very smooth, aren't they?"

I peered out the window. The tunnel walls were indeed unbelievably smooth, like polished marble or the unbreakable stone pillars of the Ancients. The tunnel was so well-lit that I saw mineral deposits snake through the smooth surface.

"Very impressive. Thanks to the fussiness of a past king? So intent on perfection that he also forbade mining the ore?"

Lenz shook his head. "This is not man-made. There *is* a law against mining here, that much is true, but it is to preserve the evidence."

"Of?"

"Creatures."

"That is very scary and unclear."

"Go up into the turret and take a look at the tunnel's ceiling. It's just as smooth, despite how difficult that would be for humans to carve effectively. It's a very high ceiling."

"In Masovska, they have these things called ladders that—"

"If you can see the ceiling's center, you will notice a further indent running the full length. That's from the ridge of the thing's spine."

I must have looked skeptical.

"This tunnel was fully formed deep in the rotrock when humans discovered it long ago, burrowed by some sort of creature. There are more throughout Rotfelsen: all the same size, with the same spinal indent at the top. Old texts say that, before these tunnels got carved up by a thousand carriage wheels, the floors carried the indents of a million little feet, each no larger than your index finger."

"You just like for me to know how smart you are, don't you? How many facts you amassed while others did their jobs and had lovers."

"I think it's interesting," he said with a shrug.

"Fine." I set down my book and moved toward the ladder. "Is this part of some lesson? A way to teach me how little I know, or what danger I'm in?"

"I just think it's interesting."

I climbed into the turret, and I saw exactly what he had described. The indent from some great thing's spinal ridge stretching off down the tunnel in both directions. I thought again about the possibility of Rotfelsen literally shattering. From within, this time.

The Sunset Palace

Somewhere in that tunnel I fell asleep, and dreamed of my father. It may surprise you to know that in those days, I did not dream of him often. The details don't matter, but he told me I had the Gift, and then I saw the Tetrarchia destroyed.

I was awakened by a harquebusier wrenching open the wrought iron door to the armored carriage. I blinked and remembered the carnage of my dream, knowing it to be the first bleeding of prophecy through the cracks in whatever dam had kept me useless and untalented. I felt Papa's words—that I had the Gift—deep in my chest. I did not feel sad about the violence that would come, only happy that the Gift was in me after all.

Once I sat up and the dream began to fade, I knew this was not so. It was not *prophecy* to envision what my father had already told me. Reality returned and I fought off the lingering joy.

I woke fully, and saw Lenz standing patiently outside the carriage door, sunlight shooting through the spires of his mussed hair. Somewhere, a bird chirped.

I stepped out onto a windy plateau, surrounded by armed soldiers who watched me closely. The very tired and dirty harquebusiers who had traveled with us were relieved by a small group of fresh soldiers in yellow: these carried swords, not harquebuses, and included a few women in their rank, unlike the harquebusiers.

We were up on the surface of Rotfelsen, with great gardens and manors behind us, and a clear blue sky stretching above us in all directions. Many of the buildings up here were built out of exported wood or non-rotrock stone. Those that were cut directly from the rotrock were constructed to mimic the look of regular buildings that had actually been, well, *built*, with grooves in their façades pretending at arches and bricks. I supposed Rotfelsen's government liked to pretend it ruled a kingdom like any other, rather than a maze of tunnels and caves beneath its feet. In front of us, blotting out part of the sky, was a tower hewn from solid rotrock, studded with marble and jade, that cast a long, jagged shadow.

Lenz smiled broadly and pointed up at the tower. "That is the Sunset Palace of the Rotfelsen Kings."

"Naturally."

The Sunset Palace was too old to pretend at being any other kind of castle. In fact, it was likely the oldest home in the entire Tetrarchia that had been continuously in use. Long ago, someone got to the top of Rotfelsen, found a jagged outcropping, and carved it into a fortress. Over the years, its wings were further shaped into one style or another, depending on the fashion of the time, and huge sections of iron, gold, jade, and even marble were pressed into the outer walls here or there. Outcroppings and buildings around its base, too, became smaller satellites in clashing styles.

The result was a formless, jutting, sloppy, gaudy mess. I was struck by just how much it looked as if a giant child had slapped the thing together. It seemed ready to topple under its own weight right off the kingdom it ruled. Which, I supposed, it very likely would. And soon, too. Maybe it would fall so hard that Rotfelsen itself would crack in half? Unlikely, but once I thought about it, the imagery wouldn't leave my head.

We went into that silly thing through a humble servants' entrance, which still had double doors, and hobbled our way up a narrow staircase through deep red walls. As we passed each floor, I would see a mass of windows in haphazard arrangements, many of them cracked. I felt ignored and constantly watched at the same time.

My legs and back ached from a week of sitting, relieved only by storming up and down the length of the carriage, so I didn't mind the exercise. At least, not for the first few flights of stairs. Lenz's soldiers, as always, were thankfully too well-behaved to prod me with their weapons. This did not diminish their threat.

As we trudged up the stairs, a cook's assistant knocked into me as he dashed down, leaping three steps at a time to avoid his superior. The cook herself—identifiable by a tall hat and gold trim on her apron—was red in the face as she screamed and gave chase, throwing bits of cold chicken at him.

"They're in a tizzy," I said, mostly to myself.

"The Winter Ball *is* tonight," Lenz replied.

Tonight. And despite all my reading, I knew so little of its guests. My heart began to speed up and my hands began to shake. Then I turned a corner and saw a Rotfelsenisch soldier in a uniform of rich purple leaning against a balustrade. I heard Lenz inhale sharply through his nose.

The soldier was completely still, a purple smudge against the rotrock wall. His left hand sat on his sword hilt as he watched us closely. One of our soldiers in yellow glared at him, jawbone clenching. The purple one smiled. Our soldiers regarded the one in purple, and the shuttered windows which may have hidden an ambush, until we were a floor above him.

I didn't know what a purple uniform meant: Lenz's books mentioned "the Purples" quite often, but with the assumption that a reader would already know who they were. Then I remembered Lenz's story about the Prince going incognito to *test* local soothsayers. Perhaps I'd get lucky, and he'd reveal my fraud and kill me before I had to deal with the ball and the soldiers and all of that.

I was not comforted. My hands shook, and I got much hotter and sweatier than even climbing that many stairs warranted.

PRINCE FRIEDHELM

So, after too many stairs, I ended up in Prince Friedhelm's office. By the time we got there, I was a swampy mess, which did not stop my teeth from chattering. I eyed the desk and did not see the letter opener from Lenz's story—either because Lenz had advised caution or because the Prince had opened no letters today. Or, perhaps its earlier appearance truly had been a test. What tricks would the Prince pull to test me? Would I meet an impostor Prince and be expected to know it? But I would look ridiculous if I met the real Prince and called him a fake.

Prince Friedhelm's office was as Lenz had described it, but its opulence still astounded me. There were, of course, art and books and exquisite furniture—but even his pens and paper, his collection of pipes, his water glasses, looked terribly expensive. I couldn't always pin down *why* they seemed so, but they did. It was something about their, well . . . comportment.

The far wall, toward which the desk faced, was the largest glass window I had ever seen in my life. It was the entire top two-thirds of the wall—the bottom being the only place in the room where the rotrock of the Sunset Palace was visible. A window that size gave the impression of the outdoors intruding in on the room: the expansive sky and the vistas of jagged and rolling rotrock may as well have been standing next to us. Far beyond those blooming red cliffs, I could see verdant green forests that may have been in Masovska or one of the Bandit States, I was too disoriented to know. I felt that I was flying, or drowning. I felt that the plumes and canyons of rotrock would come devour me. I felt that because I could see them, I *owned* them.

I caught my breath and turned to the wall across from the window, which had a bookshelf that was clearly a secret door, and, unlike Lenz, I found the secret peephole as well. It was behind a bunch of pink flowers in a porcelain vase that had bulls painted on its sides. Virile bulls.

I wondered how many other peepholes there were—for reasons of security more than lechery. A man entered the room with a loud slamming of the door, and walked toward us in such a way as to always leave a line of sight between myself and certain corners or pieces of furniture. I was sure there were sharpshooters hidden everywhere, ready to end me the moment I made a mistake.

This man who had entered the room certainly seemed like the Prince Lenz had described: strangely attractive despite (or because of?) his weak jaw and upturned nose. His attraction was not so simple as the pull of his power—that attracts many people, but has never drawn me. In many situations throughout my life to this point, I had possessed less power than whomever I dealt with.

Or was this *not* the Prince, and therefore powerless? He could have just been a strange man Lenz had described to me as part of a test. Whoever he was, he all but stormed into the room.

"Your Highness," Lenz began, "allow me to introduce Kalyna Aljosanovna the soothsayer."

"Yes, hello," the man said, before pivoting to face Lenz and, without taking a breath: "We have a problem."

"What sort of problem, Your Highness?" Lenz's manner toward the man certainly seemed like that of trusted underling to royalty. But of course, he was a spymaster and, I would hope, a decent actor.

"Another conspiracy against my brother, of course," grunted the man, waving a hand. "But we aren't fumbling about in the dark for petty plots this time, Lenz. They approached me a few days ago, while you were away."

"Who did?"

Lenz had gone from concerned bemusement to intense attention in a moment. This, and the way the man said "my brother" as though it was sour in his mouth, began to convince me that this truly was Prince Friedhelm, and that this crisis was real. Perhaps, if I was very lucky, this new plot against the King had broken their plans to test me.

Yes, lucky, that's what I would call myself.

"Selvosch," the Prince replied. "The oaf. He spends too much time down in the caves and mines, if you ask me. He, or whomever he is working for, seem to think they can put me on the throne." He laughed exactly one time, sharply. "Why, it's *almost* as though the court finds me untrustworthy."

I wondered the obvious question: Why not accept their offer? If he was going to be a figurehead, didn't that neatly let the Prince have the indolence he so craved? His aim, after all, seemed to be remaining free of the duties of running a kingdom. I did not wonder this out loud, and neither did Lenz.

"Selvosch," murmured Lenz. I vaguely remembered the name from my reading. "Did he say anything about whom he was working with?"

"No, no, of course not. He intimated that there were powerful people, and I intimated that I was interested, if they were indeed so powerful. I said he could not have my full support until I knew who his comrades were, and he that I could not know who his comrades are until he had my full support." The Prince wound his hands about as he spoke. "There must be someone very big involved, if they were powerful enough to make our Quarrymaster the one to out himself as a potential traitor to a royal." He grinned mirthlessly and placed a hand on his own chest. "Even if that royal is known for being 'listless,' 'licentious,' and 'irresponsible.' Which is all about half true. I'm sure the Queen is involved."

"I'm sorry, what?" said Lenz.

"The Queen. More than half of my brother's soldiers are loyal to her anyway, for some reason, and—"

"Not that part." Lenz did not seem to realize he had interrupted a Prince. "You *agreed* to take the King's place?"

For the first time since he had entered the room, Prince Friedhelm seemed to be at a loss for words. He even shrugged. "I . . . well, no. But I let him think I was interested."

"You . . ." Lenz drooped his head for a moment, and lifted his hand, as though to clasp it to his forehead. Then he thought better of it and stood straight. "You . . . may have committed treason, Your Highness."

"Well, I didn't say, 'Yes, kill my brother!'" replied the Prince. "I wanted to learn more, and I may have panicked a little. It seemed the best way to get Selvosch to keep talking to me."

"And did he keep talking to you?"

"A bit," said the Prince. "'By the end of the ball,' he told me, 'you had better have chosen a side.' I told him I would be happy to, once I knew who was on which side. Then he just waggled his finger side to side and repeated, 'By the end of the ball,' like the daft thing he is."

"Which is tonight," I heard myself saying.

"Just so," replied the Prince.

Lenz bit his lower lip. "Perhaps," he said, "you should warn your brother."

"He would not listen to me if I did," said the Prince, with great finality. "His *Skydašian* wife is competent, of course. Competent enough to command more than half of his soldiers. I would tell her, if I trusted her."

I cocked my head to the side at that. If the King could get by with so little action, so little competence, why did the Prince want so badly to avoid taking his place?

"The rest of the court," the Prince went on, "all think that I am like my brother: inactive, indolent, a living slab of rotrock. But where he is governed by no impulses at all, they think that I only act toward my own pleasures. Which, in a sense, I do, but at least I can think ahead." He clapped his hands together. "So then, how to keep him alive? Perhaps he can be convinced to spend another week or two at his hunting lodge, down in the depths, and we can break out the Twelfth Recourse?"

"Your Highness," said Lenz, clearly trying to be patient, "why don't you meet the Eleventh Recourse, first? Maybe she can help." He gestured toward me.

Well, that was no pressure at all. I smiled.

"Yes, yes, we've met," grunted the Prince.

Then he turned to face me and, to my surprise, smiled back. I saw then a bit more of how magnetic he could be, when he wanted to. He had gone, with a look, right from acting as though I wasn't there to acting as though I was the center of his world. He almost convinced me of it, except that I was quite used to making others feel the same way. It was as much in the body language as in the smile: open yet conspiratorial, as if shutting out everyone else.

"Kalyna Aljosanovna," he continued, "what will happen at tonight's ball?"

I stalled. "Well, it's hard to say . . ."

"Your foreign Gift works by proximity, yes?"

I nodded.

"Now you've been in the palace. What have you seen of tonight in these walls?"

"My Gift works in proximity to *people*," I corrected, as obsequiously as I could. "Have the guests arrived?"

"Not most, no. But you must see something!"

I tried to smile again, to find some remaining reserve of my duplicitous self, of the part of me that enjoyed the game. This wasn't a test with disguises and great ruses, but if he did not find the answer convincing, I suspected I would be killed, and Papa left in a ditch somewhere. If Papa had not already been left in a ditch somewhere.

I shook thoughts of whether Lenz had told the truth about Papa out of my head, along with anything about the violent end of the Tetrarchia itself. I tried to remember how I had spoken to Eight-Toed Gustaw from Down Valley Way.

"Well, Your Highness," I began, "I've only just arrived in your fine palace. There will be pressing crowds, of course, drunken arguments, duels, that sort of thing."

He raised a skeptical eyebrow.

I curtsied graciously and grasped for something. Anything. I would deal with the consequences tomorrow. I thought of the Prince's clear dislike of the Queen, and how readily he would eat up anything I said against her, but decided those waters were too deep to wade into—until I needed to. Then I thought of the soldier in purple on the staircase. I still did not know who commanded the Purples, but based on Lenz's histories and his reaction at the time, it seemed likely it was someone who did not much get along with the Prince and his Yellows.

"And, well, the Purples are planning *something*, Your Highness. They will be out in force, possibly more than you expect. As I'm new to your land, I admit I don't know what would be 'normal,' but I am seeing quite large numbers of them. And ulterior motives. So, I would suggest keeping your eyes on them."

I hoped that whoever commanded the Purples was not actually a good friend of the Prince's. Friedhelm looked thoughtful. He opened his mouth to speak; I held my breath, and my curtsy.

"Nice to meet you, Kalyna Aljosanovna," he said. "Glad to have you on our side."

I thanked him quietly, and the Prince dismissed us with, "Now, go save my brother!"

It took great restraint to not run out of there. Somewhere behind me, I heard the Prince clicking his tongue and muttering, "Now what will I do with all this spirit gum?"

THE ELEVENTH RECOURSE

We made our way quickly out of the palace, and into a spry little carriage with none of the amenities of the last one. The front was open and the railings that kept us from falling out were carved to look like racing horses. My head swirled with questions: Who ran the Purples? What was our next move? Where could I get something to eat? Where would I sleep if I survived the night? Where were we going right now? Was that how Lenz and the Prince normally interacted? Why didn't the Prince want to be King? Was Papa really on the way to join me and, if so, would I be alive when he got here? Would I meet someone at this ball tonight who would be directly responsible for the disastrous end of the Tetrarchia? Would *I* destroy the Tetrarchia?

There was only the driver, Lenz, two other Yellows, and myself in the carriage. Now, with relative privacy, and in Masovskani, I could ask the question that was burning inside of me the most.

"Eleventh Recourse?" I asked Lenz.

He laughed. "Really, that's what you want to know? Not who Selvosch is or—"

"We'll get to all that. What is this nonsense? I assume you create new 'Recourses' to stay useful, so he doesn't kill you."

"No, no. They are all his genius ideas." Lenz pressed his right hand to his chest, and said with mock-seriousness, "I was the Sixth Recourse."

"So they're all people, then? Strange talents he draws from wherever his fancy leads him?"

"Exactly."

"Who are one through five?"

"A few aren't dead."

"That's not an answer."

He sighed and turned to face me in the cramped carriage. "Our Prince can be a fanciful man, who sees plots against his brother everywhere. But he also is not *wrong*, half of the time. So Friedhelm wants as many solutions hidden away for a rainy day as possible. A researcher was Sixth Recourse, prophecy was Eleventh."

"What's the Twelfth?"

"That's a secret. But please do let me know if you have a vision of it, and how it works out."

I rolled my eyes.

"And," Lenz continued, "lest you think the Prince is unreasonably suspicious, this is far from the first such plot we've uncovered. It's simply the way Rotfelsen has always been! I think our way of living, squirreled away as we are, has led to a lot of interesting thought and contemplation over the years. But it has also led to a lot of strange people sitting in the dark and convincing themselves of the most outlandish things."

"No wonder you kidnapped me. No one would move here by choice."

He ignored me and rubbed his chin thoughtfully. "*This* plot is by far the most daunting yet, if someone as powerful as Selvosch isn't even its most important participant. He's the Lord High Quarrymaster, you see."

"Which means?"

"He masters the quarries."

I did not respond to that. Instead, I leaned forward, hands on my knees, and asked, "Why don't you think your Prince wants the job? Of King, I mean."

"He hasn't told me, outside of what I've already told you. He may think, as I do, that these conspirators would eliminate or lock up their figurehead as soon as possible."

"So that's *these* conspirators. But what about generally? It doesn't sound as though the King is saddled with too many weighty decisions or great responsibilities."

"Prince Friedhelm does not deign to share his reasons."

"Well, if he told you he *did* want to supplant his brother after all, would you help him to do so?"

Lenz was quiet. I stared at him for a moment, but he just looked out the window. I continued to stare at him, hoping to make him uncomfortable.

The two Yellows sitting with us, a man and a woman, did a very good job of not looking surprised, curious, concerned, or anything of the kind. They were both tall, broad-shouldered, and blonde: a very Rotfelsenisch look. The man was leaning forward to watch the road ahead, and the woman was absentmindedly cleaning or sharpening her dagger—absolutely unafraid of a possible bump in the road causing her to lose a finger.

"Kalyna," Lenz finally sighed, "I take no pleasure in imprisoning you, but look around: autumn is so mild up here and our winter will be nothing like Masovska's. You have food, lodgings, and luxuries that your family will share, all while you are paid in gold marks directly from the royal coffers."

"I had no choice in it."

"Did you ever make a choice to be what you were? A roving prophet living a life of mistrust better suited to a charlatan?"

Charlatan.

"My family," I said, "were never meant to be court seers for two simple reasons." I stared fixedly at gardens going by out the window and continued quietly, from memory. "First, it is our duty and burden to give our services to all classes of people; this is how we have thrived since millennia before any kingdoms of the Tetrarchia were founded." It seemed I spoke in my father's voice, from when I was a child perhaps, or from before my birth. I heard his deep, confident resonance shake my inner ears and my jaw. I felt his pride in a job well done, and my own at a job well faked, as though the ghost of the man he had been stood before me.

"Second," I continued, "just as we are the first murdered when things go wrong in a community, the seer is the first executed when things go wrong at court. But escape is easier from one than the other. Slipping out of a town in the night is difficult; escaping a *palace*"—I put up my hands to indicate all around me—"is impossible." I almost said "nearly impossible," but decided to sound more resigned than I was. "This is how we have *survived* since millennia before any of the—"

"Yes, yes, I think I know that part," said Lenz.

I folded my hands in my lap and looked at him.

"Well," he said, "you at least deserve better food and lodgings, and you will have them. Comes with the job."

A more comfortable life, until the Prince got me killed. Or *had* me killed.

"Do not pretend this is for my benefit," I said.

"Never. Your benefit is a symptom." He smiled and leaned forward, lifting his stiff left leg with his hand and grunting as he uncrossed it from his right.

We were done talking, for the moment. The Sunset Palace had gotten at least slightly smaller behind us, and before us were rows of wooden buildings, separated by hedges and gardens. We were taken to one of these, a four-story wooden servant house, surrounded by pleasant gardens and tall walls, blocking all the rest of Rotfelsen's surface except the top of the palace, which still towered above us to the west. It was all very cozy, if wreathed by yellow soldiers. One could have never guessed we were on top of a giant rock full of people.

Lenz ushered me into the servant house, and up the stairs to a chamber on the top floor. No soldiers followed us, for once, but a quick glance out a window showed that they surrounded the building. The room, which I was told was mine, had something of the quaint country home to it, if polluted by ornate luxury; as though this house was where the palace stored its leftover furniture.

A small woman was standing in the corner. She held a handful of string and looked very anxious, tapping her foot pointedly as I walked into the room. When I stopped, she snapped her fingers at me four or five times.

I ignored her and leaned against the wall, crossing my arms like an angry child. Lenz sighed. He did not lean against anything, and I could tell that this was a painful weight on his bad leg. Good. He nodded to the anxious woman, and she scurried over to me. A bird chirped on the windowsill, a pleasant little puffball preparing for winter. Why had birds bothered to fly all the way up here, I wondered. Or had they been imported too? To give the borrowed trees and grass the right ambiance?

"Very nice," I said, to Lenz, who was standing in the doorway. We were still speaking Masovskani. "And when will my father arrive?"

"Maybe another week," he replied. "With your grandmother, too, of course. I did not want them, with their frailties, to be forced to hurry."

"Do you know—" I began, before the woman jammed her hand into my armpit. I glared at her before I could stop myself, but she ignored me anyway. I looked back at Lenz and tried again: "Do you know how cruel it is to make my father go through his nightly fits while I'm not there to help him?"

"Your grandmother—"

I laughed loudly and sharply. The anxious woman, who had been counting under her breath and pressing a long string against my leg, flinched and lost her place. I leaned down and smiled at her, putting a hand lightly on her shoulder. She flinched again.

"I didn't mean to scare you," I said in Rotfelsenisch.

She coughed and went back to measuring and quietly counting.

I tried again: "I notice you're counting in Sugavi." Sugavi had once been the language of the lower eastern sixth or so of Rotfelsen.

She glared up, seemingly mortified, then looked back down to continue counting.

I sighed. "Well, I see you have not put me in a cell," I said to Lenz, back in Masovskani.

"You have free rein of this agreeable little servant house, with its unbarred windows and innocent denizens. The guards will stay outside, mostly."

"And my family?"

"Will be kept rather far away from you, most of the time."

In order to glare at Lenz, I had to look around the anxious woman's head. She was measuring my collarbone, it seemed. If she understood Masovskani, she hid it well. Lenz scratched his unruly hair.

"Will they—" I stopped when the woman wrapped a string around my thigh and nearly yanked me off balance. I almost yelled at her, composed myself, and looked down again, smiling at her and trying Rotfelsenisch again.

"Hello. My name is Kalyna Aljosanovna. What are you doing?"

"She is measuring you, Kalyna," said Lenz, still in Masovskani. "The ball is tonight, remember?"

"Why can't she tell me herself?" I asked, still in Rotfelsenisch.

The tailor coughed loudly.

"Because her job is to measure," Lenz sighed. He had now switched to Skydašiavos—just for fun, I supposed. "Not to chat or listen in. To be discreet, especially when making clothing in a great rush for a mysterious stranger."

"She'll be making a ball gown in a day?" I joined him in Skydašiavos, although I don't know what I was proving.

"A guard's uniform." He smiled. "You will still *be* guarded, and you will not be armed."

"Fine."

"And you will be trained on how to comport yourself."

"Before tonight?"

"Don't slouch, don't hide, don't hurt a noble. Try not to get killed by the other soldiers. There, you've been trained."

"Why will soldiers try to kill me?"

"Did you *actually* read my books?"

"There's a lot in there, Lenz. You should be very proud. Will my family know they are prisoners?"

"I hope not. But they *are* prophets."

"Not professionally," I said. The tailor pulled roughly at my waist.

"Besides"—Lenz loosened, trying to put me at ease, as though he would walk in and clap me on the shoulder any moment now—"they will share a building with our best doctor. You will be glad I came along, eventually. Your father might even improve." He did not actually walk into my room, however, which I appreciated. A little.

I considered what he had said about the "best doctor," but continued to scowl. Sunshine streamed into the room, which was larger than any of our tents. Comparable in size to the carriage Lenz and I had shared, in fact. And this whole room would be mine?

The tailor, who had never said a word beyond whispered Sugavi numbers, stood up straight and nodded curtly.

I still only had Lenz's word that my family were on their way at all. Perhaps they'd been left to freeze, or had their throats slit. A jailer does love to dangle false hopes and then snatch them away—just ask the Quru warden who insisted the accusation of conjuration against me was "being reviewed," every day for a month, when I was twenty-two. (I got a sort of revenge on him eventually.) But now, as much as I loved and worried for my father, I also desperately wanted to wring him for new prophecies.

"Anyway"—Lenz turned slowly away from me on his good leg—"I do have preparations outside of you. Do nothing stupid, Kalyna Aljosanovna. It is beneath you. And besides, there is very nice liquor in the cabinet. Courage juice."

"I thought you wanted me *not* to do anything stupid."

He shrugged and turned to leave. "Tonight, Kalyna," he said in Rotfelsenisch. "I hope you'll be ready."

"You must be as sick of me as I am of you," I said.

Lenz nodded emphatically before limping down the stairs with uneven thuds, followed by the tailor, who looked miserable.

Here is what I thought at that point in my life: people only give each other liquor to make them do things they will regret. I did not open the cabinet.

TURAL

My room in the servant house was the largest I had ever inhabited, and from its windows I could see over the walls to other, similar servant houses. The looming tower of the Sunset Palace, glittering in the sun and always in view, made everything feel very small. I could also see the sprawling manor houses of the nobility, which made a line in front of the palace, defending it like cannon fodder. The palace grounds were essentially their own city, complete with transplanted trees and bushes to line walkways, larger roads for carriages, and soldiers' barracks at the edges, color-coded for each of the four armies of Rotfelsen. But there was a real city, Turmenbach, below it, full of poor people, normal people, the types I'd worked for (and run from) over my life. They lived largely within the rock, not up here in a false garden. How did they view us?

My room had two chairs, a bed, a desk, and a bookshelf. The books were all general sciences, histories, religion, and the like, alongside copied volumes of Lenz's secret history. These last volumes, he assured me, had been cleansed of "the juicy bits," lest a maid get too curious.

I knew well enough that I needed to continue studying royals and nobles and soldiers, and all the other powerful types who would be at the ball: all those people who might want to topple the King. But after a week shut up in that carriage, with Lenz looking so damned *proud* of himself, continuing to study was the last thing I wanted to do. I decided that I would figure it out as I went—I'd always managed before —and chose to explore my new domain and prison. I was sure there would be no secret escape hatches, hidden doors, or unguarded tunnels through the rotrock, but it seemed like a fine idea to check. I could not escape until my father had arrived, but best to have a plan.

I listened at my door to make sure no one was in the hallway. The entire fourth floor of the sunny house seemed quiet. I stepped out and walked slowly, hearing the squeak of my boots, which still carried Masovskan dirt in their crevices. I felt as though I was sneaking through a hostile land, invading a fortress, even though there was nothing *wrong* with simply exploring one's new home. They didn't have to know I wanted to escape their country before everyone died horribly.

Six steps from my door, something appeared in the corner of my eye. I turned to see a man sitting perfectly still in the room next to mine, watching me.

He wore a white smock stained with green and orange, and a black cravat tied lazily at his neck. He had one leg crossed over the other on a high stool, and was sipping from a glass of water. When he saw that I had seen him, he leaned forward, raised a thin black eyebrow, and wound his free hand as if, I thought, to say, "Go on . . ."

I turned to face him, arms flat at my sides, and raised one at the elbow in an awkward wave.

"Hello," I began, "My name—"

"Oh!" he cried. "Ohhhh!" He looked at the ceiling, as if to ask why it had forsaken him, and his shoulders fell.

"—is Kalyna Aljosanovna. Are you hurt?"

"You are new," he said. "You are new. Come in, please. Please. I'm sorry." He waved me into his room.

It was nearly identical to mine, but lived-in. Every surface or cloth was stained with different colors, and on the walls were still life paintings of glistening fruit.

"I am sorry. Sorry," he repeated. "Everyone on this floor keeps quiet when I conjure. I got angry. But you are new, and it's unfair of me besides."

"Conjure? Are you a—"

"A chef. Yes, a chef."

Chef would have been my last guess in the world.

"Of course," I said.

We introduced ourselves to each other. Tural, for that was his name, was a wiry sort, with an intense stare, shining black hair, and a thin mustache. Upon closer inspection, he was younger than he acted, somewhere around thirty-five. He was Quru, as you may have guessed from his name. But if you don't know, Quruscan was the mountainous kingdom in the northeast of our Tetrarchia, which had been historically (somewhat) safe from Loasht due to a lot of very treacherous mountain roads, which the Quru were in no hurry to maintain.

"You live next door?" He pointed to the wall we shared.

"For the moment, yes."

"You work in the palace?"

"Sometimes."

"Ah!" He set down his water and stood, looking knowingly at me. He was almost exactly my height.

"Are you . . ." I asked slowly, "the *Head* Chef of the palace?"

"Head Chef?" Tural laughed. "Who wants to be Head Chef?

"I don't follow."

"Head Chef," said Tural, "is a tanner who is also a cooper and a chandler and a tailor and a blacksmith. Does many things; good at none. *None of them.* Head Chef means living up in the palace, not out here, only being good at sucking up to the royal family." He smiled. "I can be good at that, when I must, but not my job."

"I . . ."

"I am a specialist! The Master of Fruit! Specifically and exclusively." The volume of his voice rose and fell in that Quru way, even as his Rotfelsenisch pronunciation was perfect, if oddly phrased.

The very idea of a cook who worked only with fruit seemed so excessive as to be fundamentally inhuman. I must have looked mystified.

"Do you think this is strange?" asked Tural.

"Well, yes."

He smiled. "Not wrong. But do you know, Kalyna, how many *tons* of food the palace's kitchens produce?"

"I don't."

"Yes. Yes. You are new." There was no judgment in his voice. I felt relieved.

"The Head Chef," he went on, rolling his eyes at his superior's title, "gives guidelines, and it is we beneath him who form these into meals for the lower chefs to create. There is a Master of Breads, a Master of Cakes, a Mistress of Fowl, a Master of Rice, two acrimonious Sub-Masters of Noodles, and so forth."

I almost asked how many of these could be necessary, but then suspected I would be trapped in conversation for hours.

"I," he continued, "know every fruit that grows in the Greater Eastern Tetrarchia, and many from beyond. But it is a lot, so I must conjure."

"Are these food masters normally . . . sorcerers?"

He laughed a strained sort of laugh. "No," he said. "No, no, no. A sorcerer cannot simply 'conjure' fruits from the air. If they could, I would be homeless. No, I . . . Well, you see . . ."

He put a finger on his chin and thought for a moment. Someone stirred in the hall; hearing Tural's voice must have let them know that he was no longer "conjuring."

"Look," he said. "Krantz is the Master of Pork, you see?"

"Yes, I think. Does he also live in this building?"

"What?" Tural was shocked. "No! You cannot make food masters live with one another—they would murder. One feast day, *I* would be the King's pork, you see?"

"Yes."

"No, no, no. Ha. Me to live with . . . ha. No."

"Of course."

"Krantz is the Master of Pork." He held up a thin finger, gesturing at nothing. "If Krantz wishes to see whether a certain pork cooked in a stupid pork way will go nicely with the chard of the Mistress of Leaves, or with the Master of Breads' tangy Skydašian bread, all he—Krantz—must do is kill one of the palace pigs. There are always pigs."

I nodded intently.

"Now. Say the palace is planning, during the winter, for a feast in spring. 'Tural,' they say, 'we want fresh berries with this tart!' Where am I to find the berries that will be fresh in spring when it is winter?"

"You can't."

"Precisely! Even with our alchemy and our hothouses, we cannot grow things so out of season. How am I to know if a tungenberry compote would go with, say, the Master of Cakes' sweet-mushroom cake, or the Mistress of Tarts' spring mint tart? How am I to know that a different berry would not be better?"

"I do not know." At the time, I did not even know the difference between a cake and a tart. Grandmother would have said I was better off that way.

"I must have silence and conjure them," explained Tural. "I must sit very still, cleanse my palate"—he pointed to the water glass by his velvet-slippered foot—"and imagine, unaided by taste, the flavors of the berries, or any other of a hundred, hundred fruits. I simply imagine them, you see—remember. *Conjure* their memory, like you do the smell of an old lover's hair, or the sound of your long-gone grandmother's voice."

If only.

"After all," he continued, "we do not have *berries* living in the stables year-round, grunting and eating slop. I am not some . . . *pork* master."

"But the Winter Ball is tonight. Don't you have your fruit?"

He laughed. "If only those unpacking the Masovska peaches cared as much as you do! But yes, tonight is all sorted, and my underlings are working at it. I have nothing left to do, for tonight. I am planning ahead, for a King's Dinner next week."

"That is very . . . industrious." I reflected upon the fact that I felt entirely unprepared for tonight. "Well, I'm sorry I disturbed you."

He smiled. "You are new. You are new. What are you? I am the Master of Fruit. Also on our floor is the Master of Pillowcases, the Chief Ethicist, the Lavatory Captain, and such. Each high-ranking, but none of us report to royalty, and the menials here serve us. You are similar?"

I tried to hide my shock at the fact that there were people here who would serve *me*. I chose, instead, to look more confident in my new position.

"Well," I said, "I *did* meet the Prince today. But he barely spoke to me."

"Ah! Well, you are no chef, philosopher, or janitor because they know better than to board disciplines together. What are you?"

"An intelligence officer." I had spent a moment imagining how the house and its inhabitants would react to a soothsayer, how many fortunes would be requested, how many chances for exposure there would be. The lie came naturally.

"Ah! Those soldiers—the Yellows—they are to protect you?"

"The ones out front? Yes."

"Protect you from those *within* the palace?"

"Perhaps."

"Ah." He touched the side of his nose, as if indicating secrecy, but then immediately continued: "These palace Rots, they love their intrigues and their paperwork."

"Is that so? I've never been this close to the Sunset Palace before, so I suppose I wouldn't know."

He nodded emphatically. "Oh yes. Intriguing and backstabbing, but everything must be backed up by three manifests signed in triplicate and so-and-so's seal pressed into such-and-such assassination order and so on."

I couldn't tell how much of this was a joke and how much was true. Tural clearly liked talking, and I began to wonder what I could draw out of him. Despite how tired and worried I was, I slipped into a playful bit of attempted charm and leaned in closer. "Assassinations?" I asked. "For the Master of Fruit?"

"What? No! Only Krantz would want me assassinated, and not *really*. I am exaggerating. It's just that, back in Quruscan, people keep to themselves, and trust one another. Rots are too much in each other's business. And fancy themselves too far *out* of the rest of the Tetrarchia's business."

"Do you have trouble here?" I asked him. "You know, being Quru around all these Rots?"

"No, no. Not up here. The court likes to appear cosmopolitan, you see. Although, I admit, I rarely go down into Turmenbach or any other caves. Perhaps that makes me a bad guest, but they scare me. Up here feels better: more like being in the mountains."

"So, you like it here? Even though it isn't Quruscan?"

He grinned. "Well, sometimes Quru keep *too much* out of each other's business, for my taste."

There was the lightest tapping on the doorway behind me. An apologetic maid, standing in stocking feet with her shoes in her hand, stood there.

"Ah, Master Tural, may we . . . ?" She trailed off and motioned her head vaguely toward the rest of the floor.

"Yes! Yes, yes. So sorry," he said. "I'm done for now."

She nodded, smiled, and slipped her shoes back on before clacking away. I supposed the tapping of her shoes as she walked would have disturbed Tural's "conjuring."

"I scare them. I don't mean to," he sighed, looking past me. "They live on the bottom floor and work to serve this house only. We are their masters as the King is ours, and theirs. They never see the inside of the Sunset Palace, and do not realize how unimportant we are."

I coughed and wiggled my eyebrows, nodding in the vague direction of the palace.

"Well, I am. *You* saw the Prince on your first day at the palace." He gave me a pleasantly conspiratorial look, which I returned.

"So, Tural," I began in, I must say, perfect Cöllüknit, "what do you know about who will be at tonight's ball?"

He looked a bit dazedly surprised at my switch to his native tongue, and then became thoughtful. He snapped his fingers. "Kalyna, I can give you an exhaustive list," he began, in Cöllüknit, "of which Rotfelsenisch nobles are allergic to stone fruits. I can tell you which royals, from *all four* kingdoms, mind you, have a sweet tooth, or have an aversion to the smell of citrus, or just don't *like* berries because of how they burst in one's mouth, and so forth. But beyond that . . ." He shrugged.

"Well, I may want a list of who's allergic to what. Later." I winked.

"Oh! I . . . Well, I don't know that I would actually be allowed to . . ." He trailed off.

I laughed and waved my hand at him. "Of course not, Tural! Of course not. Joking."

He seemed relieved and smiled. There was a ball to prepare for, an escape to plan, and who knew what else. I needed to go.

"Thank you," I continued in his language, "for sharing with me your mysteries."

That is what I literally said, but in that language of Quruscan, "mysteries" have a particular meaning. A mystery can be one's trade, one's personal feelings, one's deep religious observances, or any number of other personal things. It acknowledges that a great confidence has been given. Of course, it is generally diluted by casual use, and I meant nothing by it, really, beyond proof that I spoke his language and knew its intricacies.

I could not remember the last time that someone looked so happy to see me. Not my Gift, not a daughter to give comfort nor a young woman to give pleasure, but *me*. Tural smiled widely and waved me good day with a brown hand stained with purple. I did not know what to do with the warmth in my belly. I smiled back with a truly genuine smile, and then left quickly.

I walked to the ground floor of the servant house very slowly, and found no hidden passages or unguarded windows.

JÖRDIS

All my other neighbors, it seemed, were busy preparing their own small domains for the Winter Ball, so I went back to my room. Loath to read yet more of Lenz's serpentine histories, I paced back and forth for an hour. I should have been pondering how to manage the ball itself, because I would have to survive into next week to escape with my father. If he was truly on the way here. Instead, I formulated, and discarded, a hundred different ways to take Lenz hostage, or kill him, during the ball. None were feasible, but all were satisfying to imagine. I was particularly fond of the one that included a long dive down the stairs.

Finally, I got the sinking feeling that I should actually sit down and try to learn more of what was going on in this ridiculous kingdom. A few decent prophecies would, I hoped, please Lenz and keep me alive long enough for my family to arrive (if they were indeed on their way). Begrudgingly, I took one of Lenz's histories off the shelf, and spent some time staring at it, deciding whether to read it, put it back, or tear it apart. I opened it.

Rituo, it read, *is the largest of the Bandit States that directly abut Rotfelsen itself, and as such, it is the one with which we have the most history, good and bad. When things are good between us, Rotfelsenisch officials pretend they don't see all of the Bandit States as one great mass with no differentiations. When things are bad between us and Rituo, we conduct massacres, and not only in Rituo. The Tetrarchic mind is too caught up in itself and Loasht to ever be capable of imagining interrelated, yet independent, small countries.*

I knew that I should move to something more apt for tonight, but those cascades of Rotfelsenisch names were so impenetrable. I yawned and flipped a few pages to read more about the loose conglomeration of city-states to the south.

Skoagen is probably the largest of all the Bandit States. It has been the largest, as far as we can tell, for the past ten years, as they consistently bend, break, twist, split, and absorb. We know very little of the place—the last time High General Dreher and his army penetrated that far, on a punitive mission, Skoagen's people seemed to melt away from us into hills and caves.

There are some officers in our army who, when no one of import is listening, suggest that the recent spate of attacks by smaller Bandit States are somehow orchestrated by Skoagen's leaders. This, though the Bandit States have *never* managed to work together before, is—

I was interrupted by a knock, and opened the door to see a maid. The sun was beginning to set outside, and my room had turned bright red. The light hit the expanses of rotrock and bent around the Sunset Palace, which was named that for a reason, before it got to us. When did balls normally begin? Were people already on their way in? Was I late?

"Master Felsknecht," the maid began, "has requested that you take your tea in your room."

Requested indeed. He wanted me to continue all that studying of his brilliant life's work. So I sat at my desk as I was served, and picked at food I didn't notice, while drinking tea and pointedly reading nothing. The maid left the door open.

It began to occur to me that, in the eyes of Selvosch, the Quarry-master who had approached Prince Friedhelm, and his plotters, I was on Lenz's side, no matter how many fantasies of his death I entertained. Was I being watched by Lenz's soldiers? Was I being watched by his adversaries? Could I trust even the butlers and maids in our servant house? I was not used to having so many people around me at all times, even while I had so much space to myself.

I spat out the bite of food I had just taken, as though it would save me from poison.

"That bad?" asked a Rotfelsenisch voice from my doorway. I jumped in my chair, and snorted loudly.

I saw a short, round woman with a pile of blonde braids atop her head, in impeccable imitation of a local peasant girl style. Maybe it was just the early sunset, but she was positively rosy cheeked.

"No, I choked," I said as I stood. "Kalyna Aljosanovna." I wondered if I should extend a hand, or curtsy, or cross my arms over my chest, or . . .

She scuttled up to me and bowed at the most precise angle I'd ever seen.

"A pleasure," she said. "Jördis Jagloben, Chief Ethicist serving beneath His Brightness Otto Vorosknecht, Court Philosopher of Rotfelsen. Pleased to meet you, Kalyna Aljosanovna. I'm your neighbor!" She pointed to my wall.

It occurred to me that the Master of Fruit was wiry and severe, and the Chief Ethicist playful with a libertine's figure. Palatial Rotfelsen was strange indeed.

"You have a beautiful name," she continued, "although you don't look Masovskan."

"I . . . Thank you?"

She smiled broadly. "I'm sorry, Kalyna Aljosanovna, was that rude? I think it was." Jördis dropped her courteous demeanor and put a hand on her hip. "That's why I do ethics, not etiquette."

"Ah."

Even in her casual stance, she turned, perfect as gearwork, to look around my room. "And speaking of etiquette, the rest of the house was having tea together. A last sendoff to get good and full of tea mania before the Winter Ball begins."

"Yes, sorry. Work." I waved at the half-eaten food and closed book on my desk.

"Indeed. You work for the tall one who was here earlier, with the mustache and the limp, yes?"

"I do, yes. Lenz." I immediately wondered if I should not have given his name. Well, if he was trying to be secretive, he should have told me so.

"You're a Yellow, then! I suppose that makes me a Purple." She pointed her finger at me and wound her wrist in a circle in imitation of a rapier maneuver, before jabbing forward toward my stomach. "Better watch out or I'll *get you*." She laughed heartily.

"Yes," I said.

I was still not sure who the Purples even were, but I had already implicated them to Lenz and the Prince. Were they soldiers of *ethics*? That couldn't be right. Had I branded this perfectly nice woman a traitor without thinking?

"So, what *are* you two?" she asked.

"Intelligence officers."

"Is that the same as a spy?" She was acting very excited about the whole thing. Too excited, in my opinion at the time. But then, I didn't much take to excitement.

"Much duller," I replied. I returned her smile, although with perhaps a quarter of the intensity. I got the impression that Jördis was working very *hard* to be so smiley and friendly, and felt that she might react well to a calmer conversation partner. I pretended that I was at ease.

"A pity," she replied.

"You seem disappointed that nothing untoward or dangerous is happening here."

"A touch, perhaps. It seems this house is full of dull subjects."

"Well," I began, pointing to the other wall, "Tural is—"

"Oh, Tural isn't dull, but his *subject* is. He just manages to be decent despite it. But devoting your whole life to fruit is almost as boring as doing so to ethics."

I truly wasn't sure how to respond to that, so I chose to change the subject slightly. "Jördis," I began, putting on a look of worry, which I didn't particularly have to fake, "you said before that you're a Purple, yes?"

She rolled her eyes and made a big show of deflating. "Yes, I suppose I am. I can leave now, if you'd like."

"No, no!" I laughed. "What I'm trying to arrive at is, well, that I'm new here, and I am not entirely sure what that *means*."

Jördis was quiet for a moment, her brows furrowed, and then smiled again. "You really *aren't* a spy, are you? If you don't even know that?"

I nodded and hoped I did not look entirely too stupid.

"Well, the Purples are the soldiers of my . . ."—the next word seemed to sicken in her mouth—"*boss*, the Court Philosopher."

I suppose I should have looked more knowledgeable, appeared more aware of what was going on in this kingdom where I was now practicing intrigue. But I couldn't help being surprised to hear that the Court Philosopher had an *army*. This must have shown in my face.

"Rotfelsen's philosophies need their defenders as much as the King, the Prince, and our borders do, I suppose," Jördis explained. "Or so it's said. Many Purples are simply soldiers for the gold marks, but quite a few really believe."

"Believe what?" I asked.

She opened her mouth and made a strange noise for awhile, which eventually crescendoed into, "Look, we'll be here all night if I get into that. Kalyna, it was a wonder to meet you. And so nice to see this room in use again after the *incident* with the Butler of Anointing Oils for Lesser Nobles."

I never did learn what this "incident" was. Some spy I was.

I continued not studying. My position at the moment was as mortifying as *everything else* that had beset me recently. The death of our horse, the mercenaries of the Gustavus brats (was my Gustaw still alive?), the benign tyranny of Lenz and his master, a philosopher's army, and now . . . Planning for tonight while upholding a half-formed false identity (non-soothsayer) that was itself covering a false identity (soothsayer). Not to mention the fall of the entire Tetrarchia.

I had none of the giddy enjoyment of a confident, well-prepared lie fluttering through my innards. I couldn't even enjoy my spacious new home.

ONE OF THE YELLOWS

It was almost entirely dark when Lenz returned, with the tailor and my hastily altered guard's uniform. As I have mentioned, the expectations placed upon women changed considerably throughout the Tetrarchia, while remaining frustratingly similar in certain ways. In

Skydašiai, for example, about half of all violent and physical jobs—soldiers, handler-mages, blacksmiths, so forth—were held by women, but this was not the case anywhere else in the Tetrarchia. In Rotfelsen, women could have a number of professional roles, such as a tailor or a doctor—so long as they were decently deferential to their male peers—and there were a good number of women soldiers, which meant I would not look implausible at the Winter Ball, outside of my supposed foreignness. But in all of the Tetrarchia, to whatever extent women were allowed to work at "manly" occupations, it had to be accompanied by a masculine bearing, or wardrobe. Being a man was seen as something to *aspire* to.

Even I, growing up in my strange, nomadic family—a family that put stock in no mores that did not directly serve us—found myself thinking this way at times. And so, my Yellow uniform made me feel powerful. It had brown leather trousers and sleeves, with a red sash across the chest, while the doublet, hat, gloves, and cape were the yellow of a daffodil. This marked me as one of the Prince's Guard, though there was no loop for a sword on my belt, hindering my ability to *guard*. The doublet was wool, cut exactly to my figure like nothing I had ever before owned. Having something fit me so perfectly was a bit intoxicating.

I felt a thrill go through me when I learned that the tailor would also be dropping off more clothing cut perfectly to me in the next week or so.

I went downstairs alone, adjusting my gloves and feeling very dashing. I daresay the color of the uniform was more flattering on me than on those pink Rots. Then I saw another Yellow and my confidence evaporated. Lenz had told me they would stay *outside* of my new home, but this one was sitting on a stool in the servant house's kitchen.

When my footsteps stopped, the Yellow slowly turned her head to look at me. The look on her face was thoughtful, intense. I had seen this soldier before, when Lenz and I took a small carriage from the Sunset Palace to my new home, only a few hours before—she had been playing with her dagger. She was darkly blonde, tall, and lean, tapering down from broad shoulders. Sitting as she was now, she seemed entirely at ease in her uniform with a weapon at her side, in a way that suggested she could move from leisure to violence in a heartbeat. Her mouth was shut tightly, and she looked at me in a way I took to be cold, appraising. She was quite terrifying and compelling. In front of her, on the kitchen counter, was a plate with a torn apart loaf of crusty brown bread and a pat of butter.

"Are you—" My voice went too high, and I cleared my throat. I tried again. "Are you here to take me to the ball?"

She nodded.

"Great. Well. Let's go. What's your name?"

She garbled out something that sounded like "Dugmush" through a mouthful of bread and butter.

She had not been, just now, particularly thoughtful, or appraising: she had simply been trying to chew. I was sure her name was not actually "Dugmush," but I was now too embarrassed to ask again.

She swallowed her bread and winked at me. "Don't you look sharp?"

I felt myself flush slightly. She was my guard, ready to commit violence to keep me from escaping, and yet I preened at the compliment. A base fear of her mingled with a desire to have her self-assurance, particularly while we wore the same uniform.

"Off we go!" she said.

I was then whisked off to the Sunset Palace under the close watch of real soldiers. It was time for the Winter Ball.

PARTIES

I found the Winter Ball to be disgusting.

Everything was draped in jewels, carved with the faces of past royalty, circled by ice sculptures to suggest a "winter" that had barely hit Rotfelsen. Men and women sweating into silks and furs discussed skirmishes and marriages and taxes and land-grabs, while scarfing the most carefully prepared food and getting very drunk. But none of this excess, these things I could never possess, were what disgusted me; at least, not directly. What disgusted me was that everyone there had friends, acquaintances, spouses, lovers, the freedom to gossip without being murdered, to rut without much worrying how a child would tie them down. They could have a drink or two because guards and civilization meant they were not always in danger, and they could eat because they knew the food would not run out by tomorrow morning.

Of course, this safety was an illusion, even without the destruction that was coming for the Tetrarchia. Perhaps the Turmenbach masses would rise up and crush them: this was an end to the Tetrarchia I found more palatable. Yet, imagining these thoughtless nobles as starving refugees in the coming months, preyed upon in the Bandit States, did not make me feel much better.

The first time I ever drank alcohol had also been the last time (until later that night). I had been fifteen, and a pretty girl in a Skydašian village offered me a sip of her father's liquor. I laughed, stumbled, fell.

I woke up in pig shit, at the back of a barn on a side of town I did not know. When I found my way back to my family's camp, Papa was babbling. Grandmother cursed me and beat me with a belt, and then a stick, for leaving my father to be tormented by the girl and her friends. They had thrown rocks at him from afar, and with each impact he had apologized. When I, covered in offal and bleeding, held him, he cried for my mother, Dilara.

When I saw those nobles guzzling spirits, laughing, plopping red-faced onto fainting couches, I envied them their leisure, and the freedom of their stupidity.

THE WINTER BALL

Oh yes, the ball.

I, idiot that I was (and mostly still am), had assumed a great, royal ball would take place on the ground floor of the palace. It would be easy for guests to find the party and, as the buttressed entry hall was the largest room I had yet seen in my life, I assumed it was the most impressive one the palace had to offer. Surely, it could fit everyone.

It absolutely would not have fit everyone. No, the entry hall was indeed only for *entry*. The rich and indolent passed through it, marveling loudly and insincerely, before leaving their attendants to mill about by the staircase, or outside, while they ascended to the royal clouds. How many of them, I wondered, had emerged blinking and disoriented from their caves deep in Rotfelsen—had traveled farther vertically than horizontally to get here? Perhaps emerging onto the surface and seeing so many stars was the first bit of glittering royal excess they beheld.

The main stairway was wide enough for a carriage, with railings of pure emerald gemstone, imported (I had to assume) from northern Skydašiai or Loasht. I think that if anyone tripped, they would not have grabbed that railing, for fear they might scratch it. One noble was carried up those stairs on a palanquin, although he did not seem particularly weak. A squat woman, who was clearly not Rotfelsenisch, made a big show of being annoyed by him and trying to get by.

This great palace, those huge and gaudy stairs, it all seemed so frivolous and yet so inviolate. As though this noble fancy was too big, too *stupid*, to ever be broken down and removed from the land on which it sat. But I supposed I knew better: it was all going to crumble, physically or metaphorically. This staircase would tumble onto itself, perhaps, crushing these royals just as well as it crushed their servants and hangers-on.

At the top of those stairs—and only half as far as Lenz and I had climbed up the cramped servants' stairs earlier that day—were King Gerhold VIII's Royal Party Apartments. This was their official name. I never did learn how many rooms were in this suite: there always seemed to be another and, as far as I could tell, the in-demand monarch was always one room away. It seemed everyone wanted to see him, and no one ever did.

Wreathed through the guests, and crowded at every door, were groups of guards: most in red, many in green and purple, a few in yellow. They were more interested in circling each other than watching the guests, and the Yellow who had brought me wanted to join them, so I was left to my own devices.

So, I tried to figure out which guests were plotting against the King. Or, failing that, to make up my own plot, accuse someone of it, and convince Lenz it was the truth. I simply had to survive until my father got here, then we could run away and leave Rotfelsen to crumble into dust.

Telling fortunes without the Gift, to those that want to hear them, is relatively easy. When a customer wants to believe, one can be vague. "I see you covered in a sheet" can be a death shroud or a comfortable bed, "I see your mother having a revelation" can be about your greatness or your terrible secrets, and so on. The customer shapes the vagaries to fit what they expect, if they even slightly believe you to be the real thing. And I must give myself credit for being good at acting like the real thing. So good that a master of secrets had not yet caught onto mine.

But *extracting* futures from assembled nobles and merchants was an entirely different set of skills. They did not *want* to believe I was prophetic, and in fact, it was better they not suspect. At best, I would be playing my game of setting up open statements to catch Lenz's assumptions, but even that meant actually *watching* these drunk idiots. An hour in, all I had prophesied was gout and burning crotch.

"Why don't you have a sword, soldier?"

I had not seen the speaker walk up beside me, as I had been standing in a corner, focused on a pale man with a thin beard and mustache. He had been speaking to a little curve of people, and I had gotten the idea he was important.

I turned slowly toward the speaker, a blonde and beardless Rotfelsenisch lord of no more than twenty-two years. The rapier at his side had a jeweled handle that almost tricked me into thinking it was never used. But the jewels on the pommel had been scratched many times, as had the guard, and he wore only one ring, so as to make gripping his weapon easier.

"I am not that sort of soldier," I said to him.

"Oh? What sort are you?" He smiled, and it occurred to me he might have been *flirting* with me. I was as used to unwelcome advances as most women, normally of the less genial kind, but, armed or no, I was in the yellow of a Prince's guard, sternly watching those around me. I could not see how he thought this was a good idea, unless he wanted to get into the Prince's business through me. I almost laughed at the thought.

My uniform *was* form-fitting, in a sense, but in service of emphasizing power: a triangle wide at the shoulders. The shadow I saw against the wall *was* mine, but it was a me who looked stern and implacable, which did not tend to be what men who leered at me wanted. Usually, *that* was wild, sensual exoticism—"feminine like a she-lion!" a man told me once. Had I possessed such a wildness to offer him, I still would not have. How ridiculous.

I will say that this youth did not leer, at least.

"The sort who does not need a sword," I told him. I looked back at the man holding court.

"Now you are being circular."

"Not my job to be friendly. There are attendants for that." I probably should have been less rude—after all, he could have been someone powerful (or the son of someone powerful), but I got the feeling this fancy boy would respond well to being neglected, just a touch. And if I were wrong, what would he do, imprison me?

"Is your job to stare at the Lord High Quarrymaster?"

In that moment, my skill at deception did come in handy. Because, upon learning that the man I had been looking at was, in fact, the same Selvosch who had approached the prince about supplanting the King, my heart jumped, but I did not so much as bat an eye.

"Maybe," I said. "That's certainly *their* job." I inclined my head toward the half-circle of eager listeners around Selvosch.

"Just a hobby, I assure you," said the blonde. He looked out at Selvosch and his admirers.

"Is he so entrancing to listen to?" I asked. "He does not seem so from here." It was a chance to betray so much ignorance, and be flippant to boot, but I had let the blonde set our tone. If I could learn anything useful about Selvosch, the only confirmed member of the plot against the King, I could maybe coast on that until I got a chance to escape.

"Entrancing?" the blonde laughed. "Oh my, no. But he is powerful, and rich, with a . . . captivating unpleasantness. But you could say that of most anyone here"—he trained his gaze on me—"except the soldiers. So! Perhaps you're a new type of sharpshooter? Or some sort of *magic* soldier, perhaps? I know the sorts old Friedhelm likes to recruit. A foreign mercenary? From Quruscan, perhaps? Or . . . farther?" He would not even mention Loasht by name. "You clearly aren't—"

"Rotfelsenisch? I am, but not entirely."

The blonde was fully facing me now, and certainly flirting. He was not badly formed. He had a dueler's body, lithe and narrower in the shoulders than myself. High cheekbones and piercing eyes. I was not, however, interested in flirting just then. I was also unsure whether *I* was what he wanted, or a means to some end. How many networks of spies were there? How many alternate spymasters were darting around, looking to confound Lenz?

"Meaning," he said, "that you are watching everyone, but you are a foreigner unaware of who everyone is?"

"If you like. And who are you?" I continued to stand straight, hands clasped behind me, like a soldier. Even as I spoke to him, I kept an eye on Selvosch, to be sure I did not lose him.

"Martin-Frederick Reinhold-Bosch."

"That's a lot of names. Couldn't your parents make up their minds?"

"Not really, no. That length conveys that my line is old and royal."

"Is it?"

"Well, yes, but the royal part is not so old. My grandfather was allowed to marry into unimportant royalty, you see, after distinguishing himself somehow." An exaggerated shrug. "But he was able to set up a better match for my father, and now here I am!" The false modesty was stifling.

"Here you are where, exactly?"

"Why, living up in the light rather than down in our ancestral caves. Knocking about the palace, watching for lecherous Uncle Friedhelm's treachery against Uncle Gerhold."

"You do see that I'm wearing yellow, don't you?"

"Well, one can hardly blame you for that. I know a man in my position *should* be looking to meet wilting, noble flowers—but I'm always drawn to a woman in uniform. The martial type."

I rolled my eyes, and let him see that I was doing so. I had a feeling that would only make him try harder.

"Well, I hate to disappoint you, ah . . ." I trailed off, making a show of forgetting his name. "But I'm not terribly martial. No sword, remember?" I grabbed at the empty space on my belt where a sword would have been.

He grinned and lowered his voice again. "But what *can* you do? It must be something."

I smirked. "Who are you asking for?"

"Myself."

"Well, I hardly know you. Who else?" I let my stance falter slightly, in order to gesture to his clothing in an . . . aggressive fashion. "You aren't wearing a color I recognize." His doublet was an inoffensive midnight blue, which flattered his complexion.

He laughed at that. "What if I said High General Dreher?"

"What if you did?"

"Would you tell me what sort of soldier you are, if it was for him?"

"Perhaps, but I'm not speaking to him, am I?"

"Not yet."

I began to suspect that this Martin-Frederick Reinhold-Bosch (I had in fact remembered his name quite well) had nothing more to offer me tonight. But I would keep him in mind: a royal with a way to the High General could come in very handy.

"I," I said, "am going to go over there now, and stare at people from a different angle. Thank you for the information."

The little blonde laughed and told me his name once more. He seemed quite sure he would run across me again, and he was right. Sometimes it seems everyone is better at seeing the future than me.

I walked past Selvosch as he was loudly demanding everyone agree with him that someone was a filthy, three-legged swine. They all agreed.

THE LORD HIGH QUARRYMASTER

I had passed Selvosch, the Lord High Quarrymaster, in order to better hear him for a moment, and to move away from the young blonde. Soon after that, I stood in another corner, still watching who spoke to Selvosch, and trying to see if any of them seemed conspiratorial about it. Of course, everyone was so coquettish and playful that it was quite hard to tell. Selvosch took his leave of the group, and I followed him into a small side room. My hope was to learn enough about him to craft a believable vision that could keep me alive until my father arrived.

If Papa was indeed being brought here at all. If he wasn't, if he had been killed or left behind to starve, what would I do? Still try to escape before everything came crumbling down so soon? Perhaps I would purposefully speed and aid that destruction, as some sort of terrible vengeance—it did not feel beyond me, just then.

But, for now, I watched laughing revelers in their silk doublets, too-tight hose, and enormous dresses cram themselves against each other on plush chairs and couches. It was early in the night, yet already these dresses and hose were crinkling into one another. The walls were adorned with bas-reliefs of various styles. I am no historian—and was even less one then than I am now—but even I knew these were each from different places and times. Some were of marble or onyx, some of rotrock that was separate from the room's own red walls, and a few were of that unbreakable stone of the Ancients, somehow. Any story these bas-reliefs told was unintelligible to me.

The nobles didn't care about me, and no other soldiers were visible. I slunk into a dark corner and felt relief.

"Hello, Kalyna Aljosanovna," said Lenz.

I don't know where he came from, but I managed to hide my shaking hands and turn calmly.

"Were you watching me, or Selvosch?" I asked.

"Neither. But the Party Apartments fold in on themselves. A ball can have thousands of guests, and yet one will keep seeing the same dozen people again and again. A marvel, really."

"Yes, marvelous," I said. "I suppose they wanted to imitate the confusing, twisting tunnels below."

"Wanted to, or could not help doing so," he replied. Then he dropped into Masovskani: "I am wondering why you're following the Quarrymaster so closely."

"Isn't he part of the plot against the King?"

"Yes, and he also knows that the Prince knows that he's part of that plot. I would prefer he not be followed by anyone in a yellow uniform." He sighed. "Trust that I have people with eyes on him, while you see to reading the futures of *other* powerful people, to learn who else is involved."

I sighed in false exasperation.

"Lenz," I said, "If I catch a few moments of every possible future in this palace, it will simply be a jumble. I must know whom to focus on."

"Well, if you had paid more attention to my histories . . ."

"By the gods, Lenz, there are things in your daft books about what the Ancients were and which areas they may have over-planted! Forgive me for not immediately finding the most important morsels while I was being *kidnapped*."

He shrugged, which I decided was the most I would get out of him on this.

"Tell me," I continued, "what the Lord High Quarrymaster actually *does*. Officially. This may give me an idea of who would be connected to him."

Lenz grunted in consternation and looked away for a moment. We watched the room idly, and I focused on a group nowhere near Selvosch, which seemed to be made up of important people. They were all laughing together on a couch shaped like the horseshoe of Fántutazh Lake, where trees float. Others streamed in and out of the room constantly—on their way somewhere, or looking for a place to sit. I could hardly believe how many people; it never stopped.

"Can you imagine . . . *I say*, can you *imagine*," one man was yelling to a group, "what would happen if we ever *did* go to war with Loasht?" He was trying to sound witty, and enjoyed the jolts of shock from his audience at the mention of that terrifying power to the north. "I say, can you imagine?

All those soldiers, from all four kingdoms, lined up in a row: Masovska hussars next to Quru mountaineer irregulars next to Skydašiai's puffed up Yams and so forth, all yelling in their own doggerel, with their own sets of maneuvers! Even our High General Dreher couldn't wrangle them: he'd have his hands full just telling our Purples what to do!"

A woman chimed in. "They would all fight each other before"—whispered, now—"the Grand Suzerain's forces even got to them!"

They all laughed at the *hilarious* image, convincing themselves it wasn't real. They suddenly quieted as a man went by in a tall flash of purple, followed by a stream of Purples.

"That's the Court Philosopher," said Lenz. "You said his Purples were up to something. Why don't you follow him?"

I got a quick look at the Court Philosopher's angular face and very tall hat, which jutted straight up. His soldiers glared at us as they passed. Once he had left the room, it began to buzz again. Selvosch did not seem to react one way or another.

"I rather think his men would notice," I said. "Is the High General here, too? I've heard he's rather important."

Lenz shook his head. "He doesn't do parties."

"I see. As to the Quarrymaster," I said, "I am sure he does not oversee production. Too low for someone like him."

"So you didn't *see* him with your Gift, then?"

"Not yet. Give me context."

"You are astonishingly unhelpful."

"I never said I'd be helpful. You assumed it when you *kidnapped* me."

He sighed, but did not turn to me. "The Quarrymaster," Lenz began, staring forward, "does not so much run Rotfelsen's many, many, *many* quarries as he rules them."

"How do you mean?"

"All the laws about what can be extracted: rotrock is a quite useful building material for the other kingdoms, although they usually like to paint it other colors so they don't 'look like Rotfelsen.'" He smirked. "And exporting the stuff also gives us more space for new homes and tunnels. We mine and sell a great deal of metals and gems as well from our beloved home. The Quarrymaster controls all of that, dictates where one can't dig, how much to take, which equipment is lawful, even worker safety." He laughed at this last one, at the very idea. "All go through Selvosch."

"No wonder everyone surrounds him."

"Most Rotfelsenisch landowners have quarries, because it's all that can be done with their property. Some also sell potatoes and other cave plants."

I smiled to myself at the thought of how little Selvosch would rule, if my father had been literal about those shattered remains. But I could not hold onto that smugness for long, as thoughts of the Tetrarchia's impending doom ran wild through my head once more. Would another Tetrarchic kingdom become fed up with living next to a big rock full of jewels that were slowly portioned out? Perhaps Skydašiai would finish their work of centuries ago, and simply crack the thing open to take what they wanted. Then there were the tens of thousands of miners who toiled deep in the dark to keep this place running: I would not blame them for rising up and crushing their masters. Or perhaps they would simply be unthinkingly directed to overmine the rock's foundations during the Council of Barbarians, and it would fall in on itself.

All the revelers became not just disgusting, but deeply stupid. How could they dance and drink when the country they ran was collapsing? When their way of life was going to end when winter did? *I* didn't know what would cause it, but shouldn't those in power see the end coming?

Or was it Rotfelsen's own aggression, or conquest, or infighting that would cause all of this?

Either way, no matter how stupid I told myself they were, I imagined their deaths in an avalanche of rotrock and wanted to cry.

"Well," said Lenz, "please don't allow me to distract you, my prophet. See what else you can see."

I bowed insultingly.

He repaid it with a similarly sarcastic bow and turned to leave, before stopping and turning back. "Oh, and Kalyna, do be careful."

My breath caught in my throat. "Of . . . ?"

"Earlier, some inflated Purple bumped into me, blamed me for it, and spent a *great* deal of time trying to goad me into a duel." He smiled. "It was all very transparent, and I'm sure that if I cared for that sort of honor, he'd have killed me."

"Pity."

From my first moment at the ball, it had been clear that the night would include duels between military doublets of different colors: they seemed positively twitching to do so. Already I had seen them jostle, side-eye, and spit on the floor when those of another color passed, much to the delight of the nobles.

"You'll be largely on your own if they make trouble for you," said Lenz. "Most Yellows are in the Prince's apartments, guarding him during his private, ah . . . let's say *adjunct* party."

"Keeping track of the Prince's conquests?"

"He's quite capable of that himself—the numbers aren't as high as he likes to pretend."

"Inspiring. So," I began to count on my fingers, "the Yellows are us, of course. The Purples are the Court Philosopher's army of idealists, yes?"

Lenz looked pleased with how much studying I'd supposedly done. "Yes, although I don't think they're all idealists. I certainly hope not."

"Fine. And the Greens are whom you used to be a part of: you know, the *actual* army."

"Yes." He looked irritated at that, which I liked. "They're the largest of the four, but are stationed throughout the country, not just up here."

"And lastly," I continued, "who are the Reds?"

"The Reds, Kalyna, are supposedly King Gerhold's own guards, his personal army, dressed in the color of Rotfelsen itself."

"'Supposedly'?"

"Despite being Skydašian, Queen Biruté has become quite popular. Probably because she has a personality." He shook his head. "The Reds are, I'm afraid, quite split between those loyal to the King and those loyal to the Queen. Unofficially, of course, but it's quite clear."

"And so, if a Red or a Purple or whoever comes for me, I can simply ignore them?"

"That worked for me, Kalyna, because I have a little power and am a man. It may not work for you."

"Then what will? I have far *less* power than you. What's the code of conduct here?"

"You *did* read my books, didn't you?" asked Lenz.

Then he left.

Phlegm caught in my throat, and I almost spat it onto the rug, which was made from the furs of hundreds of animals.

SKYDAŠIAN DUELS

Simply ignoring the Purples would not work for me, I learned, because no one would try to dispatch me through a duel in the first place. Although I could be a soldier in Rotfelsen, I could not fight a duel. The very idea of women dueling—with each other, or with a man—was seen as laughable in Rotfelsen, and in Quruscan as well.

In Masovska, I have heard, it had long been legal for a challenge to be issued between man and woman (still not between women), but the man had to fight up to his waist in a hole in the ground, in order to "balance out her infirmities." I never saw such a duel, and a man could demur without disgrace. It never occurred to lawmakers that a woman might have a sense of honor to affront, but then I've never really understood why honor was a thing that mattered to *anyone*.

But in Skydašiai, a man or a woman could challenge the other to supposedly equal and open combat at any time. A nice idea, insofar as any legal brawling is, but it seldom worked in practice because Skydašian women were consistently discouraged from learning the use of arms outside of those military branches that would have them. Most sword masters would not teach a woman, and most women would be shamed for the learning—unless, again, she was a soldier, in which case dueling was forbidden to her. All of this may serve to explain why I was in the habit of carrying a discreet sickle.

So, while the law of Skydašiai suggested that a woman could redress her grievance against a man (or, indeed, a woman) through lawful and godly combat, the reality was that such duels took the form of victimization. A man felt a woman had laughed at him, rejected him, slighted him by her presence, or otherwise shrunken his phallus, and in retribution, he challenged her—she who had never held a sword in her life, on pain of ridicule—to sabres at noon. She was then almost invariably killed or maimed to his satisfaction. It was to escape just such a duel that my family once fled Skydašiai, and I count myself not untalented at cutting men. Telling a spoiled, young fencing prodigy that you are not interested could be deadly there, in a way that was fully legal and public.

There is a sort of folk hero of Skydašiai, Aušra the Cleaver, who received army fencing training and then dropped out in disgrace before her first day as a soldier, due to being unmarried with child.

Fifty years before my birth, reputedly, she roamed Skydašiai, waiting for just these sorts of brutes to challenge her: she never had to wait long, never had to incite or delude them to it. She would traipse out onto the battleground, in a dress, wobbly and unsure, nearly tipping over when she drew her sword. She would then give her opponents a deeply unpleasant surprise by moving into a perfect fencing stance, and proceed to kill or maim them. The maimings were *very* specific.

I could kill and maim, but had never dueled nor learned the sword. I am no Aušra the Cleaver.

MULTICOLORED, DUEL-HAPPY YOUTHS

Unsure of what to do next, I passed back into the room where I had met young Martin-Frederick. The groups of revelers had spread out a bit, as there was no Selvosch figure to flock toward. Music was playing from somewhere that I couldn't see, and laughter was becoming very shrill. A Red and a Purple were shoving each other, while a group of refined gentlemen seemed to be placing bets.

A hand was clapped onto my shoulder hard enough to hurt. I turned to see another group of Reds, grinning at me. Their leader leaned down until his face was even with mine. His cheeks still had baby fat, and he seemed entirely sober.

"I hear," he said, "that the Prince can't sleep at night without first sucking the High General to completion."

"The Prince sounds like a considerate lover," I replied.

Not having a response, he shoved me hard, sending me reeling backward. I'm sure I looked very powerful and martial flailing my arms and spinning around. I crashed fully into another reveler, who yelped and spun down with me. For a few moments, all I could see was the lace of her dress as it wrapped around my head.

The Red kept speaking, more to his comrades and the onlookers than to me, so I couldn't hear the specifics. I was too busy struggling to get out of those skirts, and babbling, "Pardon me," over and over again to the woman I'd barreled into. When I finally got free, the noble-woman was red in the face with laughter as a gentleman helped her up.

"What do you say, miss?" the leader of the Reds was asking her, over my shoulder. "Surely, this Yellow filth gave you a grave offense." He leaned toward me, hand on his sword pommel.

"Oh yes, certainly!" she laughed in reply. It was only a game to her, and to the other spectators.

The Reds stepped toward me, four in all. Armed, of course. I fought the urge to look around for people to run behind, for possible help, for an escape. Instead, I looked directly in the leader's eyes, and told my body to relax, to seem calm, above it all. I remembered something the young blonde had said earlier in the night, and my own thoughts when I was in the Prince's apartments that morning. I summoned all the trickster's confidence and tried to steady my voice.

"Be a shame to ruin our guests' fine outfits," I said. There was still definitely a tremble in the last few words.

The leader looked confused. This was good, because if he didn't get confused enough to ask, he could just kill me, easily. The Reds hung there for a moment, silent. My heart felt ready to burst.

"What do you mean?" he asked.

I smiled widely. I had him, at least for a moment, and knowledge of that flowed into me, let me feel I controlled the situation—whether or not I did.

"Don't you wonder why I'm not armed?" I asked.

"No," said the leader.

"Why?" asked one of the Reds behind him.

I thanked a few of my favorite gods, thinking the names that I could not say aloud, and cannot write here.

"Because I'm a sharpshooter, naturally. A harquebusier. Do sharpshooters duel?"

The lead Red looked directly at me, but his comrades, back where he couldn't see them, couldn't help looking around. Especially up above.

"It's bad form to walk amongst our guests with a harquebus," I continued. "But if you think the others don't have eyes on me, and you, at this very moment . . ." I trailed off on purpose.

"But," the leader began, "women can't be sharpshooters."

I did not know this. But now that I thought about it, there had been no female Yellows among the harquebusiers who had traveled with me from Masovska. I felt my heart seize in my chest.

"Let's go," said one of the Reds in the back.

"Women can't be sharpshooters!" the leader repeated, to his compatriot.

"Are you sure?" I asked.

"Maybe the Prince allows it," said one of the Reds. "Being a deviant and all."

"Not a chance," said the leader.

"She's not Rotfelsenisch, so who knows how it works where she comes from?" added another.

"Are you even sure I'm a woman?" I asked. At this point, I was simply trying to confuse them.

"Let's not risk it," said a Red who was looking very insistently in one direction.

I glanced that way, too. There was just a large painting—perhaps he had reason to think sharpshooters often hid behind it?

I winked at the painting.

"You don't really think—" the leader began.

"Why else wouldn't she have a sword?" yelled another of his men. "Come on, there's no shame in it."

They almost pulled their leader behind them, but they left. There was a general air of disappointment from the crowd, and one man even *booed*, first at the disappearing Reds, and then at me. I shrugged and walked up to him, grinning.

"You're next," I said, only because I was angry and relieved, and just maybe enjoying being the villain.

Who was in charge of all this? Rotfelsen hadn't had a real war in years, yet these soldiers were all young and angry, and no one seemed to mind their killing one another. Did they all go mad when they came to stay up in the palace's barracks, away from their tunnels?

The man in the last room, suggesting that the Tetrarchia's armies were too divided to fight Loasht, hadn't seemed to realize that even Rotfelsen's was too divided to get much done. Or perhaps, in their ignorance and violence, these multicolored, duel-happy youths would even be the doom of the Tetrarchia.

Had these men (or boys) been the Queen's Reds taking part in a plot against their King? Even worse, were these the King's Reds after me because they *thought* the Prince was indeed trying to overthrow his brother? Perhaps we would be mistakenly murdered by the King's protectors, while whoever wanted him dead skipped toward victory. Wouldn't that be a tragic and contrived ending to it all?

But what did I mean by "we"? Let the fools kill each other, I was getting out. I just needed to survive until my father got here. If vicious infighting would end the Tetrarchia, then there were no invaders to be feared. I could escape right into the disorderly, warring cities of the Bandit States while they picked at the Tetrarchia's carcass from the south.

I was brought back to the present when the party guest who had been booing me suddenly stopped. Then he laughed.

I wondered why he was laughing, right until something beige fluttered over my eyes. Then I was struck in the stomach and dragged away.

VOROSKNECHT

"Is this the one?" grunted a voice.

"It had better be," said another.

I knew those Reds had come back with reinforcements to kill me. That they were taking me somewhere unmenaced by the Prince's sharpshooters. I actually laughed bitterly at them going to all this trouble for me, the poverty-stricken, broken, mystic outcast, who knew that the end was coming soon. I do hope my laughing unnerved them.

When the bag was torn off my head, my eyes were assailed with brightness. The soldiers above me were nothing but menacing sunspots. As my eyes returned to normal, I saw one color overwhelmingly, and it was not red.

Everything, from the walls to the furniture to the uniforms, was a near-blinding purple. This must have been the Court Philosopher's suite. Had he already learned, somehow, that I had implicated him to the Prince when I was desperate for a prophecy about tonight?

The Purples grabbed me by my shoulders and dragged me through a hallway, past more purple rooms. The Court Philosopher's suite was just *slightly* smaller, and just *slightly* less opulent, than Prince Friedhelm's in every aspect.

"I am beneath you, O Prince," the suite proclaimed, "because I choose to be."

The Purples stopped before a large, purple door.

"Why does he need an army anyway?" I asked, bolstered by assuming I was already dead. "Whom do you people fight?"

If I hadn't put up my arms in time, they would've opened the great doors with my head. I was thrown into a study, and in its center, watching me, was the Court Philosopher. My neighbor, Chief Ethicist

Jördis, was with him. She looked unhappy. The doors slammed shut behind me.

The Court Philosopher of Rotfelsen was a tall, thin man in a tall, thin hat, as though a temple column was growing up from his skull. This, along with flowing purple robes, made him the perfect picture of a great king of the Ancients, as they have been depicted in paintings. Tetrarchic artists had no idea how the Ancients looked, and so fabricated a long extinct refinement based on nothing.

A book I once read, instead of one of Lenz's, quoted a woman who spent decades exploring ruins: she swore by all known gods, demons, and planets that the Ancients had not even been human.

But this is beside the point. The Court Philosopher looked like a fashionable painting. In his angular face and carefully groomed gray-brown beard could be seen all the self-assurance and serenity of those painted Ancients, who knew they were the pinnacle of humankind.

He stood behind his desk, caressing the skull of a skeleton that was posed on a stand. It looked like some sort of dog or large rodent, with extremely long and sharp fangs. The bones were dyed purple.

I started to curtsy, but realizing I did not have a dress, turned it into an awkward bow. My stomach and arms hurt. I imagined he was planning my beating, humiliation, or death. I didn't really understand how court intrigue worked (I still don't), so I decided to try obsequiousness. I did not know his name but, thankfully, there was a large bust of him next to his desk, and its base said "OTTO VOROSKNECHT" in large letters. The statue was purple.

"His name was Meregfog," said Vorosknecht, looking at the skeleton with great affection. "A wonderful pet."

I waited.

"His glands, they secreted something when he was unhappy. Something very painful."

I waited, and made sure to widen my eyes in interest.

"So!" said Vorosknecht, turning from Meregfog's poor skeleton. A dutiful Purple dashed up and wiped Vorosknecht's hands vigorously clean with a wet rag that smelled relentlessly tangy. "Kalyna Aljosanovna," the Court Philosopher said.

I stood still. Expectant.

"Kalynaaaaa Aljosaaaanovnaaaaaa," he repeated. "You don't look Masovskan."

So I've heard, I managed to not say. I dipped my head respectfully.

"Meregfog was a good pet," he said, "because he could—theoretically, you understand—cuddle or poison someone for me. I couldn't well be held accountable for the actions of an *animal*."

I nodded.

"Ethicist Jagloben," Vorosknecht said to Jördis.

"Yes, Brightness," she replied from behind him.

Jördis seemed to be half of Vorosknecht's height, even though this was not possible (it must have been the hat). Gone was my gleeful neighbor, and in her place was a worried woman with a creased brow and a large purple sash, hands clasped tightly behind her back. I wondered if this was how I had looked around Prince Friedhelm.

"You know this Kalyna Aljosanovna?" asked Vorosknecht.

"Yes, Brightness. We just met today."

"Where does she come from? What is she? The viper disguised as a tree branch? Or the insect disguised as a peony?"

Jördis took a long breath. Since her master did not face her, she rolled her eyes. I wanted to smile at her, raise my eyebrows, or otherwise share the moment of annoyance with her, but I dared not. I didn't know her so well to rule out whether this was a trap. Perhaps making such a face was exactly what he was waiting for, as an excuse for his soldiers to gut me.

"I do not know, Brightness," she said.

"Well now, she must be some sort of dishonest, chameleonic creature."

I heard the Purples shifting behind me, weapons clanking.

"I . . ." Jördis faltered. "Must she, Brightness?"

"Why, Ethicist, did you know that your foreign neighbor here is a Yellow?"

"Brightness," I finally said, indicating my uniform, "I've hardly kept it a—"

"Ethicist Jagloben," Vorosknecht interrupted as though I'd said nothing at all, "did you know Kalyna Aljosanovna is a psychic?"

Jördis coughed and looked at me. "No, Brightness, I did not."

Vorosknecht smiled very widely and stepped out from behind his desk. He passed the bust of himself and approached a large glass cabinet full of small liquor bottles. The glass was stained purple. He poured himself a drink into a delicate, purple glass. I watched him do it, feeling intense relief that on his fingers were gold rings holding jewels of some other colors, just as a break from the monotony.

It really was a shame, because I *liked* purple. If I escaped this bad dream of a kingdom, I would wear it again.

"Our good Prince Friedhelm," said Vorosknecht, "has hired himself a psychic, Ethicist Jagloben, right under your nose. I wonder why." He downed the drink and replaced the glass, which a Purple then began to quietly wipe clean behind him.

"Why don't you ask the 'psychic'?" I asked, adding, "Brightness," and another bow.

Vorosknecht raised an eyebrow at me and said, "Huh."

I waited in mid-bow, trying not to shake.

"Ethicist Jagloben," he continued, "why do you think?"

"Well, Brightness . . ." Jördis struggled. She seemed to feel caught, the way it was for me when asked about a future I couldn't guess. It was clear Vorosknecht had a very specific answer he wanted to hear. "Well, Brightness," she said again, "I . . ."

"To *tell fortunes*," I said, standing up straight. "For the Prince. I kept it secret so as not to be pestered for the future of every neighbor in my house. That's the answer."

"Hm," said Vorosknecht.

"Would you like to know yours, Brightness?" Another dip of my head.

"Why not?" he replied.

He clearly thought little of my Gift (and who could blame him?), so I decided there was little point in trying to convince him of anything. Better to learn something, if I could.

"You and High General Dreher will soon be at each other's throats," I said. "Quite viciously."

Vorosknecht laughed derisively out of the left side of his mouth. "Oh, very good. Why, it's almost as if we have *never gotten along*."

Well, it wasn't a great revelation, but at least now I had an idea of where Rotfelsen's two armies *not* commanded by royals stood.

"Meregfog," said Vorosknecht, pointing to the purple skeleton, "was a tool. Prince Friedhelm also collects such tools."

I smiled nicely, but blinked too many times.

"You had some distinguished predecessors, psychic," said Vorosknecht. "There was the cooper who made hidden weapons, the chandler with the poisonous vapor candles, the, ah, 'dancer,' the librarian, the clown, and now this squirrely Lenz character, who is *also* a clown." He laughed. "I may have the order wrong. All tools. All more expendable to the Prince than this dumb animal," he said it with affection, "was to me."

At least he was speaking to me directly.

"But a psychic," he continued. "Ethicist, what are the *ethics* of using a psychic?"

"That would depend on how they are used, Brightness," said Jördis.

"Wrong!" He spun to face her, as though catching a child stealing sweets. Jördis jumped only slightly. "Ethics," Vorosknecht said, "as they stand, alone from all else, only dictate the uses of power, yes. But ethics alone cannot fully dictate whether something is right or wrong, is that not so?"

Jördis looked deeply unhappy. She was meant to agree with her master, but could not bring herself to. Her face turned red; she may have even shaken. She opened her mouth, closed it, looked away, looked back, and then Vorosknecht mercifully spun away to face my general direction.

"Of course it is!" he said. "Because the Ethicist and, say, the Godcounter are separate viscounts of their own provincial, philosophical lands, aren't they? They live in the proverbial caves of thought—important, but siloed. You, Ethicist"—he waved a hand behind him at Jördis, who was standing very still—"can concern yourself with the use of power, but not the morality of that power's origins."

Jördis made a noise that was perhaps intended to sound like agreement; or she was releasing steam.

"The Godcounter," Vorosknecht continued, "keeps track of the gods—knows their caprices and hatreds—but does not understand how those divine preferences can be misinterpreted. I"—he placed a hand on his own chest—"of course, live beneath the bright sky of full understanding. I comprehend the intricacies, details, and intersections of *all* our disciplines. And, with such a perspective, I counsel the court and enact laws that protect our people's morality. But also"—he turned to me—"*from* this perspective, Kalyna Aljosanovna, I see that any use of your power is deeply, philosophically troubling."

"How do you mean, Brightness?" I asked.

Was he using my supposed Gift as an excuse to have me killed?

"Your powers are a curse, a moral travesty, setting you apart from other human beings, placing you—in the eyes of *some*—above even philosophers, kings, and other thinkers."

"I don't place myself—"

"You peer into what should not be the realm of man," he seethed. He began to pace, purple robe fluttering about him. "Only the demigods should see what is to come; it is for mankind's greatest thinkers"—he did not actually point to himself—"to extrapolate and interpret!"

"And yet, Brightness," I asked with my best innocence, "didn't the gods give me this Gift?"

"What?" He seemed disappointed that I could think such a thing. "Either gods cursed you or demons blessed you, which round out to the same thing."

I took a deep breath. "Why, Brightness," I said slowly, "can't this be a gift from the gods?"

Vorosknecht smiled serenely. "Because if humans were meant to see the future, why would the holder of that power be a mongrel nomad? Such a gift would be given to those who could put it to the best use, or it would be given to everyone like smell and taste. The gods don't hand out extra senses on a whim."

"What about all the old stories of a god's chosen champion or martyr who—?"

"A sky-chariot? The strength to move mountains? Or the power to die over and over again? Honestly."

He began to pace again. I shifted my weight to one side. I was tired of standing at attention.

"That," Vorosknecht continued, "was back when the gods were at war with each other; now we live in the glorious days when they are at nominal peace. This is why the past is full of stories of such heroes, and the present is not."

I always felt this was because gifted heroes born into our era would have been run out of towns or burned. In fact, I had quite a few well-supported arguments along these lines that I had thought up during long trips, but I felt that sharing them wouldn't help me just then.

"Well," I said instead, "I also see the present, Brightness, and yet I have known men and women who could see nothing. You can walk, but my father can't. How is this different?"

Rather than being angry, Vorosknecht only seemed put upon, which was so much worse. "You fail to grasp." He demonstrated this by grasping at the air with long fingers. Then he closed his eyes, pressing the bridge of his nose until those fingers turned white. "The blind are made that way because the god who dwells in darkness cursed them; those who cannot walk were cursed for hubris by the god of the hunt; do you see? This is all simply laid out if you can only understand the world around you."

I nodded. Waiting for the knife in my back that was surely coming.

"Similarly," he continued, "you have been cursed by something that taunts you, that makes you think you're special."

I blinked back a tear. I would not let him know that he had mistakenly pricked something within me. I began to wonder if I could somehow hold him hostage, drag him out of the Purples' sphere of influence, and then *murder* him.

I couldn't, but at least he would die in two months with everyone else. This whole, gaudy room would be a great purple stain in a mass of rotrock.

"Brightness," said Jördis.

Vorosknecht jumped. I almost did too.

"Yes?" he asked.

She looked right at me. "It's unfair of you to expect her to meet you as a debater." I read nothing but mercy in this supposed insult.

"Yes. Yes, of course," said Vorosknecht. "I'm forgetting my purpose tonight." He glared at me, and I heard the heavy boots of Purples step closer behind me. "Ethicist Jagloben," he continued, "please leave us."

With my eyes, I implored Jördis not to, but of course she had no choice. She passed me, and I heard her footsteps echo until the door was closed.

"Kalyna Aljosanovna," he said. He didn't pace now, but stood still, looking me in the eye for the first time, unblinking. "Your Prince does not worry me. Your lame spymaster does not worry me. Your curse bothers me, personally, but it does not *worry* me."

He snapped his fingers. A Purple grabbed each of my arms. Here it came. My breath began to quicken as they lifted me. Perhaps I could fight my way out if—

"I don't like you. I don't like your kind. I don't like your curse if it is real, and I don't like frauds if it is not."

I took a very deep breath.

"It used to be," he sighed, "that the Purples existed to round up and punish mystics, heretics, and others with wrong ideas. That their ranks were filled only by the *faithful*; those forged deep in our darkness, full of strong ideas. But those beautiful days were before my time, and though my soldiers are quite loyal to *me*, and to the rule of logic and reason, I cannot simply wield them however I like. Having you killed would mean a day's worth of paperwork and hassle, because you are the Prince's new toy. Don't make yourself worth that hassle. I'm very busy." He smiled, then looked away from me, to someone behind me. "Instead, I recommend you tell your Prince that he can stop wondering what sort of powerful people are working with Selvosch, because it is the sort with a very loyal army."

He looked at me hard, as though I would miss the significance if he did not spell it out for me. I obliged him.

"Don't tell me that *you* are plotting against the King, Brightness!"

"Vulgar, stupid thing, aren't you? I am telling you because no one could ever mount a case against me on the word of a mongrel like you. Tell your little Prince, who has suddenly decided to pretend he has a backbone, and then keep entirely away from me and mine, until the Prince tires of you and you are kicked out or killed. I have wasted enough of my time with you."

The Purples' grip on my shoulders tightened.

"She clashes with my color scheme," said Vorosknecht, waving me away languidly.

I was lifted bodily and carried out through the door by my arms. Another bag over the head, another long walk.

A BALL MUST HAVE DANCING

As I was marched along with a sack over my head, the surrounding noise went from empty hallways, to crowds, to deafening music. I was being jostled from all directions, and it took me a moment to realize that the men who had been leading me along were gone. I removed the sack to find myself in a cavernous ballroom, filled with hundreds upon hundreds of dancers.

I *tried* to find a way out of there, honestly, I did. But a group of drunken dignitaries spun toward me with such violence that I wondered if, after surviving the Reds and the Purples, *these* were actually my assassins.

They spun in circles, and I was buffeted between a set of flushed, laughing faces. I burst out of the circle of faces toward what turned out to be the dead center of the dance floor.

No great lover has brushed so many crinolines as I did while caught in that ballroom and knowing no dances. A jumpy, brass-heavy music pounded from a great dais so far at the end of the room, it seemed miles away, even if the instruments sounded as though they were inside my ears. The guests' dances became more and more elaborate around me: each time I thought I had an idea of which step would come next, they did something else.

And so, I, certainly not dancing and clearly not a guest, was whirled through the crowd as I tried, in vain, to not bump into *everybody*.

I looked to the orchestra to orient myself, trying to keep its location in mind as I was battered about. Sweat streamed down my forehead, and I turned to see a second dais with a *second* orchestra. I soon lost track of which one I had been using to find my way, and I could see no doors. I felt more lost in this crowd than in a vast, barren steppe, as though I'd wander through these dancers forever. I'm not proud of it, but I *hated* their happiness so much.

I saw a glimpse of yellow through the crowd and stumbled toward it. A Prince's guard stood at the base of a set of stairs that went I knew not where. He was watching me, confused. I had never been so happy to see one of those uniforms.

I twisted between a pair of dancers who were trying very hard to look like they weren't groping each other. Past them, I recognized the Yellow from the Masovskan forest, and the top of our carriage where he had ridden. He said something to me, and I shook my head and pointed to my ears. He motioned me toward the staircase, and though it seemed a request, not an order, I followed.

"Enjoying the royal hospitality?" asked the Yellow, once we were far up enough that some of the din had softened. I felt strangely relieved in the presence of a man I'd seen daily during the last week. Even though he was one of my jailers, he was familiar to me by now.

"Better than I did yours," I said nonetheless.

"I hope you know I was only—"

"Following orders, yes. I know the feeling."

At the top of the stairs was a catwalk cut from the walls' rotrock, from which we could watch the guests conduct their elaborate dances.

The Yellow put out his hand to grasp mine in a greeting that superseded chivalry and hand-kissing, because I wore a uniform the mirror image of his. After we shook, he saluted and I, a moment later, did a poor imitation.

"Sharpshooter Behrens," he said, smiling. "I shot the man bearing down upon you back in the Masovskan forest. The night we picked you up."

I took a deep, long breath, and then said, "Thank you. A moving man in the dead of night must have been a difficult shot."

The compliment clearly tickled him. "Only doing my duty. Shooting that man was easier than huddling behind a railing against Masovskan winds."

Behrens' given name, small, pointed beard, and accent all spoke to a lifetime in Rotfelsen, but his brown skin and tight curls suggested a family of mid-to-north Skydašian extraction. He may well not have even spoken Skydašiavos, but I suspected his insular Rotfelsenisch fellows still called him "the Skydašian," or worse. Perhaps behind his back.

"I've had quite the time tonight, so far," I said. "First almost killed by Reds, then roughed up by Purples."

"Ah, sorry to hear that. If I'd seen any of it . . ." He mimed shooting his harquebus. "Sharpshooters don't generally duel, of course. So I'm free to assist Master Lenz while the others puncture duelists outside." His actual harquebus was leaned haphazardly against a far wall, although he was also wearing a sword.

I considered telling him about the exact ruse I'd used to get away from the Reds, but decided I'd best keep my capacity for deceit to myself.

"Is it true that women can't be sharpshooters?" I asked instead. "I heard such a thing earlier tonight."

Behrens looked a little sheepish as he replied. "Well, yes. Back when our harquebusiers were first formed, guns of any sort were still in short supply here: sold only by shifty Loashti merchants to unsavory types on our side of the border. My forebears decided to pretend their scarcity was a strength, and so constructed rituals and mysteries: sharpshooters in each of Rotfelsen's armies became rather silly, but intense, 'brotherhoods.'"

"You don't sound like you much agree with it."

He shrugged. "Maybe not, but I would lay my life down for my 'brothers' just the same. You know how it is."

I did not.

"Whether or not *I* agree with it," he continued, "the Yellows, Reds, and Purples only began accepting women into their ranks out of necessity. The Greens were snapping up most of the best fighting men. Some think they still are." He grinned and winked. "But we'll show them."

"Will we?" I asked. "I'm rather new to all this soldierly infighting. Are there . . . rules to it?"

"Sure!" he laughed. "Duels must be fought in certain places, violence must not touch the nobles—"

"But they watch it intently."

"Well, yes! But it's self-policing. If a noble is threatened, the guards involved are fair game."

"Or if the Reds *pretend* one is threatened?"

"Sure, of course. And a duel cannot be backed away from—"

"Unless you're a sharpshooter. Or don't care much for honor, like Lenz. Or a woman."

"Naturally, naturally." He screwed his lips to the side in thought. "Violence is, of course, forbidden between two soldiers of the same army."

"And when the King's Reds and the Queen's Reds are angry at each other?"

"Well, they do fight, yes."

"Does every rule have exceptions?"

"There are always extenuating circumstances, and sometimes one army changes its rules, and the others don't know immediately . . ."

"So no one knows the rules of engagement."

He smiled and shrugged.

This whole kingdom slept while its soldiers drove it into the ground.

"And what's a sharpshooter doing up here?" I asked. "Picking off Reds mid-dance?"

"Just keeping an eye open." He made a show of tapping underneath his right eye.

"So you must know who all these nobles are."

He laughed and scratched the back of his head, pushing his hat forward. "Here and there, one or two. I've spent the season closer to them than if I'd been on a Masovskan hill, but only just."

Even on the catwalk, which seemed reserved for guards and amorous couples, an attendant with a trough of food passed us. He carried little towers of crushed green ice, each on its own individual plate and encrusted with pieces of peach, embedded like cannonballs that had crashed into a fortress and remained lodged in its walls. Now this quieter luxury, away from the crowds but still attended to, appealed to me. I may have looked too eager when I grabbed up a little tower for myself.

"What?" I asked Behrens, through a full mouth, as the attendant padded away.

"Has Lenz been starving you?" He frowned.

"I wanted to try the Master of Fruit's work," I replied. "He's my neighbor."

I admit it all only tasted like sugar and water, to me.

As I chewed through the ice, I enjoyed watching the drunk, dancing fools below. I pointed to one, a woman who was tall and stately, and seemed as popular as Selvosch. The current dance involved switching partners regularly, almost constantly, but the partners never touched, nor did anything suggestive. This woman was in high demand, with dancers sometimes tripping over one another to be her next partner. They did not even seem to speak to her when dancing— too busy concentrating on the strange steps.

"Who?" asked Behrens. The whole group kept twirling and shifting away from where I pointed. At that moment, they were all doing some sort of crab walk.

I managed to swallow my ice. "The tall, popular one," I said. "With the burgundy dress, and the, er . . . prow."

"Ah? Ah! Edeltraud von Edeltraud, Mistress of the Rotfelsen Coin."

Now this name I remembered from reading Lenz's books on my ride to Rotfelsen. I recalled that she had a lot of suitors, but had seen no information on what the "Mistress of the Coin" actually did.

"That sounds cushy," I replied. "Why is she so nervous?"

Behrens crinkled his nose. "Is she?"

She most certainly was. Even from the catwalk I could see that her many dance partners did nothing to make her happy—as clear as if she screamed, "Leave me alone!" with each pass, each kick, each extend of the tongue. Edeltraud von Edeltraud's stress was clear from her clipped movements, her darting eyes, and the red marks she left on the bare arms of female partners with whom she spun.

"And here I thought you were supposed to have good eyes," I needled.

"Well, now . . ." Behrens laughed.

"Is mastering the coin particularly stressful?"

Behrens thought this over. "I suppose it's a lot like being on guard duty, which is to say, long periods of inaction, during which one must be alert. In case it's ended by emergency."

"What sort of emergency?"

"Would you like to know Rotfelsen's most wasteful law?" Behrens smiled and leaned close, as though with a great secret.

I slipped into a playful smile. "Oh, yes."

"You see, whenever Rotfelsen's ruling monarch dies"—he paused and put out his left hand in a sign of warding off evil—"be it the will of the gods that such not happen in my lifetime—the Mistress, or Master, of the Coin must travel throughout Rotfelsen, with workers, to re-stamp *every single gold, silver, or copper mark in the kingdom* with the new monarch's face."

"Terrifying."

"They are given a year: a single mourning period. Bad luck to use money with a dead king on it, which, of course, does not stop many paranoid citizens from assuming the government is coming for their savings, and refusing to turn over even copper marks. Not unfairly: it's common to receive the wrong number of re-stamped coins. Hers is a job that many clamor for when the king is young and healthy, but if the position is left vacant in the reign of an old, wizened king . . ."

"They must catch officials with a net."

"Just so. Used to be that Masters of the Coin would lose their heads if the turnover didn't finish in time, because the wrong coinage could anger the gods. Nowadays, they would simply become an outcast and never again have an appointment."

So it was not everyday stresses of the job weighing on Madam Edeltraud, what with a young king. Perhaps Edeltraud, along with the distasteful Court Philosopher, was one of Selvosch's conspirators, and therefore expected the King to be replaced soon. Imagining the effort and resources involved to do this for an entirely new government, and the anger it could stoke from the people, put new possibilities in my head for what exactly would *happen* in just two and a half months at the Council of Barbarians.

I felt a numb fear at the violent end of the Tetrarchia, and a wave of excitement as convincing half-truths began to form in my head. This would merit a prophecy.

Edeltraud von Edeltraud finished dancing and started toward a side door.

"I wonder why she's so nervous," I said. "I'm going to follow her."

Behrens nodded approval.

I did not know how much he was in Lenz and the Prince's confidence, but as I started down the stairs, I hissed, "Tell Lenz that Vorosknecht is working with Selvosch!"

I did not see Behrens' reaction. I got down into the thick of the dancing once more, and began to push my way toward where Edeltraud had gone.

Edeltraud von Edeltraud

I followed Edeltraud von Edeltraud into a small room with padded walls. She stopped and leaned against a wall, catching her breath after all that dancing, while I wandered the room picking up snatches of conversation and trying to look normal. Thankfully, it was the time of night that saw everyone too drunk to modulate their voices.

"—when the Council of Barbarians—"

"—I'll march right up to that arrogant goose and—"

"—is it true one of those southern armies got *inside the stone*, before High General Dreher repelled them?"

I stopped for a moment, to listen to that last one. If this unnamed drunkard at a party was telling the truth (and who could ever doubt *that*), if the Bandit States had amassed a force that punctured the rock even a bit, and if the High General was indeed covering it up, then something was *very* wrong. Unsubstantiated though it was, this was one more possibility for the Tetrarchia's demise. And, if the Bandit States united and invaded, running south with my family was right out.

"The High General insists it's untrue, of course," the drunk continued, "but surely *you* . . ."

"I'm sure I wouldn't know," someone replied.

I peeked around the corner and saw a drunk noble talking to a squat, pale, muscular woman who wore wool trousers and what looked to be the sort of frilled shirt some noblemen would wear, but cut for her figure from a scratchy peasant's linen. She held a long wool coat over her back and the shirt's sleeves were rolled up. I realized I had seen her on the stairs earlier in the evening.

"Well, but you're from Rituo, our only friends to the south," said the noble, dipping his head.

So she was a guest from our sometimes, sort of, kind of ally in the Bandit States.

"I'm sure"—she yawned, lifting her hand to her mouth and purposefully flexing her arms as she did so—"I wouldn't know." I wanted to introduce her to young Martin-Frederick Reinhold-Bosch, who so loved "martial" women.

"They say," the drunk noble stage-whispered, "there's a great Warrior Queen uniting your neighbors! And that she has sword arm thick as a tree and a—"

"I haven't the faintest," said the southern guest. She winked.

Was she here gathering information for a united invasion? Or working with Rotfelsen to stop it? Or was she simply a merchant, using her foreign status to toy with paranoid locals?

Whoever this woman was, Edeltraud von Edeltraud seemed to have her strength back, and I watched her leave the room. I counted to twenty before following her, and found myself in an annex with crystal walls and eight different doors. The Mistress of the Coin was no longer visible—in fact, there was no one else there, somehow.

A bit mystified by this place, I made a circuit around the empty crystal room, opening each door and looking down each hallway. These halls were all dimly lit, with vague silhouettes I could not make out, each looking nothing like the woman I was following. Thankfully, down the seventh hallway, I once more saw the recognizable shape of Edeltraud von Edeltraud.

I strode as naturally as possible into this hallway. Edeltraud von Edeltraud seemed to be looking for someone, but in the way of a drunk who wishes to seem sober and act as though they certainly are not lost. She didn't ask anyone anything, only looked anxious and purposeful.

Could this confused woman be part of a plot to destroy Rotfelsen from within? Or would the army rivalries spill into war? Or would the Bandit States invade? Why did I assume Papa's prophecy had anything to do with Rotfelsen in the first place? Possibly just because that's where I was. Certainly, most people in the Tetrarchia expected our end to come by way of Loasht, sooner or later.

I followed her into a room filled with flowers, organized in terraced troughs along the interior wall. There was also a vine in the center that writhed as though it were trying to escape the palace: at least this vine understood me. The far wall was one huge window, and the two walls that angled away from it were half bay windows in themselves. In the daytime, this room must have protruded right out into the sunlight. Besides the lamps, an eerie blue glow lit the flowers for guests to see— had I not spent so long reading *Bohdan's Botanicals*, I would not have known that this was because the top row was iridescent Quru moonblossoms. Edeltraud von Edeltraud glanced about this room, bit her lower lip, and left through another door a minute later. She paused only to take a dessert from the table by the door. It was sugar melted into flower shapes. I did not see any fruit in it, so I didn't take one.

After this, Edeltraud von Edeltraud disappeared down a long hallway. I started after her, but realized I was so close I could hear the shifting of her skirts. I stopped to wait, and prayed there wouldn't be too many doors for her to disappear through, this time.

Once a minute had passed, I continued toward where I *hoped* Edeltraud had gone. The hallway was dark and constantly twisting. I walked a long time before there were any doors. I still don't understand where in the palace it all fit: it must have writhed its way around many rooms, gradually traversing floors, and curving while seeming to go straight. After my audience with Vorosknecht, I felt that there were Purples around every corner. The hall did, at some of its turns, have alcoves: sometimes from these came giggles, running water, or low, seemingly inhuman, growls.

Then I came to a row of open doorways, and through them it appeared the party continued, even though the hallway had been nearly desolate. I glanced through each door I passed, as I hoped a guard on duty would do. I saw many soldiers in them, but not a single Yellow.

Some rooms that I passed: a maroon-lit room in which an ochre substance was being crushed into brandy and drunk by laughing guests; a chamber planted with short trees in which a round merchant stood on a table to regale bored nobles who thought him less than dirt; a nearly dark room in which a very intimate private dance was taking place between a number of couples, but none of them had my (self-appointed) charge's silhouette; a cave, essentially, in which a woman scantily clad as a boar chased a man dressed as a bird wearing a sorcerer's cap; and a series of rooms in which various games of cards, tiles, sticks, balls, and terrains were being played by screaming and laughing guests, between walls that matched the color of each game's primary component.

This was the top of Rotfelsenisch society, nobles and rich merchants who held the purse-, shoe-, and bodice-strings of the rock-bound kingdom. These were the people giggling like children as disaster loomed, whether from within or without. They were enjoying luxuries I'd never have imagined, while I was living in a *house* for the first time in my life, and while poorer Rots down in the depths drank brown cave water. I did not see Edeltraud von Edeltraud, nor did I see King Gerhold VIII. I felt sick.

The hallway ended abruptly at a chamber of natural rotrock, with a fountain in the middle whose water came from . . . somewhere.

In the corner, a crowd gathered around two noblemen who were being fanned. One had a bloody nose, the other blood trickling into his eyes. They were grumpy, but the cause of the fight seemed forgotten. Those surrounding them were attempting to talk them either into or out of an ensuing duel. I looked about the room: low mutters twisted amongst towers of fruit and meat that blocked out half the room, a liveried boy of about twelve stood in the center singing softly, and a magician was performing sleight-of-hand silently with minimal flourish. I did not see the Mistress of the Coin.

I stepped around a spire of pork (with a giant, wild boar's head on top, its fan-shaped ears brushing the ceiling) and slunk over to the window for air. Far below, in the courtyard, I saw small groups of soldiers posturing and fighting each other: tiny drunken figures lunging awkwardly, blades glinting. Greens against Purples, Yellows against Purples, Reds against Reds.

I felt a pang of protectiveness toward the Yellows, whom I did not know and probably would not like. Curse the power of a uniform.

I was about to turn back from boyish duels and the fresh night air, in order to look once more for Edeltraud von Edeltraud, when I heard Masovskani mutterings.

Masovskani is, I think, a beautiful language, which is easy to pick out even if you cannot catch the meaning, as it seems that every word has at least one "sh" or "tz" sound in it. So I heard the noises but not the words, creeping around the great tower of pork. I moved toward the sound, and the words became clearer.

"But if the King . . ." muttered a voice in halting Masovskani.

"What do I care for the King?" asked a second voice.

Something unintelligible.

"But if we are not careful—"

"The hammer will fall on him whether or not—"

"'The hammer'?" laughed a third voice, which sounded familiar. "So dramatic."

"Dramatic or not," was the reply, "we must be ready—"

"Never marry a man with a distinctive face!" a woman near me piped up *very* loudly. It was all I could do to not cough pointedly.

"Whyever not?" asked her companion. "I like the look of a face with some *character*!"

"If you marry a man with a distinctive *face*," the first replied with the unerring tone of one who gives advice because they have two years of experience on the other, "he will know immediately that the baby is not his. And even if he is too in love to see it, everyone else will, I assure you."

"But—!"

"And don't you take a distinctive lover either!" she added.

These two women had finished walking past me, but the damage was done. I finished circling the great spire of pork, and hoped the Masovskani speakers would have more to say.

Behind the meat was one last cluster of nobles, taking food from a small kitchen alcove with a serving window. There was also a lute-player relaxing on a divan, many rich men making verbal contracts that surely were *completely binding*, and a small curtain in the corner behind which some kind of rutting was likely taking place. Edeltraud von Edeltraud was there, speaking to two Masovskans, a man and a woman. They were dressed in almost-Rotfelsenisch clothing, but with puffy fur accents, and the woman, whose elegantly pinched face I could see, had the sallow skin and deep-set eyes of Masovska.

Two men entered the room, with a large group of Reds, and a smaller contingent of Yellows, but they were mostly blocked from my view by the pork. Everyone else in the room made a show of not reacting to them. Regrettably, one of these Yellows saw me and limped over.

"Well, hello!" laughed Lenz. "So nice to see you again, Kalyna Aljosanovna." He nodded at the lute-player, who began to play, masking our words. The music also masked the Masovskans' conversation, unfortunately.

"Hello," I said, looking at Edeltraud von Edeltraud. "Why aren't those Reds and Yellows fighting?"

"This is a Red room," he replied. "The *King's* Reds, mostly. A Purple would be barred outright, a Green would be 'allowed' in, but the guests would quickly disperse. Yellows are permitted, if they behave, because they serve the Prince."

Lenz said this in Masovskani; I quickly switched to Cölluknit.

"It's good Purples can't come in here," I said, "seeing as how Vorosknecht kidnapped me not long ago."

"Is that so?" Lenz took the hint and also dropped into Cölluknit. "What for?"

"Wait, is the Prince here?" I asked.

Lenz nodded toward the two men who had recently entered, surrounded by Reds and Yellows: they had moved more fully into my view, and I saw that one of them was our own Prince Friedhelm. The other one was unremarkable—Lenz told me that he was the King.

If inbreeding had rendered Prince Friedhelm's face particularly strange, it must have been because all those features had waited for him in the Queen Mother's womb, after sliding completely off of King Gerhold's smooth personage. The King was bland and characterless, a face that could be forgotten moments after being seen. If the Prince radiated power and a kind of sick charm, only the rounded gold lumps on a large necklace told anyone of the King's import. And thus, I beheld King Gerhold VIII.

"That's it?" I muttered.

"Why, he's positively beaming today," replied Lenz. "What did Vorosknecht want?"

"He wanted me to know he doesn't like me. And that he's working with Selvosch."

"Wait, he—"

"But right now," I interrupted, "I am *trying* to hear what the Mistress of the Coin is saying to those Masovskans. To make sense of a vision."

"Ah." Lenz snapped again at the lute-player, whose tune slowed and softened. "Then let us walk the room," he whispered, "and make conversation."

We began to walk toward Edeltraud von Edeltraud. For a moment, her companions were blocked from my view by a pair of rangy men in gold buttons making plans for a marriage of children.

"I suppose you know your Yellows are fighting outside?" I said to Lenz.

"They aren't *my* Yellows, and of course they are."

We curved around the rangy nobles, and I got a good look at the Masovskan man. It was Klemens Gustavus, the tyrant of Gniezto whose mercenaries I had fought Down Valley Way, when he tried to dispossess his eight-toed cousin. He looked awfully smug.

Your Lovely Rock

The other woman with Klemens Gustavus, I realized, shared many of his features. She must have been Bozena, the only daughter of old Gustaw Close-Hand.

"What?" whispered Lenz. "What is it? Do you see something?"

"I have seen them, in my visions, and I . . ." I blinked many times, for effect. "I see more now . . ." My eyes were closed.

I already suspected Lenz hadn't sent anyone into the courtroom that day in Gniezto, and so I gambled that he didn't know the Gustavuses.

"Those are changing bank magnates from Masovska," I said. "Their names are Klemens and Bozena . . . something. They have a third sibling as well. Brother or sister I cannot yet see."

"And what of them?" he asked.

It occurred to me that the Mistress of the Coin would have a great deal to discuss with the owners of the Tetrarchia's largest changing banks, and that Edeltraud von Edeltraud's nervousness may have been due to simple economics. Perhaps there was nothing sinister here. Then I saw the uncaring smirk on Klemens' face and remembered the mercenaries in the forest on their way to Eight-Toed Gustaw from Down Valley Way. I remembered being nearly killed.

"They plan to kill the King," I said.

Lenz straightened suddenly, started to reach for his sword, then stopped himself. "Here? Now?"

I put two fingers to my forehead and "thought" very hard.

"Tonight. I see it. Very soon."

"I must tell the Prince," hissed Lenz. His belief in me was intoxicating.

My hope, at this point, was that when Edeltraud von Edeltraud and the Gustavus brats were put away, and there was no attempt on the King, I could claim that I had stopped it with my prophecy. Of course, Selvosch had intimated to the Prince that *something* would happen tonight, but if it did, I could just claim that arresting these three hadn't been enough. If I was lucky, Edeltraud and the Gustavuses would act very close-lipped and suspicious because they were actually up to some good old economic chicanery together. If I was *very* lucky, they would actually be part of a plot. Whatever the case, I could probably keep suspicions going until I was able to escape.

Unfortunately, Edeltraud von Edeltraud and the Gustavus brats seemed to have finished their deliberations. Lenz and I spoke nonsense to appear as if we were not listening.

"I'm afraid I must retire back to Turmenbach," Klemens yawned.

"We look forward," Bozena began, loudly, in Rotfelsenisch for all to hear, "to the rest of our visit to your lovely rock."

Klemens looked bored.

"Don't we, *brother*?" she growled.

"Oh yes," he said in stubborn Masovskani. He began to look idly around the room. "After all, it is so very . . . you know . . . here it is just so . . . so . . . stone."

Bozena shrugged and smiled at Edeltraud von Edeltraud. "The boys," she said in Rotfelsenisch, "will always be the boys."

Klemens was not listening. He had made a show of looking around the room, until he saw me. His eyes narrowed.

Lenz's back was to the conspirators, and I fought to keep from doing anything so damning (and pathetic) as hiding behind him. Klemens had seen me, and either he recognized me, could not remember where he had seen me before, or found me strange looking. I told myself I appeared very different in my uniform, which was true, and that Klemens had been too disdainful in court to notice his audience, which was likely.

But he had certainly noticed Ramunas.

I forced myself to look back at Lenz. "Edeltraud is preparing to leave," I said in Cöllüknit. "I will—"

"You stay with the twins. Warn the Prince."

"They aren't twins."

"Stay with them." Even in Cöllüknit, he made sure to avoid any word for Masovskans. "You have followed her enough; she may notice. I'll go."

I didn't tell him I was worried Klemens had recognized me. It would mean admitting the Gift was not how I had learned of the brats, and I would negate a beautiful chance to extend my myth. A chance that had fallen into my lap.

I nodded. Lenz turned as though getting ready to leave, and rubbed his bad leg. Klemens whispered to his sister. Edeltraud von Edeltraud began to bustle toward the door. Was it my imagination, or was she glancing toward the King and the Prince? But then, who wouldn't?

Lenz disappeared through the doorway, and I backed toward a wall, hoping I would be out of Klemens' view. Then everything fell apart.

SMOKE

I am still not entirely sure what happened next. There are a few possibilities, although I suppose specifics hardly matter. After a few minutes of watching the Gustavus brats make some other goodbyes around the room, brown smoke streaked with blue began to billow out of the little kitchen.

Guests wondered at a parlor trick, laughed at what must have been the accident of a clumsy cook, and then became uneasy when the smoke continued to move toward them.

A strapping young man, finding the thousandth way to prove his manhood that day, was theatrically not bothered by the smoke, and let it surround him while others backed away. Then he spun and dropped to the floor in a fit of coughing. He stopped moving. Someone screamed. The Reds and Yellows all began to yell at once.

Everyone flattened against the wall, glasses broke, the lute stopped. One woman threw herself against the window so hard I thought she was going for the short way out. She hovered there instead, sucking in fresh air.

Soon the smoke overtook us all. I could not see whether the brave young man was dead or unconscious. I heard coughing, moaning, and pleading all around me. At the far end from the kitchen, near the window, the smoke was not quite so thick, and I could see outlines of the people around me. I didn't see Bozena and Klemens.

I think I vomited? I am not sure. I know I suddenly tasted Tural's peaches, but the flavor was corrupted, bitter, and twisted into something wicked. My insides burnt and I retched, and my joints seized up.

"You used too much!" someone said in Rotfelsenisch.

"Just hurry!" hissed another.

If there was more, I didn't hear it over my own coughing.

I turned to the window, and the woman who had been hogging it was gone, although I may have tripped over her. I threw myself against the sill and took a deep breath of night air. The dueling guards below did not seem to know anything was happening. They would learn soon enough, as I definitely vomited this time.

I heard a thump, footsteps, voices that were not hindered by coughing. I heard a sword leave its scabbard.

I looked back and saw nothing but smoke. Tasted it again as well.

A NOXIOUS MIXTURE

The squirming Skydašian skrogdti plant, when cut, dried, and combined in an alchemical pot with burning jadestones and Loashti fogwort, which only grows in the warmest of climes and takes its "fog" moniker ("ukungukuru" in Loasht) from the blue sediment that it discharges in every direction, converting the most brutal desert scene to something like a burning evening lost at the Cold Sea—creates a thick soup of smoke that is best characterized by its deep brown color, similar to the bark of a healthy pine tree, strung with streamers of sky blue. This issue, which secret societies of criminal eveningmen put to dastardly use and colloquially dub "pukevapor," creates the most unkind reaction in the humors, and any who breathe it in eventually cough, cry, and vomit until they have coughed themselves into a deeply painful unconsciousness. Many times, Adomas the Scoundrel has made use of it in order to steal the work of others.

In order to inhale this noxious mixture without such a reaction, one need only treat a wet rag with . . .

SAFE OR MISSING

At the time, I did not stop to think where this quotation had come from, but of course it was a bit of *Bohdan's Botanicals* that had wound its way into my brain.

So, I knew that this smoke alone would not kill me, only cause extreme pain and unconsciousness, which is nowhere near as easy to turn and face as armchair swashbucklers would have you believe. Pain, vomiting, and unconsciousness are best avoided even when there isn't obscured violence going on in the midst of it, which there was. I heard, amongst the coughing, more struggle, the clang of swords, and the dull cutting of flesh.

The King was in this room, and the smoke must have been in aid of an assassination. I should have stayed by the window, but my mind kept screaming: *Assassination. King. Collapse. Gustavuses. I want to see Papa.*

In that moment, it made complete sense to me that I would have to do my—or Lenz's—job if I ever wanted to see Papa again.

The result of all this frantic thinking was that I leapt into the smoke, waving my arms. I was trying to stop someone from doing something.

I remember brown and blue, then darkness as I closed my tearing eyes. I couldn't breathe, someone hit me, a blade grazed my side, my knuckles creaked as the blade's owner got punched in the head. The assassins, whom I fancied to be the Gustavuses' hirelings, could breathe where I could not, but we were all just as blind.

More flailing, more hitting, more sounds of stabbing, something was sideways, all was dark, and then I sat up in a carriage. The smoke was back in the palace, many floors above me, and there was a clicking in my ears.

"The Prince is shaken up, but safe," said Lenz, pushing a blanket under my chin. My uniform was torn, and I was cut in more places than I remembered, but lightly. He looked worried.

"The King?" I coughed.

"Safe. Or missing."

I sat up, pushing the blanket off me. "What does that mean?"

Lenz sighed. "There was some sort of attack in a room containing the King, the Prince, some Reds, and some Yellows. All of the Yellows who were in the room are dead: run through." He raised an eyebrow. "Except us. The few surviving Reds insist the King was taken to safety, but that could be a lie. Either as part of a plot of the Queen's, some other plot that has Reds in on it, or a flailing attempt to cover their own incompetence."

"And there were the Masovskan merchants, too," I grunted.

Lenz nodded. "The official story: a fire in the kitchen, the King fell ill, and was whisked away to his rooms, while the Yellows died of smoke. We don't know the real story yet."

I slumped back down against the seat, numb. The carriage rolled between noble estates toward the servant houses. The night seemed quiet, peaceful. I groaned and twisted to look out the window. The Sunset Palace was as dark as it got (not very dark), and there was a wreath of smoke still twisting out one window and over the moon.

"Next time," I said, eyes watering, "you send me in *armed*."

Lenz nodded as if to say he would consider it.

"You're cut," he said.

"Because I tried to stop them." I coughed. "A fool idea. I hope this doesn't make me too *involved* in what's going on," I added. "You know that if I'm too close to what's happening, I will not see it anymore."

Always hedging my bets; always preparing for future lies.

Lenz didn't reply. I sat in the carriage, wondering if the King had indeed been abducted, or killed. Wondering if I'd just witnessed the start of the end of the Tetrarchia.

THE AFTER PARTY

In the carriage, through the palace grounds, and entering the servant house, I blinked in and out of consciousness. I felt as though I simply appeared at a dinner table on the third floor, like a fruit conjured into Tural's head. In fact, Tural was sitting across from me when I realized where I was. He looked worried.

"Have you wakened to the world?" he asked in Cölluknit.

Lenz, who was standing and leaning over me, putting his weight on the back of my chair, did a very good job of looking as though he did not understand Tural's words. The knowledge that he certainly did reminded me not to confide in *anybody*.

Tural held out a cup of something. I took it and lifted the cup to my lips, only to smell acrid alcohol, and put it back down. I was shivering. I noticed I had been rudimentarily bandaged.

"Too good for Skydašian pear brandy, are you?" said Tural, in Rotfelsenisch. I think he was being playful, but it was hard to tell.

"I told you, she doesn't drink," said Lenz. His voice thudded somewhere too deep in my head. I wished for him to back away. I felt as though I were chained to him.

"Yes, yes, right," said Tural.

Skydašian pear brandy sounded, to my inexperience, like a quality liquor, rather than what would be hauled out for medical reasons. I blinked until the world around Tural bled back into place. That was when I saw that the table was full.

The room was dark, lit only by the warm glow of candelabras at each end and a large window coaxing in moonlight. Jördis the Chief Ethicist was there, her cheeks deeply rosy, and nothing in her face showing that she had been present during Vorosknecht's confrontation. They had all been drinking, and the table was strewn with plates of half-eaten Winter Ball leftovers: mostly dried fruit.

"What? Why?" I muttered.

"I was helping you upstairs after the maids patched you up," said Lenz, a little surprised I didn't remember, "and when we passed the party, Tural offered a drink, hoping it might help you come to yourself. You said—"

"No, no, no. Why . . . party?" I gurgled. I was immediately embarrassed and wanted to hide my face.

"Well—" began a stout bald man next to Jördis.

"Because?" Tural stammered.

"Why not?" said a small woman at the other end of the table.

Jördis smiled and leaned over the table toward me. She jostled a pile of raisins on the way, but didn't notice. She was so chipper and, well, normal, that I wondered if my audience with Vorosknecht had been a dream.

"Because the Winter Ball is over," she said, "and we can relax. No couriers with sudden moral quandaries, no emergency plum shortage, no night soil *situation*."

"And what's more," cried Tural, "leftovers!" He flourished toward the tabletop.

"Yes, yes," said the stout bald man, whose back was perfectly straight even while sitting. "Does anyone mind introducing us?"

I did not have the energy, but I did not need it. Many chimed in, even though Tural and Jördis were the only two I had met before: I was a soldier, a spy, a consultant, a hero, a researcher—someone even suggested I was an assassin. Not in such words, of course. Jördis did not give me away for a soothsayer.

"Charmed, Kalyna Aljosanovna," said the bald man, who looked around thirty years. He stood and leaned forward, to lightly reach across the table and take my hand, which he lifted as though to kiss, but did not. He was Rotfelsenisch to the core, but his pronunciation of my Masovskan name was flawless. "And since no one has introduced *me*"—he cast a side eye at Jördis, who just laughed—"I am Vondel, Tenth Butler to High General Dreher."

"I thought Dreher didn't do parties," I said.

Vondel nodded solemnly. "Correct. Neither does he keep much exciting food in his household. So, thank you all, for sharing your leftovers. I'm sorry to have missed the ball."

"No, you aren't," said Jördis.

Vondel allowed himself the barest, most ethereal, whisp of a memory of a laugh.

I nodded and tried to smile, and he was very good at pretending as though I was being gracious while he sat back down. Overwhelmed as I was in that moment, I made sure to remember this man—a butler to the High General could be a useful font of information, even if he was only the tenth one. (How many butlers did the General have?)

After a moment's silence, I gulped. "Please, all, continue what you were doing before I arrived. I need to let the world become real again."

Jördis laughed. "So you do not drink, but what *did* you do?"

I kept my weary, ingratiating smile, but stared directly into her eyes. "Very little. But I had some uncomfortable audiences."

She smiled back. "I can only imagine."

"Kalyna," said Lenz, "was caught in the kitchen accident." He squeezed my shoulder hard. "It vacated the King's upper floors."

"Oh yes," said Vondel. "It was something quite noxious, wasn't it?"

"Yes. Something," said Tural. He seemed quite unconvinced that it had been a kitchen accident.

They all talked for some time after that. Maybe it was twenty minutes or two hours, I don't know. I learned that supposedly every piece of the Winter Ball had almost not worked, that numerous last-minute fixes, and amazing feats of strength and ingenuity, were responsible for each nonpoisonous drink, each ice sculpture that did not impale, every pair of rivals who somehow did not run into each other, each morsel of food that tasted right, and every window that someone did not tumble out of. These, at the table with me, were the people who had made the night's festivities possible, to hear them tell it. Of course, to hear *them* tell it, their own underlings were all bunglers and idiots. I suspect a different story was being told in buildings yet farther from the palace, or by exhausted workers descending back into Turmenbach.

For what it's worth, Tural—whom I had decided was my favorite—was not so dismissive of his subordinates, and Jördis—who was becoming my least favorite—did not seem to have any. Apparently, her job at the Winter Ball had been to prepare the Court Philosopher himself for any ethical questions posed by high-ranking nobility in light conversation. I wondered what her ethics said of covering my head with a sack and throwing me into his study.

The night's conversation ambled on. Someone asked where I was from, of course, and everyone seemed interested in the answer. ("Everywhere.") Eventually, thankfully, they got off the subject and back to the ball. The Master of Pillowcases was surprised at how few couples had used beds without permission; the Mistress of Periodicals was frustrated by dog-eared copies that had clearly not been read, only held open by those who wished to look engaged; the Woodwind Leader was pleased with everything; and the Lavatory Captain had to put up with my giggling, apologizing, and giggling some more. He graciously told me he was used to the reaction, and I was just happy for anything that kept me from worrying about the King. These were my new neighbors, whose work touched royalty in important ways that went unnoticed—and they liked it that way. Vondel was not, it turned out, one of my neighbors: he lived in a different servant house, but was friends with Jördis.

The laughter came easily, the leftover brandies and vodkas and ales flowed contentedly, and the shutter was eventually pulled down, only to rattle with cold winds, of which we felt the fingertips. More than once, Lenz suggested I get some sleep, and each time I surprised both of us by deciding to stay a little longer, and eating more fruits and nuts and pretzels. My body ached, and I felt exhausted, but not at all sleepy, and I found myself fascinated by the insights of the Master of Fruit on toilets, or the Lavatory Captain on ethics, or the Chief Ethicist on pillowcases, or . . .

Many toasts were drunk, and only the most perfunctory were to the King, Prince, High General, or Court Philosopher. I winced slightly at the mention of the King, and put him from my mind. There was a loud stamping and "Hear! Hear!" when we toasted Biruté, the Skydašian-born queen of Rotfelsen to whom many of the Reds were loyal. She certainly seemed popular. Perhaps Rotfelsenisch suspicion of one's neighbors and political enemies can overcome even

Rotfelsenisch insularity. Or, perhaps, she was pretty and had a personality. (Both true, I would learn.)

Quite a few toasts later, we were simply raising our cups to "a job well done." My companions became so friendly and their pride so strong, and I so beaten down, but also comfortable, that I joined in on the third "job well done" and downed my pear brandy.

It burned and I coughed, which I had done *quite enough of that night*. I readied myself to be laughed at for such a reaction, but nobody cared. I waited for my brain to turn stupid, and nothing happened, except that I felt *warm*. Not just physically, in my fingers and toes, but in my . . . well, my feelings. It was nice, and I liked the people around me so much.

Then I caught myself thinking pleasantly about Lenz, and there was a cold snap in my chest. My face fell into something neutral.

"I'm going to bed."

Lenz reached to help me up. I ignored him.

"Vondel," I said, "if you please."

Always ready to do the proper thing, Vondel hooked my arm in his and walked me up to my room. He said good night, and by the time the door was closed, I was in bed. I got halfway through thinking, *I hope Papa will be*—and fell asleep.

WAKING

I woke up the next morning into what seemed a beautiful reality, in which I believed everything previous was the dream. Not just the Winter Ball, not just Lenz and Friedhelm and Vorosknecht, but the entire world as an imperfect place for unhappy people, *that* was the dream. I had simply spent a night in fitful sleep, wherein I had imagined war, starvation, rape, hatred, my father's illness, my grandmother's evil, my failure, Lenz's kidnapping, the Winter Ball's smoke, the King's disappearance, everything, and I had woken to the correct world, where all were happy, and things were as they should be.

Of course, then I woke fully and knew which world was real. I knew this because my jaw ached from grinding my teeth.

PART THREE

THROAT CUTTING IN AN ALLEY

Five days later, I learned to be wary of Lenz in a new way, when I saw him run his sword through a woman's throat, causing her axe to swing wide.

I was a few feet away, blinding a man in one eye. I am no slouch.

I realized then that the limping veteran, the spy who avoided combat and preferred dishonor to duels, was not so immobile as he let on. But I suppose I should explain why we were killing goons in an alley dusted with Rotfelsen's first snow of the season.

THE PRINCE'S BATHS

The very day after the Winter Ball, the Prince was, as I'm sure you can imagine, in a bit of a snit. Lenz looked almost as exhausted as I when he came to get me, and we were whisked back to the Prince's apartments. Specifically, to a small, hot, windowless room of tile, where Lenz handed a report he had written to a servant. We waited next to each other at a sort of soldier's rest, hands clasped behind us, facing a little round porthole door. Lenz began to sweat.

"This is a strange office," I said.

"Yes," Lenz replied.

The porthole door opened. Steam lurched out, and the Prince's voice echoed into our chamber, telling us to come in. We had to duck through the door.

Even after the ball, Prince Friedhelm having a series of private baths in his suites was a level of luxury that surprised me. This was not a tub next to a shitting hole, but a large marble chamber pocked with pools of different alchemically-enforced temperatures, rising steam, statues of nude figures (gods in the Ancients' stone, perhaps?), and a small army of attendants. There were no Yellows visible, and their uniforms would have been unbearably hot, but there were stands and statues and modesty screens that must have obscured doors hidden in the stone. I'm sure I could have been shot dead at a moment's notice.

Scattered throughout were small stations, often a table and stools, each with its own amenities. There was a food station, a liqueur station, a shaving station, a skin station, and an especially coy, hidden "relaxation" station. At the far wall, there was a huge, glorious opening that was blocked not just with a glass window, but two sheets of glass enclosing water. Between them, schools of small fish swam back and forth among lake plants, doing their best to avoid the larger fish also in residence. All the light in the baths came from this massive window, filtered through quivering water and the life swimming in it.

I felt a strange sadness for those poor fish, suspended in glass, who would be so confused if this whole place toppled around them, their glass shattered, and they fell out into the air before slamming into stone. Why I felt worse for them, in that moment, than anything else living in the Tetrarchia, I couldn't say. But then, maybe our country's end would simply be a massacre of human beings, and these fish would happily swim for whoever took over the Prince's baths next.

The Prince was sitting naked by a pool, being toweled dry by an attendant while he rubbed at his own shoulders with a piece of volcanic rock. Rippling shadows of fish flitted over his pasty skin, and he was shivering, so I supposed this was a cold pool he had just come out of.

"I still feel that smoke on me," he growled, to himself or his attendant. "And in me. It stinks of death, and it won't come off."

Lenz cleared his throat loudly.

"Ah, Lenz Felsknecht. Kalyna Aljosanovna." The Prince smiled with a friendliness betrayed by the split second in which he slammed down the volcanic rock onto his marble table. He stood up from his oak stool, and his attendant continued to towel him.

The urge, of course, was to stare at his nakedness. But I suspect he liked showing that even at his most vulnerable he had power—over life and death, over an army, over his attendants, over how comfortable or not we were—and so I gave him a cursory once-over, as I would have were he dressed, and then fixed my eyes on his clavicle. His heart didn't seem in it anyway.

"First of all," Prince Friedhelm continued, "thanks are in order. Kalyna, I believe you saved my life."

This was news to me, but I decided not to act surprised.

"Ah, how's that, Your Highness?" asked Lenz.

"She was right there in the fighting," the Prince explained, "when all the other Yellows in the room were dead. Yet I'm still here."

I nodded. "Your Highness, I only wish I had seen a vision of those attackers sooner, in order to save more lives."

Lenz looked unconvinced.

"However," the Prince continued, his smile fading quickly, even as he raised his arms so the attendant could towel off his sides, "I have not seen or heard a thing of my brother. The *Reds* say he was taken back to his rooms, but that can't be trusted."

"Your Highness," said Lenz, "let's not be hasty. Your brother may simply be resting after an ordeal."

"Or," replied the Prince, "the Queen's Reds have taken him somewhere. It may be time for the Twelfth Recourse."

"Your Highness," Lenz began, "I really think it's early for—"

"Well, I don't like it," interrupted the Prince. "People are starting to talk, and if he doesn't show his face soon, the talk may well concern putting me on the throne." He shivered at the thought, or at the cold. "It seems I did not do whatever it was Selvosch wanted in order to show that I was on his side, because they came for me as well last night."

"We don't know whether that's true, Your Highness," said Lenz. "There was a great deal happening at once, so perhaps you can still salvage your . . . erm . . . *relationship* with Selvosch, Vorosknecht, and the rest."

"Ah!" replied the Prince. "So now you recognize that it was a good idea for me to lead them on. Let them think I could be their pliable figurehead."

"No, Your Highness. I most certainly do not. But this is where we are."

"Mayhap," continued the Prince, ignoring Lenz, "Queen Biruté and her Reds are in on this, with Selvosch and the Court Philosopher. *Mayhap*, their plan was to marry me to the queen, let her be the real power."

"I . . . doubt it, Your Highness," said Lenz.

"Well, she's pretty enough, at least," said the Prince.

I rolled my eyes, but no one was looking at me. I stood as still as possible, both to ignore further attention, and because I was beginning to sweat considerably in this steam-filled room.

"Your Highness, let's stick to what we know," said Lenz. "Selvosch and Vorosknecht may not have turned on you yet. Perhaps, Highness, in last night's confusion—"

"Hang the confusion!" grunted the Prince. He turned and lifted his foot, to kick the stool he had been sitting on, but stopped, I suspect, because he was barefoot and it would have hurt a great deal. "They want me dead. Selvosch, that purple idiot, and whoever else!" He put his foot back down, then simply nudged the stool over with his knee, into the nearby pool. It didn't look very satisfying.

"Well, Your Highness," I chimed in, "I think I know who else." I curtsied.

"Will another round of names even help at this point?" the Prince seethed.

"It will," I replied, holding my curtsy, "because they will be easier to get to than Selvosch and Vorosknecht." I stood up straight and smiled.

I told the Prince of Edeltraud von Edeltraud, Mistress of the Coin, and of Bozena and Klemens Gustavus. I fabricated visions of them plotting together, talking about what would happen once the King was gone. Edeltraud would be about as hard to get to as Selvosch, but the Gustavuses, as important as they were, could only be Masovskan bankers in a Rotfelsenisch noble court. Though rich and powerful in their little world, they had only been such for two generations. If I could keep suspicions trained upon them, I could remain useful and alive, until I was able to escape with my father. Or avenge him. I did not feel much guilt at the deception.

"Lenz," the Prince began when I was done, "some of the attackers' bodies were left behind as well. See if you can find anything damning on them, now that we know this. And do put someone on Edeltraud. Selvosch and Vorosknecht will be expecting it, but hopefully she will not."

Lenz nodded and looked thoughtful. My heart pounded in my chest at the possibility of *nothing* being found to implicate any of these people. What if the Prince and Lenz spent all their time and effort following people who were not involved at all, while the real plotters got to the King—if they did not already have him—and set into motion the bloody end of the Tetrarchia? For neither the first nor the last time, I began to wonder if I would *personally* somehow be responsible for the great disaster looming.

Well, all the more reason to escape. Both to save myself and my family, and to take myself out of such a sensitive position where I could affect so much. I admit that I did, in that moment, manage to convince myself that my escape would partly be for the *good* of the Tetrarchia. But no matter my reasons, Prince Friedhelm was convinced I had saved his life, so it was a good time to ask for a little more leeway.

"Your Highness," I said, bowing slightly, "I assume you're aware of my Gift's reliance on greater context? In order to make sense of my visions?" I dropped about halfway into the level of obsequiousness I had used when dealing with Court Philosopher Vorosknecht. It felt right, with the Prince, to pretend a little less.

"Yes, yes, of course," he replied.

"Well, I was hoping to be given a touch more freedom: to be able to roam the palace grounds at will." Lenz opened his mouth, and I quickly added, "Unarmed, of course. This will allow me to get closer to more people, and to better understand their places at court."

"Lenz?" asked the Prince.

"Can't she be accompanied by a guard?"

"I recognize that I stand out," I said. "But I will stand out even more if I always have Yellows with me."

"I don't like it," said Lenz.

I turned to Prince Friedhelm. I did not say to him that I had (supposedly) saved his life and named more members of the plot: I gave him a look that said I trusted him to know that on his own.

"I don't see a problem with this," said the Prince.

Lenz sighed. "No weapons, and you will check in with the Yellows at your servant house every . . . let's say two hours."

"Of course." I curtsied. "Besides, my family isn't here yet. Where would I go?"

Lenz grumbled.

"Good," said the Prince. "Whom are you going to look into? Did you get any other useful visions at the ball?"

"I'm afraid I don't know yet if they are useful."

The Prince, still naked, looked at me expectantly. Waiting for more information. I supposed what I'd already given him only went so far.

"Something about the Bandit States, Your Highness," I said. "Some people seem to think their little nips at our borders have actually pushed into the rock itself, and that the High General is covering it up."

"That would be quite large to cover up," murmured the Prince.

Lenz shrugged. "But not impossible. The Reds manage our borders, after all."

"I haven't seen yet whether it's true," I said. "I was going to look a bit into the High General's underlings, as well as whatever I can glean from that delegate from Rituo, the woman who . . ."

"Andelka," Lenz offered. "I believe she's staying at Royal Inn of Ottilie's Rock."

"That's the one." I had never heard the name before. "And thank you."

"Fine, fine," said the Prince. "If you can bring me more plotters like these Masovskans and the Mistress of the Coin, then all the better."

Prince Friedhelm dismissed us. I had certainly set something in motion, for good or ill. Now I needed to hope that either Edeltraud and the bankers *were* against the King, or that I could pass them off as such until I escaped. And if they died for my lies, what did it matter? Everyone around me would be gone in two and a half months.

THE ROYAL INN OF OTTILIE'S ROCK

That night, while Lenz put his Yellows to work looking into the Gustavus siblings and Edeltraud von Edeltraud, I used my slightly longer leash to do a bit of my own investigating. I left my servant house about an hour past sundown, casually saluting the Yellows on duty at the front door.

"If I'm not back in two hours," I said, "it will mean I'm dead or captured, not that I ran away. I promise."

They looked annoyed at my flippancy. I winked and strode off with much unearned confidence.

As soon as I was out of the Yellows' sight, I changed my bearing significantly. I did not feel particularly *safe* running around the palace grounds alone at night, unarmed, and so I affected the quick movements of a harried servant running some errand. At least, in the dark, it would be harder to see how un-Rotfelsenisch I looked. I made my way toward the Royal Inn of Ottilie's Rock. Out on my own, at night, I realized that even Rotfelsen was getting quite cold now, particularly up on top of the rock where the winds could absolutely howl by. In a day or two, it would even start snowing—I could feel it in the air, or so I fancied.

Even after the previous night's excesses, I had managed to be surprised when Lenz told me that the palace grounds had their own inns: three in all. I had assumed that guests stayed in Turmenbach, the city below. It seemed those in the palace would do anything to pretend those beneath them did not exist.

The Royal Inn of Ottilie's Rock was just to the southeast of the barracks that housed the Greens up here on the surface—although the largest Rotfelsenisch army had stations throughout the kingdom. (So, too, did the other three armies, but very small and only in particular places.) I had used the inn's location near the Greens as further proof to Lenz that I shouldn't bring any Yellows with me. I was there to learn about our good friend from the Bandit States, not to start duels.

The inn itself was easy to find, as Ottilie's Rock itself was a huge, jagged outcropping that pushed up out of the ground, about as high as a small building. The inn sat on top of that, four floors dotted with inviting lanterns that illuminated patches of its brown wood. It looked precarious, but in a cozy sort of way: like it was the last outpost of humanity in some inhospitable place. In truth, it was only a short walk from the barracks, a servant house, and what appeared to be a cobbler's shop.

It was at this inn that, apparently, Andelka, the squat, muscular woman from Rituo, whom I had seen egging on drunken nobles the previous night, was staying. So I made my way up the stairs that had been carved into the rotrock, and made dangerously smooth by years of use. A gust of cold wind picked up and almost knocked me clear off Ottilie's Rock, which would have been a painful fall indeed. I wondered how many people had died on their way to, or from, this inn. Despite the cold wind, I felt a strange heat radiating up through the soles of my boots.

The first thing I noticed upon entering the tavern on the first floor was the warmth: it was warm beyond the fire cracking in a corner, steaming even. It was not dissimilar from the steam in the Prince's baths, except that a sort of pungent mineral smell hung in the air. The wooden tables and chairs were all nicely lacquered, I assume to keep from falling apart in the steam, and currently held only a smattering of patrons. I did feel that there was something very comforting about the tenor of the lanterns in that place, and the windows clattering from the wind, but I may have been prejudiced by seeing no *soldiers* for the first time in a week.

I did not see Andelka either, and there were only a few patrons scattered about, so I chose to lean awkwardly at the bar and attempt to get the attention of the keeper behind it. The bar itself was the only thing in the place that betrayed our position on the top of Rotfelsen, for it was a part of Ottilie's Rock that jutted up through the wooden floor, which had been built around it. The bar was long and mostly straight, although it had a few odd moments of curvature. Like the stairs outside, it had been worn down to a smooth sheen. When I leaned against it, the bar also generated a very light and pleasant heat. The keeper was a surprisingly tall man—hunching and bald, with a beautiful smile—who loped over to me.

"Good evening!" he said. "I don't believe you're lodging with us. Here for the ambiance?" His voice was surprisingly soft.

"It certainly is something. Where is all this coming from?" I waved away some of the steam.

"You didn't know? Ottilie's Rock has a natural hot spring inside of it, so downstairs there's a nice little cave with a sauna." He stretched his arms almost alarmingly far backward as languid steam hung about. "Even up here, it limbers up the muscles!"

"Marvelous!" I replied, smiling quite charmingly, I'm sure. "My name is Kalyna, what's yours?"

"Gunther. What'll you have?"

I supposed it was too late for a "normal" person to order a black tea, and less aggressive teas weren't popular in Rotfelsen: they wanted the tea mania, more than the flavor or ritual, to which I could relate. Given that, only the night before, I had drunk alcohol for the first time since childhood, I certainly didn't know what one was supposed to order at a "royal" inn.

"Well, Gunther"—I leaned forward—"what would you suggest?"

He smiled broadly, and twisted his body to grab a bottle from behind him without looking at it. His movements were both graceful and awkward, like a young cormorant that has learned its footing, but not yet the length of its legs. He brought up a small mug carved from rotrock and poured a clear liquid into it.

"I'm sure you have too discerning a palate for our ale," said Gunther.

I laughed. "Quite sure!"

I took a careful sip, and tasted something lighter than the previous night's brandy, with a greater number of flavors. I did cough, but he seemed to view this as the correct reaction, and nodded sagely.

"Starka," he said.

"Starka?" I coughed through another sip.

"Liquor from a simple potato, or other good, Rotfelsenisch root, thrown into a barrel with apple and lime leaves, or whatever else is to hand. The process is started at someone's birth, and the barrel is then hidden away in a cave, or buried in dirt." Gunther mimed this with his hands as he described it. "When that little baby grows up, the result is served at their wedding—or coronation. But, nowadays, some people make a lot more than they'll need and sell it." He shook his head. "I don't know whom this bottle was originally for."

"It's delicious," I said, truthfully, despite another cough.

"That mug was free because I knew you'd like it." Gunther winked, in a purely friendly way. "A silver mark for the next."

So expensive, but I supposed that was normal up here, so near the palace. Earlier that day, Lenz had begun to pay me, so I dropped two silver marks onto the bar, where they clunked pleasingly against the rotrock.

Gunther opened his mouth to protest.

"This is for the *next two*," I assured him.

He smiled and refilled my cup. "Now I know you aren't a courtier: they don't have taste, they only want whatever's expensive. So that's what I give them. But this"—he tapped the bottle—"is better." He stood up straight, and his great height was still surprising. "So, what brings you here?"

"Court, I'm afraid," I replied with mock humility.

"Well, isn't that a shame," he joked. "For the Council of Barbarians, I assume." Because, *of course*, I couldn't be Rotfelsenisch.

"Naturally. You see, Gunther, I represent a patron who is looking for a place to stay during the Council."

The keeper maintained his friendly manner, but I saw something in him changing, as he tried to figure out who, or *what*, I was. His smile remained, but his eyes grew distant.

"I'm fully convinced this is a fine place," I added, holding up my mug before downing the rest of my second helping. "But I'm tasked with finding out whether anyone will be staying here who might be, ah, dangerous to my patron."

Gunther screwed his face to the side, obscuring his lovely smile as he poured my third drink of starka. "I don't know that I can help you here, my friend. We don't discuss our lodgers. Boss' orders, you know."

"Oh, I certainly do know." I rolled my eyes to show that I entirely understood. Lenz was really the only *boss* I had ever had—unless you counted Grandmother—but I could empathize with someone who felt downtrodden. Never mind that this man poured liquor for minor nobles, and must have been paid well for it. I'm sure a keeper down in Turmenbach would have considered his struggles laughable.

Gunther's smile returned, and he poured himself a cup of starka before offering me another. I finished what I had and plunked down another silver mark. This seemed dangerous for one so new to drinking, but what else was one meant to do in the face of inescapable collapse and calamity? Drink, and try to escape—I was working on the "escape" part. I just needed to know whether the Bandit States would be a very bad place to run to.

"Perhaps," I continued, "I can ask you a few questions, at least. They may be slightly leading."

"Lead away."

"I was wondering if anyone from the Bandit States has been staying here. I'm sure it won't surprise you to know that my patron, like so many others, feels uncomfortable about our *friends* from Rituo and the rest."

He brightened a touch and poured himself another. He could

really put it away, and I needed to make sure I didn't start trying to match him if I wanted to get anything useful done tonight.

"Well, who doesn't?" he replied. "And I don't much mind telling you because, you see, this is common knowledge, but our tavern is often crawling with those people."

And there it was. My uncomfortable, ironic stress on "*friends* from Rituo" had encouraged him, shown him that even though I was clearly not Rotfelsenisch (even if I partly was), I was certainly not of those people to the south. Now we were in agreement, which I didn't much like. The worst part was, he still had a very nice smile.

"Well, Gunther, as I'm new here, why don't you just tell me what everyone knows."

He laughed. "If someone from the Bandit States needs to a place to stay up here on the palace grounds, they are always foisted upon us. Like this one." He nodded toward the upper floors. "She comes down once a week to make a big show of spending money, then spends the rest of her time in her room, living *cheaply*."

I leaned closer, creating a conspiratorial air between Gunther and myself. He was good enough to oblige me by bending down.

"But why do they all stay here?" I asked.

"So the Greens can keep an eye on them, of course." He then stood up straight, no longer telling secrets. "That's the prevailing theory, anyway. No one can fully trust them, after all. I suppose an individual can be as good or bad as anyone else, but the way their little countries are always shifting and changing, you never know who's, well, on *our* side and who isn't."

Unlike, I thought, the extremely stable Tetrarchia, which was on the verge of violent collapse from an unknown source. Not to mention Rotfelsen's four armies, which were in *total* harmony with one another, and seemed as likely to bring the whole place down around our heads as anything else.

But if it was true that High General Dreher and his soldiers needed to keep an eye on Andelka, the woman from Rituo, perhaps these were normal precautions; or perhaps it was true that Bandit State armies had penetrated Rotfelsen itself recently, and the Greens wanted to be sure their ally from Rituo wouldn't go telling anybody. Or perhaps even Rituo was no longer our ally, aiding in this invasion, and Andelka was a scout or a defector.

Was Andelka as much a prisoner as I? It sounded as though she seldom left her room. Perhaps, if I could get to her, not only could I discover the Bandit States' part in the Tetrarchia's looming demise, but also find an ally against our captors—one who could help my family and me escape.

I asked Gunther a few more questions that went nowhere, and stood up, with the intention of sneaking upstairs and finding Andelka. But when I stood, my head reeled at all the starka I'd drunk. I chose to stumble back to the servant house. I was less worried about walking around alone at night on the way back, although not for any good reason.

The Yellows on duty were angry when they first saw me, as they had just been rounding up a search party. But when they noticed how I was stumbling up to them, they laughed it off.

THE KING REPAIRS TO HIS HUNTING LODGE

I woke up the next afternoon with my first real hangover. I regret to tell you it would not be my last. Another flesh-alchemist patched up my small cuts from the smoke-filled excitement of the Winter Ball, and told me again and again that, no, he could do nothing for a hangover.

The following three days (before that scuffle in an alleyway that I have mentioned) were a bustle of activity, in which I took little part. I spent them reading more of Lenz's secret histories, trying to find underlings of High General Dreher I could influence, and making regular visits to the steam-filled Royal Inn of Ottilie's Rock, hoping to set my eyes upon Andelka. She did not make herself known, and only being able to leave the servant house in two-hour increments made it impossible for me to lay in wait very long. I did become quite familiar with the schedule of Gunther, the tall, gentle-voiced barkeep.

Besides that, I spoke to my neighbors in the servant house, but learned little of note, just yet. I managed friendly chats with Jördis, but was loath to ask much of her. Who knew what she would take back to her master, the Court Philosopher? I also began to just barely appreciate food and drink far better than what I was used to.

I fell into a rather agreeable routine. I started to feel that the luxuries I was enjoying—solid walls, food and drink, well-fitted clothes, trips to the tavern—were something I was tricking my captors out of.

These rich nobles and sneaky soldiers thought they were keeping me around for their plots, but then I would escape them with whatever I could carry. This was at least how I rationalized enjoying myself a bit.

Outside of the tavern and my little house, the Gustavus brats were apparently staying in Edeltraud von Edeltraud's mansion, which was nestled right near the Sunset Palace itself. Edeltraud and Bozena didn't show themselves after the Winter Ball, which was helpful to me in making them seem suspicious. Also helpful was that one of the attackers from the ball, who had been killed in the scuffle, had been found with Masovskan lesser grivnas in his purse. Carrying money from another kingdom was not unheard of, but neither was it normal: most businesses wouldn't accept it. Perhaps my wild guess had been correct.

Klemens was regularly seen returning to the Edeltraud mansion, although never leaving. I told Lenz I had seen a vision of him down in an enclosed city, which I assumed to be Turmenbach, the capital city just beneath us. This was, of course, because at the ball I had heard Klemens mention retiring "to Turmenbach." One of Lenz's operatives (simply a Yellow out of uniform) plied one of Edeltraud's servants for information, and learned that Klemens had a mistress stashed down in the city.

Apparently, Bozena also had a lover nearby, but the servant had no information on their whereabouts. I could have told Lenz that for free: in a land like Rotfelsen, a woman must keep lovers very secret because her consequences will be more dire. Klemens could be a cad, could sire bastards, and so forth, but Bozena would be at best upbraided and forcibly married, even if she was the real power of the Gustavus family (which I began to suspect). Lenz was none too happy that he had spent money on any information, however. Wasn't that my job?

I hoped I made up for it by "seeing" other facts about Klemens, Bozena, and their brother, Bernard, who had stayed home: full names, that they had just come into more money due to their father's death, that Klemens had killed a vagabond for fun. Lenz dutifully wrote them all down in his little books. Safe for all time—all two months of it.

The official word, during this time, was that the King was doing much better, but had repaired to his hunting lodge in the caves to the south, where he was stalking the giant coypu rats, wide as two burly men side by side, that lived there. He was apparently quite fond of doing this with no notice, leaving his Queen and most retainers behind. Besides, everyone would see him again at the upcoming King's Dinner, wouldn't they?

While the King enjoyed his constitutional, Lenz and I looked for Klemens down in Turmenbach, which was built into the rotrock itself, and was accessed by bridges and ramps that wound down from the surface.

Turmenbach was a series of caves, sprawling in all directions from a central cavern that was itself larger than some cities I have seen. The rich mostly lived in huge manor buildings carved right out of the cave floors, which were generally as close as possible to the few great cracks in the surface that let in shafts of natural light—although there were also a few gigantic side caves that were entirely the home of this or that noble.

The rest of the city lived their lives in crowded streets or small networks of pockmarks up and down the walls. They traveled by pulley and catwalk, striding streets cut into stone and sometimes hopping over small crevices. Commoners would be knifed in small, dark tunnels that crossed only feet above private ones owned by nobles. Everyone there lived their lives as though such a place was entirely normal.

THE POPPYHOUSE

Hidden off to the side of Turmenbach's great, central cavern was a dirty little neighborhood made up of a mishmash of stone and imported wood buildings. The kind of place, apparently, where visitors stashed their secret lovers. Those streets, I was told, had once been *nice*—before the nobles hollowed out bigger and grander spaces—and so the neighborhood still sat beneath a sliver of sky. When I visited, that sky was dropping the season's snow into Turmenbach.

So, on the fifth day since the Winter Ball, hours before I saw Lenz kill an axewoman twice his size, he and I came to that rundown neighborhood and sat in a Turmenbach poppyhouse. It was little more than a cave with windows and a sign, really, where customers lay about on cushions, drinking poppy milk and dreaming poppy dreams.

We did not partake; poppy milk would have made our business there far less productive (though far more entertaining). Drifting through a poppyhaze while everything around me fell apart had a certain appeal, and the last few days had seen me relax my rules against alcohol, at least. But alas, we sat sober in the Reconstitution Room, which was placed at the front of the poppyhouse to show the street a respectable face. This was where customers recovered from their poppyhaze by sitting upright, drinking lots of water, and eating small, salty things. The fact that my jailer and I had been seated at the Reconstitution Room's window for nearly six hours was worthy of no one's notice. Lenz assured me that so-called poppy geniuses sometimes spent that long or longer reconstituting, in preparation for their next go-round. A morning haze and a dinnertime haze were normal bookends to their day.

If, as I often worried, the very rock of Rotfelsen would somehow crumble in the cataclysm to come, I envied these poppy geniuses who would know, deep down, that the ceiling and floor caving in were only part of the haze.

Lenz and I sat and ate olives, pretzels, pickles, nuts, and dried beet slices as we looked out a small window onto a cavernous Turmenbach street—more an alley, really. Through the window, all sorts of illicit customers turned the light snow on the ground to acrid slush. Winter had finally come to Rotfelsen, sort of.

In the Reconstitution Room, a girl of perhaps eight played a xylophone. There was no tune, just a simple and soothing rhythm loud enough to drown out the mumblings of the next table. No poppy genius wanted to realize, when he started to come down, that he had been blathering and now his neighbors knew the flavor of his illusions. The girl had been there as long as we had, and looked very bored. Lenz explained to me that she was the granddaughter of the proprietor (whom Lenz knew), and that she was being punished. This explained the hastily scrawled sign in front of her that read, "NO TIPS, PLEASE."

Through the window, I could see loiterers at both ends of the street. I knew them to be incognito Yellows, Prince Friedhelm's soldiers ready to enact a quite illegal secret arrest on our behalf. Lenz and I were simply there to oversee, to point out the right man if he ever showed his worthless face. We were bored and on edge all at once.

Lenz had once said we would "sit comfortably far from the dangers we see," after all. Ha ha ha.

"Just four," I said. "We should have brought ten."

"The Prince would not allow it," replied Lenz. "A small force is less likely to be seen. Secretly arresting a Masovskan magnate, based on a prophecy, isn't something the Prince wants to be known for."

"Well, if he does not trust my prophecies, I can leave."

"And yet here we are. Although it would certainly help if you could see a little *more*."

"If only I had seen you coming in the first place," I muttered.

Lenz stared out the window. The girl's plinking slowed as she got tired of pounding the xylophone. The man at the counter, her uncle, began to clap loudly at her, exhorting her to pick up the pace.

"The Prince trusts, Kalyna, but does not want to be seen if things go sour."

"Unlike you and I, who are so excited to be in the middle of it."

Lenz shrugged and shoved a fistful of almonds dusted with pepper into his mouth. Then he grunted, rubbed his bad leg, and fussed about repositioning the rapier in his belt so it didn't scratch the floor. A tired man at the table next to us got up and walked shakily toward the back cave for another haze, his second since we had arrived. The Reconstitution Room was luxurious by the standards of the neighborhood, but my days in the servant house had already spoiled me such that I found it dirty. I hated myself for this: the end was coming—with fire and sword and shattering—while I allowed myself to soften.

"You know," I said, "if the Prince were as careful about ruling as he is about *not* ruling, he might make a half decent king. Why doesn't he just . . . let this plot happen?"

"That is treasonous," Lenz grumbled.

"Arrest me!" I chuckled, arms outstretched.

He grumbled some more. If Lenz were particularly on edge, it may have been because after I nearly died in the pukevapor, he had allowed me to arm myself for this little excursion. My beloved sickle was at my side that day. He knew that I knew better than to attack him here and now, but it was one more small thing outside of my kidnapper's comfort. Something I could cling to, until the Yellows who were almost always watching me confiscated it again.

"Honestly," I said, "our Dutiful Prince is so dedicated to avoiding work that he has given himself huge amounts of it—being king would only pile a little more on his shoulders, I think."

Lenz said nothing.

I turned my stool to face him directly, staring at his left ear and gray temple. "Lenz," I said, "if the Prince decided he *did* want to supplant King Gerhold, would you help him? Or is that where your loyalty ends?"

He looked at me and said in a very slow whisper, "This is the second time you've asked me this. Do you *see* something?"

"No," I answered. Deadpan, to make him wonder. "Just curious."

Lenz's gaze returned to the window. Someone in the back cave had a coughing fit bad enough to be heard in the Reconstitution Room, over the girl's xylophone.

"You are," he mumbled at the window, "insane if you think I can answer that."

"Lenz, Lenz, Lenz!" I laughed, slapping his bad knee to rattle him. "It's an intellectual exercise!"

"In case you haven't noticed," he said, "the very fact that the Prince *refuses* to take the job is why we're in this . . . mess."

"So then you would help him to do so? Make your job easier, wouldn't it?"

"That is extremely not what I said. But I do think our good Prince could do well to be less cagey. He *is* a libertine, but would it be so difficult to show that he cares, at least a little, about keeping our kingdom afloat? Even if it is for selfish reasons."

"What monarch has nonselfish reasons?" I asked.

Lenz did not answer, but he did not disagree either.

"And what," I continued, "do you think Vorosknecht, Selvosch, Edeltraud, and the Gustavuses care about?"

"Power for Vorosknecht. Money for the others. If I were to guess."

I blew out a long breath, flapping my lips irritatingly. "But if the King does so little, why do they need to even supplant him? Why can't he be their figurehead?" He glared at me, and I shrugged, adding, "Context, Lenz."

"I would guess that they want more than one army on their side. High General Dreher has never struck me as hungry for power; he seems to relish living well within his means, and he knows how exhausting it is to use what power he already has. He seems most invested in maintaining the status quo. So the Greens and the Reds won't bow to the Court Philosopher. And now they know that neither will the Yellows."

"Well," I said, "old Friedhelm *tried* to trick them. He thinks he is very clever, doesn't he?"

"Yes," Lenz sighed. "That's why he hired us, after all."

"Hired you."

"Sure."

"And I still wonder whether he might not try to grab that power for himself."

Lenz shook and sat up straight. "Do you really think the Prince would have hired a soothsayer—"

"*Kidnapped* a soothsayer."

"—if he had plans to do . . . that?"

"Maybe he has no plans. Maybe"—I emphasized each word by wagging my finger—"he does not yet know he'll do it!"

"So you *have* seen—?"

"No, no. Not yet," I said.

Then I looked out the window for a long time, acting oblivious to Lenz's study of me.

Outside, at the far right corner, were two incognito Yellows, a squat man and a tall woman. They looked bored, and the novelty of seeing each other in off-duty clothing had long since worn off. Besides, there was only so long they could believably "loiter" before having to move farther down the street, and then later circle back.

The woman was the same tall Yellow who had taken me to the Winter Ball, whose name I had misheard as "Dugmush" because her mouth was full. It now felt too late to ask for a correction. Through the window, I saw her fiddling with her dagger, likely still frustrated at not having a sword; a "normal" Rotfelsenisch woman in a dress was not supposed to be so well armed. When she had been in uniform, I had found her strangely compelling, and also hoped that I, in my uniform, looked a bit like her. In a dress, however, she seemed uncomfortable.

The two disguised Yellows at the other end of the street had wandered away again, to avoid suspicion. This "street" was an enclosed tunnel, and its "buildings" were outcroppings and caves in the rock wall. I was never quite sure how any snow got in there. Across from the poppyhouse were apartments, and we had it on good (well, passable) word that in one of them lived the Turmenbach mistress of Klemens Gustavus.

"He's got to show eventually," Lenz mumbled. "Libido springs eternal."

"Until it doesn't," I added.

"Until it doesn't," he agreed.

"Feh," I grunted and slapped the table. "If only we knew where one could kill vagrants for fun, we'd have him by now."

Lenz smiled. "And do *you* have a lover waiting for you somewhere?"

I laughed and laughed and laughed. A man sitting near us, resting his chin on his hand as he watched visions dance away, jostled and fell onto his table. He looked at me, angry and horrified. I ignored him.

"I'm relieved you were so obvious," I finally said.

"Yes, well, no one's written a treatise on your love life."

"But you will?"

He shrugged.

"In the days since the Winter Ball," I said, "you have been respectful and decent. You've let me roam, within reason, you haven't pried into my affairs or shown off all you already know of them—so genial and comradely that I began to worry I wouldn't notice it when you became yourself." It was good to have these reminders. To know that I was a prisoner, always watched, even while living comfortably.

"I am always myself."

"Of course," I said, patting his hand mockingly, the way Grandmother would have. "I was worried about a subtle campaign of wheedling out my secrets. Thank you for your bluntness."

He cocked his head to the side and put his face in his hand. "So . . . *do* you?"

"What?"

"Have a lover?"

"Why?" I sneered. "You want to *fuck*?"

Lenz scowled and sipped his water.

"Naturally, it's no business of yours," I said.

"Perhaps there's a moonstruck someone waiting for you, then. Raising your child, perhaps?"

I turned away and kept my mouth shut. If I had someone waiting for me, I would have told Lenz I did not. As it was, I decided to let him believe in such a fabulous person of whatever gender. I fancifully imagined Lenz sending lackeys to all corners of the Tetrarchia only to discover, after years of searching, that I hadn't had a real sweetheart since I was twenty.

After years of searching indeed. The Tetrarchia had two months until breaking, violence, and death. Was I escaping south from a

Loashti invasion? North from the Bandit States? Into the depths of Rotfelsen to escape squabbling nobles? Or would a starving peasants' rebellion sweep through and see me as another royal tool? Perhaps the other three Tetrarchic kingdoms would decide they just didn't *like* their insular neighbor. Or perhaps these would all happen at once. I was spoiled for terrible options.

Lenz yawned. "What, ah . . . what language do you and your family speak with each other?" he asked.

"You know," I sighed, "you can just stop prying, rather than coming up with such questions."

Truth be told, we spoke a sort of jumble, and in my thoughts, I changed languages based on my moods. Cöllüknit when I was sad, Masovskani when angry, Skydašiavos when happy, Rotfelsenisch when pragmatic. Sometimes I sang to Papa in Loashti languages.

"Just curious!" laughed Lenz.

"Well then, bring my family to me and you can find out."

"That reminds me," Lenz began, "I received word this morning: your father and grandmother arrived sooner than I expected."

"What?" I slammed my hand down on the table. "Why haven't you told me until now?"

"Wait, look!" Lenz hissed. "Klemens! Finally!"

MONUMENTAL GOONS

The youngest Gustavus brat was indeed across the street, leaving the building of his mistress. This was surprising, as we had expected to catch him *entering* it. Lenz looked perturbed, but not worried: the street only went in two directions, after all, and Yellows were at each end. There would be no mistaking Klemens, either, even if he had not been alone, and wearing his Masovskan furs.

Lenz knotted his brow and further mussed his unruly hair. "I thought he would have a bodyguard."

Klemens, calm and smiling, turned toward his right and began to walk down the street very slowly. The two Yellows behind him, at the far corner, did their best to not look like they were watching. From where Lenz and I sat, the other two—whom Klemens was walking toward—were hidden from our view by the poppyhouse's rotrock window frame. Still, they couldn't have been more than a few yards away. Why didn't they pounce?

Lenz yawned theatrically. "I think . . ." He yawned again. "That I need to stretch my leg a bit before it seizes up, you know? Let us take a stroll, Kalyna Aljosanovna."

"Don't think this conversation is over," I grumbled.

"What more is there to say? Your family is here. You're welcome. We can go see them once Klemens is good and trussed."

As we moved toward the door, we got a better view down the block: Klemens was still walking alone, followed by two Yellows. The other two, who should have been in front of him, were nowhere in sight. Klemens was whistling.

"Where the devils *are* they?" hissed Lenz.

We did not try very hard to exit the poppyhouse inconspicuously: it was the owner's professional duty not to notice strange things, and the customers' hobby. As the girl's soothing plink-plunking faded away, the other two incognito Yellows, the man and woman, sloshed across the snow in front of us, in too much hurry to be careful.

Lenz calmly watched them pass, but his calm evaporated when he looked where they were going: Klemens had an empty stretch in front of him, and then disappeared to the left, down an alley. Or was it another street? In Turmenbach, the difference between an alley and a street felt academic. The disguised Yellows who had passed us followed him into it and vanished.

Lenz moved quickly toward them. I didn't care for intrigue, but I needed to gain Lenz's confidence to effectively escape the country's death. Running headlong into danger at the ball had gotten me my sickle back, after all. Off I went, past my boss-captor, slipping my sickle into my hand. At least this time I wasn't guaranteed to vomit, but anything could happen.

It's good that I did. Run, that is, not vomit. I skidded into the alley, slipping on mushy snow, to find where Klemens' bodyguards had been waiting for us. Three of our disguised Yellows were there too, in a bent and bloody heap, one with his entire face laid open. The fourth, the Yellow who had taken me to the Winter Ball, was alive, held by her wrists with a knee in her back, as Klemens delighted in kicking her. She was then dumped over to join her comrades. Klemens had his sabre out, ready to hack at her prone body, but I fumbled in, and he stopped to look up. Her death mattered as little to him as her life.

I was now, effectively, alone in a narrow alley with Klemens and his three bodyguards, while Lenz limped somewhere in the street behind me. For however much use (I thought) he would be when he got here. The Yellows had surely been ambushed, while I at least *saw* my enemies, so I had that going for me. Klemens looked as maddeningly comfortable as ever.

"And who are you, madam?" he asked. It sounded cordial, even as he nodded his bodyguards toward me: two women and a man, all huge, all with huge axes. Next to those axes, my sickle felt like a toy. I brandished it anyway, and tried not to feel too ineffectual.

And here I had hoped coming down to Turmenbach, out of the hands of Vorosknecht and his Purples, would keep me safe. Ah well.

"I don't suppose it would help to throw the Prince's name at you?" I replied.

"Unsurprising," said Klemens. He shrugged.

A monster of a woman with long black hair loomed up in front of me. Her double-headed axe blade, end-to-end, seemed as long as I was tall. This couldn't have been true, but in that moment, nothing made more sense. She lifted her axe, blocking Klemens from my view.

The gigantic axeblade slammed into the snow and stone with a crunch. I had avoided it ably enough, but was too scared to move in and attack. I backed toward the mouth of the alley instead.

She stepped forward and wrenched the axe up out of the ground. Almost cut me in half with the motion. Yes, *double-headed*, right.

The male bodyguard had a golden beard that made him easy to spot from the corner of my eye. He approached my left side, and the third, a woman with a thatching of scars on her arms, was right behind him, each wielding their own unsettlingly large axes. The open street was to my back, but getting out of their reach seemed impossible.

"Lenz!" I yelled. I did not really want to warn him, but it seemed the best option. I choked it back as the axeman swung across at me. The blade screeched against the walls, and I ducked beneath it.

"Yes, yes, ambush," said Lenz as he limped into sight, rapier in hand.

The man's axe skidded off the rotrock wall and swung wide to his left. The black-haired woman who had come at me first was nearly shoulder-to-shoulder with him in that space. She had to skip forward like a child to avoid his wild swing, which made her look less dangerous. A narrow alley was not the place for such monumental goons.

The black-haired woman turned her skip into a run, past me and toward Lenz, as though this had been her intention all along. The man and the scarred woman both eyed me, stepping forward and back, nearly bumping as they traded places, not sure who should try first.

A light snow began to fall in through a nearby opening in Turmenbach's rotrock ceiling, adding to the slippery layer of brown slush beneath us. The alley was small and awkward, the bodyguards big, so I took a chance. I dashed diagonally at the axeman, head down, praying to someone. He paused before his swing, expecting me to check my momentum, but I abandoned my fate to the slush and skidded past him in the snow while his axe was still raised.

I slid uncontrollably toward the scarred woman. The man fumbled and half turned toward me, getting tangled in his comrade. In a moment I would hit the wall behind her, giving her a chance to cut me down. On my way past her, I flailed my sickle wildly. The axeman was still trying not to hit his comrade when she collapsed in a heap, her stomach opened by my sickle. He was very confused.

I rushed behind him, but the axeman managed to turn with me. Behind him, at the mouth of the alley, Lenz was peppering the black-haired woman with his rapier. He was much more mobile than I had expected. She avoided his attacks, but had no chance to respond.

The man facing me kept swinging, his blade clanking against walls and ground. I hoped his reach was too wide for Klemens to feel safe coming up behind me. I felt wind from the axe as I jumped back to escape, falling painfully to the ground. Sliding backward on my shoulders, the top of my head crashed right into Klemens' shin.

Surprised, he shoved me back toward his lackey. I suppose everyone was surprised. I managed to straighten up, twist past the axe and, using Klemens' gift of momentum, bring my sickle down across the man's face and into his left eye. He fell screaming and grabbed my knees, it seemed, for comfort.

At the same time, I saw the black-haired woman stopped in mid-swing by Lenz's rapier through her throat. She then crumpled to the ground.

I looked back at Klemens.

"Well." Klemens shrugged. "I guess . . ."

He broke into a run, bursting down the alley, past me and toward the street, hoping to get by Lenz and escape. I lifted my sickle as if to throw it, which would have been useless.

Lenz looked tired, and was heavily favoring his bad leg. Klemens ran past, sword flailing ahead of him to clear the way. Lenz stepped aside and thunked the Gustavus brat on the base of his skull with his pommel. Klemens dropped, groaning.

I kicked the half-blind axeman in the face to dislodge myself. I felt no guilt over taking his eye, but this felt wrong to me.

"You may be a better thug than soothsayer," Lenz called from the other end of the alley.

Was this a joke? Or was I not good enough at my job?

"Help me with these Yellows, will you?" he added as he limped toward me.

THE PRISONER

Three of the Yellows were dead. Now, my sickle confiscated once more, we rode back up through the city with an angry cargo, fastidiously tied and gagged in a compartment below our feet.

The only remaining Yellow was my "Dugmush," who was bruised but insisting she was fine. I found myself feeling simultaneously sorry for and scared of her. Her comrades had been killed, as she nearly had, and yet she seemed almost entirely calm, with something terrifying lurking beneath the surface.

But no amount of prisoners, murders, or tall women mattered enough to keep me from needing to see my father—I had never before lived apart from him.

"Where is my family?" I asked Lenz as the carriage began to creak its precarious way up to the surface.

"Safe. On the palace grounds," he grunted.

"Take me to see my father."

He coughed. "We're a little busy at the moment, Kalyna. Just now, we have two prisoners"—he stomped on the floor with his good foot—"one soldier, one soothsayer, and myself. We'll need to get Klemens good and squared away, and interrogated, not to mention gather whatever prophecies about him you can muster. I cannot spare you, or the Yellows to escort you."

I began to wonder again if Papa was alive at all, or if the possibility of his existence was being dangled in front of me, waiting for the perfect opportunity to break me by letting me know he was dead in a Masovskan ditch.

In silence, we ascended to the open air, where the snow had stopped, and the sun was out again. Lenz spent the time scribbling onto a piece of paper pressed against his good knee. Once we had lurched onto the surface, we rolled toward the giant walls of the palace grounds, and through them to that vast complex.

We were taken to where Lenz lived, in the officers' quarters of one of the barracks that circled the edges of the palace grounds. It was a squat brick of granite: painted yellow, naturally. In front was a pleasant little filigreed table and chairs, so that officers could pretend they were at a café. The carriage deposited us at its door, where we met Behrens, the sharpshooter, and a group of Yellows. Lenz explained what had happened, and they were all made suitably angry.

"We have the brat, and another," sighed Lenz. "No matter your inclinations, don't hurt them. Just put them away, *separately*. And once that's done, Kalyna and I will speak to our honored guest."

"Of course," said Behrens.

Klemens Gustavus' surviving guard was taken away, and I never did see him again. As he was just some mercenary, I hope that he was simply held for a bit and let go. Klemens had a bag thrown over his head and was marched right up into the barracks, where all the Yellows who saw him simply glanced at him and then turned away. They did this very purposefully, as if clearly signaling that they knew he was never here, and would not be surprised to never see him again. I found this terrifying, and I certainly did not forget that Klemens was only here because of my lies.

Lenz and I followed him upstairs through the barracks, lagging behind as Lenz's leg was greatly bothering him. By the time we got to Lenz's horribly messy office, I had entirely lost track of where Klemens had been taken. My jailer sat at his desk and began scratching away with a pen. I shoved some papers off a couch, sat down, and looked around.

What I could see of his rooms were less a study and a bedroom than they were two identical rooms that each played both all at once. Books, clothes, tools, cots, couches, bundles, all of these could be found in each room, scattered haphazardly. I suspect that before we worked together, weapons had been scattered about in the same fashion. The next room over had a real bed, and therefore must have been the bedroom, despite both rooms showing signs of having been slept in. I kicked over a pile of books, but Lenz ignored me and kept writing.

After maybe fifteen minutes of this, the Yellow who had survived our encounter down in Turmenbach—Dugmush, as I was now officially calling her in my head—reappeared. She was back in uniform, and appeared a completely new person; the bruises on her face only made her seem more formidable. She crossed to Lenz's bedroom and closed the door after her. I opened my mouth to ask, but decided against it. After another half an hour or so, I got too bored and angry that I wasn't with my father.

"What are you doing?" I grunted.

"Finishing up about our little adventure."

"Isn't that, you know, secret?"

"No more so than my theories on the King's virility, and the rest." He gestured unthinkingly at the pile of papers I had displaced on the couch.

"And if you're going to just sit there and write, why can't I go see my father?"

"Don't worry. You come across valiantly."

I sneered. "I'd rather be left out."

"No such luck." He finished writing with a big, theatrical flourish, and then stood up. "Well, let's go talk to our prisoner."

"Where exactly is Klemens Gustavus locked up, anyway? In your rooms?"

"Sort of!" he laughed. "We can't keep him in a prison when the state doesn't admit he's a prisoner."

Lenz walked into the bedroom, and I was curious enough to follow him. He asked me to close the door and, rolling my eyes, I did so. I saw no sign of Dugmush here. Lenz put both hands against the base of his bed, pushed, grunted, and almost collapsed.

"This . . . stupid . . ." he grumbled. He pushed again and collapsed, again, rather than push too hard from both legs. "Could you help me, Kalyna Aljosanovna? The *Prince*'s rooms have perfect hidden doors that glide like greased knives, but I am not the Prince."

"You have a secret passage?"

"I wanted to slide it open and surprise you, but it is tricky and my leg is bum."

I stood above him, considering possible bludgeons in the disordered room around me. Then I sighed, got on my knees, and pushed. The bed groaned and swiveled out: the head was bolted to the floor, and the foot moved to reveal a rotrock staircase.

"These stairs are the only way to where we're going," said Lenz.

"That you know of."

"You first, please. It's quite steep, and I'd rather you not push me."

"Foiled again."

The stairs twisted so often I quickly lost track of how far down we were. Could one hide from a war here? Not if Rotfelsen's great rock was going to shatter, of course. Our footsteps echoed loudly, and I had to raise my voice over them to continue insulting Lenz.

"You aren't married," I said.

"Oh?"

"You took such an interest in my love life, it seems fair to pry into yours. No one who loved you would let you keep your rooms like that."

"Well," he said, "I'm young yet."

I prepared some other crack, but was interrupted by the muffled, hoarse, agitated screaming of a man with filled with rage, and with too much confidence to be scared. Yet.

"—and you fat, ugly, smashed-tomato-faced Rots wouldn't hear the rumble of your doom if you could get your fathers' cocks out of your ears long enough to—!"

At the bottom of the room were two bored Yellows in wooden chairs trying not to stare at a barred cell in the corner. In that cell was Klemens Gustavus, and in the whole chamber was his voice. I wondered if the "rumble of your doom" part was a normal threat, or proprietary knowledge. But how could he know anything? He may not have even been involved in the plot: I had invented a role for him out of my own childish anger, hadn't I?

"—go bathe in your auntie's menstrual blood in the summer home you built in your brother's ass, you—!"

"Seems a little sore," said Lenz. He was calm, but he had to yell to be heard.

"—slice up your pisshole so it opens like a peony in—!"

"He ran out of good things to say in Rotfelsenisch a few minutes ago," said Dugmush, "so he has moved on to Masovskani." She smiled brightly, reclining against the wall, with her hat halfway over her face, entirely relaxed despite the day's excitement. "I don't know what any of it means!"

"—flung from the top of the Sunset Palace dangling from your intestines—!"

"He's run out of good things to say in Masovskani too," said Lenz.

There was one lone torch on the wall, near the cell, and we stood mostly in the dark. I hoped that Klemens had not recognized me in Turmenbach, and would not do so here either.

"—may your ancestors rise from the grave in a thousand years to violate your descendants and— Oh." Klemens looked at Lenz and dropped his voice to normal, saying in Rotfelsenisch, "You have a limp. The one who cracked my skull."

"If only," said Lenz.

"This will all go much easier," suggested Dugmush, "if you let us jostle him a little now and then." She smiled again. An easy smile: the implication was troubling, but I couldn't help smiling back.

"No," said Lenz.

"Not shatter," she clarified. "Jostle. I owe him after he killed the others, and kicked me a thousand times."

"Five times," said Klemens.

She shrugged. "Lucky for you I'm unaccustomed to fighting in a skirt, and only had a dagger."

"I'm sorry," Lenz told the Yellow, "but no jostling."

She shrugged again and made a "well, I did what I could" expression, which she trained on me, then her compatriot, who shrugged back, and then Klemens.

"You're all going to die," said Klemens, pacing. "Not—not how everyone will die," he clarified, stuttering his Rotfelsenisch in anger. "I mean . . . I mean everyone in this room who is not me will die soon and ignominiously. That is what I mean."

The Yellow who had said nothing so far grunted.

"You do not do this to *me*," continued Klemens, grabbing the bars. "You won't kill me, and you won't keep me."

"Oh?" asked Lenz.

"I'm too important. You Rots, unable to see outside of your

depressing kidney stone of a kingdom, may think that no one outside it matters, but I am not some provincial Masovskan merchant. I run the biggest changing banks in the Tetrarchia."

"Yet you've already disappeared," said Lenz. "It'll make no difference how lasting that absence is."

Klemens seemed to have not considered this until now. He fell onto his cot and put his head in his hands.

And there was my guilt. I should have felt nothing close to sympathy for Klemens, a terrible man who killed because he could. But it's hard for me to keep seeing through the eyes of the helpless—I am just so used to seeing through my own. Here was a ghastly young man who could easily end up assassinated and never found based on my need to cover my own failure. Even he did not deserve to be a casualty of my fraud. Did he?

"Klemens Gustavus," said Lenz. "We know who you are, and we know that you, your sister Bozena, and Edeltraud von Edeltraud are involved in a plot against the throne. You can tell us what happened the night of the Winter Ball now, or you can suffer the consequences."

Lenz and I stepped closer to the cell. The guards sat up straight. Klemens dug his fingers into his greasy hair and looked up at us. He started to laugh.

"Against the throne? *Against*?" He laughed again, edged with desperation, and he began to shake.

We stood unmoving, silent.

"A plot against the throne? Tell you? Oh . . . oh hell, you're going to kill me." His voice strained and tears began to roll down his face. His hands shook, and he didn't think to sit on them—just moved them up and down as though looking for somewhere to put them. His sallow complexion began to turn red, and he began sobbing, then gulping for air.

"Just tell us," said Lenz. "Then you live."

If Lenz felt guilty, it did not show in his body language. I hoped it did not show in mine either. I had been nearly killed by Klemens' lackeys Down Valley Way because he had preferred assassination to sharing any part of his wealth. I hated him. Why couldn't he have the decency to strut and gloat? I wanted him cowed by his loss of power, but not so thoroughly that it was unsatisfying. Instead of a sadistic plotter, here was a sobbing man-child who reminded me of every time in my life I'd been caught and threatened, every time I'd been accused of impossible things, told to explain the unexplainable.

"Tell you?" Klemens laughed again, hysterical. "You kill my guards, hide me here, demand secrets I don't have about a plot *I am trying to stop* and—!"

"Trying to stop?" grunted Lenz. He moved forward, leaning against the bars. "What do you mean?"

Klemens muttered the defining traits of several Masovskan gods into his hands.

"Klemens," said Lenz, saying each following word slowly and carefully, "tell me what you've been trying to stop."

"Your Prince," Klemens sobbed. "And the Quarrymaster, and I don't know who else. They want to kill the King." He looked down as he spoke. "We planned a counterattack, to kill your damned Prince. But we failed, and now the King is missing."

Lenz made a noise deep in his throat, but otherwise did not seem to react much to this. "What," he ventured, "convinced you of this plot's existence?"

Klemens simply began to blubber, then hiccup, then shake his head. He seemed either to not have an answer, or to be entirely unable to speak out of fear. He raised his hands, as though to motion toward an obvious answer, but still no words came.

"Think it over, Klemens," said Lenz. "You may be able to save yourself. Perhaps your sister, too."

He turned to leave. I followed, and hoped I had not completely bungled everything.

MORE LIES

I had always thought that one's joints aching with the weather was an invention of Grandmother's. Or that if it were real, it was only for the very old. But as Lenz and I sat in another of his rooms, I could see that the cold outside caused pain in his left leg, although he was no more than thirty. He rubbed it, groaned, kept moving it up here, then down there, then back up again. He didn't seem to be exaggerating, although I harbored no doubts that if he needed to spring up and kill someone again, he could.

"That," grunted Lenz as he shoved papers off a chair in his suite, "was not what I expected."

I stood and said nothing.

"What *exactly* did you see?" he continued. "What exactly of Edeltraud and the Gustavuses planning to kill the King?"

I was in deep now, and the only way I saw out was more lies. What was I supposed to do, tell him I was a fraud who had lucked into a role in the highest court? The assumption would be that I was a spy from somewhere else—Loasht perhaps. These Rotfelsenisch always assumed Loasht because they couldn't place my background, and had very little actual experience with the Loashti. I decided the best way out was anger. I got up and stood over him. Lenz stared at me, unblinking.

"I saw three rich and powerful people who had orchestrated an attack, and I saw the King!" I waved my hands above my head. "What do you want from me? I see things, but I must also *interpret*. You drag me away from my family, whose years of experience can help me understand my visions, throw me in front the most bizarre and circular court, and tell me that there's a plot against the King!"

Lenz said nothing. I steeled myself, put my hands on his shoulders, and looked straight into his eyes. "I was ready to see plots against the King everywhere, and I must have seen their attack on the Prince, *who was standing next to the King*. What, by all the gods, did you expect?"

There was silence for a few moments. Lenz looked thoughtful.

"Can you tell me anything else?" he asked.

"Their plan, whatever it is, was called 'the hammer.' Or, at least, Edeltraud called it that." I smiled a bit. "Klemens thought the name was overdramatic."

"Hmm," said Lenz. "I suppose I agree with him on that, if it's true. Anything else? Anything *solid*?"

I glared at him. "Solid? No. For all the reasons I have just given you. But I've been visiting the inn on Ottilie's Rock, and learning some uncomfortable things regarding the Bandit States."

"Can you, ever, be more specific?'

"It seems the Bandit States have indeed been invading the rock itself, and that the High General has covered it up." I wasn't sure I believed this, but it seemed possible, and I needed something.

"Really?" Lenz scoffed. "Surely someone would have noticed that."

"How often does anyone up here speak to those on the outposts of your kingdom? How much power does the High General have over the people who live there?"

He looked thoughtful.

"For that matter," I continued, "couldn't a High General order massacres of his own people to cover up previous massacres by his enemies?"

"Is this something you have seen evidence of?"

"No, Lenz, I am making guesses. Something that even *I* must do. Let me get closer to Andelka to be sure. Some time near the High General wouldn't hurt either."

"Very well," he grunted. "I'll see what I can get out of Klemens."

There were a lot of ways my many, many deceptions could all come crashing down, but I still felt the satisfaction of having bluffed my way to safety, for at least the next hour.

"At least he wants to protect the King," I offered.

"At the expense of Prince Friedhelm, unfortunately. I don't know how we can convince him we're on the same side, now that we've killed his bodyguards, trapped him here, and cannot find the King."

"Hmm, yes, what a bother," I said. "So, take me to my family."

"We must report this to the Prince right away."

"After I see my family," I said. But he didn't even seem to hear me.

THE TWELFTH RECOURSE

And so we were whisked back up to the Sunset Palace once more. Lenz seemed almost as unhappy about it as I was. Soon we were in the Prince's study, and Lenz told him all that had happened today: about capturing Klemens, and what he had said in his cell. Lenz did not tell him about the poppyhouse, which was my personal favorite part of the day, but some people simply don't understand what matters in life.

Once he was done, the Prince shot up and began pacing intensely enough to wear a hole in his polished floor. This was the first time I'd seen him since our interview in his baths, and he did not seem to have spent the last five days in a good state. His fine clothes were disheveled, his eyes were bleary, and he was furiously smoking a pipe full of something that was not calming him down. He went on pacing for some time, and I found I could not care much for how unhappy he may have been. I just wanted to see my father.

"You know, Lenz," said Prince Friedhelm, finally, "I was already thinking it's time. But with what you've told me about Klemens, it is certainly time."

"Time, Your Highness?" asked Lenz. He sounded very much like he knew what that meant, but was hoping he was wrong.

"Yes, time! They're trying to kill me, it's almost the King's Dinner, and my brother is off *hunting*, supposedly. Such was my thinking over the last few days, but this Klemens character has decided me fully. If he's truly trying to *stop* these plotters against the throne, we need him on our side. And I only see one way to do that."

"But, Your Highness," began Lenz, "if your brother truly is off hunting, and he comes back—"

"He isn't, I'm sure of it. But if he *is*, we shall have an awkward reunion. Which is fine. We've never much liked each other." The Prince moved over to his bookshelf, and yanked one of the books so hard that it came off in his hand, revealing the hidden lever that controlled the hidden door.

I almost laughed. The Prince pulled the lever angrily and the door swung open, revealing a long staircase. These Rotfelsenisch loved their hidden passageways, I suppose.

"Hurry up!" Friedhelm yelled down the stairs. Then he grinned mirthlessly; Lenz put his head in his hands.

Soon enough, footsteps could be heard coming up toward us, and then an extremely bland-looking man appeared at the top of the stairs, huffing and puffing.

"Well . . . phew, quite the climb," he grunted. "I say, well, I made it, finally." He braced himself against the false bookshelf and smiled a clever little smile.

"What . . . ?" I asked, looking to Lenz.

"Meet the Twelfth Recourse," he sighed.

I looked back at the man. His smile disappeared, and his face became smooth, forgettable, vacant. I blinked four or five times as I felt the pang of recognition. He looked exactly like someone I had seen speaking to the Prince at the Ball: he looked exactly like the King.

He stepped toward me, his face that same vacant mask, then he broke back into a smile and bowed to me.

"I don't believe I've had the pleasure," he said. "Name's Olaf"—he winked—"but you can call me Gerhold VIII."

Lenz flopped back onto Prince Friedhelm's couch. Probably because of his leg, but it also carried with it the whiff of a great lady fainting in surprise.

"I cannot believe you're actually doing it," he grunted. He then quickly added, "Your Highness."

The Prince grinned. "And why not, eh?" He seemed very pleased with himself.

"And that you have now told Kalyna, as well," Lenz added.

"Well, if my brother has been kidnapped, how is she supposed to find him in her visions if she thinks that Olaf here is him, eh?"

"Just so," I said.

"I suppose," murmured Lenz.

I moved closer to Olaf, squinting at him. "How . . . ?"

"Flesh-alchemy, of course," sighed Lenz.

"But . . . like this?" I reached out, and almost grabbed Olaf's cheek to see if it would come off.

"Oh, far more than your garden variety alchemy," laughed Prince Friedhelm. He leaned back on his desk, seeming relaxed for the first time since the Winter Ball.

Olaf nodded at me. "Go on."

I pinched his cheek like he was a child. It felt real enough.

"We spent quite some time," said Lenz, "finding someone bodily similar enough to the King who also had . . . well . . ."

"No real ties," laughed Olaf. "No one will much care that I'm gone, you see."

"A drifter," added the Prince, "found living from ditch-to-ditch in the deepest caves. But a lucky drifter, in the scheme of things. He'll get to live like the King for a week or two."

"Until I'm poisoned or stabbed, or found out and *then* poisoned or stabbed," added Olaf. He hardly seemed sad about it.

Lenz grunted and threw his leg up onto the side of the couch, putting himself on his back. "After we found Olaf, we had the best flesh-alchemists spend weeks studying the King from afar, studying paintings and sketches of the King, studying even the gold marks that bore his face. Each focused on one part of his face, supposedly to reconstruct in case he ever had an accident, and then taught *those features* to other flesh-alchemists, without telling them whose face they belonged to. Everyone was sworn to secrecy, of course."

"Of course," echoed Friedhelm, absentmindedly.

"I've never heard of such a thing," I muttered, finally taking my hand away from Olaf, who smiled and became some semblance of himself again.

"Of course not!" laughed the Prince. "It's never been attempted before."

"The sad part," said Olaf, "is that if I survive this, they'll change me to not-the-King, but they won't be able to turn my face back to how it was." He shrugged. "No one ever spent weeks and weeks studying *my* face. No sketches, no paintings. A pity: I was quite handsome!"

Lenz dipped his head slightly in agreement.

"And you've lived down in a hidden room . . . ?" I began.

"For some time," laughed Olaf. "I can't very well go walking around like this. But the room has a window, so I could get used to the sun. It was torture at first, but now I rather like it. What's more, I had time to learn the King's manner. It mostly involves thinking of something else and looking far away." His eyes went vacant.

I absorbed that, and his seeming nonchalance about the whole situation. It was impossible for me to imagine this plan *working*.

"You must have spent that time learning how to be a king, yes?" I finally asked. "Polishing up on duties and such?"

Olaf snorted. "What duties? All I have to do is show up where I'm told, smile, nod, and not say anything *too* idiotic."

I opened my mouth and closed it again. Then I looked at Prince Friedhelm. He still seemed quite pleased with himself, so I decided now was as good a time as any to broach something that had been on my mind.

"Your Highness," I began.

"Mm?"

"If there are no real duties involved in being King of Rotfelsen—no complex decisions that must be made, no crushing responsibilities— why are you *so* insistent on avoiding the crown?"

"Kalyna . . ." Lenz warned.

I quickly added a curtsy and an, "If you please," so as not to seem too presumptuous.

Friedhelm was surprised at my forwardness, but then the corner of his mouth curled up, as though this was also something he *wanted* to tell. As though he thought he was about to be very charming.

"Why, Kalyna Aljosanovna," he said, "because it is *boring*. Crushingly, terribly boring."

Lenz looked up at this.

"For a man like Olaf, with no other prospects, it's the good life. But for me?" Friedhelm began to pace. "State dinner after state dinner, after state *luncheon*; presiding over fencing tournaments; staid little"—he yawned—"drinks with staid little functionaries; the opera, but always with some morose outer noble singing his own little aria about the taxes into my ear; siring absolutely, positively, *no bastards*." He made a face and shook his head. "Absolutely not. I shall have the privileges of royalty without *those* responsibilities. Let Olaf here"—he patted the man's shoulder—"handle the boring parts until we find my brother."

"And if your brother hasn't been kidnapped?" asked Lenz.

"Lenz, I tell you again that he *has*," said the Prince, leaning on his desk again. "And now his kidnappers will be trapped and confused. They'll want to prove that I've put a double on the throne, but won't be able to accuse me without exposing themselves." He grinned and clapped his hands together. "Meanwhile, you two will figure out where the real King has disappeared to. This will teach that ridiculous little Selvosch and that pompous Vorosknecht to turn against me."

"But," Lenz tried again, "Your Highness, if your brother is simply hunting—"

"Then mayhap this will teach him not to disappear like that. And when he comes home, I'll make a big show of re-changing Olaf's *pretty face*. After brother Gerhold is back on the throne, perhaps I'll lend him one of my bastards, since his *Queen* is unable to give him one."

"Are you sure," began Lenz, carefully, "you're not doing this *just* to see the look on her face?"

The Prince pushed off his desk and stood very straight, looking down at Lenz. "I have given you a very free hand, Lenz Felsknecht," he said quietly. "Don't you go and force me to rein you in."

Lenz spun to sit up straight, wincing as his bad leg was jarred in the motion. "Yes, Your Highness."

"And get off my couch," said the Prince. "You are dismissed."

So we were hurtling toward having two identical kings. If we couldn't have the fool, we would have the drifter with a death wish. Without either of them, we'd have the *Prince*. Gods, it was like I was seeing how everything would fall apart right in front of me, but with no way to change it. Unless I made it worse.

Lenz and I began to leave. I opened my mouth to remind him that *now* I needed to see my father, before the Prince spoke up again.

"Oh, and Lenz, please take Kalyna with you to the watchtower right away. I've hired someone else who should be able to help you find the King: You remember Chasiku, yes?"

"Oh. Yes, Your Highness," said Lenz.

We began to leave. Olaf waved cheerily, with seemingly no idea of the violent doom he would probably cause.

"I look forward to working with you!" he sang out.

THE WATCHTOWER

Soon I was back in a carriage with Lenz once again. He looked very irritated.

"This plan," I ventured, "seems ill-advised."

"I wouldn't go so far as to call it a plan," Lenz grumbled. "His Highness has a bad habit of throwing new ideas at a problem and just . . . seeing what lands."

"Like hiring a soothsayer," I said.

Lenz looked up at me. "You could say that." Then he broke into a laugh.

"What's so funny?"

"Chasiku," he laughed. "He's hired two of them, now."

"Two what?"

"Soothsayers," he replied, smiling.

I was quiet for the rest of the ride, until we reached the watchtower, which was made of rotrock bricks. Lenz talked to me, but I acted as though I wasn't listening.

This watchtower, Lenz explained, was one of the oldest structures on the palace grounds, and hardly in use anymore. It had been built in pre-, pre-, pre-Tetrarchic days, when Rotfelsen was a collection of small states, many of which planted capitals here on the surface: a confusing time, when who ruled which outcropping, or which tunnel, was never clear. The watchtower had originally been built to keep a lookout for armies on the surface, and was not high enough to look into the forests beneath Rotfelsen's bulging sides. In our modern, civilized age, it was for punishment: a good place to send a loud soldier for a day or two, where they could watch for absolutely nothing. It had apparently been easy for the Prince to requisition the watchtower for the use of his newest human bauble.

"A second soothsayer," I said as I stepped out of the carriage.

Lenz nodded.

"So the Twelfth Recourse wasn't enough?"

"I suppose this is Eleventh Recourse, Stroke Two," he sighed as he led me and a Yellow into the small circular tower. "Her name was brought up in our original search, and I even visited her in North Shore Skydašiai, but she said no. I suppose she changed her mind, and the Prince accepted."

"She got to say *no*?"

"Well, it was earlier in our search."

"In that case, will you be—"

"Letting you go? No," he said quickly. Then he grinned. "That isn't how Friedhelm operates. And besides, he seems to think you saved his life." He chuckled at the thought.

"Lucky me," I grunted.

"A second King, a second soothsayer," sighed Lenz. "We had better find Gerhold before the Prince replaces me, as well."

I snorted a bit at the thought. "Or before he brings in a juggler, and a dramaturge, and a bard, and—"

"Don't even speak that into existence!" said Lenz. "I doubt it is beyond him."

Well, this was a terrifying new wrinkle. Lenz likely thought little of my supposed Gift after that Klemens debacle, and this new fortuneteller was probably a fraud, like all who claimed to see the future outside of my small family. A more skilled fraud than me, likely enough. She would, I expected, do everything she could to discredit me. Or, at best, her lies would run counter to mine. And when I became even more useless than I already was, I would become only a prisoner who knew about a false king. Not a long life expectancy there, I suspected. How long had the Prince allowed those flesh-alchemists who cobbled together Olaf to live? Not long, I'm sure. My heart began to positively pound.

"As far as I know," I said, "only my family has the Gift." Best to start discrediting her *now*, rather than later. I hoped I would escape soon, but it's always good to plan for every possibility.

"Families grow and separate," said Lenz as he walked toward the center of the watchtower. "You might be surprised at your relatives."

"I have two relatives."

The watchtower was only as wide around as a big room. It was dark, with one guttering torch visible from the ground floor, and around the walls, there was a small, twisty staircase with a lot of bricks missing. A small pallet on a rope hung in the center.

"More stairs? You're not making your job easy, Lenz."

He smiled grimly and sat on the pallet. There was a wrenching sound above, and the pallet shook and began to rise.

"It's meant for supplies," said Lenz. "You'd better jump on now or take the stairs." When he finished talking, he had already risen past my waist.

I took the stairs. The Yellow followed me, to make sure I didn't try to cut the rope somehow.

At the top, the staircase curled around a system of pulleys and weights. The pallet was just surfacing, and a rope reached all the way down to the bottom, with some sort of counterweight hanging from it.

Lenz grunted as he flopped over onto the floor next to me, quite undignified. He pulled himself up. The top of the watchtower was a small open platform that led right out on all sides to a railing from which the surface of Rotfelsen could be viewed. We were up much higher than the nearby barracks or my servant house, yet the watchtower was hardly noticeable when it shared a stage with the Sunset Palace. There was one walled-off room up here, and the rest was open to the air. The room had a small wooden door, which was the only new-looking thing here, besides the pallet and its ropes.

That door was open. The small room had bedding on the floor, a few bags of what I took to be clothes, and no other openings except for a matching open door that led out onto the walkway that circled the watchtower. There was a figure in the room, sitting on the bedding, staring out that open door, with her back was to us. As I have mentioned, her name was Chasiku, and she was from North Shore Skydašiai.

A VERY SHORT HISTORY OF THE PRE-TETRARCHIA

Have I explained to you, whoever may be reading this, Skydašiai and its two shores? It would have been the strangest kingdom of the Tetrarchia, were it not for the other three.

Long ago (but long after the Ancients and all that), a wandering tribe of sallow, pale people came to what would eventually be the Tetrarchia, and for some reason, settled in a frozen forest (Masovska). Soon after, they were supposedly followed by a sort of sibling tribe of stocky people both related to, and distinct from, that first group. This second tribe, smartly, settled in a pleasant seaside land next door (roughly half of Skydašiai).

These two tribes squabbled and split off for some time, until a host of entirely different peoples arrived, darker than any descended from those two tribes, and speaking languages like nothing that had been heard in the region before. They trickled into the nearby mountains, and these became the Quru.

Rots liked to think that they arrived fully formed, but this is of course untrue. The pink cheeked and often blonde people who came next gravitated toward the great rock nearby, for some ungodly reason, and fought amongst themselves within it for centuries.

These four groups were soon hundreds of small nations and city-states. Over time, they congealed down into roughly four, fighting and trading amongst themselves. But one more element was required for them to become the four groups that existed in my time.

The Skydaš Sea (or whatever it was called back then) cut off the north of our continent, except where the Quru mountains curled around its eastern end. The northern shore of the sea was visible from the southern, hanging golden in the distance. The not-yet-Skydašians on the southern shore sometimes sailed across to hunt and forage, but they never stayed. Monolithic Loasht loomed to the northeast, already ancient and sitting upon its guns; trading across the water, with no desire for new neighbors.

Then perhaps a thousand years ago, the *other* Skydašiai came. They wandered into the region from somewhere in the lands northwest of the Skydaš Sea, and settled right at its shore. The word "Skydašiai" did not exist yet, and these new settlers, with their deep brown skin and tightly curled hair, did not look like their new neighbors. This people happened to arrive during the lowest point in Loasht's most recent Era of Waning (which some whisper will soon end), and so were able to avoid being expelled or absorbed. They traded, fought, set down roots, and built cities.

There was no singular moment when the North and South Shore folk merged into one kingdom: their union was more gradual than the carefully negotiated formation of the Tetrarchia, centuries later. The two became symbiotic, with the North Shore providing a military bulwark against Loasht, while the South Shore grew abundant produce and became a trading hub. People began to intermarry, and rudimentary trade languages expanded into greater complexity. By the time a royal marriage was made between the two shores, their unification was a foregone conclusion.

Later, when the Tetrarchia was formed, Skydašiai (a word combined from two old languages that have long since merged and rendered the term gibberish) was a single country with a single language and set of laws. The North Shore and South Shore remained somewhat distinct groups through the centuries—with different physical characteristics on the outer ends, blending toward an almost homogeneous center around the sea, and with different customs throughout, depending on local specialties—but Skydašiai is Skydašiai. It is as much a land of wandering peoples settling down next to each other as is the Tetrarchia itself.

CHASIKU

She did not turn to face us. Skydašians of both shores tended to be a friendly, physical people—they liked to *hug*, but not Chasiku. She was sitting straight as the watchtower itself, with her legs pointing out in front of her. Cold morning light peeked in around her head from the door through which she looked. Her hair was cut extremely short, and I could see where the nape of black hair faded into the dark brown skin of her neck. She kept her back to me when she spoke.

"Good to see you again, Chasiku," said Lenz.

"Pleased to meet you," I offered.

"The limping spy I've met," she said. "But you're new. Average height. Some sort of mutt. Long, loose, curly hair, big nose. Scar on the upper lip."

"Uh-huh," I said.

Her back was still to me, naturally. A basic trick: she had either stolen a glimpse before I saw her, or pieced together clues from what Lenz, or Yellows, had told her.

"Pleased to meet you, too," I repeated, loudly and slowly.

She nodded her head slightly, toward the open door. "Kalyna Aljosanovna Tsaoxelek," she said.

"Kalyna Aljosanovna," I replied. "You must be confused."

"Oh!" She curved forward, away from us, like a tree that grows in heavy wind, then shook her head. "I apologize. That is not your name yet. It may never be."

I turned to Lenz and trained a *very* incredulous sort of look on him. Did he really believe her?

But then, he believed me. Didn't he?

"Maybe you will come around to her," he said.

"It's true," said Chasiku. "Maybe."

"That," I growled, "is just about enough of that." I stomped around the room to look into her face. "You may not need to look at me, but I prefer to see the person I'm talking to!" In order to better form fake prophecies about them.

I had expected that there would be a theatrical reason why Chasiku didn't show us her face: blindness (real or pretended) or great scarring. But no, when I came around, and stuck my head between hers and the door, she looked up at me uncaringly. Her face was smooth and unblemished, with high cheekbones; her eyes were large. She seemed willowy and hardy at the same time, if that is possible. As though you could easily snap her body in half, but she, head against her own rear, would only shrug and ask if you could do no better. She was attractive, I suppose.

"Yes. All right," she said, looking me in the eyes. "This is better?"

"Where do you come from?"

"Skydašiai."

"Yes, but . . . I mean, where did Lenz find you?"

"Skydašiai. Months ago. I turned down his offer, but have since decided I could use a change of scenery."

I looked up, past her, at Lenz. He looked back at me, but said nothing.

"You are giving me a headache," said Chasiku. "I feel the pounding of your death between my temples."

"Oh, really?" It was a stupid thing to say, but all that came to me.

"The Prince has told me about your family," said Chasiku, "and what you call 'the Gift.' You are all extremely lucky."

"*Lucky?*"

"My family," she said, "live on the outskirts of Kalvadoti, a great city. Even from so far away, where we see no one but those who come for our services, we are assaulted by the trembling delicacy of the people crammed into those buildings and streets. So many people, so many possibilities, every choice they may or may not make: it is all amplified, a constant thrumming behind everything. We have never called this a 'Gift.' It is a burden."

"That is all very sad, if true," I said. "My father is beaten by nonsensical imagery from across the world, so you will forgive my not crying for you. It also seems that your family has homes."

"I don't care to play at whose life is harder," she sighed. "The closer anyone is, the more of their futures dance before me. This whole place quivers of death more than most, as though none of you exist at all. It must be all these soldiers killing each other."

"And you feel my death, too?" I asked, trying to sound as unconvinced as possible.

Chasiku nodded.

"I thought," I said, grinning a little, I admit, "that I was going to marry this Tsaoxelek person, whose name I don't recognize. Now you say I'm to die soon."

Chasiku wrinkled her brow and cocked her head to the side to look at me, as though I had tried to get the better of her by pointing out that the sky was not blue, but *sky blue*.

"Sometimes," she said very slowly, as though to a child, "there may be *different things that can happen*. Is that so complex?"

I narrowed my eyes and stood up, back to the cold sunlight, arms crossed. "Yes, thank you. My family sees whatever is most likely."

"'Most likely'? What is 'most likely'?"

I shrugged. "Whatever we see."

She actually looked thoughtful for a moment; her eyes wandered over to the single decoration on her wall: a hanging tapestry that, to my view at least, was entirely abstract. I glanced at Lenz again, but he was watching her.

"Death, then," said Chasiku. "Death soon is what I see the most. Kalyna the wife of a man named Tsaoxelek is far less likely."

I wondered, was this woman a fraud trying to scare me, or planning to kill me? Or was she the real thing, and seeing, in her own roundabout way, the same ending of the Tetrarchia that my father had picked out of the future. Was all that death she saw because we had two kings? Or because Loasht would invade? Or because an earthquake would break Rotfelsen like an egg?

I looked at Lenz again, trying to intimate that if he believed her, he was a fool. He betrayed nothing of what he thought, unfortunately.

Chasiku melted back into the position she had held before. Her legs were still stuck straight out, across the bedding and the floor, pointing toward me and the door to the watchtower's platform. She stuck her arms out behind her and leaned on them, but remained almost entirely straight. She blinked again, closed her eyes longer, opened them, and sighed.

"And has she told you anything helpful yet?" I asked Lenz, over Chasiku's head.

"She only just got here," he replied.

"I am truly not interested in arguing with you," said Chasiku. "Your very presence here hurts me."

"Convenient," I grunted. "Privacy means fewer chances to say the wrong thing, more time to think out your 'visions.'"

Chasiku fixed her gaze upon me with a look that seemed angry and pleading all at once. I expected the anger, but the absolute desperation unbalanced me. There was something in her eyes that seemed to beg for my understanding.

"I need you to leave now, and take him with you. I am not so lucky as to have my mind pick and choose what it sees, as yours does. Even your father, it sounds to me, sees one thing at a time. To have you here, with all of your possible courses of action, and the things that could be done to you, oozing out of your every pore, it's as though I'm trying to read a book in Loashti while you yell Skydašiavos curses in my ear. Do you understand?"

I glared at her and repeated, "Very convenient."

The set of her jaw was tight, her eyes stared into me, seeming to beg for understanding while being disgusted at my very existence. After a lifetime of trusting what I observed in people—because how else could I have done my job?—it seemed almost believable that her power was real. Her pain certainly appeared so.

Chasiku would be fun to work with. Oh yes, a regular joy. All the more reason I needed to get out of this place. I reckoned my life had become cheaper than ever to Lenz, now that he had a newer, better soothsayer. Perhaps it was *her* false prophecies that would bring about the violent end of the Tetrarchia. There was a comforting thought, in a way.

"Let's go," said Lenz, turning toward the door we had come through.

I stepped back around her and followed him toward the door. Apparently, on our way up, Chasiku had been the one to release the counterweight and thereby propel Lenz's pallet up to the top of the watchtower. Because she had known when we would be there, *of course*. From the top, Lenz could get the contraption working himself. I watched him go and wished he would crash.

Supposedly our presences, not our words, bothered Chasiku, but nonetheless we didn't speak anymore until we were out of the watchtower and in our carriage.

I Concoct a Desperate Plan

I was bone-tired as the carriage rumbled beneath me. Today I had killed, captured, interrogated, met a false king, and found that I was in danger of being replaced. I knew where Klemens was kept, and who Olaf really was, so there was no way being replaced would mean I could go on my merry way. I desperately needed escape.

"So," I began carefully, "my family . . ."

Lenz watched me silently for a moment, then yelled something to the carriage driver, and we turned.

We said nothing as the carriage pulled up in front of a five-story building on the palace grounds, wider and taller than my servant house, but similar in design. On my way out of the carriage, I looked at Lenz once more, trying to read him. Was I truly, finally going to see my father? It almost felt impossible by now. I hadn't seen him in almost two weeks—a lifetime. My hands shook as I went inside. I ran up a flight of stairs, and it occurred to me again that this could have all been a con on Lenz's part to string me along. Would I round the staircase to see more guards? Was it all a trick to root out any vestiges of hope? I shook and slowed my walk, not wanting to reach the top.

At the third-floor landing, a large man in a burlap apron leaned against a railing and scribbled furtively on a piece of paper. When I looked at him, he seemed not just annoyed and distracted, but angry that I was there. Who was this? What was going on?

"Oh, you must be the daughter," he grunted. "In there."

I felt a deep, and sudden, need to distract myself from uncertainty with violence. I wanted to hit him. At least then *something* would be clear.

But then I heard, "Is that you, freak?" and "Kalynishka!" and I stormed through Grandmother's room to my father's, giving him a hug.

I did my best to hide how tired I was, how ragged after nearly dying twice in the last five days. I acted as though I had picked my family's uncomfortably large rooms out myself, after a thorough inspection of the building. Grandmother insisted on knowing what I was *actually* doing, and why there were nosy doctor's assistants everywhere. That was who the man in the apron had been, and there were more of them, always scratching away with their pens, constantly underfoot. To get some privacy, I had to yank one such assistant out of my father's room and deposit her into the hallway. She yelped along the way.

Grandmother asked what my scheme was because there was no way, of course, that anyone would hire me to do anything. I was not fit to wipe the asses of elderly merchants. I ground my teeth further and didn't argue. Papa was proud, beaming even, though he knew no more than she.

"When are you planning to explain what's *really* going on here?" Grandmother yelled from her room, where she sat in a chair that she must have purposefully torn up in order to feel at home. "You ungrateful little—"

I slammed the door to shut her up. The noise scared Papa, and he began shaking like a baby mouse. I ran to him and patted his hand to calm him down.

"They have put our things in that closet, Kalynishka," said Papa.

"Yes. They'll be safe there."

"Oh, we have nothing worth taking, Kalynishka," he sighed, patting my hand. "The fish in Fántutazh Lake have changed, Kalynishka."

"Oh?"

"The stew tasted different this time than when I was younger; the lobsters must be dying off."

"I see."

"I'm so glad we're up here, not down in the depths again."

I nodded.

He let go of my hand before looking up at me and smiling. "You look well, Kalynishka."

"You always think that."

"Do I? Well, it is always true."

I smiled. We were both quiet for a few minutes, and I could not tell if this was the sort of comfortable silence shared by those who are at ease, or if there was something I *should* have been saying. Papa stared off into space, then suddenly snapped his fingers and looked at me, as though he had remembered where he left something.

"Kalynishka, the Tetrarchia will fall, do you remember?"

"I . . . Yes, Papa, I remember."

"It will crumble and topple."

"Literally?"

"I . . . don't know, Kalynishka. It's all so mixed up. But something will happen."

"Well, Papa, I do remember."

"Oh! Good, good." He patted my hand. "Soon, you know."

"I know. In about two months."

"So soon?" he mused as though he had an appointment.

"Yes, Papa."

"Oh, my. Well, do not forget."

"I won't."

"Also . . ."

"Yes?"

". . . our things are stored in that closet, remember."

"Yes, Papa."

We were silent again. I tried to calm myself down, to stop thinking about death and destruction, about unavoidable doom.

Looking at my tired father, I suddenly knew how fanciful any thoughts of a quick escape had been. He and Grandmother weren't going to just disappear in the night with me. I needed to work with Lenz until I had a real plan for escape.

And then, just such a plot began to roil in my head. We sat quietly in each other's presence a little longer, as I thought it through. It was a terrible idea, but worth a try.

"Papa," I hissed under my breath, grabbing his right hand in both of mine, which were so much more calloused than his. I could not afford to let Grandmother hear this.

"Yes, Kalynishka?" His loving gaze turned to one of sudden

fear—fear that had not surfaced while he discussed death and destruction.

"Papa, I need your help with something."

His eyes widened. He looked excited that I needed his help, but also seemed terrified of failing me. I felt deeply guilty. He nodded firmly.

"A man is going to come up here in a few minutes and meet you. My master, I suppose. I need you to tell me if you *see* anything about his future."

"What kind of—?"

"Anything at all!" He started, and I immediately felt like a monster for interrupting him. "Even the most mundane thing may be useful." I just needed leverage.

He bit his bottom lip and nodded his head once.

"But Papa, it's *very* important you tell no one about this. Not the man, Lenz, not Grandmother, not *anyone*."

He nodded again, and I thought my heart would break. He always wanted to be useful, but the stress of pinpointing real things in his miasma of visions was so taxing. If only I were not so broken; if only escaping this country were not so vital; if only Grandmother did not adhere so firmly to her own cruel principles.

"If . . ." I stammered, patting his hand. "If you see nothing . . ." I was going to say that he shouldn't worry, but I needed to use whatever I could to escape. Or perhaps I just wanted to get the best of Lenz so badly.

"If you see nothing," I repeated, "*try harder*."

He nodded again and seemed to understand, bless him. I would ruin him for our escape, and yet I still didn't know where we would *go*.

FATHER AND JAILER

I asked Papa to wait a moment and left his room, passing Grandmother and slamming the door on her. On my way downstairs, another assistant asked me what we had discussed. I ignored her.

I found Lenz on the ground floor, talking to a Yellow. I smiled at him and suggested he come up and meet my father.

"Why?" He seemed leery.

"I told them I work for the Prince, and though I didn't exactly lie, a corroboration might help keep Grandmother quiet."

"Kalyna . . . that's a lot of stairs." He looked down at his bad leg. "It's been a day."

"You've kidnapped me, forced me to work, put me in front of assassins and thugs, and involved me in . . ." There were Yellows and doctor's assistants around, so even though I was saying this in Masovskani, the next word was simply ". . . Olaf. The very least you could do is look my father in the eye."

Lenz sagged to one side and rubbed his chin. "Your father has the Gift, yes?"

"The Gift has him," I replied.

"Hm."

"Don't."

"Mm?"

"Don't try to make my father 'see' things for you."

"Whyever would I? I have you and Chasiku."

Was he sarcastic? Did he suspect I was a fraud?

"He sees nothing useful," I said, "and it would . . . it would cause him great pain to try." I choked, thinking of all the times I'd pushed Papa to see visions so that I could better cheat our customers. Thinking of what I had planned for today.

"What about your grandmother?" he asked.

"*Please do* ask for her assistance."

"I'll go," he sighed, and followed me up the stairs.

Lenz looked truly harried by the time we got to the third floor, as Grandmother loudly described his "lame, syphilitic leg." His limp was more pronounced than usual as we both perched by Papa's bed. Grandmother continued spewing invective from the other room.

"Pleased to see you again, Aljosa Vüsalavich," he said.

I tried very hard not to look surprised. Papa blinked up at Lenz with no recognition in his face.

"Lenz Felsknecht. We spoke in Masovska."

Of course they had. I imagined him asking my poor father a hundred questions and felt my face burn.

"Lanso, was it?" murmured Papa.

"Lenz. And I"—he raised his voice, half yelling through the door into Grandmother's room—"*serve our Highness Prince Friedhelm!*"

"Our highness of balls!" replied Grandmother.

Papa beamed at me, looked back at Lenz with fear and concentration, muttered a response, and nestled into his pillow.

Lenz ignored Grandmother and attempted small talk with my father:

"Your daughter has been extremely helpful in the Prince's service," he lied.

"Yes," said Papa. He was deeply focused upon his lack of focus, and did not seem to know what he was agreeing with. "Yes, yes," he continued, "and the green crests of the Skydaš Sea scoop up skeletons of antennaed sharks that lived before humanity."

Lenz coughed and made his goodbyes.

"I'm heading back to my office, to try and straighten out the Prince's . . ." Lenz stopped himself and eyed my father, then said, ". . . business. You may stay for a bit. The Yellows will take you back to your house when you're ready."

When he passed through Grandmother's room this time, she sat silently with her lips pulled together, following him with her eyes until he was going down the stairs.

I looked at Papa, who seemed to be attempting to stare hard at something behind his own eyes. He noticed me, seemed frightened that I was there, nodded seriously to let me know he remembered what I'd asked, and then smiled, as though only just realizing the person in front of him was his daughter.

"Do you see anything?" I asked under my breath.

"Lots," replied Papa. "Lots and lots and lots."

"About Lenz?"

His smile faltered. "I don't know yet, Kalynishka. It's all so . . . so . . . so *much*." He pressed his hand to his forehead. "I will try to sort through what I've seen today, but it may take time. You know how my mind is."

"Not really, no."

He smiled again at that. "I won't forget."

"I know."

"And don't you forget either." He wagged his finger playfully.

"About the—?"

"Encroaching doom, yes," he whispered, as though gossiping about a neighbor. "Remember."

We embraced. He shivered less than usual, and I still felt guilty. I left the room.

Broken Shitworm

"*What* won't your poor, beleaguered father forget?" asked Grandmother as I passed her.

I had considered the window, rather than going through her room yet again, but it was a long drop to rotrock. I kept walking and said nothing.

"Tell me what is happening, you wretched girl," she snarled. "What are you doing to my poor son, now? Haven't you ruined him enough?"

I stayed quiet as I approached the door to the stairs. Grandmother stuck out her foot as if to trip me, but pulled it back when she saw I would not stop.

"Tell me, you broken shitworm. What's going on?" She began to sound . . . concerned?

"If you must know," I said at the door, staring out, "why not use your *own* Gift to see?"

"My time with the Gift is done. That's your job, half-a-brain."

"Yet you still have the Gift."

"Of course I do. I am no sliver of a human being like you. I chose to carry on our legacy, and then when your father took over, I rightly chose—"

"But why can't you—?"

"*Because I should not have to*! Don't you understand that, you miserable thing?"

I turned to leave.

"You would not *dare* leave while I'm speaking to you!"

I was at the door. I *was* actually leaving, and it felt marvelous. I was a prisoner, but my jailers were more powerful than Grandmother. How could she stop me?

"If you don't come back," she yelled, "I will *tell them!*"

I stopped. I wanted to cry. I padded slowly back into her room.

She was in her chair, looking smug with her eyebrows raised, crinkling the tattoo above her left eye. I slammed the door, then passed her to shut the door to Papa's room. Grandmother slowly replaced her unlit pipe, clacking it between her teeth. She was so, so small.

"Why don't you sit, girl?" She pointed to the floor in front of her. "Not right to look down on your grandmother like that."

I did not sit on the floor, clean though it was.

"Tell me," she said calmly, "what's going on here."

I looked at her a long time, then said, "If it could save our lives, would you use the Gift?"

"It should not be *my* job to save our lives."

"If it could save our lives."

"Pray tell me, child, from whom we need saving."

"If I tell you what's going on, will you at least consider using your Gift to help?"

"Are we in mortal danger?"

"Will you *consider* it?"

Grandmother sat back and blew out a long gust of smoke-less breath through her pipe. She coughed and looked thoughtful.

I bit my lip and then stopped. I didn't want to look desperate. Something flapped by the window.

"No," said Grandmother, sighing. "No, I don't think I will consider it. What is mortal danger, anyway? Our line is done."

"You were deciding whether or not to lie to me."

"And aren't you *glad* I chose truth and honor, little fool? As I always do?"

Had I been on the floor, in her reach, she would have pinched my cheek.

"Always," she repeated. "I always tell the truth, regardless of what is 'safe' or 'considerate.' If that is uncomfortable, it is your fault for being so weak. You could get us out of any silly scrape if you were half the soothsayer your father was in his prime." She pointed at the closed door with her pipe.

I gripped my forehead to keep my skull from falling out. "Of course I'm not *half* the soothsayer he was." This next part came out very slowly, giving each whispered word its space: "I do not have the Gift." And then I started yelling. "Have you *forgotten* somehow? How can you hold me to the same standard?"

"Your father and I—"

"Have a Gift from the gods," I hissed, flailing at her, "which . . ." I wanted to yell it, let the Yellows and the doctor's assistants know, but of course I whispered again, "which I don't! I have done everything I can to keep us alive—"

"And a fine job of it you're doing," she said.

"You *are* alive, aren't you? Eating better than you ever have!"

"Eating too well. This decadence will poison us, like some . . ." She actually spat on the floor. ". . . *aesthetes*."

"It is a magnitude more than *you* have done! I must—!" I cut myself off to lower my voice and begin again. "I must lie, cheat, and fight to keep us going in the way you and your blessed ancestors saw fit, while you squander your Gift and insult me."

"I have to insult you," she said. "No one else knows how defective you are."

"But why in the world won't you *help* me?"

"It is not *my* fault *you* are broken."

"Your blood's in my veins, demon. Perhaps it *is* your fault."

Grandmother looked hurt. I had actually hurt her in a way beyond simply existing. I had cut through her armor and injured her. Her eyes filled with sorrow and her pipe fell.

I wanted to cheer and dance, to caper about the room, laughing and pointing at her like a five-year-old. Then I felt guilty for thinking this about my own grandmother. *Then* I got angry at myself for growing so soft toward the old demon, who had never given me reason to be kind to her. I looked into her angry little face and knew I wanted to hurt her more.

Or perhaps it wasn't you, I considered adding, *perhaps my mother was the broken one. The one to blame for me.* I had never met my mother, what would trampling her memory matter?

I did not say this. It was too blasphemous toward a woman who may not have been the goddess my family described, but did not deserve to be used as a cudgel.

Now Grandmother and I both felt terrible. She told me to lift her and put her on the bed, repeating herself three times until I finally did as she asked.

"I might drop you, you know," I said as I felt her angry, gnarled little body curled into my arms.

"Won't be enough to kill me, *you know*," she said.

I put her on the bed.

"Why are you inflicted upon me?" she asked. "I always told your father that he should have had another child. Maybe that one would not be shattered inside."

"Anyone raised by you would be shattered inside," I mumbled.

"Eh?"

"I said he never wanted another child." I pulled her chair up to the side of the bed, just out of her reach, and sat.

"Never forget," she replied, waving a finger at me, "that continuing *our line* was always more important than whom you love or what you like or who you are or what you have. But much to my shame, you chose to ruin that."

"I did not *choose*—"

"My great-grandmother Aytaç's wife could not give her a child, so Aytaç found a man for a night and bore my grandfather Huso," she began, as though I did not know the family history by heart. "Married in the eyes of our family, but by no priest, they raised Huso together. When he was grown, Huso met my grandmother, who bore my father, Mildo."

I nodded and waited for her to finish.

"Mildo bore me, I bore your father, and your father found your wonderful mother, who bore you."

"I know."

"You then killed her—"

"I *know*."

"—and as punishment, the gods made you our end. Instead of seeing the future, you *cause* it. Now I get to watch my son die slowly, and know that it is all over. You know, for a time, I thought you might still have some sliver of the Gift, useless but *there*. But it is clear you do not, or that you have chosen not to access it. You're too old to fix anything now."

"I am only twenty-seven," I growled, as I wondered why I was arguing on her terms.

She ignored me anyway. "Why couldn't you be more like your great-grandfather Mildo?"

I wondered the same thing.

"He never complained. He may have had complicated feelings around bearing a child, but he never complained." She sighed. "I am too good and kind a person. Sometimes it still hurts me to think that I caused my father so much pain."

She shook her head, and the next cough may have doubled for a sob. She stared at the ceiling.

"So much," she moaned. "I hurt my father so much." Another broken sob. Then she turned her head to me and grinned through it all. "But," she said, "at least I did not *kill* him."

I left. Her chair slammed to the floor behind me.

REGARDING CHILDREN AND
SUCCESSION IN MY FAMILY

As far back as is known, the rule in my family has been that there is one child in a generation. A second is purposefully conceived only if the first has died. So, yes, when Grandmother said Papa should have had a second child, she was essentially calling me a corpse. Dead inside, at best.

This rule of only children existed, we were told, to keep the Gift from being split between multiple children, diluted. The logic of this escapes me, but then so does the logic of my physically resembling Grandmother more than my mother, as she has been described to me. It could be our ancestors simply didn't want the family to split into competitive branches with different customs, or were worried about what some great Soothsayer Conglomeration could get up to. I wondered if Chasiku was part of some long-forgotten offshoot, perhaps even the catalyst for our rule.

This rule did not mandate monkhood. There are root concoctions and gall bladder sheaths and the like that can stop conception, and still allow for a man and a woman to rut if they have tired of alternative activities, but they are not foolproof. Neither did the rule require relationships to be one man and one woman. My ancestors would bear a child with whomever they could have a child with, and raise that child alongside whomever they could stand to travel with—these did not need to be the same person.

In my teen years, I learned that I had neither time nor freedom for loving or sexual attachments. A boy is too likely to decide I am his, to insist I settle down, to expect Papa to survive on his own or happily move in with the new "us." They were often good enough people, I suppose, but they had no idea their happy future would completely alter the girl they found so alluring. Women were often easier to get along with, but I found it was a lot of work keeping track of which parts of the Tetrarchia fully frowned upon such relations, and which saw them as just two (or three) girls being "good friends."

I desired as much as anyone, but soon realized I couldn't afford to be with anyone while so much depended on me. So I kept my own company, with my own fingers.

This may have been ill-advised because, as a descendant of an old family of soothsayers, it had been my *duty* to have a child to carry on tradition. I put it off because no man would be willing to travel with us (Grandmother insisted this had been no obstacle for her), and caring for a child would mean so much time when I'd be incapable of caring for my family or doing my job. Then, around age twenty-five, I was lucky enough to have Grandmother decide that my childbearing days were over before they'd started. She chose to give up hope and revel in the misery of our line being over.

To my mind, at the time, these were the only reasons not to do my duty. Now, in hindsight, I recognize that deep down, I was terrified of having a child as broken as myself. A child without the Gift. How would Grandmother treat such a child? How would I?

A GALIAG ZIGGURAT

Behrens, the sharpshooter, saw me back to the servant house. We chose walking over yet another carriage ride. The thin layer of snow on the ground was already melting, and the flowers and hedges were still bright. A far cry from how frozen the Great Field in Masovska must have been, just then. This made me feel thankful for Lenz's interference in my life, and I had to drive that feeling right out.

"Been in a share of scrapes since you joined us," said Behrens.

"You could say that, yes."

"I begin to wonder," he went on, appraising me, "what would have happened had I missed that man in the forest. The night we followed you down toward the valley in Masovska, I mean."

"I would be dead."

"Is that . . ." He touched his temple. "Your professional opinion?"

"Common sense. Past possibilities are rather beyond my senses."

"Hmm. I don't know. I wonder what else our master saw in you that night."

"I was just starting to like you, Behrens," I said.

He threw up his hands. "Sorry! Just a curious sort."

"Most are."

He nodded.

"It seems I'm not quite enough for the Prince," I added.

"Oh, you mean Chasiku? Odd sort, isn't she? But, you know, the more the better, yes? I'm not the only sharpshooter in the army, either."

I thought on that for a moment, but decided I didn't much like the idea of being part of some coterie of soothsayers very much at all.

"Behrens, what do you think of all of the Prince's . . . *plans* and *experts*? Do you think the man knows what he's doing?" I kept it purposefully vague because I didn't know whether Behrens was aware of Olaf.

He laughed and made a show of looking around, to ensure no one was listening. We were out on a footpath, with no one close by. I could see the Royal Inn of Ottilie's Rock in the distance, and wondered whether Andelka was having a friendly conversation with a Green whose job it was to ensure she didn't escape.

"I try not to think about it too much, if I'm being honest. I'm in Lenz's good graces because I am very observant, but care for little but my sharpshooter brethren. This means I'm privy to a lot of strange information, and I think that if I showed too much of an interest in it, things might go bad for me."

"As in, you would be gotten rid of?"

"Or given a more important job."

"Do you care deeply for keeping the King in power? For keeping Rotfelsen and the Tetrarchia together?"

He shrugged. "Only insofar as it seems better than not doing so. If I wanted to be a soldier who *cared* about something, I'd be a Purple. And we see how that's working out for them."

"It may work out quite well," I replied, "if they succeed in taking power. Do the Reds or Greens feel anything for their charges?"

"I think that the Greens care about protecting our borders, and the Reds care about keeping either the King or Queen safe. But you'd have to ask them. As for the Yellows, our duty is to guard the Prince, but I don't believe many of us *care* for him."

"How scandalous," I replied in a clearly sarcastic monotone.

"Quite. I suppose most of us want, generally, to keep the palace grounds, and therefore the kingdom, quiet and safe. Relatively."

I wondered whether "quiet and safe" for the palace grounds really did mean the same for the people who lived beneath it. I decided not to voice this.

As we walked up to the servant house, Behrens concisely changed the subject: "A lady Yellow will accompany you to your room to make sure you didn't bring back any souvenirs."

I nodded. "Behrens, what would you do if the Court Philosopher ordered you, directly, to bring me to him?"

Behrens thought this over. "Well, I can't *directly* disobey Vorosknecht, but—"

"A good question, that!" chirped Jördis, who was ambling about just inside the house.

We both stopped dead in the doorway.

"Oh, don't worry about *me*," she laughed. "I'm off-duty! And my master's all hot air, you'll be fine!"

I faked a smile and said goodbye to Behrens, who did not fake it as well as I did.

"A nice seat on that one," said Jördis, under her breath, as he walked away.

I told her I supposed it was true. But ogling a body lost some of its thrill when I imagined that body as meat, cut up by a sword or crunched beneath rotrock.

Two months. Two months and a week, maybe. How specific was Papa's understanding of time, anyway? I sighed and went inside.

"Maybe you could make him into a Purple," I offered. "Get to look at him more often."

"I don't think he'd like it much in the Purples," she replied. "Any more than I would, if I had to be a *Soldier for Ideas*, as Vorosknecht calls it." She grimaced. "Besides, I suspect some of them would, ah, feel a way about his Skydašian ancestry."

I decided it wouldn't quite be prudent to ask her about what the Purples' "ideas" were. We began to make our way up the stairs, followed by a Yellow I did not recognize.

"I shouldn't even be cordial with you, you know," said Jördis.

"Because Vorosknecht—"

"I honestly don't know if he wants you beaten, killed, kicked out, or subordinate to him. He tells me very little." She grinned and shrugged. "So *I* don't bother hating his enemies. I'm sorry he ambushed you at the ball, for what it's worth. He only told me, minutes before you were dragged in, that we would see 'the Prince's mind-witch.'"

"And I, of course, never told you I'm a—"

"Why would it be my business? Who cares? We're all frauds here."

I coughed. "Well, I . . . I mean, I wouldn't say *that*."

"Oh, *of course* we're all entirely the experts we are paid to be." She winked. "And you and I love and respect the men we work for."

We stopped on the landing by our respective rooms. I leaned an arm against it and looked at her. "You take so little pride in your calling?"

"'Calling'?" she laughed. "Tural has a calling. I only follow in my father's footsteps. Never much cared for it, but I don't know what else I could do."

"I'm familiar with that feeling."

"Is your father a spy, too?"

I sighed. "No. And I didn't realize one could be a philosopher who doesn't care, unless one's philosophy is one of not caring."

"I regurgitate old books for Vorosknecht. No philosophizing necessary. Which"—she shook her head—"is fine by me."

"Well then, do those books say it is *ethical*," I asked, "to kidnap someone and threaten them with violence, whether or not that person is me?" Was Jördis aware of Vorosknecht's part in a plot against the King? The Court Philosopher had sent her out before discussing that part, but that could have been for show. If the King had been kidnapped, did she know where he was being kept?

"I told you," she said, "I'm off-duty. I'm not asking you *the future*, am I?" She said it as though the very idea of telling the future was laughable.

"I think you and Behrens, the Yellow you were admiring, would have a lot in common," I replied, "in your lack of caring."

"Is that meant as an insult?" She looked up at me in a way that was, at worst, mischievous.

"Not at all. I think some people up here care far too much about their work."

"I wholeheartedly agree."

We said our goodbyes, and I went into my room, where the Yellow searched me in a gentle and businesslike fashion, and found that I had stolen no weapons during this outing. She left, and I lay face down on my bed, nose in my pillow, staring blankly into an empty future.

My bedroom had become much more homey than I would have liked in the last few days. It was a prison, but it was mine more than any place I'd ever lived. I didn't share a space with Papa, Grandmother, transients, bandits, one-legged pimps, bulletfrogs, muskrats, or anything else. Sitting by the window, I had an endless expanse of fifteen unoccupied feet to the door: an embarrassment of empty space. Here I would sit, with the windows to my right and left, my back to the wall, and take very deep breaths. I had never been so alone in the place I slept.

There had been a few times before this when my family resided between real walls and doors. On the border of Skydašiai and the Tetrarchia's northeastern neighbor Loasht, there was a city called Galiag, and every few years it would be conquered by whichever country did not own it. Who owned it now? Would it be included in the Tetrarchia's collapse?

Galiag was contentious because if the Grand Suzerain of Loasht chose to invade the Tetrarchia, that city would be the gate by which their army entered our unwieldy country. Galiag was not contentious because anybody in their right mind wanted to live there. A land of burning winds, just as enjoyable as they sound, which rip up through the valleys to be channeled right into the city. Somewhere along the way, those winds must pass over deserts or lava flows or dragons or whatever it is that makes them burn so hot.

When I was a child, my family spent a summer—*a summer!*—in this place, which was Loasht-controlled at the time. The winds were so hot that at midday, one had to cower inside to keep from losing skin, and they were so strong that our tents were bowled right over. We spent one terrible night thinking our camp would hold in an alcove below a dune outside of town, and soon everything was shaking and moving. Papa had disappeared, Grandmother was screaming, and I was being pelted with stones so hot I suspect one could cook meat on them. I still have two scars from that: a round burn the size of a child's palm on my right ribs, and a rectangular pebble mark puckering a piece of my upper lip.

So we rented a tiny apartment in a disgusting little ziggurat. For reasons that are probably clear, rooms with windows were cheaper than those without in Galiag, and rooms facing east, where the wind originates, were cheaper still. We were on the ground floor, with a window facing the eastern valley and the farts of the gods. We could only afford such a place because Papa still told fortunes.

When the winds were at their worst, the room was almost fine. Down went the heavy shutters, and they would rattle from wind and fingernails, showing human silhouettes while we huddled the farthest from the shutters we could—not huddle *together* of course, since it was very, very hot. There was something thrilling about knowing death and pain were outside, and we were in there, separated by more than a tent made of animal skin. No, the winds were not so bad, but when they abated, the room was terrifying.

When the winds ebbed, we heard everything in any room near ours through those thin inner walls. Plots, cursing, rutting, robberies, abuse—every word of it leaked into our room. All complemented by the cries of hyraxes that scuttled in the walls. Outside the ziggurat was even worse, as the destitute, torn up by the winds that had just relaxed, scratched at our walls and moaned at our window. A window we could not keep closed all day, lest we die in that thick and over-heated air. From both the neighboring rooms and the street outside, some of the people we heard wanted to get inside to us—to steal, to sleep, to rage, to talk. I didn't have my sickle yet, but that summer I gouged a man's eye out with my bare, little ten-year-old hands.

There *were* people who chose to live in Galiag. They were far from us, in the windowless centers of the ziggurats, rich and well-guarded. Perhaps they saw the sky at times, but certainly not often. Where we stayed was too rundown to attract anyone with money or power, but I did explore the ziggurat's innards a few times, when I was sick of being scared by the same people and decided to replace them with strangers. Those innards were all straight pathways that lead toward the center. The center was bronze, not brick, and the guards did not like me. That was my previous experience living between walls.

That crumbling ziggurat in Galiag came to me again as I sat by the window in my Rotfelsenisch room, looking out at a pleasant evening with pleasant snow. I noticed that I had, at some point, gotten myself a mug of brandy and a bowl of cheese curds.

I had spent five days living without Papa to care for, with servants making my food and cleaning my clothes, with space to call my own. Five measly days, and I had taken to drinking liquor and eating useless foods. I was a prisoner and I had become spoiled. Having so much space to myself had eroded what little decency I ever possessed: my clothes and books lay everywhere, curled around half-empty mugs that I had for-gotten about days previous. I always suspected I only had self-control because I needed to care for Papa and not get yelled at by Grandmother, and it appeared I had been right. What a defective mess I was.

I sighed and stood up to pour another mug of brandy, and left my domain and prison to go talk to Tural.

Persimmon Cousins

Tural opened up a thoroughly disgusting liqueur that he kept by his bed because I could not stand to go back for more brandy and have him see what a mess my room was. I described how exhausting my day had been, without telling anything of substance besides that Lenz and I did not see eye to eye. Tural, bless him, asked for nothing more.

"You and your boss seem to argue a great deal," he said in Rotfelsenisch.

"What else has a boss ever done?" I replied in Cölluknit.

He brightened and said, "Nothing," in the same language.

"Have I interrupted your conjuring?"

"Oh my, no," Tural replied. "No conjuring is needed, not today." He laughed.

"That must be why you're smiling."

He nodded and held out the plate. "The day after next, and so soon after the ball, the King's Dinner looms, and all scatter like flightless parrots, but not the Master of Fruit. Never."

"And why is that?"

"Because I may now test my fruits with impunity, because they are in season and have arrived!" He gestured to a plate on his desk. "I know exactly what is ripe and how ripe, and I can taste them whenever I require. Everyone else has procrastinated until today, fighting off their decisions as humans do, but I could not *make* complete decisions until now, and so narrowed down every possibility months ago. In short, I am prepared. And the fruits are delicious."

"That sounds like a good place to be." And the opposite of where I was.

I felt helpless, able to do nothing but wait: wait for my family to arrive, wait for my father's prophecies to fall into my lap, wait for the Tetrarchia to crumble. In the meantime, I supposed I would eat good food, drink alcohol, laze about on the fourth floor of my prison, and prove Grandmother right. I decided to try learning more from Tural, in order to convince myself I was *doing* something.

"What exactly is this King's Dinner about?" I asked, wondering just how much of society Olaf would need to muddle through. "Didn't we *just* do this?"

Tural laughed, but not at me—a laugh of agreement that the royals' social calendar was all a bit much. He had a satisfying laugh, and a light salt and pepper at his temples. Quru doctors use tattoos to mark any injuries that they treat, such as the childhood injury above Grandmother's eye, and as he leaned back against his desk, I wondered idly if Tural had any such tattoos, and where.

"We did, I'm afraid," he said. "But this is a much smaller thing. Our good King hosts and attends an endless number of small state events. These monthly dinners were started by Queen Biruté as a way for her and the King to learn more about how their kingdom is run, but it has become just the same group of people who surround him at any other time, saying the same old things." He grinned. "But the meal must always be magnificent."

"Of course." I supposed this would be Olaf's coming-out party, as Gerhold VIII. What a terrifying thought.

"But," said Tural, picking up the plate from his desk, "I have put off one decision for the dinner, so lend me your taste buds."

"They're quite useless, I assure you."

"That can't be true." Tural pointed out the two sliced up pieces of fruit on his plate. At first glance, they were almost identical, except one was a bit waxier. "Upper red persimmon, tart." He pointed to the less waxy variety. "Lower red persimmon, sweet." He pointed to the other. Both were orange in color, to my eye, if leaning toward red. "Two cousins in the same family, one grows in the open, up here on the surface, where the Rotfelsenisch live like human beings, and the other grows beneath, where sunlight slithers into the rock. I cannot decide which to serve as the dessert starter tomorrow night. It will be the first thing eaten after dinner, but before the full dessert, a Quru cake."

"Is the Master of Cakes also Quru?"

He raised an ironic eyebrow and shook his head. "Rotfelsenisch."

"Ah. Disappointing cake, then?"

He opened his mouth to speak, paused for a moment, and raised his free hand, as though acquiescing to something. "Much as I would love to demean our Master of Cakes, and pretend that my Quru nature gives me some greater insight into our food, the fact is he makes extremely good Quru cakes. Even my mother would admit so, if she ever had a bite."

"I see."

"The cake will include many syrups, which were made from fruits I provided. However, the Mistress of Syrups is badly organized, and has not yet determined which ones she will use, so the dessert appetizer must be a fruit she does not have in syrup form. Hence"—a flourish—"red persimmon."

I nodded.

"Now," he continued, "I would love to know which you prefer."

"I truly don't think I can help."

Tural did not seem to understand.

"I don't really . . . *enjoy* food," I explained.

He knitted his brows together. "How do you mean? Was your mouth injured? Burned out? Or do you not enjoy the textures?"

"No, no. Nothing like that, I simply . . ." I thought for a moment. I had never really put these feelings into words before. "I have not, in my life, had the time or the money to learn to appreciate the intricacies of flavor. I have always needed what was fast, cheap, and filling."

Tural looked at me for some time. I was worried I would see deep pity in his eyes, but he only seemed thoughtful.

"Well, now you have the time and the money, don't you?" he said. "In a way I envy you, getting to experience the joy of new tastes."

Time, indeed.

"Besides," he continued, "fast, cheap, and filling can still be quite delicious."

I did not know how to respond to this. It truly hadn't ever occurred to me. I began to wonder how much of my unformed taste was due to my circumstances in general, and how much was simply thanks to Grandmother.

"Well," I said, "be that as it may, I'm certainly no expert."

"I did not ask for an expert's opinion," said Tural. "I asked for *yours*." He then produced a small knife and reduced each slice of persimmon into half-inch pieces. "Try a small piece. Please?"

His knife was sharp by the look of it, and it had a gold handle, so he must have taken it from the more distinguished palace kitchen where he did his work. A kitchen that was not checked by guards on the lookout for missing knives taken by an imprisoned soothsayer.

But before I could take it, I had to sample this fruit. I took a piece of each persimmon and admitted that they tasted the same to me. I asked him to describe their differences, and he happily obliged as I gave the fruit another try. Tural, without condescension, suggested I chew slowly, to savor, to look for certain aspects of the flavor. I had never eaten slowly before, except when my jaw had been broken, and at first it was maddeningly boring and frustrating.

But a strange thing happened: by my third piece of each fruit, I could swear I was tasting the difference between the two. Tural's own joy at the whole enterprise bolstered me further, and I realized I really did *like* what I was eating. And not just because there was sugar in it: I actually noticed each little fiber in the fruit's body, tasted the components that Tural swore were there.

Or fancied that I did. I may have simply learned that tartness could be good, and no more. But by my last piece of each, I had made a decision.

"Upper," I said.

Tural agreed, and celebrated by eating the rest himself. He bent back his head dramatically and closed his eyes to do so. He was a little drunk, and swayed slightly.

That was when I put a hand on his arm, to playfully hold him steady as I snatched his knife from the plate, hoping he had forgotten about it in his excitement. Same as soothsaying: take advantage of distractions. I palmed it and slipped it into my sleeve.

I felt guilty when he was finished and looked back at me, but not guilty enough to admit anything. Tural either did not notice the knife's absence, or felt that it was rude to acknowledge, which in Quru custom meant essentially the same thing.

We had a few more drinks and talked about nothing, as the knife threatened to fall out of my sleeve, and soon enough I took my leave.

I felt happy when I stumbled back the few feet to my room and shut the door. I secreted the knife inside an especially large book and flopped onto my bed. My chemically-induced happiness did not give me the space to stare into what the future might hold.

Up Ottilie's Rock

The next day, I attempted to visit my father, to see if I could wring any visions from him, but was told by the Yellows outside that I was not allowed in without express permission from Lenz. Why, it was almost as though I'd escape with Papa in the night if given half a chance! (And leave Grandmother if I could.)

Instead, I chose that night to attempt a different sort of approach to the Royal Inn of Ottilie's Rock and Andelka, our delegate from Rituo, that most friendly of the Bandit States. I still had not seen her in the week since the Winter Ball, despite my many trips to the inn.

What I had gained, I suppose, was a better knowledge of Gunther, the keeper, as well as a few people staying at the tavern: lesser dignitaries staying on the second floor of the inn, in the "cheap rooms." These included a Rotfelsenisch bureaucrat representing a noble with quarries *deep* down in the rock, and a Skydašian merchant hoping to sell local politicians on a law regarding property taxes before the Council of Barbarians started. The most I had learned from them was that in addition to the second floor's "cheap rooms," the third floor housed the "good rooms," and the fourth contained the "Suzerain's Suite." This last one referred to how supposedly luxurious the suite was, such that if the Grand Suzerain of Loasht were to ever visit Rotfelsen (a thing that has never happened), they would stay in that very suite. Never mind that there were entire *mansions* on the palace grounds that could be rented out by visitors—this was beside the point. It was rather hyperbolic, but that is what the suite was called and, according to Gunther, the "Suzerain's Suite" was where Andelka was staying.

"In the grand suite, and only eating the cheapest food when she's up there," Gunther had groused.

So, this night, just a day after the Turmenbach mess, Olaf, Chasiku, and an attempt to drag new visions out of my father, I went back to the Royal Inn of Ottilie's Rock toward the later end of dinner time: when Gunther would be there and, I hoped, quite busy. Those staying in the "cheap rooms" would be drinking away their failures or toasting their successes, secure in the knowledge that they had only a short trip upstairs to their beds.

This time, I walked around to the back of Ottilie's Rock, which was shrouded in almost total darkness, save for the light from a few of the inn's rooms. Back here, there were none of the inviting lanterns, beckoning guests inside for respite from the growing chill in the air. No lights seemed to be on at the back of the "Suzerain's Suite" either.

I groped around in the dark for the servants' entrance that had to be there somewhere, and eventually found a small, rough, precarious set of . . . well, less *stairs* than *conveniently placed bumps and ledges*. The pathway here was narrower than my shoulders, and I marveled at how Gunther must have traversed it every night while full of starka.

I moved slowly up the jagged stairs, until the back wall of the building was almost close enough to touch, and then I (daftly) sped up just a hair, and slipped on the top step. I fell forward and flailed wildly at the wall, my hands hitting wood and my fingernails scraping until they stopped against a molding. I became utterly convinced that someone had heard my awkwardness, and so stayed perfectly still, legs sprawled out behind me, hands gripping the molding, midsection hovering in the air diagonally.

When I counted out a minute (and couldn't hold that position any longer besides), I pulled myself up to my feet.

I felt around the molding and found the back door, which was, surprisingly, unlocked. I crept inside to what felt like a maze of corridors that, from the smells and the noise, must've emptied out somewhere to the kitchens and the tavern, where I heard the Skydašian merchant laughing. I found my way to the servant's stairs with surprising ease, and didn't run into any maids, cooks, or other staff. Looking back now, I realize I should have thought this too easy; at the time, I was so shaken by my fall that I simply assumed the gods were balancing out my luck a bit. As though this was anything they had ever done for me before.

The stairs were dark and creaking, but I didn't seem to attract any attention, even when I alighted on the fourth floor. And when I tried the knob to what I assumed to be a servant's entrance to the "Suzerain's Suite," it turned and the latch clicked. Just as I finally began to doubt my good luck, the door refused to budge.

I held still for a moment in the pitch black at the top of the stairs, and heard nothing. I pushed at the door, and it gave slightly, but wouldn't open. It felt as though something was wedged against it.

For what felt an interminable moment, I pressed my forehead to the cool wood and tried to decide what I should do. Pushing harder and forcing my way in could make a lot of noise, but I had come so far already. What was I to do otherwise? Just turn around? I "worked" for the Prince, after all; our Bandit States visitors couldn't just kill me without causing an incident. Could they? Maybe even if I got caught, I could learn something.

I threw all my weight into the next push. There was a moment's resistance before the door opened entirely, and I found myself sprawling into more darkness, bound up with another body. We tussled, tangled up in one another, each trying to extricate ourselves. I kicked something metal that made a low clank, and I felt the person below me take a breath, as though about to yell something.

I panicked and reached out for where I hoped this person's face was. My hand brushed long hair as it clamped over their mouth—at the exact same time that I felt an impossibly strong hand cover my own mouth. Then a light shone into the room.

ANDELKA

"What," someone bellowed, "is going on here, by L——?!"

Even in that situation—caught and bundled up with a stranger, covering their mouth while they covered mine—I felt myself wince at the very sound of someone saying a *god's* name out loud. (I have, of course, not reproduced it here.)

I looked up and there, standing in a doorway leading to more of the suite, was Andelka: broad, squat, and pale. She wore a sort of armless and open dressing gown of silk brocade, and held a lantern that spilled light into the room, glistening off so many gold and silver surfaces that I couldn't quite make out anything. That light was also reflected on her powerful and veined arms, and the long, curved blade held in her free hand.

I looked down and, pinned beneath me, with his hand on my mouth and my hand on his, was Martin-Frederick Reinhold-Bosch, the young, blonde royal scion I had met at the Winter Ball. Even as I held his mouth closed, I saw his eyes widen with recognition, and then he winked.

I smiled back stupidly, before realizing my mouth was still covered. I rolled off him and we each let go of the other.

"Well," continued Andelka, "now you can talk, can't you?"

I was in a half crouch, Martin-Frederick was turning onto his knees and didn't much look like he was about to say anything.

"It was a love game," I said, almost without thinking about my lie before spitting it out.

Martin-Frederick laughed.

"You know," I continued, standing up, "*forbidden* and all that."

Andelka did not much look like she believed it. Martin-Frederick also stood, and I saw that he was armed, although his rapier was still sheathed. He began to reach down toward his belt, and Andelka waved her dagger, or machete, or whatever it was.

"Don't touch that sword!" she yelled. "Now why are you *actually* here?"

"Look," sighed Martin-Frederick, holding up his hands. "I work for High General Dreher. Yes, I was spying, but you're his guest, aren't you?" He nodded down to a piece of paper wedged into his belt, not far from his sword. "The orders are there. May I?"

Andelka stepped closer, holding up the lantern and waving her blade inches from his face. "Go on," she said.

Martin-Frederick smiled and nodded his head in thanks and began to slowly reach for the paper. Andelka nodded back. Then the young man darted backward, out of her reach, and seemed to go for his sword. Andelka yelled and swung at nothing.

Martin-Frederick laughed and brought up the piece of paper after all. He was uncomfortably at ease in this situation.

"Joking, joking!" he said, holding out the paper. "Read it for yourself. I'll wait."

Andelka snarled at him, set the lantern down on a marble and gold side table, and snatched the paper.

"You *can* read Rotfelsenisch, can't you?" Martin-Frederick couldn't help adding.

"Of course," replied Andelka. "Can *you*, little boy?"

I looked to Martin-Frederick, and nodded toward the lantern, attempting to ask, with my expression, if I should go for it: throw it down, start a fire. He gave a small shake of his head and smiled.

Andelka cleared her throat loudly and began to read in the flickering lantern light. "'Search the Rituo woman's papers for information about you-know-who. As she is our guest, try to be discreet and refrain from embarrassing her. But if she becomes a problem, you may bring in some Greens.' Signed, High General Dreher." She looked up, angry.

"And that's his seal," Martin-Frederick added. "But you know it already."

"That I do," sighed Andelka.

"My Greens are downstairs, keeping the servants quiet and out of my way in the kitchen. But now that you know"—he shrugged—"I'll call them up and they'll have a look." He bowed. "So sorry for the inconvenience."

"And what is she doing here?" Andelka waved her blade at me. She seemed to purposefully flex while she was doing it.

Martin-Frederick shrugged. "Love game. Thought it would be fun to sneak her in while I was at it."

"I shudder to think what else you people are doing in my room when I'm not here," said Andelka, not seeming to believe him.

"We'd have much less trouble if you ever left," replied Martin-Frederick.

Martin-Frederick Reinhold-Bosch

Martin-Frederick and I went down by the guest's stairs, to go have a drink in the tavern. Gunther was mostly hidden by steam, but greeted me as though entirely unsurprised I was there, which I took to be his professionalism. The tall keeper poured us cups of something he already knew to be Martin-Frederick's favorite—a liquor made from beets that I did *not* particularly enjoy—and we sat at a table in the corner of the tavern. The guests of the "cheap rooms" were being quite loud that night, and it was easy enough to talk. In the soft light, that young royal, who had once declared his interest in a "martial" woman to me, was still slim, beardless, blonde, and, I dare say, pretty.

"Well," I said, once we'd sat down across a small wooden table, "if it isn't . . . Marvin-Friedhelm?" I knew his name perfectly well, but I wanted him to *try* to stick in my mind.

"Martin-Frederick," he corrected quickly. "And I still don't know your name, or what sort of soldier you are. Or why you were up there." He leaned a little closer across the table.

"I was looking into rumors about the Bandit States," I said, answering only his third question. "But if you do work for the High General, you must already know the answers I was looking for."

He shrugged and sat back, trying to look like he didn't much care about what I wanted to know. It was the most awkward I had yet seen him.

"Perhaps," he replied.

I laughed charmingly and covered my face partially with my hand to pretend at masking it. This false laugh, intended to endear people to me, is much more musical than the snorting that happens when I laugh genuinely.

"Fine, fine," I said, through more fake laughter. "I am too tired to play around any longer." A lie, of course. (Well, I did feel too tired—but such is life.) "My name is Kalyna Aljosanovna, and the Prince *recruited* me as one of his soothsayers. The first and best one, naturally."

The young blonde marveled at this for a moment, as I had hoped he would. "I knew the Prince enjoyed surrounding himself with . . . experts"—he had clearly been about to say something less kind—"but I did not expect that. You know I'll have to tell High General Dreher about you."

I nodded. In fact, I hoped that he would. I was being forced to work by the Prince, I was very much at odds with the Court Philosopher, and the King was missing, so perhaps I could get something useful from Rotfelsen's strongest military power. Or at least learn where the High General stood.

"My turn," I said, as though Martin-Frederick wasn't the one with an official order and a band of soldiers upstairs. "What I was looking into was whether there is any truth to the rumors about the Bandit States invading Rotfelsen. That is to say, their armies actually getting inside of your lovely rock. I've heard quite a bit about it, but have seen nothing of the sort in my visions." I smiled and bowed my head. "Sometimes even my Gift needs a little help."

"Oh, *that*? Is that all?" He waved a bejeweled hand. "Not a chance. Not a chance! This whole idea hinges on the possibility that High General Dreher would rather lie to preserve his honor than do what must be done to keep us safe."

"And you don't think he would?"

"Not a chance!" he repeated. "If Rotfelsen were at stake, Dreher would publicly, clearly, ask the Prince and the King for help—perhaps even the Court Philosopher! What Dreher cares about is preserving the order and safety of Rotfelsen, not honor. Or perhaps, in *that* lies his soldier's honor. That's why he's been High General so long. And"—he grinned—"that's why he doesn't listen too much to men like me. You know"—he affected a deep voice—"'duelist adventurers' and 'royal thrill-seekers.'"

"If that's an imitation of our good High General and his favorite names for you, I'm afraid it's lost on me. I haven't had the pleasure."

"It's a gruff sort of pleasure, but I like that he treats me like any other soldier."

I sincerely doubted the High General did so.

I took another sip of beet liquor and made a face that Martin-Frederick apparently found cute. The guileless boy certainly didn't sound like he was lying about the Bandit States, and I could only take his word for it unless I could speak to the High General himself. I could always be wrong, but if Martin-Frederick was telling the truth, then I had my escape route nicely planned. Perhaps Papa's "fire and sword" would not come from the south.

From where then? But I shook that away and had another sip. It didn't matter. I just needed to get out. I was but one broken shell, in constant danger of losing my life even without Papa's doom prophecy bearing down upon us. I owed it to him to find our way south.

"Well, either way," I said to Martin-Frederick, "I would be very gladdened to meet with High General Dreher. Do you think you could arrange that? Surely, he listens to you a bit."

"Well, a *bit*, surely," he echoed, talking through a broad smile. He certainly did want to impress me. "I'll see what I can do, Kalyna Aljosanovna."

He raised his mug, and I clacked mine against his. We finished our drinks.

"Thank you, Melvin-Franklin," I said.

The King's Dinner

Unfortunately, Prince Friedhelm "requested" my presence, as well as Lenz's, the next evening at the King's Dinner. It was held in a part of the Royal Party Apartments I, somehow, hadn't yet seen. It was a long, but low-ceilinged, dining room, with around forty people milling about a table that could probably seat fifty. It was soon made clear to me, however, that only fifteen would be *sitting* at that table. The rest—like Lenz and myself—would stand behind our masters and look serious and dutiful. I hoped we would at least get to pick at the leftovers.

There was a palpable tension animating those people who milled about and tried to act casual, waiting for a king they had not seen since the Winter Ball. It was suggested, in hushed tones, that soon an excuse would be made, and everyone would be asked to leave. Neither Selvosch the Quarrymaster nor Edeltraud von Edeltraud the Mistress of Coin were there, and I did not see Andelka of Rituo in attendance either, but Vorosknecht the Court Philosopher was, and I kept my eye on him. Perhaps *some* people had seen the King more recently than they let on, after all.

I reflected on the fact that I had recently seen the King's face, at least, and smiled. I decided to go talk to the Court Philosopher.

"Oh," he said when I approached him. "You're still here?" A Purple stood just behind him, a man that I think I recognized from our interview at the ball.

"So far," I replied. "Why? Have you a good reason for me to leave?" I grinned up at him.

Vorosknecht looked more annoyed than anything else. "I thought I had provided a compelling reason, but you must be dimmer than I realized."

"Perhaps I'm not willing to give up your charming company so easily, Brightness."

He grunted and flourished toward Prince Friedhelm, across the room, who was standing with Lenz and another Yellow I had met a few times.

"Tell me, fool," Vorosknecht began, "why the Prince needs three Yellows with him tonight when I am brave enough to be here with just one of my men." He nodded to the Purple behind him.

"I apologize, Brightness," I said, with a deep curtsy. "I did not realize you would be intimidated by the lame researcher and the unarmed prophet."

"Prophet indeed," he snorted. "I only worry what new problems you will blunder into. Your master was given a chance, after all."

"That is not how I remember the ball," I replied.

He yawned theatrically, stretching his arms high above his head. "I'm tired of this, and of you. I shall take my leave: the King isn't coming."

"Are you certain of that, Brightness?"

"Positive," he laughed. Vorosknecht nodded again at his Purple and turned his back to me.

"You should avoid telling the future to a prophet, Brightness," I called after him.

Without turning, he waved a dismissive hand at me as he walked toward the door.

Others began to notice that the Court Philosopher was leaving, and the murmurs and uncertainty grew. Various dignitaries began to make their excuses to each other, and to round up their attendants. I shot a look at Lenz, who seemed mortified. Prince Friedhelm was smiling calmly and fabricating his own excuses for leaving to a ruddy, stocky man in a green doublet.

Vorosknecht coughed loudly as he approached the door of the chamber, to ensure that everyone saw him leaving the room, insulted at the King's tardiness. He looked back over his shoulder, smiling imperiously at the guests, and so walked fully into a pair of Reds, who growled and shoved him backward. Behind those Reds, stood the King.

Vorosknecht stumbled and his smile dropped. He stood, tall and unmoving, watching the King's entrance with an intense, confused stare. His Purple stepped toward the Reds, but the Court Philosopher was smart enough to put out an arm and hold him back.

"I apologize for my lateness," drawled the King, as he scanned the room with his vague, uncomprehending face. When his gaze alighted on me, there was a brief twinkle in his eye, and I knew this was Olaf.

I saw relief in the faces of the dinner guests, as well as lingering confusion about what had taken so long, and about the King's week-long absence. I glanced in the Prince's direction, and saw that Lenz and the man in the green doublet certainly look relieved. Prince Friedhelm was perhaps acting too surprised: his jaw hung open in supposed disbelief.

There was then much bustling and noise as the important people found their seats, and everyone like me tried to find somewhere to stand. The floor of the dining room was rotrock, but smoothed and buffed until it shone like red marble, and caused each heavy oak chair to squeak and groan across its surface. In the middle of all that cacophony and chaos, I watched Olaf as he sat languidly at the head of the table. For the most part, he was doing a very good job of making the serene, vacant expression that was the real King Gerhold VIII's normal manner, but every now and then he would wince as a chair tore at the floor, or look suddenly to his side when someone flopped loudly into their seat. I hoped no one but me was seeing any of this.

Olaf was also studiously ignoring Queen Biruté, who sat next to him with a hand draped over Olaf's armrest. This was my first time seeing the Queen, and I must say she seemed too beautiful to be as inbred as her husband. She was also the only person in the room, besides me, who was not a pink Rotfelsenisch type, which immediately made me like her a bit. She was of Skydašian stock—probably a most careful mix of North and South Shores, to keep the balance of power in that kingdom going. She and Olaf were each leaning away from one another, and while he did not spare her so much as a glance, she constantly shot her eyes toward him, and then away, and then toward him, and then away. I hoped that the real king was as neglectful of her as his reputation suggested, and that she was just annoyed, rather than suspicious. But of course, this was the woman our Prince most suspected, and she commanded at least half of the Reds. I also began to wonder how long Olaf would be able to ignore so handsome a woman.

Vorosknecht, at least, did not seem to pay any attention to our false monarch. The Court Philosopher had gotten into a chair quickly, and was saying something quietly into his Purple's ear. The soldier nodded, and nodded, and nodded again, asked a question, and then nodded once more before quickly leaving the room. I assumed he was off to tell Selvosch and . . . whoever else was in on their plot, about the King's appearance. I wondered where exactly Vorosknecht had expected the King to be. Scared into staying in his rooms? Locked in a dungeon, perhaps? Sick from poison? The Reds who flanked Olaf betrayed nothing of their expectations or knowledge regarding him and his missing doppelgänger.

Prince Friedhelm was sitting in front of me, chatting with the ruddy older man in green, who I soon learned was High General Dreher. The same who had recently sent Martin-Frederick to search Andelka's rooms. I mostly saw his back.

"I admit, I wasn't sure my brother would show either," laughed Friedhelm, leaning in to be conspiratorial. "I thought he had been scared off by the . . . incident at the ball, you know?"

The High General chuckled, but did not agree with the playful, almost-traitorous comments the Prince was so fond of making. "I think our King is made of sterner stuff than you give him credit for, Highness. But then, I only saw him from a distance when he was a child—growing up together may have given you a different perspective."

"That may well be, High General. I think I am too familiar with him as a brother to see him as a King." The Prince shot his eyes at Olaf for a moment, then back to Dreher, and smiled.

The High General just smiled back and shrugged. Standing behind him, I saw, even in that small movement of his, what seemed to be a great deal of pain and effort.

"Welcome all," drawled Olaf at the end of the table, about four or five seats down from the Prince. "I hope you will enjoy your . . . our . . . ah . . . dinner. Together. And please do let me know if you have any . . . oh, you know, concerns."

Queen Biruté rolled her eyes for a moment. Was that a normal part of their relationship?

I had seen the real King, but never heard him speak, so I had no clue as to how accurate Olaf's Gerhold voice was, and I wondered if he was laying on the uncaring absentmindedness a bit thick. But no one stood up and screamed, "Fraud!" so I supposed we were doing all right so far.

The first course came out, but everyone had to wait for the King to start before touching their food. In front of each person was a little cup of brown broth with a perfect dollop of something yellow in the center, emitting a pleasing steam. Olaf took a small, noisy sip and proclaimed, unenthusiastically, that he was sure it was delicious. Then everyone began to eat.

Curious about his pained shrug earlier, I decided to watch High General Dreher for a bit. He held his body in his chair as though any extra movement would be excruciating, and when he ate, he bent his arm at the elbow and leaned down to sort of catch his food. Dreher must have been around sixty, but this went beyond the normal aches of age. His pain at simple movement seemed quite acute, especially in regard to his right arm, and I guessed he had some injury, or great sickness.

My feet were already starting to hurt as I stood behind the Prince and the High General. I glanced at Lenz, who was already heavily favoring his bad leg, slumping to one side. I stood straighter and grinned at him. He pretended not to see.

Olaf was looking with glazed eyes at an official I did not recognize, nodding almost imperceptibly as she spoke to him. He seemed to be doing a well enough job, but very little had been asked of him yet. The

Queen spoke to another courtier and continued to glance back at her "husband." She even waved her hand toward him, as though discussing him. I wondered if they had spoken before joining us for dinner and, if so, what was going through her mind right now. If Olaf pulled this off, would it be because he was a great actor, or because King Gerhold VIII was so much nothing?

Then I thought about how the King could very well be bleeding and broken in a dungeon somewhere, and felt bad for insulting him like this. Even a royal is just a scared person in such a situation, aren't they? (I'm not sure.) I decided to perk myself up by seeing how angry and flustered Vorosknecht was.

I looked across the table to where the Court Philosopher was sitting, but he was not staring at Olaf with a combination of confusion and anger, as I'd hoped. No, he was lifting a fork to his mouth and shoving a piece of meat into it while looking directly at me. I admit I was surprised to see his eyes trained on me, and my surprise probably showed. He continued to glare as he chewed slowly. What was he guessing at now? How much had he figured out? His Purple returned, and he mumbled something up to the soldier, while still looking at me.

I raised my eyebrows and smiled at Vorosknecht. After all, I knew *two* things that he did not: how we'd gotten a king here, and that all of his machinations would mean nothing when the Tetrarchia plunged into chaos and death. My smugness ebbed away, and I looked back at Olaf. I wondered, again, if his very existence, somehow more fraudulent than mine, would cause our end. The false King was looking slightly more engaged, leaning forward to listen to High General Dreher across five or so other people. The High General also leaned forward, with a pained grunt.

"Your Majesty," Dreher was saying, "I promise you that the rumors of the Bandit States' incursions into our fair country are spurious."

Olaf cocked his head to the side, a little puzzled. But it was Queen Biruté who spoke.

"Our *kingdom*, you mean, High General?" she said quickly, snapping out each word. "Our *country* is the Tetrarchia."

High General Dreher was silent a moment, and most of the table went quiet as well.

". . . told him that's not how you use a—" continued someone absorbed in their own conversation, before cutting themselves off when they realized no one else was talking.

Olaf turned slowly to Biruté and smiled halfheartedly. She smiled back, angrily. Olaf took an age to turn his head back all the way to face High General Dreher.

"The Queen," he said, "is quite correct, Dreher."

I frowned at Olaf. I worried that the King was too passive, and that even this slight bit of disagreement was out of character. I wondered whether Olaf was succumbing to a pretty face.

"Our blessed kingdom," Olaf continued, "is but one of four that make up our . . . ah, what did they tell me to say . . . our quadruple-blessed country."

High General Dreher was quiet for a moment, and I could not see his face as he looked at Olaf.

"True," laughed Dreher, finally. "But of course, if the Bandit States *did* invade Rotfelsen, they would also be invading our country, the Tetrarchia, would they not?"

Olaf smiled and nodded, and everyone seemed to relax slightly. I chanced a look at Vorosknecht, but he was eyeing his plate in that moment. I believe they were on the fourth course?

"Moot either way," the High General continued. "The point is, they have done no such thing. They gnash their teeth at our borders, but between our Greens and our alliance with Rituo, the Bandit States are kept well in check, I promise you."

"Well," said Olaf, "that *is* a relief, isn't it?" He slumped back in his chair.

"Indeed, brother," said Prince Friedhelm. "We need all the soldiers we can spare for when we host the Council of Barbarians, don't we?"

Olaf waved a lazy hand at Friedhelm. "Yes, yes, but we're hardly in danger there. Our allies are as invested in the Tetrarchia as we are. Oh, there may be rumblings in some of their backwaters about separatism, but it will amount to nothing." He coughed out a laugh. "After all, we've always had the most separatists right here, and we keep them under control just fine. Always worrying, aren't you, brother?"

There was some uncomfortable laughter around the table at that. Prince Friedhelm smiled without seeming very happy, and I did not know if this was all part of the play-acting, or if Olaf was taking his role too much to heart.

I thought about what Olaf had said regarding the Council of Barbarians not being particularly dangerous and remembered my father's prophecy. What was I doing, standing around, watching courtiers eat and trading barbs with a puffed-up philosopher, when I needed to get out of this place as soon as possible?

The next course came, and a nervous little server pushed past me to put small plates in front of Friedhelm and Dreher. Bored, I looked down over the Prince's shoulder to see cut up pieces of persimmon. So this was the beginning of the desserts, and soon this interminable night would be over. I smiled to myself and thought of Tural.

Someone was expounding more upon their worries about trade during the Council of Barbarians, and Olaf was pretending to listen. Or perhaps Olaf was *pretending* to pretend to listen. Whatever the case, he had not bothered to touch his persimmon slices yet, and therefore no one else did. Prince Friedhelm, always playing the sensualist, was drumming his fingers on the table with impatience about starting his dessert. I looked at the High General's vague annoyance, at the Prince's bejeweled fingers pattering on the table, and then again at the persimmon on his plate. And that was when I began to wonder if something was wrong.

The pieces of persimmon laid out on the Prince's plate weren't cut very evenly, or displayed very carefully, which was unlike all food I had seen served in the palace at this point. I leaned closer, almost touching the Prince, and saw the waxy sheen of the persimmon's innards. Hadn't Tural chosen, based on my input, to use the upper red persimmon variety? I closed my eyes and tried very hard to remember the fruits he had shown me, what they had looked like, and which one had been the waxier of the two. I tried, in a way, to *conjure*.

I remembered Tural's smile and high cheekbones; his pleasant smell and the flecks of gray in his hair. This was not what I needed to conjure. I remembered him happily pointing to the upper red persimmon, the tart one, which I had enjoyed. I definitely remembered it being less waxy in its appearance than what was currently on the Prince's plate. Perhaps Tural had changed his mind?

I saw Olaf's hand lazily move onto his plate, pushing around the thick and uneven piece of persimmon he had been served. I looked at Vorosknecht, and he was staring at Olaf, but that hardly meant much. Did it?

I leaned forward further and tapped Prince Friedhelm on the shoulder. I hoped very much that I would not look very stupid very soon.

"Those aren't the right persimmons," I whispered in his ear.

"What?" he hissed back.

"They look like the wrong kind," I said. I shut my eyes tight, as though to not see the deep amount of trouble I was getting myself into. "I just had a vision of someone dying at this table."

"Do you *know* it's the persimmons?" replied the Prince.

"I can't guarantee that. But look at how badly they're cut."

"I rather thought the cooks were getting tired," he replied.

"What's going on?" whispered Lenz.

Dreher glanced over at us. Olaf pressed two fingers around a piece of persimmon.

"Do we want to lose a second King?" I growled, my lips touching the Prince's ear, so no one else could hear.

"No," said the Prince, still whispering. "Kalyna, I suggest you let everyone know."

My eyes widened, and I felt my heart had stopped. I thought I could just feed the Prince the information and he'd do what he willed with it. I stood up straight. Olaf had picked up a piece of persimmon. Would I let him die to avoid everyone thinking me a fool? I considered it.

I took a deep breath, and brought up all the false confidence that I could.

"Your Majesty!" I positively boomed across the table. "Don't eat that!"

Olaf looked up at me, confused. But he dropped the persimmon slice. I wondered if the real King would have trusted me so quickly.

Everyone began to yell at once, some shoving their plates away as hard as they could. One of the Reds slipped up right behind Olaf, reaching for something on the table. I felt my body seize up in fear. I looked down at the Prince's knife, and wondered if I could grab it and vault over the table in time.

I had one foot on the Prince's armrest when the Red grabbed a bottle of clear liquor, poured it on a napkin, and began vigorously rubbing Olaf's fingers clean of persimmon residue. I deflated and stepped back down to the floor. The Prince turned and stared up at me confused.

"Well, what's the matter with the persimmons?" asked Dreher.

Vorosknecht said nothing, and did not seem to react much at all.

"Poison," I said, loud enough for all to hear. I found myself very much hoping that I was right and they were poisoned, and not that Tural had had a sudden change of heart regarding which kind to serve. I began formulating lies for what I would say if it was not, actually, poison: perhaps that I actually saw someone choking on their dessert?

"Bring the Master of Fruit in here at once!" roared the Prince.

"No, wait," I began, but I was drowned out.

THE MASTER OF FRUIT

There was a whirlwind of activity then, but the result was a very confused Tural sitting in a chair, surrounded by Reds. Some of the more squeamish dinner guests had left, but plenty remained, crowded up behind the Prince, the Queen, and Olaf, who were facing Tural. These remaining guests included Vorosknecht, who stood just behind the Prince, and Dreher, who was still seated at the table. Lenz and I were over by the wall, where we were supposed to look unobtrusive. A Red's large hands were on Tural's shoulders, holding him down in the chair. He looked searchingly at me, but did not say anything.

"Master of Fruit," began Prince Friedhelm, "are you aware that—?"

"Oh, let's just feed him his own fruit and be done with it," said Vorosknecht. "A quick test, and we'll save a lot of time."

Vorosknecht's one Purple soldier in attendance grabbed a plate of the offending persimmon and pushed it right into Tural's face. The Reds neither stopped nor helped. Prince Friedhelm glared at Vorosknecht. Olaf looked passive.

"It's just the best way," agreed Queen Birutė.

Was the Queen in on the plot? Seeing her agree with Vorosknecht, especially on the unimportance of Tural's life, made me begin to agree with the Prince on that. It would certainly explain all of her searching looks at her supposed husband.

"I hate to say it," said High General Dreher, who twisted his body toward us from his seat at the table, "but it may be our best option." He shrugged and winced.

The Prince turned farther, to look back at the High General. The Prince knew, of course, what I knew: namely that Vorosknecht was definitely in on a plot to kill the King. But of course, he had no proof, and neither knew nor cared about Tural. I saw him mulling over the High General's words, clearly considering it.

"Then how would we know who hired him?" asked Lenz.

"Hired? Hired?" cried Tural. "You hired me, Your Majesty!" He flailed his arms at Olaf, almost tipping over the plate in front of him. The Purple growled.

"What is this all about?" continued Tural.

"He's foreign," Vorosknecht pointed out. "Easy enough to guess: a Skydašian plot."

"How *dare* you?" cried the Queen, reeling toward Vorosknecht and shoving a finger in his face, even though he was much taller than her. "And this man is clearly Quru!"

"Well, that's less exciting." Vorosknecht smiled at the crowd behind him. "But Quruscan isn't far from Loasht, either."

There was a hushed whimpering among the remaining dinner guests and attendants at the thought that *they* were somehow adjacent to a Loashti plot. Prince Friedhelm looked pointedly at High General Dreher again.

"He's indelicate," the High General said, "but, again, not necessarily wrong."

"It's simply the best and quickest way to find out," agreed Queen Biruté.

"These . . ." Tural grunted, looking at the plate in front of him. "These aren't my persimmons!"

"Oh yes, very good," laughed Vorosknecht. "A bit late, aren't you?"

Tural suddenly shot to his feet, getting out of the grip of the Reds for a moment. They put their hands back on him, but didn't push him down.

"Sir!" he cried, clearly at Vorosknecht.

The Court Philosopher, for his part, seemed truly surprised at this outburst.

"I have never impugned your work," Tural continued, "and here you impugn mine!"

"What's that to do with anything?" laughed Vorosknecht. "I'm the Court Philosopher, and you're just—"

"*The Master of Fruit!*" Tural yelled. "I would *never* serve something of such an ugly cut and arrangement! You can believe that if I was to poison someone, they would *never* know until they were dead!"

I put my face in my hands. This had started well, at least.

"And," Tural continued, stepping on whatever Vorosknecht was going to say next, "there is one thing I'll say for you Rots: you insist on keeping records of everything!"

Prince Friedhelm tilted his head to the side and furrowed his brow at Tural.

"Most of the time," Tural continued, "it is a great nuisance, I must say." His chest was out, as though this was his great declaration. "But *these*"—he pointed disdainfully at the plate of persimmon slices held by the Purple—"are clearly lower red persimmon. And if you look at my acquisition and disposal paperworks, you will see that I signed the order to feed the King and his guests *upper* red persimmon!"

He went on to explain this paperwork in great detail, alongside all the bureaucracy that would come to bear once the dinner was over, in order to get these lower red persimmons, which he had *not* used, into the servant houses in the shadow of the Sunset Palace. He also explained how difficult it would have been to poison the already sliced (and, he pointed out, very evenly and thinly sliced) upper red persimmon, while poisoning whole fruits and *then* cutting them would be much easier. He was deeply thorough about everything, and I will spare you the bulk of it.

"Hmm," said Prince Friedhelm, finally. "So, how do we test it?"

"Your Highness," sighed Lenz, "it's much less dramatic than making someone eat fruit that may be poisoned, but we do have alchemists for that sort of thing. They check everything before it comes into the palace, of course."

"Just as I say," said Tural. "These were poisoned in the palace, behind my back!"

Lenz sighed. He had meant to leave that part pointedly unsaid.

"Yes, yes, good idea," said the Prince. He opened his mouth to issue more orders, then stopped himself, and turned to Olaf. "That is, brother, if you agree."

Olaf seemed to be falling asleep halfway through his nod of agreement. Queen Biruté's lips were pressed tightly together, but she nodded too.

"Well then," said High General Dreher, "I will leave you to your tests. It's all a bit technical for me, and I'm absolutely exhausted." He groaned and heaved himself up out of his chair.

"And how am I to know," began Vorosknecht, "that you won't lie and say these were poisoned just to protect the reputation of your newest acquisition?" He waved a hand at me. "This psychic of yours?"

All eyes went to me for a moment, and it was all I could do to stand tall. Prince Friedhelm said nothing because he knew there was nothing to say. If these were indeed poisoned, it was almost certainly Vorosknecht's doing, but he had just thrown doubt on the very idea. The techniques of alchemy were purposefully secret and obtuse, so it wasn't as though the King, Queen, Prince, and Court Philosopher (or their agents) could watch the alchemists and verify their findings. The only way to prove to all present that the fruits were poisoned was to force someone to eat them right there, while everyone was still gathered.

I believe that the Prince chose to let the Court Philosopher have that small victory, not because he didn't want to kill some poor servant, but because he did not want to contradict himself.

Everyone began to file out. Some seemed quite disappointed that there had been no deaths; this way, it was hardly a story to dine out on in the future.

The Reds kept a close cordon around Olaf as he made his way toward me. He took my hand limply, but let a smile twitch at his lips.

"Thank you," he said. "I do believe you saved my life."

"Think nothing of it, Your Majesty." I bowed.

Queen Birutė, standing next to Olaf, looked at me for a long time, with narrowed eyes. I did my best to stand still and accept her gaze. I did not know if she was suspicious of me because she did not trust the Prince, or because I had ruined her own plot for her husband, or if she thought all soothsayers to be evil witches, or if she thought I was cute. I thought about her willingness to let Tural die as I looked back at her.

"Yes," she finally said. "Thank you."

I bowed again.

ANOTHER CONSPIRATOR LEGITIMATELY UNMASKED

The next morning, as the sun crept over increasingly leafless trees, I saw a carriage rolling to a halt from my window. It stopped in the sad, sludgy old snow that dotted the top of Rotfelsen and a Yellow ran out breathlessly. I had just enough time to throw on some clothes before he banged on my door, and I was whisked outside and into the waiting carriage.

I was surprised to see not just Lenz, but also Prince Friedhelm, sitting in the backseat. I was pushed in with them and the door was closed, but the carriage didn't start moving. Two Yellows standing outside the carriage began to have a very loud and conspicuous conversation about how the weather affected their old dueling wounds.

"Good morning, Kalyna," said the Prince. "We're on our way to a Red barracks to see how Olaf is coming along. Thought we'd stop by on the way."

"Of course, Your Highness." I managed to find some well of composure, despite being barely awake.

The Yellows outside continued to drone on—I suppose they were meant to drown us out, in case the Prince got loud.

Apparently, word had come back from the Prince's alchemists that the hastily prepared lower red persimmons had in fact been poisoned. And that the perfectly sliced upper red persimmons, which had been thrown unceremoniously into a garbage heap, had been perfectly safe. Regarding the poison's appearance, the Prince, Lenz, and I all felt quite confident that the Court Philosopher was to blame, but there didn't seem to be any good way of proving it.

"So," said Lenz, "now we will try to help Olaf manage the Reds' side of the investigation. I suppose we command two armies now."

"One and a half," corrected the Prince. "At best. The Queen's Reds must have been in on my brother's disappearance. Olaf will need to be careful—this particular rift between armies isn't helpfully color-coded." He shook his head. "That blasted woman. This is why I never married."

"Yes. Certainly. This is why," replied Lenz, deadpan.

"So," the Prince continued, "I wanted you to know all this right away, Kalyna, so that you can stop wasting your visions on the dessert man."

"You mean Tural, the Master of Fruit?"

"Yes, sure."

"Tural," I repeated. "Who almost died."

"I suppose. Now tell us who else is part of the plot!"

Just then, I could have killed the Prince myself. As though Tural were not worth a hundred times any royal on this damned rock. The Prince was already a little tyrant, and Vorosknecht was Vorosknecht, so their callousness had not surprised me, but it nurtured my distaste for them. High General Dreher, for better or worse, had seemed purely pragmatic—after all what is another death to a general? But I found myself particularly fixating upon Queen Biruté's part of last night's excitement—perhaps because I knew that Prince Friedhelm already suspected her. Or perhaps because I, for some reason, chose to hold her to a higher standard than all the breathless pink men.

"There must be someone else!" continued the Prince. "I let you run all over the palace grounds, wherever you please, to *read* whomever you like. Surely you've made something of your new freedom."

"Such as saving your life twice now?"

"But who else is working with them?"

"Oh?" I cocked my head to the side. "Is that all?"

They both looked at me intently. I had, of course, spent most of my time and energy looking into Andelka and the Bandit States, only to be led to the High General. And I was thinking of the High General, with his man Martin-Frederick, more and more as something to be used *against* the Prince. So none of those investigations had rendered anything I much wanted to tell Friedhelm and Lenz. Nor, for that matter, had I learned anything useful about how the Tetrarchia would crumble in on itself, or who would cause it. But I remembered Tural sitting in that chair, being threatened with death, and I remembered a number of sidelong glances toward our imposter King. The answer to the Prince's demand seemed clear.

"Well," I said, "Queen Biruté, of course."

Friedhelm laughed and clapped his hands in excitement. "I knew it! I *knew* it!"

"Your Highness," said Lenz, shooting a doubting glance at me, "this is hardly something to celebrate. If the Queen is—"

"Oh, we'll get her now, won't we? We'll pry those Reds away somehow."

Lenz stared at me while the Prince prattled. Finally, Lenz reminded his master that they had more to do that day, and ushered me out of the carriage.

Just outside the carriage, the two of us stood for a moment in the now days-old snow, which had so far received no reinforcements. It was mixed with dirt and dead leaves, as though autumn was still preserved beneath our feet. I shivered a touch.

"Are you quite sure you saw the Queen?" Lenz hissed in Cöllüknit. I nodded.

"Doing *what*?" he added.

I looked directly into his eyes. "Telling her Reds to kill the King," I said. "I saw it after finally being near her at the King's Dinner, so it is in our future." I shrugged. "Or it was later last night."

"The real King or . . ." He mouthed "Olaf."

"That I don't know," I said. "But either is bad, isn't it?"

"The latter," he sighed, "could mean she is on our side, but doesn't realize it. That she wants to rescue the King."

Instead of responding, I simply nodded to show the most vague, and possibly ironic, assent. I'm sure it was maddening. The lie had come so easily. But now, with a moment of quiet, the enormity began to appear in my head, even if I did not exactly feel *guilty*. I didn't need real powers of prophecy to feel that I had just put the whole Tetrarchia, immutably, on the path to destruction. That, by implicating the Queen to the Prince, I had all but assured that this rock would be torn apart beneath me.

Lenz sighed theatrically, placed his hands on his hips, and tapped his good foot against the ground. It sluiced through the old snow and did not make a satisfying sound.

"Well," he said, still quiet, but switching back to Rotfelsenisch, "I hope we'll have this all sorted before the Sun's Death."

My mind had been so stuck on Papa's prophecies that I first thought this meant the sun would actually die soon. Could the sun die? I must have looked confused.

"That's Rotfelsen's solstice, Kalyna. In just a few short weeks."

"Ah. Not another ball, is it?"

"Thankfully, no," he said. "But you've wintered here before, you must know of it."

"If you can call it winter." I kicked the watery snow.

"Yes, yes, but it gets cold and dark enough that in the middle of winter we gather, and—"

"Who's 'we'?"

"Families and friends come together in their homes, with food and ale and . . ." He trailed off. "Ah," he said, when he realized why I had not heard of the Sun's Death.

"This sounds very insular," I said. "Will you visit your family?"

"No," said Lenz. "Have a good day, Kalyna Aljosanovna." He lifted himself back up into the carriage.

I went back into the servant house, and spoke to Tural, giving him the news about the persimmons, which he took with such a calm, "I told you so" manner that he reminded me of Grandmother. But, you know, an appealing version of Grandmother.

He then grew a touch angry, but only because two good batches of persimmons had been ruined. He didn't even think to ask anything so vulgar as *who* had done the poisoning, or *why*. I found that I did not feel particularly guilty about implicating a royal on his behalf, even if he would have abhorred the idea. He never had to know.

PART FOUR

LOCK IT AWAY

The Reds spent the next few days rifling through the kitchens, and scaring the poor workers, and the Yellows spent them sniffing around Vorosknecht's and Queen Biruté's apartments, but nothing useful was found either way. I do not know how much influence the Prince and Lenz had over even the King's Reds, through Olaf, at this point, but those soldiers certainly didn't seem to be doing anything particularly useful.

But then, neither was I, at least not insofar as it would help find or stop whoever had tried to poison Olaf. My focus was still entirely upon escape. With every new wrinkle in the catastrophes unspooling around me, I imagined only the ever-growing probability of what my father had foreseen. If Martin-Frederick could be believed, the Bandit States were not, in fact, invading, and that was all well and good. But *something* must have been going on there, for High General Dreher to be keeping such a close eye on Andelka and "you-know-who." Vorosknecht was, it seemed, attempting to kill our false King, while the real King was hidden from us, and I had implicated the Queen in a (justified) fit of pique.

I did my best to ignore the continuing feeling that I was *causing* the Tetrarchia's impending collapse. After all, these powerful idiots had been undermining each other for years, so how was one imprisoned faker supposed to waltz in and ruin the whole place? (Dare I admit, even now, that a part of me felt satisfaction at the thought? That the narrative of me being plucked against my will, dragged into their court intrigues, and tearing everything down had a thrill to it? If only I could have destroyed only the monarchy, the nobility, and the armies, leaving everyone else alive and well. That, I think I would have been happy to do.)

Whatever the case, I tried to focus on my escape. I wanted to see if my father had picked through his visions to see anything useful about Lenz, but avoided visiting for the next two days. I told myself this was because it would strain him to have me asking, every day, whether he'd found something helpful, which may have been partly true. But I was also getting comfortable, and Papa and Grandmother were reminders that we were not *meant* to be comfortable. Besides, for once in my life, I did not have to take care of him myself. He was in good hands.

I had somewhat free rein over the palace grounds now (in two-hour increments) because Lenz guessed, correctly, that I would not leave without Papa, whose building was guarded. In the absence of useful information on my captor, or any word from Martin-Frederick Reinhold-Bosch, I devised schemes.

I was set on the Bandit States as our destination, as it was the closest way out of the Tetrarchia and had not, I hoped, been raiding Rotfelsen anymore than before. What's more, I knew which obscure villages and tunnels in lower Rotfelsen to take there, but how to escape the palace grounds? Even if we could give the Yellows the slip, we needed a mode of transportation for Papa and Grandmother. I considered hitching a ride with the Skydašian merchant at Ottilie's Rock, perhaps convincing him we were traveling performers, but didn't know when he would leave. I wondered if I could fake my own death and tell Grandmother where to meet me, but couldn't trust her (and couldn't trust Lenz to let them go after my death). I even prayed to my two favorite gods to deliver me, even though they were my favorites in part because they were not known for seeing devotion as transactional.

I spent a day in my room, hatching and abandoning these plans as I ate leftover Quru cake, sipped whatever brandy was to hand, and sewed some of the gold marks I'd been paid into my clothing. But soon, the chances to procrastinate became too tempting: I could read one of Lenz's books, apologize more to Tural about his near death, or try to wheedle information out of others in the house. These were all ways to convince myself I was doing something helpful, but of course, the usefulness was all in my head. I had nothing new to glean from these sources that would help me *escape*. So I did what any self-respecting plotter and charlatan would do—I repaired to a tavern.

My hope was that a change of scenery, combined with regular walks back to the servant house, through ever brisker and windier air, to let the Yellows know I had not escaped, would knock the cobwebs out of my head. What's more, I was still hoping to hear from Martin-Frederick Reinhold-Bosch, and through him from High General Dreher, one of the only people whose power rivaled the Prince. But I did not think I could just traipse right up to the Green barracks and risk being seen doing so.

I spent two days moving back and forth between my prison and the Royal Inn of Ottilie's Rock, chatting with Gunther, and plotting in that steamy room over tea, alcohol, and meals. It felt like a new low (or high?) in my decadence. I wanted to see Papa, but I was glad I could avoid seeing Grandmother, not just because she was awful, but because she would tell me I was drinking too much and lazing about. And she would be right. On the second such day, a greater snow finally fell upon Rotfelsen, and I got to experience my first time trudging home drunk through snow up to my knees. I found it strangely pleasant.

On the third day, I finally decided to see my family again. I crunched out through more snow toward the building where my father and grandmother were housed. I had felt so inactive lately that walking was far preferable to another carriage ride, no matter how cold the wind.

In the building's entryway, I met the Yellow I was still calling "Dugmush" in my head, for lack of something better. She cheerily followed me upstairs. I ignored my nagging embarrassment at not knowing her name—what would it matter in the long run?—but could not ignore her. I was beginning to find her easy confidence alluring, although whether it was a yearning *for* her, a need to be *like* her, or a morbid *fear* of her, I wasn't sure. Likely all three.

I also ignored the doctor's assistants in their burlap aprons, scurrying about underfoot as I went up the stairs. I crossed through Grandmother's room, and also ignored whatever terrible things she had to say.

At the door to my father's room, another doctor's assistant stood in front of me and said, yelling to speak over Grandmother's invective, "Your father needs rest, you know . . ."

I growled at the assistant, and she scampered away. My grandmother kept yelling, and the Yellow decided she could guard me well enough out on the landing. I went into Papa's room and slammed the door. He looked at me with surprise, excitement, and unease, but he repeated his old joke:

"Welcome, stranger, to the tent of Aljosa the Prophet! In this humble place I will untangle the strands of fate that— Oh! It's you, Kalynishka!"

I smiled and took his hand tightly. It was not as clammy as normal. He really *was* being cared for here. I looked down into his sweet face, and wondered whether it would be best to stay here, in comfort, until the end came for the Tetrarchia. Was it worth trying to escape so badly, and tearing him away from his care? Would it be so bad to haunt the crumbled remains of Rotfelsen until I was allowed into a hell?

I sat down next to Papa and touched his face. He positively beamed up at me, and I felt warm inside. He had so much trouble seeing clear visions, what was I doing trying to get him to help me? Trying to wheedle ammunition against my jailer from him?

"How are you doing, Papa?"

His eyes twinkled. "I saw a thing," he mouthed to me in a mixture of three different Loashti languages.

I stiffened. "About the . . . limping man?" I replied in Cöllüknit.

Papa nodded excitedly. "Kalynishka, I . . ."

I gripped his wrist so tightly in anticipation that, after a few seconds, he twisted slowly and moaned. I was hurting him. I loosened my grip.

"Yes, Papa?" I croaked.

"Never, Kalynishka," he whispered. I did not know what he meant. "Not even around Mother. Not around the doctor, nor her scratchy assistants who never leave me be. I didn't . . ." He looked frustrated, he wanted so badly to explain to me. "I . . . I locked it away."

"You didn't speak of it. Even during your . . ." I did not want to say "rants."

"My screaming nights, yes!" he cried, relieved at my understanding. "And I will keep it from everyone but you, Kalynishka."

I patted Papa's hand. "I know you will," I lied. "I have always been able to count on you when I need to, Papa," I lied.

He then told me what he had seen. He promised again that he would tell no one. Papa was going to hurt himself so much holding onto this secret for his ungrateful daughter.

PAPERWORK

"What are you making my poor son do for you *now*?" cried Grandmother as I passed through her room again, onto the landing.

I answered her by slamming her door. The Yellow, Dugmush, who had been waiting for me, smiled and shrugged.

"Ready to go?" she asked.

The doctor's assistant I had scared off earlier began to slip past me back toward Grandmother's room and, I assume, Papa's.

"Of course," I replied to the Yellow. "But a minute, if you please."

"You're the boss," she said, even though I was not. I found her easy trust in me a touch thrilling.

She shrugged and leaned back onto the banister, one long leg sprawled out to the side, and yawned. The assistant had her papers clutched tightly to her burlap apron, and was trying to get around me. I leaned down to look at her.

"Excuse me," I said, making a concerned face.

She looked perplexed and uttered awkward half-words. She slowed, but did not stop. The assistant was smaller than me, and only doing her job. I would feel guilty about this. Later.

She passed me, and I said, "I just wanted to talk to you about—"

This was when I kicked her in the back of the knee. She folded backward and waved her arms, looking terrified. I snatched the papers out of the air and winced when she hit the floor. The Yellow at the banister seemed to wake up and start toward me. I stepped around the assistant and, even as I heard the soldier's footsteps, glanced down at the papers in my hand.

As I thought: she had been copying down what Papa said, during his fits and otherwise.

"Just one moment," I said to Dugmush. "I'm not trying to escape."

The Yellow followed but seemed only curious. I dashed toward the other end of the landing, where a bigger doctor's assistant was poring over something. He was a thick man, heavily muscled, his voice deep and bewildered.

"What's—?"

I hit him in the nose and he reeled, then I grabbed his throat and jumped toward him, using my weight to knock him over. He was big, but not particularly fast; the muscles were to hold down injured, squirming soldiers while they had limbs cut off them. He crashed to the floor beneath me, and I let go of his throat. Leaning in the doorway, Dugmush barked out half a laugh before thinking better of it.

"Are you going somewhere with this, ma'am?" she asked. "I was only told to keep you from running off with your family, but I suspect Master Felsknecht would not appreciate all this."

I stomped past the prone assistant toward a desk, which I ransacked for more papers, yanking out the drawers. I wasn't allowing myself to feel worry, just anger. Rage at Papa's most secret moments, his pain, being put on display. The fear would come later—I could not afford it yet.

"Just a few minutes," I said. I turned to face her. "Please."

"Did they *do* something to the old man?"

"Somewhat."

I threw an empty drawer behind me with a clatter. The thick male assistant groaned. The small female one was at the doorway now.

"What are you doing?" she screamed. "Those are medical documents!" She looked at my guard. "Aren't you supposed to stop her?"

"Only from escaping," was the reply.

No one saw me smile bitterly as I continued my search. There were papers documenting the edges and silhouettes of the futures Papa saw every day. Here was a good reminder of where I stood in Lenz's clutches. No matter how many secrets I was told, I was still a prisoner.

My father had the best medical care possible, but it was not free. It was not unconditional.

How much could be learned from these papers? Had my father truly kept what he saw of Lenz's love life secret? Worse still, had my fraud been exposed? My heart positively pounded against my chest. My neck and fingertips went cold.

In a fit of childish anger, I kicked one of the wooden drawers that lay at my feet. It broke against the wall, and the small assistant yelped. I stormed back toward the stairs, and she tried to bar my way, but faltered when I got too close.

"Follow me," I told Dugmush.

"Of course," she laughed.

"What is happening out there?" screamed Grandmother.

DOCTOR AUE

Doctor Aue was a thin woman with a snub nose who barely looked at me when I burst into her ground floor office. She was standing at the side of her desk—in stockings and breeches, dressed "like a man" because she was a *doctor*—bent over a collection of medical drawings. The Yellow, whom I was still ridiculously thinking of as Dugmush, leaned in the doorway, and I felt both bolstered and threatened by her presence. Behind her was the rattled female doctor's assistant, looking anxious. The larger male assistant was, I think, I still lying on the floor above us.

"Yes?" said the doctor.

"What is *this*?" I asked as I shoved a paper into her hand. "And where are the rest of them?"

She smoothed it out over the meticulous drawing she had been inspecting of a man having a tumor drained. She sighed, rolled her eyes at me, looked down at the paper, picked it up, blinked and moved it far away for a better view, then brought it back to where it had been, and finally read.

"'There are flowers,'" she said. "'Orange hydrangeas, and a boy is running through them. His mother is on a horse. The ocean is capsizing Loashti fisherwomen. They are crying out for their gods, but they are drowning. Purple. Blue. It blinks. The walls of a fortress house a family of rats. Lights everywhere, she cannot see her father anymore.'"

Doctor Aue squinted up at me. "I don't know. What is it?"

"I suppose," I muttered, "that out of context . . ."

"Shall I go on?" she asked. "There's much, much, much more. 'The tiger is coming for him, but he is too aroused to run.' That's a good one."

I snatched it out of her hand. "My father, your patient Aljosa Vüsalavich, is very sick, and sometimes he raves. These are records of what he has ranted about under your care. Is that a standard treatment?"

Doctor Aue blinked many times. "Huh." She looked at me, looked at her assistant, and then slowly circled back to sit behind her desk. Her office was small and very cold, with every inch of wall covered in drawings, instructions, and sometimes dried innards I could not place. None of this looked like decoration; it seemed every object on the wall had been put there in a moment when Doctor Aue needed to see it immediately.

"Is that what this is, Louisa?" Doctor Aue's gaze shot right past me and my guard to the assistant out in the hallway. There was a very long silence.

"Yes, Doctor."

"Huh."

"Do you," I said, "honestly suggest this went on without your knowing?"

"A nice thing," she replied, "about being a *very good doctor*, is that I can afford to have scruples. Sometimes. My job is to help my patients, most of whom are nobility and would never allow their utterings to be recorded. What's more, since it has nothing to do with how your father *feels*, it's a waste of my staff's time and effort, and could jeopardize his trust in us, which can be dangerous."

"But . . . ?"

"But, if Lenz Felsknecht had told me, with the Prince's voice, to copy down your father's ramblings, I would have been required to do so. Lenz, I'm sure, knows that I would carry out this task while also complaining and petitioning bitterly against it, which is why he instead went straight to Louisa here." Her eyes darted back to the assistant, although I wondered how well the doctor could see any of us. "Didn't he?"

I looked over my shoulder. Louisa nodded.

"And you did the right thing by listening to him," said Doctor Aue.

I shook the papers noisily in my hand. "I thought this was a waste of time and effort?"

"And it's the duty of any Rotfelsenisch citizen to waste their time and effort on royal aims, if asked. That includes myself and my busy little bluebirds here. If he told them to do something, and told them to not tell me, that would be their duty even if he hadn't offered money. Which I am sure he did."

She looked past me for confirmation. Louisa must have nodded again because a moment later, the doctor looked at me, or my fore-head, and continued, "Yes, quite. Well. Now that I know, I will begin petitioning. But hard to say much will come of it."

I stared down at Doctor Aue for a long time. She began to trace a finger over a graphic illustration of hemorrhoids.

"Please leave those papers," she added.

I slammed them onto her desk, to which she did not respond.

"Thank you for taking care of my father," I managed to say.

Doctor Aue said nothing more, but her finger stopped tracing hemorrhoids for a moment. I walked out of the room.

I began back toward the stairs, but Dugmush moved to block my way. She did the courtesy of not grabbing or pushing me.

"Sorry, ma'am," she said, "but given all that, I don't think I should let you go up there, just now. I'm only supposed to stop you from escaping, but I think that if you told your family about all this on my watch, I'd never hear the end of it." She shrugged.

"Of course," I growled. I couldn't bring myself to thank her for let-ting me go as far as I had. I felt a wild fear begin to rise in me, but tamped it down. "Tell the other Yellows, when they look for me, that I'm at the tavern."

DISAPPEAR

I went back to Ottilie's Rock and drank too much. I was trying to make my hands stop shaking. Trying to tell myself that if Papa had betrayed my secret, I would've been dead by now. But I didn't believe it. Lenz or the Prince could have been toying with me, or using me to wheedle visions out of my family. I drank until my breathing finally slowed. Until even Gunther began asking me to slow down. Until the Yellows that stopped by every two hours to check on me began to blur together.

I woke up with what is still one of the worst hangovers I have ever had. I was also on a small couch, covered by a blanket, in a small wooden room I did not recognize.

"Ah, ma'am!" cried a maid, as she passed through the room. "You're finally awake."

I sat up and felt that my head would spin off of my body up into the sky. I wanted to cry, but worried that doing so would make me vomit.

"Where am I?" I managed.

"Just a maid's quarters," she replied. She pointed to the beds in the room, which may as well not have existed until she revealed them. "That nearest one's mine. You slept like a rock all night. It's early afternoon by now, ma'am."

I mumbled some sort of thanks to her that was, I'm sure, not suffi-cient, and stumbled to my feet. I went to the nearest window and saw Yellows outside, standing about in the snow, looking bored. Or at least I think they were—my vision was blurry enough that they may have been gigantic talking flowers. Well then, I was in no hurry to leave and report in to my captors.

I decided to partake of the sauna beneath the inn. As Gunther had told me, it was simply a cave, where a few people wrapped in towels sat on rotrock outcroppings and ignored each other's presence in steam so thick they could pretend they were alone. My first inhalation down there was painful, and the very air seemed to assault me, but by the end, I found it agreeable, despite the ongoing invec-tive of Grandmother's that ran through my head the entire time.

Loafer. Aesthete. Drunkard. Monster. If you like the steam so much, why aren't you cooking for your father?

Grandmother. Papa. Oh gods. I must have been exposed by Lenz's treachery. But was it even treachery? Or was it simply the cost of get-ting to sit in this sauna after drinking too much expensive starka the night before?

I managed to replace my stockings, skirt, blouse, and bodice over wet skin, lacing everything with fingers that hardly listened to me, and tromped back upstairs into the tavern proper, sweating profusely. And there, like a blonde, arrogant messenger of the gods, was Martin-Frederick Reinhold-Bosch, the young swordsman, sitting idly at the same table we had shared after our misadventure with Andelka of

Rituo. His eyes brightened when he saw me, but the deeply steamed nature of my joints meant that I made my way over quite slowly.

I opened my mouth, but he interrupted me: "Martin-Frederick Reinhold-Bosch," he said quickly.

"Oh, I remember." I sat, and allowed him to kiss my hand. I tried to smile. But my eyes weren't fully open.

"I was hoping I would find you," said Martin-Frederick. "The funniest thing happened. Here I had been, trying and trying to get our good High General interested in speaking to you, and being ignored!" He seemed genuinely frustrated.

"Aren't you glad he treats you like any other soldier?"

"Well, when it's *appropriate*, yes. But then, a few days ago, he calls me to his office first thing in the morning and says, 'I want to speak to that Aljosanovna woman.' Just like that!"

"Was this just after the most recent King's Dinner?"

"Why, I believe it was."

It was good to know my performance had impressed the High General. Martin-Frederick poured me some tea. It was over-brewed, but I was hungover and still breathing heavily from the sauna, so I felt as though its bitterness would somehow chase the poison out of me.

"So then," said Martin-Frederick, "would you like to meet him?"

"I would be delighted."

"Now?"

"Of course!" I said this before I even thought it through. Perhaps I should have waited until my hangover wore off, but if Lenz was reading about my fraudulence right now, I was out of time. Besides, I felt relaxed just then.

So we walked, side-by-side, out into that clear morning at the top of snow-covered Rotfelsen. Martin-Frederick was a small man, but, even while relaxed, the feel of his arm told me that he was all muscle. No matter how I felt about him, it was, again, rather nice to touch another human body—one that wasn't trying to divorce my soul from mine. The paths were mostly full of servants dashing from building to building, or heading up toward the palace on their way to a full day of carrying, tiptoeing, and being spat on.

The Yellows guarding the tavern noticed us, of course. As we walked out onto the snowy surface, the four of them bore down upon us.

"Ma'am?" said one of the Yellows.

"I get two hours, don't I?" I replied.

I vaguely recognized the Yellow who had spoken, but did not know him by name. He narrowed his eyes at us. "And where are you going?" he asked.

"It's a secret," replied Martin-Frederick.

"Master Lenz—" the Yellow began.

"What's the matter?" interrupted Martin-Frederick, looking back over his shoulder. "Don't trust her?"

My head was beginning to pound again at hearing my kidnapper's name. Surely, I had been found out. Or would be soon.

"Not about trust, sir," said the Yellow. He and his comrades came up quickly behind. "Just orders, you know?"

"Of course," said Martin-Frederick.

A troop of ten Greens appeared from seemingly nowhere. The Yellows stopped dead.

"What do you think their orders are?" asked Martin-Frederick.

The Greens glared at the smaller group of Yellows. One Green spat on the ground. I felt a thrill at power being exercised *for* me, for once in my life. It was replaced by a pang of fear for the Yellows, whether or not they deserved my sympathy. Those Yellows, caught between duty and being outnumbered, stood their ground.

"Go on," said Martin-Frederick, waving a hand at the Yellows. "Disappear."

As though this gave them permission to act on their fears, the Yellows turned away and walked very quickly, but did not run.

"We had better go before they come back with friends," said Martin-Frederick, exhilarated by the whole thing.

One of the Greens looked like he wanted to disagree, so eager were they for a fight, but Martin-Frederick shook his head, and the soldier went silent. The Greens had never hassled me personally, and, according to Lenz and his books, they were Rotfelsen's biggest, and best trained, army. The one that came the closest to actually protecting its people.

Four armies in this one kingdom, itself one of four kingdoms in a larger country, all desperate to tear each other apart. The place was trembling with potential violence—with all that death Chasiku had supposedly felt. Imagine, for example, if a fight did break out, and a stray bullet killed Martin-Frederick, or someone even more important than him. Rotfelsen was easily one duel away from exploding. I hoped this thought was simply the product of an overemotional hangover.

"I wish this was my own social call," laughed Martin-Frederick, as we half-ran eastward, toward a series of hedges and away from the Sunset Palace. I admit a part of me agreed with him. I was not terribly interested in Martin-Frederick, but who wouldn't enjoy running from a bit of trouble with a pretty boy?

Behind a hedge of orange flowers, we came to what looked like an outhouse, but it wasn't near a building. It was padlocked and guarded, built from green-painted rotrock as though lazily pretending at camouflage against the hedges and grass nearby. No one had painted orange flowers on it, regrettably.

"High General Dreher," I asked, "wishes to take breakfast with me in there?"

"Sort of," said Martin-Frederick.

"'Sort of' in a way that means 'not at all'? I try to avoid following soldiers into strange rooms."

Through most of my life, I would have done anything to avoid groups of soldiers, and yet here I was. Being yanked to and fro by soldiers was simply what one did on the palace grounds, and I'd gotten used to it already. Disgusting.

"Even if it's the first step toward getting out from under the Prince's thumb?" asked Martin-Frederick.

The Greens guarding the outhouse undid the padlock and opened the door. Inside was a platform ringed by a cage, hanging on pulleys that squeaked beneath the green stone roof. It was the sort of thing used to transport goods from the surface into the depths of Turmenbach. Martin-Frederick got in first, to show that it was safe.

"Well," I said, "that's unexpected."

Martin-Frederick flourished toward the cage around him. Perhaps the High General really would help me. The end was coming soon anyway, and I decided I'd do what I could to live a bit longer. In I went.

GLAIZATZ LAKE

I was packed in very close with Martin-Frederick and one other Green. The young swordsman was a little too theatrical about his gentlemanliness, but at least it meant he didn't jam himself against me. He would not tell me where we were going besides "down."

The cramped cage holding us plunged down through a narrow tunnel for some time, wobbling and clacking and sometimes banging the walls. This was particularly fun for my pounding, starka-soaked head. Our descent was slowed by the pulleys—else we would have died—but it *felt* like a free fall. There was a lamp clattering above us that miraculously never spilled its oil. At least it was all too loud for conversation.

We were going to Glaizatz Lake. I didn't know this yet, but I'll save you that little suspense, since the revelation likely means nothing to you. But I'd been to Glaizatz Lake before.

There is no Glaizatz Town or Glaizatz Hill or Glaizatz Region or Glaizatz Oblast, just the lake. A big, circular lake murmuring in a great cavern somewhere in the center of the red boulder that is Rotfelsen. The lake is too important to Rotfelsen as a water supply for unpredictable towns to be allowed to form near its surface, so the only people there are pulleymen, guards, fishermen with permits, Turmenbach teenagers sneaking in to look brave, and guides who lead young children and their bitter grandmothers up thin, rocky paths to see the surface of the lake itself.

When I was six, we were in Rotfelsen for a time, and Papa allowed me to visit the lake because I begged and begged and pleaded and begged. But Papa couldn't make it up those paths, not by then, and so it was Grandmother who took me. I would say she never forgave me, but I was unforgivable long before that. We saw the surface of the lake, its mossy walls streaked with thick, pointed gashes, with its pulleys and buckets, its guards, its railings for outsiders to gawp behind, the lights that flash and throb beneath its surface. Our guide was a sprightly woman, perhaps a decade older than Grandmother was, who ran up and down the rocks like a lizard.

Glaizatz Lake, I learned from the sprightly guide, does not emit patches and bursts of light from nowhere; it is filled with barely visible creatures that shine when threatened by larger fish.

"The wiggly little shrimp," she said to me in a chirp that should have felt condescending, even at six, but didn't, "bounce about in the lake together, looking for safe patches of water in which they can float, still as rocks, and contemplate the love of the gods. But when the heathenish fish that wish to eat them during their contemplations thrash up to them, the wiggly little shrimp exude a light derived from their own divine understanding. This blinds the heathenish fish and, more importantly, attracts even larger fish, with larger *teeth*"—she lunged at me, squeezing her hands like little shark mouths; I think I laughed and cringed—"who, drawn by the light and the true understanding, gobble up the heathenish scavengers and save the wiggly little shrimp. Understand?"

I nodded enthusiastically. On the way back to Papa, I had devoured half a grilled "heathenish" fish, which the guide had given me for free when Grandmother refused to pay because it was too "fancy" for me. Unfortunately, I proved Grandmother right by becoming too full, and when I complained of stomach pain, she slapped the rest of the fish from my hand.

"Now it's no one's," she hissed.

I don't know why I remember this so clearly.

Whether or not the shrimp understand the gods (and who am I to assume that they don't?), their light shows frequently succeeded at protecting them, by signaling the fishermen to kill their predators.

After all this, Grandmother dragged me back down. We spent our time in one of those towns with no sunlight that are stuck into tunnels far lower than the surface of Glaizatz Lake. The town had a spigot stuck into its eastern wall, which was one of the edges of the bowl that held the lake, with all its glowing shrimp and heathenish predators. This single spigot oozed grimy, sometimes bloody, water that needed to be sifted before drinking, and was guarded by Greens.

HIGH GENERAL DREHER

Eventually, our cage popped out of the ceiling of the cavern. After perhaps half an hour in a tunnel confined to the width of three sets of adult shoulders, a split second saw us hovering at the top of a monumental cave. Glaizatz Lake itself was maybe seven miles across, and the cavern was wider than that. Our cage felt unmoored, floating in the air above the circular lake, which was alive with the blinking lights of wiggly little shrimp, strewn with boats, obscured by buckets on pulleys, ringed with ledges on which workers slept in shacks. The whole place was eerily quiet and muffled, just as I remembered it, thanks to the soft, thick, absorbent moss that grew on every wall.

Would Glaizatz Lake crumble too? Would those in the towns at its base be crushed, drowned, or shot to pieces? Where would all its water go, then? Flooding those towns perhaps, filling up the rock. Or draining down into some hollow in the center of the world.

Martin-Frederick, next to me, laughed good-naturedly at my gasp. "Surprised? It's—"

"Glaizatz Lake," I muttered to myself, not meaning to interrupt.

"Yes. Oh. You knew?"

I nodded, holding onto the bars and looking out over it all. "I have never seen it from above before. Incredible."

Martin-Frederick looked pleased.

"What I don't know," I said, "is what this *thing* we're in is called."

"A lift," said Martin-Frederick.

"Simple enough."

Our tunnel must have been a hollow pillar right through Turmenbach. We sped down, and only when the lake reared up to slap us did we slow. Our cage clicked lightly onto a small island of rotrock no larger than my bedroom, on which High General Dreher was seated at a wooden table. Behind him was a Green.

The cage clanked open, and I stepped onto (somewhat) solid land once again, shaking from the trip.

"You'll excuse me if I don't get up," said Dreher. "Good to see you again, although I don't believe we've been introduced. I'm High General Dreher. Please sit."

I gave my name and sat across the square table from the High General, while Martin-Frederick sat around the corner to my left. The space at my right, where a fourth person would have sat, was taken up by a huge roast. The Green who had taken the trip with us stood by the open cage. There was a tall lantern on a pole stuck into the ground behind the High General, so I could only see his face when wiggly little shrimp flashed nearby.

"I know that was excessive," said High General Dreher, "but I do love to take my breakfasts down here."

I leaned forward on my elbows and forced a smile. My head was throbbing. "Right out in the open, yet this might be the most private place in the Tetrarchia, hm?"

"Exactly," said Dreher. "It's the only island on the lake, you know. Barely visible from the shore."

"There are theories that it doesn't reach the lake's floor!" chimed in Martin-Frederick. "And that there are larger creatures further below!"

"There are theories about everything in this place," sighed the High General.

Martin-Frederick and I were left to serve ourselves, and so the young man enthusiastically cut the roast for me before I could stop him. The knives on the table were quite sharp, which perhaps showed the General's trust in his guests. Or, perhaps, showed that there was nowhere to run.

The roast was tough, and there was nothing to go with it—I was now so spoiled as to be disappointed with the perfectly edible. I remembered the papers documenting Papa's ravings: all that good food I'd eaten recently had not been *free*. I should have been happy with tasteless nourishment.

Martin-Frederick took a bite of the roast before gleefully throwing a chunk into the lake to watch the water light up around it.

"So," said High General Dreher, "what did you and the old bejeweled purple chatterbox discuss during the ball?"

"Nothing interesting." I shrugged. "He just wanted me to know that he's very important, and that I should leave as soon as possible."

The High General laugh-coughed, and was then silent for a few moments. "Yes," he finally replied. "That sounds like him. But you're still here."

"And not bruised, that I can see," said Martin-Frederick.

"Impressive though his suites are," I said, "*he* didn't drop me into the center of Glaizatz Lake."

The High General looked up, concerned. "I'm not trying to impress. I just—"

"Of course," I said. "That's why you succeed."

He leaned back and groaned, looking uncomfortable at the idea of being too ostentatious: the type of officer invested in looking like a common soldier. A common soldier who ate breakfast on a private island and commanded Rotfelsen's largest army. A common soldier who commanded a young prince. A common soldier who seemed to never be called by his given name. (It was Franz, but I learned that later.)

I felt that I immediately understood the High General. He was respected and feared throughout Rotfelsen as a straightforward, no-nonsense man, and he was as much a fraud as I. The only difference was that he did not seem to realize it. No one with that much power is *common*, no matter how plainly they speak.

Another flash of wiggly little shrimp gave me a closer look at Dreher's face than I had gotten at the King's Dinner, where I was mostly behind him, or far away. It was a square and ruddy face, like it had been carved from the rotrock itself. More important than his face was the care with which he made every movement, as though always trying to minimize pain, just as he had at the dinner. That morning, I felt I sympathized, even though my movements were only painful due to a hangover.

"I suspect Vorosknecht," laughed the High General, after a few careful bites, "wants to scare you away for the same reason that I'd like to bring you closer."

I set down my knife and fork. "Oh?"

"Because you're a mind-witch!" said Martin-Frederick. He smiled at me as though the act of smiling rendered this accusation meaningless.

"Martin-Frederick," said Dreher, "please."

The young man opened his mouth to respond, and then seemed to change his mind. He smiled at me and shrugged apologetically.

The High General looked at me silently. No flashes from the lake came to tell me his expression.

"I am a soothsayer," I said.

"That seems like something the purple windbag wouldn't like," said the High General. "For reasons he would term as 'moral.'" He laughed at this, although it quickly became another cough.

Martin-Frederick moved to pat the High General's back, but was waved away.

"And what are your morals, High General?" I asked, once his cough had subsided.

"Whatever protects Rotfelsen," he replied immediately. "If I got caught up on whether things were 'right' on some higher, moral plane, I would not have an army at all."

"Vorosknecht has an army," said Martin-Frederick. I could've thanked him for pointing out the obvious so I didn't have to.

"Vorosknecht," grunted Dreher, "can afford to be highly selective about his ideals. He can have all his statues and parties and jewelry and cordials—he can be decadent because he does not need to protect our people."

"Except from bad ideas," I added.

The High General laughed at that, which was good. I was genuinely enjoying seeing the man whose soldiers had brought me to his island in a restricted cave, miles beneath the capital, call someone else "decadent." It was honestly great fun for me—I enjoyed playing along. My audience with Vorosknecht had been difficult because I could not tell where his beliefs ended and his fraud began. Dreher seemed to truly believe his own nonsense, which endeared him to me, in a sense.

"Personally," he said, "I'd much rather your abilities—be they curses or gifts, I hardly care—be used for the good of Rotfelsen. I'm glad Vorosknecht doesn't recognize their utility, but you are wasted on princely intrigues."

"Perhaps," I allowed.

"Whose fortunes do they have you telling?"

"Whoever's the Prince requires."

"Mine?"

"If you like."

"No, thank you," Dreher said quickly. "I mean, did the Prince ask for my fortune?"

"Not yet, no. Or I could look at the future of your battles against the Bandit States."

"No. No, thank you. Unnecessary. Our relationship with Rituo has only been improving."

I cleared my throat, glanced to Martin-Frederick, and then back to Dreher. "Even when taking into account, ah, '*you-know-who*'?"

Dreher let out a long, irritated breath and looked at Martin-Frederick, who gave another apologetic shrug. The High General made a dismissive gesture with his hand.

"I am a straightforward man," he said. The kind of thing straightforward men *always* say. "The rumors of some Warrior Queen in the Bandit States are true, in that a few little states, farther south, have been knitted together by someone. But she's no real threat—not now, anyway. We're simply keeping an eye on her, and ensuring that Rituo continues to help us destabilize her."

"I see."

"Do you *like* telling fortunes for the Prince?"

I could imagine most any answer to this going wrong, but given the fights I had seen between Yellows and Greens, I made my choice. "Of course not."

"Do you need *help*, Kalyna Aljosanovna?"

"I don't follow."

"Look," said the High General, "it's clear enough that Friedhelm and his lackey are holding you against your will. At the dinner you were in uniform, but unarmed. I don't know what they have on you, but when he tires of and discards you—if you live that long—who will protect you from Vorosknecht, I wonder?"

I grinned. "A High General, maybe?"

He laughed. "Maybe. I feel for your position, truly, but sympathy alone isn't enough for me to risk helping you. I'm sure you understand."

"I do." I appreciated Dreher's upfront nature, no matter how many layers of artifice it required.

"I think," he said, "that I could use your help to maintain order here in Rotfelsen. And that, if you helped me, I could do far more than protect you from the Prince."

I pondered this for a moment, which he graciously allowed me to do. There were clearly things he was not telling me. But then, who could blame him? We had a false King under his nose—I wondered how his desire for order, for maintaining the peace, would conflict with that.

I considered what I could gain from the High General, in this moment, if I told him about Olaf. Perhaps he would rescue me right now, but perhaps, with no reason to think I was loyal, he would have me killed and then start a war with the Yellows. I decided to hold onto that piece of information, for now.

I leaned forward with both hands on the table. "Can you help me escape Prince Friedhelm?"

"I'd like to try."

I sat back. If the High General treated me like a normal underling, and not a prisoner, it would be much easier to disappear in his service. Although I wondered if I'd feel guilty about running out on someone I found a bit pleasant, despite everything.

"I like the sound of this very much," I said, letting real excitement and relief bleed into my voice. "But how do you know I don't actually love the Prince's service? How can you trust me?"

"What's the most you can do if you're lying? Tell the Prince I don't like him? Hardly a revelation."

"Well then, what can I do now, to prove that I can be helpful to you."

"Do you know why the lights of Glaizatz Lake are so mysterious?" asked Dreher.

I kept silent, expectant. No one spoke for a long time. Everything we ate and drank was cold, and somehow there was a draft in that cave, yet I sweated out liquor and steam.

"No, no," said the High General, laughing, "that wasn't rhetorical, I'm really asking. You're a prophet; I thought you might know."

I laughed with him. "Sir, I only see images, and they are often useless without context. Please go on."

"Meaning that if you know the mystery, you may be able to learn its answer."

"You see, General?" said Martin-Frederick. "I told you she'd be useful! Before you even saw her at the dinner, I told you!" He flourished at me.

"You did," Dreher conceded. "I'm glad to know you have an eye for talent."

Martin-Frederick seemed pleased by this.

"Kalyna," said Dreher, "I've been told that there are mountain pools and steppe bogs in farthest Quruscan with creatures similar to these, who carry in them tiny flames to light up their predators or prey."

I nodded. This was true, I had seen them, but they were nowhere near as bright or numerous as the wiggly little shrimp in Glaizatz.

"Have you been there?" he asked. "Is that where you're from?"

"Yes, I have. And only partly."

"Well, do you know the difference between those in the steppe bogs and these?" The General pointed down at the water. Shrimp flashed accommodatingly nearby.

"No," I said.

"The sun." He did not point up. "The ones that flit around in Quru pools have the sun above them half the day, like most decent creatures."

I nodded. It seemed inopportune to point out that most of his fellow Rots seldom saw the sun. That even his soldiers were mostly drawn from such people. That we were currently in a cave.

"The, ah, explanation that most who pay attention to these things give—for the Quru shrimp, I mean—is that half the day they pull the sun's light into themselves. Just enough, or their tiny translucent bodies would burst. They hold this inside in order to release when necessary." He laughed quietly. "Of course, who's to say this theory is trustworthy? It's also said that when they release the light, it actually burns their enemies, which seems unlikely."

"Wouldn't water douse their flame?" asked Martin-Frederick.

"So, the answer that I wonder if you know," continued High General Dreher, "is this: If their Quru cousins receive light from the sun, what illuminates the little ones down here?"

"The divine love of the gods?" I offered.

Dreher coughed appreciation at that, which was satisfying.

"In a way," said Martin-Frederick, trying to be cryptic.

The High General shot him a look. "No one knows," he said, "but there are *theories*. Does that jog the slivered future in your brain?"

"Not yet."

"Hmm," he said. "Hmmmm."

"No one knows what's at the bottom, you know," said Martin-Frederick. He was leaning far forward. "Some say there isn't one. The lake just keeps doing, down through the middle of the rock, and into the ground below it."

"Well," I said, "I will grasp for new visions and find your answer."

"That would be lovely," said High General Dreher. "When you do, tell Martin-Frederick here. Then we'll plan your extraction."

"I'll do you one better," I replied as I cut another piece from the roast. "Come get me and my family from my servant house on the night of the Sun's Death. Everyone will be tired, and full, and I will certainly have something for you by then. If you aren't satisfied with what I tell you"—I shrugged and gestured upward with the skewered piece of meat—"you can drop me right back with the Prince, or wherever else you like."

I had no idea what I would say when this time came, or how long I would work for the High General, but I was giving myself an ultimatum: have a plan by the Sun's Death or die with the Tetrarchia.

Dreher looked at me, silently, for a good long time. Then he smiled. "Wonderful."

I smiled back and nodded and ate the chunk of roast I had been waving about. It was still underwhelming, but my alcohol-wrung body cried out for nourishment. "Thank you," I said when I'd swallowed most of it, "for the liberation, and for the breakfast."

High General Dreher nodded and looked off across Glaizatz Lake, rubbing his right side with his left hand.

Martin-Frederick chattered at us as we continued to eat. I don't remember what he said, as I was too busy trying to think of what answer to this strange question would most please Dreher.

He was certainly my best chance for escape, and I was now even more confident that fleeing south into the Bandit States was the way to go. What's more, with Lenz poring over Papa's ramblings and clearly on the brink of learning my secret, the sooner the better.

Dreher was the most likable source of power I'd yet met in this rock, but that was because I felt I immediately understood his flaws and desires. He was personally likeable, but still a general, and no general can be a good person. The Tetrarchia saw no large-scale wars these days, but border towns carried bad memories of what men like Dreher were capable of.

Still, it was difficult to connect the man in front of me to that. I did not understand enough of armies and politics to know whether High General Dreher oversaw carnage or only stuck pins into maps in his office. Which of these is worse is its own question.

No matter. It couldn't hurt for me to make up something about the bottom of Glaizatz Lake and see what I could get out of it. I would use anyone as a means to escape the Tetrarchia before spring.

MOLDERED LUNG

Breakfast was finished quietly, goodbyes were grunted, and soon Martin-Frederick, the Green who had come with us, and I were back in our small cage, or "lift." The Green yanked a cord, and we were hauled up toward the surface. It was slower going (and quieter) in this direction, but whatever pulleys and counterweights and buckets of water were doing the pulling made decent time. I wondered about what poor villages we were passing through—what people might be just on the other side of the shaft's stone walls.

Martin-Frederick made little conversation on the way up, mostly compliments on my ability to charm Dreher and my prophetic powers. When the sun became visible above us, and I knew we were nearing the surface, I said, "I do hope the High General will be healthy."

"What do you mean?" asked the young swordsman.

"Well, a fighting man suffering from moldered lung, it must be frustrating for him. His days of charging embankments are long past."

The sound of the old general's cough, and the movements he could and could not make, had been as clear as day to me, and guessing at a man of action's frustration was just as easy. The biggest gamble had been deciding to not try impressing Dreher directly with my insight. Best to let the lackey do the talking: the High General did not seem the type to appreciate a show-off.

"How . . . ?" For a moment, Martin-Frederick was stunned at my insight, before muttering, "Oh, yes. Of course. The future."

I grinned. "On the subject of the future . . ." I began.

"I feel we've hardly discussed anything else," Martin-Frederick interrupted. "But I suppose that's true of most people. Until they're old, then they discuss the past."

I nodded as though what he was saying was wonderfully profound. The lift clanked closer and closer to the surface.

"But yes, what about it?" he asked.

"Well, as I mentioned to your High General, my Gift requires context, and I'm afraid I won't be getting down to Glaizatz Lake very often."

"Oh, you mean because of my uncle, the evil prince who's keeping you captive?" he laughed, as though this very true statement were something from a play.

"Yes," I replied. "So if I had a better idea of *what exactly* High General Dreher wants me to see, then I would know when I have seen it."

"Or not seen it."

"Just so."

The cage clanked to a stop in the green outhouse and I stepped out, less wobbly this time. Martin-Frederick followed, and I stopped just outside, breathing in the fresh air for a moment.

"Then context you shall have," he said, smiling at me in the morning light. He was at least nice to look at, if not to talk to. "But don't tell him I told you . . ."

"Why would I?"

"Well, if what I'm about to explain comes up in conversation, maybe you could tell him that you saw it . . . You know, in one of your prophecies?"

I knotted my brows. "I don't lie about my abilities. It is like a duelist's honor."

"I see. Shall I not, then?"

"Tell me."

He laughed. "Finally, I have something that *you* wish to know. Well, High General Dreher is convinced that the very Soul of the Rotfelsenisch Nation lives in that lake."

I was quiet for a moment, and leaned back against the outside of the little hut that enclosed the lift.

"The *what?*" I finally asked.

"The Soul of the Nation. Some silly idea the High General picked up that every nation—"

"Rotfelsen is not a 'nation.' It's one-quarter of a nation."

Martin-Frederick waved this away. "You may not understand. But you've been to all corners of our Tetrarchia, and so you know it isn't so simple. Each of the Tetrarchic states still sees itself as its own nation with its own people."

He was stating what was, to him, fact, and I suspected my disagreement would invite more explaining, so I nodded. Of course, citizens of the Tetrarchia didn't go around thinking of themselves as "Tetrarchic" every moment. But neither did most people think of themselves as Rotfelsenisch or Quru or Skydašian or Masovskan most days. If my travels had taught me anything, it was that people were far more likely to identify themselves by their geography, their town, their neighborhood, their politics. Only those in the corridors of power (or, like Martin-Frederick, aspiring for them) thought the world was defined by the broad lines the Tetrarchia had painted across the grasses all those years ago.

I nodded.

"And each of those nations," he continued, "are supposed to have their own individual 'Soul.'" He snickered at the thought. "Loasht, too, and everywhere else. Maybe a multiheaded monstrosity for the Bandit States? I don't know. The ideals and archetypes of a nation bound up in some spirit that guides its fate, you know."

"How abstract," I replied. "I always heard of spirits as being rather straightforward and small: a dead person's memory, a wind-sprite in a mountain, a source of courage, that sort of thing. A small part of everyday life."

"Exactly!" he laughed. "Whereas this Soul of the Nation is the sort of theory fanciful scholars come up with on long boring nights, while taking many different substances and trying to make sense of their people's history." He shrugged and shook his head. "But history doesn't make sense—it's just things that happen!"

"Well, those drug-addled 'fanciful scholars' you describe don't sound like the High General."

"No. He's a pragmatic type whose highest calling has always been protecting our kingdom. But theoreticians can hook a man like him if their fantasies are told the right way. Particularly if he's led to believe he can *guide* this Soul."

I cocked my head to the side. "But it sounds to me like the Soul of the Nation is a rhetorical exercise more than a—"

"Mostly, yes. But, you see, there's a . . . sect."

"Naturally."

"A small group of deranged—if you ask me, but don't tell Dreher I said so—thinkers who believe this Soul of the Nation is a real thing that actually lives in the stone. Or beneath it."

"Perhaps they're just too literal minded."

"Now *that* sounds like our beloved High General," he sighed. "So many hours spent staring at Glaizatz Lake and its mysteries—strange shrimp, singular moss, ancient lacerations up the walls—has led our good Dreher to the inevitable conclusion that the Soul of the Nation is a real thing, which lives at the bottom of that lake, deep in the rock, or below it, feeding the shrimp their light."

"The love of the gods after all," I said. "He should talk to the tour guides."

"Oh, he has! Although he doesn't think of it as a god, exactly. Whatever it is, he thinks that *pleasing* it, if it exists, will benefit Rotfelsen. So he hopes you'll prove its tangibility without his pushing, in order to prove him right."

"And yet you tell me . . ."

"I hope you'll be able to give him proof to the contrary. I think that his fancies are beginning to get in the way of his aims. Chasing phantoms does not protect our borders, you know." He made a face. "And he thinks that this 'Soul' is disgusted by all of the 'decadence' going on above it. Personally, I rather fancy nice things."

"If he's so obsessed, he may not believe me."

"I maintain hope that our High General can be reasonable in this, as he is in most things."

I thought for a moment, tapping my chin. "And, of course, there are plenty of strange creatures in the world: What if he's right?"

Martin-Frederick laughed and threw up his hands. "I'm not against the idea of the thing existing. If you prove it, I will happily prostrate myself before it, offer sacrifices, or whatever one does. But his hope is that you'll find it, while mine is much more mundane: I hope to take you to the opera."

"That"—I grinned—"would be much easier if I were liberated."

"I agree," he said. "First, your rescue from the evil Prince. And then, down in Turmenbach, there will be a production of *The Leper's Five Tits*, a wonderfully popular comic opera! Performances will begin near the end of winter, when dignitaries are beginning to stream in for the Council of Barbarians. The Grand Opera House will be filled up to its brim."

I bowed slightly and tried not to think about the Council, and how it had to be related to Papa's apocalyptic vision. I intended to leave the Tetrarchia behind me before this opera would begin its run, anyway.

"I would be delighted," I said. "Have a fine day, Martin-Frederick Reinhold-Bosch."

"And yourself, Kalyna Aljosanovna. I look forward to seeing you again soon."

Two Greens were ordered to escort me back to my servant house, but when I asked to go somewhere else instead, they happily complied. At least I was not *their* prisoner as well. Once the Yellow barracks were in sight, the Greens let me walk the rest of the way by myself, rather than start a fight.

SURVIVE TO TELL THE TALE

I marched right up the stairs to Lenz's rooms. I played in my head, again and again, how I would yell at him when I got there. I tried not to think about my need to escape, about what he might know; I just wanted to be angry at him for what he'd done to my father.

I also tried not to think about whether this even was something done *to my father*, so much as something that terrified me because it could lead to my entire fraud being laid bare. Because it reminded me that I had not given Papa a doctor, a room, and good food; they had been granted to help me forget that I was a prisoner.

On top of everything else, my head was still pounding with that hangover.

But one foot in front of the other, I stomped up the stairs and into Lenz's messy rooms. There were papers everywhere, as usual, and I wondered which ones might contain what my father muttered in his most private and vulnerable moments. Through a door, I saw him sitting on the bed in the next room, speaking to someone I could not see. My face was twitching with how badly I wanted to throttle him.

"Lenz!" I bellowed as I moved toward him.

He turned and looked puzzled. I opened my mouth to say more, just as Olaf's stolen face appeared in the doorway and he smiled at me.

"What?" I gurgled.

"Well, hello!" laughed Olaf.

I entered the room, and saw that Prince Friedhelm was there as well. So-called Dugmush, the Yellow who had guarded me when I discovered Lenz's surveillance of my father, shut the door and waited outside. All the thoughts of what I would yell at Lenz drained away. For now.

"Yes, Kalyna?" asked Lenz, still seated.

"What . . . ?" I began, but was unsure how to continue.

"What am I doing here?" laughed Olaf.

I nodded. I wondered the same about Prince Friedhelm, but thought better of questioning him. The "King" was here, but the Prince was everyone in the room's boss. Seeing the Prince and the "King" in Lenz's messy bedroom seemed *wrong* somehow, like a city guard out of uniform, or a calm god painted hovering above an ancient scene of destruction.

"Well," said Olaf, "the King and the Prince are beginning to spend a bit more time together. Mending our relationship! It gives me an excuse to get away from the Reds for a bit, since we don't *quite* trust them." He shrugged. "And who knows if they trust me?"

"The more Yellows we can have around Olaf, the better," added Lenz.

"So far so good!" laughed Olaf. "I've never had a more comfortable bed, finer clothes, or better food."

"Except for the persimmons," added Prince Friedhelm.

"I never expected to survive this adventure, but it's nice to get a taste of the good life beforehand. I must say I hope we find Gerhold, or that I die, sooner rather than later—I was not prepared to keep up this charade for more than a few weeks."

I looked at Olaf, studying his stolen face. What life had he left behind to be so cavalier? He certainly seemed to be enjoying himself. As someone with the extremely gauche and commonplace need to *survive*, I truly could not understand his thinking.

"Running out of things to tell the Reds?" asked Prince Friedhelm.

"Oh no," replied Olaf. "They're used to silence from me. It's the Queen."

"Speak to her as little as possible," said the Prince. "I foolishly used to think she only disliked my brother as much as I do, but it is clear now she is part of this. She is trying to expose you."

"That's not the impression I've gotten," said Olaf.

"Oh really?" Lenz replied. He glared at me.

"Well, perhaps I am too simple to understand," Olaf conceded. "But so far, she has simply been reminding me that she and I—that is, that she and the King—have been trying to have children."

"Olaf," snapped Lenz, "you haven't . . ."

Olaf threw up his hands. "By all the gods, no!" He shook his head. "And not just because we could sire all kinds of bastards. That would be an awful thing to do to anyone, wouldn't it?"

Lenz nodded. The Prince smirked.

"She is just trying to fluster you," said Friedhelm. "Goad you into admitting the truth, probably where you can be overheard. Having your baby wouldn't help her cause any more than if she bore some other bastard."

"Well," I cut in, "we had better find the King so you can survive to tell the tale."

Friedhelm glared at Olaf. "You had better never tell the tale."

Lenz stood up and grimaced slightly. "Why don't we go find out what our friend Klemens Gustavus knows, yes? That *was* the original reason you brought Olaf here."

Prince Friedhelm nodded absentmindedly, and we got started on moving Lenz's bed to once more reveal the secret stairway. It was good that Dugmush helped because the royalty—even the false royalty—were not about to lend a hand.

COUNTER-CONSPIRATORS

So, the five of us—Lenz, the Prince, the false King, the Yellow I called Dugmush, and myself—all went down that same winding staircase to the secret cell where the spoiled little Masovskan murderer Klemens Gustavus was held. I damned the vertical, rock-bound kingdom, and its many sets of stairs, under my breath. I also damned Lenz, again and again, as I waited for my moment to have him alone.

Lenz and I entered the little room first, where another Yellow waited outside the cell. As before, the light was mostly on Klemens, and we were in shadow. Prince Friedhelm stepped out behind us.

"Back to kill me?" sighed Klemens. He was standing, leaning forward, with his aggravating little bully's face squeezed against the bars.

A thought occurred to me, and I glanced back to where I knew Olaf must be, at the bottom of the staircase, hidden from view. I am at least decent at theatricality, and so motioned to him to stay out of sight, hoping he saw it. Lenz and Friedhelm either did not notice, or played along.

A moment later, Dugmush emerged, meaning she must have passed Olaf. I smiled, which Klemens took as confirmation that we would kill him now. Then the Prince stepped forward enough to be in the light. Klemens reeled backward and made a strangled sound somewhere in his throat.

"Well?" screeched Klemens. "What do you want? Do you want me to *apologize* for trying to kill you before you kill me?" His Rotfelsenisch seemed to crumble around the words he wanted to say, but he puffed out his chest with, I suppose, a kind of bravery. "You like to see your enemies die, Prince? I swear I will haunt you until the end of your days!"

The Prince chuckled quietly, not arguing with anything the brat was saying. Klemens' nerve seemed to already be flagging.

"Tell me again," Friedhelm finally said, "why you and your conspirators wanted me dead."

"*Counter*-conspirators!" Klemens growled.

"Rather a mouthful," I said.

"*We*," Klemens continued, "were trying to stop *you*, Selvosch, and the rest from killing your brother."

Prince Friedhelm said nothing. He just stood there and smiled.

"Did . . ." Klemens gulped. "Did . . . I . . . did we succeed?"

Prince Friedhelm now laughed louder. Louder than I had ever heard him laugh, or speak, and it echoed through the room. It was deeply sinister, I must say. As he laughed, the Prince turned toward the staircase and nodded at it. Olaf emerged into the dim light, his face as vacant as the real King's. Klemens blinked many times.

"You . . ." he stammered. "You are the King?"

"So far," said Olaf, with a nod.

"Huh," said Klemens.

"Despite the rumors," Friedhelm began, "my brother and I get along well enough. For siblings."

"There was an attack on me that night," said Olaf, "though it did not come from my brother." He stepped closer to Klemens. "Thank you for saving my life."

Friedhelm cleared his throat loudly, and I suspected he didn't much care for that improvisation. Klemens laughed triumphantly, and I immediately hated the rich monster all over again.

"But *unfortunately*," Friedhelm continued, "your attempt on *my* life threw us somewhat. So we would very much like to know who you are working with, and what you know about our enemies. Who are also *your* enemies."

Klemens nodded enthusiastically.

"Kalyna," said the Prince, "will he behave himself?"

I had rather forgotten that I was there for a reason, and jumped at my name. I nodded to the Prince and stepped forward into the light, right up to the bars, staring into Klemens' face. He looked very pleased with himself.

"He will," I said. "Today, at least."

A Yellow unlocked Klemens Gustavus' cell and, with that, he was free. Freer than I, in fact.

It occurred to me then that Prince Friedhelm had created a false King who obeyed his orders, and was presently using that tool to extract the names of Klemens' fellow counter-conspirators. What a terrifying man I worked for—did he *really* want his brother to return to his throne? Was this purely momentum?

Whatever the case, Klemens fell for it fully, and I did enjoy how stupid it made him look to me.

So we all went back up to Lenz's apartments, where Dugmush got a flame going in the fireplace. I hadn't noticed just how cold the winter had become until I felt that warmth.

Klemens sniffed at the state of the place, and made a big show of finding it disgusting and common. That he was only seeing it at the royals' mercy did not seem to cross his mind. Then, in those messy rooms, Klemens Gustavus laughed about the whole "misunderstanding," and happily told the "King" about his counterplot. Now that he was free, he also treated Friedhelm and Olaf as, at *best*, equals. The Masovskan banker also enjoyed pointing out what good terms he was on with King Lubomir XIII of Masovska. Friedhelm seemed to find this amusing, and Olaf did not react.

I will spare you Klemens' self-aggrandizing and long-winded explanation, and simply tell you that Klemens and his sister, Bozena, were working with Edeltraud von Edeltraud, the Mistress of the Coin, whom I had followed at the Winter Ball. Edeltraud, it seemed, had been approached by Selvosch, much as Prince Friedhelm had been. It seemed also that, like the Prince, her desire for immediate comfort had outpaced her hunger for power. Edeltraud had been promised a high place in the new government—although who would *rule* that government had been left vague—if she could ensure that, after the King was overthrown, Rotfelsen's money would keep flowing as it always had. The offer that had been meant to sway her was that, once King Gerhold was out of the way, the Rotfelsenisch coinage would only need to be collected and reminted *once*, replacing the royal face with a yet-to-be-chosen symbol, and then never altered again. Edeltraud von Edeltraud had been too shortsighted to see past this first overhaul, which would still have to take place within a year. If she failed, she would have to explain herself to an overzealous and unstable new government.

Selvosch had also told her that "someone with an army" would be on their side. This had probably meant Vorosknecht, but for *some strange reason*, Edeltraud had suspected the King's scheming, degenerate brother, *simply* because he was the kind of man to hire spies, prophets, and doubles. So, Edeltraud had reached out to some business acquaintances, and she and the Gustavus siblings had bought some assassins of their own for a counterattack. These would-be assassins had been paid in Masovskan money from the Gustavus coffers, hence the lesser grivnas found on one of their bodies.

"We were in such a rush to arrive in time for the Winter Ball," Klemens sniffed, "that we did not have time to stop at one of our *own* banks. Cleaning up some legal nonsense back home, you see."

Klemens was questioned on who else his "counterconspiracy" knew to be part of the plot against the King, but he knew less than we did. He was not told that Court Philosopher Vorosknecht was part of the plot, nor that Queen Biruté supposedly was.

I kept quiet through most of this talk, partly because I worried that Klemens would recognize me from Masovska, and mostly because I was waiting for a chance to get Lenz alone. Klemens, sitting languidly across one of Lenz's chairs, warming his feet by the fire, had barely glanced at me.

"But," I finally said, "why do you and your sister care what happens in Rotfelsen? The new marks would spend the same."

"We run the largest changing banks in the Tetrarchia, Loashti," he said.

"I'm not—" I began.

"So our trade depends on the four kingdoms . . . oh, you know, playing nice."

"What does one King or another matter to that?" I asked.

Klemens furrowed his brow and cocked his head to the side. "Loashti," he said, "these people want to *leave* the Tetrarchia."

A LOT OF YELLING

So that was it. The end of our country. It had to be. There was no doubt in my mind, but I still didn't know *how* it would all happen.

We stayed in Lenz's chambers for some time, discussing the fact that Vorosknecht and Selvosch wanted Rotfelsen to back out of the Tetrarchia entirely. The Prince was shocked and affronted at the very idea.

"Separatism?" he cried. "*Separatism*?! That's supposed to be for sad bumpkins in forgotten corners who speak outmoded doggerel languages! Not for nobles in the very seat of power! What could they be *thinking*?"

Lenz, despite his own surprise, kept trying to describe the long historical view on such things to Friedhelm, who truly could not care less. Olaf kept his face blank.

Eventually, it was clear that the discussion was going nowhere, and that Klemens was eager to be on his way. So off he went.

A few minutes later, Friedhelm and Olaf were donning their "royal disguises" in order to get back to the palace, where they belonged. These disguises were just a pair of ratty wigs, clearly meant to signal that it would be shameful to admit to whatever they were up to, but also shameful for royalty to try *too hard* to fool anybody. The hope was that people would begin to notice that the Prince and the King were closer than everyone had thought.

Soon, Lenz and I were alone in his rooms. Dugmush was out in the hall, and we didn't even have a prisoner below us. Lenz deflated into a large wooden chair shaped like a raging hawk. I began to pace.

"This sort of nationalism seems to have been born in our own depths, but has since been popping up in all corners of the Tetrarchia," he sighed. "The idea is that backing out of the Tetrarchia will make a people stronger. More *themselves*."

I kicked over a particularly tall pile of folders, made up my mind, and stomped toward him, grabbing one of his books on the way.

"I shudder to think what would happen if our country's ties were simply broken in such a way," he said.

I had no strong personal feeling that the Tetrarchia needed to remain unified, but such a violent withdrawal, during the Council of Barbarians, simply had to cause the destruction I'd been dreading. These people were rushing right toward my father's prophecy. But I had Papa's other prophecies on my mind.

"I've heard of similar things in—"

I threw a book at him; it clipped his shoulder.

"Kalyna, what is this?"

"Have you heard from Doctor Aue yet today?" I asked. Picking up whatever was to hand: a pile of papers.

"No," he replied as he stood up. "Should I?"

I threw the papers at him, but they sputtered out into the air and floated to the floor.

"Of course!" I growled. "Why pay for his care if you can't also use him?"

"Ah, I see." He grabbed a folder and waved it in my face. "I'm ending that little project anyway, because this"—he threw it into the crackling fireplace—"is nonsense."

"I told you it would be."

"And now I know for myself." Lenz began to pace, slowly and unevenly.

"My father is sick, and you—"

"Gave him the best care he has ever had."

"You betrayed him. Kept him prisoner, held his life over my head."

Lenz put himself right in my face, then. "Because you are a prisoner," he hissed. "Of course your father is held against your good behavior. And your behavior has been as underwhelming as your prophetic powers."

Did he know? Had Papa betrayed me? Or was Lenz truly angry that nothing useful was in those records? Nothing of my fraud, nothing of what Papa had learned about him, nothing of the end of the Tetrarchia.

Whatever the case, I would keep bluffing until I knew for sure. It was all I could do.

"Is this about those damn Gustavuses again?" I growled. "I told you that—"

"Vague," Lenz spat. "Everything you see is so vague. I'm still not sure the Queen is against us, but now the Prince—"

"I would see more *clearly*," I said, "if you hadn't dragged me so far into all this palace intrigue in the first place!"

"Oh yes, that's right," he laughed, "if you're too involved in a future, you cannot see it."

"Yes, and—"

"*And*," he continued, "you have to be near a person to see their future. Very convenient way to explain never seeing anything."

I said nothing. Those were the actual rules of the Gift, for those who really had it, but there was no way to argue *that*.

"Talking to Chasiku, and seeing how her powers work, has been enlightening," he said. "Your father's Gift is unfocused, but I begin to doubt whether *yours* even exists."

I felt cold. I could not feel my fingers. "I did not ask to be your personal psychic!" I sputtered. "You don't drag Chasiku all over this damned rock. Use her and let us go!"

"Chasiku," he replied, "doesn't *need* to be taken everywhere to be useful. And you know too much to be let go."

"That's just it!" I cried. "You knew from the start I can't see things that involve me, yet you have dragged me into this . . . this nest of ridiculous intrigue! Of course I don't see enough for you."

"Pathetic."

"If there ever can be an 'enough,'" I continued.

"Pathetic," he repeated.

"You"—I lowered my voice, working very hard to push confidence back into my words—"are not the only one who can pry into another's relationships." I remembered what Papa had seen about Lenz.

Lenz laughed bitterly and reeled away from me. "How hollow. Now I know you have nothing."

I shrugged. I wanted to blurt out what I knew, but I still planned to abscond with the help of the High General during the Sun's Death, so I said, "I am fickle and capricious."

"You," he said, "are more trouble than you're worth."

"Then have me dragged out and killed!" I shouted, loud enough for Yellows in the hallway to hear. I ran up and waved my hands in his face. "Do it, if I'm too much trouble! Have my family slaughtered and stop worrying!"

I had caught him off guard, which was, of course, the point. Lenz blinked many times and leaned away from me.

"Kalyna Aljosanovna," he said. "I, too, am a prisoner here. The Prince—"

"You have resources! Money, carriages, secrets. You could run!"

"I cannot leave the King to . . . wherever he is."

"I don't think much of you, Lenz, but even you should be smart enough to not care about something so silly as royalty."

"I—" he began.

I clapped my hands loudly in his face, interrupting him. I only had one thing left, so I used it.

"What does *one worthless king* matter?" I hissed. "This will all be rubble in two months!"

There was a long silence. An orange-and-sky-blue butterfly landed on a nearby windowsill.

Lenz opened and closed his mouth a few times, then took a deep breath. He composed himself, sat down, crossed his bad leg over his good, and set his back straight.

"I'm sorry, Kalyna Aljosanovna, what was that?"

So I told him.

THE FALL OF THE TETRARCHIA

I told Lenz that *I* had seen the fall of the Tetrarchia in terrible violence, and that *I* could see nothing of the cause. That was the only fabrication.

No weak skirmishes and redrawing of borders, war will pour in like a deluge, change will come to all with fire and sword. To the whole Tetrarchia. The survivors will not live the same lives beneath different flags, they will be ruined and enslaved, or strung out beneath the sun with their entrails stretched across the landscape and their children thrown into the Quruscan steppes or among Rotfelsen's shattered remains. It will crumble and topple.

I quoted Papa almost exactly, and hoped that the specificity, the belief in my face and voice, would be clear. I sat slumped on a bench piled with books, my elbows on my knees. As I spoke, I stared at a book on the floor and memorized every squiggle in the marbling along the edges of its pages.

When I finished, Lenz sat still for a few moments, his eyes wide. Then he leaned toward the door and yelled for Chasiku to be brought to us.

"Why didn't you mention this earlier?" He spoke softly, not even angry.

"What reason have I had to be forthright with you?"

"But this . . . this is no simple kidnapping or palace coup, this . . ."

"Exactly. What would it matter to tell you? It will happen."

"How fatalistic."

I laughed. A different false laugh—the mean one. "My family rather tends toward fatalism. This is coming, and"—even now, I couldn't ignore an opportunity—"this has loomed so large in my visions that it's made seeing anything else difficult."

"Well, if you can't see past two months!" Lenz stood up and paced awkwardly again. "But . . . why is changing this any different from changing other prophecies? You and your family make a living giving people fortunes that *can* be changed."

"This is bigger."

It seemed that Lenz was taking me seriously now. Perhaps it was the conviction in my voice, combined with having just heard what Vorosknecht and his conspirators were up to, but Lenz was talking as though the end was real.

Papa had not betrayed my secret. Not once. He had screamed and twisted in the night, tormented, without me there to hold him, but he had said nothing about my fraud or what I'd asked him to do. I wanted to cry.

"But can't we stop it?" Lenz wasn't really asking, so I didn't answer. He was just talking as his mind twisted around. "If this were immutable, you and your family would have seen it years ago, your father would have seen it before you were born. It's possible *now*, and it can be made . . . impossible, but we need to know more. This plot against the King must be a catalyst . . ."

He was right that here, in the seat of power, there was a chance that we could change the thing. I began to think that I should simply come clean to him, sell myself as the translator of my father's ramblings. It would make my life easier (if I wasn't killed for it), and make it much less likely that the Tetrarchia would fall based on some false future I made up to get out of a situation, like the Bandit States invasion that I no longer expected, or the Queen's part in the plot (which still felt quite possible to me).

I am a fraud, my father saw the doom of the Tetrarchia, please don't kill me, came to the front of my mind. I moistened my lips to speak.

At that moment, a Yellow announced Chasiku. Her arrival immediately curdled any desire to unburden myself. Maybe it was to keep her from being smug, or maybe the moment had simply passed. Either way, current discomfort won out over abstract future dangers. I hoped my cowardice had not doomed us all.

Chasiku looked even more uncomfortable than me, however. The newer soothsayer, my replacement, was shivering when she came in, and had a scarf almost entirely around her head. Lenz moved to help her to a chair, and she slapped his hand away before stumbling over to fall into the farthest possible seat from us. Most of her face and body was covered, but that bending, long-limbed physicality was still visible, hidden beneath.

"It's not *that* cold, is it?" I asked her.

"This is not cold," she growled from beneath her scarf. "Why have I been dragged in front of all these dying soldiers? It pounds at me, destroys me from within. It's been like this for *days*, and bringing me here makes it so much worse."

Lenz opened his mouth to explain, but I stood up and spoke first. "You did say that everyone here stinks of death, didn't you?"

"Yes, yes, including you," she spat.

"Hmm, interesting," I replied. "Could that be, oh I don't know, the imminent destruction of the Tetrarchia?"

Chasiku clawed the scarf off her head to look up in my general direction, although not directly into my face. Seeing her face again, I was still surprised at how put together, and unblemished, she was. I suppose I assumed that all soothsayers ran from mobs, had scars from Galiag windstorms, and learned to cut men down when it was needed.

She blinked many times in quick succession. "Could it?" she murmured.

"Of course, you *see* so much," I said, "and yet—"

"When I got to this sad little kingdom," she interrupted, "I was accosted by so much, *including* images of shattering rotrock. I thought that was a normal occurrence here, but I begin to wonder if it was"— she waved her arms about—"the whole place."

Lenz stepped forward. Chasiku, eyes closed, became tense all over. She no longer shook.

"Was that Rotfelsen itself . . . ?" she muttered.

"It will be," I said. "*That* I have seen."

I felt myself fill with confidence at my ability to pass for prophetic. This confidence was wrung from the doom that faced us all, but I felt no worse because of it. I am that terrible of a person, I suppose.

Chasiku glared up at Lenz. "Why did you bring me here and not tell me of this?"

"I just learned it a few moments ago," he replied. "Why didn't *you* tell me? When you agreed to come here, you didn't see that this was looming?"

"No," she replied. "But it explains a great deal. Part of why I chose to leave Kalvadoti, was that most of what I saw was getting confusing, brutal, and short. My family just accepted it, but I thought a change of scenery would show me other possibilities . . ." She trailed off.

I made an obnoxious flourish with both hands. "Surpriiiiiiiiise."

She did not seem to notice or care, so I said, "Well, you wouldn't have escaped it in Skydašiai anyway. Rotfelsen may crumble. But the rest of the Tetrarchia has its doom just as assured. Armies, chaos, and the like."

"Then why didn't I see this before?" she sighed. "My family and I *have* had difficulty seeing clearly lately. I need more time to consider this."

"I'm so glad we have lots of time," I said, turning to look idly at some books on a shelf.

"Thankfully," said Lenz, grinning in a sickly sort of way, "we have two soothsayers to figure this thing out. You two can work together."

"Only two?" said Chasiku. "I thought you had a whole family."

"Aljosa is not well enough to help," said Lenz. "And Vüsala turned me down."

I stood up straight so suddenly I hit my head on a shelf. "What?"

"I offered your grandmother a position when we first moved them into their new home. She . . . rejected it."

It was good to laugh. I wiped away a tear of joy when I was finally able to speak. "I would give so, *so* much, just to have seen that rejection."

Lenz smiled weakly.

Chasiku looked uncomprehendingly from me, to Lenz, to me, to Lenz, and said, "Can I *leave*?"

"Yes, of course," said Lenz. "But I *expect* you two to look into this together. And soon. Perhaps each one's visions can help illuminate the other's, if you can put your egos aside. Maybe Kalyna's . . ." He waved his hands, looking for the word. ". . . proximity will help? Either way, I can't have you two at each other's throats at a time like this."

Chasiku ignored him and growled, "Why can't anyone make decent *coffee* in this forsaken rock," as she all but ran away. She slammed the door.

I glanced at where she had been, and wondered why she got more freedom than I. Possibly because she wasn't actively trying to escape, which reminded me . . .

"You should come to my servant house for the Sun's Death," I blurted out.

This surprised him, and Lenz turned to look at me. "The Sun's Death? Why?"

"It might be nice. And you can convince the others in my house that we're friendly. That I'm not a prisoner."

He looked skeptical.

I grunted. "Fine. I would like to see my family, and if they come to my home, you'll want to keep an eye on us, won't you?"

"I'll think it over," he grunted.

"And that's all I ask," I said with a very large grin. Then I paid him an ironic salute. "Until then, I will see what I can see," I sighed.

"This isn't just about where King Gerhold is being held," said Lenz. "I know you don't much care for Rotfelsenisch royalty, but everyone—"

"Don't play moralist against me *now*," I growled. "If," I continued, "I could save Olaf and Tural and every farmer and cook and prostitute and merchant and barkeep in our drawn and quartered country, I would. They are *all* my people, remember? Even the Rotfelsenisch. But I cannot save everyone."

Because I am broken, I thought.

TEA IN THE ALCOVE

It felt like weeks since I'd last been in my servant house, even though I had only left it the previous day. Since then, I had terrorized some poor doctor's assistants, plunged down to Glaizatz Lake to eat with High General Dreher, learned a secret about Lenz, visited a hidden prisoner with the Prince and the "King," and told Lenz that our terrible end was nigh. It was starting to get dark, but it wasn't really evening yet: the Sun's Death indeed.

The servant house had a little alcove on the first floor: a windowed bulge popping out of the building's side. As I walked up toward the house, I saw Tural sitting there with a teapot, looking out at the snow, which sat in patches, mere inches from the alcove, so close it looked as though Tural was sitting outside. He seemed far too content to be conjuring his fruit flavors.

I waved to him, and he nodded very slightly. I went inside, took off my coat, and turned directly to the left of the door toward the alcove.

"I know this time is yours," I said in Cölluknit, "but would it disturb you to have company?"

Until I spoke, Tural had looked like an artist's rendering of a man in deep thought: lean legs crossed, elbow on his knee, chin on his fist. Only the slow steam rising from his teacup had told me this was not a painting. When I spoke, he turned to me and smiled broadly.

"It would please me to share."

Tural reached into a shelf in the tea stand and pulled out another cup, which he then flipped right side up with his thumb. He poured me tea, and I did the slow, steady, open-palmed hand gesture that the Quru sometimes preferred over saying "thank you."

"No!" he said, in guttural Rotfelsenisch. "No, no, no, no, no. None of that, now. We aren't in the steppes, and you needn't flourish for every word. I certainly don't."

I smiled and sat. The tea was radiant snow-cave leaf, a dark green drink that was nowhere near as blunt in its power as the black Masovskan tea I was used to. Its very smell warmed me.

"Delicious," I said.

Tural thanked me with a hand gesture, and I chastised him for it.

"No fruit?" I asked.

"My great joy in fruit was drained years ago," he said, back in his native Cöllüknit. "A *tragedy!*" He clasped his hand to his chest.

I had noticed that his white chef's jacket was unstained and there were no seeds in his cravat. I also noticed (for the first time?) that he was handsome.

"But," he went on, "right now is almost the best part of the Rotfelsenisch year: when it becomes beautiful to live in this half-burst pimple filled with blood."

I made a face at the image. "Winter? Why is winter so great here?"

"I left my home," he began, raising his voice, "because there is hardly any fruit alive there, half the year. Too cold, everything freezes. What appears in spring gave me my love, but every year I dreaded when the mountains would heave with snow, and the bushes would lose their leaves. So I traveled to escape that time, and to learn more. Nothing to me is so sweet, varied, and wondrous as fruit, you see. Nothing else shows the fingers of the gods through the world in its every little line, strand, and membrane."

"Vegetables?"

"Well, yes. But I also have a sweet tooth. So! I traveled, landed here where winter is mild, and stayed."

"Winter is even less oppressive in Skydašiai," I offered. "And nonexistent in some parts of Loasht."

"Too little winter for me," he said. "Skydašiai produces most of our fruit, of course, but I like a little cold, in the air *and* in the people. They are too friendly."

"And this is the dark story of how you left your home. But you haven't told me why winter is the best part of the year, here in the bloody pimple."

He grinned. "I used to dread winter, now winter is wonderful. I still must work, I must sit and conjure, but the Sun's Death is the one meal I needn't prepare for. No one wants *berries* at the Sun's Death, they want lamb and ale and hard brown bread to soak in stew." He smiled wistfully and looked back out at the snow. "It's marvelous."

"That's sad. You came out here for the love of something, and now you hope for its absence."

Tural shrugged. "I still love fruit. I love it as one loves the family member whose presence is longed for, and then whose absence is a relief."

"I know just the one. And what family do you share the Feast of the Sun's Death with, then? Or do you take the opportunity to go home to Quruscan?"

"I don't, you know," he laughed softly, "visit my family very often anymore. They feel I have been 'Rotfelsenized.' Or even"—he lowered his voice—"what some call being 'Tetrarchized.' You know, taking this great, silly experiment we live in as an identity." He laughed at the thought. "No, a few of us in the servant house with nowhere else to go have a little meal here. At this point, I would not miss it."

I must have looked very pathetic because he quickly added, "You will be joining us, of course?"

I nodded and thanked him, my mind turning over possibilities for escape to the south. Could I somehow bring Tural with us? I did not want him to die when the great pimple fully burst and collapsed. (This way of seeing Rotfelsen was now seared into my mind, it seemed.)

I leaned forward with a playfully conspiratorial air, and began, quietly, to speak in a Cölluknit dialect specific to the far Qoyul Mountain, at the very edge of the Tetrarchia. Many who knew the language of Quruscan, but were not native speakers, would not understand me. To Tural, I must have sounded like a bumpkin.

"Lenz also needs somewhere to go that evening," I said.

Tural nodded sagely.

"I would like to organize for him a surprise, as he has been working too hard. But because of my duties, I can't leave the palace grounds."

"Oh?" He raised an eyebrow and leaned closer, quizzical. Winter or no, he still smelled of berries; they must have soaked into his skin.

"Could you do me a favor down in Turmenbach?" I asked.

Tural sat back, and unfortunately, I couldn't smell him anymore. He looked out the window and scratched the nape of his neck under the cravat. He looked at me again, hand still on his neck, and his sleeve fell slightly. I saw a Quru medical tattoo, jagged like broken bone, on his wrist.

"I suppose I could, now that I am in my slow period," he said. "But considering the last time I found myself in a room with Lenz and yourself I was nearly fed poison in front of the King, I worry that this is more of your . . . intrigue."

"I promise you that it is not more palace intrigue." I very purposefully added the world "palace."

"Well, that's good. Sometime soon, I hope you will explain to me what you and your boss are really up to."

This was the most prying he had ever done, bless him.

I nodded and said, "Thank you." I put a hand on his shoulder in a most Rotfelsenisch way. "You are remarkably calm, in your off-time."

He laughed. "I will be fed up with it soon enough, and I will yell and scream for more to do."

Then I explained my *surprise* for Lenz. Well, part of it.

SOMETHING WRONG IN YOU

My next step, if I was to escape with my family during the night of the Sun's Death, was to learn more about this "Soul of the Nation" theory that, according to Martin-Frederick Reinhold-Bosch, had so captured High General Dreher's imagination. In this, I did not seek *truth*, partly because I took the idea itself as fanciful garbage, but mostly because truth did not serve my purposes. Whatever "truths" I offered about the Soul of the Nation could then also be enhanced by the quite damning truths about Prince Friedhelm's little masquerade with Olaf.

All I needed was to tell the good High General enough, one way or another, for him to take me into his services—at least for a day or two. Once I knew the lay of the land in his service, where I would hopefully not be a prisoner, the rest would come to me. (I hoped.)

I considered asking Jördis, the ethicist in my servant house, if she'd heard of this "Soul," but I did not trust her. Dreher and Vorosknecht did not seem to get along, and letting the purple windbag know that I was courting the High General's favor—and through philosophical theories, no less—seemed like a clear road to failure. Besides, Jördis was as mercenary as I.

I spent a day in my room, combing through book after book to see if I could find anything on this Soul of the Nation concept, but came up empty. Neither Lenz's own secret histories, nor the other volumes he had placed in my room for me, so much as mentioned the thing.

The next day, I considered taking a trip to the Royal Inn of Ottilie's Rock, but quickly admonished myself for this: Did I *really* think Gunther and his regulars would be able to help me with such an esoteric concept? Of course I didn't, I merely wanted an excuse to do something nice, for a change. I shook the thought out of my head, sighed, and decided to go talk to Chasiku, the Prince's second sooth-sayer. Lenz had insisted we "work together" after all. I let the Yellows in front of my servant house know where I'd be.

"If I'm not back in two hours, come find me there."

I did indeed hope that Chasiku could help me make sense of what was going on, but also her very presence was nagging at me. A second soothsayer was a constant threat of my fraud being discovered. Not the biggest threat I faced, but one that I could actually confront, unlike the Prince and the Court Philosopher and the onrushing doom of the Tetrarchia itself. She was a danger to me, but I did not have nightmares about her. So while part of me hoped to get real informa-tion from her, another part wanted to get one over on Chasiku, before she did the same to me. It was petty, but it felt like the only way to have some measure of control over my life.

So I went up the stairs of Chasiku's tower, to see her out on the walkway, leaning against the railing in the cold, with a mug in her hand. It was a cold, sunny day, the trees were all bare, and the only bright colors I saw were my own powder blue and persimmon orange dress, and Chasiku's patterned shawl of two-tone gold, green, and black. She did not turn toward me.

"Someone may think unkindly of seeing you in green," I said.

"I prefer for no one to see me at all." She sighed and motioned for-ward with her mug, toward the view, as though she were looking at me. "Well, you're in trouble. What *are* you planning?"

If one can grin without smiling, that is what I did. "Don't you know?" I replied.

Chasiku seemed only weary in her reply. "I see the *future*, Kalyna, not the past or present—beyond what I am seeing right now." She gestured again toward where she was looking, off the very edge of Rotfelsen itself.

I moved closer and glanced down. It was bright up here, but below, where Masovskan forests must have been sitting in the shadow of this great piece of rock, I saw only the top of a heavy fog. Rotfelsen may as well have been a pebble floating in a cloudy sky. Off in the distance, I saw the curved backs of creatures that never showed themselves on a clear day, only ever half visible, slithering through the fog. I felt a bit dizzy and stepped back. Chasiku turned to look at me.

"And now, all I see is an insecure fool," she said, motioning toward me with her mug, and then taking a sip. She made a face. "The coffee here is execrable. I've started making it myself, but the beans are so stale by the time they get here." She drank some more anyway.

"It's like that everywhere in the Tetrarchia besides Skydašiai," I said. "If they have it at all."

"Awful," she said, then took another sip. "I am getting bits of your future that are ever more ridiculous. Still death, but stranger, and at whose hands, I cannot tell. You have truly stepped in something. What's wrong with you?"

"What's wrong is that this place is falling apart and I'm trying to—"

"No, no. I don't mean what's wrong with you right now," she interrupted. Chasiku trained her eyes on mine, perhaps because she remembered I preferred it. "I mean, what's wrong with you, in general."

I narrowed my eyes.

She seemed confused. "There's something wrong *in* you. Something broken."

"Why do you say that?" I asked as evenly as I possibly could.

"Because I see bits of your future, and when it isn't death, it's all staring into space or apologizing to your father. Whatever is corroding you is so distracting."

I took a deep breath, and told myself that she was making this up to undermine me. "And so it is only me that you see? Nothing about the Prince, or the King, or our High General, or Vorosknecht?"

She looked down. "I am trying, but you cause so much . . . so much noise. And the King has been difficult to get a grip on. I met him, for a moment, but things seemed off. Like he existed, but also did not."

So she had been introduced to Olaf as the King. That she saw something wrong did not prove her powers to be real, however, as she could easily have noticed something off about him—to be a false prophet, one must be very observant. I wondered, too, whether Friedhelm and Lenz were revealing secrets to *her* that I was not made privy to.

"The destruction of this place is knocking around my mind," she continued, as though each word were a painful grasp at making me understand, "sweating death from every pore. I agreed to come here because I wanted to get away from Kalvadoti, that terrifying and bustling city. Now I've learned that I'm not just doing new work, I am, *apparently*, all that stands between the entire Tetrarchia and destruction."

Was she, I wondered? Was that the position I would leave Chasiku in, if I managed my escape? (Or, for that matter, if I botched it and was killed.) Well, it was too late to start worrying about her now, so instead I reacted to the insult.

"'*All* that stands between'? Now wait, I'm here, too—"

"You are worthless," she said. "Lenz will listen to you more than you realize, and he will assassinate, will throw armies at this plot, while the end only becomes more likely. Your power is empty, your whining threatens to overcome even me, and whatever you do, the end *only becomes more likely*. And your . . ." Her jaw clenched, her body shook. Chasiku seemed to be in pain: not the sharp pain of a cut, but the quivering ache of trying to thread a needle with a sprained wrist. "And your family of diluted psychics will continue to pick away at my concentration with your hatred of each other and yourselves, unless you, Kalyna, *tell me what is wrong*."

"I am sorry to inconvenience you," I said.

She stopped. "Wait," she muttered. "How did that all sound to you?"

"How do you think?"

She looked at me again. "I don't know? I was trying to help."

I stared at her for a long time. Was that true? I could not make sense of her.

"Look," I finally said, "I came here to ask you about something specific. Think you can manage that?"

Chasiku drained her terrible coffee, made a face, and then bowed sarcastically. "Come into my chamber then."

THE SOUL OF THE NATION

Chasiku's room now had a desk, a real bed, and a stack of books of its own. The only ornamentation was still the tapestry on the wall, which seemed to just be a mass of colors.

"Have you heard of something called the 'Soul of the Nation?'" I asked her.

"I believe the phrase may be used in some old poems," she replied, leaning forward over her desk, with her back to me. Its top was mostly empty, save for a few stacks of paper and a quill. "But it rings a bell," she added, shuffling through the papers. "Have I heard it in the jumble running through my mind recently? Or perhaps it's simply in those somewhere." She waved the other hand backward, toward the stack of books.

She continued her shuffling, and I looked through her volumes. These were different than what was in my room: secret histories of Lenz's with titles like *Supplemental* and *On Separatist Movements*, alongside books by others such as *Quarry Economics Vols. I–VII*, *The Foolishness of Utopian Thinking*, and *The Tracts of Rotfelsen's Godcounters*. Some of these volumes seemed as slapdash in their binding as Lenz's histories, and others did not even have titles written on their covers. They looked like the sorts of dissident literature that I had seen in Hidden Markets, such as the one where I'd bought my sickle treatise.

"Heady stuff he's left you," I said.

Chasiku nodded. She was still riffling through her own scribblings at her desk.

"Yes," she said. "I think he hopes it will further clarify what I see in my visions." She snorted. "I have been reading them when I need a break."

I squinted at a book with a very long title whose pages seemed to have been adhered with spit. It seemed Lenz thought much more of Chasiku's intelligence than mine, as I had no lofty works of political or theological theory in my room. I did not let on to her that I was insulted, and besides, Lenz wasn't exactly *wrong* in this—I found even the titles mystifying.

But I sat down on Chasiku's bed and began to page through them anyway, hoping I could find something. Chasiku eventually sat at her desk, and began alternating between looking through papers and staring off into space. It was almost companionate. At one point, a Yellow came to check on us, and I waved him away.

After a few hours, I was flipping through *On Separatist Movements*, trying to make sense of it, when a pamphlet fell out: *The Secret of the Soul of the Masovskan Nation: DO NOT COPY! DO NOT QUOTE! BURN THIS IF YOU SEE A SOLDIER!*

Well, who could resist that? I gave it a read and, other than this pamphlet clearly having been written by Masovskan dissidents, about the supposed "soul" of Masovska, I did not learn much beyond what Martin-Frederick had already told me. Until the very end:

Once more, please be exhorted to NOT ever for ANY reason share these great truths with the authorities. Even if you think those authorities MAY be sympathetic.

A popular trap they will lay for you: "If a nation can have a collective 'soul,' then ours must be for the whole Tetrarchia, as that is our nation."

DO NOT FALL FOR THIS! If you agree, you will anger the SOUL OF MASOVSKA. If you disagree, they will lock you up as a TRAITOR. Avoid the issue entirely by NEVER SHARING THIS DOCUMENT WIDELY. Our time will come.

Martin-Frederick had told me about this Soul of the Nation idea so casually, but then he didn't believe in it. It made sense that the theory, whether taken literally or metaphorically, would be criminalized: I had read no poems passionately composed to the Tetrarchia, seen no singular identity applied to its people. It, collectively, was no one's motherland.

"Do you mind if I keep this?" I asked Chasiku, holding it up.

"Yes, yes, fine," she replied, as though we had not just been silent for hours. "Have you received any new details about it?"

"About the Soul of the Nation?"

"The what? Are you still on that? No, no. The violent end of our Tetrarchic Experiment."

I tucked the pamphlet into my blouse. "Afraid not," I replied. "A pity about all that awful death on the way: I'd let the whole structure burn down, if we could save the people." It was an imprudent thing to say, but I wanted to better understand where Chasiku stood.

She looked at me and nodded very slightly. "I shall have to try re-summoning the vision of shattering rotrock that I saw," she said. "Perhaps I can figure out what causes it. It's all well and good to worry about plots, but it may be a simple natural disaster, right when the Council of Barbarians is taking place. We have earthquakes up in the North Shore, do you have those here?"

"*I* didn't grow up in Rotfelsen. But I can't imagine they do, or else . . ." Well, or else it would all crumble, wouldn't it? Neither of us bothered to voice it. Instead, I stood up and said, "I shall leave you to conjure."

When I moved away from her bed, Chasiku all but pounced from her desk onto it, as though I had been hoarding it from her. She lay back, head propped up, hands behind her head, staring at her tapestry.

"If your family," she began, "only sees what's 'most likely,' then seeing everyone's futures changing like this must have been confusing."

This had not actually occurred to me until she said it. I wondered what hells Papa must have been going through the last few months. I even started to think on how this may have affected Grandmother, but thought better of it.

I opened my mouth to thank Chasiku for the surprisingly sympathetic words, but she continued before I could:

"No wonder you are all such fools," she said.

I sighed and turned to go. But then I had a thought.

"Chasiku, if you want to help out a poor fool—"

"Helping fools is the only thing I have ever done consistently."

"—perhaps I can ask you one more time about this 'Soul of the Nation' thing. I promise I will be specific."

She rolled her eyes.

"Have you seen anything beneath us? Down where the caves and the lake—"

"Oh, is *that* the underground lake I've been seeing in your futures?"

"In *mine*?" I gulped. "What did you see there?"

"I saw you in the waters, and something beneath you. Glowing."

"Beneath me?" The glowing little wiggly shrimp stayed near the surface, as far as I knew. "What was it?"

She shrugged. "Some very large glow. It isn't what kills you down there, if that's what you're wondering."

"I wasn't."

"Or is it? It's so hard to tell these days. But I think it will be the drowning or the bullets, or the many large fish."

"Thank you," I muttered.

"Any time." She actually smiled. Was this her way with customers, a genuine desire to connect with me, or glee at my death?

LEINGARDE'S COMPREHENSIVE GUIDE TO BANNED COMIC OPERAS

The next day, I sent Martin-Frederick Reinhold-Bosch a copy of *Leingarde's Comprehensive Guide to Banned Comic Operas* that I found on one of the shelves in my room. (Chasiku got complex theory, I got warbling "crafty servant" archetypes.) With the book was a very kind note, saying that it had made me think of him. Inside the book, at the first page about *The Leper's Five Tits*, was crammed a second note, saying, "I look forward to seeing your carriage at the Sun's Death. I have found what you need."

I hoped this was not too blatant, lest a Yellow find it. I also hoped it was not too subtle, lest Martin-Frederick miss it.

I heard almost nothing from anyone for days. No Martin-Frederick to confirm or deny getting my message. No Prince Friedhelm discussing his plans to ensnare the Queen, or take over the Reds. Nothing from Lenz about the end of the Tetrarchia, the King, whether my erstwhile jailer would even come to the Sun's Death, or whether my family would be allowed to attend. He did send a little extra payment for the "visions" of Papa's that had been written down during his screaming nights, along with a note saying how pleased he was that Chasiku and I were "working together." It was decent of him, in a way, but I needed him to come to the Sun's Death if I was ever to escape.

I was questioned by a couple of Yellows about my jaunt with Martin-Frederick and the Greens. I told a lot of truth: that after the King's Dinner, High General Dreher had wanted to meet me, and that he wanted my prophetic opinion on a boring personal matter. If they thought it was something more sinister than that, it was their own fault for always getting into fights with the Greens, wasn't it?

My escape plan was set, so I spent much of that time waiting for Yellows to be free enough to escort me to my family, since I was still not allowed to visit them on my own. Once there, I tried my best to pack their things in a way that did not *look* like I was packing their things, and assess my father's ability to travel. He desperately wanted to leave, but he was also "so comfortable, Kalynishka. Just so comfortable here." At least I was finally able to keep him company when the Gift came for him again, a duty that I had been neglecting for weeks (as Grandmother continued to remind me). He saw nothing new that I could use, but the important thing was that I was there for him.

"Is Dagmar with you this time, Kalynishka?" asked Papa, one night.

I cocked my head to the side. "Who?"

"That would be me, ma'am," said the Yellow in the next room, who had graciously been allowing Grandmother to scream at her for a bit, instead of me.

Yes, this was the tall, striking blonde woman I'd thought of as "Dugmush," and had decided it was too late, and too embarrassing, to ask her name. I felt that I would die, just then, and spare everything congregating around me the trouble.

"Ah!" I finally said, turning to look at her. "Well, good to meet you, Dagmar."

"Likewise." She winked at me.

But I didn't want to start learning the Yellows' names *now*, particularly not one I found rather attractive. I was on the cusp of escaping and leaving them to their deaths, if I was very lucky.

The two weeks until the Sun's Death stretched into those voids of seemingly infinite darkness that happen near the solstice. I spent them in my head, reading histories that had not been written by Lenz. I read of ancient, pre-Tetrarchic societies because, while those times were no more savage, modern historians were much more eager to describe their savagery. All the better to cry, "See how humanity improves!" Dark, old things seemed right for those days. Besides, if Masovska could survive the Year of Massacres, Rotfelsen the Jackal Disaster, and Quruscan the Decade of Avalanches, perhaps we could survive the coming catastrophe.

Or *they* could. I would be in the Bandit States. I wished very much that the pale, pink, hidden Rots hadn't decided to name their solstice "the Sun's Death."

THE SUN'S DEATH

The day of the Sun's Death had *some* light: the morning burst into terrible brightness for what felt like a few moments. In that time, the servant house bustled with activity as a feast was prepared, and the big, third floor dining room was decorated.

Everyone I encountered as I ducked beneath dead branches, and stepped around carefully composed piles of earth, assured me this would be an embarrassing shadow of what a Feast of the Sun's Death should be. They were all quite disappointed it would be my first.

"Only five main dishes!" a cook exclaimed, taking a break because five main dishes afforded him infinite time to chat.

"No new coats of paint on the walls," mumbled a maid as she decorated the dining room. "Closer to the palace, there would be a new coat over the walls, just so someone with *talent* could adorn them." She shrugged. "Down here, there are no great tableaus or grand old trees dragged up thirty stories, just some branches and my scribblings."

She insisted I not call her an artist. As she spoke, she was engaged in painting, on the space between two windows, a golden sun body with the orb of the sun for his head. He (that is, the personified sun) ran terrified through a wood lit only by himself, as star-headed wolves bayed and chased him, each wolf an individual, each one facing the sun from a slightly different angle. All this while the moon looked gleefully on from above, using his hands to block his own light from confusing the wolves, although moonbeams peeked out between his fingers.

But she was not an artist, she said, and this was nothing compared to the murals that would cover whole walls at a "real" Feast of the Sun's Death. Her lifetime ambition, it seemed, was to someday work in one of the nearby noble houses, dabbing in the smallest details at the House Artist's direction. The Sunset Palace, which loomed just out the window, right next to her painting, was further than she could ever imagine going.

And all this work, which the first- and second-floor servants insisted was the lowest of the low, was being done for *us*. I had met the Prince, the Court Philosopher, the High General, and the King (sort of), and seen the rich at play at the Winter Ball, and so had come to see Jördis, Tural, and the rest as plain, normal, working folk. But they were not. Breaking their backs to give us a nice feast were the menials who lived below us, and who, here on the palace grounds, lived lives that I, through most of my own life, would have seen as luxurious.

Whether it was guilt about my new station, or revulsion for the nobility, I felt a deep need to show the servants that I, too, knew how to do real work. They laughed in a friendly way and sternly forbade me from helping.

"It is nothing. Nothing!" cried the servant house's head butler. "This is hardly even a dinner to us, I promise you. Certainly nothing close to the *Feast*."

I was idling in the dining room as he inspected every surface. It was now just about time for the sun's, well, death, which is to say it was early afternoon and the sky was red.

"Well, what did your family do for the Feast of the Sun's Death, Johann?" I asked. "Paintings a mile high, whole trees, runners of red fabric as far as the eye can see?"

Johann coughed to cover a laugh and turned to face me. He was prim and perfect as a head butler should be, but for the scar down his face, which meant he was not presentable enough to be head butler in a more prestigious place. He could, I had been told by a cook, make a hefty sum as a third or fourth butler in a noble's house, but felt it was beneath his experience.

"Of course not," he said. "Of *course* not. But that is different. We are on the *palace grounds*, and what's more this is your *first* Feast of the Sun's Death. I wish it could be more satisfactory."

I shrugged. "But I won't know it's meager if no one tells me."

This line of reasoning did not please him.

The smell of old wood around us was only slightly noticeable mixed in with that of food from below. I had been down there recently, before being shooed away, and it seemed there was only paprika and butter and sweat to breathe, with no air left at all. Up on the third floor, it was pleasant, and light reflecting off the red silk that was hung everywhere made it seem that the paprika had actually floated up here physically, in one big cloud. Some of the old branches had been picked for their perfect gnarls and twists, while others had been broken into shape, but every branch, while quite dead, seemed to yearn for the sky, for the sun that was not there. Circling everything were the maid's paintings of the personified sun figure's life, death, and rebirth. These were small, none wider than my shoulders, but I appreciated the intimacy of them. I don't claim to know art, but I do know that the sun felt warm when I gazed at him, and his absence was chilling. I was told these would be painted over tomorrow.

The long table where I had eaten so many times was draped in red. This was the sun's . . . I don't know, blood, I suppose. Eight places were set, all around one end of the table for ease of conversation, while the other was covered in variously sized decorative plates, which were empty.

Eight seats. I didn't know how many people were originally meant to be at dinner, so I couldn't tell if my *surprise* had been planned for, or if Lenz or my family would join. We would see.

Candles, hundreds of them, were stuck onto any part of a branch that would hold them. A boy of maybe fourteen, who looked both bored and terrified, stood in the far doorway holding a metal bar taller than he was, with a douser on the end. He was our bulwark against burning the whole place down. The candles were mostly red or blue, with a good number that were a swirl of those two colors. Scattered about were also a few with a dark brown and tan check pattern right in the tallow, and a smattering of your average yellow-white candles.

I remember the candles so well because I idled about, staring at them, for some time. They had been lit hours ago and were already leaking multicolored globs.

"So sorry, ma'am!" chirped the douser boy in a cracking voice.

"For what?"

"The white candles, ma'am." He looked at the floor. "We were out of the other colors, you know. And we usually have a smattering of purples, yellows, and greens, you know, just in case someone—"

"Oh, I hadn't even noticed!"

"Nice of you to say, ma'am," he said to the floor. Then he seemed to remember that he was meant to the watch the flames and looked up, terrified.

I wanted to sit at the table until dinner began, but suspected this would alarm the staff. I leaned back against an open window and felt a cold winter wind on my back, which was nice in that building of paprika and steam. I smiled at the douser boy, and he gulped.

I didn't want to sit in the quiet of my room, so I stood there awhile longer. I thought about the season and the comfortable servant house, I listened to the bustling around me and watched the douser boy glare about the room, from one candle to the next, endlessly. If I went to my room I would only think more about my plan, and it was much too late for *that*. I had considered and reconsidered and re-reconsidered my impulsive, devious, and cruel plan. The conclusion I had come to was that it was our best chance, even though it was terrible and would likely get us all killed.

Besides, what was there to do in my room? I had already packed what I could.

The Feast of the Sun's Death, Almost

At first, four people milled about the dining room, feeling that, with eight seats, we needed at least one more diner to be seated. These were myself, Tural, Jördis, and, again, her friend Vondel, the stout, bald Tenth Butler to High General Dreher, whom I had met after the Winter Ball. Most of our neighbors were off with their families, and the dining room was all so quaint and friendly, so free of the divisions that were always felt at court. So very nice and, if everything went as planned, I was going to ruin it.

Seeing Vondel again allowed me to compare him to our servant house's own head butler, Johann: Vondel was younger and less experienced, but worked in the Sunset Palace, and therefore was prestigious enough to sit with us while Johann bustled. Vondel seemed to have endless poise, which Jördis found amusing.

After a few more minutes, Lenz arrived. He looked uncomfortable, but I was happy he was there at all. I must have smiled when I greeted him because after that, he looked *much more* uncomfortable.

He was followed by two fully armed Yellows whom I knew by face but not name. I found myself wishing that one had been Dagmar. They planted themselves at far sides of the room.

"Kalyna Aljosanovna," said Lenz. "When you have a moment, I have some news for you regarding our"—he glanced sideways at the others—"business."

"Subtle!" laughed Jördis. "Careful, Lenz; you've got a High General's man and a Court Philosopher's woman standing right by you." She jabbed a thumb behind her. "And also Tural."

"My work is too lofty for one master," sniffed Tural.

"Yes, well," said Lenz, "deep down we are all King Gerhold's, aren't we?"

"That," said Jördis, "is a toast. Down, everyone, find your seats!"

We did, all five of us bunched around one end of the table. I sat with two empty chairs to my left and Tural to my right, next to him was Jördis, then Vondel, an empty spot, and Lenz, who was across the table from me. Lenz was almost a rival for Vondel at sitting bolt upright, as though about to run off at any moment, but it was nowhere near as graceful in him. His discomfort did not please me as much as I had hoped.

Jördis leaned over Vondel and patted Lenz on the hand. "We need to get some ale into you, I think."

"Yes," said Lenz, smiling.

Jördis smiled back sweetly, turned to the main doorway, and took a deep breath to scream for ale.

"What? No!" Vondel interrupted. "Not yet, Jördis; you are a monster."

Tural chuckled, Jördis rolled her eyes. I am sure I looked confused.

"This is the only reason you bring me, isn't it?" sighed Vondel. "To keep you in order."

"And here I thought we were friends," said Jördis.

"Everyone join hands," said Vondel, raising his own. "Unless we're waiting for . . ." He pointed to the empty places.

"No, no," I said. "They won't mind."

"Excellent." Vondel inclined his head toward me at just the right angle to communicate, *If you say so, but I do not believe you.* I was amazed at what he could convey with such subtlety. Like Klemens Gustavus in a Gniezto courthouse, if he were pleasant and friendly.

We all joined hands with our neighbors. Tural's was surprisingly soft.

"O sweet sunlight," Vondel began, "bleed through the night and cut down through our rock where even daytime finds you scarce, deliver us from . . ."

Thus began the Feast of the Sun's Death. Vondel hardly seemed interested in what he was saying, but he took great satisfaction in saying it. He went on for some time.

After what felt like ten minutes: ". . . you grow up the cave-barley that makes our ale, and now we drink deep of that ale so we may pass the time of your death all the quicker, and wake into your new life and warmth very soon.

"Now," he continued, to Jördis, "you may call for—"

Casks of ale slammed onto the table, and the plates and mugs jumped. Butlers began pouring the thick, black liquid into our goblets. This was an entirely new sort of alcoholic beast to me, and I admit that to my untrained tongue, the first taste was of bitter mud. But, as usual, I saw others enjoying it and soon grew accustomed. Surely they knew better than me.

At some point, while Vondel spoke, the plates covering the other side of the table had been piled high with roasted root vegetables, strings of anemic greens, hunks of lamb, egg noodles, and much more. After coughing down a few draughts of the ale, I reached toward a plate of carrots.

"I suppose we can supplement this ale with—"

Vondel stopped me with a glare. "The guest," he said, "must be taught the Order. We do not eat anything yet, and not the carrots."

"Oh."

"*Certainly* not the carrots."

I hadn't even been particularly hungry. I put my hands in my lap and waited.

There was much more after that. Vondel had a long speech about the sad vegetables and springtime—complete with a rote comparison between the green of the vegetables being served to eat and the Greens that he served. This was followed by a bracing tradition that had us all up and walking circles around the table to see who was the drunkest. I honestly thought this had to be made up, until I saw how easily even Lenz, with his bad leg, went along with it. Why, he almost seemed to enjoy himself.

All the ceremonial food that had been laid out ahead of time was meant to be eaten as part of the Order; we were nowhere near the meal. When we finally got to those sage-buttered carrots ("These that feel your great light even when they are in the dark and beneath the world, like so many of your people"), a third Yellow tromped into the room and stood at attention.

"Two more to dine," he said. "Aljosa Vüsalavich and None of Your Damn Business."

I smiled.

"Show them in," said Lenz.

Slowly, up the stairs, came the sound of a woman peppering

someone with curses, interspersed with low mutterings of "yes, ma'am" and "of course, ma'am" and "uh-huh, ma'am." Then a large Yellow came through the door, carrying Papa in his arms, crushed to his chest. Papa was in his best silk brocade caftan from the days when he still ran the business, and his arms were wrapped around the soldier's neck. Grandmother was right behind them in a stunning array of Quru scarves over a many-layered dress. She was yelling.

"Be sure you don't bump his head against— Oh, it's you."

In all my years of fraudulence, I don't know that I have ever faked so good a smile.

"Grandmother! Papa! So glad you could make it!" I ran to them, embracing both. Grandmother, for all her bile, was too suspicious of the surroundings, and my affection, to fight me off. I don't think I had hugged her in more than twenty years.

With a strained smile, I introduced everyone to Aljosa Vüsalavich and Vüsala Mildoqiz. "I don't believe either of them has taken part in this feast before," I added, "but I hope you will be charitable."

Papa's face broke into a huge smile as he looked around the room.

"This! These branches and cloth and candles, and the *carrots*! Oh, the carrots!" he cried. "I have *seen* this. Again and again, caught between sharks and robberies and ladies walking to town! I have *seen* this in so many homes of pink-cheeked people, like some of you, but only in flashes, in silhouettes: I never knew what it was!"

He reached out, and the Yellow took him over to the nearest decorations. Papa ran his hand over a silk stream of red, and touched the dead branch. The douser boy looked very uncomfortable.

"All along it was the Feast of the Sun's Death I saw," Papa continued. "I never knew because we have not passed a winter in Rotfelsen in some time. Some time indeed."

There was a very long silence then. Eventually, I had to answer the expectant stares.

"Yes, well, uh . . . Lenz and Jördis already know this, but, ah, I am a soothsayer. So there's that. My father and grandmother are, too. Yes." I think that I rubbed my hands nervously as I said this.

Vondel, professional that he was, seemed to note the information same as he would my middle name, had I one. Jördis remained confused by Papa's gibberish. Tural almost fell out of his chair.

"What!" he cried. "And you did not tell me!"

"Vorosknecht called me a 'psychic' at the King's Dinner," I replied.

"I was not paying great attention," said Tural.

"No wonder they've kept you around," growled Grandmother. "No one knew what you are."

"Well," Tural went on. "Well. I am sure you have had reasons."

"Thank you, Tural," I said.

"Have you," stammered Papa, "have you already walked around the table?"

"We have," said Vondel, standing. "But there is much more to come, Aljosa Vüsalavich. I am so glad to share this time with you." He moved to Grandmother, took her hand, and before she had a chance to say anything, he was off to Papa, bowing. The Yellow did a nice job of dipping Papa in a mock bow right back.

"But you must be cold," continued Vondel. "Please sit. The carrots are warm, and the ale is warm enough."

"Oh!" laughed Papa. "Oh yes, thank you!"

I saw now that his cheeks were red, his hands shaking. I had been too preoccupied to notice. Too busy looking to see if Lenz had any inkling what was coming. Too busy trying to look calm before my moment came.

Eventually, we did get them seated, with Papa between Grandmother and me, thankfully. Three of the on-duty Yellows stood against the wall, one behind each member of my family. It was clear who the prisoners were here, and Tural furrowed his brow at me. None of the Yellows present were Dagmar, possibly because she had allowed me to assault the doctor's assistants, and was now on first-name basis with my father. None of them were Behrens, my sharp-shooter friend, either. I felt sure this was on purpose.

So, on went the Feast, in which so far there had only been light nibbling. Vondel began the first song, "Blood-Green Pastures of the Rotfels," which seemed less like a prayer than a drinking song. Grandmother shocked me by joining in. She even knew all the words to the verses, which were complex and easy to mumble through until the rousing chorus.

"What?" she snarled at me afterward. I had said nothing.

Everyone at the table had gotten very good at pretending Grandmother was whispering inaudibly when she insulted me.

"I didn't realize you knew this song."

"Monster, monster," she sighed, shaking her head. "I know the Order inside out. I did have a life before you two were born."

"Pity you still do," I mumbled into my ale. Papa smiled at me.

"Now," said Vondel, "who can tell me, and our guests, wherefrom came the red cloth that adorns the dead trees of—"

"Hello?" came a voice from the stairwell. "Hello? Third floor, is it? The third floor?"

Lenz stiffened. I grinned.

"Yes! Yes!" called Tural. "Right up here!"

A slight, chestnut-haired man burst into the room, red-cheeked and breathing heavily, but not hard. He had the easy movement of a martial bearing that had relaxed over the years: coordinated, but not stiff. Clutched to his doublet of unaffiliated gray was a large bag, at his hip a rapier.

"I am so sorry to be late," he laughed. His voice was musical. "Hellishly difficult to find paste-breads today; I should have put in orders a week ago, but what's done is done." The man smiled at everyone, looking at Lenz last.

Tural smiled with recognition at the newcomer, then turned his smile toward Lenz. Lenz's eyes were wide, his lips pulled together, his face the mottled gray of the sky before a torrential rain. He looked like he was going to burst. The Master of Fruit then glared at me hard, with a disapproval I felt in my stomach.

So this was Lenz's lover, whom my father had strained himself to find in his visions.

SURPRISE!

Gabor was a handsome man, if boyish for my taste. He appeared to be around twenty, in the moments before one saw the crinkling at his eyes betray him for closer to thirty. Lenz had done well for himself. Gabor could have done better.

I knew, from what Papa told me, that Lenz visited Gabor in Turmenbach regularly, at the home they used to share. I suspect no one in Rotfelsen—possibly including Gabor and Lenz themselves—would have considered them to be spouses, but "husband" was the word Papa had used. What part, I wondered, had this relationship played in putting Lenz so closely under the Prince's thumb?

"Kalyna . . ." said Lenz from across the table.

"What? I learned that your friend here would be all alone on the Sun's Death, and I thought that sounded very sad."

He narrowed his eyes as though trying to see my very brain. "You *learned*."

I smiled sweetly.

"Didn't you hear I was coming?" asked Gabor, cocking his head to the side to look at Lenz.

"No," said Lenz.

"You've been so busy lately," I said. "It's been hard to get hold of you."

Gabor crossed over behind my back, toward Lenz's side of the table, dropping his bag into the hands of a waiting servant as he did. On the way, he clapped a hand on Tural's shoulder and begged Vondel not to get up. He approached Lenz, and I saw no awkward almost-kiss, no longing embrace. Gabor grabbed Lenz's shoulder much as he had Tural's, and gave it a good, hearty pat. He then plopped down next to Lenz, smiling, and Lenz nodded brusquely back, keeping his eyes trained on me. I did everything I could to not look out the window—to not check if Martin-Frederick was out there yet.

Gabor introduced himself to the rest of us informally from across the table. Vondel was uncomfortable about this, but Jördis ribbed him into relaxing.

"Please, please," Gabor said, arguing the point playfully, "in the shadow of the Sun's Death, we're all family! Otherwise we freeze!"

This was, I gathered from Vondel's smile, a reference to a prayer in the Order. Probably a bit we had already done.

Gabor claimed to know me through Tural, and acted almost as though the two of them were old friends. They had only just met, after I had asked Tural to find and invite him.

"Now," said Vondel, once introductions were done, "as I was saying: Wherefrom comes the red cloth that—"

"Ooh!" cried Gabor, pouring himself ale. "We're almost at the meal then."

Everyone gave this a laugh, the sort that showed it was a joke made every year, with the only surprise being who would make it. Yes, everyone had a good laugh except for me, who still did not know what was going on. Even Papa and Grandmother, the people with whom I could always share my alienation, knew these stupid words Vondel was saying, and understood the meaning of the red cloth or dead branches or why the carrots were so different from the . . .

Good. This was good. I didn't want to get too comfortable. My hands twitched and I thought about violence. About the use of small violence to escape great violence. This was my neighbors' last chance for a decent Feast of the Sun's Death—next year's would happen in refugee camps or Loashti prisons, if it happened at all—and here I was to desecrate it.

Vondel had apparently been giving his speech about the significance of everything around us, with others joining in. I hoped I looked like I was listening, but I didn't absorb a word of it. As Vondel spoke—sonorously, I must add—Jördis smiled the smile of warm nostalgia. Papa showed inklings of understanding, Grandmother glared at her plate but chimed in, and Gabor took a moment to smile at me.

Lenz continued to stare at me hard. His mustache twitched. He was trying, I think, to figure out how and why I had done what I had done. He wanted to know what my plan actually was.

What My Plan Actually Was

Well, it wasn't to expose Lenz's secret relationship to the world, although I'm sure he suspected otherwise. I do not *think* I am that cruel, but why would anyone believe me?

No, my plan was to get my family into a coach provided by Martin-Frederick Reinhold-Bosch, which would take me to the High General, whom I would then regale with visions of Glaizatz Lake and the truth about Olaf, Prince Friedhelm's pet pretender. This may well start its own war, but this place was on the verge of destruction already, and *that* could not be blamed on me. Could it? I felt bad about what this meant for Olaf, but he seemed to welcome death.

When everyone was nice and relaxed near the end of the night, I meant to retrieve Tural's knife from my room and hold it to Gabor's throat. I would keep him hostage in the carriage to ensure Lenz's good behavior. Then, once I was safe with the High General, I would make plans for my family and me to escape him as well. He would be busy, and I would earn his trust with lies about the Soul of the Nation, and the truth of the imposter on the throne.

It was a plan likely to end in my death, I grant you, but it seemed my best option. Most guards got the Sun's Death off, and Martin-

Frederick would vouch for me. Besides, Gabor was smaller than me, and if I could get my hands on him, we would see just how strong Lenz's sense of loyalty to his master was. Would he let someone who knew about Olaf go, to save his beloved's life?

This was my terrible plan. It had a lot of possible failings, and I had just found a new one: I *liked* Gabor.

THE FEAST OF THE SUN'S DEATH

The meal was finally underway. The steam that rose from heaping plates of meat and grains, the twinkling light of hundreds of candles, and the alcohol in my body, gave the whole room a gauzy feeling. It seemed Jördis' laughter was taking physical shape in the air, like a warm fog.

And I wasn't even drunk. I had sipped when the Order told me to drink deep, and I had nursed a mug of ale in between so as to not seem suspicious. I wanted to be sober when it was my turn to play kidnapper. I couldn't afford clumsiness or warm feelings.

"So!" Gabor yelled a little too loud. He had a low tolerance, which was good. "What goes on in the Sunset Palace these days? You all must know who's been skewered, and which mouthy viscount's been thrown from a window, yes?"

"Our Kalyna here fought off an *assassination* attempt," said Jördis, pointing across the table's corner at me and smiling.

"It was a *kitchen accident*," I murmured.

"Oh?" said Gabor, sitting up straight and looking over at me. "Who was the victim?"

"A roast," I said.

I made a show of being very full and needing to move, so I stood up and began to pace. Papa looked at Gabor and blinked a lot.

"We," said Vondel, almost puffing up his chest, "do not *know* at whom the assassination-that-was-not was aimed. Perhaps we could be enlightened?" He raised an eyebrow at me and smiled with exactly one-eighth of his mouth.

"Kitchen accident," I repeated, moving idly toward the window, which wasn't far from Lenz and Gabor.

"Do I . . . ?" muttered Papa.

"It was a kitchen accident," echoed Lenz. He had finally stopped staring at me every second.

"Oh, please!" laughed Gabor, patting Lenz on the back.

Lenz closed his eyes when he was touched.

"The stories trickling down to Turmenbach were good enough for you before, Lenz," Gabor continued, "but now you know the inner circle!"

Lenz sighed. "But there are so *many* inner circles." He almost smiled. "Piled on each other like pangolin scales."

"When you lived together?" asked Papa out of nowhere.

"I'm sorry?" asked Gabor.

What little relaxation Lenz had found disappeared. I did not risk looking out the window for Martin-Frederick and his coach.

"You two," said Papa. "You lived together."

"Oh! Yes," answered Gabor. "We fought together in the army, and afterward pooled our meager pensions to buy a property neither of us could have afforded on our own. Why do you ask?"

I waited for Papa to answer, and my eyes may have been as wide and horrified as Lenz's. Gabor's calm was amazing to me, and without him there, I suspect Lenz would've been bleeding from the nose and eyes.

Papa cocked his head to the side and blinked a few more times at Gabor. Then he sat up straight and said, "Just curious. You seem to be great friends."

I fancied that the exhalation of pent-up breath from Lenz and myself could have put out every candle in Turmenbach.

"We are!" said Gabor, seemingly unfazed. "You are very observant, Aljosa Vüsalavich, you know that?"

Papa turned on the charming little "you can trust me" smile that I had not seen on him in at least a decade. It was an expression I practiced in the mirror almost daily. "I suppose it's a gift," he said.

Lenz actually smiled and looked up at me quizzically. I tried to look reassuring. Perhaps I succeeded, perhaps he was simply exhausted. Papa began to babble across the table at Gabor, who listened intently and asked many questions.

Ale flowed, food was shoveled, the night wore on. I made it over to the window and glanced out. There was a small coach there that did not belong to the Yellows. I couldn't see who was in it.

If Lenz was no longer tense, neither was he personable. He spent the rest of the night slumped in his chair, trying to extinguish something in his chest with alcohol. Jördis, Gabor, and Papa did most of the talking, and no one seemed bothered by Papa's nonsense. He even managed to sneak a few sips of ale without Grandmother yanking it away from him. I moved back to my seat.

I never forgot my plan, but it had fallen so far back into my head as to be a vague buzzing when Lenz lurched unsteadily to his feet.

"Kalyna Aljosanovna," he said, "I know it is . . ." He choked and gurgled, cleared his throat, and continued. "I know it is the Sun's Death, but may we, you and I, speak business privately?"

"Yes. Of course." I stood. "My room is yours."

I gouged my palms with my fingernails as I waited to see if he'd go for it.

He trod slowly and loudly across the room, staring downward. Everyone was silent, even though they didn't know what was happening. Gabor looked very concerned, and I felt a pang of guilt.

The Yellows guarding the room (and fastidiously removing all knives from the table the moment we finished with them) began to follow and were waved away. Lenz pointed at Grandmother and Papa and mumbled something. The Yellows stayed. My heart began trying to jump out of my chest. It was my chance. A better chance than kidnapping Gabor, perhaps.

I followed him up the stairs to my chamber.

You Can't Play the Hero Now

"It wasn't fair of them, you know," said Lenz.

He was sitting in my chair. The one against the wall and between the windows, where I felt the most safe and could view my whole room. On his way to it, he had not lit any candles, but had grabbed one of my half-empty mugs of day-old (at best) brandy, sniffed it, and taken it with him. I stood over him, but my eyes wandered toward my bed. Tural's knife was under the pillow.

"What wasn't fair?" I asked. "Not fair of me to bring Gabor—?"

"Did I say 'you'?" he spat. "I am not that drunk." He sipped. "It wasn't fair of *them*."

"Whom?"

"The army. Rotfelsen's army."

I said nothing. He wanted to tell me whatever it was; there was no need to ask.

Lenz's face was barely visible, but starlight quivered in the windows behind him. Most of the servant houses were dark, but the noble manors and Sunset Palace beyond them were lit up in nearly every window as the Feast of the Sun's Death played out. I became very aware of the fact that Lenz could probably see my face in that light, so I crossed over and sat on my bed to his left, in shadow. The hilt of the rapier on his belt glinted a foot away from my knees.

"They encourage it, you know," he said.

"What?"

"Men."

"Oh?"

"For morale," he said.

It seemed that this was meant to illuminate for me the entire tale that was in his head. When I didn't respond, he finally clarified.

"For morale," he repeated, "many armies encourage their soldiers to rut in the night, hoping that, being lustful, sentimental youths, they will be quicker to trust and protect one another when battle comes with the morning. The Greens are entirely male: they think women will fail on campaign, and no one wants pregnant soldiers."

I nodded.

"Can you imagine?" he laughed, pushing back his hair, which managed to fall over his face and stick straight up at the same time. "Can you imagine how the minds of comfortable old commanders can justify eagerly throwing fit young men at one another when in the army, while soundly condemning the same activity so much as a second after discharge?"

"Of course I can."

"It's chivalrous when our boys are youthful and the army is out in the world," Lenz continued, "but past twenty-two years of age, it's disgusting and childish. Because 'old' men—and I am not so much older than you—are disgusting, no longer lithe and beautiful. Two grown men together are considered either so arrested as to be fools, or entirely amoral. So"—he pointed at nothing—"the *army* gives men like Gabor, like myself, a taste of what we will miss for the rest of our lives. It's all so . . ."

"Arbitrary. Yes."

"A policy for dilettantes!" he seethed. "For men who wish to try new things and throw them away. Or men like Friedhelm, who simply wish to scandalize by *pretending* they try such things."

"I can see how that would make you angry."

"Of course you can. That's why you brought *him* here."

I sighed loudly—perhaps a touch theatrically—and said, "*That* is not why I brought him here." It was considerate of him to phrase it this way, so I didn't have to lie. Not that I mind lying.

"Oh, really?" said Lenz, halfway between sardonic disbelief and a desperate need to believe.

"Really," I said.

"*Saw* him, did you? Saw me visiting him."

I nodded. "Many times. At the house in Dunkel Cave, with the lattices and the orchids. It's nice."

He coughed loudly. "It was my house, too, before the Prince yanked me up here to work for him."

"So you have often said to Gabor when you look around the place." I shrugged. "Or will."

"How melancholy," he grunted.

I leaned over across my bed, propped up on my right arm. And if the fingers of my right hand happened to slip underneath the pillow, what did it matter?

"It certainly doesn't bother me if you flout Rotfelsenisch conven-tion," I said. "I only wanted to show you that I, too, could put my enemy's loved ones under my power."

"Are we still enemies then?" he sighed.

I took a deep breath and let it out in a long sigh. I supposed I *had* taken advantage of Lenz's need for secrecy, even if that made me queasy. If others could know about Gabor, Lenz would surely have brought a Yellow or two into my room.

Lenz tried to see the palace grounds through the window over his right shoulder, but seemed uninterested in turning far enough around. I wondered if Martin-Frederick was out there in that coach, if Lenz might see him. Then Lenz looked at me again, waiting for some sort of explanation.

I gave him one.

I shoved myself up with my right hand, the knife glinting out in the open as I moved off the bed. Every part of me pushed toward him at once. I pivoted on my left foot, lifted my right, and stepped on the hilt of his sword. The small, gold-handled knife stopped against his throat.

Lenz didn't look scared or angry, yet. He showed only a dull surprise as the mug slipped from his fingers. I caught it in my left hand.

"Let's not make any noise," I said.

The knife blade was quite sharp, and when he nodded it shortened the stubble on his neck. I put the cup, carefully, on the desk. I loomed over him, left hand on his shoulder, right hand holding the knife to his throat, right leg pushing down his rapier.

"So," he rasped, "you brought Gabor for him to be here when you finally kill me?"

"Killing you is the contingency plan. I just want to leave."

"You'd leave the Tetrarchia behind to rot when you could save—?"

"I can do nothing. Nothing but escape. You seemed well convinced of my uselessness recently."

"Look, I'm sorry I said—"

"I don't *care* what you said." I leaned in closer, his sword pivoting under my foot, my weight pushing against the blade. "Just let me go. You have my replacement."

He shrugged as much as he could without being killed. "I can't. I need you."

"Let Chasiku do my job."

"Chasiku," he gurgled, "hasn't saved Olaf's life. Besides, if one was enough, I wouldn't have brought her here in the first place."

I pushed the knife harder against his skin. It was sharp enough that a small red line began to show beneath it.

"I've already been compromised by my soft heart tonight," I said. "Let me go or I kill you."

"I can't stop you now," said Lenz. "You may kill me and try to leave. The Yellows are too trusting of you as it is; you might make it. Before Gabor hunts you down."

"Then why not save your life in the process?"

"Because I need you to stay. I cannot force you, so I will ask." He swallowed carefully, and I moved the knife a fraction of an inch away to avoid cutting him further. "If it were only about finding King Gerhold"—he gulped—"I would let you escape and face the consequences. I swear I would."

I could not tell if this was true, but I could feel the possibility digging into my resolve.

"Please," he said. "Please stay. I'm begging you. I need all the help I can get to save everyone from what you've seen."

"Maybe I was lying."

"If you were not in a hurry, you would plan a better escape. Please, help me save the Tetrarchia."

"It is not your job to save the Tetrarchia."

"What you foretold will happen right when the Council of Barbarians meets in *that tower*!" He pointed behind himself with his thumb, at the Sunset Palace, without moving his shoulder. "That is not coincidence."

I felt myself begin to buckle as I imagined *something* happening at the Council, and then the whole rock crumbling. Then I got angry. I put my weight on my right foot, pushing his sword further down and pulling his belt into his stomach—because I couldn't press the knife farther without killing him.

I had to fight to keep from yelling. "You abducted me, put me in danger, and held my father to keep me in line. You can't play the hero now!"

"Fine," he said. "Both of us have—"

"No! Not 'both of us.' This hasn't been some equal arrangement where I gave as good as I got. Whether or not you *enjoyed* having power over me, you had it."

"Then let's make it one."

A long pause. "One what?"

"Equal arrangement."

"You're joking."

"I am too terrified to joke."

I was about to call this into question, when I realized he was quivering beneath me.

"Go on," I said.

"You agree to stay until we have either unmade the disaster, or been crushed in it—you agree to do all you can to help the Tetrarchia's *people* survive. You get full freedom of movement: no checking in, no limits, armed to the teeth if you like."

"And my complete freedom from this rock once it is all over?"

"That is up to the Prince, but if we survive, I will try."

"How can I trust that you won't throw the Yellows at me the moment I let go of you?"

"Tell me what I can do to convince you."

I didn't know, but I was tempted. The comfortable living, the care for my father, the fact that it was probably too late to get out in time: if I were given my freedom, these would be good reasons to live up to the bargain.

And perhaps it was only repetition, but Lenz was beginning to chip away at me, to make me believe that *I*—monster, broken shit-worm, failure—could save the people of the Tetrarchia. I did not want those who had been beaten down as much as I, worse than I, to suffer all the more. My family had been chased out of every part of that quartered country, but I loved its peoples even so. They were motley and divided, but they were, all of them, *my* people.

The four monarchs would be in one place, so near, when everything fell apart, when this rock broke and the rest of the country was subsumed by war and chaos. He was right, damn him, that wasn't a coincidence, and I was close enough to do . . . what?

I had already risked my life just to get Eight-Toed Gustaw from Down Valley Way his inheritance, and my family would have died without me to support them. The end of the Tetrarchia was so much larger, and yet I was risking no more. Perhaps dignity, but what is dignity to a fraud? I had risked my life for less so many times, and now I was going to run when I could save *everyone* in all four kingdoms? Or rather, when there was even the slimmest chance that I could save them?

I pulled the knife away, but not too far, and maintained my position of power over Lenz.

"I hate this," I admitted. "It feels like you're *granting* me freedom."

"I came here to grant it," said Lenz, slowly rubbing his throat. "But last I checked, you took it at knifepoint instead."

"You would have already been dead by now," I said, "if I hadn't come to like Gabor in the last few hours. I'd hate to see him a widower, even if he has made a terrible choice with his life."

Lenz smiled. "I like him, too."

Some part of me wanted to smile back, but I fought it. "Again, how can I trust you?"

He sighed and looked thoughtful. My knee was getting sore, so I moved my foot from his rapier handle. But I held the knife near his left arm, ready to cut him if he reached for it.

"Neither of us," he said, "want a scene while Gabor is here. I don't want him to know I'm your *jailer*, and you don't want him trying to help me."

"Really?"

"I met him in the *army*, Kalyna."

I sighed.

"I will leave, with my Yellows," he said, "and your family will stay here tonight. It will be monumentally easy for you to fly before dawn. If you don't, then meet me at my barracks, first thing tomorrow. We will have a civilized conversation about where we stand, and Chasiku's role, and this whole blasted mess."

"I meant: How can I trust you the moment I let go of you?"

"Ah," he replied. "I am still quite drunk."

"Will you even remember granting this to me in the morning?"

"I will." He burped. "You have scared my mind into some kind of lucidity, even if my body is still sluggish."

I stepped away from him. I didn't know what else to do. I still disliked him—possibly hated him—but I felt damned inconvenient sympathy for him. Not for his position in this moment, but for how the Prince's service had wrenched him from the one he loved.

Lenz stood, swayed, fell across my desk, and stood again. His hair went in all directions.

"Maybe," I said, "we should not meet first thing in the morning. You'll be hungover."

"I'll manage," he said. I could see him in the light from the windows now, and his left eye seemed trapped in a permanent squint, even though he was not looking at anything. There were glittering bubbles of spit in his mustache. "I will see you in the morning."

"If I don't run away."

"Will you?"

"I think I will."

Lenz smiled weakly and inched his way toward the door, hands against desk, shelf, wall, whatever would hold him up. When he got to the door, he yelled downstairs: "Get my coach ready! And bring Kalyna Aljosanovna's"—another gulp—"bring her sickle up! It's in the backseat compartment!" Then he turned and shrugged at me. As he stumbled down the steps, I also heard him mutter, "And stop hiding the silverware from her. It's embarrassing."

The night wrapped up quickly after that. Lenz and Gabor left together almost immediately, and Papa seemed very tired, so Jördis, Tural, and Vondel all took the hint and retired. The servants had already made up guest rooms for my family in the servant house.

I could hardly believe I was doing it, but once the Yellows were gone, I ran outside to where I had seen the small coach through the window. It sat just outside the walls, in shadow, seemingly empty, but when I approached, a blonde head popped up and Martin-Frederick Reinhold-Bosch opened the door, leaning out into the moonlight. Behind him was a Green. I squeezed my fists until they hurt: escape was right in front of me.

"Things have changed," I hissed. "I can't leave now."

"What have they done to you?" The young blonde leaned farther down, his face inches from mine.

"Nothing! Just a change of plans." And then I added, as though it was a favor to him, "But you are correct: the High General's 'Soul' does not exist."

Martin-Frederick stared at me for a moment, eyes wide.

"Don't tell him yet," I added. "We'll meet again soon, and you and I can decide how best to break it to him. But, for now, you need to leave before you're seen!"

He screwed his mouth to the side. "A pity. I want to know more, and Dreher had a task for you and me to do next. Together. Ah well." He grinned. "Until our next meeting, Kalyna Aljosanovna."

He leaned forward, as though expecting a kiss. When he did not receive one, he bowed theatrically and nodded to the Green.

A whip cracked and the coach rode off, with Martin-Frederick gripping something inside and hanging out of the open door, continuing to bow. I could see his white teeth in the moonlight.

I laughed at myself as I went back to my room. I was not going to escape tonight, with Martin-Frederick or otherwise. I had decided it. I wanted to stay and, well, *save* the Tetrarchia. Ludicrous as it was, I began to think that, while I would likely fail, I had as good a chance of success as anyone else. This made me feel powerful.

Unfortunately, I was not going to have a nice, civilized meeting at Lenz's barracks the next morning—in fact, I would feel quite powerless right away. Of course, I did not know that yet.

PART FIVE

I DID NOT RUN

I slept with my sickle clutched against me, like the good luck charm Grandmother threw away when I was nine. ("Garbage. Nothing can fix *your* luck!") I felt safe, even though I was doomed. I had an ally—I didn't like or trust him much, but I believed what Lenz had said to me that night.

Until I was awoken, violently, by a couple of Yellows I had never seen before. They shook me, yelling something I could not make out, and I knew I had been betrayed. I continued to know this all the way to the Sunset Palace, in hastily thrown-on woolen stockings and a nightgown, beneath a large coat and scarf, shivering in the cold as I still clutched my sickle. They had not taken it away from me, but what would one sickle matter against an army? It was still dark, and the Yellows kept yelling, but I was barely awake and could not retain any of it other than "Prince," "Lenz," and "now."

And, soon enough, I was in the Prince's study. Prince Friedhelm was lying on his back on the couch, flanked by nude statues and covering his face with his hands. Lenz was leaning awkwardly against the Prince's desk, even more disheveled than usual, one hand playing idly with the letter opener, next to a large, round-ish bundle in purple fabric.

When I stepped in, the Prince quickly twisted to look at me, then groaned and resumed his position. Lenz hardly looked at me at all, and I began moving toward him, in order to kill him.

"Oh," Lenz finally mumbled. "You're still here. That's one small bit of good news this morning." He sounded very unenthusiastic.

"Well, if I'd known you were lying," I growled, inches from him now, fingers tight on the handle of my sickle, "I'd have—"

"No, no," he sighed. "You misunderstand. We have a . . ." He could not find the word, and weakly indicated the bundle next to him on the desk.

The bundle was sloppily wrapped, the purple cloth distributed uneasily around it. I became curious enough to give him a reprieve, and warily moved my sickle under my armpit, pressed to my body, and moved toward the bundle.

"Go on," moaned Prince Friedhelm.

I had to pick it up to begin unwrapping it. It was heavier than I expected. I pulled part of the cloth away and saw a blank human eye staring up at nothing. I admit I gasped.

"Keep going," grunted the Prince.

I didn't really want to, but I continued. I saw flesh that was pale and waxy even for Rotfelsen, and then I began to see familiar features. I saw Olaf's face.

"Olaf!" I gulped out as I dropped the dead, heavy thing. A door creaked.

"Yes?"

I turned and, standing in the hidden doorway in the Prince's bookshelf, was the King's face, smiling and winking.

I looked back down at the head, which was rolling along the floor, then back up at the man standing in the doorway. The head thunked sickeningly against a foot of the couch, and the man in the doorway looked down at it. Uncomprehending, at first.

"King's dead," I said.

Olaf finally realized what he was looking at, and began to retch.

A FIGUREHEAD

Once Olaf's breakfast had been cleaned up, he sat on the Prince's couch, staring at the floor. But definitely *not* staring at the head that shared his face, which had *not* yet been cleaned up. Prince Friedhelm sat next to him, and did look down at the head, pushing it lightly back and forth with his foot. They almost looked like brothers, that way.

"No, no, no, no, no, no, no," muttered Olaf.

"There was a note," said Lenz. "Not signed, but the cloth is purple, and . . . well, who else would it be?"

He handed me the note, which, like the head it had been bundled with, was oddly bloodless. The note read:

"WE DON'T KNOW WHAT YOU'RE PLAYING AT WITH YOUR FAKE, SO WE STARTED ON ONE GERHOLD, AND SOON WE'LL GET THE OTHER. WE CAN'T PROCLAIM HIM TO BE A FAKE, BUT NEITHER CAN YOU TELL ANYONE ABOUT WHAT WE'VE DONE. WE NEVER NEEDED HIM, OR YOU, AS A FIGURE<u>HEAD</u>."

Head was indeed underlined. Vorosknecht thought he was very clever, I'm sure.

"Maybe it's a fake," I said.

Lenz and the Prince looked up at me. Olaf didn't move.

"You made one, after all." I waved a hand at Olaf. "Maybe they found some flesh-alchemists to do the same."

Lenz shook his head. "One thing we could not change in our good Olaf, was the teeth. A very trusted doctor took a look, and *that*"—he pointed to the head, which lolled between Friedhelm's feet, staring at the ceiling—"certainly has Gerhold's teeth. It seems Gerhold has also been dead quite some time, and the head was, ah, preserved."

"Oh gods," moaned Olaf.

"He may well have died the night of the Winter Ball," added Lenz.

"Why did you rewrap it?" I asked.

"Because we didn't want to *look* at it," sighed Lenz. "It's King Gerhold VIII."

"No," said the Prince. He clapped a heavy hand on Olaf's back, and the false King seemed about to vomit again, but held back. "*This* is King Gerhold VIII."

"Your Highness!" cried Lenz, standing up straight. "This is really too much!" He limped over toward where all the royalty in the room, alive, dead, and false, was concentrated. "This is ridiculous, you simply can't! Retire Olaf and become King. We can change his face today, get a little loose with the timeline of your brother's death, and then still pin it on Vorosknecht. Somehow."

Olaf nodded quietly.

"It's time to end this farce," Lenz concluded.

"The farce," said the Prince, "would be me throwing the rest of my life away rotting on that throne! I know it's hard for you people to understand, but royalty are *divinely appointed*, each for their own uses. Women like my mother to continue the line, men like my brother to bear the burden of rule, and men like *me* to enjoy its fruits."

"With no consequences," said Lenz.

"Yes!" replied Friedhelm. "When have consequences ever come into it? And you have the gall to tell me to 'end' the 'farce.' I hired you to save my brother's life, didn't I? A fine job you've done!"

"Hired? *Hired*?!" Lenz yelled, putting his hands on the Prince's shoulders and shaking him. "Coerced, blackmailed, kidnapped. Not hired!"

I couldn't help smiling a bit at that. It was like hearing myself speaking to Lenz.

Prince Friedhelm, however, had had enough of Lenz's insolence. He pushed aside Lenz's hands, stood up, and backhanded the spymaster across the face. Quite hard, it seemed. I lost my smile.

"Last I checked," said the Prince, "you were in the army, and I'm a gods-damned prince."

"And princes eventually have to be kings, don't they?" growled Lenz.

There was silence for a moment, as the two men glared at each other. I coughed loudly, and could hardly believe what I was about to say.

"Lenz might just have a point, Your Highness," I suggested. "What's more, your duty aside, our jobs would be much easier without so many layers of fakery folded atop one another."

The Prince reeled to face me, and he seemed an entirely different man than the one I'd first met. *This* gnarled, twisted, angry, petulant face—this was the face of a man about to have someone killed. Someone most people wouldn't miss, even if they knew about her. I calmed myself by remembering that the moment I decided to help Lenz rather than escape the Tetrarchia, I had essentially signed my life away.

So, I continued: "Whatever the morality of blackmailing him, and kidnapping me, think of how much time and effort would have been saved if Lenz had not spent the last month and a half trying to keep me from escaping, and . . ." Deep breath. Why not? ". . . I had not spent it trying to escape. Why, I even told him I thought the Bandit States were invading." I laughed. "A lie to cover my escape. Your brother would still be alive, had you gathered underlings who *cared* to be in your service."

"It sounds to me," said the Prince, "like you two are traitors."

Lenz opened his mouth to speak. But the Prince interrupted him: "And don't say anything about *earning* your allegiance, Felsknecht. I am royalty, remember?"

"You are royalty when it suits you," said Lenz.

I fancied that, by bringing Gabor to the palace grounds, I was responsible for this surge of courage and impudence in Lenz. I liked that.

Prince Friedhelm stared at him for a long time. Olaf moaned to remind us all that he was there.

"Well," said the Prince, turning away from Lenz, "true enough. And it still suits me little. So much time wasted doing a King's piddling chores." He shrugged. "Olaf, you are now royalty, too. King for life, my man." He patted Olaf's back hard. The false king burped.

"Olaf as your figurehead sounds like an awful lot of work," I said. "Why not just take the throne?"

Friedhelm laughed and shook his head as he turned to face us. "He won't be a figurehead. We'll get rid of the Queen and replace most of the Reds, so Olaf can hold dinners, kiss babies, and find a new Queen. Then he and that Queen can secretly have a bastard child of mine, to keep the line going. Lenz will teach Olaf more about politics, and it will be out of my hands." He clapped them together to show this.

I shook my head in disbelief. The Prince hardly seemed to mind. The urge to have us killed seemed past.

"Now," he said, "you two have saved *this* King from a plot before, so please do try to continue doing so. And find out who Vorosknecht's allies are so we can kill the whole lot of them, eh?"

Lenz nodded numbly, I shrugged, and our interview was over. I hardly knew where to start.

A TASTE OF FREEDOM

Olaf, unsteady on his feet, went back through the secret entrance to the King's—well, to his chambers. Lenz and I left as well, through a normal door. When we left, Lenz spent the whole way down the Sunset Palace's many, many stairs cursing under his breath. Once we got outside, he took a deep lungful of crisp, winter air, and looked at me.

"Despite my leg," he said, "I think a walk will do me good. Will you accompany me?"

I was still in my nightgown, but I had a big coat on over it, and a walk sounded nice, so I agreed.

For the first ten minutes or so, we spoke very little. Now and then, Lenz would say something like, "I can't believe him," or "this is a nightmare," and then I would laugh quietly to myself and shake my head. As far as I knew, we weren't going anywhere in particular, and this suited me fine. I was walking with Lenz, but there were no soldiers with us, and I could simply *leave* if I wanted to, and walk somewhere else. What a heady feeling it was. Why, I could have kicked him in the shin (the good one; I'm not that monstrous) and run away, had I desired to do so just a bit more than I already did.

And I must say the surface of Rotfelsen looked beautiful that day, or perhaps choosing to stay put me in a better frame of mind to enjoy it. It was finally, truly winter up here, but not a bitterly cold one, if one was properly bundled. It was snowing again, lightly, but green grass and rotrock still burst out here and there, seemingly reflected back and forth between sun and snow forever, until the colors were dazzling. Winter flowers in light blues and purples could also be seen, beneath barren bushes and surrounded by broken lines of variously sized paw prints. It was all so delicate. Which, of course, then made me think of how *delicate* Rotfelsen itself would turn out to be, along with the whole Tetrarchia. I took a deep breath of sweet air and tried not to think about it too much.

"You don't seem to have told the Prince about my doom prophecy," I said, after we had been walking for some time.

"Sometimes," Lenz replied, "our bosses do not need to know everything."

I suppressed a laugh, but could not help snorting quietly.

"It's true!" he added, looking at me and smiling slightly. "I suspect that if Prince Friedhelm knew, he would try to run, with an entire retinue of servants and soldiers and lovers, causing a panic. I fully believe that the plot we're up against is tied in with the end of the Tetrarchia, so if we have him focusing on the conspiracy, he can remain blissfully ignorant on the rest."

"Or," I began, "escape can still be on the table. You and I, Papa, Gabor." Maybe Tural.

"Your grandmother?"

"Why ruin a perfectly pleasant and harrowing escape?"

"Well," said Lenz, "honored as I am to be included in your escape plans now—"

"Only because I suspect Gabor wouldn't leave you."

"—I still meant everything I said last night, about working together to save this . . ." He looked around at the snow and the rotrock crags and all that. ". . . beautiful, stupid place."

"Now you're getting into the spirit," I said.

"So, I suppose if we must protect the, ah, King, then . . ." The words were souring in his mouth.

I shrugged. "You know how I feel about royalty. But I like Olaf, so if anything, I am now *more* inclined to—"

"Please don't finish that thought, Kalyna," he begged. "I'm sure I know, and I'm sure I do not want to hear it. I'm shaken enough as it is."

I shrugged. I *did* like Olaf, and yet the thought of him remaining as King seemed easily like another path to destruction. But what other options were there? The Evil Prince?

Martin-Frederick also came to mind. He was, after all, in line for the throne. Perhaps a silly young man, who still had room to grow in his life, would be a better choice.

"Now," said Lenz, "let's talk about something nice, like how you certainly meant to kill me a few minutes ago."

I grinned at him. "I thought you had betrayed me."

"An auspicious start to our partnership."

"Don't be silly!" I clapped him hard on the back, and he coughed. "The *start* of our partnership was when you kidnapped me in the middle of the night! Let me handle the auguring—it's my job, after all—and you focus on whatever it is you're good at. Then we save the Tetrarchia."

Lenz sighed. "Have you seen that?"

"Oh, gods no," I laughed. "We will have to bring it about our-selves. So, now what?"

Lenz, still walking slowly beside me, stared down at me. "I was going to ask *you*. As you say, that's your job. Partner."

I wondered for a moment if we were on good enough terms for me to be honest about the Gift, and my original fraud. I quickly decided that this partnership was much too shaky for that.

"Well," I said, "we could always try assassination?"

"Of Selvosch, maybe. But Vorosknecht and the Queen may be too difficult to get to."

In all that had happened, I had almost forgotten how I had impli-cated Queen Biruté. I considered telling Lenz that had been some-thing I made up on the spot, but then reconsidered. After all, who was I to say that I hadn't accused her based on my own intuition? She ran half the Reds, and had been quick to agree with Vorosknecht at the King's Dinner, after all.

"What about the Greens?" I asked. "They're the largest army by far. High General Dreher wouldn't much care for the Court Philoso-pher and the Queen banding together to depose the King, would he?"

"Unless Vorosknecht can expose Olaf, or at least cast doubt upon him. Last I checked, our good High General Dreher is no great fan of Prince Friedhelm. He groups him together with Vorosknecht, as a decadent, soft aesthete."

I looked up, and noticed that we were nearing the Yellow barracks where Lenz lived.

"I may be able to help with the Greens," I ventured.

Lenz narrowed his eyes and looked down at me. "How?"

"Dreher," I began, "and his underling, a little royal named Martin-Frederick Reinhold-Bosch, may have been interested in . . . liberating me from your grip."

Lenz laughed sadly. He lifted a hand, as though to press it to his forehead but, having done that a great deal this morning, scratched his cheek instead.

"And why was he interested in that?" he asked.

"Firstly"—I held out a finger—"because he hopes to learn from my Gift, and I *was* trying to escape. You remember that. Secondly"—another finger—"because, as you've mentioned, he hates the Prince."

Lenz groaned.

"*But*," I continued, louder, "that is because he, like everyone, thinks Friedhelm wants to replace his brother."

"Which he has," sighed Lenz. He sounded very tired.

"Well, we won't tell the High General *that*." I waved it away. "Perhaps, rather than a spy, two prophets, and a doppelganger, our good Prince should have hired a propagandist."

"Oh, he did," muttered Lenz. "Quite dead, now."

"But," I continued, "if I can convince Dreher of the truth—"

"*Part* of the truth."

"Of course, of course." I did not explain to him just how comfortable I was with untruths. "Have you spoken to Chasiku about . . . all of this, yet?"

Lenz shook his head. "The Prince doesn't want her to know about Gerhold. *You* were already in too deep to not tell you."

"See if she figures it out herself," I said. It was a terrifying thing to imagine them doing *to me*, but I suggested it nonetheless. This is why it's awful to begin feeling comfortable: you'll do anything to keep that sliver of comfort.

Lenz grunted noncommittally.

"Why are we at your barracks?" I asked, as we were now quite close. Perhaps a handful of yards.

"Are we?" Lenz looked up. "Oh! I was just wandering, must have been drawn here. Gabor, ah, stayed over last night." Lenz smiled, slightly, in spite of everything. "I hope he hasn't left yet."

"He's too good for you," I said.

"I know."

And that was when someone began shooting at us.

ON GUNS

I admit I hadn't yet interacted with guns much in my life—the people who wanted to kill me generally couldn't afford them. Guns had only been available to the Tetrarchia, in any noticeable numbers, for perhaps a hundred years, and only by the grace of Loasht. Their design schematics, the best ways of making them, and gunpowder itself, all came from that country looming in our north, who sold them to us for a nice profit. Unfortunately, up on top of Rotfelsen, the people who wanted me dead were of a quite better class than I was accustomed to.

Many theorized that Loasht sold us guns in order to push the Tetrarchic kingdoms toward killing each other; others suspected that we were only sold terribly out-of-date models, leaving us defenseless against shiny new firearms; and some believed that the guns had spells woven upon them, so that they could be made to jam, or even explode, from miles away by Loashti "sorcerers." Personally, I think that Loashti merchants only wanted to make money off the strange and combative country to their south, and hardly cared about whatever plots their Grand Suzerain may have been concocting. But this, of course, went against the popular idea of a monolithic, decadent, and inherently sorcerous Loasht bent on our destruction. (Loasht had its own uneasy relationship with so-called "sorcery," but that is another conversation.)

The point is, I wasn't very used to guns. In my time in Rotfelsen, I had *seen* them quite a lot, carried by soldiers, but had hardly ever heard the report of such a weapon since Behrens and his comrades shot up goons in the Masovskan forest. So, when the first shot rang out at Lenz and I, as we were walking idly back from the discovery of a regicide, I simply froze. Startled and confused, I stood completely straight, and stayed completely still.

Lenz's body flopped to the ground, and I looked down at him from where I remained standing, puzzled by his odd behavior. Then I looked behind me and saw puffs of smoke blooming from a small copse of trees, one of many that dotted the surface, pretending that Rotfelsen was a normal kingdom with normal ground. I heard more of those terribly loud noises, and what I now know is the sound of a bullet whirring quite near one's head. I flinched, but did not think to duck.

"Lenz!" called a voice from somewhere in front of me that sounded miles away, with all the noise around my head. I turned back to gawp at the barracks, where Gabor was in the process of dropping from a second story window, twisting, grabbing a windowsill, and then landing on the little filigreed officers' table in front of the building. He broke some crockery and fell into a run along the rotrock ground, drawing his sword.

As Gabor ran in a sort of zigzag toward the trees, a group of eight or so Yellows appeared in and around the barracks door, tripping over each other, tangled up as they tried to draw swords or load harquebuses. Gabor was far ahead of them, untouched by gunfire (as was I, but I didn't realize why just yet), when one of those Yellows took a bullet beneath the eye and fell back against the yellow wall.

Finally, I thought to drop to the ground. It was Gabor's unthinking anger at the thought that Lenz had been shot, and the dead Yellow staining the wall, that made me realize what was going on around me. In my defense, it had only been scant seconds since the shooting began. I turned to Lenz, to see if he had dropped on purpose, or been hit.

"Gabor, be careful!" he cried.

Gabor reached the trees, seeming not to have heard Lenz. The hidden attackers became much less hidden then, bursting out into view and beginning to run from the copse. They wore no uniforms, nor colors of any particular allegiance, and were masked; but I had my suspicions. One of the masked men tried to reload his harquebus as he ran, so Gabor stabbed him, and he fell lifeless to the imported dirt. The rest, perhaps six of them, were out of Gabor's reach.

"Are they *all* running from him?" I asked. "I know he was a soldier, but—"

"Are they what?" Lenz grunted. He craned his head around, then looked back at me. "They're running *toward* us."

I hopped back up and saw that a group of Yellows was still bungling forward to intercept our assailants, but would not reach them before the masked men reached us.

"Kalyna . . ." muttered Lenz. He was still on the ground, trying and failing to pull himself up. This was something much more than his normal limp, but I did not have the time to ask.

I growled at him, which I know I should not have done, before reaching for his hand. He grabbed mine tightly, and I began to pull. Just then, someone grabbed my other *hand*, and yanked at me. I turned and saw a slender man with his face hidden behind a white silk mask, covering all but his eyes. I gurgled something out as I tried to release myself from his grip, still pulling up at Lenz with the other hand.

I was stuck in a very silly looking position, I am sure: bent toward Lenz, my arms out in both directions, feeling dragged between these two figures. I decided to remedy it by kicking the masked man very hard in the gut. I made sure to throw myself into it enough to yank Lenz upward. Both men groaned in pain at the same time, but neither let go. The masked man did double over, however, which put his head near my waist. So—my arms still held between both, like in some circular peasant dance—I decided to knee him in the face.

He pulled himself back up just in time for me to look like a fool, kneeing at the air and going off balance toward him. The masked man had also gotten his breath back, and began to speak.

"No, no, no, no, Kalyna!" he cried. He lifted his other hand, which held a bejeweled rapier, and used the tips of his fingers to pull off his mask. "I'm here to save you!"

It was Martin-Frederick Reinhold-Bosch, and he was grinning at me, his face flushed with the excitement. From his expression, it immediately became clear to me what this whole fiasco was in his mind: the righteous rescue of a downtrodden woman from an evil prince and his lame underling.

"Oh. Balls," I said.

This was about when the Yellows crashed into the masked men, and it all became a great mess of yelling and fighting. The only person with any sense of clarity seemed to be Martin-Frederick himself, whose attention was entirely trained upon me.

"I don't need saving!" I tried to yell over the battle.

Martin-Frederick was about to respond, when Gabor twisted his way into the skirmish and swung his sword at the back of the Martin-Frederick's head. How the young man knew to duck is a mystery to me, but he did. He let go of me and turned to parry Gabor's next few strokes, hopping sideways, the grin never leaving his face.

Lenz's hand was still in mine, and I tried to pull him farther from the fighting. Gabor, still looking furious, attacked Martin-Frederick a few more times. The young man laughed and leapt entirely out of his reach.

"Away!" yelled Martin-Frederick. "There are more coming!"

And with that, the masked men (who I now realized were Greens) began extricating themselves, although none did so as gracefully as their leader. The Yellows cursed them for cowards, while Gabor spared Martin-Frederick only a fleeting glance before he ran over to Lenz. More Yellows were indeed running to join us from the barracks, too late to do anything besides shake their fists.

Once it was all over, there were only two dead: the Yellow shot as she exited the barracks, and the masked man Gabor had killed. There were quite a few light cuts and scratches amongst the Yellows, and Lenz had been shot. I don't know if it was particularly lucky or unlucky that he had taken the bullet in his bad leg.

HONOR

There was a great deal of fussing after the attack, and we helped Lenz over to the officers' table outside the Yellow barracks. It was perhaps a touch too cold to sit outside, but we all had our blood up from the excitement, so it seemed comfortable enough, for the moment. Beneath Gabor's skeptical eye, a Yellow was conducting rudimentary field medicine on Lenz's leg, to staunch the bleeding while we waited for the flesh-alchemist.

Once Lenz's patching was finished, he sat very still, breathing in and out slowly, while Gabor sat near him and tried very hard not to hold his hand. I stood over both of them, and decided to speak in Skydašiavos, just in case. The Yellows near us kept watch, but gave us space to talk.

"They were trying to rescue me," I said to Lenz. "That was why their shots never hit me."

"From whom?" asked Lenz, in the same language. It sounded like he knew the answer.

"From the *Prince*," I said, letting that word stand in for, *the evil, scheming Prince who has coerced us into his service and supplanted his brother.*

"Hm," said Lenz.

Gabor hardly seemed to mind that we were speaking over his head. He was thinking his own thoughts.

"What a mess," I grunted. "Remember how we wanted to make them our allies?"

"Who?" said Lenz.

"That was Martin-Frederick Reinhold-Bosch," I replied. "I suppose that he, or High General Dreher, decided to speed things up. To 'help' me."

"Dreher?" Gabor said suddenly, looking at me. "What about Dreher? In Rotfelsenisch, if you please."

Lenz leaned over and said quietly to him, "I suppose those were Greens."

"I killed a Green?"

"Most like," said Lenz. He looked sad.

"Well," sighed Gabor, "isn't that a pity? As a retired Green myself, I don't much relish the thought of fighting more of them." He shrugged. "But there's nothing for it, yes?"

"Nothing for . . . What do you mean?" I asked.

"Their leader, the young one"—Gabor smiled warmly—"I'll need to fight him again."

"What? No!" I gasped, running around the little table to Gabor's side. "He was trying to help me, he thinks that our boss is attempting a . . ." I silently mouthed the word "regicide." Then I continued: "We're on the same side, so we should—"

Gabor shook his head. "First he shot Lenz, then neither he nor I had a conclusive victory."

"Gabor, I'm fine," said Lenz. "Just a wayward bullet lodged in flesh that's already thickened and scarred. It isn't as though he was after me, and even if he was, it was a misunderstanding. And he certainly wouldn't know that you and I are . . . what we are."

"Not the point," laughed Gabor. "Lenz, it's not even about you, really. We crossed swords and all that."

"I'm sorry, is this about *honor*?" I hissed. "What a ridiculous thing. We are trying to—"

Gabor turned to me and grinned. "Yes, but don't worry about it. Why, when I was younger, some of my closest friends were those whom I'd fought first. I may well bind your alliance!"

"And if one of you dies?" I asked.

"Then one of us dies." He shrugged and smiled. "That's a swordsman's life, you know?"

Gabor seemed entirely at ease. I looked at Lenz imploringly, but he was too busy staring at Gabor with a mix of affection and irritation.

TSAOXELEK

Lenz insisted that I be escorted by Yellows at least for the rest of the day. So far, my new freedom had involved one trip with Yellows to the palace, where the King was dead, and one trip back, with Lenz, during which he had been shot. Now I did not feel particularly free. One of the Yellows that escorted me was Dagmar, and she seemed eager for more trouble.

"I heard about *this* whole fracas too late," she bemoaned, pointing a thumb backward at Lenz, whom Gabor was helping up. "You need to stop having so much fun without me."

Dagmar's presence was welcome to me now. That lean body would enact violence to protect me. She felt like safety.

I hoped very much that Lenz and Gabor were going to go have it out, and that Lenz would talk Gabor out of trying to fight the annoying young Martin-Frederick Reinhold-Bosch. I still wanted to make High General Dreher our ally, and I also did not want either Martin-Frederick or Gabor to get killed.

I felt strange when I returned to my servant house, like the world around me was vibrating, but no one else noticed. There were no longer Yellows stationed outside the house, and Dagmar and the other left entirely once I'd entered. I supposed this was freedom.

Everything inside was quiet, as it was the day after the Sun's Death, and it seemed all the residents were milling about or sleeping off their food and drink. Unfairly, I found it distasteful that people could go on about their normal lives when the King was dead, an impostor was on the throne, and everything seemed to point, unerringly, toward the most awful collapse.

Jördis must have been up at some point because she was napping in the first-floor alcove. I looked down at her, and wondered what she knew about what her master was up to.

I lay down in my bed and tried to think of what in the world I should do next, but it all just seemed too big, and my onrushing end seemed assured. There was a knock, and I sat up to see Tural standing in the doorway. I had not even closed the door to my room.

"So," he said in his brusque Rotfelsenisch, "what was I a part of last night? Eh?" He was a sinewy thing, leaning a shoulder on the doorframe. Was he always so handsome, or only when he was quiet?

I laughed weakly and sat up. Last night seemed so long ago.

"First there was the King's Dinner," he continued, "and I asked no questions. Then you asked that I bring your boss' friend, and still no questions."

I nodded wearily. He was right to be fed up with me.

"But, I bring him and then . . . something strange in your boss, yes?"

"Yes," I agreed. "Lenz has . . . kept me a prisoner here, until now," I said. "And I brought Gabor in as a way to threaten and control him in return." I smiled awkwardly until my cheeks hurt. "And that is that."

Tural looked unhappy, concerned, disapproving.

"But," I added, "we've sorted it all out, and I'm no longer a prisoner. Everything is fine, and Gabor is safe!"

"Really?" he asked.

"Yes. I promise."

"If you're a prisoner, I'll—"

"I'm not."

"All right," he said. "Good. Because I am not sure how I would have ended that sentence. All right. Yes. All right. The next time you need something from me, even if it is just to talk, Kalyna . . ." he grinned. "Just *tell* me."

"I will. And Tural?"

"Yes?"

"I stole your knife."

"Yes."

"Sorry. You can have it back."

I somehow pulled myself to my feet and picked the knife up from where I had dropped it the night before, after deciding I wouldn't open Lenz's throat. I walked up to Tural and tried to hand it to him. He did not smell like fruit today.

"Keep it," he said. "But next time you need something that's . . . not right, you tell me, yes?"

"I will."

"Good nap." He turned to leave.

"Tural?"

"Mm?"

"What's your surname?"

He stopped. In Quruscan, surnames were often secret from any who were not close to one's family. Descriptors and nicknames were used to tell people apart, not unlike certain Masovskans, such as Eight-Toed Gustaw from Down Valley Way.

"Why?" he asked. "You've spent time in Quruscan, you know better than these Rotfelsens."

"Are we friends?" I spoke Rotfelsenisch, but used a Cöllüknit word for friend.

He sighed. "We are."

"And I am also Quru, and you know mine."

He laughed. "Aljosanovna is different, and you know it. But I'm Tural Tsaoxelek."

I had suspected.

"Thank you, Tural Tsaoxelek."

"Tural will do," he said. "Good nap." He left.

Tsaoxelek. The Quru name Chasiku had claimed to see appended to mine in one possible future. Were she a fraud, like me, she would have needed to find out that Tural and I had been very lightly flirting, and then somehow discovered his secretly held surname. I was more and more inclined to think she was the real thing, which led me in some troubling directions. First, that there *was* some sort of great light beneath Glaizatz Lake, playing into whatever High General Dreher believed, and contradicting what I had told Martin-Frederick. Second, that I was probably going to die down there. And third, that there was indeed a whole other family (or even collective of families) of people with some other version of the Gift, while I was still bereft of it.

None of this convinced me to jump on Tural the next chance I got. In fact, it made me more wary. The weight of possibilities. But if Chasiku's Gift was real, and did in fact see futures in a different fashion than Papa's did, there was at least a small chance of a future stable enough for Tural and I to both be alive and married. If so, how could I make such a world possible, whether or not Tural and I became joined within it?

Romantic entanglements, and something beneath the lake, together led me toward one place: Martin-Frederick Reinhold-Bosch. If I could convince him (and through him, Dreher) that we were on the same side, then we would have a civil war of Yellows and Greens against Purples, probably with the Reds split. I didn't much like the idea of a war at all, but if this could happen before the Council of Barbarians, perhaps the end of the Tetrarchia itself could be avoided.

This was when my mind fully seized upon the idea of putting Martin-Frederick on the throne. After all, between the false king and the evil prince, why not someone who at least had potential? He was young yet, but that meant he had time to become someone better, and he certainly knew more about the workings of the court than Olaf. Not only was he likely the best choice, but how better to get the Greens onto our side? Surely Lenz could put together some family trees that would nicely paper over the succession, if Friedhelm allowed it.

With the possibilities buzzing in my head, I wrote to Martin-Frederick.

I hope you will give me a chance to explain.

—*Warm feelings, K*

I summoned a courier, but those who served my house had grown accustomed to not being called on by me, and he gave me a blank look for a long time before finally dashing off. Then I fell into a dreamless night's sleep.

GABOR

"Just how good are you?" I asked Gabor.

"Great!" he laughed. "At what?"

"With a sword. How good with a sword?"

"I get by," he said, with a smile that suggested he did more than get by.

In Papa's original vision of a meeting between Lenz and Gabor, he had seen every detail of the house deep in its cave, with its lattices and orchids. Specifically, he had seen a sign that said "DUNKEL CAVE." This is how, after some time with a map of Turmenbach, I had been able to tell Tural where to find our guest for the Sun's Death.

Now I was in the home Gabor had, until recently, shared with Lenz in the (I thought) whimsically named Dunkel Cave, well underground on the south side of Turmenbach. Gabor and I were sitting out on his veranda, which was lit with blazing torches and looked out over a garden of cave plants: huge mushrooms, multicolored mosses, wrinkled liverworts, and broad green leaves that somehow caught trickles of sunshine, or something like it. Snow was piled up in the corners, though I was unsure how it had gotten there.

Gabor was in a very large housecoat that had almost certainly been made from a rug and, despite giving off a sort of languid noble air, had served me tea himself. I saw no one else in the relatively clean house. Lenz must have decided not to tell Gabor that I had planned to bargain with his life at the Sun's Death, because Gabor seemed happy to see me.

"You get by?" I asked him.

He nodded. "I got through the 'Skirmishes,' fought off Bandit State raids many times, and these days I do little but garden and practice swordplay." He looked out at his mushrooms and smiled, then opened his mouth to continue and hesitated, looking a little embarrassed.

"I . . . come from an aristocratic background. Strictly minor, but nonetheless I grew up expecting to spend a few years under High General Dreher and then, you know, live on family money forever." He shrugged, and stretched out the next word far too long. "Buuut being disinherited for . . . well, you know"—he winked—"doesn't suddenly change one's habits. Working every day comes naturally to Lenz; I tend to live off our pensions and what he makes, and when things run scarce, I hire out my sword, here and there."

"You're that good?"

"I hope so. In all honesty, most jobs only require a basic competence."

It occurred to me that if Klemens Gustavus had not been so insistent on hiring giant protectors, Lenz and I might have met Gabor in the alley by the poppyhouse. That would have been interesting.

"How much do you charge for a little light stabbing?" I asked.

"Oh, I'd never charge a friend."

I felt a pang of guilt, took a deep breath. "You *do* know Lenz and I aren't friends, yes? We work together and don't get along."

Gabor raised an eyebrow. "Did I say anything about Lenz?"

I wasn't used to someone being so quick to call themselves my friend; it made me uncomfortable. What did he want from me? Where was the catch? Was this how life went for people who were able to live in nice, clean, safe buildings? I expected to wake up covered in pig shit again, still drunk, still fifteen.

"We *are* friends, aren't we?" Gabor added.

"I . . . suppose so."

"Good, good!" he laughed, patting me on the shoulder. My tea spilled. "Now, Lenz has told me you're no slouch yourself. Why do you need me for your skewering?"

"I don't. I was hoping to talk you *out* of stabbing someone."

"Why, who?"

"The young Green. Martin-Frederick Reinhold-Bosch."

He deflated slightly, but kept up his smile. "Oh! That one. I don't plan to stab him. Just a few nicks."

"Must you fight him at all?"

"I'm sorry, Kalyna, but we have already had this conversation. And I'm sure the young man would understand as well."

"Perhaps. But he hasn't been in real war, you see."

"This isn't about *war*, Kalyna." Gabor sat back, thoughtful. "Technically, I've never seen war either. Just the Skirmishes with Skydašiai because the Tetrarchic kingdoms can never go to 'war' or the whole thing would fall over. Just, you know . . . slap-fights between brothers." He laughed at the phrase, and then his smile dropped away. "But slap-fights in which I *slaughtered* my Skydašian countrymen, sometimes while they begged for mercy. Because I was told to do so. And we were all so young: children, as I would measure it now. Younger even than this Martin-Frederick."

He became quiet, staring past me and pulling at the brown hairs of his eyebrow.

"I'm sorry, Kalyna, where was I?"

"Your fight with Martin-Frederick isn't about war."

"Oh! Yes, quite right. *War* would be hunting him down and slaughtering him. Like I slaughtered the man who first shot my poor Lenz in the leg." He clicked his tongue distastefully. "This is honor, a duel, a challenge. You may find it silly, but men like Martin-Frederick and I, who get by on our swords, just like to know whether or not we're better than each other."

"But, Gabor, you must understand, not only are the Greens an important ally for us to have, but Martin-Frederick is also my friend." Was he? I wasn't sure.

"And, as I told you, after this he may well be mine. It really does often work that way. There's something *intimate* about a duel. And they hardly ever really end in death. Usually a cut, some scars."

"Did you and Lenz ever duel?"

Gabor let out a laugh from deep in his gut, quite unlike the pleasant one he usually had. "Gods, no! He never would have stood a chance. That's not the kind of intimacy I mean." He screwed his mouth to the side. "Well, *sometimes* it was. Before I met Lenz." Gabor leaned forward and patted my hand. "But I promise you, Martin-Frederick is too young for me."

"He is not that kind of friend." But I was thinking more and more that he might be a halfway decent king, compared to the other options.

"Yes, of course," said Gabor. "But you'd prefer I not kill him."

"Very much."

"Well, I don't intend to."

"But can't you—"

"We will fight, Kalyna. And it will work out for you. You'll see."

I sighed and looked away for a moment, admiring his garden. Then I looked back, brow furrowed.

"How did you mean '*see*'? Lenz has told you what I am?"

"Of course! A soothsayer."

I smiled as I felt myself slip into lies, confidence games, and false charm—as surely as if I'd been back in our tent. Gabor had been so quick to tell me about himself and his past, he seemed almost desperate to know what I thought. Somehow (I can't imagine how) he must have gotten the idea that my opinions *mattered*. What's more, as Lenz still believed my great fraud, so too did Gabor. Doubly so, perhaps, as he hadn't spent weeks failing to get useful visions out of me. I wondered if Lenz had told him about Chasiku.

"Gabor," I continued, "the better I know someone, the weaker my Gift becomes concerning them. If we *are* to be friends, this may well be the first and last time I can tell you anything of your future."

He nodded and leaned forward. I put out my hand and took his; it was calloused and lined.

"You want to know whether you win."

He nodded. I could tell from the set of his jaw that a disastrous future vision would not stop him from what he felt he needed to do. The duelist, sellsword, and soldier in him did not particularly fear death, or killing.

"Well, I admit that I have been trying to see it, and it's been hazy. Part of why I came down here, Gabor, was to see if I could 'part the mists,' so to speak."

He was hanging on my every word.

"It could be," I continued, "that your own indecision has been causing the future to be cloudy. Perhaps, even as you told me it would be a harmless duel, you also saw young Martin-Frederick as a man who'd tried to kill Lenz." I did not tell him how close *I* had come to killing Lenz.

"Well . . ." he muttered. "Well, of course. And Lenz has been kept up there, away from me, all this time."

"But I do believe you have firmed up your resolve, Gabor. After all, I'm seeing much better now."

"And?"

I smiled broadly. "Gabor, I will not tell you who wins. That would take the fun out of it. But I will say that, if you go easy on the boy, you two will indeed come out of it with just a few scratches, and as life-long friends."

Gabor slapped his own knee and sat back, full of wonder. It had been almost too easy. When was the last time someone had gone into a reading trusting me so much?

"Well, that's lovely, Kalyna! So good to know neither of us will die."

I hoped very much that I had made the right choice.

A BRIEF GLIMPSE OF LOVE

I spent the way back to the surface imagining Gabor and Martin-Frederick as fast friends after a few sword exchanges, followed by a future in which Martin-Frederick was king, and Gabor his right-hand. I tried very hard *not* to think about what would happen if Gabor, puffed up by my "prophecy," decided not to take the duel seriously.

I went back to the servant house, where my family were being moved into new lodgings: Lenz had used the Prince's name to empty out two rooms on my floor; the Lavatory Captain was unhappy about leaving, and I missed him.

I needed to speak to Papa, and the sun was already setting in the early afternoon when I went into his new room, which was on the other side of Tural's from mine. Grandmother's was far at the other end of the floor because Lenz was merciful.

I didn't knock before entering. Papa was propped up in his bed, wearing his coat and three layers of blankets.

"Welcome, stranger," he cried out in Masovskani, "to the tent of Aljosa the Prophet! In this humble place I will untangle the strands of fate that— Oh! It's you, Kalynishka!"

I felt the warmth of a real smile in my cheeks and took his hand. "You are peppy today, Papa!"

"Of course!" he chirped. "We stay in these new rooms tonight, and then we leave Rotfelsen tomorrow!"

I felt my face tighten in an attempt to not frown, as showing my feelings would only make him feel worse.

"No, Papa, we will not be leaving tomorrow."

His face fell. I was a monster. He slumped down and lay on his side, and I leaned down to look into his face.

"When will we leave?" he asked.

"When I have saved the Tetrarchia." *If Prince Friedhelm allows it.*

He looked thoughtful, and this overrode his sadness. "That sounds like a big job."

"Not everything about the Tetrarchia; just from the great doom that you saw."

"Oh. Oh! That, yes." He smiled now, from his sideways head. "I still see it, you know. Now and then. Is it soon?"

"Very."

"Oh, good!"

I knotted my brows at him, and Papa actually noticed my reaction.

"Good because that means we will leave soon!"

"If I can stop it."

"Oh, you will, Kalynishka." He struggled and wrenched his right hand out from under the covers to pat mine with it. It was warm and sweaty. "I know you will."

"Have you seen that?"

"Oh, no!" he chirped. "Just death and destruction. Entrails, shattering, so on, so forth, so good. But I know you will because you are my Kalynishka!"

I felt warmth and happiness and quickly doused them both. I had no right.

"Perhaps, Papa, but I need more of your help, if you can give it," I said. "It should be much easier than last time!" I added quickly.

Papa nodded. He still smiled.

"The man you saw before, whom you met at the Sun's Death? Gabor?"

It took him a moment, but then he nodded. "Gabor. Yes. Yes. I do hope I did a good enough job before with finding what you needed, and keeping the secret."

"You did wonderfully, Papa." I embraced him. "You were as focused and wily as you have ever been. It was a joy to see." I meant it, too.

"Why . . . why thank you, Kalynishka."

I moved back, hands still on Papa's shoulders.

"Gabor will be fighting a duel soon," I said. "Can you see it?"

Papa bit his lip and rolled his eyes up into his head. Unfortunately, this was when Grandmother opened the door and shrieked.

"You! You little . . . little . . . *shirker!*" she cried. "Get away from him. *Get away from my son!*"

She walked up slowly, but I sat unmoving and stared at her, like a fish blinded by the light of a wiggly little shrimp. I didn't move or react until she slapped my face with her leathery hand. I blinked and continued to stare at her. Then Grandmother removed her pipe and hit me on the top of my head with it.

That was when I stood up. My cheek stung more from affront than physical pain, but the top of my skull ached, and I couldn't help rubbing it like a chastised child.

"Do your job yourself, you broken thing, and trouble my son no more!"

She then let loose a stream of Cölluknit curses that I will spare you. Cölluknit curses, you see, are too long in their original forms to be used effectively, and so are shortened when screamed. This means that a literal translation, without the context that comes with knowing the language *and* the people, is inoffensive and nonsensical. She screamed things like, "Green shoe blue rock dead fish old king," in rapid succession, a total of maybe one hundred words. I, of course, knew that just two of them (you may guess which two!) were enough to mean I was made of feces scraped from the backside of Quruscan's greatest pervert. The economy of it all is stunning.

She stopped when someone else who understood what she was saying interrupted.

"What *is* happening in here?" yelled Tural, also in Cölluknit, from my father's doorway. "By all that is just, I've been trying to conjure for the past hour!"

"And who are you?" screamed Grandmother.

"Grandmother, you've met him—"

"Kalyna, is your family going to be this loud—"

"I will be as loud as I—"

I actually put my hand over Grandmother's mouth. I held it firm. She tried to bite me and yank down on my arm, but failed at both.

"Tural. Sorry we disturbed you, but *out*." I pointed to the door with my free hand.

Tural left. He looked angry, but he always looked angry when he conjured, and this was my family, so I didn't much care just then.

Speaking of my family: having given up on biting, Grandmother licked my palm to make me let go. I did so, recoiling and wiping my hand on her scarf.

"You will rely on my poor son for nothing else, monster," she muttered.

"Even if it kills us?"

"Even if it kills everybody."

I looked down at her for a moment. Had she seen the end? If so, she would never act on it. I strangely admired her restraint.

"Fine," I said. "I'll find this future another way."

She raised a thin, white eyebrow, and the tattoo above it crinkled. "What other way?"

I couldn't help grinning. "You and Papa aren't the only ones up here with the Gift."

Wonder came into her face. So neither of them had seen Chasiku, it seemed. No great surprise; they had never been near her, and they already knew me too well to see my future.

"Not the only . . ." she mumbled. "You don't mean that you . . . Kalyna, have you . . . Kalyna my child, have you awakened . . . ?"

Then I saw it in her eyes. She thought I had the Gift at last, and with that thought there was hope, as well as something else. Something I had seen moisten Papa's eyes many times, but never Grandmother's . . . except, when she was looking not at me, but at her son. I almost gasped.

Love. She was filled with it; seemed to stand up straighter.

"No," I said. "There's *another* soothsayer here."

Grandmother slumped into the chair I had left. The love left her eyes and she stared at the wall.

I must admit that I *savored* this moment. It's foul, but I did.

"No," she said. "No no no, that's impossible."

"But true," I replied, leaving. I began to laugh at her in an ugly way. A real laugh.

"Impossible. Throughout history there has only been our family, one at a time, through the generations."

"Now *that*," I said from the doorway, "is impossible. A line like that could be wiped out so easily. There must have been someone else." I continued laughing at her, from my gut.

Grandmother looked up, her face twisted with anger and crumbling, poisoned love. "Take me to this fraud."

"No."

"Freak! Monster! Take me to this faker now!"

"No, Grandmother."

I slammed the door on her because Grandmother always brought out the best in me. When I walked by Tural's room, his door was closed.

I did go ask Chasiku about Gabor and Martin-Frederick.

"Why?" she snapped. "Don't you worry about *your* death, about what will kill everyone around us? Why these two?" She was sprawled across her bed, on her stomach, talking into a pillow.

"Because a lot depends on it. Can't you just try?"

"Yes. Yes. Fine." She was silent for a moment, then, "No, afraid not. I can't pick two ridiculous Rot men dying out of the hundreds that I see all the time."

"Great. I am glad you tried so hard. What uniforms are those hundreds that are dying wearing then?"

"All colors. I say, don't you see *anything*?"

"My Gift is being stubborn."

"Sounds like a good problem to have."

And she would say nothing more to me that day. I hoped this counted as "working together" enough for Lenz.

When I returned home, I had a note from Martin-Frederick. He apologized for having been so busy lately, and asked that I join him in a bit over a week in Turmenbach, at the Grand Opera House. If I could just get him, and through him, High General Dreher, on our side, then we would have Rotfelsen's largest army. We could save the Tetrarchia. Then we could accuse Vorosknecht of (genuine) regicide, and the Prince could abdicate in favor of Martin-Frederick, saving Olaf from continuing his charade. We could save my father.

I wrote him back to say I'd be delighted.

A Battle Written in Stone

Rotfelsen had finally, truly found its winter. Snow was now piling up and the winds chilled the bone, although it was nothing like what must have been happening in Masovska's Great Field just then. Down in Turmenbach's stage district, only slivers of sky were visible, and yet the streets were piled with snow. I gazed idly out the window of a carriage that I had hired myself, passing lanterns and snowdrifts. For the first time, I realized Turmenbach was beautiful, in its way. Pity.

The thin crack of sky became a rough circle above as the carriage splashed into a great rotrock cavern. The door opened, the driver said, "Ma'am," and flourished, and I stepped out into the cavern that served as Turmenbach's Grand Opera House. It was somehow far colder than the surface, and the walls were covered with great divots in no clear order or pattern. At the far end was one great craggy outcropping, which I would soon learn was the stage. All throughout was the clanking of the shovelfolk doing their thankless duty.

Shovelfolk were teams of men and women dedicated to keeping everyone from getting buried. They hauled away snow, melted it with torches, carved out walkways, hacked at ice, and were ignored by the people around them. To the citizens of Rotfelsen, they may as well have been alley bats snatching up mice. If Rotfelsen ever saw *real* winters, the shovelfolk would have been heroes of the realm. Instead, it was a seasonal vocation forced upon the destitute, excepting a handful of nobles who "selflessly" joined this group to feel like they were in charge of *something*, the way a noble was supposed to be.

Groups of shovelfolk were guiding the snow into a great pit on the right-hand side of the stage, where another group had torches to melt it. Up on the stage, holding a shovel that was only used to point while giving orders, was Martin-Frederick Reinhold-Bosch. He wore a doublet of red, green, purple, and yellow, all very shiny and gaudy and spreading over his torso in various patterns. The four colors of Rotfelsen's government gamboled up and slashed through his doublet in perfectly equal amounts, except for pinpricks of green that littered everything. It was all quite impressive. He also had a cadre of four Greens keeping an eye on him.

"Ah!" he said when he saw me. "You came!" Martin-Frederick vaulted down from the stage, and I admit I was impressed to see him not slip on the sludge. He threw aside his shovel, and the rest of the shovelfolk continued to work just as well without his supervision. His was a vanity position to show how much one of Rotfelsen's royal sons cared about the people.

I put out my hand for him, as I forced a smile. "Yes, well, I am free to come and go as I please."

He kissed my hand. Then the young man stood up straight, still holding my hand, and looked me over for a moment. "I think I like you better in a uniform."

"And I like you better when you aren't shooting at me."

"They were *never* shooting at you," he replied, still smiling. "And I would never touch a harquebus myself. Beastly Loashti things."

He then led me in a stroll, arm-in-arm, around the outer edges of the opera house, under the fiction that he was showing me the place. Huge piles of snow were wedged up against the walls, sagging toward us and waiting to be melted.

"Do you mind," I began, once we were farther from other ears, "telling me what exactly it is you think you're doing?"

"Naturally," replied Martin-Frederick, with a grin. "I am supervising the shovelfolk!"

I sighed. "I mean your *attack*, Martin-Frederick. What were you thinking? What was that all about?"

"But I told you, Kalyna Aljosanovna, it was a rescue!"

"And I told *you* at the Sun's Death that I did not—"

"Well, you know, I thought old Uncle Friedhelm had you under some sort of greater duress than before: that he had forced you to say what you did the night of the Sun's Death. So I talked Dreher into giving me some men to liberate you and put a bullet in the spymaster."

I ground my teeth, closed my eyes, and tried again. "But if I had been under greater duress, why would that have *changed* by the very next day?"

Martin-Frederick raised his free hand and mimicked a gun. "That's why a 'pop' in the skull for the spy, yes? Pity he was only wounded. It all went rather Skydaš after that."

I must have looked confused.

"Old Green talk," he clarified. "Gone Skydaš—gone bad, like that fermented bread they eat. You understand."

Now that I had begun to appreciate food, I had another reason to hope the Tetrarchia would remain: I needed to try this bread.

"Fine," I said. "*Thankfully*, Lenz is still alive."

He stopped walking, almost yanking me backward just by standing still. "Now, Kalyna, I say! I almost begin to wonder if I shouldn't have tried to rescue you at all!"

I let go of his arm and turned to face him. "You *absolutely* should not have. That—!" I realized that my voice was echoing, and the Greens were looking my way quite intently. I continued, quietly: "That is what I have been telling you, over and again. What I don't know is why you would not listen to me until now."

Martin-Frederick Reinhold-Bosch put his hands on his slim hips and looked at me, incredulous. "So you'd prefer I left you in Friedhelm's clutches?"

I sighed. "I would prefer that you listened to what I told you, and showed some trust in me."

"And if you were under some sort of, I don't know, spell?"

"What do you know of spells, Martin-Frederick?"

"That some strange person, wreathed in bones, can, from miles away of course, mutter and imitate your downfall. He will burn herbs and chant, and tear at his greasy hair, until you follow the exact routine he is demonstrating for you."

"That is not how spells work," I said, even though I had no idea at time. (In truth, I can say now, he wasn't far off.) "*I'm* the 'mind-witch' here, remember?"

"Well now, I don't think of you as a . . ." He trailed off and, for the first time, his smile seemed to falter a little. Martin-Frederick knitted his brow and looked at the slush beneath. "Kalyna Aljosanovna, I'm sure I'm sorry. Please do understand that I only wanted to help."

I smiled very nicely and told him I forgave him. Then we chatted a bit about nothing much, and I felt very strange walking casually, arm-in-arm with some kind of prince, inspecting the strange shapes in the walls, while destitute men and women shoveled and carried and cursed all around us.

"You should see this place when it's full of people," sighed Martin-Frederick.

I looked at him, and then at the shovelfolk who were, currently, all around us. I echoed his sigh, but for my own reasons. I supposed it was too much to ask that Martin-Frederick be a better king to his people than any *other* monarch was, but I still hoped he could be improved—molded.

"Your average drama or mummery only half fills the place," he continued, "which leaves space for milling about, and some benches are often brought in. But *The Leper's Five Tits* will fill the place!"

Just in time for its walls to crash down, perhaps. Although physical collapse wouldn't even be necessary if soldiers hemmed in the audience. I suddenly imagined tens of thousands of Loashti soldiers, all with guns more powerful than what they sold us. They could shoot or burn or let trampling do most of the work. In an attempt to stop thinking about *that*, I leaned over to inspect a dip in the wall as Martin-Frederick kept talking.

These dips and gouges and outcroppings slashed throughout the walls played the parts of benches, catwalks, and even elevated private boxes for the rich, complete with velvet pillows. I looked at a shallow dent in the wall near the ground: it looked just like the impressions of spinal ridges that graced the roofs of so many of Rotfelsen's tunnels.

Across one section of this dent was a vertical shape taller than me, driven deeper into the stone, and I tell you there is no way it was anything besides a claw mark. I looked up at the other shapes in the wall, some deep enough to use, some only decorative, and began to see the truth etched out across them: a dip where a head or tail had sunk into rotrock like it was butter, a line where a long body had been whipped across the side, a series of gouges where a grasp had come up with only stone. Everything that could be reached and used by humans had been worn down over the centuries, but the shapes still told a story.

The Grand Opera House had been carved out by a fight between two or more of those thousand-legged burrowers, and . . . something else. Now, thousands of years later, it was like seeing huge, unknowable creatures fight in the darkness through brief flashes of far-off lightning.

Did any of these things still exist? Was worrying about conspiracies a waste of time?

"It is marvelous and powerful to be surrounded by so many people, all enjoying something together," said Martin-Frederick.

"Ah?"

"I have a box reserved for us."

"Yes, of course," I muttered, glancing at an oblong nobles' box far above his head. Its bottom half was smooth from use, but its top half still showed lines like sections of a giant caterpillar. Those sections were interrupted by deeper lines that could only have been teeth; the mouth that held them, when it whipped its prey about and slammed it into the rotrock, must have been circular.

"Martin-Frederick," I began, "did you ask me to meet you all the way down here just to show me where we'll be seeing the opera?"

"Yes! And thank you for accepting," he said. "But I also wanted to show you the Grand Opera House itself." He leaned in eagerly. "Do you wish to know its origins?"

This time, unlike on the way to Glaizatz Lake, I didn't step on Martin-Frederick's chance to tell me about where I was. He expounded upon the major theory of the Grand Opera House's forming, which I had just guessed, and felt extremely smart telling me about it. I nodded and smiled because I was trying to make the Prince and the High General into allies, and possibly Martin-Frederick into a king. He could be a bore, but that certainly seemed our best option.

"And *that* is the only reason you brought me here?" I asked when he was finished.

"Not only," he sighed. "I also rather fancy you, if you hadn't guessed."

"I did not need my Gift to see that," I said. "I'm quite glad you didn't burn our bridge entirely and kill Lenz."

"As am I, now, I must say. But what to do about Uncle Friedhelm?"

"And why can't Prince Friedhelm be your ally?"

"Well . . . I was told that he . . . hmm . . ."

"Besides," I continued, "I never did get to tell you *why* I canceled our first escape."

"It would be quite decent of you to do so," he laughed.

I had a lie prepared for this. A lie to convince the pretty blonde and his boss that I had been feeling out the Prince's true allegiances, and that now I had them, and they were to the crown. Then we would present the High General with Prince Friedhelm and Olaf together, much as we had for Klemens Gustavus. What's more, Olaf would then say that, as he was unable to have children, he was now adopting Martin-Frederick Reinhold-Bosch as his heir. I opened my mouth to begin it, but no one heard me.

"You there, boy!" cried a voice from the entrance, echoing through the Grand Opera House. "Are you ready to give me satisfaction?"

It was Gabor.

A DUEL

"Satisfaction?" Martin-Frederick yelled across the Grand Opera House. "For *what*, pray tell?"

Gabor hopped over a stream of melted snow running out of the cavern, his every movement and every moment of stillness showing great control. It was amazing to watch. This friendly, small man communicated so much that was threatening in a twitch or a blink, and when he steadied the rapier on his hip, it somehow said he wanted nothing more than a fight. The Greens went for their swords. The shovelfolk ignored him, and continued melting piles of snow.

"We didn't finish our last engagement," replied Gabor.

Martin-Frederick, for his part, was equally skilled at showing disinterest. A stifled yawn, loose movements, a wandering eye. I took this to be all part of the game these sorts of genteel duelists played. (I was more familiar with back-alley brawls and the like.)

The Greens who were there to guard Martin-Frederick started toward Gabor, ready to draw their swords. He smiled at them as they stood between him and us.

"Ah, hiding behind Greens again?" sighed Gabor, beginning to remove his left glove, finger by finger.

"Of course not," replied Martin-Frederick. "Do we have some quarrel, sir?"

The Greens did not move out of Gabor's way, but neither did they draw their swords. Gabor removed his left glove entirely, smiling past the guards at Martin-Frederick.

"A disagreement. We crossed swords. I'm sure you remember—after all, *I* was not masked."

Martin-Frederick laughed with what seemed to be genuine humor. "And so you wish to kill me?"

I managed to bite back a protest. This was not supposed to turn deadly: I hoped it was all posturing.

"I wish," said Gabor, "to see who is better."

With his left, ungloved hand, Gabor made a rude gesture. Then he threw the empty glove to the stone ground. Quite a way behind him, on the far wall, the gouges from a great set of ancient claws seemed a wreath about him.

"Then you shall have satisfaction," said Martin-Frederick.

"This doesn't need to be deadly," I hissed at the blonde.

Martin-Frederick Reinhold-Bosch looked at me and laughed. "Of course it doesn't need to be!" He looked at his guards and waved a languid hand. "Out, all of you. Shovelfolk, too. I won't have it said that my loyal underlings helped me to kill this fool."

The Greens grumbled, but looked like they understood, and began to leave the Grand Opera House. The shovelfolk left with much rolling of their eyes, which Martin-Frederick did not seem to notice.

Within a few short minutes, the whole of the great cavern had only three people within it: Gabor, Martin-Frederick, and me. Suddenly I found myself very cold in there, with the snow in huge piles, melting all around our feet, and so few bodies about.

Gabor had done nothing to agree with, or refute, Martin-Frederick's talk of killing. Was this a normal part of the back-and-forth of these things? Was it about cowardice?

"Gentlemen," I implored, moving between the two men. "You are both my friends, and this is all a misunderstanding."

"Then he should apologize for his comment about my being masked," said Martin-Frederick. "I was, after all, trying to save his *friend*."

I bit my lip to stop myself from calling Martin-Frederick a child. That never discouraged a young man from being childish.

"Masked or not, what does it matter?" said Gabor. "I don't care what you get up to, young man, but we never finished our fight. My fingers ache at such a lack of resolution. It is, well . . . unsatisfying."

"But you're on the same side!" I pleaded. "Try not to kill each other."

Martin-Frederick turned to me and shrugged, as though he could do nothing to change the situation.

"I'm sure," said the young blonde, "you won't mind if we dispense with seconds. I am at your service this instant, and Kalyna Aljosanovna will bear witness."

"Naturally." Gabor's voice rose musically.

I haven't seen many duels in my time. I suspect that, had there been a greater audience, these slight, deadly men would have shaken hands, crossed swords, gone back six steps, twirled, or what have you. As it is, they stripped to their shirts, unceremoniously drew their rapiers and, within a second, Gabor had circled to the left and lunged at Martin-Frederick.

The boy pivoted his blade only slightly to deflect this. I learned just how slim my understanding of swordplay was when I assumed, in that moment, that Gabor was off-balance and had lost. He recovered instantly, and neither seemed surprised. He had not expected to hit his mark so early, I realized: he had been giving Martin-Frederick a jump.

And they were off, faster than I could follow. The two men circled each other, swords rebounding. I could not tell the difference between an attempted cut and slapping someone's sword aside. Their eyes never left each other's blades, and yet both stepped effortlessly over and around piles of sludge, or cracks in the rotrock floor.

Within a minute, they had quickened. Each of Martin-Frederick's movements became faster, harder, more controlled, matching Gabor well enough. I had expected the boy to be easily riled and overwhelmed by a professional, but I suppose there was a reason Dreher kept him around.

Martin-Frederick advanced, and Gabor gave ground with each riposte, finding less time for his own thrusts. Gabor began to slip in the melted snow. Martin-Frederick's back was to me, and he seemed a faceless machine. I could see every line of worry on Gabor's face, or at least fancied I could.

I began to have the sinking feeling that this bore greater similarity to a knife fight in an alleyway than I originally thought.

The younger man feinted to the right and then slipped back to the left, bashing against Gabor's defense. He pivoted, striking from one side and then the other, left, right, left, left again. Gabor's back was now against the wall.

My lips were dry, my throat cracked. I had told Gabor that neither would die; *I* had told him to "go easy on the boy."

Again and again, Martin-Frederick's blade was deflected from Gabor's body by only a hairsbreadth. Gabor ducked a stab at his chest, but it cut across the side of his neck. I gasped. He rolled backward to avoid the next, into a low gouge in the wall that held a loveseat. Martin-Frederick seemed annoyed as he jabbed at the rolling figure.

Gabor got to his feet and shoved over the loveseat, which set Martin-Frederick back for perhaps a half second. The younger man jumped forward again, blocking my view. I saw only Gabor's shoulder as he leaned forward, and both men stopped moving.

I rushed up, and saw Gabor's blade sliding away from Martin-Frederick. The young blonde slipped backward, falling into a sitting position on the wet stone. I felt a rush of relief as I saw him there, legs out and back straight, elbows on his knees. He looked like he was catching his breath.

I rushed to Martin-Frederick to see how badly he had been injured. I sat beside him, bracing his back with my hand, as he sat there.

"Martin-Frederick, where did he get you? Are you alright?" The hand on his back came back covered in blood.

"Oops," said Gabor, winding his right shoulder. "Maybe next time."

Martin-Frederick was dead.

BEFORE HIS BLOOD DRIES

Gabor rocked back on his heels. "Sorry about that, Kalyna. I tried!"

I shook Martin-Frederick's body with numb hands. I felt all our chances to ally with High General Dreher, to save the Tetrarchia, going up in smoke. I felt the absence of a young man who had been vital and alive moments before. An arrogant one, surely, but he could have become a better person someday (unlike me), and even a good king. His body was limp. I *missed* him.

Gabor stepped forward to wipe his blade on the front of Martin-Frederick's shirt. I must have looked affronted because when he saw my face, he seemed shocked and said, "I tried to go easy, like you said, but he got me in a difficult position, Kalyna. I couldn't help it. Did you care much for him?"

"Not really," I said to the back of Martin-Frederick's head.

"Well, at least there's that, eh?"

"Gabor?"

"Yes?"

"Run."

"Excuse me, Kalyna?"

"Run. There must be a service entrance in this place. Get out of here and go to Lenz's barracks. He has a secret chamber. I'm going to call for help."

"Now?"

"Before his blood dries. They're right outside, and I need to—"

"I really am sorry that—"

"Later. Go now."

And Gabor was gone, silently into the darkness at an alarming speed.

I took a series of deep breaths, counted to twenty, put both hands right in his blood, smeared some up my arms for good measure, and screamed my lungs out. Screamed like I couldn't gather the faculties for the word "help." Screamed like I was the one dying. I hoped I sounded terrified, as though a man I cared for had been killed by a violence I didn't understand. I hoped I did not sound like I was screaming with frustration at the end of my plans. I hoped that I could twist this into something useful.

I screamed until the Greens were peeling my bloody fingertips from the corpse's clothing.

A CLEAR CASE OF ASSASSINATION

High General Dreher's office—the one *not* in the center of a subterranean lake—was at the top of a Green barracks, and only two rooms larger than Lenz's. I wondered how many secret chambers it had, but perhaps he didn't need them: he had Glaizatz Lake. In all, it was the sort of suite I expected: consciously pared down and near the soldiers. Did the Greens love him half as much as he wanted them to?

The small ruddy man was at a desk covered in papers and knives, and whenever he opened or closed a drawer in his desk, I heard a clink of heavy glass: I'm sure there were many medical ointments and potions in there. The remains of a roast sat at one end of the desk, looking as dull as the one I had eaten on the lake with him and Martin-Frederick. How many of these sad roasts had the young swordsman eaten with the High General? To think that they had been among his last meals was deeply depressing.

Dreher looked at me sternly, but not harshly. He was trying not to scare me, and I was trying very hard to look scared, because it helped me to seem raw from Martin-Frederick's death. I was depending quite a bit on the camaraderie that can be found amidst loss and high emotion.

"So," said Dreher, "his name is Gabor. I know that much because apparently you called him such before . . . Martin-Frederick sent the Greens away." He said the dead man's name as though he was irritated at himself for being irritated by Martin-Frederick's stupidity. "Do you know his family name? Anything else about him?"

"No," I said, shaking my head. I realized I did not actually know Gabor's full name, so that, at least, was not a lie. The rest would be.

"Do you know why he attacked Martin-Frederick?"

I noticed his use of the word "attacked" rather than "challenged," or "dueled."

"I believe," I said, carefully, "he was involved in the, ah, fracas the other day, when Martin-Frederick tried to rescue me."

Dreher sighed and sat back, grunting in pain. "Damn young fool, I never should have let him do it. So this Gabor is a Yellow?"

"I don't believe so, High General." I was unsure, as yet, how far I could go in incriminating Gabor to get Dreher on my side, if I needed to do so. But I knew for damn sure I would not reveal his relationship with Lenz.

"And why didn't you want to be rescued, Kalyna? I could still use your Gift over here, with the Greens."

I leaned in closer, both hands on Dreher's desk. I let my very real desperation at how everything was spiraling out of control, at how it felt that everything I did led toward Rotfelsen literally crumbling around us, bleed into my voice and he looked truly surprised.

"Because I have gotten in good with the Prince!" I growled. "Because I know his plans, and I think you will be surprised. And I have seen something *glowing in Glaizatz Lake* besides! Something strong." I added that last part onto Chasiku's vision: if he thought it was Rotfelsen's Soul, then of course he would want it to be strong. Whatever that meant, for a glowing something or other.

Dreher opened his mouth, then closed it and looked thoughtful. He leaned forward as well, until his face was inches from mine, his fingers steepled and his elbows on his desk.

"Kalyna Aljosanovna, I think you are shaken up by what's happened today."

"I suspect so, High General, but—"

"Please call me Franz. And let me ask you: Did you much like Martin-Frederick, Kalyna? I know that he was fond of you."

I nodded. "He was brave, and kind to me, and pretty. I—" I stopped myself, seeming unable to get out the words, before starting again. "I allowed myself to hope he might keep me as a mistress."

"I think he would have," said Dreher, patting my hand. "Do you think he was assassinated?"

"Gabor is not a Yellow."

"That's not what I asked you. Was it a fair duel?" It was clear from his tone that High General Dreher already had an opinion on this question: he thought it was his enemies coming after him. What he wanted, what he *needed* for me to gain any modicum of his trust, was a confirmation of what he already "knew." And I happily threw Gabor to him.

"Well, Franz," I said, "the fight was *technically* legal and honorable, but he was an older, more experienced duelist who goaded Martin-Frederick to anger." I gulped. "He gave the young man no choice, pretended at little skill, and then cut him down. I believe he was a professional swordsman." This last part was, of course, true. I felt the words curdling in my mouth as I said them, but my old need to say what a mark wants to hear was too strong. I am proud and sickened to say that none of my distaste showed.

High General Dreher sighed for a long time, and it seemed to pain him. "Martin-Frederick," he finally said, "was young and impetuous, but he had so much potential."

I nodded.

"What's more," he continued, "no one assassinates my officers with impunity. We will capture this man, with your help, I hope."

I nodded again.

"Please go home and get some rest. We shall talk more tomorrow."

The High General poured us two mugs of a Masovskan pine liqueur. Very foreign, I thought, for a man obsessed with the Soul of Rotfelsen. Almost "decadent."

As though he'd read my thoughts, he sheepishly said, "It's my one vice."

He lifted his mug, and I did the same.

"To Martin-Frederick," he said.

"Martin-Frederick Reinhold-Bosch," I sighed.

We drank. It warmed me down to my stomach. Or maybe I was warmed by knowing that I had hooked High General Dreher. And all it had cost me was the betrayal of a friend and a pretty young man's death.

CHANCES DWINDLE

"You did what?" sighed Lenz, the next morning.

"Gained High General Dreher's confidence."

"There is a manhunt on for Gabor, who is trapped beneath my room."

"Well, he *did* kill Martin-Frederick. After we both asked him not to fight the duel. Does he mind it?"

"Not as much as he should," grumbled Lenz. "He's mostly worried about his plants."

"Something needed to be done to get the High General on our side," I said. "We're all dead if we can't stop this. So I made the most of a bad situation. And now you can have him near you."

"How did you end up using my lover twice? While I have found none of yours?"

"He was convenient, and I'm too unlikeable to have lovers."

"Untrue," said Chasiku. "Surprisingly."

We had been traveling up to the top of her tower on the pallet as we argued. I had told Lenz about Gabor and Martin-Frederick's duel, of course, but also about Dreher's belief in the Soul of the Nation, and Chasiku's vision of something glowing, which, whatever it was, could be used to manipulate the High General. Chasiku, now, was sitting in the open air, with her back to the view and her head against the metal railing, her arms hanging over her knees.

"Well," I said, stepping off the pallet. "No lovers recently."

"Yes," said Chasiku. "But that can change soon, if you lie."

"I don't care enough to lie," I lied. "And how does your family procreate, Chasiku? If you can't stand to be around people?"

"What do you two want?" she asked.

"To know how your family—"

"What is she up to?" Lenz interrupted me, pointing in my face as the two of us walked out to the railing.

"Why not ask me?" I offered.

"I have." Lenz turned to Chasiku and specified, "Where is she going with this?"

"Hard to say," said Chasiku. "Cause and effect are chasing each other around in my head. There are thousands of actions that she, or you, may take, but our chances of surviving the next month only dwindle. The short version: I don't think she knows where she's going."

"Sounds right," I said.

Then Chasiku looked thoughtful, and added, "Well, *our* chances are dwindling, Lenz. Yours and mine. Kalyna's odds of survival seem to be improving."

"That's . . . interesting," he said, turning to me. "Planning to run out on us?"

I wasn't, but I shrugged. Was I?

"Anything else?" he asked Chasiku.

She shook her head.

"Your Gifts," said Lenz, "have a great number of limitations."

"If soothsayers could pick out the future perfectly," I began, "the first one would have been kidnapped by a king millennia ago, and that king's family would still rule the whole world. Why do you think we suffer in obscurity?"

"Kalyna," said Lenz, "do you really think you can gain Dreher's confidence? Convince him that we're on his side?"

"I do. He likes me, and thinks I could be useful. More fool him. I'll probably tell him some secrets and prophecies to get his full trust."

"What kind of secrets? About Gabor and me?"

"About the Prince, Lenz. Dreher doesn't care about you."

"Fine. Tell him all about Friedhelm for all I care, just don't tell him anything about the King. Do either of you have anything else that can be helpful?"

We didn't, so I went back to my servant house to ponder. Instead, I spoke to Tural for a bit. He was deeply anxious about the Council of Barbarians, which was now only a month away. He had been the Master of Fruit four years ago, the last time the Council was in Rotfelsen, but he only remembered a blur of frantic activity.

He and I then played a strange game where I gave him the names of fruits, and he muttered long sentences about them in return. He imagined different ones together, and wove long histories of each, how they interacted with the culture and times of their land of origin. To hear Tural tell it, none of human history would have happened without fruit. Did you know that the beginning of trade between the North and South Shores of Skydašiai was for apples? This may be entirely untrue.

We talked into the night, and near the end, I found myself wanting to kiss him. I remembered what Chasiku said, and did not do so. As I fell asleep, my thoughts were instead on High General Dreher.

DINING WITH THE HIGH GENERAL

I began to regularly visit High General Dreher for dinner, and we always consumed the same sad, bland roast. It reminded me of myself before palace living spoiled me, but Dreher had access to *so much* good food, which he happily ignored.

On the first day, after some pleasantries about the hunt for Gabor, Dreher began to speak about his vision for Rotfelsen itself, in vague terms. So, I gave him a little push by telling more of what I had supposedly seen beneath his lake. I took what Chasiku had seen, something glowing at the bottom, and embellished.

"Something is down there: something alive and glowing bright that will soon stir. It waits in repose for . . . I'm not sure what."

There was a very long pause. When Dreher rasped, "When?" he was barely speaking.

"Soon. I don't know more, yet." I brought out the old prophetic classic of looking off into the middle distance, as if seeing something there.

"But you said yesterday that it was 'strong.'"

"I did. It cannot be fully viewed, but it looms large behind all I see." Arms crossed, I flicked my eyes back to Dreher's. "The Soul of Rotfelsen," I said.

High General Dreher pounded on the table and jumped out of his seat in excitement, and then moaned in pain, but hardly seemed to care. "I knew it!"

He huffed his way around the desk to me, putting a large hand on my shoulder, and said some nonsense about how even my foreign Gift saw the greatness of the Rotfelsenisch people. I did not disabuse him of the notion as I should have. When I considered a corrective, I pictured the Greens and Yellows killing each other, each thinking the other were regicides, and then the Purples swooping in (probably with mercenaries, as well) to take out the Reds and topple the Tetrarchia. It seemed a likely cause of our country's doom, so I smiled and flattered Dreher regarding the special place of the Rotfelsenisch people in this world. Insensible love of one's kingdom never made much sense to me, but it must have included love of the King, and that was what I needed from Dreher.

Over the next few days, I fed him more about the Soul of the Nation, and about the importance of Rotfelsen as a kingdom. It was easy enough to get Dreher to spend his meals with me, easy enough to show I agreed with his view of the world. I may not know the ways of courtly intrigue and politics, but I have always been a manipulator. Every time I saw him smile at a comment, every time he asked me to come dine with him again soon, I felt a warmth like that of love and friendship. It feels so good to play a role, to feel smarter than the other person, to appear to them as someone who is not *me*.

The strangest part of it all to me was that, even as I listened to Dreher's assertions of the Rotfelsenisch peoples' pride of place in the world, of how the Soul would cure them of foreign corruption and vices, I never stopped finding Dreher personally pleasing. He came across as humble, attentive, and interesting, even when I *knew* he was, at best, our begrudging ally, whom I was deceiving. But then, what did I know? Maybe that *was* the Soul of the Nation down there. The gods have created so many strange and wondrous things in the world.

One evening, I broached the topic of Prince Friedhelm.

"You may," I said, "be surprised at where his priorities actually lie."

Dreher took another bite of his sad roast and laughed. "Are you trying to tell me that our Prince is not an evil schemer?"

"I . . . well, that isn't entirely inaccurate. But a schemer can be useful, and he thinks that the King—"

"Is a fake," Dreher interrupted. "A fake that the Prince has put there. Did you know that?"

I did not have to fake my stunned silence. I knew about Olaf, of course, but was not sure how Dreher had found out, or why he was telling me. One particularly terrifying possibility began to nag at me.

"I . . . did not, High General."

"Franz."

"Franz, I must say, it's hard to believe. Why are you telling me this?"

"Because I want you to understand what your master is capable of, and I want you to use your Gift to help my cause, instead."

"And what is your cause, Franz? I thought I knew, but I begin to wonder." I felt a sinking feeling in my gut.

"Rotfelsen, of course. I have never pretended it is anything else. You have seen its Soul, and so you understand its greatness."

I nodded. I was not sure what else to do. High General Dreher stood up and moved to the door of the office.

"Kalyna Aljosanovna," he said, "I would like you to join myself and some others in an after-dinner drink. The Greens will show you the way while I collect our friends. Please do not call me 'Franz' in front of them."

Our friends. Oh, this was bad. Whatever was going on here, it was troubling.

"Oh, and Kalyna," he said, "Martin-Frederick once told me that your Gift showed you my . . . condition. If tonight you are asked for a demonstration of your powers, use something *else*."

"Of course."

He gulped and looked away, out the door, embarrassed. "Do you know . . . ? That is, how long do I have?" His voice quavered not, I expect, from fear of death, so much as from fear of seeming weak.

"Your condition won't end you any time soon," I said, sagely and with great confidence.

He sighed and nodded, though he didn't turn to look back at me, and left. I was led out of the High General's suite by two very deferential Greens, and had no way of letting anyone else know where I was going.

PLOTS AND PLANS, POTS AND PANS

That night I was wearing a sky blue dress with a dark green (*total coincidence*) bodice, and my sickle, which the Greens let me keep, was slung at my side like a sword. I was taken out of the High General's barracks, and to one of the large mansions near the palace. The Greens were still deferential, but answered no questions.

I was then left alone in a chandeliered parlor full of plush chairs with landscape murals on the walls, but no windows. I listened to the pleasant clink-clank of kitchenware from the next room. Pots were being stirred, and something was being fried. Who was I about to see, and what was Dreher's goal? I had a strong suspicion, but tried to talk myself out of it because, if I was right, the odds stacked against me were overwhelming.

When Dreher arrived, the first thing I saw behind him were great swaths of green and purple. My fears were correct, and I managed to act unsurprised when Court Philosopher Vorosknecht ducked his ridiculous hat through the doorway.

Filling out the room was a group of very rich nobles. One was Selvosch, others I vaguely remembered from the Winter Ball: a woman who had been just a little too drunk, a man who had gotten too excited when someone sat on his lap, and those sorts. So these were the regicides: thirty or so powerful people and their bodyguards. I was introduced to royal advisors, magnates, and priests of a few disparate gods. Vorosknecht did not look happy to see me. Even less happy to see me, almost hiding behind him, was Jördis.

"What is *she* doing here?" the Court Philosopher asked the High General.

"Lending us her power," replied Dreher. "I hope."

Vorosknecht scoffed as though he could not get full words out. I grinned at him.

"Kalyna," said Dreher, turning to me and looking very serious, "you must understand that, though I like you, your life depends on these next few minutes and these fine people."

Vorosknecht almost said something, but bit it down.

"I," continued Dreher, "am going to give you privileged information now. You see Kalyna, we all—you are giving me a look."

Now or never. "You are the regicides. You kidnapped and killed King Gerhold, and now are looking to get rid of his false replacement, along with the Prince, and take over Rotfelsen, removing it from the Tetrarchia entirely."

"This is your prophet, isn't she?" someone squeaked.

"She's a devil," said Vorosknecht.

"Do we succeed?" someone else asked me.

I smiled in that general direction, although I didn't see the speaker. "Looks that way. But things can change."

Jördis was very intently studying the floor.

"I cannot believe you have done this, Dreher," said Vorosknecht. "What does she have to gain through loyalty to us? Put her *below* and forget her!"

At the word "below," many people cringed.

"Wait, wait, wait!" cried Selvosch, pushing his way forward. "Do you . . . truly have the *Sight*?"

I almost laughed at his wide-eyed intensity, but I nodded. "I do. And besides my problems with the royal family—for example, a prince who kidnapped me—I submit to His Brightness Vorosknecht that seeing the future makes me predisposed to side with the winners."

Vorosknecht scoffed, but no fortuneteller or swindler has ever starved by telling someone they're a winner. I smiled and did a very good job of looking at ease.

"So what now?" exclaimed Vorosknecht. "Tell her our secrets—"

"She already knows our secrets," someone said.

"—and induct her into our mysteries—"

"Vorosknecht," said Dreher softly. "She's seen it."

"What?" spat the Court Philosopher.

Selvosch, who was still leaning over me, knew exactly what this meant. His eyes widened.

"*It*," repeated Dreher. He pointed down. "The Soul."

"You can't possibly think—!" As suddenly as he had yelled, Vorosknecht stopped. He pursed his lips very tightly before grunting, "Go on."

I smiled graciously. All my power went into not appearing scared; everything else needed to convince them would flow from that. I told them there was something glowing beneath the lake, in the deepest parts of Rotfelsen. Reactions were mixed; clearly this Soul of the Nation cult was not the only reason for regicide. Some looked bored, some shrugged it off, but Dreher, Selvosch, and some others looked as I must have as a child spending my first winter night in the Ruinous Temple: hearing the low murmur of wintering merchants, looking up at lanterns and animal skins heavy with snow far above me, feeling that it was all quite magical. Vorosknecht looked intently at Dreher.

"Are you sure?" blurted Selvosch. This man who had wielded so much social power at the Winter Ball now seemed so fragile, as though his every belief in the world hung upon what I—whom he'd just met—would say.

"I can't guarantee it's what you're hoping for, but I saw what I saw and would not tell you if it were otherwise."

High General Dreher turned to Court Philosopher Vorosknecht and hunched in his direction, arms out, inviting a response. The Court Philosopher glared, but did not refute me.

"I suppose," he said, very slowly, "the gods would not allow a cursed and deluded devil to see such divine truths. If she has seen it, and seen it *correctly*, which it seems she has, we must believe her." The words were moldy vegetables in his mouth.

I smiled sweetly. A few others let out sighs of relief. No one in the back grumbled, because if anyone disagreed . . . well, they could take *that* up with the Greens and the Purples.

Dreher nodded at a nearby Green to offer me his arm in order to help me up. The High General shrugged apologetically at being too weak to do so himself.

"Now that we are all done standing around and determining that you will not be sent below, let me explain."

Brandy Slings

We all moved into the room where I had heard the melodic preparation, and the conspirators spread out to chat, served drinks by men in green livery. Given the company and the atmosphere, it was no different from a small chamber during the Winter Ball: powerful, well-dressed people talking, laughing, and drinking, surrounded by stunning art none of them looked at.

"Lovely to see you here!" I said to Jördis, a bit too loudly.

It appeared that even her well-honed smile could not match my own false friendliness because she faltered and laughed awkwardly. "Yes, yes, you too, Kalyna."

"It's good that I have finally found something that you truly care about, Jördis." I winked at her. "Or did you just find yourself here, following in your father's footsteps? Perhaps you're hoping it can all pass you by."

She coughed loudly and looked around her. "Well, I . . . I don't know . . . I mean that is . . . Excuse me please, Kalyna."

She showed me that perfect bow again, and scuttled off. I continued schmoozing, and learned more of these peoples' plan.

The plan was that all Tetrarchic monarchs (including Olaf), as well as their advisors, would be killed at once at the Council of Barbarians. The Reds, split between the Queen and false King, and exhausted from preparation for the Council, would be easily overtaken, along with the Prince's degenerate Yellows. The coup would be sprung, and a new age of independent Rotfelsenisch glory rung in to the sounds of clanging swords and harquebus blasts. The deaths of every leader at the Council would break the Tetrarchia entirely and make Rotfelsen a sovereign nation.

But, beyond this clear plan, was a garbled sense of the *why* of it all: there seemed to be little shared by the group beyond "overthrow the government." Everyone had their own reasons: Martin-Frederick (I was told) had in fact *wanted* to be king, Selvosch wanted complete control over all mining with no oversight, Dreher wanted a militarized Rotfelsen free of "corruption," and Vorosknecht wanted "a country based in reason." It was hard to imagine a military dictatorship with an unprepared king and a long list of philosophical rules standing up on its own, all while making less off its mines. Everyone wanted power, but after the breaking up of the Tetrarchia, all their ideas diverged. Did every single one plan to betray the rest? Who would replace Martin-Frederick now? What's more, half of them were mesmerized by tales of a magic being in the lake that would somehow represent all of the cave-bound pink people. Perhaps the only common cause was nationalism at the expense of all else.

But the viability of these peoples' ideal government had little to do with how dangerous they were. I simply didn't want the great, big pimple to pop while I was on it, and for the rest of my home to eat itself.

Given the Rotfelsen-centered nature of their cause, it didn't terribly surprise me that Queen Biruté was, in fact, entirely uninvolved. A Skydašian import was not in high esteem here, so she was meant to die with the other kings and queens. I hoped it was not too late to untangle the mess I'd made by accusing her.

It was cold that night, and I drank what was called a hot brandy sling (which tops brandy with hot water, sugar, and spices), and ate fried slices of reindeer cheese as Dreher explained that he would sweep out decadence and rot. Vorosknecht was visible behind him, gleaming in purple and jewels as he communed with a Purple: a man of about my size with a too-easy and mirthless grin. Jördis tended to hang about behind them. After some time, Vorosknecht approached me.

"And you aren't loyal to this Prince? Or his limping spy?" he asked, loudly.

"You mean the men who kidnapped me?" I laughed.

"Yes, them. How *did* they replace the King?"

I shrugged. "They did that right under my nose, and now I trust them even less, if that is possible."

"Amazing powers you have."

"The fake looks the same in the future as he does in the present," I sneered. "I'm afraid this is all new to me. But at least I can look forward to seeing Prince Friedhelm and Lenz being—ah, what was it High General Dreher said?—sent below, yes?"

Someone behind me choked, just a little, on their drink.

Vorosknecht glared in the direction of the choking, and it stopped. Dreher smiled uncomfortably.

"Ah, Kalyna, there are many here with delicate sensibilities," said Dreher.

I lowered my voice and smiled at him. "But what exactly does it mean?"

A bit of silence, and then Vorosknecht said, "Oh please, High General, you've told her everything *else*."

Dreher shrugged. "There's a building down by Glaizatz Lake. It used to be a prison, nothing too strange about that. Belonged to the Court Philosophers, who could put the wrong-thinking down there."

"What a glorious time," sighed Vorosknecht.

"When control of Glaizatz Lake came to me," continued the High General, "it became mine, but I had little use for it, and it fell into disrepair." He made a short motion toward the Court Philosopher. "But then Vorosknecht told me about the Soul, and we began working together, and put it back into use. Secretly, of course."

"And who goes in there?" I asked, although I felt I knew the answer.

"Our enemies," said Dreher. "It's where Gerhold went, when he was alive. We have others down there who have gotten in our way—Greens and Purples who would not fall in line, that sort of thing—and it's where Martin-Frederick's assassin will go as well. It's always good to have more—we'll use them."

"Now, I feel like this is a stupid question," I asked, lowering my voice, only speaking to Dreher, "but use them for what?"

"Come down to the Lake with us, and we'll show you."

"I would love to. When?"

"You'll know when it's time," he said

"Well, that's all very spooky and ominous," I laughed, letting others hear me. I was happy to play the uncouth commoner: I wasn't going to fool anybody by acting noble or Rotfelsenisch, and it allowed me to ask probing questions.

Dreher seemed pleased with me, and Vorosknecht insulted me a few more times. I didn't learn anything else useful.

"Kalyna Aljosanovna," said Dreher as we were leaving. "Welcome to the New Rotfelsen."

I smiled magnanimously.

SHUDDERINGS

When I got back to my bedroom, daylight wasn't far away. I had smiled and laughed all night, been free of visible fear or discomfort; I had understood the people I was with implicitly, and they had been lucky to have me and all my great power.

I slowly lay down in bed, and proceeded to hold myself and shudder uncontrollably until midmorning. I had to let out every feeling I'd missed. Two extremely powerful men who I'd thought at cross purposes were, in fact, allies. The leader of Rotfelsen's largest army was aligned against me in ways that were entirely irreconcilable. He not only wanted to take over the kingdom, he wanted to destabilize the entire Tetrarchia, no matter how much death and misery it caused.

I could not imagine what chance we had to prevent utter destruction, and once more, I considered running. But I had made my choice. Knowing Dreher and Vorosknecht's ridiculous reasoning only made me want to stop them more.

Apparently, as I lay shaking, Grandmother yelled at me from down the hall, and Papa had one of his spells, in which he cried out and writhed and saw hundreds of unconnected images. That night, once again, I wasn't there for my father.

When I was up, I almost avoided him again: I had gotten so accustomed to not seeing him every morning. But now he was mere steps away, and I made myself go say good morning.

"Oh! Oh, Kalynishka," he sighed from his bed. "Did I miss you last night? I don't remember if you were there."

I almost lied. "Sorry, Papa."

"I know, I know, but you're very busy these days. Running around, seeing people. Today I think you'll hear something important from . . ." He lowered his voice and looked around for Grandmother. ". . . the *other* one."

I raised my eyebrows. "You mean the other sooth—"

"Shhh! Shhhh shh shhh!"

"You aren't bothered by her presence?"

"I'm overjoyed, Kalynishka. She will do your job, and we will leave here."

"Soon, Papa."

"Except for the disaster that will end everything," he said, as though realizing he had forgotten a hat. "That is soon."

"Yes. Papa, do you remember Glaizatz Lake?" I smoothed his forehead; it was dry and warm.

"Of course! I didn't get to visit myself, but you and Mother did."

"Do you . . . know if there is anything beneath it?"

"Like what? I don't believe there's much. The water keeps going down, I've seen that. Down into an ever broadening emptiness. Does that help?"

"Perhaps. Are there spirits there?"

My father was quiet for a long time, leaning against the headboard. He looked out the window, at the wall, leaned over to look at the closed door. We had been speaking a mélange of all the languages we knew.

"Quiet this morning," he said. "Where is Mother, I wonder."

"Father. A spirit? Do you see it?"

"I don't like to look for spirits, Kalynishka. It ends badly."

"How so?"

"Badly."

He would tell me nothing more, and eventually I left. It was eerily quiet as I did so: Grandmother's door was closed, and I heard nothing from her room. I hoped she was sick or dead.

I knocked on Jördis' door, and heard nothing. I knocked again, louder. Still nothing. I thought to myself, *How would Dagmar knock on a door?* And pounded relentlessly, throwing my strength into each impact. Still nothing.

"Jördis? I just want to talk!"

Not a thing. So I went out and walked to Lenz's barracks, flanked by Yellows, for my protection.

TEA COOKIES IN A DUNGEON

When I got down the winding stairs from Lenz's bedroom, into the hidden dungeon where we had once kept Klemens Gustavus, the door of the cage was open wide, and Gabor was performing pull-ups from the bar atop the doorway. At a small folding table, looking over a plate of mottled yellow and brown tea cookies, sat Lenz and Dagmar, the latter of whom was watching the stairs and looking intent.

"Kind of you to join us," said Lenz.

"Well, I've been busy," I replied. "But I couldn't think of anywhere else to go for cookies."

"A gift from Tural," said Lenz.

"We're old friends now!" laughed Gabor, his voice heavy with exertion.

"No tea?" I asked.

"Couldn't get it down without spilling," garbled Dagmar.

She had been so still when I came in, had looked so focused: this had been because of a mouth full of cookies. I began to suspect that she never had serious thoughts, but only wished to do violence, relax, and eat. I envied her that, and realized in that silly moment that I *wanted* her. In some capacity, anyway.

"I hope you've been productive," Lenz sighed. "Did you get the High General on our side?"

I laughed and laughed. "Oh, my sweet Lenz," I said, slumping into a chair. "High General Dreher will never be on our side."

"Hates Prince Friedhelm that much?"

"Well, yes, but that's not why. He's been in with Vorosknecht the whole time: one of the other 'powerful people' Selvosch mentioned to Friedhelm." I let my head fall back against the chair, staring up at the dark ceiling. "It feels like a lifetime ago. Our Dutiful Prince probably should have just joined them."

"Oh," said Lenz. Then: "Oh! Oh gods. Oh no."

I nodded.

He slumped back in his chair and looked at the ceiling. "I never thought he had that sort of lust for power."

"He doesn't," I replied. "He thinks he is doing it for the good of Rotfelsen."

Lenz groaned.

"At least," I added, "there is good news." This was the best way I could think of to frame another one of my great mistakes. "Queen Biruté is *not* part of their plot. You were right, Lenz: what I saw must have been her suspecting us of being *against* the King."

Lenz turned to glare at me. "I knew it," he said.

"Friedhelm said the same thing when I told him the opposite."

"Friedhelm is a fool," Lenz replied.

"Hey!" Dagmar bellowed through more cookies. "Watch what you say about our Prince!"

Lenz froze.

Dagmar swallowed, stared at him intently, and then broke into a laugh. "You should see your face! Of *course* Friedhelm is terrible."

I wondered if she was just having fun, or deflecting his ire from me.

"So then," huffed Gabor, still doing pull-ups, "at best, we are looking at a civil war with the Greens and Purples on one side, and the Reds and Yellows on the other?"

Lenz seemed to sag at the thought. "If we can convince the Queen to join us. And even then, I don't much like the odds. The Greens are so large . . ."

"No," I said. "We will end this before it becomes a war." I grabbed a few small cookies, each about the size of a child's thumb. "I want to avoid as much death as possible." I punctuated this by popping a cookie in my mouth.

"Whoops!" laughed Gabor, dropping down to the floor. "I suppose I shouldn't have killed the young man."

"It's fine," I said through crumbs. "It has ended up making my life easier, and apparently he meant all along to supplant the King in favor of Dreher and Vorosknecht and their ilk." I sighed and closed my eyes. I felt I was already forgetting Martin-Frederick's face. "I know he didn't believe in everything Dreher does, but what a disappointment that he was happy to let them destroy everything." I opened my eyes and looked at Gabor. "How is my assassin?"

"Bored!" Gabor replied. "I think I'd rather be up there where everyone is looking for me than safe down here. At least it would be interesting. I think that he"—Gabor pointed at Lenz—"keeps me in this prison because if I came upstairs, I'd clean his rooms. I'm not the most tidy, but without me, this one lives like an animal."

"That's enough," said Lenz.

I ate another cookie. "Martin-Frederick's death has been useful, but I'd still rather avoid more."

"Well," said Lenz, "we must nonetheless prepare for war and death. Do they trust you?"

"I think the High General does, and Selvosch. I have encouraged their . . . religious feelings."

"Their what?" asked Lenz.

"Gabor, Dagmar, do either of you speak Masovskani at all?" I asked.

They both shook their heads. I smiled apologetically. "Sorry, spy things. You know."

I gave Lenz a brief report of all that had transpired the night before, in Masovskani, to keep Olaf a secret. I did not see any glimmers of recognition in the others' eyes.

"This is an entire mess," Lenz sighed afterward.

Gabor, full of energy, began to run back and forth across the small room, jumping up against each wall and vaulting off it to run toward the other. It was tiring to watch. I laughed at myself for ever thinking I could have held him hostage. Dagmar's eyes followed him disinterestedly.

"When will you learn more?" asked Lenz, switching back to Rotfelsenisch.

I ate another cookie; they were lemon-hazelnut. "Can't say. They seem more interested in grabbing me when they want than in giving me a clearly drawn schedule. They want to show me something with the prisoners, down at the lake."

"So secretive!" laughed Gabor.

"We *are* in a hidden dungeon," offered Lenz.

"But with cookies," replied Dagmar.

"And they have a secret dungeon, too," said Lenz. "At Glaizatz Lake."

"Why can't we just assassinate the lords high and get it over with?" mumbled Dagmar.

"I'd love to," I sighed. "But they're always squirreled away with a host of guards. Perhaps when they next grab me, I can kill Dreher, and possibly Vorosknecht too, before I'm murdered, but there are more of them than those two. Did I mention Jördis was there, too?"

Lenz grunted.

"What if," Gabor puffed, walking over to the table, "you had help?"

"What? No," groaned Lenz. "We're going to prepare for a quick, decisive war. Maybe I'll ask Edeltraud von Edeltraud and the Gustavuses for help. If they can use their considerable fortunes to hire mercenaries, we'll have three armies, and we might even win."

"Let them capture me," said Gabor.

"What." Lenz glared back at him.

"Let me out," said Gabor. "Kalyna can turn me in to gain more trust, and then when she's taken down to Glaizatz Lake for one of their secret meetings, she releases me, and we kill all of them."

"Releases you," said Lenz, as he stood up, "from the secret underground prison? And then *you* kill *all* of them? Will you listen to yourself?"

"Dreher did say that many of the prisoners already down there are Greens or Purples who didn't want to betray the Tetrarchia," I said.

"Why, that's perfect!" laughed Gabor. "I can spend a few days in there, getting them riled up, you release us all, and there you have it!" He clapped his hands. "Dreher: dead. Vorosknecht: dead. The rest of their fools: dead."

"Absolutely not!" cried Lenz. "This is ludicrous."

Gabor narrowed his eyes, and I decided it would be good to end this argument. I changed the subject: "We should go speak to Chasiku."

"I agree," said Lenz. "*You* stay here, Gabor. Someone will bring you books."

"Not the ones you wrote, I hope," said Gabor.

"I knew I liked you," I said.

TELL THEM EVERYTHING

I appreciated that Lenz was coming more and more to Chasiku with his questions about the future because it might mean he was thinking of me less for that sort of thing. I wondered if I should make everything easier and come clean, but that went against my very nature. I was a terrible, broken, failure of a soothsayer, but what would I be without even that?

When asked what she saw now, Chasiku said, "They will come for you soon, Kalyna."

"Who?" I asked.

"The big men: the sick one and the liar, you know."

"Who's sick?" asked Lenz.

"Dreher," I said. "Quite sick, in fact. How will they come for me?"

"To take you down . . . down there again, where it's dark and bright. To induct you into their mysteries. Or to kill you. Depending."

"When?" Lenz asked her.

"Soon. In the coming weeks. Maybe."

"I can use this to dismantle the regicides," I said. "With Gabor's—"

"No," grunted Lenz.

"Maybe," added Chasiku. "But your actions so far have only made destruction more likely." She said it as if it were obvious.

I was about to respond when there came a shrieking from the bottom of Chasiku's watchtower.

Lenz was surprised, and even Chasiku seemed baffled. I felt myself sag, my neck droop, my insides go numb. It was Grandmother.

"You let me up there right now, you worthless nothing!" Down at the bottom of the watchtower, Grandmother was a dot: a scarf with its hands on its hips. "You are a waste of your mother's life and my son's juices, and if you don't lower that thing right now I will—!"

"What?" I cried, leaning over the precipice, the pallet floating by my head. "You will *what*? Come up all those stairs by yourself, maybe?"

"I will tell them things about you!"

"Things?" murmured Lenz.

I wondered again if I should tell Lenz the truth about my Gift, get the game over with so I could focus on my new persona of reluctant spy.

I lowered that pallet. Grandmother glowered the whole way up, but I stared right back.

Once she was up there, Lenz began, "Nice to see you—"

"Quiet. This is all your fault," she snapped.

Lenz sighed.

"I," proclaimed Grandmother, a finger in the air, "have known my share of frauds—"

I winced.

"—and *you*"—she pointed at Chasiku—"are the most brazen I have ever seen!"

"Oh?" said Chasiku. "Please explain."

"Where do you come from, faker?"

"Kalvadoti on the North Shore of Skydašiai. My family is large and has been there for generations."

"You're a liar," said Grandmother. "No soothsayer stays in one place, none has so many children."

"You must have split off from us centuries ago," said Chasiku.

"*We*! From *you*!" Grandmother sputtered and gave her a look she had never given even me. "We trace our line back thousands of years."

"Humanity is old and so are you, but . . ." Chasiku looked puzzled.

"What?" I asked.

Chasiku's finger sort of spasmed as it pointed to Grandmother again and again. "Does she know about the end? She must."

"*She*," I said, "has foresworn her Gift."

"But does she know?" repeated Chasiku.

"Oh!" cried Grandmother. "The great-great-grandfather of all tricks! 'I know a thing but will not tell you.' Of course. Who are your bastard father and whore mother, fraud?"

"My family hate being around people too much to make rutting our profession," said Chasiku. "My parents cannot stand each other, and this"—she waved her hands around the room—"is already more people than I would ever like to be around at once. Someone must leave. I think it is you."

"That's not how the Gift works!" screamed Grandmother.

"Then I don't possess it. Leave."

"Kalyna," said Grandmother, "you are not to associate with any of these people again." She shook a fist at everyone; the joints in her arm popped. "This playing at intrigue and politics, or whatever you're trying to cram into the emptiness inside you, will make your father cry. Come, now!"

I looked at Lenz, annoyed, and Chasiku, bemused.

"No," I said. "I'm busy."

Grandmother was already halfway to the pallet when she realized what I said. She turned, spat, and glared at me with a look that still, in my adulthood, terrified me.

"If you don't stop this nonsense," she said, "I will *tell them*."

I stood very still. "Tell them what?"

"You know what, you freak, you waste of the gods' breath."

I stared at her and hoped I was not shaking. "Go on."

She put a gnarled hand to her forehead; a puff of air whistled out the end of her unlit pipe. "You stupid, *selfish* girl, I am trying to *help* you. Why do you never see that?"

I sat in silence. Everyone else was purposefully looking at the walls.

"I am trying," she continued, "to help keep you away from these . . . these *charlatans*! I did not think you could tarnish our family's legacy any further, but I was clearly wrong."

"Then go on," I said. "Help me. Tell them. Tell them everything about me. Go on."

"My own granddaughter . . ."

"Now. Tell them."

Grandmother narrowed her eyes, turned around to look at everyone else, one by one, then back at me. Her mouth tightened.

"You threatened to tell them," I said. "Do it. Do it or I'll never take you seriously again."

Her whole face puckered. She was at war with herself in a way I had never seen.

She said nothing, turned, and stormed out to the pallet. I heard her release the rope to descend. I hoped she'd fall too fast, and break everything.

Part of me was disappointed she hadn't told them.

"Well," said Lenz, "what was she going to tell us, hmm?"

"How should I know what a 'dark secret' is to a woman like that? Could have been anything: the first person I slept with, that time I stole a bauble when I was five, anything."

"Hm," he grunted. "You shouldn't let her treat you like that."

"It's fine," I said. "She'll die soon."

Chasiku coughed.

"Do you see her death on the edges of your vision too?" I asked her.

"Everyone I have seen in Rotfelsen has the stink of near death on them," said Chasiku. "Except her."

There was silence.

"When everything falls apart," Chasiku continued, very slowly, "when we fail, in every way we fail, *that one* will somehow survive."

I looked at where the pallet had been.

"The old demon will outlive us all," I sighed.

"And in one possibility," Chasiku continued, "she escapes on your shoulders, after you abandon us."

"I think I would rather die," I said.

DISPASSIONATE

After this, I was exhausted, and I slept for what felt like a day or so. I was awoken by Dagmar in the late morning of the next day.

"Up with you," she said. "Lenz has been talking to the Prince, and wants you to join them." She gallantly turned away while I got dressed.

As we left, I glanced at Jördis' closed door. In a carriage on our way to the palace, Dagmar, with one leg up across an empty seat, threw a sheaf of paper at me.

"Lenz wants you to read this on the way."

It was a new draft for Lenz's ongoing life's work, his secret histories, dated to the previous day. The ink was still wet at the end, and it was full of misspellings, from which I will spare you. The final draft would also probably involve Lenz himself much less. It read:

Today I told the Prince about Aljosanovna's discoveries regarding the identities of our regicides: he easily believes Dreher's part, but has not, of yet, managed to stop suspecting Queen Biruté. After that, he and I, with Olaf, who is now King Gerhold VIII, had a sad little meeting with Bozena and Klemens Gustavus, the Masovskan bankers. They were very obsequious, spoke a great deal about how honored they were to be "favored" by the King, and told us they were on our side without promising anything. It was a waste of time.

After that, Olaf took me to his apartments and asked for my help. Seeing him as the King, I said yes before knowing what he needed.

"Lenz," he said, "I have told Queen Biruté who I am."

I made quite a few exclamations. After Olaf convinced me to sit back down, I asked him why.

"Well, she and the King were hardly close, so she didn't mind how little we spoke to one another, but they were trying to have children, remember. When she first got suspicious, I said just what you told me: that I was worried I couldn't have children at all. But she's quite invested, after all and, with the real Gerhold dead, I couldn't just say 'I don't feel like it' forever, could I? She had begun replying with things like, 'Well, neither do I. But it's what we must do!'"

He spoke as though he was my underling, begging me to forgive him.

"Now Lenz, you see what a position I was in? It isn't often that a person is so straightforward about these relations, but when they are, how is one to respond? Keep turning her down and make her more suspicious, do her a great injustice by sleeping with her falsely, or tell the truth? What would you have done?"

I said something about ignoring her entirely.

"But we must attend so many functions together!" Olaf continued. "And besides, I thought that if I could get her to understand, perhaps we could unite the Reds. So I told her. I had to. I told her that I was meant to just be a quick replacement for a few weeks, and how out of my depth I felt now that I was King, and I admit I broke down a little bit."

He was quiet for a bit, and I asked him what she had said in return.

"She said, 'I have never had someone come up with such a lie to avoid sleeping with me.'"

"I'm sorry, Olaf. What?"

"And then she said that she knew it was a bad time for jokes, but couldn't help it."

Note: I must be sure to include this in my file on the Queen.

"Then," Olaf continued, "she got very serious and asked me what I looked like before. I didn't take her meaning, so she explained that if we're to have children together, and they look off, she'll be the one accused of adultery. Flesh-alchemy is too new for us to know whether it would make my . . . issue look like Gerhold or me. I told her I didn't think I had any great, hereditary disfigurements."

I was pulling out my hair at this point, but managed to tell him that she was not, in fact, one of the regicides.

"Oh good! That's very good. Because after that we had dispassionate relations."

"Fools," I said once I'd finished. "They're all fools. And so am I."

"I haven't read it," said Dagmar, "but I agree."

THE KING AND QUEEN REPAIR TO THEIR HUNTING LODGE

When I entered the Prince's study, I was greeted by the sound of someone screaming, "No, no, *no*! I will not allow it!"

It appeared that Prince Friedhelm was yelling at Olaf, who was sitting calmly on the couch. Lenz was at the Prince's desk, watching.

"I'm sorry, brother," replied Olaf, who looked entirely calm as the Prince stood over him, fuming, "but there's nothing to allow. It's decided. Unless you outrank both myself *and* the Queen."

"The fraud and the traitor, you mean!" cried Prince Friedhelm. "Lenz, talk some sense into him!"

Lenz shrugged.

"Don't you want a niece or nephew, brother?" sang out Olaf. "I'll be back soon! Or at least in three weeks, for the Eve of the Council."

"Olaf," asked Lenz, "what exactly are you and the Queen planning?"

"A vacation!" laughed Olaf. He looked right past Friedhelm, at us. "Do you know of Lady Starost, by any chance?"

"I believe I've written about her," said Lenz. "There were rumors about her and the Queen."

"All true," laughed Olaf. "They're quite in love and have been for years, but always with the understanding that Biruté would also be, ah, intimate with the King. For the sake of heirs."

Lenz clapped a hand over his eyes, as though trying to not see what was happening before him. "Did you tell this Starost about . . . ?"

"About me? Oh no, of course not!" Olaf laughed. "Biruté is keeping our secret. But she told Starost that she and the King—which is me—are beginning to . . . get along much better. Lady Starost was overjoyed because she had been worried about the lack of an heir, and suggested we all take a trip together, to get away from palace life and be a bit freer. Lady Starost also invited along a man she knows whom I've found quite handsome, and—"

"This is a travesty," muttered Prince Friedhelm. He began to pull at his hair. "The bastard child of a fake, a traitor, and possibly two degenerate, childish nobles will doom the Tetrarchia."

"I thought you wanted the King to have children," I said.

Friedhelm rounded on me, glaring wildly. "*Royal* children. *Rotfelsenisch* royal children. Our family is divinely appointed."

"Biruté doesn't wish to adopt your bastards, brother," said Olaf.

"Of course not," spat Friedhelm. "Because she wants to usurp you and control the kingdom."

"Not at all!" laughed Olaf. "And we can worry about that later. This will just be a nice time: like one of those Skydašian farces, with all the running around and slamming of doors, except that we'll all know why we're there, and no one will be jealous! I hope."

"That sounds," I began, "like so much more fun than what I will be doing."

"Oh? And what's that?" asked Olaf.

"Does no one else care about what is happening here?" cried the Prince.

"Infiltrating a cult," I replied to Olaf. "But not a fun one. They just think Rotfelsenisch people are better than everyone else."

"Ew," said Olaf.

Friedhelm walked over to his desk and sat down, glaring over it.

"You," he said to Olaf, attempting to be calm, "are the King of Rotfelsen. The King simply cannot have this sort of scandal." He pressed his hand to his face, massaging his eyelids and letting out a long grunt. "If he could, then, well . . . I would be King."

There was silence at that. The implications were lost on none of us. Olaf, finally, stopped smiling and looked seriously at Friedhelm.

"There will be no scandal," he said, "Your Highness. The King and Queen will be on holiday together to reconcile themselves to one another, and therefore better represent Rotfelsen at the Council of Barbarians. The only whispers will concern the ways in which the royal union was weak before, but is now strengthened." Olaf sounded positively responsible.

"Honestly, Your Highness," Lenz added, "with everything we now know about the regicides, having Olaf and Biruté away from the palace is a good idea. Safer for them."

Friedhelm was quiet. Thoughtful. I wondered if he was thinking of having us killed. I thought again of the flesh-alchemists who had "made" Olaf, of the doctor who had looked at the teeth in poor Gerhold's disembodied head, of all of the Prince's earlier "Recourses" who were no longer alive.

"This once," Friedhelm grunted.

Olaf stood, and nodded.

Just then, Queen Biruté came in and sang out, "Dearest, we're ready to go!"

"*Sister*," said Prince Friedhelm, "please keep the royal reputation in mind."

Biruté looked him in the eye. "That, coming out of your mouth, is truly the strangest thing I have ever heard." She took the hand of her husband's doppelgänger. "But I always do."

"See you at the Council," said Olaf, as they moved toward the door. "We've told the Reds, jointly, to listen to you in all things related to security, Your Highness. Tell everyone we'll be at the hunting lodge, shooting giant rats."

"And where will you actually be?" asked Lenz.

Biruté put a finger to her lips, and the two left, chattering. At least someone was happy, in all this.

If we could get this all sorted out, and save the Tetrarchia, I rather envied the new life Olaf would have in front of him. But of course, living outside of what was normally acceptable was much easier for a king: Lenz and Gabor only wanted to live quietly together, and that had been interrupted by the Prince. And yet Lenz and Gabor still had the protection of their ranks, and could live their lives much easier than many others. All I had to do was think back on women I had known to begin feeling resentful of Olaf and his luck.

The Prince immediately turned toward me, as a new outlet for his anger. "Well?"

"Well what, Your Highness?"

"What Lenz told me: that you're in good with Dreher and the regicides, and that *she* is not one of them. Is this true? I begin to believe I can trust no one."

"It is," I said.

"Tell me everything that happened."

So I did, including Chasiku's visions of my soon being down in Glaizatz Lake with Dreher, Vorosknecht, and the rest. I only left out the great, terrifying, encroaching doom that was beating down the doors of the Tetrarchia.

"Well," said Friedhelm, "find a way to get someone else down there!" He was sweating, his hair flopping everywhere. "And *kill them*! Do I have to decide everything for you?!"

Lenz nodded curtly, and we left. On the way out, Lenz managed a smile.

"I convinced Olaf that the vacation was his idea," he said. "If he told the Queen, who knows who else he might tell."

"I was worried about that," I replied. "What if he tells his traveling companions after all?"

"Either," said Lenz, "the Tetrarchia will be crushed and it won't matter, or we'll be in a better place of power to protect our secrets."

"*Your* secrets. If we succeed, you're letting me go."

"If it is at all possible."

It felt silly, meaningless even, to discuss what we would do after we won. I certainly felt the crushing weight of our inevitable failure bearing down on us, and I had to believe that Lenz did as well. Now, I would just try to enjoy the ride.

KNOW YOUR PLACE

That evening, I was attacked.

Now that I could traverse the palace grounds armed, I admit I had gotten too comfortable. Certainly, violence sometimes broke out in the vast flat gardens and uneven crags of the surface, but it was always of the dueling or partisan brawl variety, and it wasn't as though Martin-Frederick would have a group of Greens start shooting now. The same comfort that had led me to get used to a bed and walls, to alcohol and good food, told me that this was a place where I was relatively safe, up until the rock would shatter beneath us all. Besides, there were Reds everywhere, trying to clear out the troublemakers for the Council of Barbarians.

The point is, I was not being as careful as I would have been, for example, on my way to Gniezto from the Great Field. When I heard running, I assumed it was just a group of Reds on their way to do something important, to the extent that I thought about it at all. So I passed, unthinkingly, behind a great, high wall of shrubbery and was punched in the left side of my face, wobbled, and was shoved to the rotrock below.

"Not the face, horse-fucker!" someone hissed. The voice jumped at "fucker," suggesting it belonged to the person delivering the kick to my ribs.

I twisted and caught the next kick in my hip. It wasn't dark, but I could barely see my attackers: five or six, pink skin, brown clothing, a flutter of purple here and there. They kept kicking at me as I tried to pull away.

One of them leaned down to grab me, and I kicked their chin with both feet. I turned this into a painful roll backward, pressing my spine hard into the rock below, but managed to move up into a weak crouch and draw my sickle. I held it above my head, looking up at them through the curve of its blade.

The five attackers were dressed normally but their purses, pommels, and various other trimmings and accessories tended toward purple. One near the back was holding his chin, which made me smile.

The man in front was familiar, but I didn't place him immediately. His hand was on the purple tassel that hung from his rapier's guard.

"Listen," he said in the voice that had grunted *horse-fucker*, "we don't like you much, and we are here to knock you around. But you come at us armed, and we will have to do the same, and then you might just die. We don't mean to kill you."

"Just 'knock me around,'" I spat.

He nodded, and laughed at nothing.

My breathing came with difficulty, my body already ached, and I felt as though my lips were swollen, whether or not they were. Then I remembered where I'd seen him.

"You're one of Vorosknecht's," I croaked. "I saw you at the lake. You were never more than two feet from him."

"Sure, sure, but I am off-duty."

"Of course you are."

"Well?" He drew his sword an inch from its sheathe.

What a terrible decision he had given me. Vorosknecht wanted me to know he had sent these soldiers to humble me, and to know he had *officially* done no such thing. I ground my teeth and gripped my sickle tightly. The urge to crash amongst them and cut up their faces was strong. They had attacked me. Why not take every possible retaliation? Maybe I could even win.

But these were not bulky henchmen in a too-small alley. These were trained soldiers who had been chosen for this, and I was already hurt.

My hand shook as I lowered my sickle. I sneered. Even then I considered stepping forward and raising it back up into their leader's gut. At least he would be done with.

I dropped the sickle.

Need I tell you what happened next? I acquitted myself as well as can be expected from one who's been beaten and chased all her life, in every corner of our land: I punched and kicked and bit and threw myself upon them with great tenacity. They followed their directive to avoid my face as best they could. At one point, the man whose chin I'd kicked got frustrated enough that he pulled a dagger, and the leader punched him in that same chin for it.

But don't let me sound appreciative. They beat me savagely, and though in the end some had bruises, bloody faces, and (I hope) cracked ribs, I was the one on the ground, holding my stomach, coughing and moaning. I couldn't speak, I felt as though I'd never again move or breathe. My knees were pulled up, my arms were around my midsection. I stared at the soles of their boots.

"There we are," said the leader. "Now you understand, we simply do not like a mind-witch. You see?"

I gurgled.

"Our master, of course, knows nothing about this and would not condone it if he did."

I coughed. In my mind, it was an insulting laugh.

"But," he continued, "if somehow he *did* know, and somehow he *did* condone it, and wanted me to give you a message—and let me remind you that he does not—that message would most certainly be:" He leaned down, his mouth by my ear, and I prayed for the strength to turn and bite him. "'Know your place.'"

I coughed many more times. I wanted to say that the message was clear enough without words. I also wanted to threaten this man's mother with murder. I couldn't speak. They left.

DAGMAR

"Well, they certainly knew their business," said Doctor Aue.

It was the day after my beating, and I was sitting up in bed against a wall of pillows while Doctor Aue dabbed at my ribs and stomach. Lenz had insisted on bringing his favorite doctor, and he now stood a few feet behind her, his mustache matching the frowning line of his mouth. At the door stood two Yellows: Behrens, the sharpshooter who had saved me back in Masovska, and Dagmar, the tall one. They assured me that Jördis was not home next door.

"What do you mean?" Lenz asked the doctor, before I could.

"You said," she answered, to me, "they were meant to send a message, and not to damage you irreparably. They wanted you to be presentable, yes?"

I nodded, and somehow even *that* hurt.

"Well, I think they have at most broken one rib. I think! Hard to say without opening you up!" She laughed at this. "I'll bind it, and you should be reasonably well in a few days, if very sore. As I say, they knew their business." She smiled at my stomach, not my face.

"Well, good for them," I croaked.

"Quite! You will heal entirely. Eventually. I expect."

To this day, the middle finger on my right hand is regularly sore and easily hurt. I think I tried to block a boot with that hand and failed. Aue was a good doctor, as far as I could tell, but a doctor is no more a prophet than I.

"Gentlemen must turn their heads," Doctor Aue called out in a singsong. Lenz and Behrens did so as she lifted my nightshirt farther to inspect my chest. She made a pained inhalation and said, "This will hurt for some time."

I nodded.

"But only bruises. Deep bruises," she added. Doctor Aue dropped my nightshirt back down and tucked it into the covers around my thick wool stockings before singing, "All done, gentlemen!"

Lenz and Behrens looked at me again, and both seemed worried. I thought they were being silly: I wasn't dead, after all, and I had taken worse beatings in my time.

"Rest," said Doctor Aue, "rub this on it." She set down a jar of dark green gunk strung with lines of pink. "You will know to put on more when your midsection stops smelling terrible. Also, avoid spirits, which thin the blood, rich foods, which thicken the blood, and dark tea, which quickens the blood. These indulgences tell the gods you don't care about your health."

I nodded blankly. Doctor Aue leaned forward to pat my shoulder affectionately and, though I was dressed, her hand touched the one spot that wasn't bruised. She was a good doctor.

"Really," she said, "you'll be fine. They wanted you to know that they *could* break you, but they didn't want to, yet."

"Is it surprising that this doesn't make me feel better?"

Doctor Aue looked reassuringly in my eyes, and then away. "I suppose not, but you'll be alright this time."

"Thank you."

"And you *might just* have had this coming, after what you did to my poor assistants."

I said nothing, but she smiled in a friendly fashion.

As Doctor Aue got up to leave, there was a knock on my door. It was Tural, pushing Papa in a chair that glided (and spun, and teetered, and got stuck) on little wheels. When I saw Tural, I began, casually I hope, to lace up the open front of my nightshirt. I didn't want him to see me blotched with bruises.

"Nice to see you again, Aljosa Vüsalavich," said the doctor as she passed my father on the way out.

"Yes, yes, you too," he replied, with no idea who she was.

"Kalyna," said Lenz, "your subterfuge isn't working."

Papa was rolled up to my bed to hug me. I saw Grandmother glaring in through the door from the hallway. She stood there, silent and unmoving, like an angel of death.

"What do you mean?" I replied to Lenz, "The doctor said I'll be fine!" Papa nestled into me as I spoke, gripping me intently.

"And next time?" said Lenz.

"There won't be a next time. I have everything planned." This was a lie. "Tural, do you mind giving us the room?"

"I am sure I don't want to know," he said.

As Tural left, he tried to talk Grandmother into leaving with him, but she remained in the door, still as a statue, and glared. Finally, she slowly lifted her arm and pointed at me, before silently mouthing the words, "Got what you deserved."

Dagmar, at the door, looked at me inquisitively, as if to ask whether Grandmother should be shut out of the room. I almost shook my head, before realizing that I did not have to say no.

Is this warmth in my gut what power *feels like? Or am I bleeding internally?*

"What you deserved," Grandmother repeated, this time making just the rattling beginnings of sound in her throat, and dragging out the last syllable. She trained that evil look on me, sucking air in through her nose. Papa still held me tightly.

I nodded slightly at Dagmar, who looked down at Grandmother, shrugged, and moved into the doorway, blocking the old demon from view entirely. Then she closed the door, slowly, in Grandmother's face.

Gods and hells and Ancients and monsters, did that ever feel *glorious.*

"Unsettling," said Lenz.

"I can do nothing about her, but I have everything else planned," I said. "All of this"—I indicated my midsection with both hands—"is proof I've shaken up Vorosknecht." Papa hugged me tighter and my body ached, but I wasn't about to stop him.

"Shaken him up?" asked Lenz. "Wasn't he supposed to trust you?"

"He did this because he's intimidated by my influence over Dreher, not because he suspects. He's scared of me, so I can force him into a compromise."

"Influence," said Lenz, bracing a hand on my bed and leaning over it, to get the weight off his bad leg, "that you can use to unobtrusively learn their plans in order for us to counteract them. When we have our war."

"Well yes, *if* I fail at stopping all this first." I grinned. "Trust me. We're partners!"

Papa finally looked up from hugging me and declared that he needed to sleep. When the door was opened, so that Tural could come and get him, Grandmother was gone. The door closed, and I was now alone in the room with the military types.

"Well, *partner*," said Lenz, "will you please stay home and recover?"

"I need to do something first. Then I'll rest."

"Fine," said Lenz. "I would like you in relative working order on the Eve of the Council."

The Eve of the Council was the night before the first official meeting of the Council of Barbarians. It was marked by a feast, and its full name was The First Hallowed Evening Proclaiming the Future Thaw Upon Which the Divine Monarchic Council of Pure Blessed Blood for the Furtherance of the Greater Eastern Tetrarchia as a Bulwark to Its Devious Neighbors and a Net Spread to Catch the Dropped Blessings of Its Gods, Will Meet and Present Themselves, Weaponless and Free, for Inspection Before Falling Upon Food and Drink with Great Strength. It was when we supposed the regicides would strike, and it was about three weeks away.

It was also when the very Tetrarchia would crumble, and everyone I knew would die. And we still did not know exactly *how* it would happen.

"I intend to stop them before that," I said.

"Well, good for you," he said. "Did you know two of the other three Tetrarchic monarchs are already in Rotfelsen?"

I did not.

"We've received word," Lenz continued. "Their unwieldy

entourages are already dragging their way through our tunnels, stopping at cities, shopping for the fête, bickering with one another."

"Great," I said.

"Kalyna, stopping this on your own, beforehand, is *stupid*. Our armies are the solution."

"That's not what Prince Friedhelm told us to do."

"He's a fool."

"I know."

"Whatever you do, Kalyna, I'm not letting you run around without protection anymore, and *that* is final. You need a bodyguard."

I think he expected me to protest, but I was very sore. "That sounds lovely," I said.

Lenz smiled very genuinely. "Dagmar," he said, "please keep an eye on Kalyna."

"Why not?" said the lean, broad-shouldered Yellow leaning against the door. She winked at me again, and I prayed she would never know I had gone weeks knowing her only as "Dugmush."

"Dagmar is very good," said Lenz, "and isn't known to be *mine* more than any other Yellow."

It was easy to see why: Dagmar always seemed too relaxed for power games. Yet here she was.

"And you, Dagmar," I said, "you're already all caught up on the . . . ah . . ."

"Destruction of the Tetrarchia because we don't know why, ma'am?" she said, smiling. "Yes, ma'am."

"Good," I said, tripping over possibilities in my mind. "Good, good. If you, Dagmar, can act as my loyal guard, who would happily go Green with me, then they might let you come down to Glaizatz when the regicides meet. If I have someone who can fight—"

"Kalyna," said Lenz, "I'm giving you a bodyguard, not an assassin."

"Are you sure?" I asked.

"Whichever," yawned Dagmar.

PURPLE HALLWAY

Later that same day, not long after rubbing Doctor Aue's pungent goop all over my bruises a second time, Dagmar and I stood in the purple hallway outside Court Philosopher Vorosknecht's study in the

Sunset Palace. I hadn't seen the place since I was dragged there during the Winter Ball.

"Is it true," asked an on-duty Purple, leaning toward Dagmar, his voice dripping with his intentions, "that Prince Friedhelm is trying to quit his addiction to young boys? Or is he as ravenous as ever?" He grinned widely.

"Why should I know or care?" asked Dagmar.

The Purple was confused by her answer for all of a half second. Then she broke his nose with her fist. I liked Dagmar more and more.

The Purple slid down the wall and sat on the floor, moaning and holding his nose. It had twisted in a new direction before he grabbed it, trying to keep it on his face. The other Purples surrounded Dagmar, who threw her hands in the air and laughed. It wasn't a mean or cruel laugh: very genuine.

"What?" she asked. "Isn't this how it works? I'd ask for all your dueling cards in a line, one after the other, if I could, but your master must change the laws first. Women can't duel, so I broke his nose." She shrugged. "Seemed fair."

The Purples grumbled to one another but did nothing else. I, in my blue dress, and with no yellow accents, pushed right past them and pounded on the door to Vorosknecht's study, since we hadn't yet been announced to him.

The door was opened by the man who had led my beating the night before. His gasp was suitably satisfying. We pushed past him, to where Vorosknecht stood behind his desk, next to poor old Meregfog's skeleton. The man who'd opened the door ran back to stand at the Court Philosopher's other side.

"Kalyna Aljosanovna, what a pleasant surprise," sighed Vorosknecht.

"You're a fool," I said, walking right up to his desk. Dagmar stood behind me.

"Whatever do you mean?" asked Vorosknecht.

I put my hands on his desk and leaned over it, getting my face much too close to his. "That you're a fool, Your Brightness."

His face twisted as he smelled the awful goop smeared on my bruises.

"Kalyna Aljosanovna, I don't—"

"I am one of Dreher's advisors now. You don't want me as your enemy."

"What are you talking about?"

I looked at the Purple behind him. I could remember him kicking me, could remember seeing that face obscured by his fists. I grinned, which I'm sure looked ghastly. "What's your name, soldier?"

Silence.

"Oh, come now, I'll learn it anyway, the next time we regicides are all together!"

"Keep your voice down!" hissed Vorosknecht.

"You're his personal guard, I'll know you soon enough. Your name."

Vorosknecht nodded.

"Alban," murmured Alban.

"I'm sorry?" I said, leaning toward him.

"Alban!" he said louder.

"I *am* sorry, I don't hear you. Vorosknecht, your man doesn't know how to speak to one of High General Dreher's adv—"

"Alban, *ma'am*!" yelled Alban.

I stood up straight and smiled. I'm sure Dagmar also smiled.

"You should have Alban here killed for assaulting me," I said. I lifted my right hand in a supposed sign to Dagmar, although we had worked out nothing of the kind. "My woman will do it for you, if you like." I heard her step forward. Alban flinched.

So *this* was how having a henchman felt! No wonder everyone up here liked it so much.

"What is this all about, Kalyna Aljosanovna?" asked Vorosknecht.

"Well, either your man and his friends assaulted me for no reason, in which case we have them executed, or you sent them to do so. We both know the answer, of course, and it was an idiotic thing to do."

"Why?"

I breathed out in exaggerated annoyance. It was a good way to cover wincing from the pain of my beating. "Because *I* am the only person capable of wresting Dreher from your control over that Soul of the Nation garbage."

Vorosknecht stood still and straight as Chasiku's watchtower. "Go on."

"What's to go on with? You told him about it, I have *seen* it. Maybe he'll listen to you over me, but we all know the fanciful theorist and the no-nonsense leader will be at odds once the King is deposed. I'm the safer option. Especially because I haven't got an army."

Vorosknecht grinned. "Saw it, did you?"

"You don't believe me?"

"You weren't the first to visit me today," he said.

He wasn't still anymore. In fact, the Court Philosopher began to walk idly along the side of his desk, toward the purple bust of himself and the glass liquor cabinet. He was comfortable now. What had I missed?

"Well," I said, "that stands to reason."

"As a matter of fact"—he drew out his words interminably—"you weren't the first *of your family* to visit me today."

"Oh?" I managed to squeak.

"Your grandmother had a very interesting story to tell me about you."

She wouldn't, I thought.

"I admit," sighed Vorosknecht as he wheeled toward me, "even *I* never thought you were so bad as a"—he cleared his throat—"'broken shitworm who killed her own mother.' Did I get that right?"

She had told him. The old demon had really told him.

LIE TO EVERYONE

One day when I was seven years old, we were camped somewhere that may have been Masovska, and may have been Quruscan. We were traveling from one to the other, and had stopped for the night, setting up camp a good distance from the road, using the same tents that would be packed up in Papa's room at the servant house twenty years later.

Back then, I had no idea my father was holding the pieces of himself together just enough to care for me. In my memory, he was as strong and smart as anyone I have ever known; stronger and smarter, really. I remember helping him pitch camp as he walked around on his hands, hands with which he drove each stake into the ground with one blow (or so I recall it).

I remember that after the work of setting camp was done, I jumped onto Papa's back and loudly insisted he gambol about with me. He plucked me off. His beard was still brown then.

"Oh, Kalynishka, Kalynishka, no. Papa must rest!"

"Did you always not have legs, Papa?"

"Now, Kalynishka," he laughed. "You know you should not ask people questions like that."

"I know!" I cried. "I did not ask 'people,' I asked *you!*"

He patted my head. "Kalynishka, I did once have legs, but I don't remember them."

"And you don't miss them?"

"How could I miss what I never knew? And I can still beat you in a race, Kalynishka!"

I suspect my father would still have been faster than me when I was twenty-seven, if his mind had not fallen apart in the intervening decades.

At seven, I jumped up and down. "Let's race!"

"Not now, my love, not now."

He walked on his hands over to a rock beneath a tree and lay down to rest. This exchange, innocuous though it was, has always stayed with me, and became a particularly potent memory after Papa stopped pretending he was fine. As I look back now, it seems he probably *was* just tired that day, but to myself at, say, thirteen, it was a horrifying presentiment of what was to come, heavy with meaning that may not have been there.

On that day when I was seven, it had been only two weeks since Grandmother first told me I killed my mother. Of course, at that age, two weeks is a very long time, so I felt I had been wrestling with this my whole life, and also that Grandmother *must* have forgotten the conversation.

This was why, later that night, I took a walk out in the nearby grasses, thought for a long time, and then came running back, shouting excitedly.

"Papa! Grandmother! Papa! Grandmother! I'm fixed! I'm fixed!"

Papa, sated, was taking a second nap by the fire. Grandmother sat nearby and grabbed my shoulder when I was close enough. Her fingers gouged and hurt me.

"Quiet! Don't wake my son with your nonsense games!" she hissed.

"But, Grandmother," I said, trying to lower my voice, but each word ending higher than it had began, "I have the Gift! I was out in the field and there was a buzzing in my head like a bee was in there, but it was not a bee, and then I fell down and saw a vision and I have *the Gift!*"

Papa slept through my excitement. Grandmother looked down at me, puffing smoke through her pipe.

"Really," she said.

I nodded.

"What did you see?"

"I saw that . . . next year, Gniezto will have great rains!"

"Really?" She smiled, relaxing her grip. "That's good!"

I grinned and nodded. I felt a wave of relief: she believed me, and now I would be normal.

"For how long?" she asked, still smiling. "Will it come in from the north or the south?"

"Uh . . ."

"Go on, girl, will it be just enough to help the crops, or so much that it washes them out? Will there be thunder and lightning? Wind? Hail? Will it be early or late spring?" Her smile was hard.

"Well . . . that is . . ."

"When you felt this," she continued, shaking me, "did the 'bee' in your head seem angry or placid? Did it hurt? Did it feel nice? Did you lose your balance or decide to lie down to better concentrate?"

"I . . . I don't know, Grandmother, I—"

Her smile finally dropped, and she slapped me hard. I almost fell into the fire.

"Don't ever waste our time and our hopes with this nonsense again, useless child," she said through her teeth. She hit me again. "To survive, you must lie to everyone. But not to us."

OTTO

Twenty years later, in the Court Philosopher's study, it seemed Grandmother had actually told someone else the truth.

"What do you have to say about that, Kalyna Aljosanovna?" asked Vorosknecht. "Going to deny it, defame your ailing old grandmother?"

Ailing, indeed.

Vorosknecht walked right up to me, exploiting his height to make me look up. Which I did, right into his eyes.

"No," I said. "I never had the Gift. It's a sham. My father and grandmother do, but not I."

I had considered continuing my lie, no matter the evidence, as I always did. But the Court Philosopher had made up his mind, and I didn't need us to spend the next ten minutes arguing. Better to turn this new wrinkle toward my original aim.

Besides, even to someone I hated, it felt *good* to say that out loud.

Dagmar, unflappable as always, did not seem to react to this.

"Ah-ha," said Vorosknecht slowly. "Ah-ha." He drummed his fingers on his desk. "How did you know about the persimmons?"

"I guessed. You're not very subtle."

"Subtle or not, I've outed you."

I shrugged. "And? It changes nothing."

"Unless I tell Dreher."

I grinned. "And deprive him of his greatest proof that the Soul of the Nation, which will guide Rotfelsen into his hands, exists? You know he's clinging to that mightily now—you made him too great a fanatic, *fool*. Now you just might lose him."

Vorosknecht looked irritated, but he no longer looked smug.

"Listen, Otto," I sighed, putting a hand on the Court Philosopher's shoulder, and shaking him. Alban stepped forward, as though I were attacking his master. "Otto, Otto. We're a pair of frauds, you and I, and we're also the pillars bolstering our great High General's faith in *a magical lake spirit that will lead the pink men to glory*. A ridiculous notion, but at this point, if either pillar is shattered, well, his belief may never return."

Vorosknecht pulled his shoulder from my hand and backed away.

"Oh, Otto! Don't be like that!" I laughed.

"If you didn't leave this room alive," he said, "the High General could still believe you had seen it."

Dagmar stepped in front of me. I rested a hand on my sickle, which was on my right hip, and the other on a rapier, which was on my left. I didn't know how to use the sword, but it looked good.

"In that case," I said, "Dagmar here could just kill you. She can do it before Alban gets over the desk."

Dagmar's hand was on her sword, two inches of steel showing. Alban didn't move.

"You would both be executed for it," said Vorosknecht.

"But Your Brightness," said Dagmar, "once I'm caught, I'll tell the tribunal, honestly and truthfully, that I lost control of myself when you questioned my mistress' honor." She smiled. "I will swear up and down that she called on me to stop, even as I butchered you like a hog. Oh, I'll be executed, but Kalyna will face no consequences, and you'll have traded your life only for *mine*."

I could have kissed Dagmar. Vorosknecht looked angry, and genuinely shaken.

"Stand down, Dagmar," I said. "I want His Brightness to be my friend. We have the same purpose: we want to keep Dreher in the dark."

Vorosknecht chewed his lip.

"Well," I said, "not my *friend*, but you know."

"What do you *want*?" asked Vorosknecht.

"When last I saw you, you said something, mockingly, about inducting me into the mysteries of your Soul of the Nation cult."

"Yes . . ."

"Induct me!"

"Dreher is already planning on it," he spat. "Even though our mysteries are *currently* limited to Rotfelsen's best, brightest, and richest. You are not they."

"Lucky me. I expect it will come in the middle of the night?"

"As it did for him, yes," said Vorosknecht. He was wary, but he was answering me.

"Then don't fight him on it. Warn me ahead of time when it will be, prevail on Dreher to let me bring my woman here"—a thumb back toward Dagmar—"for protection, and prepare me for the mysteries, so that mine will be *particularly* auspicious. Then I will *see* the Soul of the Nation, way down in Glaizatz Lake, ordering its servants to . . . well, whatever you like." I grinned.

Vorosknecht rubbed his beard.

"*And*"—I sweetened the pot—"I can give you Lenz and the heretical works about the Soul in his library, which may undermine your own . . . interpretation."

This was probably a cruel offer. I made it nonetheless.

"Alban here told me to know my place," I said. "Well, I do. It is beside Dreher."

"So the mysteries, your thug here, my trust, Dreher's trust, secrets, the schedule," grunted Vorosknecht. "And then the Soul of the Rotfelsen Nation will certainly want our victory over the Tetrarchia, and a return to true Rotfelsenisch philosophy."

I nodded. "Yes, sure, whatever that means."

"Anything *else* you need from me, fraud? Or will all of that be enough?"

"Just your understanding that if Alban ever comes close to me again, Dagmar will kill him."

"Happily and easily," said Dagmar.

Court Philosopher Otto Vorosknecht, His Very Brightness, looked at me for a long time.

"I may do some of this," he said, "if it suits me."

DAGMAR AND I

As we walked in the shadow of the Sunset Palace, I cleared my throat loudly, and Dagmar said nothing. The rush was leaving me, and I was in a lot of pain.

"Dagmar," I finally began, "the truth of what I admitted in there, about myself . . ."

"I don't much care, ma'am," said Dagmar.

"Don't call me 'ma'am' when we aren't putting on a show. You work for Lenz, not me. And you can be honest."

She turned to me as she walked and grinned. "In that case, I don't much care. I *was* being honest. I became a soldier for gold and excitement, and had little of the second until you showed up. I don't care what you are or aren't." She winked at me.

"You have got to stop doing that."

"Is that an order, ma'am?" She did it again.

"No."

"Good."

We walked back in silence.

PERFECTLY SAFE

"Dagmar!" snapped Lenz. "I thought you were supposed to keep her safe!"

"She's fine!" laughed Dagmar, presenting me with two open hands as though I were a pie she had baked. "Perfectly safe!"

"Well, what's done is done. Now you can be inducted into their mysteries and learn more about their plot."

"I can do more with Gabor."

"You mean his silly notion about getting arrested on purpose?"

Normally, I would have gotten uncomfortably close to Lenz, to make him uncomfortable. But I knew I smelled bad, and we were now on the same side.

"Yes," I replied. "He's already in danger; let's make use of his danger."

"Seems to me," said Lenz, "you already have. Martin-Frederick's death has benefited you very much."

"It's benefited *us* very much, Lenz! And with more of Gabor's help, we can stop this before it starts. We can save *everyone*."

"We get Gabor arrested, and he goes into that secret prison."

"As opposed to the one you have him in now? And we'll wait for Vorosknecht to tell me when I'm being inducted, so Gabor will only be imprisoned for a few days! He's a strong man, and it was his idea. The Tetrarchia's doom concerns him as much as it does us, and you are not his father or his master."

"I should never have told you how formidable he is," said Lenz.

"You two have a secret love; you don't get much chance to brag about him."

He smiled at that. "Kalyna, I want what you're proposing to be possible, I do. But Gabor isn't enough." He sighed and shook his head. "This would be a much easier decision if it were our only choice, but if you fail at this, and then we *win* a battle on the Eve of the Council, I must face a life alone."

Lenz wasn't used to discussing these feelings. He didn't tear up, and his voice didn't quaver, he just stared forward and spoke softly. I felt guilty.

"Then let's even the odds," I said. "We'll have him arrested with, say, ten Yellows. Dreher said they can always make use of more."

"'Make use'? Gods, what will they do with them? Why can't you just risk your own life? Mine would be harder without you, but I wouldn't miss you."

"Well, you should not have—"

"Kidnapped you, yes. And you'll never let it go."

I nodded.

"But," said Dagmar, "if he hadn't kidnapped you, none of us would know what was happening, and I'd be guarding a bathroom right up until the Tetrarchia crumbled."

I couldn't very well argue with that. I still wished that I had been in the Bandit States this whole time.

MY RECOVERY

Since Vorosknecht and I were now allies in fooling Dreher, I didn't want the High General to see that I'd been beaten up, so I finally went home. The hope was that I had done enough to be allowed a few days' recovery before diving back into my stupid plan. I could wait for other people to respond to *me*, for once.

I eased myself carefully into bed and began to rub Doctor Aue's terrible goop onto my torso. Then what I most feared came to pass: Grandmother barged into the room.

I readied myself for a long string of invective, followed by a story, followed by what exactly she had told Vorosknecht and why, along with how she had thought to go to him in the first place, and how she had gained an audience.

Instead, Grandmother simply glared and said, "We are leaving now."

"No," I said.

"You deserved that."

"What?" I asked with feigned innocence.

"Having your flawed nature exposed to the purple man."

"No." I shook my head.

And she barged right back out.

I felt my whole body relax at her absence. Let her continue betraying me. I didn't care anymore. (Of course I cared, but less.)

Doom, war, destruction, and who knew what else was coming, but for three glorious days I padded about the servant house, slept a great deal, spent time with Papa, hardly saw Grandmother, flirted with Tural (or at least thought I was), and did not go outside. I communicated with anyone who didn't live in that house by messenger. Even without brandy, dark tea, or heavy foods, it was delightful.

Jördis was barely at home during this time, but I did manage to catch her, and she smiled as though nothing had happened, even after I closed the door to her room, and we were alone.

"Your boss doesn't much like me," I told her.

"Well, we already knew that, didn't we?"

I opened my blouse, which was an incredibly uncouth thing to do, and showed her how bruised I was.

"*Ouch*," she said. "I am sorry, Kalyna, but you know how he is. He doesn't much like being challenged and, well, your involvement in his affairs may be more challenging to him than when you were officially his enemy."

"Don't you mean *our* affairs?"

Her smile finally dropped, but she still seemed quite calm. "I only go where my master tells me," she said. "I have never lied about how much I care for his ideals."

But she also, apparently, had not cared enough to expose his treason months ago.

"I am sorry he had you beaten, as I was genuinely sorry when he ambushed you at the Winter Ball. But I'm not sure what you expect to get from me, beyond an apology."

I let it go after that, and Lenz began putting incognito Yellows on Jördis. She was spending most of her time in the palace.

On the second day, I received a visit from an extremely uncomfortable man whose clothing showed no affiliation. But I recognized his face as one of those Purples who had beaten me alongside Alban. I had been bundled up in the chair in my room, but when I saw him, I immediately found the energy to be up and about, bustling and folding papers, and pouring myself radiant snow-cave tea and generally showing that I was *just fine*. He sweated a great deal, and handed me a small piece of paper that only said: "TEN DAYS FROM NOW. EARLY MORNING. YOU WILL BE DUNKED. YOU CAN BRING YOUR YELLOW." Vorosknecht gave no more details, but I had drawn *something* out of him, and he was not currently having me beaten or killed.

On the third day, a Yellow brought a note from Lenz, that said, "Fine." It went on to tell me that ten of the hardiest Yellows had volunteered—the types who dared each other to do dangerous things, or hit each other for fun—to be arrested with Gabor. They would be caught carousing in the Royal Inn of Ottilie's Rock, which was conveniently very near the Green barracks. I would make sure that they were particularly irritating to Gunther, the keeper there, which would make them quite easy to find, as he would tell anyone who asked about them. I felt a little bad about it.

I burned Lenz's letter.

GABOR'S ARREST

"I have found Martin-Frederick's murderer," I hissed under my breath to High General Dreher. I was sitting in his study in the Green barracks, nervously tearing at a small piece of paper. The bruising on my face was almost entirely gone now—at worst I looked a little puffy, like I had been crying and not been beaten.

He sat forward so quickly it must have set something in his torso out of sorts because he began to cough, and finally wheezed, "Truly, Kalyna Aljosanovna?"

I nodded, and then looked about as though I was deeply disturbed. "Yes. I . . . I saw glimpses, in my head, of this man laughing with his cronies, celebrating his success. They're hiding the assassin in the closet of their rooms on the third floor of the Royal Inn of Ottilie's Rock."

"Are they armed?"

"Yes. Ex-soldiers, I think."

"Hmm." He sat back and rang a little bell on his desk.

"But," I said quickly, "do try to take them alive. So we can learn more."

"Of course, Kalyna. We always want more able bodies in our prison."

"You still haven't told me why."

"Soon, Kalyna. I promise."

I smiled. A smile of haggard relief at justice being done. High General Dreher grunted as he got to his feet, and came around to the desk to take my (artfully quivering) hand.

"Thank you, Kalyna. I have never . . ." He shook his head and smiled. "I have never had reason to trust someone not of Rotfelsen before."

It was two days before my initiation. A week after that, everything around us was due to end. But we still did not know exactly how.

A HOLLOW PROMISE

"Are you ready for this, Kalyna?" asked Lenz.

I was in my bedroom, stinking of Doctor Aue's ointment, with everything cleared out of the room's center so I could clomp up and down the floor with my sickle, now and then glancing at the desk.

Lying open upon it was my sickle fighting treatise, showing page after page of old drawings of dismemberment. I sliced at the air.

"Of course not," I said.

"Well, it doesn't matter. Gabor is down there, and I'm sitting up here and imagining it."

"As am I," I said. "But I promise you, Lenz"—another slice, up through the air—"that if I survive tomorrow, I will make sure Gabor does, too." It was a very nice promise that I had no way to keep.

"And you're sure High General Dreher said he was arrested without incident?"

"Oh yes. He and his 'friends from the war' all gave up right away; there was no fighting."

"Good." Lenz looked like he wanted to pace, but my practicing kept him still, lest he walk into the blade. "We should have taken Jördis prisoner," he added.

"*That*"—I raised the sickle and spun—"is your answer to everything."

"And look how it turned out. You're telling me what to do now." Lenz actually smiled. I don't know what Gabor told him before running off to be arrested, but it must have been reassuring.

"Besides," I added, "we would make the Court Philosopher suspicious if we did that. Where will you be tomorrow?"

"Up with Chasiku." Lenz pointed up, above his head. "Hoping she can give me an idea how our chances change with your . . . actions."

I nodded. "I hope Olaf is staying hidden."

"I'm sure he's fine," said Lenz. "Between what he, Biruté, and whomever else are enjoying, it feels awfully unfair that Gabor's down there."

"At least you have someone." I was breathing hard now, and I set down the sickle to start stretching.

"Are you still hurt?" he asked. "Can you even do this?"

"As you said, it doesn't matter if I'm ready." I spoke to my ankle as I tried, and failed, to touch my toes.

There was silence as I stretched more.

"Tomorrow, huh?" he said.

"Tomorrow."

"And you really think you can—"

"Yes," I lied. "I wouldn't do this otherwise."

"If it works, what will we do?"

"Move on."

THE NIGHT BEFORE MY INITIATION

"Kalynishka," said Papa, "you are going to do something."

"Yes." I leaned over his bed.

"I'm not seeing your future," he clarified. "I am not *that* far gone. But I see things happening around you. Large things."

"I hope so. Do you know what?"

He shrugged. "Fighting, death, anger, eyes."

"Thank you, Papa."

"You are going to do something."

"Yes."

"Do it well, Kalynishka."

I nodded. "I'll try." I sighed and took his hand. "But you never like it when I hurt people."

Papa nodded as many times as I just had, his head moving as far up and down as mine. "Of course not, Kalynishka, but sometimes it is what you do. Sometimes you do it for me and your grandmother. Necessary?"

"I'm not sure tomorrow is necessary."

"I *am* sure that if you think it might be, it is," he said, patting my hand. "I will see you tomorrow."

I didn't have the heart to tell him how likely it was I would die tomorrow.

Grandmother never came out of her room, and I did not go to see her.

I tried to go to sleep. It was still relatively early, although the sun had, of course, been down for hours. I lay awake, staring at the ceiling, heart racing. There was nothing for me to do until tomorrow.

After what must have been an hour, I got up, padded down the servant house's hallway, and knocked on Tural's door.

He was wearing belted silk pajamas in a deep blue, with buttons running up the side. He looked annoyed and then smiled when he saw me. His whole body moved as one to invite me in, but I stayed in the doorway. After the King's Dinner, and having him bring Gabor to the Sun's Death, I had kept Tural out of all of my plots. He had almost died at Vorosknecht's hands once, and he deserved the chance to just focus on his fruit. But I had to say *something*.

"I may not survive tomorrow," I said.

He blinked quite a few times at that, and then looked at the floor. "You told me to just *tell* you, next time."

"That I did. Do I want to know why?"

"If you'd like," I replied. "But it's complicated."

He nodded and looked at me again. "Best not get into it, then. You probably need your sleep."

"I suppose." I smiled. Warmly, I hope.

He smiled back and nodded. I hung in the doorway, my body sort of swaying in and out of the room. It was all very awkward and teenaged.

Finally, I took a breath, closed my eyes, and I said in Cöllüknit, "Tural, will you come to my bed tonight?" Even though I was still sore, still had fading bruises, still could not get the smell of Doctor Aue's goop off of me.

When I dared to open my eyes, he was still there, and so was his smile. This was a good sign.

"Kalyna," said Tural, "I would like to very much."

I think I smiled too widely then. I felt pleasant jitters rise in me.

"*But,*" he continued, "I cannot. I don't care for propriety, but I know I've never slept unattached with someone and not awoken with a stinging need to be, well, *attached.* Whether or not it was a good idea."

I felt the flutter in my chest die down.

Tural continued, "I don't say that if we do this, we must be married. That would be silly—we're too old for such illusions. But I know that, for my sake alone, if we do this, and if you survive whatever is going to happen, I would need to know we would make a try at *finding out* whether or not we could be married."

Kalyna Aljosanovna Tsaoxelek, I thought.

"Does that make sense, Kalyna?"

I nodded numbly.

"Can you, Kalyna, promise me we would try to find this out together?" he asked.

I liked Tural very much, and I knew, from my own feelings and Chasiku's vision, that our marrying was something that could, *conceivably*, work. But I knew, instantly, that I did not want it to. Whether what I felt could become love was not the point: my duty was to my father, and he could not survive staying in one place. Not any more than I could imagine Tural leaving Rotfelsen to travel the world with us.

For that matter, even without my father, could *I* survive staying in one place? Could I, broken as I was, put so many of my hopes for security and happiness into one person? Tural was handsome and kind, but also persnickety and set in his ways—and how those flaws would *grate* upon me if I changed my whole way of life for him.

But what could it hurt to tell him "yes," I wondered. I would surely die tomorrow. If I did not, there was the good chance that we all would soon enough. And if somehow my plan worked and everyone, myself included, was saved? What then?

I could still leave with my family once it was all over. I could avoid Tural, or tell him I changed my mind, or even admit I'd lied. What did it matter? I would soon be gone. I could lie tonight, and then do my duty to family and Gift by attempting to become pregnant by him—perhaps I would even succeed, to Grandmother's shock. Or I could lie to Tural, and limit myself to the great world of things a man and a woman can do together that will not conceive. Whatever the choice, with so little chance of a future, why not lie for an exciting tonight? It would be far from the worst thing I had done on Rotfelsen's surface. Far from the worst lie I had told.

"No," I said. "I can't make you that promise."

He nodded and smiled sadly. "I assumed as much, but I would have kicked myself had I not made sure."

"Thank you for your honesty."

"And yours, too."

"Good night, Tural. I'm going to . . . Good night."

"Sleep well, Kalyna."

When I turned to go, Tural almost said something: I heard the sound of his mouth opening, a slight inhalation. But there was nothing, so I went to my room.

I considered finding an attractive Yellow (such as Dagmar, or a stranger), but decided against it because they might see me as a superior to be pleased no matter their will. So I lay on my bed and used my hands. Looking back now, I wonder if Tural did the same that night. At the time, I didn't think about Tural at all.

Once I was done, I still couldn't sleep. With lust somewhat sated, all I had left was fear, and it would not let go. I grumbled to myself, and tossed and turned in my bed.

Then I wondered idly if Prince Friedhelm would sleep with me if I prostrated myself before him. I imagined this and laughed myself to sleep at last.

PART SIX

MY INITIATION INTO THE
MYSTERIES OF THE SOUL OF THE
ROTFELSENISCH NATION

They came for me early the next morning, a group of three Greens who inquired respectfully after me at the door of the servant house. Dagmar brought me downstairs, and we met the Greens at the front door. I made sure my nightshirt was laced up so they couldn't see my bruises.

"Why wasn't I told about this visit?" I demanded.

The Green in front sighed and said, in the voice of rote memorization: "The Mysteries of the Nation do not warn, and they do not wait. You will come with us now." He then inclined his head and added his own "Ma'am."

They waited outside the servant house as I got dressed. I did it quickly; no need to keep anyone waiting. I had laid everything out the day before. A simple wool skirt in bright blue, the same sort I had spent my life wandering, fighting, and prophesying in. Beneath that were warm wool stockings tucked into the knee-high boots I'd been given for my short stint as a Yellow. I wore a yellow blouse covered by a thick leather vest that would not stop a blade, but might at least make it rethink its direction, and atop that a heavy green wool coat and orange scarf. From a belt on my waist dangled my sickle, which was expected, strapped to my left thigh was a long dagger, and in my right boot was Tural's knife with the gold handle. My hair was up as much as it could be, although curls fell everywhere.

I had spent a half hour the night before practicing at throwing knives, but only ever managed to hit my desk with the handle. The gold handle was dented when I gave up.

I took a deep breath and left. On the way out, I didn't see Papa, Grandmother, Jördis, or Tural. Only maids and butlers going about their morning duties. Dagmar followed me silently.

Outside the servant house, there was a large carriage with black curtains over its windows. I almost laughed at how melodramatic it was. The Greens helped me in and seemed unsurprised by my sickle, or by Dagmar, which was a good sign. We were blindfolded, even though the curtains were opaque, and off we went. The morning was quiet and chilly.

The carriage rumbled awhile, and I suspect we went in circles. Every time it bounced, my ribs hurt. When we stepped out, I found it rather cute how intently the Greens pretended they weren't putting me into a lift down to Glaizatz Lake, even as we descended. When we landed, I was still blindfolded, but I knew we were at the edge of the lake. The quiet lapping of the water, and any other noise, was muffled by the moss that ran up the walls

As we walked by the lakeside, I heard splashing and saw, through my blindfold, the light of the wiggly little shrimp. I suspect they were being purposefully riled up for my benefit: soldiers tromping in the shallows, kicking at the water.

Then there was a rustling of cloth and the lights disappeared, although I still heard muffled splashing. I was led upon the stone in a great series of twists and turns, spirals and circles. Back, I suspect, to exactly where I'd started.

"Kalyna Aljosanovna!" boomed a voice. "Soothsayer and prophet of far-off lands, you are in the presence of the hidden chosen!"

The voice was almost certainly Vorosknecht's, and the urge to say, "Is that you, Otto?" was strong, but I fought it. I waited quietly for them to continue their farce.

"Do you know why you're here?" he said. He was forcing his voice into a lower register, but it was definitely the Court Philosopher.

"To submit myself to the mysteries of the deepness beneath Glaizatz!" No one had told me exactly what would need to be said, so I guessed.

I heard some muttering, and then my blindfold was removed with a flourish.

I stood in a black silk tent, the top higher than I could make out, and the sides wide enough that one draped wall fluttered over a corner of the lake itself, bringing water inside. In that water could still be seen the odd blinking light of shrimp, but they were no longer being provoked. All that tiny bit of light served to show me was the soldiers standing in a circle around the silk walls, in purple and green uniforms. I could see nothing else; all was darkness.

Were they truly going to induct me, or was this a secret execution? All I knew was that Dagmar and I were surrounded by enemies in the dark.

"Kalyna Aljosanovna," said a different voice. Quarrymaster Selvosch's, I think. "Is it true that you, *even as a foreigner*"—a good thing about darkness is no one can see you roll your eyes—"believe in the purity of the Rotfelsenisch nation and the truth of the spirit of light, built from our goodwill and strength, that resides beneath our very feet, guiding the fate of our great stone?"

"Not only do I believe it," I said, taking a long pause for effect, "*I have seen it.*"

More murmurs, from in front of me. I heard a strange rasping somewhere behind me.

"A being beyond god or demon," I continued, "beyond physical form. Swirling warmth and light, made from, and maker of, the goodness of your people."

The lie was easy, but I almost choked on the word "your."

"Seeing," said Vorosknecht, "is not enough."

Some sort of sign must have been made because torches were lit in the hands of four soldiers, and the rest of the enclosure flickered into view. I still couldn't see the top: it must have been hanging from Glaizatz Lake's massive ropes and pulleys far, far above.

There were probably twenty soldiers visible here, equally split between Purples and Greens. Among them were some faces I recognized, including an angry-looking Alban.

In front of me was a great dais of what looked like heavy onyx. I didn't know how they had gotten it down here. Behind it were ten figures: one had a tall hat, another was hunched. I assumed those to be Vorosknecht and Dreher. It was not as many as I'd met before, but these were only the people involved in the regicides' religious aspect. I must say, a part of me felt relieved that I certainly did not see Jördis' outline amongst them, although I wasn't sure what difference that actually made.

At least no one had made a move to kill me yet.

To my right was the water, and to my left I could see, through the tent, the outline of a lit up building, which must have been the prison. I looked behind me and saw what the rasping noise was: perhaps twenty-five people, all kneeling in rows, with ropes binding their wrists and connecting them to one another. Their clothes were tattered, and their mouths were gagged. I fancied that one of them looked like Gabor, but in the darkness, it was hard to tell.

As the torches grew brighter, I looked back in front of me, and saw more faces: many I didn't have names for, along with Dreher, Vorosknecht, and Selvosch.

Someone to Dreher's left growled, "There's a Yellow here. And they're both armed."

Dagmar grunted with exertion. I turned to face her, just as she was theatrically tearing off her yellow jacket and throwing it on the rotrock beneath her. In a show of extra zeal, she stomped on the jacket. Then she looked up, grinning, in her shirtsleeves and darker yellow trousers.

"I could take the rest off too, but I don't think it would be decent," she said.

I smiled at the audience. Some of them laughed, which I took as a good sign. I looked back at her, and used it as an excuse to look past her, at the prisoners. Their heads were bowed, and the soldiers surrounded them.

"Commendable," said a begrudging Vorosknecht. "But we still need to disarm you."

"Of course." I bowed.

Soldiers came and took my sickle and Dagmar's sword. Naturally, we both had hidden weapons, but we were their allies, and it would have been an affront to search us. I casually scratched my left leg with my right boot heel, to remind myself that a dagger was there.

A soldier with a torch walked closer to the dais. Dreher had the smile of a proud sponsor or teacher, or perhaps pet owner. I winked at him, and he smiled wider.

"Kalyna Aljosanovna," he said, resting his elbows on the dais, which, despite its appearance as heavy stone, wobbled, "I have recommended you for this honor not only because of your exotic Northern Gift, but because of the dedication you have shown to us, our cause, our Soul, and a great people to whom you don't belong."

I curtsied.

"Kalyna Aljosanovna," he continued, "of Masovska and Loasht and places foreign"—I gritted my teeth—"are you prepared to submerge yourself in Glaizatz Lake and bring yourself closer to the Soul of the Rotfelsenisch Nation? To endear yourself to its goodwill as a righteous subordinate? To cleanse yourself of foreign corruption in its pure waters, before they are muddied with our enemies?"

I curtsied again and nodded.

"Advance," said Vorosknecht.

I began to step forward, and stopped when I realized he was speaking to his partners, not me. They circled out from behind the dais (which shook some more as they bumped into it) and proceeded with the ceremony.

I won't bore you with the whole thing. There was a lot of walking in circles and call-and-response chants amongst those Ten Noble Regicides (who were supposed to be called The Ten August Nobles of the Soul). Quite often, one would turn too slowly, or forget to turn and bump into another, or a few lines of response chanting would be mumbled nonwords except for "Soul of the Nation" and "Ten August Nobles of the Soul," or someone would hiss "no, no, skip that part." *These* were the people in grasping distance of toppling our nation, of somehow killing untold thousands. Vorosknecht, of course, was perfect in his movement and enunciation, and never stopped letting me know, with his eyes, that he wished I were dead.

The worst part of this ceremony was when a soldier was sent to scoop up water from the lake, and I had to drink it, blinking shrimp and all. They were too small for me to taste, and I barely felt them, but I somehow felt guilty, even though I ate meat regularly. Why do we feel any of the silly things that we feel?

"Are you ready," Vorosknecht asked me, *eventually*, "to drop your body into the waters of Glaizatz Lake, Kalyna Aljosanovna? And to emerge reborn, or *drown*?" His preference was clear.

I nodded.

"And do you," the Court Philosopher continued, "with the power of your sight, see that the Soul of the Nation, which dwells beneath, wishes to begin being sated on the blood of its enemies?" He waved a hand at the tied-up prisoners behind me.

I was both aghast and unsurprised that these ridiculous nobles, with their made-up cult, had gotten all the way to human sacrifice. Vorosknecht stared at me hard, willing me to remember that I had agreed to say that the Soul saw whatever he wanted it to see. I'm sure he had a plan to expose me, or at least murder me, if I did not.

I nodded again, and prayed that I had not just, personally, condemned Gabor and the others to death.

Dreher came right up to me and whispered. "You must swim out a bit and let yourself drop deep. Remain underneath for as long as you can before you swim to the surface. If you think you can do better, go up for air and try again. Don't be afraid to stay so long that you pass out. We'll haul you back. If you feel a pull on the rope and you aren't done, give a pull back. If they feel nothing in return, out you come."

I felt myself begin to overheat under all my layers of wool. "'Swim'? You mean I don't just, I don't know, dunk my head?"

"Oh no," he said in my ear, "we try to get as close to the Soul as we can. Without dying, of course." He laughed.

"Did you do this, General? Even with your . . ."

"Condition?" he whispered. "I had Greens swimming alongside to help, but you're a healthy girl from a wild place."

I nodded. "Thank you. I'll do my best."

"And when you're back, we'll start on the prisoners!" he said. He seemed cheery about the whole thing.

Suddenly I very, very, very much wished I hadn't dressed in wool and leather for combat, and was not burdened with hidden weapons.

I removed my wool jacket and leather vest, laying them by the shore of the lake. I took off my boots carefully, desperately willing Tural's knife to stay inside the right boot as I lay it down. I still had a great deal of heavy wool on, but there was no way to remove my stockings or skirt without everyone seeing the dagger strapped to my thigh. I would simply have to do my best.

A rope was tied around my waist and fastened to a metal spike that had been driven into the rotrock ground. All of the Ten Noble Regicides crowded around the piece of lake that sat underneath the silk tent, and seemed rather at a loss for how to act, now that they did not have a chant or an order in which to stand. I wondered if anyone planned to mention this to Vorosknecht in the future: "Wouldn't the Submersion be grander if . . . ?"

These ten were mostly men, and I hoped none of them were getting in close just because I was (barely) undressing. They did seem eager; maybe they wanted to see how foreigners floated.

Many of the soldiers also crowded in behind them, and the rest watched from where they stood guard over the prisoners. What else did they have to do? I looked back, planning to give Dagmar a meaningful look, but she was already creeping away from the crowd.

I stepped into the water slightly, and saw that at this part of the lake, there was an immediate drop-off to great, murky depths: there would be no wading in. Standing with just my toes in the water—well, my toes in thick wool stockings, which were soaking in the water—I looked down into that great expanse, lit only by guttering torches behind the Ten Noble Regicides and wiggly little shrimp below. I turned back to look at everyone watching me.

"Do I . . . say anything first?" I asked quietly.

There were chuckles. These dangerous fools felt quite smart in the presence of someone even more ignorant of the Mysteries than they.

"No, no," said Dreher, in a benevolent fashion, with a hand on my shoulder. "To this group, your words will mean very little until you've done it."

I nodded and looked back into the water. I wondered if Vorosknecht had ever done this or if, as the founder of this little cult, he had been exempt. I stared into the dark waters.

"Well," I sighed, "off I go."

It was a stupid thing to say. I took many deep breaths to saturate my lungs and dove into the water.

I am lucky enough to be a good swimmer, ever since that boy at Fántutazh Lake showed me how to perch in the water-bound trees and catch the fish that eat the moss there. Following his tanned legs through the water was a great motivation to learn. But I've never taken much pleasure in swimming for its own sake. What's the point if you aren't doing it in order to kiss a boy in a tree?

I decided to give them a show. The longer I was in there, the closer they would think I was getting to the Soul of the Nation, and the longer Dagmar might have without being noticed.

Swimming beneath the surface of Glaizatz Lake was quite the experience. It was so dark, above and below the water, that it was easy to become disoriented. The shrimp blinked all about, and a part of me always wished to move toward them. Sometimes much larger creatures brushed my legs, unseen outside of a scale or an eye appearing in the light of a shrimp's fear. Swimming in a wool skirt isn't easy, but at least it gave me a barrier against those things I couldn't see.

The rope meant I had a decent idea of where I was in relation to everything else, although it also meant I couldn't go too far. Staying near the surface, I was able to move out from under the edges of the black silk tent, and see dots of light quivering through the water. I also saw torches near and far that went up the walls of the great cavern, illuminating them better than I had seen before, showing the moss that lived there, and the great, pointed gashes in it that I remembered from my childhood.

It all seemed blissfully removed from, well, *me*. I was in the quiet and dark, decorated with little shrimp who blinked in and out of my field of vision. Anything could have been happening above, really.

When my lungs began to hurt, I straightened myself perpendicular with the surface and allowed my body to slowly, carefully float toward the top of the water. My nose and mouth eased above the surface, and I took a series of breaths, hoping no one would see or hear the water breaking. I caught a strange smell, but assumed it was just another of the lake's oddities. After this, I slipped back down and swam around a bit longer. There was a tug on the rope, I tugged back to let them know I was alive. I went up once more, only nose and mouth, and took more breaths. Again that smell, like burning hair, but I slipped back down and swam longer.

There was another pull on the rope. Before I could respond, I was being yanked back toward the tent. As I looked out through the water, I saw the torches flickering in and out of view.

I pushed my head into the air, smelled burning hair, saw smoke everywhere, and heard yelling and the clashing of metal. The tent was burning and, in the way silk does, emitting huge amounts of smoke. My heart quickened.

My rope was still being pulled, so I curved about under the water and slipped out my dagger, struggling with the waterlogged rope, sawing at it. Whatever was going on up there, the shrimp had noticed, and they began to pulse and shine faster and brighter than before. Fish and eels thrashed about me on all sides. I don't think Glaizatz Lake had ever seen a battle by its shores.

I felt myself dragged toward the shore, faster, then slower, then faster: whoever was reeling me in had other things to do. Once I sawed through the rope, I was so close I would have been inside the tent had it still been standing. Silk burns terribly fast.

I didn't want to go above, to put myself in danger or see my plan failing, but my lungs were sore, and I tasted metallic streams of blood snaking through the cold water. I pushed up, and popped my head and chest out, immediately feeling how heavy I was.

Here is what I saw: a battle in smoke between those in uniforms and other, harder-to-see figures. A lot of flashing steel, quite a few prone bodies, and Dagmar in the thick of it, in her shirtsleeves and more than happy to attract our enemies' attention.

I also saw Gabor, haggard, but spry as ever. In the moment I was watching, he jumped over one blade in order to stab the owner of another; it was quite impressive, and I wonder if anyone else who survived that day saw it. I must be blessed. What I could make out of the fighting seemed furious, and many bodies were already floating halfway into the lake, turning the waters murkier.

There was a group huddling by the dais that I took for the Ten Noble Regicides, but it was hard to say. A soldier was thrown back into the dais, and it broke, gushing tan splinters and revealing the black-painted spruce frame it had always been.

I saw this whole tableau in perhaps two seconds, but it looked, by the gods, as though this plan was *working*.

Then a Purple saw me and yelled something, and there were harquebuses leveled. I dove, leaving Dagmar and Gabor to their fates.

I didn't hear the reports of the harquebuses, but the bullets that punched down into the water spiraled past me. I panicked and swam away from them, which meant not only across the lake, but further down, into the depths.

Everywhere a shrimp brightened, I now saw other creatures, some dredged up from depths and caverns humans never saw, twisting and swimming in all directions. Confused as their fish minds could be, torn by bullets from above, clouding the waters with their innards. I saw stray fins, tentacles, and eyes float past me.

None of this mattered to me at the time. My mind had, for some reason, decided to prioritize safety from bullets over air, and down I went.

The agitation of the lake creatures grew, and I tasted blood again and again, which I doubt was human. My lungs began to ache, and I was buffeted on all sides. I didn't see bullets anymore, so the need for air took hold, and I began to swim frantically in the direction I thought was up.

I will tell you now that it was not.

LIGHT

So I swam toward what my stupid body took to be the surface. Maybe if I had the Gift I would have known better.

Soon the fish and eels and whatever-else of Glaizatz Lake were so thick around me I could hardly move. Battering me, getting caught in my hair and my dress. My lungs burned, and I knew I would die. I had expected to die today, but not like this, not without even *knowing* if we had saved the Tetrarchia.

Would I go to one of the hells that tortures you by letting you see how the world goes on without your presence? Or one of the hells that tortures you by refusing to show it?

Then I saw light peek out from between the fins and arms and tails and tongues. It was to my left: I had been swimming sideways, not up, toward the far walls of the lake. I turned and swam toward the light as my body felt like bursting. That light had to be the surface.

As I went, the creatures of the lake began to clear out, which I assumed was because I was nearing the air. The light grew brighter, larger, until it was impossible that this could be the cavern's torches. I don't know why I kept swimming toward it; perhaps I was so far gone I thought it was the sun.

The light was white, yawning bigger and bigger, and I finally realized that in swimming toward it, I was swimming straight down, away from air. The light seemed to fill the entire bottom of the lake.

The lake, need I remind you, was seven miles across.

Was this the Soul of the Nation?

A sort of blot appeared at one of its edges, and slid down over the light. A dark circle moving toward the center; a miniscule dot that was far larger than I. I was fascinated. I floated in the water, entranced, staring down. My head, deprived of air, began to think this dot was the beginning of a cancer on that Soul, caused by me and my actions.

Then I realized it was the pupil of an eye.

Some deep foreboding gripped me (finally), and I began to swim up, away from it. But even as I did, I looked down, watching this great eyeball that was the very size of Glaizatz Lake itself, if not larger. In that eye, I searched for intelligence, for benevolence, for, I suppose, a soul. The pupil centered itself and then began to move again. It flitted here and there, tracking each thing in its domain, up, across, down, with no reason or purpose beyond an animal's alertness when it smells blood.

I saw reflected in that eye an empty and singular mind. As you see in the face of a fish that has been drawn from the water and does not yet know it's dying, glassy and emotionless, but feeling pain.

Glaizatz Lake had no floor: it only tapered down to this, something living in a cavern below Rotfelsen, or in the very depths of the world. A great, blank, cold-blooded animal peering into our little rock, so much larger than anything that had dug tunnels through Rotfelsen, or fought in what was now the Grand Opera House. A creature of a size that could destroy this entire rock and all its people with a swish of its tail, if it had a tail.

I swam faster for the surface. Every part of my body pained and waterlogged. I am sure that, though I was but one speck in Glaizatz Lake, this great eye locked onto me and me alone for half a second, and I have never been so scared before or since.

As I neared the surface, the lake's creatures seemed to have calmed, and the pupil rolled away again, back to the edge and out of my sight. Soon after, the great eye closed, the lake darkened again, and I burst out of the bloody and body-clogged surface of the water. I was coughing, sputtering, and, I think, crying, although with so much water and blood everywhere, it was hard to tell. I swam for the nearest shore, heaved myself onto it, and passed out. If someone came and killed me, what did I even care? At least it would not be that thing.

MOVEMENT

I was shaken violently, but my eyes wouldn't open. I heard clashing and yelling, and a great thrumming beneath it all, but there was a clicking in my ears that obscured everything. I wasn't touching the floor; mostly dry hair brushed my face.

"What . . . ?" I burbled.

"Not now!" grunted a voice by my head, vibrating my cheek. My face was buried in someone's neck. I smelled sweat.

I got my eyes open. There was a Green, his face straining with exertion, his sword falling toward me. I screamed, but it came out a croak. His sword was stopped by another blade. I was gripping something tightly; was it a sword? Was I waking up in the middle of fighting? The clicking in my ears began to fade.

"I said not now!" yelled Dagmar.

The Green's sword was stopped again, and I felt myself lurched toward him. A hand that wasn't mine pushed his face away, and then he was run through by the sword that I thought I'd been holding. I wasn't. Something dashed across my vision, and I thought it was Gabor.

The Green fell to the floor, and my world finally expanded, but not by much. I was in a small, enclosed lift cage; the rumbling I heard was its ascent. The rushing walls of the rotrock tunnel came into focus, as did the wildly shaking lanterns above us. Purples and Greens crowded in on us, the lift swaying and tipping, but I bounced even more. My feet were dangling, whipping about; my arms were over a strong pair of shoulders, gripping a vest for dear life. To my left, Gabor was fighting.

Dagmar was also fighting, and I was on her back, whipping around with each of her movements.

"What's happening?" I said into her ear.

"We're fighting," answered Dagmar, spinning as she exchanged sword strokes with two men who were each hardly a foot away.

Gabor slammed into the wall to our left, grunting as his sword flicked out and opened a Purple's cheek. Then Dagmar killed the soldier, and I felt her shoulder slow for a moment, as her blade hit resistance in his body, and then quicken as it slid the rest of the way, and back out.

"Yes!" cried Gabor, pushing himself off the bars. "We're fighting!"

"So we didn't win?" I asked.

"Not as such," said Dagmar. "Now shut up."

I complied. My legs felt like wet yarn, dangling as Dagmar carried me, leaping through the small space, stepping over bodies to create more of them.

Moments later, it was over. Gabor breathed hard, smiling and wiping off his sword, and Dagmar lowered me, gently, to the floor in a corner of the lift. I counted six dead soldiers on the floor—I could hardly imagine how they, and the three of us, had even fit in this space, let alone fought here.

Not that *I* had done any fighting.

Dagmar crouched down in front of me, like she was speaking to a child. She even wiped my wet hair out of my face. I think I sort of chirped.

"How're you doing?" she asked, arms resting on her knees.

Gabor came up behind her and dropped my boots, jacket, and leather vest to the floor near me. His clothes were ragged, his face bruised.

"Fine?" I gulped. "You did all the work." I shook the water out of my head. "I saw you fighting and dove right back into the water."

"So?" said Dagmar. "We were fine, and there were at least four harquebuses pointed your way: to come out would have been suicide."

I couldn't meet their gazes anymore, so I looked at the floor, where the empty, dead eyes of a man stared up at me. He must have been younger than twenty-five. I kept looking at him as I fumblingly fit my wet stockings into my dry boots.

Going back in the water may have been the smart thing, but I knew that wasn't why I'd done it.

"What happened?" I gulped.

"Dagmar set the tent alight, and then cut us loose," said Gabor.

"I had to knife a few of their soldiers on the way," added Dagmar.

"Oh," I said. "Good." I had one boot on when I finally looked up at them again. "Is . . . is that good?"

"Yes!" cried Gabor.

"Eh," added Dagmar.

"Did our plan work?" I coughed.

"Well," said Dagmar, "Gabor, his friends, and some other imprisoned workers all put up a good show, for how little they must have been fed."

"Very little," Gabor agreed.

"We fought, and we killed many, but seven of the ten regicides got away. Including Dreher and Vorosknecht."

"Oh."

"They're ahead of us in another lift, on their way to the surface," said Gabor. He shrugged.

It would be some time before our enemies reached the surface, but we could do nothing, warn no one. This had been as terrible as all my plans. What I would have done for Ramunas' messenger lammergeier now.

I put my head in my hands. We sat in our lift full of corpses, with no idea where on the surface we would emerge. Somewhere below us, the freed prisoners were finishing up with the enemy soldiers. I hoped they wouldn't kill them all—it wasn't their fault, really. Was it? My only booted foot slid out, and I mistakenly kicked the dead soldier near me in his dead face.

My heart pounded, my head throbbed. It was all over, and I had failed. The whole point had been to kill the ringleaders, and instead I had revealed my allegiance, and they'd gotten away. I suppose we'd saved the prisoners, but this was still the end. With nothing else to do, I tried to wring the water out of my clothes. My hands quivered. In my mind, I saw the great, white eye. Now I knew from where the wiggly little shrimp drew their light. The lift screeched against the tunnel.

"Did you see the light?" I murmured. "Did it reach you from the water?"

"What? Like their Soul?" laughed Dagmar. "I think I saw some of the shrimp sync with one another for a moment . . ."

"No. Not like the Soul or the shrimp. Something else."

"A near-death illusion," said Gabor. "I've had them myself."

I shook my head. "Can't we go any faster?" I moaned.

"No rush!" laughed Dagmar.

"Indeed," added Gabor. "They must be waiting for us at the top."

"What if we get up there," I sighed, "and it's already war?"

"Then we'll fight," said Dagmar.

I shook my head. I never was cut out to be a soldier.

They began to regale me with how the fight I'd missed had happened. Dagmar and Gabor seemed awfully calm, and I half-listened as I tried to not pass out from fear. One of the regicides had been killed, two more taken prisoner. The lift dragged us ever upward. I nodded aimlessly.

Gabor laughed. "You see! I told you she'd want to take prisoners."

I nodded again.

Dagmar rolled her eyes and put a copper mark in his hand. "I wanted to kill them all; Gabor said you'd be angry if we did."

I nodded again.

Then they had found me and fought their way to a lift. They told the story as if we weren't all doomed.

How could they be so calm? I felt sick, I was sore, my lungs hurt, and I was shivering with cold, soaked through as I was in late winter. People have faced war in better shape. The lift kept screeching and dragging us upward.

"How many of ours died?" I asked.

"No time to count," said Dagmar. "Plenty."

Another thing to feel guilty about. How many had I led to death?

There was a loud burst above us, and a corpse in the back of the lift shook. Someone was shooting at us.

SHARPSHOOTERS

Dagmar extinguished our lantern to make them shoot into the dark.

Leaning over the mouth of our tunnel, with the sun blazing above them, were two silhouettes, and whenever one started to reload, the other fired. We did our best to flatten against the sides of the small lift, which shook and hit the walls of the tunnel.

"Do you have that little knife?" asked Dagmar.

I popped Tural's gold-handled knife out of my boot and gave it to her. Dagmar flung the knife upward, her body snapping up, leg kicking out. One of the figures above made a choked noise and disappeared. Moments later, a harquebus fell amongst our feet.

"Show-off," I grunted.

The other outline disappeared. They must not have realized none of us knew how to reload the gun.

Gabor, sword in his right hand, hefted the harquebus in his left for show. We all crouched as we hit the open air, which I had been sure I would never see again. It was midmorning. Blindingly so.

This lift didn't have a little building around it, unfortunately, but popped up into the air beneath a gazebo. There were high hedges around us, and off to our left I saw Chasiku's watchtower, reaching far above, which at least gave me my bearings for the few moments I expected to live.

The man Dagmar had killed with the knife was a Purple, as was the other shooter who was, inexplicably, also dead. There was a Green's corpse as well, and otherwise, no one we could see. It didn't *sound* like the surface had exploded into war, but how else to explain the dead bodies?

"Well," said Gabor. "I'm glad they weren't waiting for us, but this is all a bit eerie, isn't it?"

I nodded as we stepped out of the gazebo. We were all so exhausted; it was certainly preferable that we get into no more fights. Then, of course, there was a yell, and ten more Greens came running around the hedges toward us. I heard a moan and realized it came from me.

This whole day had all been my stupid idea, so I took the lead in front of the two trained soldiers, sickle raised, and ran forward, expecting to die.

At least I wouldn't be killed by the creature below the lake.

A tall man with a scar and a sabre in his hand was in front of his men. We met, his sabre dropped toward me, and then he jerked to the side and was dead before I had done anything.

"Ha!" Dagmar cried.

The rest of the Greens looked confused. Another dropped.

I stood still, confused, until Dagmar and Gabor leapt past me. I shook my head to clear it and joined in.

Grunts and impacts sounded around me, and I was quite lost in it all. If there's a good thing about being outnumbered, it's that you can flail and trust you won't hit a friend.

But then, we hardly got a chance to *hit* anyone. Gabor and Dagmar did a bit of cutting, but the Greens kept dropping of their own accord. I fancied I heard distant shots.

One particularly large Green had been absolutely within inches of killing me, executing a perfect lunge entirely outside of my weak defense, when he had suddenly spun like a dancer and died.

I looked up to see puffs of smoke coming from Chasiku's watchtower every few moments.

When there was one Green left, he pressed himself against the hedge to our left, to hide himself from the watchtower. He looked so confused and terrified that I felt for him. Then he was shot *through* the hedge, and died.

"Not complaining," said Dagmar, "but what's going on?"

"This way," I said between heavy breaths, pointing toward an opening in the hedge.

But first I went and retrieved Tural's knife.

BANG

"Did you see that?" yelled Behrens as he bounced down the last few steps of Chasiku's watchtower. "Did you *see that*?"

"Yes, yes!" I laughed as he hugged me. "What was I seeing?"

"Something amazing!" he said.

At the top of the watchtower, a group of Yellow harquebusiers leaned against the railing and looked down at us. They were clean, their yellow uniforms smooth and sharp. Dagmar, Gabor, and I were rumpled, dirty, and stained with blood, my hair a scraggly mess. I smelled of lake creatures, and I was shivering. We must have been a sight.

"Miss Chasiku," said Behrens, "she comes to my barracks and asks for me, you see."

I had an idea of how difficult it must have been for her to leave her watchtower and go deliberately to a place full of soldiers. I nodded at Behrens to continue.

"And she tells me that soon you'll be killed, unless I bring, ah, 'a gaggle of your shooting friends.' Once we're all lined up on her balcony, she—well, ma'am, I knew that she was a soothsayer, like yourself, but I didn't expect anything like this. Half of us, we didn't even see whom we hit. She just stands there, you see, with her eyes closed, and she points.

"'No, no,' she says to me. 'Why are you aiming, idiot? Point. Bang. Point . . .' and I say, 'Bang, miss?' and she nods, you see?"

I saw very well now. Behrens and his sharpshooters had gone one after the other: Chasiku, eyes closed, would point, and the sharpshooter would aim right along her arm and fingertip to shoot. This was how they hit targets they couldn't see, or that were in the middle of a mad dash.

Targets. I mean people, human beings.

I thanked Behrens, who loudly insisted he didn't deserve it. I tried to enjoy his excitement in victory, but I couldn't stop thinking of what else might be happening, where else the Purples and Greens were going. Yet even *that* was a welcome reprieve from that great eye, which was still throbbing in my mind, like when you stare at the sun and then close your eyes. It was lurking somewhere beneath the lake, in Rotfelsen's depths.

"Did she see anything else?" I asked, failing to keep my voice down. I nearly screamed it.

"Yes," he said. "Miss Chasiku saw that the regicides were going to do something, so she sent Lenz off to your servant house."

My scalp prickled. I began to shake worse than when I'd been on Dagmar's back.

HOSTAGES

As many Yellows as chose to follow me hopped into a carriage, and when we got to the servant house, I leapt out and ran inside screaming for Papa. Johann, the head butler, got in my way, demanding to know what was going on. I ignored him and went up the stairs three at a time, with the soldiers all trailing behind me.

I threw myself into my bedroom, and saw two dead Yellows and one living person. Sitting in my chair, feigning calm, with one leg crossed over the other, was Selvosch the Lord High Quarrymaster.

I was inches from stabbing him when Behrens grabbed me and held me back. The Quarrymaster's supposed calm drained away. The Yellows filled the doorway and the hall outside, keeping anyone else out.

"Kill me," shrieked Selvosch, clearly hoping that I would not, "if you want the hostages to die!" He said these bold words even as he shivered.

"Where?!" I managed to scream in his face. I must have looked like actual death to him, crusted over with blood, eyes wild, trying to twist out of Behrens' hands.

Selvosch managed to grin. "With us. And if I don't join the others within the hour, they die."

I finally stopped straining against Behrens' hands. He did not quite let me go, just yet.

"It will take us longer than an hour to bring up the regicides we captured down in Glaizatz Lake," I said. "You need to give us more—"

"Keep them," said Selvosch. "Or kill them. They believe in the Soul of the Nation, and they'll die before they talk."

"Then what do you want from us?" asked Dagmar, stepping forward.

"Bring us your false King," said Selvosch, "and you can have them back."

"We don't know where he is," I replied.

"I doubt that."

"We don't," I pleaded. As far as I knew, no one left on the palace grounds had any clue as to where Olaf, Biruté, and their paramours had absconded to. "And he likely won't be back for a week. Not until the Eve of the Council."

Selvosch shook his head and stood up. "Bring him to us, and you get them back. Try to intrude upon the palace, without that supposed King in tow, and they die."

He began to walk toward me, and the rest of the Yellows, expecting us to part for him. When we didn't, he went around, and squeezed out into the hallway. I stared straight ahead, at where he had been. Then I slumped into the chair, hearing Selvosch's boots on the stairs. I began to cry, and they were big, ugly tears.

"Did they get Lenz, too?" hissed Gabor. He looked down at the dead Yellows, who must have accompanied Lenz there.

I just shook my head and shrugged because I couldn't speak.

"Why do you think Selvosch called the king 'false'?" asked Dagmar.

"Who knows?" said Behrens. "Soul of the Nation garbage to delegitimize him, I'm sure."

There was a thump in my closet, and Dagmar ran over to open it, sword drawn. Her sword's point, and the barrels of two Yellows' harquebuses, met the figure that tumbled out onto the floor.

It was Papa. He lay limply on his back.

I knocked them aside as I ran to him, still crying, grabbing him, blubbering incoherently as I held his rigid body. Then he blinked.

"Can I move now, Kalynishka?" he muttered in my ear.

"Yes, of course!" I cried, hugging him. He relaxed into a heap in my arms, and we sat in a pile on the floor, surrounded by Yellows. I told him how much I loved him in perhaps three different languages.

"Your friend with the mustache, Lanzo?" said Papa. "He came here with his men and told us to keep quiet, said we were in danger. Well, you know, Mother began screaming and screaming at him, and at his soldiers, daring them to kill her. So he put me in there and said to stay very still. Until it was safe to move."

"But, Papa, if you're here . . ."

"Yes!" he cried, grabbing my clothes, hands turning white, as though he had just remembered. "They took Mother, and your friend!"

I blinked the tears away many times, and then I laughed. Genuinely, but evilly, I think.

"Lenz and Grandmother," I choked out. "They only took Lenz and Grandmother!"

I pulled myself up, giggling, and started toward the door. Gabor grabbed my arm.

"Kalyna, where are you going?"

"To kill Selvosch, of course!" I said, grinning like a mischievous child. "They only took Lenz and Grandmother! I'm going to go kill them."

Gabor yanked me back violently.

"You may not care for your grandmother," he hissed, "but we will have a plan before we go and get Lenz killed. Is that clear?"

His handsome, youthful face, which had been so full of joy even during all the carnage earlier that day, was suddenly hard in a way I had not seen before.

"He doesn't deserve someone caring about him so much," I grunted.

"Neither do I," he replied. "But he also saved your father. What do *you* deserve, Kalyna?"

I shrugged and went back to Papa. Behrens and Dagmar helped me sit him up in my chair, and I sat on the floor next to him, stroking his hand. I reflected upon the fact that Lenz had saved my father from being taken, and knew that I had to rescue my kidnapper. If nothing else, I refused to owe him.

THE DELEGATIONS BEGIN TO ARRIVE

Selvosch had been right about the two regicide plotters we had captured: they wouldn't say a thing. Dagmar asked if she could *convince* them, but I did not let her. I suspected no one was offering Lenz the same kindness. The captured regicide soldiers didn't seem to know very much, and it would be very easy for their masters to deny any accusations that came from them. So, we shoved them, seven in all, into that one cell beneath Lenz's barracks, and convinced some Yellows to feed them regularly. We did not know what to do with them, but at least they were very uncomfortable.

As far as we could tell, Vorosknecht and Dreher were curled up in the Sunset Palace, with a coterie of regicide plotters and loyal soldiers, holding their hostages—who may or may not have included Prince Friedhelm—and making sure that we came nowhere near them without Olaf. "We" in this case was myself, Chasiku, Gabor, and any Yellows not already in the palace. So, without Prince Friedhelm, whom we had not heard from since Glaizatz Lake, and so must have been trapped in the palace; without Lenz, who was at best a prisoner; and without even King Olaf or Queen Biruté, we were all that was left. No available royalty also meant no one could get the Reds on our side, and they were busy keeping the peace for the Council of Barbarians. Jördis, for her part, had entirely disappeared: her clothes and furniture were still in her room, but her papers and books were all gone.

The day after our battle at Glaizatz Lake, Gabor, Dagmar, and I found ourselves in Chasiku's tower, trying to formulate some sort of plan. Everyone kept looking to the two prophets in the room, for obvious reasons, but Chasiku kept seeing Rotfelsen falling apart, and all I could think of was what I had seen in Glaizatz Lake. Or *beneath* the lake. Papa had seen an "ever broadening emptiness" down there. How big could the thing be? What sort of shape took up that space? Every time I considered it, my mind reeled, and I felt almost drunk.

So we sat around with no real leaders, reminding me of a play I saw in my youth, in which a town lost all of its adults, and the children had to lead themselves. I believe it ended with the children being slaughtered by an invading army: it was a morality tale.

After we had said a great deal with no actual progress, I was leaning against the railing of Chasiku's tower, idly watching streams of dignitaries make their way up from Turmenbach, and into the Sunset Palace. I believe I was seeing a Quru delegation of some sort, based on the enthusiastically waving flags of almost prismatic colors and patterns, and the deep red robes. It certainly wasn't large enough, or elaborate enough, to be Queen Sevda of Quruscan, but was likely some group of mountain officials. They were chanting, "Barbarous! Barbarous!" in Cölluknit, and many were laughing.

"Remind me why we can't just sneak in with them and murder our enemies?" I asked.

"Everyone's being checked at the door," muttered Dagmar, "by Greens and Reds. Someone would tell our friends hiding out in there."

"There must be someone who can get us in," said Gabor. "Tural's been going in and out, right? Couldn't he, I don't know, pack us in barrels of peaches or some such?"

"He doesn't have access to those until they're already in the Palace," I sighed. "Besides, I doubt he would even have time to listen to us right now." And I wanted to keep him out of danger, to the extent such a thing was possible.

"This is interminable!" cried Gabor, tearing at his hair. "We're just sitting here, and Lenz may be *dead* by now."

I laughed. "No, no, he's the spymaster, they'll keep him alive to help them catch the King and the Prince. But Grandmother has probably made them angry enough that they've killed her already."

"You're probably right," Gabor mumbled. Then he realized what I'd said and looked up at me. "Gods, I hope not!"

"Then you're the only one," said Chasiku.

I nodded.

"But I've still never seen her death," Chasiku added.

"Well, great," I growled, turning my back to the railing and staring at the three of them.

Chasiku was sitting straight on her bedroll, drinking her home-made coffee with a grimace, Gabor was against a wall, and Dagmar was actually lying on her back on the hard floor, her hands behind her head. This was who I had: the woman I had called a fake, the man I had planned to kidnap, and the guard whose name it took me weeks to learn. By the gods, I actually missed Lenz.

And now it was about a week until the Council of Barbarians would begin, and everything would crumble. But how?

I thought again of the eye beneath Glaizatz Lake. It had intruded around the edges of my thoughts all day, and it was easy enough to imagine its connection to the shattering of Rotfelsen. But how would these deluded nationalists cause it to destroy us? I opened my mouth to speak, but couldn't bring myself to. The others would either find me mad, or be faced with something they could affect even less than the regicides.

"Have you seen anything useful, Chasiku?" I asked. "Or are you only not seeing my Grandmother's death?" And then, I very quickly added: "And obviously *I* haven't seen anything useful."

Chasiku just smiled and shrugged.

We all stood around for awhile, as more pieces of Cöllüknit wafted up from below.

"The Masovskans are supposed to start showing up tomorrow," said Dagmar, stifling a yawn. "At least that's what they tell me."

"Oh no," I said.

"Oh no, what?" asked Gabor.

"Dagmar, with me," I sighed. "I know who can get us into the Palace."

THE EDELTRAUD MANSION

Dagmar and I found ourselves approaching a sprawling and decadent mansion, one of many that were in a nice little line just in front of the Sunset Palace. Poor, departed King Gerhold VIII's grandfather, Gebbrandt II, had convinced (or forced) his major officials and lesser relatives to come live in this part of the palace grounds, where he could hold them beneath an imperious eye. All these estates were of Masovskan wood, not rotrock, so that they would not become fortresses.

The particular one we were about to enter had a metal gate that looked impressive but would stop very little, surrounding a couple acres of gardens with a mansion in the center. As we came closer, the building seemed to consistently reveal itself to be larger than I expected.

This was the home of Edeltraud von Edeltraud, Mistress of the Coin, and friend—or at least begrudging host—to the Gustavus siblings. A butler with the nose of a boxer welcomed us and led us into a drawing room filled with paintings, sculptures, and couches of stone housing voluminous cushions. On one of those couches was Klemens Gustavus, the spoiled scion of the changing bank, who had tried to have his own cousin killed in Masovska a lifetime (or a few months) ago. And who, of course, Lenz and I had kept locked up for a bit. Everyone makes mistakes.

Dagmar spent most of the way there telling me not to trust Klemens, and that I should let her kill him.

"Let's not forget that he killed my comrades," she hissed. "And kicked me many times."

"We *had* ambushed him," I replied.

She only harrumphed.

Klemens was having tea with Edeltraud von Edeltraud herself, whom I had not seen in person since I followed her around during the Winter Ball. Upon seeing me, she stood up, welcomed me, and then began to leave.

"I want no part of whatever you will discuss," she said. "I don't want to be involved!" And she disappeared, as though she had never been there.

"Please sit," said the young banker in halting Rotfelsenisch, motioning to a small stool that was, pointedly, lower than the couch he was on. Klemens seemed delighted to see me, which I took as a bad sign.

If I was positioned lower than Klemens, Dagmar, standing behind me with her hands on her hips, cast a shadow over both of us.

"Kalyna Aljosanovna!" he continued, once I had sat. "My old jailer! Looking beautiful as always."

I could not help laughing at that, but I think he took it as modesty, which it was not.

"I'm sorry again about our misunderstanding," I said. Being forced to look up at him made this apology feel particularly infantilizing.

"Oh, don't even begin to speak to it!" he laughed. I had only ever seen him be dismissive or frightened, and so this friendliness was disarming, no matter how false. "It worked out, we are on the same side, and we have kept the King alive so far."

There were a few things wrong with that last phrase, but I said, "Yes. He is alive and happy at his hunting lodge."

"Truly?"

I nodded.

"Then all is right with the world! Why, I'm so happy with how things have turned out that I do not even blame you for that mess back in Masovska."

"I couldn't possibly know what you mean."

"Of course." Klemens sat back, and crossed one leg over the other, and *there* was the hateful, dismissive child from the Masovskan courtroom.

Dagmar coughed. "I don't know what this is about, but do I need to hit him?"

I shook my head.

Klemens laughed. "You needn't worry. I'm not so dull as to start killing advocates in Gniezto. My cousin can have his little windfall, and *you* can give me direct access to the King!"

"What are you doing?" snapped Bozena Gustavus, in Masovskani, as she stormed into the room.

I heard Dagmar's sword clank against her hand, but she did not draw it. Bozena stomped up and looked ready to hit her brother, but she did not do so.

"Why don't you just tell her everything, you fool!" she cried, still in Masovskani. She glowered at him for another moment before turning to me, and switching to Rotfelsenisch. "What do you want from us, witch?"

"Watch your tone," said Dagmar.

"Oh, come now, sister!" laughed Klemens. "She is our august ally, and she sees the future!"

I opened my mouth to answer Bozena's question to me.

"She is not our ally!" She sneered at him. Despite the rest of us, she had gone back to Masovskani. "She is a royal tool with no power."

"Keep it to Rotfelsenisch, please," grunted Dagmar. "So I know whether you're threatening to murder us."

"If I may!" I all but yelled. "All I am looking for is passage into the Sunset Palace."

"Into?" grunted Bozena.

"*Our* enemies," I said, "have hostages, have taken control of the palace, and are keeping us out. The King is blessedly away, but he will be back soon. Just because you have no longer been involved in trying to stop the regicides, does not mean they are done. If you do not want the King, as well as the King of Masovska, and the other monarchs besides, to be *assassinated*, we must get into the palace."

"Things got away from your spymaster, did they?" laughed Klemens.

"Yes," I snapped. "Clearly."

"You should have left it to us," replied Klemens.

I smiled and nodded.

"And what do we get in return?" asked Bozena, back in Rotfelsenisch.

"An unbroken Tetrarchia, for one," I answered, "in which you can continue to do business. And your lives, besides."

"But you understand we would be putting ourselves in danger for you," she said.

"We are all in danger."

"Not good enough," said Bozena. "We have only your word on that. You will kill these regicides, if you get in?"

"Or throw them in a dungeon forever."

"In that case"—she flourished a hand at her brother—"we will need a new Court Philosopher, won't we?"

"You're not suggesting a Gustavus?" I replied, coughing out the name.

"And why not?" asked Klemens. "I've always had a philosophical nature."

I laughed at them. I had been a conniving fraud long enough to recognize the simplest games when I saw them.

"And maybe Bozena as the High General?" I asked.

"Oh? Will they need one of those, too?" asked Klemens.

"I would love," said Dagmar, "to see you try to get siblings, and Masovskans at that, into those titles."

"Maybe we should get rid of both positions altogether," I said.

"Well then," sighed Klemens, "what about Selvosch's quarries? Who will take those?"

There it was. He had started out high and outlandish to make this seem plausible. Bozena nodded her agreement.

I found imagining the government of Rotfelsen overrun with Gustavuses to be at least a little entertaining, and smiled.

"I am not the King, of course," I began, "but with him away, and the Prince and spymaster trapped in the palace, I can only say that I'll do what I can." I grinned. "Which is a lot. I've grown quite close to the King, you see." I leaned forward, elbow on my thigh and chin in my hand, staring straight into Klemens' eyes. "So, if you can get, say, twenty of our people into the palace, then the King will be very grateful, and I will do all I can to encourage him." I sat back. "If not, then I doubt any of us will survive the Council of Barbarians."

Klemens looked up at his sister, who was standing beside him, gripping his shoulder. She sighed and nodded almost imperceptibly.

"Capital!" said Klemens. "You and your Yellows can come in with us."

"Thank you." I bowed my head.

"Then I shall see you again on the Eve of the Council!" he said.

I started. "The Eve? That's a week away! What about tomorrow? I thought the Masovskan delegation—"

"The *royal* Masovskan delegation," Bozena corrected. "Merchants who can afford to take part in the Council and petition the clerks and politicians, we all show up right before it starts."

A whole week. How much damage could they do in a week? And a week knowing that the eye was . . . down there. But then, had it *always* been down there? Was Rotfelsen that precarious? Was the world?

"Can Edeltraud get us in earlier?"

"Oh my, no!" laughed Klemens. "She's terrified of being seen in there again, ever since she first turned down Selvosch and the regicides. Why, she's hardly left the house!"

I sighed and took my leave. I did not see Edeltraud von Edeltraud anywhere along the way—she had disappeared.

"See you in a week, Kalyna Aljosanovna!" called Klemens.

"Don't trust them," Dagmar muttered. "We should kill them and be done with it."

I shrugged and shook my head.

WAITING FOR THE COUNCIL

The following week was awful, and largely uneventful besides. It was almost spring, but Rotfelsen was actually hit with its biggest snow yet, on top of everything else.

Every day of that week, Tural would come back from long hours in the Sunset Palace, with nothing to tell us beyond kitchen gossip, most of which was only kitchen-related. We did learn from him that no one in the palace had seen the Prince, which was worrying. He also told us that whenever Yellows had tried to enter the palace, as they normally did, the Greens would not officially bar their way, but always provoke them until particularly egregious brawls broke out. Purples would then jump in, outnumbering the Yellows, until the Reds would disperse the fight, sending the Yellows back to their barracks.

The full force of the Yellows was in flux, running drills and patrolling the palace grounds at the behest of their extant commanders. Those who had been part of Lenz's espionage, at least, would listen to Dagmar, Chasiku, and I.

"It is almost as though," I said, "having four separate armies in one place is a bad idea."

"I suppose I never thought of it that way," said Gabor.

I then thought about how much better *no* army would be, but I did not say this out loud.

That was the extent of what we got out of Tural. Gabor hired someone to go take care of his plants, and then spent most of the time pacing in what had been Grandmother's room, and sometimes coming to chat with Papa. Dagmar never left my side.

I spent a good deal of that week with Papa, both because I was quite sure we would all die in a few days, and because I hoped against hope that he would see something new and useful. He did not.

However, Chasiku did.

On the night before we were set to infiltrate the Sunset Palace (if the Gustavuses hadn't forgotten), a Yellow I didn't recognize woke me up and told me Chasiku wanted me to come over to her right away. I roused Dagmar from where she was sleeping outside my door, threw on a big scarf, and off we went. As soon as we were up in Chasiku's tower, Dagmar sat down against the wall and closed her eyes.

"Wake me if someone's killing us," she said. Then she began to snore, lightly.

Chasiku was out at the railing, looking off into the darkness. She was shivering, but hardly seemed to care. I joined her, and began to lift my scarf onto her shoulders. Chasiku whipped her face around to glare at me.

I froze for a moment, then continued to put the scarf over her. She grunted.

"Well?" I asked.

"You saw something down in Glaizatz, didn't you?" she said. "I knew it when I was seeing your future before, and you have been very reticent to talk about it."

The eye in the bottom of the lake had continued to haunt me. I nodded.

"I didn't want to scare anyone," I whispered, slipping into Sky-dašiavos.

"Well," she said, "if you don't tell me, I shall be driven mad by seeing pieces of it with no context."

I sighed, and I told her. I told her about eye that had glowed, that had looked at me, that was definitely not some Soul of Rotfelsen, just a large, dumb creature in the depths of the rock. Or below even that.

"That . . . likely explains why the whole rock will fall apart," she said.

"I have tried not to think about it, but yes. It's the only thing I can imagine causing that."

She nodded.

"But," I ventured, "if Rotfelsen has stood all these years, what would cause that thing to . . . thrash about beneath us now? Has it always been there? Does it travel around through the depths of the world? Are there . . . *more* of them?"

"One thing at a time," said Chasiku. "I saw something new tonight, Kalyna. I saw soldiers in purple uniforms marching what seemed an unending number of prisoners down to Glaizatz Lake and, down there, slaughtering them. Over and over, for what may have been days." She blinked her eyes, not looking at me, and I fancied I saw tears there. "Thousands dead, and I saw every single one. Each silent or pleading person, every single face in its last moments. I saw them all in a *moment*, Kalyna."

I had nothing to offer. I simply nodded.

"Then," she continued, "I saw the crumbling again, the rock coming apart. I saw soldiers in purple startled by it, and then crushed in the midst of their endless murder."

A thought appeared somewhere in the back of my head, a glimmer of an idea. Then it grew and grew, and I had a sickening feeling.

"Were they throwing the bodies into the lake's waters?" I asked.

She nodded.

"That was their plan with Gabor and the rest, some kind of human sacrifice for what they *think* lives down there," I continued. "But we stopped it. When I saw the eye, our battle had already filled the water with some small amount of bodies and blood."

"You think that clouding the waters with blood and bodies, with pieces of humans, will . . . irritate it?"

"Chasiku, I saw no thought behind that eye. It was blankly panicked. If the water is clogged with dead, the fish will begin to thrash and die, they will not be able to see or hunt, it will simply change their lake, and their little fish minds will be confused."

"And so perhaps that great, big fish mind will also be confused, and alarmed," she said. "Or at least inconvenienced or irritated, like someone spat in its eye. Or it may feed on those fish, somehow, either when they come down into its depths, or when it reaches up into our lake."

The thought of it *reaching up* made my skin crawl. And I remembered those great gashes in the walls of the cavern. Which I had seen as a child, and again when I went down there to be "initiated."

"And if it's irritated, or can no longer hunt here," I muttered, "it may just decide to leave for somewhere else and . . . turn around."

I bent over until my forehead touched the railing with a muffled clang. I stared at my feet and began to breathe very fast. Neither of us said anything for a few minutes.

"Sneak me in with you tomorrow," said Chasiku. "It would be torture for me to be in the palace at its normal capacity, let alone during the Council, but I can't just sit here and trust . . . *you* to fix this without me."

I snorted. "What could you possibly do?"

"Tell the stupid boys where to shoot."

I stood back up. "Fine. Give me back my scarf."

She did so.

THE EVE OF THE COUNCIL

I woke up on the Eve of the Council expecting something to happen, but, at first, nothing did. The Council of Barbarians proper would begin the next day, but there would be the Opening Invocation tonight. I still felt quite certain that those invocations would be when our regicides would make their move, as it would be the first time all four monarchs would be in the same place. Unfortunately, by that morning, I had heard nothing from Olaf and Biruté, and nothing from Bozena and Klemens Gustavus.

At midday, I was sitting in my chair, with my feet pulled up and my knees against my chest, grinding my teeth and staring into space, when a messenger came from the Gustavuses. Half an hour later, myself, Dagmar, Gabor, Behrens, a beleaguered Chasiku, and fifteen loyal Yellows were outside the Edeltraud mansion, all hidden in a large carriage. We were well armed, and I had decided to wear trousers that day. For violence, whether or not it made sense.

Outside the mansion, in the surprisingly bitter cold of late winter, was a huge crowd of people, maybe a hundred. Klemens Gustavus was standing on top of a pile of crates, yelling and pointing, but no one seemed to be listening to him. Dagmar, Gabor, and I left the carriage and made our way to him.

"There you are! Finally!" snapped Klemens. "What are you waiting for? Get in!"

"Get in where?" He did not hear me over the crowd, so I repeated it, yelling.

Klemens jumped down in front of me and pointed behind him. "Into the crates! You and your flunkies!"

Dagmar barked out a laugh. I looked at the crates, blinked, and looked back at Klemens.

"What a miserable man," said Gabor.

"You have a hundred people here," I said, "can't we just blend in? Throw cloaks over the uniforms until we're in the palace?"

Klemens' eyes looked like they would pop out of his skull, and his sallow face went red. "A hundred people, Kalyna, with *a hundred* Council passes stamped what feel like *a hundred times* by the correct dignitaries, Kalyna! They do not make a habit of letting just anyone in, do you understand that? These aren't just our retinue, some of these are from our sister changing banks in other parts of the Tetrarchia. And everyone had to be verified by someone in their place of origin *and* here." He flung an arm off to the right. "We are even *trying* to expand to the Bandit States, so we have a group from Rituo. *Rituo!* Do you know what a nightmare it was to get papers from the Bandit States! If I knew what was right for my *business*, I would have skipped that, thrown them into these crates, and *you* out on your asses!"

I let Klemens regain his breath before I smiled and patted his shoulder. "Thank you so much for your help, Klemens Gustavus. Your ability to pull this whole retinue together just shows what a fantastic quarrymaster you will be."

"Thank you, Kalyna Aljosanovna. Now get in the crates."

Dagmar stared hard at Klemens for a long time. Gabor shrugged and began to climb into a crate.

"I don't think we should do this," whispered Dagmar, so close I could feel her breath.

"We have to get in there," I sighed. "We have to find the Prince, ally with the Yellows trapped in there, and stop the regicides before they ruin everything. And I am out of ideas on how to do so."

Dagmar shrugged. "Well, you're the one who makes tricksy plans. So."

In we went. My crate was full of musty, but pleasant, Masovskan furs. It wasn't as though I thought Dagmar was *wrong* exactly, but I had not found another way in. Dagmar's shin was pressed against my face, and Gabor's head was against my stomach. What would happen would happen.

"Just in case," muttered Dagmar, as she pulled out a dagger and almost cut Gabor.

Our crate was nailed shut, sealing us in and almost gouging my shoulder. I could hear the rest of our people climbing into the others, as Klemens was screaming, "And don't any of you tell anyone that there are people in the crates, if you value your jobs or your lives! It's for a *surprise!*"

That it was. I hoped.

After what felt like forever, we were lifted up by angry men who kept grunting Masovskani curses into our ears, and loaded onto something. For the most part, all I could see was Dagmar's leg, but it was sometimes dappled by the midday sun peeking through the boards of our crate. I could feel puffs of cold air from outside, now and then, but crammed in with other people and heavy furs, I was sweating awfully. I hoped I did not smell too bad, first because it would make the others in my crate miserable, and second because I began to fancy it would somehow give us away.

We were close to the palace, but the ride felt interminable. I wondered what Dreher and Vorosknecht were up to, if Grandmother had gotten herself and Lenz killed yet, and whether the King and Queen had arrived, or were still off in their love nest.

The same cursing men lifted us back off the carts, and began to carry us into, I hoped, the palace. Something was blocking out the sunlight, now.

"Who're you?" came a disdainful voice.

"The Gustaw Gustavus Changing Bank," said Klemens, "and affiliates, with gifts for—"

"What kind of gifts?"

"Furs and fish, mostly."

I was thankful that I had not been put in a crate of fish.

"Let me take a look."

"My good man, the crates are nailed shut."

"Well, I still think we should—"

"Hey!" another voice cried. "Who are they?"

I felt Dagmar tense. Her dagger had been out and ready the whole way, and she began to reach for her sword with the other hand. I suppose she wanted to pull it out the moment the crate opened, but mostly she just kicked me in the face a little.

"Just more affiliates, my *good man*," growled Klemens.

"Did you bring hangers-on from the damned Bandit States?!"

"Well, yes! We're trying to open a bank in Rituo."

"Andelka and the Rituo delegation have already—"

"But this isn't—"

"You can't just—"

"You there, Rots!" cried Bozena, from somewhere behind me. "You come and take a look at their papers, and tell me whether or not they're in order, yes? Rituo is our *ally*."

"Watch your tone, Masovskan."

"Come look at their papers, first."

Inspection of their papers took a long time, and there was much complaining about some parts being in the language of Rituo, which the soldiers certainly did not know. The inspection of everyone else's papers went on even longer, and Dagmar remained tense throughout. Sometimes she muttered, "I'll kill him. If nothing else, I will kill him."

Finally, I heard a soldier murmur to another: "What about the crates?"

"We'll probably have to read a series of gods-damned *books* in five languages detailing everything in there. We've wasted enough time, and have plenty more to check in. Let them through."

"Yes, sir. Besides, the way those fish are smelling, I'd rather not let any more stench out."

And in we went. The noise of soldiers yelling, birds chirping, people screaming that they had papers, all melted away and became the bustle of the Sunset Palace in utter disarray before a big event. A cheery butler told the Gustavuses where to put us, as a much less cheery one screamed at a group of people who were, I think, mopping the floors.

I kept listening for Tural's voice, even though I knew we couldn't be near the kitchens. I did not hear him.

We were carried a bit longer before we were set down. Dagmar began to writhe in anticipation. I heard low voices that I could not make out, and we were lifted again. This time, there was no cursing, just grunts and jostling as we were carried. We went like this for some time, and the bumping became worse.

"Something's wrong," grunted Dagmar.

"Just keep quiet," hissed Gabor.

Dagmar arced her foot upward, almost kicking me again, and began to slam on the top of the crate.

"Stop it!" I whispered.

Voices finally came from outside the crate, grumbling something in Rotfelsenisch. Dagmar kicked again, and the wood began to give. The crate was dropped to the floor, and my teeth cracked together from the impact. Dagmar kicked again, and the top of the crate broke outward.

In a moment, her sword was out, slicing through the furs, and she was on her feet. Then she didn't move.

When I managed to pull myself out of the crate, at first all I saw was Dagmar's yellow uniform against a vast ocean of purple. I blinked a few times.

The three of us were surrounded by Purples, with their swords and harquebuses pointed at us. The walls behind them, and everything else in view, was also purple. There were no other crates or allies or bankers in sight. It seemed the Gustavuses had indeed betrayed us.

"I knew it," growled Dagmar.

THE GRAND SUZERAIN

Dagmar, Gabor, and I were led down another purple hallway to a small door that opened into a room that was now familiar to me: Court Philosopher Vorosknecht's study. There was the purple couch, the great desk, the gaudy paintings, the glass liquor cabinet, the bust of the Court Philosopher himself in purple-stained marble, and the skeleton of poor old Meregfog. The door closed behind us and became one of the paintings.

Ranging about the large room, and out into the adjoining halls, were about twenty Greens and twenty Purples, including the ones who had brought us there. Some sat, some stood, two Greens in a hallway were even throwing a small Loashti rubber ball back and forth. Vorosknecht stood, looking smug, but harried, behind his desk, with Alban at his side. Slumped into the great purple couch was High General Dreher, surrounded by Greens who looked quite out of place against the room's predominant color. Selvosch sat near Dreher, on a little stool, shaking with . . . some sort of feeling, I'm sure.

In the center of the room, were three figures, bound and gagged. Lenz and Prince Friedhelm were covered in bruises, from what I could see. Lenz seemed to have had the worst of it, with old blood crusting in his mustache, and one of his eyes so swollen I was not sure he could see out of it. Grandmother was there as well, but she did not seem to have been beaten. She seemed to be trying to bite off and swallow her gag, in order to be free or to choke to death in spite.

"Well, hello everyone!" I chirped, because I could think of nothing better to say. Grandmother glared at me, and I grinned at her.

We were divested of our weapons and shoved to our knees near Vorosknecht's desk, with our hands hastily tied behind our backs. In those few moments, I saw so much of what the last week must have been like for the leaders of the regicides. Dreher was breathing hard, as though even that movement was painful, with his hands braced against his knees. It seemed that he would have bent over entirely, with his face between his knees, if he was not keeping his red, unblinking eyes fixed on Vorosknecht. For his part, Vorosknecht's beard was unkempt, and he could not stop drumming his fingers on his desk. He also glared across the room at his partner. The High General and the Court Philosopher didn't seem too fond of each other at all.

"Perhaps now we can get some answers," sighed Vorosknecht. "And if not . . . oh well."

"Answers would be ideal," snapped Dreher. "After your Chief Ethicist disappeared right when she could have been useful."

Vorosknecht shrugged. "Alban, I believe the High General had words for our witch."

Alban grabbed me by the rope around my wrists and dragged me across the floor until I was in front of the purple couch, where Dreher leaned forward and slapped me. It was surprising, but it didn't hurt much.

"How *could* you, Kalyna?" he said. His red face was full of anger; his bottom lip quivered.

I looked up at him. "So, they haven't killed you for bringing me into the fold yet?"

"We were all taken in by you," said Selvosch. He seemed on the verge of tears. Such love for the Soul of the Nation, I suppose.

Vorosknecht cleared his throat behind me, as though he very much wanted to dispute that "all" of them had been taken in. But he said nothing.

I had gotten to them. I was captured, I would probably have my throat slit any minute, but I had gotten to them and that warmed my heart. The anger in that room was so thick and palpable. What had they screamed at each other during the past week? How many attempts, or perceived attempts, at undermining each other had there been? How miserable and sleep-deprived were they and their men? I felt a tingle just imagining.

"Well, now you have me," I said. "I suppose you win."

"We won when we had the Prince," sighed Vorosknecht. "He led us on a merry chase for days through all his hidden tunnels and whatnot, but we got him in the end. And in here, no one else in the palace can hear him or the spymaster scream."

"Now, we just need one of you to tell us where your false King is," sighed Dreher. "I'm honestly surprised at how well the Prince has held up."

"That's because none of us know," I laughed. "He and the Queen have disappeared. Beat us all you want, we still couldn't begin to tell you."

I remembered that Olaf had promised to be back for the Eve of the Council. If he kept his word, he would be delivered right into their hands.

"And if we began on your grandmother?" asked Alban, from behind me.

I craned my neck around painfully to look at him, and grinned. "Please do."

"Disgusting," grunted Selvosch. "To care so little for your own family. No Rot would ever—"

"Oh, stop it, Selvosch," moaned Vorosknecht. "I'm sure even the pretender will be back for the Council, so let's just kill them and wait it out. The worst-case scenario is we kill *three* monarchs and take over the palace."

I heard Alban, still standing behind me, draw a knife.

"Not yet!" cried Dreher. He leaned forward closer, his red face inches from mine.

"First, Kalyna, why did you do it?"

"Do what, *Franz*? Exploit your beliefs?"

"Have this . . ."—he waved a stubby hand at Gabor—"*animal* kill Martin-Frederick. Tell me you saw the Soul of the Nation. Make me look like a fool. All of it!"

Alban snorted. "'Look like'?"

"Quiet, Alban," laughed Vorosknecht.

Dreher glared over my head. "Quiet!" he screamed. Then he looked back at me. "Kalyna," said Dreher, "A little spying is one thing, but to play with our beliefs like that. Why did you do it?"

"Because it was fun, Franz," I replied. My own grin became infectious, and very genuine: I couldn't stop it. And I was not entirely lying.

Dreher raised his hand to hit me again.

"Let me, High General," said Alban. He stepped across and backhanded me hard enough to knock me onto my side. I tasted blood. From there I saw only boots, and the purple-stained wood of the floor.

"Oh, that's cute," I said, my cheek pressed into the floor. "Hit me for the High General: that will convince everyone that the Purples and the Greens are one big group of friends."

Dreher wanted some sort of absolution from me, and that could buy me a few minutes, but for what? Would Chasiku and the others come save us? Most likely, they were in a dungeon or dead. I could try to prolong my death, but either way, these men would win and the whole Tetrarchia would fall. Crushed by the whim of some great . . . *fish*. I felt like the condemned man who chews his last meal slowly: taking up time for the sake of one more breath. My mind raced for other ways to stall.

At least they hadn't gotten Papa. He would be safe and comfortable until the end.

"What do you mean?" groaned Selvosch. "What do you mean about a big group of friends?"

"Exactly what I said. You're all waiting to betray each other, and you act like friends. It's cute."

"An easy lie," said Vorosknecht. "Alban, bring her here."

"Come up here, Loashti," grunted Alban.

I was dragged up to my feet and over to Vorosknecht, so I could look him in the eye.

"Tell us where you hid your pretender," he said, looking down at me, pointing with his long fingers. "This is your last chance, before Alban slits your throat."

"I told you what a fool you were before, Otto," I laughed, making sure to get some spittle flecked with blood in his face, "back when you and I planned to string Dreher along with this Soul of the Nation garbage. But even *I* didn't realize just how blitheringly stupid you are."

"What?" roared Dreher behind me. It was followed by the sound of him wheezing.

"Now wait, High General, wait," stammered the Court Philosopher. "This is clearly a trick. Alban, kill her."

"Don't you dare!" shouted Dreher. "If you want her dead so quickly, maybe there's truth in what she's saying." He had moved closer.

"Come now, High General," groaned Vorosknecht, pressing his hands to his eyes in consternation. "Haven't you believed enough of her lies?"

Dreher's voice was right behind me. "What are you saying, witch?" I fancied I could smell the bland, sad roast on his breath.

"You honestly believed," I began, "all of Vorosknecht's stories about a powerful Soul of the pink people's nation, one that would be pleased by human sacrifice? You really think we weren't stringing you along?"

Dreher shoved me aside to get in Vorosknecht's face. I slammed against the purple bust of the Court Philosopher. To my left were the purple-stained bones of Meregfog, his old pet.

"Is this true?" cried the High General.

"Of course not. She is just trying to get to you, High General. We've learned all she knows, and she's trying to stay alive."

I pressed harder back against the cool marble of the statue, feeling for any rough edges I could use for my ropes. It was quite smooth. Maybe Vorosknecht often rubbed it for good luck, or some such. I needed more time.

And then, all at once, the best way to keep us alive a little longer came to me. If I survived, I knew I would never stop feeling I had betrayed myself. I started to laugh again. It was a laugh calculated to sound threatening, cruel, evil, but the truth is, it started deep inside me, in a well of self-loathing.

Both men stopped yelling at each other and turned to me.

"What?" ventured Vorosknecht.

"What I know hardly matters," I said. "You *should* be wondering what the Grand Suzerain knows."

That shut them up for a moment. The Court Philosopher understood it first, and his eyes widened.

"The Grand Suzerain of Loasht?" he whispered.

I grinned. I think there was blood on my teeth from when Alban had hit me. "And he knows *everything*." I leaned forward, eyes wild. "Do you truly think that assassinating your four little monarchs will make you safe? That conquering this backward rock will *make you safe*? What do you honestly think will happen when this ailing, sectarian, four-part government crumbles?"

Dreher looked shaken. "The Rotfelsenisch nation," he began, "will rise and—"

"The armies of Loasht," I interrupted, "will swarm through this broken experiment and crush you while you're weak. More soldiers than you can imagine, with guns like you have never seen." I laughed some more. "Rotfelsen is not so strong a fort, and there are more of our soldiers amassed at the border than there are pink idiots within this rock."

"No," said Dreher.

I nodded. "Oh, yes. Whom do you honestly think I've been spying for in Rotfelsen all this time? Lenz? *The Prince*?" I turned and spat in the direction of the bound and gagged captives. Prince Friedhelm's eyes were so wide that I wondered if he believed me.

I could tell from the faces of Dreher and Vorosknecht that they certainly did. The second easiest thing to make a customer believe, after what they *want* to be true, is what they *suspect*. To them, this was the pieces falling into place: Loasht was always the great threat, looming and unknowable, and I was *foreign*. There is much more Rotfelsenisch in my blood than there is Loashti, but what does blood matter anyway? Mine doesn't even bother to carry the Gift.

"Quiet, witch!" yelled Alban.

He stormed up to me to hit me, even as I saw fear in his eyes. I acted as though I wanted to avoid being hit, and moved into a position where, I hoped, it would look normal for me to stagger off to my left. Then I let him strike me, and did so. I laughed some more, a laugh of pain at betraying myself, and of gleeful satisfaction at conning them all. I hated myself, but it was *thrilling*.

I turned to my left and right and continued to smile ruefully, now at Dagmar and Gabor. They looked appropriately horrified.

"Kalyna? You can't be serious!" cried Gabor. He overplayed it a touch, but no one else noticed.

I stumbled back until I felt Meregfog's pedestal behind me. "Pathetic." Now I tasted even more copper, so I smiled in Vorosknecht's direction with a bloody mouth. "Still think it's a good idea to work behind Dreher's back, Otto?"

"She's lying, of course!" yelled Vorosknecht.

"Why would I lie now? You're going to kill me, and I know it. But I will go to meet my reward with the ancient Lords of Loasht in their fortresses. I will die knowing I brought Loasht glory."

Alban drew a dagger. "Then I suppose it's time to—"

"Stop!" yelled Dreher, walking over and pushing the Purple away from me. "Every time you plan to kill her, you convince me that she's right about you."

"Come now, High General," groaned Vorosknecht, crossing the room to us. "You aren't really going to listen to this—"

"You traitor!" Dreher continued. "You agreed that she was seeing the Soul! You must have been in league with her, and with Loasht!"

I laughed and laughed, and pressed my ropes against old Mereg-fog's fangs. I hoped very much they were no longer poisonous. As the two men yelled at each other, the Greens and the Purples in the room began to amass, glaring and murmuring.

"Really now, this is too much!" Vorosknecht growled, throwing his hands up in the air. "You're going to believe the professed Loashti spy over me? You don't think she may have hoodwinked me as well?" He waved an arm at me.

I stopped trying to cut my bonds, as they were looking at me once more. I could not tell if I had made any progress.

"Why not? I'm a soothsayer," I laughed. "I did see your country's puny soul, but the Loashti one is so much *greater.*"

"Do you honestly expect us to believe you are a Loashti spy *and* a soothsayer?" snapped Vorosknecht.

"If they have them," said Dreher, "then who better to use as a spy?"

This next lie played so heavily on vile beliefs that I almost couldn't bring myself to say it, but I did: "Loasht has deep and ancient magics borne in our very blood, you fools. Where do you think my Gift comes from?"

"She's a fake!" yelled Vorosknecht, looking back at Dreher.

"Oh?" I sneered. "Is there *some reason* you think I'm a fake, Otto? Some reason you knew, but never told Dreher? Perhaps my grand-mother can enlighten us!"

Vorosknecht was silent.

"Believe me or not," I sighed. "But I know you're each planning to have the other killed once the assassinations are finished."

They were both quiet then. I don't know if either of them had spe-cific plans for the other one's end, but there was no way they could both create the Rotfelsen they wanted while working together, and they knew it. They must have known it during this whole week spent at each other's throats, with nothing to unite them but getting to tonight's invocation. What's more, their most loyal soldiers and com-manders—here with them—must have also known it.

As a matter of fact, it was not the leaders who broke first: it was a Green who drew his sword. The epaulets on his uniform suggested he was one of Dreher's commanders.

"You!" he cried, leveling his sword at Vorosknecht. "First you seduce our High General with your fairy tales—"

"No!" yelled Dreher. "It's not a fairy—"

"—and then you plan to assassinate—!"

Alban knocked the man's sword aside, and clubbed him over the head with the pommel of his dagger. A group of Greens drew their swords. Purples loyal to Alban drew theirs. It was all very quiet for a moment. As everyone else stood still, the Green who had been clubbed wheeled about awkwardly, trying to catch his balance.

Then, as he turned, he inadvertently sliced Selvosch's arm with the tip of his rapier. No one was on Selvosch's side, but someone had been cut, and they all exploded.

ALBAN

The room and its adjoining hallways became an unbalanced blur of green against a great canvas of purple, and soon there were splatters of red as well. Dreher and Vorosknecht were yelling at their soldiers, but no one could hear them. I backed up against Meregfog and began desperately trying to cut my bonds on his teeth, thinking how silly I would look if I poisoned myself and died.

A Green backed up toward me, and ducked beneath a Purple's wild sword swing. To avoid it, I threw myself backward, crashing to the floor with the stand and the skeleton beneath me. My back hit the stand hard, and I lost my breath. I heard the crunching of bones and hoped none of them were mine.

I had never noticed before that, on the ceiling of the study, there was a large painting of Vorosknecht bowing before the gods of wisdom. I laughed hysterically at the look of quiet dignity on this gigantic version of the Court Philosopher, even as I reached desperately for Meregfog's fangs. I could no longer see the fighting, I could only hear it.

I managed to wrap my hands around a long fang. One side was so sharp that it cut me, and I felt my hands become slick. The fighting got louder. Somehow, with my bloody hands beneath my own body weight, I managed to cut the rope apart. I rolled onto my side, and found myself with the use of my hands. I scrabbled around for a better look at what was going on.

I turned just in time to see High General Dreher punch the Court

Philosopher in the face. The two began to fight, and I felt an inescapable glee. Throughout the room, the forty or so soldiers were hacking each other to bits, yelling about betrayal, and generally making a mess. Lenz and Friedhelm had scooted off, beneath a far table, trying to stay out of the way. Grandmother, it seemed, had already rolled to some other part of the room—I did not see her. Closer to me, Dagmar writhed against her bonds, while Gabor lay on his back across a prone Green, trying to grab a weapon with his bound hands.

I hopped up, shakily, with the long fang in my right hand, like a small knife. That's when Alban, through all the commotion, saw that I was free.

He roared something and ran toward me. I reached for the closest thing, and hurled Meregfog's skull at him. It burst into pieces against his forehead, and he staggered. Then he was attacked by a Green.

I turned to Dagmar, quickly cutting her free with poor Meregfog's fang.

"Finally," she grunted as she shot up to her feet.

She turned to Gabor, but he had already freed himself with a dead Green's sword, while I took the corpse's dagger. Gabor avoided four or five blades that weren't exactly aimed for him, and skewered a Purple who had been distracted with someone else. He snatched her sword as she fell, and threw it behind him, to Dagmar.

"Get behind the desk," I hissed. "I would rather they kill each other and we just mop up whoever's left."

"Not without Lenz!" Gabor called over his shoulder. Then he plunged into the battle.

"I'm going to help him," grunted Dagmar. She became a daffodil blur in that purple room.

Well, *I* went behind the desk. I cowered there and felt very silly with a dagger in one hand and an old fang in the other, peeking over the surface to watch everyone else fight. The Greens and Purples were really going at it, and I felt confident that many of them had expected this confrontation to come. Just not for another day or two. They were cutting each other to pieces, knocking over all of Voroshnecht's fine furniture and art, pulling down tapestries, and spraying blood everywhere. Gabor was weaving his way through, toward where Lenz and Friedhelm were huddled under a table, not even aware that Dagmar was protecting his back, letting no one get close. That woman was like iron: it was inspiring, terrifying, and enticing.

At one point, in a far corner of the room, I caught a glimpse of Grandmother. She was hiding behind an armchair with a fiery look in her eyes. It was the worst thing I'd seen all day.

"Oh gods," I mumbled to myself. "What do I do?"

Suddenly, on the other side of the desk, Dreher and Vorosknecht popped back up into view. The High General had the Court Philosopher in a headlock, and was dragging him backward, yelling and cursing. Selvosch stared at them from behind a statue, shaking.

Two Greens started toward them, to help Dreher kill his rival, until one of the Greens was very surprised by a sword poking out through his chest, and the other took a dagger across the throat. Alban burst between the two of them, sword and dagger in hand, and began trying to pull Dreher off Vorosknecht.

I ducked down beneath the desk and hoped no one had seen me.

"Loashti charlatan!" was suddenly screamed inches above me.

Selvosch was sprawled atop the desk, his head over the side, in front of mine. He was gesticulating wildly toward me.

"She's here! The witch is here! It's all her fault, we need to stop—"

I jabbed Meregfog's fang into his shoulder, and he howled and slid away, tumbling off the desk into some other direction. Regrettably, he took the fang with him.

So much for hiding. I popped up and began to run for another corner of the room. I could no longer see where Gabor and Dagmar were through the wall of Greens and Purples. For a moment, above it all, I saw a Purple standing up on the couch, laughing and fighting someone off, until he was run through from behind by a Green. The table beneath which Lenz and Friedhelm had been hiding had long since collapsed, but I had no notion of whether or not they were still under it.

I ran behind the statue of Vorosknecht and waited a moment, looking for the next safe spot in this chaos. I saw the large glass liquor cabinet, and went for it. I was almost touching it when Alban tackled me.

I managed not to be knocked over, so instead we did a sort of dance together: me stumbling backward as he stumbled forward, our arms entangled, unable to get at each other with our weapons. My flailing leg kicked over the liquor cabinet as I went. I heard it crash, but never saw it, which is rather a shame.

Our strange little dance ended with me crammed into a far corner of the room, but too close up against Alban for him to bring his rapier to bear. I grabbed his sword arm with my free hand, and knocked it against the wall until the thin blade bent, and he dropped it. I tried to stab him with my dagger, but he jumped back and avoided it. Over his shoulder, I saw the battle raging on.

Then, I did a very stupid thing: I threw the dagger at him. In my defense, I knew I was not capable of hitting him with the blade. But I knew he'd see a metal *something* flashing toward him, and I followed just after it, hoping he'd flinch.

He did, holding up his arm to protect his face as the harmless handle of my dagger hit him. Moments later, I was upon him, both of my hands gripping his wrist, trying to shake his last weapon out of his hand.

Alban hauled back his free hand and punched me in the face. My mouth was already very bloody, and I grinned.

"I already know how hard you hit," I choked out.

A quick moment of surprise was enough to get his dagger out of his hands. Unfortunately, it practically flew away, behind him, and now there was just the two of us and our fists, alone in this room of violence.

I didn't want to back away, so I allowed him to hit me again. I hooked my left arm around his body, my face next to his, chin over his shoulder. Our cheeks touched. I punched him in the stomach three times with my right, hooked my leg behind his, and shoved him back. He fell, but grabbed the front of my blouse to pull me with him. Rather than trying to pull free, I put out a foot to stop myself, and stomped on his chest.

None of the other fighting mattered now. Not Dreher and Vorosknecht, not Gabor and Dagmar, not Lenz, and certainly not Friedhelm and Grandmother. I stomped on him again.

Alban swung a leg up and caught me in the chin. I staggered back, and he turned over, crawling toward where the dagger had fallen. But he still thought a simple kick to the jaw was enough to stop me. I am not the strongest or the fastest, but I've been hit a lot in my life. I didn't spend a childhood being walloped by brigands and townsfolk and competitors for nothing.

He had barely moved by the time I was sitting on his back. I slammed my hands as hard as I could against both sides of his head, smashing his ears and, hopefully, bursting his eardrums. He cried out, and I grabbed his ears tightly, and began to slam his face into the wood floor, again and again.

"How good are you without six of your men, Alban?" I shrieked. He couldn't hear me.

He struggled and reached backward for me, turning his head as far as he could. I saw half of his face, and his eye socket looked wrong, shifting beneath the skin. I punched him, and he went limp. I held his hair in one hand and kept punching him anyway. I was beyond thought or care. I didn't even hate Alban: he was just a cruel man doing his cruel job, but he was here to be hit.

I wasn't even listening to what was going on around me. If a Purple had decided to come up behind me and slit my throat, I could not have stopped them. All I heard was noise, and all I did was continue to beat this man with my bloody hands. Until, finally, I was too tired, and I just stopped. I sat on top of him, panting and shaking.

My hands quivered until Dagmar grabbed them, and yelled something to me that I didn't hear. I shook my head. There was nothing in the world but Alban and my bleeding hands. Dagmar yelled it again, and pointed.

I turned, and saw a great wave of Yellows streaming into the room. Behind the first row of them was a group that carried a sort of palanquin made from the top of a crate. Perched upon it was Chasiku, pointing feebly with a hand shaking as much as mine.

AN AUDIENCE WITH THE KING

I mumbled, or yelled, I don't know, as Dagmar held me tightly, pulling me away from Alban's limp body. The Yellows who had come into Vorosknecht's apartments were quickly followed by an even larger group of Reds, who yelled and pointed weapons until everyone was still.

I was standing up, leaning against a wall, covered in blood and surrounded by broken furniture, when Olaf entered the room. He looked pristine in his ermine and scarlet silk, a ceremonial sword gleaming at his side.

"I say!" he laughed. "What in the world is going on here?" He looked around, seemingly tickled more than anything else. Until he saw me and ran over. Olaf bent over to look into my face, putting a hand on my shoulder. "Kalyna, are you alright?"

"Did we win?" I whispered.

"Well, I hope so!" he laughed. "But what happened, are you—?"

Queen Birutė appeared at his side. She was in immaculate dark blue robes, and placed a delicate hand on his shoulder.

"*Your Majesty*," she whispered. "The Reds are watching."

Olaf smiled at her and stood up straight. In a moment, I saw his face change to that blank Gerhold expression.

"Well," he said. "My, my, you've all made quite a mess." The King and Queen then wandered off to inspect the Court Philosopher's apartments.

I saw Chasiku being laid out on the purple couch, which was now stained with blood, and I staggered toward her. Dagmar followed, ready to catch me if I fell.

"Chasiku. Chasiku!" I didn't mean to yell, but I still had panic sitting somewhere deep within me.

Chasiku did not move.

"Did we win?" I cried. "Do you see the . . ." I looked about at everyone in the room: scores of Yellows and Reds, as well as captured Greens and Purples. I switched to Skydašiavos. "Do you see the shattering? Did we stop it?" I grabbed her shoulder and began to shake her.

"Kalyna," she moaned, her head swiveling toward me. "I can't see Rotfelsen shattering anymore, in any future. At least not this year. We won. I am in so much pain. Leave me be!"

I let go of her and slumped to the floor. I did not even care that I was wedged between Green and Purple corpses.

THE INVOCATION

Eventually, I was pulled up off the floor and cleaned up. When all was said and done, about seven Greens and Purples had survived the fight in the Court Philosopher's apartments. There was not a single dead Yellow, as they had burst in just at the end, when the others had done most of the work on one another. It turned out that Chasiku, Behrens, and the rest of our secret invasion force had been taken to a storage room. There they were let out of their crates by smiling Gustavuses, who, of course, had *no idea* how one crate had been misplaced. It seemed the bankers had hoped *I* would die, but that Chasiku and the rest would save the Tetrarchia.

Chasiku had indeed led those Yellows, from her palanquin, to where the battle would take place. There were Purple guards out front, but with Chasiku's guidance, their legs were shot out from under them before they saw anyone. This commotion in front of the Court Philosopher's apartments was what brought more Yellows, the Reds, and eventually the King and Queen.

Gabor and Dagmar had indeed saved Lenz and Prince Friedhelm, although Dagmar took a few small injuries protecting Gabor as he untied them. Neither Lenz nor the Prince was able to be particularly helpful after that, as they had spent days being beaten.

While the room was being cleaned up and inspected, a visibly shaken Gabor took me aside and told me that he had seen Grandmother slit an unconscious Green's throat. No one else had seen it happen, and Gabor hadn't the slightest idea what had driven her to it. Grandmother, of course, refused to say anything beyond insults: at me, at Lenz, at the Prince, at her captors, and so forth.

The surviving Green and Purple soldiers from the battle were arrested, as were a blubbering Quarrymaster Selvosch and a stoic High General Dreher. Court Philosopher Vorosknecht—the one I would most liked to have gloated over—was dead. The High General had expressed his martial courage through a table leg, and stove in his onetime ally's skull. When I heard this, I looked up at the purple bust of Vorosknecht, still standing and untouched, and thought of what a shame it was that his end hadn't come by being crushed beneath it.

Alban also survived, by the way. He was thrown in prison as well, of course. I heard later that I had permanently deafened him in one ear. I felt neither guilt nor joy: really, we had both been doing our jobs. His just carried the requirement of being a bad person, while for mine, being a bad person was a nice extra.

Chasiku was carted back out to her tower, and I was thrown into a yellow uniform and dragged to the evening's invocation, which would preface the Council of Barbarians. Lenz was excused from duty that evening, in order to convalesce.

The Feast of the Eve of the Council took place in a great hall that had, somehow, not been used for any part of the Winter Ball, nor anything else I had attended. Months spent as a royal pawn, and I could still get lost in that damn palace. The room had a ceiling, hung with wreaths, that was higher even than that of the Grand Opera House.

I stood with a group of Yellows up in the rafters, watching a priest of the goddess of springtime drone on in front of a great crowd of courtiers, dignitaries, advisors, minor royalty, their spouses, and whoever else was able to get in. The front row of this audience was conspicuously empty, with no Dreher, no Vorosknecht, no Selvosch, no Edeltraud, and a very heavily bruised Prince Friedhelm, still resplendent in yellow. Behind the man giving the invocation sat Queen Sevda and Consort Kagiso of Quruscan, King Lubomir XIII and Queen Thora of Masovska, King Alinafe of Skydašiai, and King Gerhold VIII, lately Olaf, and Queen Biruté of Rotfelsen. Besides the empty seats, and the overwhelming presence of Reds, in the near-total absence of Greens or Purples, it seemed that nothing had changed.

I kept waiting for shots to ring out, for battle cries to sound, but the old man just droned on. I imagined the creature with the eye in the depths of the world ripping through us all with its tentacles, or fins, or hands, right through the great hall and the rotrock itself. But nothing of the kind happened, and the old man just kept blathering. We had avoided the end of the Tetrarchia, had avoided civil war, and had even kept the battle to a small group of rooms and fewer than a hundred dead. So why did I feel like a failure? I'd nearly died, and killed, for the broken and unwieldy Tetrarchia, and the similarly ruptured Rotfelsen, to continue on just as before. I had fought for sameness and stagnance, and that was what we got.

I sighed and looked over the monarchs again. Some looked intense, some bored, and I think it was Lubomir who was asleep. Olaf maintained the blank expression of his forebear, with empty eyes looking at nothing. But every now and then, a small smile would appear at his lips, as though he was fighting a laugh at what a strange place he was now in. He wasn't looking at me, but I could not help smiling back. That was something.

A GREAT DEAL OF CLEANUP

The Council of Barbarians continued along its way, and I had very little do with it. Those of us who worked for Prince Friedhelm were rather busy.

I had this beautiful idea of winning a moral victory by going to

Dreher and convincing him that his plot had been wrong all along. In my mind, he would realize I was right and tell me everything, letting us hunt down the rest of his compatriots. But the ex–High General had nothing to hold onto but pride, and refused to say a word. Three days into the Council, he killed himself. We never did find out where he got the poison, and it seemed that his last words were whatever he yelled while crushing the Court Philosopher's skull. Perhaps it is silly, but I was glad he lived long enough to learn that I was *not* in fact a Loashti spy.

Jördis, it turned out, had been in hiding at the servant house of her friend Vondel, Tenth Butler to High General Dreher, who had not been important enough to be involved in anything. Jördis, true to her nature, had wanted to see who "won." She had apparently remembered my little bluff about a soothsayer siding with the winners, and so once she realized I was not, in fact, on Dreher and Vorosknecht's side, she had decided the best option was to disappear for a bit. When it was all over, she allowed herself to be arrested, along with many promises to help however she could.

It seemed that old Meregfog's skeleton really was all out of poison, as Selvosch grew quite talkative. Not to me, of course; he hated me. It was Lenz's idea to send Jördis in to speak with the Quarrymaster, as she seemed so keen on proving her trustworthiness. So, Selvosch saw Jördis, a high-ranking subordinate of Vorosknecht's, as clear proof that the movement was gone, and we didn't tell him otherwise. He didn't need to know how little she cared for ideology. Selvosch told her who else was in on the plot, as well as that the other Greens and Purples had, largely, been expected to fall in line once the coup began, without being given time to think much about it. Jördis did not demand a full pardon based on this, but heavily suggested she would do whatever *else* was necessary to obtain one.

Selvosch also babbled about when Vorosknecht had first brought up the Soul of the Nation, and I couldn't help feeling that this moment, and whatever was in the Court Philosopher's own head, and whatever chance encounters he had, must have been what redirected Papa's futures from stretching for decades toward, instead, an imminent doom. I think we would need to read Vorosknecht's mind to know for certain what he had done and what he believed, but that mind had been splattered across his carpet.

Most of the regicides were tried in royal tribunals that I was not privy to. I don't even know if I wanted them to be treated well or harshly, only that royal tribunals make me nervous by their very nature. Give me a muddy Masovskan courtroom, full of gawkers.

Doctor Aue had quite a few sounds to make over Lenz and Prince Friedhelm's injuries, but they were nursed back to health. Lenz felt that he had been particularly ill-used in the past few weeks, and I supposed I could not disagree.

It seemed that we had saved the Tetrarchia. In the long term, of course, something terrible lived beneath us. In Rotfelsen, or beneath Rotfelsen, or beneath the entire Tetrarchia.

Oh yes. I also went alone to see *The Leper's Five Tits*. Not as some honor to fallen Martin-Frederick, the would-be nationalist king, but his tickets were given to me, and it seemed like a good thing to do. It was funny!

KING GERHOLD VIII

"I hate this," said Jördis. She was draped from head to toe in purple, but of a more reasonable style than Vorosknecht had worn. And no hat for Jördis. It was the fourth day of the Council of Barbarians.

Two Purples were straightening her caftan, until she waved them away. We were in a small room in the Sunset Palace, along with Lenz, who still looked viciously bruised, and Dagmar, who hung behind me.

"You asked what you could do for a pardon," said Lenz, "and we need a Court Philosopher immediately. The role will be stripped of its real power, and you'll hate the duties, so I think it works out."

"Rotfelsen will be well-served by a Court Philosopher who doesn't want the position," I added.

"Well, you've got that," grumbled Jördis. "My father would be *so proud*." She glanced at the mirror and sighed. "I look like a grape."

"But not a prisoner," I said. "And you have soldiers now."

"Not a full army, of course," she replied. "Which is fine. Maybe this will keep the soldiers from all fighting each other all the time." She did not sound hopeful.

A great shift had taken place, and a forced exodus. Along with Jördis, there was a new High General: an oblivious young man named Engel, who had simply been the most likable officer to have no part in Dreher's treason. Now he and Jördis both commanded Greens and

Purples who were mere shadows of themselves: the first a small honor guard, and the second about half its original size. I suspected that, in five to ten years, the Yellows would be the next great threat to the Tetrarchia. I would have to ask Papa.

"Jördis," I began, "do you . . ."

"Have anything to say to you, Kalyna? No, not that I can think of. Other than that I could have been a better neighbor. But I saw the light, didn't I?" She grinned.

"I suppose."

Prince Friedhelm appeared in the doorway. The bruises were starting to fade on his face, and his yellow robe was so long that a pageboy carried the end of it.

"Lenz, Kalyna, come with me right away."

We all moved to follow him, and he pointed at Dagmar.

"Not you, Yellow, stay here," grunted the Prince.

Dagmar clicked her tongue and leaned against the wall.

Lenz and I went with the Prince to his study, where Olaf was waiting. He was sitting on Friedhelm's desk, grinning from ear to ear.

"It's all such nonsense, isn't it?" he laughed. Olaf threw up his hands, waving them around. "Everything! All of it! Why, just today I swore, by the gods and my royal blood, that I would protect the, ah . . . Oh, what was it, brother?"

Friedhelm slammed the door behind us. "The Freitabranden Moss Caverns in the southeast district of—"

"Yes, yes, I'll learn it all," laughed Olaf. "Eventually. I'm King now, aren't I? Time to push me out of the nest, I suppose. I've gotten very good at thinking about fun things during long speeches."

"I would like nothing better. Now why did you request *my* remaining Recourses?" He sneered. "Other than you, that is."

"Oh, because they're going to be mine now, brother. You don't need them anymore."

"Yours?" I groaned.

"With the option to leave entirely, if you wish," Olaf added quickly. "After all, you saved my life and my kingdom!" He giggled at this last word. "And, Friedhelm, I believe you only needed them, and me, because Gerhold wouldn't listen to you about all the threats to his reign." He hopped off the desk and walked toward Friedhelm, his hands clasped behind his back. "Well, I promise you that Gerhold is now *very* aware of them, and would like the tools to fight further threats. What could you possibly need them for?"

"Well, I—"

"You want me to stay alive on the throne, yes? To take over all these boring functions, so you don't have to? Well, lay the responsibility at my feet." He winked. "Brother."

Prince Friedhelm stood still for some time, then he exhaled very slowly. "You will pay me for them."

"Of course, of course! I have a whole list of your people I want, and what I think they're worth." He clapped Friedhelm on the back. "You won't be disappointed! I'll be the best King you ever installed."

Olaf then pushed past Friedhelm, to put a hand on my shoulder, and another on Lenz's. "Well, you're both free to stay in my service, or leave!"

"I will . . . stay," said Lenz, weighing each word, "if I can live down in Turmenbach again."

"Granted!" Olaf clapped his shoulder.

"I'm already gone," I said.

"Of course! But I hope you'll let me send you along with some payment, and a few useful gifts to remember me by."

"I . . . sure, why not."

"Splendid, splendid!" Olaf spun about and walked back to the desk. "Now, brother, I've brought the paperwork, so we can just take a look right now." He pointed to a sheaf of papers with the King's seal still dripping upon it. "You two may go. But Kalyna, I'll definitely want to talk again before you disappear!"

Prince Friedhelm continued to stare at his new "brother" for some time. Perhaps he was planning to supplant Olaf after all, someday, but it wouldn't be *my* problem. Lenz could deal with that. Although I did also wonder if the Prince wanted me dead, now, to keep his secrets.

In the doorway, I looked back at Olaf. He bugged out his eyes at me and mouthed, "Isn't it *mad?*" before turning to business.

BLOOD COMRADES

"You put some little fat woman into the Court Philosopher's chair!" cried Klemens Gustavus. "If we had known women could hold that position, we could have tried Bozena after all!"

It was the fifth day of the Council of Barbarians, and I was in the mansion of Edeltraud von Edeltraud, Mistress of the Coin, with a good ten Yellows besides Dagmar. I had not fully left the Prince or the King just yet.

"What's done is done!" said Edeltraud von Edeltraud, who was sitting in a large chair. "I'm just glad it's all over and done with, without real bloodshed."

"And that the King is young and will live a long time," sneered Klemens. "So you won't have to mint all-new marks."

"That does not hurt," said Edeltraud.

"Neither will those quarries," added Bozena.

"I do not have Selvosch's quarries yet," said Edeltraud.

But she would, as I had already heard. Better than the Gustavuses, perhaps.

"This is all academic," I growled. "Klemens Gustavus, do you want to tell us how I ended up in the Court Philosopher's hands?" I knew the answer, of course.

"Oh?" He cocked his head to the side. "You mean when we smuggled you into the palace, specifically so that you could kill him, and then you found him and did exactly that?" He shrugged. "Who can say? The world is full of mysteries, you know."

"Quite mysterious indeed," I said.

Klemens smiled and moved toward me. Dagmar thrust her body at him in a feint that made him jump. Then she laughed. Klemens took a deep breath and extended his hand to me.

"No hard feelings, yes? It was a whole mess in Masovska, of which you only saw the end. Then here in this awful place, we thought we were on different sides, and you killed my men and kidnapped me, but still we came together." He clasped his fingers to show this, and then extended his hand again. "I know we were only doing our small part for the Tetrarchia, but you could not have saved thousands of lives without our help. We are blood comrades now." He said the last sentence in Masovskani, in which the term "blood comrades" had a particularly strong meaning.

I stared at him for a few moments. I was a killer, it's true, but Klemens was a *murderer*, and I, at least, saw a difference. We had needed his help and that disgusted me, but I suppose these are the sort of allies one must make when playing with the fate of a country. I hardly even cared whether he had betrayed us: that at least was understandable, with how we had treated him. But I could not look at him without seeing the men who had been sent to kill Eight-Toed Gustaw from Down Valley Way, and imagining those who had been sent to other inheritors—the men I hadn't stopped.

I looked Klemens right in the eyes, smiled, and shook his hand firmly.

"Blood comrades," I said in Masovskani. Then in Rotfelsenisch, "Allies, now and forever. All is forgiven."

Klemens smiled genuinely, and Bozena seemed relieved.

Perhaps it was hypocritical of me to give my forgiveness, and what amounted to a serious Masovskan oath of alliance. Perhaps I should have spat in his face, told him what I thought of him, stormed out. But it's always best to avoid making enemies, until you come for them in the night. I am a liar, after all.

GOLDEN KNIFE

That same day, I stood in Tural's doorway once again, as I had so many times. We'd hardly had a chance to speak since my "initiation." He was conjuring a flavor, but when he saw me, he snapped right out of it.

"You're leaving soon," he said in Rotfelsenisch.

"I plan to," I replied in Cölluknit.

"Are you sure?" he asked in the same.

"No. But I will anyway."

He nodded and looked down, then walked up to me, smiling. There were slight creases at the corners of his narrow eyes. His mustache looked like it would have felt nice.

"I had hoped we would get along well," he said.

"We do. And could have gotten along even better, were I more selfish."

He sighed. His breath smelled like earthy tea.

"Did I tell you," I began, my hands shaking as I avoided his eyes, "that in one of the futures Lenz's other soothsayer saw, I had your surname?"

He smiled and shook his head, as though I had told him something endearing. "No, you did not. Ha."

I tried to take a deep breath. I felt the very real possibility of future love hanging there in the air between us like dust, and disappearing. It was the closest I think I've ever come to seeing the world the way

Chasiku did. But I simply could not allow it to happen, not with the way that I needed to live my life. Spending all this time up here with Tural, and even Martin-Frederick, had made me realize how lonely I was, but it was not right to subordinate my entire life to escape loneliness. Better to find someone who could assuage my loneliness on the road—who would expect very little from me.

"I still have your knife," I said, holding it up. "Would you like it back?"

"Someone was killed with that knife, weren't they?"

"Not by me."

"Please keep it."

Stupidly, I had already started trying to hand it to him. He put his hand on mine and gently pushed it back toward me.

"Please keep it," he repeated.

I am sorry to sound maudlin, but his hand on my hand was the longest amount of time that Tural ever touched me. Out in the hall, Dagmar was whistling very loudly, in order to not hear what we were saying.

THE EYE

I never told anyone but Chasiku about the great eye I had seen at the bottom of Glaizatz Lake. What was the point in telling Lenz, or the Prince, or Olaf? What would they do, shoot at it? Who was to say there weren't things like this under every mountain and lake in the world? People live in all sorts of dangerous lands, and a great rock was always going to be strange and precarious.

I hoped that its presence in my thoughts would lessen, but to this day, I often think of the moment it glanced at me. And when I do, I want to cry.

On the sixth, and penultimate, day of the Council of Barbarians, I went to speak to Chasiku about it. She shrugged it off.

"I'm always seeing terrible things," she said.

"And are you going to stay here?" I asked in Skydašiavos.

"I will," she said. "When I saw the Purples slaughtering all those people, down in Glaizatz, it was honestly one of the worst futures I have ever beheld. It's stained my mind."

"Then why—?"

"Because, Kalyna, sometimes, in new visions, or even in person, I see those people. The same faces that were begging for mercy, cruelly cut down and discarded, I see them living now: smiling, grumbling, cursing, *alive*."

"That's wonderful."

"Often it still hurts," she continued. "Seeing them reminds me of that vision, reminds me of their deaths. But I will stay. I'm working directly for the King now, apparently."

"I never thought you'd stay anywhere in order to be around people."

"Kalyna," she said. She still didn't look at me as she spoke. She was leaning against the railing of her balcony, staring off the edge of Rotfelsen into a clear early-spring sky. "Where I come from, my family is . . . well . . . Imagine your grandmother and her expectations, if she were thirty people."

I shuddered. Though Chasiku was not looking at me, she laughed.

"Have you worked in North Shore Skydašiai before, Kalyna?"

"Many times."

"In the big cities?"

"We often avoid big cities."

"Well, my family are a perfect example of why you do. We're a business: a great, stifling, powerful business, that forces out competition."

"Ah," I said.

Chasiku turned, ostensibly to face me, and leaned her back against the railing. But she looked above me. "Detachment is forced upon us from a very young age. Your grandmother may be terrible, but at least she yells at you, and that is emotion. Believe it or not, Kalyna"—she grinned—"I chose to get away from my family because I am *friendly*, comparatively. I wanted to be near people." She spread her arms and continued to smile the most I had ever seen. She had a lovely smile, really. "This is me being friendly."

"Chasiku, you're a much better soothsayer than I am."

"Or will ever be," she added. Not being mean, just frank. I couldn't tell whether she had learned the truth about me. "But it's because of you that this place no longer beats me with the deaths of thousands— at least, no more than any other place. I could not have done my part without yours."

"You're welcome for that, I suppose."

"Oh, and Kalyna?" She trained her face on mine, but still her eyes wandered.

"Yes?"

"Someday you will not be a soothsayer. I promise you that."

This might be the greatest thing anyone has ever told me.

SPRINGTIME

I was in Papa's room on the final day of the Council of Barbarians, packing up the tent rolls. It was one of those sunny days that comes in the early spring, still cold, but promising more. I even heard chirping again. My hope was that if we left right away, we would not be caught in the great surge of traffic that would leave the palace grounds tomorrow morning. Papa was buoyant.

"Are we leaving, Kalynishka?" he asked from his bed, for the fifth time.

"Yes, Papa. Soon. Didn't you like it here?"

"Oh, I did. I did! But, you know, a prophet must wander."

I nodded and folded his clothes. I was smiling.

"But Kalynishka," he asked after a few moments, "did *you* like it here?"

I sighed. "I suppose I did, Papa. Parts of it, anyway."

"Would you want to . . . to stay?" He sounded terrified of the idea, but thought he was putting on a brave face for me.

"Well—"

"Don't you spoil your daughter, Aljosa!" cried Grandmother, bursting into the room.

"Well now, Mother," said Papa. "Don't say it like that. If you are too angry about it, she *will* want to stay."

"She *does* want to stay," growled Grandmother. "She wants to stay and rut with the fruit-man. She wants your grandchildren to smell of durian, my boy."

"She does *not*!" cried Papa.

"Grandmother," I asked, "are you packed?"

"You want an old woman to pack her own bags? You've been off the road too long. You'll do it."

"In a moment," I sighed. "Maybe."

The door to Papa's room was open, but Gabor knocked on it anyway.

"Kalyna!" he cried. "Lenz is on his way up, but I ran here first to say goodbye! I think he wants to talk to you about, you know, spy things."

Gabor gave me a hug, which was odd. He had killed a number of people because of me, starting with Martin-Frederick, but now he was only a slight man wrapping his arms around me.

"You will let me know if you come by Rotfelsen again, won't you?" he asked. "Even if"—he lowered his voice—"you don't let *him* know." He motioned his head back toward the door and winked.

I nodded and patted his shoulder. "And I'll let you know if I need more stabbing done."

"And I you, if I need someone beaten to a pulp!"

"Not so loud, please."

Lenz appeared at the doorway, leaning on a cane, which Doctor Aue had promised him, by the grace of many gods, he wouldn't need after a month. He and Gabor glanced into each other's eyes for one short moment, and it was perhaps the most demonstrative I ever saw them. Then Gabor laughed and rushed through a beam of sunlight to go say goodbye to my father.

"How are you there, Aljosa?" he asked, and they began to talk.

"Hello, Kalyna," said Lenz.

"Good morning," I said.

"Kalyna, I really am sorry that I—"

"If I ever see you again, I will still bother you about the kidnapping, but in the end, I suppose . . ." I sighed. "Well, you were also the Prince's prisoner, and we both did distasteful things in his employ. And I *suppose* it was all for the best, what with saving the Tetrarchia."

"Saving the *what*?" screamed Grandmother. "What did you people *do*?"

"Now, now, Granny," said Gabor from where he sat on Papa's bed. "Come over here and talk to your son and me. You'll be leaving soon, and I want to know *everything* about your strange family's history before you do."

Grandmother looked angry and doubtful, but couldn't resist the chance to give a younger person a lecture about the perfect lineage that I had besmirched.

I walked over to Lenz. "I still haven't packed my things," I said as I left the room.

In the hallway, we passed a chair where Dagmar dozed lightly.

My bedroom was brighter than my father's. Even though it was very cold out, I had left the window open overnight because I needed to remind myself how it felt to shiver in my sleep. I began gathering up a few volumes: ancient histories, *Bohdan's Botanicals*, and the like.

"You can keep those," said Lenz, as he hung in the doorway. "Just don't take any of the ones I wrote."

"Oh, come in already," I said.

Lenz did so.

"Kalyna, is Olaf sending you off with enough gold marks?"

"Too much would make us a target," I said. "I only asked for what could get Papa put up somewhere with walls and a doctor, now and then. More importantly, he's giving us a good carriage and some horses. But not a carriage that *looks* too nice, I made sure of that: something the army got sick of. We're negotiating what else I can bring with me, to keep us safe."

"Good, good." He looked about and poured himself a drink from a bottle on my desk. "You threatened my life in this room," he said.

"I threatened your life a lot; I got the closest here." My back was to him as I tried to make as many books as possible fit in a case.

"Are you *sure* about leaving?" he asked.

"I always have been."

"Yes, but . . . now you could stay of your own accord. You could have walls, a ceiling, mild weather. Olaf would be delighted. Doctor Aue is here, and Dagmar and Tural."

And the eye.

"I know what's here," I said.

"Kalyna," he said, "you hate being a soothsayer."

I wondered if I should just tell him the truth.

"And?" I asked.

"If you stayed here, you could work for me."

"I've had enough fighting."

"Not fighting. You figure people out, and understand how to . . . how to . . ."

"Take advantage of them."

"Well, yes! And that makes my job much easier, and much less violent."

I began to laugh.

"Don't laugh at me, Kalyna," he said through his own chuckles. "Yes, we killed some people, but you did an amazing thing. I know you don't much like royalty or our government, I know you don't much like me—"

"Well, in that company, you're not so bad."

"—but you like Olaf, don't you? And think how much better your life, and your father's life, could be if you stayed here."

"You finally learned to leave Grandmother out."

"We were locked up together for a week."

"Well, she'll be gone soon."

He came closer, crossing the small room. "Does no part of you want to stay and do something different?"

I finally turned to face him. "It doesn't matter what I want. It doesn't even matter what's best for my father's health because Doctor Aue can make him comfortable, but she cannot cure his mind. He *needs* to travel, he needs to continue in the world the way he has, watching me practice our family's calling because he does not know how to handle anything else. Every time he sees me, Lenz, he asks me when we're leaving." I ran my hands through my hair and then gripped it at the nape. "I think I *want* to stay," I admitted as I stared at my boots. "I want to sleep with Tural and talk to Gabor and keep an eye on Jördis in her new position and have Dagmar as my body-guard so that *I don't have to fight ever again.* I even want to work with you, Lenz, because I've gotten used to it. But until my father . . . until later, what I want doesn't matter. There will come a day when I will be devastated, but also freed."

"And now you'll go out and . . . sell your Gift."

I wanted to be angry, but in Lenz's eyes I saw only sadness and pity. He still thought I had a Gift to squander. I took a deep breath. All this time I had kept the secret, except from Vorosknecht, who was dead; Alban, whom no one would listen to; and Dagmar, who didn't care. But here was Lenz, with whom I had been through so much, still under the influence of my fraud. And saying it out loud to those others had been so satisfying.

"Lenz," I said. "I need to tell you something."

He leaned on his cane and looked down at me with an open, mys-tified expression, that wiry hair stuck out in all directions. This was a man whose presence and knowledge I'd feared, and now he hung upon my next word. And I wanted so badly to unburden myself.

"Lenz," I said again, "I honestly will miss you. Even though I don't like you."

He smiled and shook my hand.

Of course I didn't tell him that I was a fraud. Of course. What in the world would that have accomplished?

EPILOGUE

We wandered throughout the spring and did many things. I still sat at Grandmother's feet, still brought her food, and she still cursed me, but it bothered me less and I didn't let her hit me. It was easier to see the regard in Papa's eyes, to remember it in Tural's, Olaf's, Gabor's, Lenz's. I don't tell you I was, or am now, a happy person, but I will say that now, as I write these words, I am more content than I ever thought possible. That year was when I started inching toward who I am today.

The following summer, we returned to the Great Field, north of the town of Gniezto, in the kingdom of Masovska.

"What are you doing, freak?" cried Grandmother one balmy summer night. "If you go and get cut open, you will kill your father."

I wore leather trousers, my hair was up, I had the sickle on my right hip. A warm breeze shifted the field's grasses as we sat just inside the open tent.

"Don't you do this, shitworm," Grandmother continued.

I stood up, my hair brushing the tent, and kissed her on top of her ancient head. "Shut up."

I stepped out of the tent as she yelled through a mouthful of sage-buttered carrots. To my left, Papa waved from the fire pit, where he sat in his wheeled chair, laying out batter into a sizzling pan. He preferred cooking this way to the alchemically warmed pot. A lantern burned far above him, hanging from one of the turrets of our carriage.

"See you in the morning, Kalynishka!" he said.

I buckled on a sword and walked past the other tent to the edge of this year's hill.

Olaf had been happy to send someone along with us, for our protection, so now we were four. Six, if you counted the horses.

"So"—a laugh—"who is this man again?"

"Some petty extortionist working for the Gustavuses," I replied. "We're starting small."

"Well, that's better than nothing." Dagmar cracked her knuckles. "Traveling with you three has been better than guard duty, but just barely."

I looked up at her and feigned insult, mouth agape.

"Oh, settle down." She patted my cheek.

"Do you think our little assault lies within the King's orders?"

She shrugged. "My orders are to keep you safe."

I nodded.

"And *then* Skydašiai?" she asked. "I've never dueled before."

"Sure. Skydašiai."

"Finally. Shall we?"

Dagmar leaned down and kissed me intensely. She never expected more from me than this: a kiss, some time alone, light words, a bit of excitement. Once we managed to disengage, I nodded, and we walked down the hill into the warm night.

ACKNOWLEDGMENTS

It is wild to me that so many incredible publishing professionals have thrown their weight behind some silly ideas I came up with ten years ago, and I can't thank them enough.

My agent, Hannah Bowman, has been a tireless advocate for my work and an invaluable guide to publishing for my *extremely* neophyte ass. She was also a huge help in improving the book: please guess which major character, and entire related subplot, came from conversations with her.

Erewhon felt like the perfect home for *Soothsayer* even before I knew that their editor, Sarah Guan, was interested. Sarah has done amazing work to make this book the best that it can be, and I was overjoyed when her first comments were along the lines of, "But could we have *more* of the politics?" (Yes. Yes we could.) As I write this, promotion has just started, so I've only seen the beginning of what Martin Cahill is capable of on the marketing side, but it's already staggering.

Sasha Vinogradova's cover is stunning, and elegantly captures so many aspects of the book's vibe and iconography. Cassandra Farrin's interior design expertly conveys both the gravitas and lightness that I was going for in *Soothsayer*. Copyeditor Lakshna Mehta has done an exemplary job of fine-tuning the language while maintaining Kalyna's voice.

That voice of Kalyna's, and her very thought process, would never have existed without Ed Park's course on writing in the first person. (Or, for that matter, without Charles Portis's *True Grit*, which was assigned reading.)

As to friends and family: My spouse, Brittany Marie Spector, has been the first reader of my work as long as we've been together, and has never been content to just tell me it's good and pat me on the back. Simon Leaver-Appelman, Martine Neider, and Anna Bristow were all extremely helpful early readers for *Soothsayer*. Long before this book, Simon was also indispensable in helping me develop my writing style.

I'm also a fourth-generation writer. My father, Lincoln Spector, has been a freelance humorist and tech journalist for much of my life, with side projects in film criticism, poetry, and Purim spiels. My mother, Marilyn Kinch, has been a fanfiction author for decades. My grandmother, Rebecca Newman (her memory is a blessing), traditionally published one novel, self-published another, taught writing for years, and even hosted a public-access TV show on writing.

I never got to meet my great-grandmother, Sarah Spector, but I identify strongly with her. When she wasn't distributing leftist literature in her old folks' home, she was writing an (unpublished) novel based on her experiences growing up in the shtetl and immigrating to New York. The half-remembered, and mostly obliterated, Yiddish world passed down from her part of the family is deeply important to the themes and milieu of *Soothsayer*.

I also have to thank the friends and partners who make up the strange, bicoastal Venn diagram of found families in my life. My fellow artists, queers, leftists, and diasporic Jews, as well as the fine folks who are none of those things but tolerate us.

And you. Thank you for reading my book. I love you.

FURTHER READING (AND VIEWING)

Secondary-world fantasy settings don't spring fully formed out of an author's imagination. Unfortunately, I wrote the first draft of this book around a decade ago, so I hardly remember most of its influences. (For example, I can't for the life of me find where I learned that sickle-fighting treatises were a real thing in medieval Europe. But they were, I promise.)

Nonetheless, here are some references of note I do remember:

Vanished Kingdoms: The History of Half-Forgotten Europe (sometimes under the much less romantic, and greatly inferior, subtitle *The Rise and Fall of States and Nations*), Norman Davies (2011)

    Nothing influenced the world and larger plot of *Soothsayer* more than this book. It explores European nations that completely disappeared from the world and, through them, how nebulous our modern ideas around national identities and borders really are. It's also a history book in which the author is clearly subjective, and sometimes grumpy, which I love.

With Fire and Sword (Polish: *Ogniem i mieczem*), Henryk Sienkiewicz (1884; I read the 1991 W. S. Kuniczak translation)

    "Alexandre Dumas–style historical adventure novel set in Eastern Europe" is a concept that narrowcasts to me so intently as to be almost parodic. This book is also how I first learned about the Polish-Lithuanian Commonwealth, without which the Tetrarchia absolutely does not exist. (But beware: it's from the nineteenth century and, unsurprisingly, offensive at times.)

The Thirty Years War, C. V. Wedgwood (1938, revised 1957)

Another great bit of history on how shaky the seemingly set foundations of modern Europe are. This book taught me a lot about the strange way the Holy Roman Empire was run, which was also a major influence on *Soothsayer*. Wedgwood has a real gift for quickly sketching each individual in a long procession of historical figures.

F for Fake, directed by Orson Welles, cowritten by Orson Welles and Oja Kodar (1973)

A dizzying, rambunctious, and insightful treatise on fakery and expertise, edited together in a way that feels thirty years ahead of its time. I would often watch scenes while writing this book, just so I could soak in the rhythm of Welles' speech and editing.

CHINA
UNDER DENG

CHINA
UNDER DENG

Edited by
Kwan Ha Yim

Facts On File
New York • Oxford

China Under Deng

Copyright © 1991 by Facts On File, Inc.

Facts On File, Inc.
460 Park Avenue South
New York NY 10016
USA

Facts On File Limited
Collins Street
Oxford OX4 1XJ
United Kingdom

Library of Congress Cataloging-in-Publication Data

China under Deng / edited by Kwan Ha Yim.
    p. cm.
    Includes index.
    ISBN 0-8160-2315-8 : $24.95
    1. China—Politics and government—1976– I. Yim, Kwan Ha.
DS779.26.C47354 1991
951.05—dc20   90-42164
                                                  CIP

ISBN 0-8196-2315-8

Facts On File books are available at special discounts when purchased in bulk quantities for businesses, associations, institutions or sales promotions. Please call our Special Sales Department in New York at 212/683-2244 (dial 800/322-8755 except in NY, AK or HI) or in Oxford at 865/728399.

Composition by The Maple-Vail Manufacturing Group
Manufactured by The Maple-Vail Manufacturing Group
Printed in the United States of America

10 9 8 7 6 5 4 3 2 1

This book is printed on acid-free paper.

CONTENTS

PREFACE

In 1980, Facts On File published *China Since Mao*, which covers the period immediately after Mao Zedong's death in 1976, to 1979. This volume is a sequel to it. What is attempted here is an "interim history" that tells the remarkable, and in some ways, tragic, story of China's post-Mao transformation achieved under the aegis of Deng Xiaoping: "socialist modernization."

The narrative begins in January 1979, with the rise of Hu Yaobang, Deng's protege, to key positions of the Chinese Communist Party, and closes with the tragic events at Tiananmen Square on June 4, 1989. Implemented between these two historic events are a series of daring reforms in China's economic and political structure which were to have dramatic effects on the lives of the Chinese people. The Chinese were drawn out of their pursuit of ideological purity and introduced to an alternative life-style above the line of general poverty, a new form of socialism that rewarded private entrepreneurship.

Deng Xiaoping, the architect of these pragmatic reforms, was not the most logical candidate to step into the shoes of the late Chairman Mao. Deng and Mao were complete opposites. Where Mao had been tall and charismatic, Deng was short and seemingly shy. Mao had been a romantic, a visionary who indulged in poetic license; by contrast, Deng was a realist, a deal-maker and a consummate practitioner of the art of the possible.

Mao had believed that China could achieve the goals of a truly communistic society ahead of any other country, including the Soviet Union. What stood in the way were inertia, old habits, feudal values and bourgeois attitudes. In the last years of his life, Mao, the "Great Helmsman" sallied forth at these citadels of human frailty by leading teenage gangs, the Red Guards, against his erstwhile colleagues and the leading members of his own party. Some 100 million people are said to have been affected by the Cultural Revolution. An official estimate of those who actually lost their lives runs to over 35,000—including the former head of state, Liu Shaoqi.

The passing of Chairman Mao was, therefore, greeted with a secret sigh of relief. Deng, with his diminutive and common-sense approach ("It doesn't matter whether a cat is black or white, so long as it catches mice.") appealed to the mood of post-Mao China. Instead of mouthing heady slogans, he spoke of raising the standard of living. He despised ideologues and railed against their dogmatic conservatism. He stressed the need for modernizing China's defense, agriculture and industries by acquiring knowledge and technology from the West. He struck a responsive chord in the minds of the vast numbers of people who had lived through the furies of the Cultural Revolution years. Deng Xiaoping was in his time.

Deng was born in 1902. After his secondary school education in his native province of Sichuan, where he came into contact with French missionaries, he went to France in 1920 under a work-study program. It was while there that he became a Communist and worked with China's future premier, Zhou Enlai, organizing communist movement among expatriate Chinese student-workers.

In January 1926, he traveled to Moscow to enroll in the newly established Sun Yat-sen University of Working Chinese. His stay in the Russian capital was relatively short—a mere 18 months. He returned to China to work on the staff of a nationalist general, Feng Yuxiang. That, too, was short-lived, as the Nationalist-Communist united front broke up in 1927. Deng went underground, trying his hand at organizing communist cells in Shanghai and later leading guerrilla fighters in Guangxi. In the early 1930s he joined the Communist forces in Jiangxi and, with Mao Zedong, went on the Long March.

During the Sino-Japanese War, Deng Xiaoping distinguished himself as the political commissar of the redoutable 129th Division. His rise in the Communist Party hierarchy was rapid. By 1955, he was already a member of the Chinese Communist Party politburo and the general secretary of the Party.

Deng fell on hard times with the onset of the Cultural Revolution. He was denounced by the Cultural Revolution faction as the second most detestable "capitalist despot." He was hounded out of his office and made to kneel on the ground in front of raging Red Guards. He was banished to the remote province of Jiangxi. He was called back in 1974, apparently by Mao himself—to assist the ailing premier, Zhou Enlai. More trouble awaited him. The radicals around Mao's wife, Jiang Qing, had him purged again shortly after Zhou's death in January 1976, but he was able to make a comeback in less than a year. Mao died in September of 1976 and Jiang Qing and her followers, the Gang of Four, made an abortive coup attempt that resulted in their arrest and incarceration.

Deng regained his position as vice-premier and the chief of staff of the army. From this power base, he rallied civil and military officials (pragmatists) against both the remnants of the Cultural Revolution faction and the more moderate Maoist "whatever faction," supporting Mao's hand-picked successor, Hua Guofeng. A veteran of many intraparty factional fights, Deng reckoned no peers. One by one his rivals fell by the wayside. He was clearly in charge by 1980.

Deng used his power to steer China in a new direction. A series of reforms, which he inspired, opened China to foreign investment and trade. Its economic makeup underwent radical restructuring to allow a greater scope of market forces. Younger and better-educated people were brought into the higher echelons of the Communist Party, replacing the aging leaders. Incompetent and corrupt officials were ferreted out by the millions. All of these reforms, which passed under the generic title of the open-door policy, testified to Deng's unspoken faith in the twin cure for any stagnant economy: the global market-place and private entrepreneurship.

No one can deny the impressive record of China's achievements in the first part of the 1980s, under Deng's leadership. Chinese economy grew at a breathtaking pace. China normalized its relations with the United States and the Soviet Union, pretty much on its own terms. China moved ahead with its modernization programs, scoring impressive results and thus emerging as one of the principal players in international politics.

The success, however, created its own problems. Deng was able to use the centralized political structure of his country to press forward with his reforms. But his liberal reforms were antithetical to the monopoly of state power by the Communist Party. To put it in Marxist terms, the socialist superstructure bound and shackled the new productive forces unleashed by the infusion of a capitalist economy. Deng had made light of the difficulties involved in fostering private entrepreneurship within the framework of the Communist state. He made the same mistake as had the Chinese statesmen of the 19th century, who had thought that China could adopt Western technology without overhauling its social and political structure. The conflict manifested itself in the confrontation of prodemocracy activists and armed soldiers of the People's Liberation Army at Tiananmen Square on that fateful night of June 4, 1989.

Facts On File has published accounts of these and other momentous developments in China, in its weekly summaries of world events, based on the information its diligent staff culled from a multiplicity of contemporary sources, including official press releases, newspaper accounts, broadcasts and expert analyses. This volume brings together in book form the previously published materials, organized in such a way that the reader may be able to see individual occurrences in the context of broader trends. The editor is responsible mainly for the organization of the materials. Facts are presented here with scrupulous regard for objectivity.

Kwan Ha Yim
Valley Cottage, New York

1

MANAGING THE TRANSITION

HU YAOBANG GETS KEY PARTY POSTS

In December 1978, the Chinese Communist Party's 11th Central Committee adopted a new ideological line, "seek truth from facts," which implicitly repudiated rigid adherence to Maoist principles. Deng Xiaoping scored a significant victory, but there lay ahead many difficult tasks for his pragmatic reform programs. His new policy to revitalize China's economy by putting profit, not politics, in charge was still heresy in terms of orthodox Marxist-Leninist practices. It left the Communist Party's ideological fringe, "the Cultural Revolution group," deeply skeptical, if not outraged.

Deng sought to strengthen his position by placing his trusted lieutenants in key positions of the Party and the state. It was reported on January 4, 1979 that Hu Yaobang, one of Deng's close associates, had been appointed secretary general of the Chinese Communist Party and chief of the party's Propaganda Department.

The post of secretary general was revived after having been abolished at the start of the Cultural Revolution in 1966, when its last incumbent, Deng, was purged. Hu was also ousted at the time. It was presumed that Hu would relinquish his job as head of the par-

1

ty's Organization Department, a position to which he had been appointed in 1977.

As secretary general, Hu, who was 62, was regarded to be in a good position to compete for the eventual succession to Deng.

Like Deng, Hu was a strong supporter of practical policies aimed at speeding China's economic development. Hu reportedly had been a leader of the campaign in November 1978, to downgrade the image of the late Communist Party Chairman Mao Zedong and had assisted in the publication of recent articles calling for greater democracy in China.

Hu was believed to have been appointed to his two new posts at a meeting, in December 1978, of the party's Central Committee that also promoted him to membership on the politburo. That session also was said to have demoted Wang Dongxing, a deputy chairman of the party, who reportedly opposed Deng's moves to downgrade Mao. Wang reportedly was ousted as head of the party's General Office, commander of the 8341 unit and editor of Mao's writings.

The General Office handled internal party communications. The 8341 unit was an army division charged with security for downtown Beijing, where Chinese leaders lived and worked.

"LET THE PEOPLE SAY"

The new Party line manifested itself in Beijing's tolerance, if not encouragement, of people's right to express their views. The Communist Party newspaper, *People's Daily*, January 3 strongly supported the right of the people to display wall posters to express their opinions.

Alluding to some of the recent placards calling for democracy, the newspaper's editorial said: "Let the people say what they wish. The heavens will not fall. A range of opinions from people are good for a revolutionary party leading the government. If people become unwilling to say anything, that would be bad. When people are free to speak, it means the party and the government have strength and confidence."

Meanwhile, a group of students and workers was said to have produced two issues of a new newspaper called the *People's Forum* and posted copies on walls around Beijing. The second issue of the four-page mimeographed sheet carried an article saying that "in the age of computers in the world, the feudal imperial system still exists in China."

It did not take much encouragement from the Party or the government to bring demonstrators out onto the streets of Beijing. On January 8, several thousand persons marched around Tiananmen Square demanding democracy, food and work.

The rally had been called ostensibly to commemorate the third anniversary of the death of Premier Zhou Enlai. While others paid homage to Zhou, the demonstrators carried banners which read, "We don't want hunger. We don't want to suffer anymore. We want human rights and democracy."

Political wall posters also appeared. One placard demanded the review of the case of three men from Canton who had been jailed for writing a wall poster in 1974 criticizing the Communist Party as a new elite class.

A group of 100 to 200 peasants from various parts of China arrived in Beijing January 14, in an unsuccessful effort to present their grievances to government officials. Police barred them from seeing Deputy Premier Deng Xiaoping or Communist Party Chairman Hua Guofeng. The peasants carried banners with the slogans, "Persecuted people from all over China," "We want democracy and human rights," and "A plea for help from Deng Xiaoping."

Many of the marchers shouted, "We're tired of being hungry" and "Down with oppression." The demonstrators drew a crowd of about 1,000 onlookers. They quietly ended their protests January 15.

Lest people's protests get out of hand, the Chinese government issued warnings. The February 12 *People's Daily* said that while some people had legitimate grievances, they should "bear in mind the country's overall interests and work wholeheartedly for modernization." Demonstrators "deliberately creating trouble that has serious consequences" would be punished, the newspaper said.

The warning was prompted by violent disturbances reported in Shanghai the previous week and by demonstrations in Beijing in January. The Xinhua news agency on February 10, had quoted a Shanghai official as saying that since the end of January "there has been a small group of young people blocking traffic, damaging public property . . . , assailing cadres and stopping moving trains."

Foreign visitors to Shanghai had told of protests by thousands of young people who had been resettled in the countryside under the Cultural Revolution's "Youth to Countryside" program, which was being phased out. The young people had denounced their assignments and poor living conditions.

Many of the demonstrators either had left the rural villages to which they were sent and drifted back to the city, or had complained that the factories to which they had been assigned after finishing their terms on farms were too far from their homes in Shanghai, it was reported.

In the spring of 1979, the Chinese government resumed its crackdown of dissident groups. On April 14, the Beijing police arrested four human rights activists attempting to post protest placards.

The four, all members of a group called the Human Rights Alliance, were seized after they tried to put up wall posters criticizing the government's "bureaucratic system" and its "masters." The posters were in response to recent articles in the *People's Daily* terming human rights "a bourgeois slogan" and assailing the activists as "reactionaries and counterrevolutionaries."

Protest posters continued to appear in Shanghai on April 15, despite the government's ban. There was no apparent attempt by authorities in the city to remove them.

One mimeographed message charged that "The Shanghai Public Security Bureau [the police] is the real criminal in Shanghai." It said, "The people of capitalist countries can discuss human rights; why not those of us in this socialist China? If the people do not have freedom of speech, what is the difference between us and wild animals?"

According to radio reports, the Shanghai protesters also had blocked traffic, attacked high central government officials and beat up police.

In Zhejiang province there had been an attempt by "counterrevolutionary elements" in March to seize power, according to official provincial broadcast transcripts that had become available to Western sources in Hong Kong in mid-April. The broadcasts told of an unsuccessful effort by "a few people" to create disorder and oust the Communist Party committees in the province.

A Beijing wall poster, written by an imprisoned Chinese dissident, said that many of China's high-level political prisoners of the past 10 years had been incarcerated in a jail near Beijing where they were frequently tortured and deprived of food and visits from relatives, the *New York Times* reported from Hong Kong on May 6.

A copy of the poster (dated March 3), obtained by the *Times*, had been written by Wei Jingsheng, who had been arrested several weeks after it appeared. Wei's description of another political prison near Beijing had appeared earlier in an underground newspaper in Beijing.

A Hong Kong magazine's article on the first prison cited by Wei said the Gang of Four, including its leader Jiang Qing, were being held there. Among the others who had served time there and were later released were Wang Guangmei, the widow of former head of state Liu Shaoqī; Peng Zhen, former mayor of Beijing, and the Panchen Lama, the second highest spiritual leader in Tibet.

Wei said that "as a result of prolonged torture" during her imprisonment, Wang had gone temporarily insane.

This was the first report that disgraced top-level Chinese officials had been imprisoned rather than held under house detention.

The *Washington Post* on May 29 reported that the Communist Party cadres in the southeast province of Hunan openly took issue with Deng Xiaoping. In a series of broadcasts heard during April and May, they questioned his policy toward the Soviet Union and his agricultural policy. These broadcasts surprised analysts who had assumed that Deng had solidified his position at the Central Committee meeting of December 18–22, 1978,

The Hunan broadcasts were considered significant because the province was the birthplace of the late Communist Party Chairman Mao Zedong and the political base of the current chairman and premier, Hua Guofeng. The criticisms of Deng were broadcast openly and were considered to have the backing of influential political figures in Beijing, according to the report.

A broadcast in April was critical of indications that China considered improving relations with the U.S.S.R. Moscow had indicated in April that it was willing to reopen talks with Beijing on border disputes and other conflicts.

Beijing had not rejected the Soviet request out of hand, leading to speculation that the harsh line toward the Soviet Union might be changed. The Hunan broadcast warned that China should not "beg" for a change in relations but should rely on "the strong power of the proletariat."

In May, the *Post* reported, Hunan radio broadcast a tribute to the village of Dazhai, an agricultural collective often praised by Mao. Deng's supporters had recently criticized Dazhai for preventing its peasants from cultivating private plots and for ignoring individual initiative. Sinologists noted that it was the first public praise for Dazhai in several weeks.

Meanwhile, Deng and his supporters had begun a campaign to respond to the criticism. Press articles called for unity with the current party policy and criticized Deng's opponents for relying completely on Mao.

The pro-Deng articles refuted claims that Deng's call for democracy had resulted in protest wall posters and unrest. "Of course, some places have gone a bit astray in various ways," said a broadcast cited on May 25 by the *New York Times*. "However, the emergence of these problems is certainly not caused by the party's policies themselves, but by variations in their execution."

Deng, himself, replied to his critics, according to a report released by the Taiwan intelligence agency. In a speech thought to have been made in March, Deng said, "We should let people put up posters . . . We will be able to avoid making the masses angry."

THE CULTURAL REVOLUTION VICTIMS
REHABILITATED

Deng Xiaoping and Hu Yaobang, both of whom had been victims of the Maoist-inspired Cultural Revolution, made it the first order of business to rehabilitate their fellow victims.

The Xinhua news agency reported on January 25 that the government would return property seized from businessmen during the Cultural Revolution to enlist their support in the drive to modernize the country.

The news agency said that Ulanfu, a politburo member, had told a gathering of 200 former industrialists in Beijing January 22, that the Communist Party's Central Committee had decided that businessmen's assets and bank deposits, confiscated since September 1968, would be given back with interest. Their professional titles would be restored, and their children would not suffer discrimination in jobs and schools. The government also would permit members of the business class to return to their requisitioned homes and would grant political advancement to those who excelled in productive labor and business.

Ulanfu blamed former Defense Minister Lin Biao, who had died in 1971, and the purged Gang of Four for having unfairly characterized the Chinese bourgeoisie as "monsters and demons and reactionary capitalists."

The Central Committee's reforms, Ulanfu said, were designed to undo the harm caused by the "untruthful charges" leveled against the Chinese business community.

Many Chinese industrialists had fled the mainland with the Chinese Nationalists after the Communist takeover in 1949. Those who remained were stripped of their property, money, titles and status in 1966, at the start of the Cultural Revolution.

The Beijing press reported on August 3, that the Beijing Communist Party had restored to favor a group of editors and writers purged during the Cultural Revolution because their work had been considered critical of the policies of Mao Zedong.

The leaders of the group were Wu Han, who had been deputy mayor of Beijing, Deng Tuo, who had served as secretary of the Beijing party committee and editor of its publication, *Frontline*, and Liao Mosha, also an official of the party committee. Wu and Deng had both "died under persecution," according to the official Chinese press agency. Liao, who was 72, was given the right to take part again in party activities.

The leaders had already been rehabilitated as individuals. The new action rehabilitated those others who had been persecuted for their connection to Wu, Deng and Liao. The editorial boards of the *Beijing Daily*, the Beijing *Evening News* and *Frontline* had been disbanded in 1966 and their leaders punished because the publications had carried articles by Wu, Deng and Liao.

The Gang of Four and the late Defense Minister Lin Biao were accused of arranging the 1966 purge. The Xinhua news agency quoted the Beijing Communist Party as saying, "These outrageous frame-ups by Lin and the gang, to serve their criminal purposes of usurping top party and state powers, should be completely redressed."

More purge victims were rehabilitated as the Communist Party Central Committee announced on September 28 that it had added 12 persons, all of whom had been victims of the Cultural Revolution.

One of the 12, Peng Zhen, was named also to the party's ruling politburo. Peng had been a mayor of Beijing before he was ousted during the Cultural Revolution. Also promoted to the politburo was Zhao Ziyang, the party first secretary of Sichuan province.

Both Peng and Zhao were considered close allies of Deputy Premier Deng Xiaoping. The promotions were seen as a continuation of the policy of adding supporters of Deng to the politburo without removing those who might be considered Deng's opponents.

The persons promoted to the Central Committee included Zhou Yang, a former cultural commissar, Bo Yibo, an economic planner, Yang Shangkun, mayor of Canton, and Lu Dingyi, a former propaganda official.

In addition to announcing the promotions, the Central Committee said that it had unanimously endorsed a plan for accelerating farm development. The plan called for the government to pay peasants higher prices for grain and had been "warmly welcomed by the peasant masses in their hundreds of millions," the committee said.

In a speech on September 29, commemorating the 30th anniversary of the People's Republic of China, to which foreign diplomats and journalists were invited for the first time since 1949, Communist Party Senior Deputy Chairman Ye Jianying described the Cultural Revolution of the late 1960s as "an appalling catastrophe suffered by all our people."

Ye listed a number of errors the Communist Party had made in the late 1950s and the 1960s, and emphasized that China must now "seek truth from facts," or, in other words, adopt a pragmatic, non-dogmatic approach to matters. The late Communist Party Chairman Mao Zedong was described as a great man whose leadership was vital to the success of the revolution before 1949. But, Ye added,

Mao was not a god. Mao's thought, Ye said, was "not the product of Mao Zedong's pesonal wisdom alone. It is also the product of the wisdom of his comrades-in-arms."

Although the late head of state Liu Shaoqi was not named by Ye, his speech appeared to approve of Liu's actions and take a step toward Liu's posthumous rehabilitation. Liu was purged in 1968 during the Cultural Revolution.

Ye said that the Eighth Party Congress, which took place in 1956 and at which Liu had presented the political report, had been completely correct. That meeting had been denounced at the next party congress, which was held in 1969 during the Cultural Revolution.

He went on to say that the campaign against right-wingers, which followed the short-lived Hundred Flowers period of political liberalization in 1957, had gone too far. Of the Great Leap Forward in 1958, Ye said, "We made mistakes in giving arbitrary directions, being boastful and stirring up a communist wind." Liu had opposed Mao on that movement.

A Hong Kong newspaper had reported in November 1978, that Liu had died of pneumonia in 1969 while being moved during his detention at the close of the Cultural Revolution.

Liu's death was confirmed by the Chinese government. The Xinhua news agency, without saying when or where Liu had died, acknowledged his death by reporting that Wang Guangmei, widow of Liu Shaoqi, had appeared the previous week at a Beijing party celebrating the Chinese New Year. Among the government officials attending the affair was Communist Party Chairman Hua Guofeng.

The Central Committee of the Chinese Communist Party, February 29, 1980, made a formal decision to rehabilitate Liu. The decision rescinded the Central Committee resolution of 1968 that expelled Liu from the party for life and deprived him of all positions. The communique said that "an appraisal on the eve of the Cultural Revolution," which had claimed that Liu had headed a "bourgeois headquarters" within the party, "was contrary to fact . . ."

In addition to rehabilitating Liu, the Central Committee meeting ousted four members of the Communist Party's politburo who had risen to power during the Cultural Revolution. They were: Wang Dongxing, who had been ranked sixth in the party hierarchy; Ji Dengku; former Beijing Mayor Wu De; and General Chen Xilian, whose post as commander of the Beijing military region had been turned over to Qin Jiwei.

Two followers of Deputy Premier Deng Xiaoping were promoted to the Standing Committee of the politburo: Hu Yaobang, head of the party's Propaganda Department, and Zhao Ziyang, first secretary of Sichuan province.

Hu also was named secretary general of the party. The elevation of Hu to the party post led some observers to suggest that Hu, 64, had been chosen as the successor to Deng.

ECONOMIC PLAN REVISED

The Fifth National People's Congress had adopted, in March 1978, an ambitious economic development plan, which was aimed at pushing China into "the front ranks of world economy" by the year 2000. Prepared under the auspices of Hua Guofeng, the plan gave priorities to heavy industries over light industries and consumer goods. Its critics, among whom was Deng Xiaoping, regarded it as overly ambitius and unrealistic. Serious doubts about its practicality were raised, because of China's economic conditions, which, in 1979, were experiencing numerous difficulties.

According to a newspaper report published in Hong Kong, Vice-Premier Li Xiannian told a Beijing conference in April 1979, that 20 million Chinese were unemployed and 100 million did not get enough to eat. He added that the government faced a budget deficit of $6 billion.

Li indicated that Beijing would have to cut back on government spending and channel money into agricultural production instead of industrial development. "China has a poor economic base," Li was reported as saying. "The sabotage done to the state's economy by the Gang of Four cannot be repaired in a short time."

The government deficit reportedly resulted from compensation paid to purged officials who were rehabilitated, as well as from too-rapid industrial development. It was also said to have grown out of a 1977 pay increase for industrial and clerical workers and a series of bonuses for higher productivity.

On May 6, Chinese Foreign Trade Minister Li Jiang announced that China was cutting back on its ambitious economic development program, a move that involved retrenchment in heavy-industry imports of capital goods in the immediate future.

Despite the change, Li said, China was not abandoning its campaign of Four Modernizations (China's developmental priorities)— in agriculture, industry, science and technology, and defense. Nor did it wish to end cooperation with the U.S. to achieve those goals, he said.

According to Li's explanation of the new policy shift: "The readjustment of our economy undertaken at this moment is exactly for the purpose of concentrating our efforts in the most needed projects and quickening the pace for the Four Modernizations."

Li made his statement in a toast to U.S. Commerce Secretary Juanita Kreps, who had arrived in Beijing on May 5 for a two-week visit to help restore normal trade relations between the U.S. and China.

Chinese Premier and Communist Party leader Hua Guofeng acknowledged on June 18, that China's economic goals for 1979 had been too ambitious. Echoing Vice Premier Li Xiannian, Hua said China would have to cut back on some of the development plans adopted in 1978.

BUDGET PROBLEMS AND LEGAL REFORMS

The National People's Congress, China's nominal legislature, met in Beijing during the final weeks of June 1979. In a speech to the opening session of the congress on June 18, Premier Hua admitted that "some of the measures we adopted (in 1978) were not prudent enough." He said three years would be required before China could embark on a program of high-speed economic development.

Hua told the 3,300 delegates that expansion of light industries would proceed more quickly in 1979 than development of heavy industry. He promised more consumer goods, increased salaries and increased exports.

For the first time since the 1950s, Hua provided figures on China's past economic performance. He said grain output for 1978 was 304.75 million metric tons, a 7.8% increase over 1977. (A metric ton is 2,204.6 pounds.)

Total industrial output, Hua continued, had increased 14% in 1978 over the year before. He said steel output had totaled 31.8 million metric tons, coal output 618 million metric tons and crude oil production 104 million metric tons.

China's projected income and expenditures for 1979 were reported to the National People's Congress on June 21, by Finance Minister Zhang Jingfu and state planning commission chairman Yu Qiuli. It was the first time in more than 20 years that the Chinese government had made its budget public.

Zhang said revenues were expected to total $70.7 billion, about the same as in 1978. Expenditures were estimated to equal revenues, but Zhang indicated that a deficit was expected.

In presenting the economic plan for 1979, Yu promised a 20% increase in the price paid by the state for grain. Prices for other farm products would be increased by almost 25% to encourage agricultural production. The 1979 plan, according to Yu's report, called for farm production to increase by 4% over 1978. He said government investment in agriculture would be 14% more than last year.

Total industrial production was targeted to increase by 8%, Yu continued. Investment in heavy industry (machinery, steel and chemicals) would be sharply reduced from 1978, to 46.8% of total investment from 54.7% of total 1978 investment. Light industry would receive 5.8% of new investment, an increase from 5.4% in 1978.

Besides increased farm prices, Yu said factory workers would receive higher wages. He added that funds would go to creating new jobs, especially for unemployed urban youth. An experimental fund would be set aside for individual factories to use as they wished, Yu added.

Yu forecast a 24% increase in foreign trade in 1979 to $27.7 billion. He predicted that China would borrow $2.5 billion in 1979 to pay for imports.

In a speech to the Congress made public June 29, Finance Minister Zhang also said China's military spending in 1979 would total $12.64 billion, an increase of $2.1 billion over 1978. Foreign aid expenditures in 1979 would total $625 million. The increase in military outlay was necessitated by the February–March border war with Vietnam, Zhang said. This was the first time in nearly 20 years that China had publicly disclosed its military budget.

The National People's Congress ended its two-week session July 1 by appointing three economic specialists as deputy premiers. This brought to 17 the number holding that post. The Congress also created a new government agency and carried out major changes in the country's legal code and governmental structure.

One of the new deputy premiers, Chen Yun, also was named head of the new agency, the State Finance and Economic Commission. Chen was a member of the politburo's Standing Committee.

The other deputy premiers were Bo Yibo, a former finance minister, and Yao Yilin, a former commerce minister. Both had been purged during the Cultural Revolution in the 1960s and later rehabilitated. The newly appointed deputy premiers were thought to be close supporters of Deputy Premier Deng Xiaoping, the *New York Times* reported on July 2.

In addition, the Congress appointed former Beijing Mayor Peng Zhen as a vice-chairman of its Standing Committee, a post also held by Chen Yun.

Among the major governmental changes enacted:

- The governing revolutionary committees in counties, districts and provinces were to be replaced by new local governments with personnel elected or appointed by people's congresses.
- The people's congresses at the county level were to be elected directly, instead of appointed from above as in the past. The dis-

trict, provincial and national congresses, however, would be indirectly elected by the congresses at the level below them. The candidates for these posts could be nominated by the Communist Party or by noncommunist organizations and individuals, as long as they were seconded by at least three people.

Under a new criminal code, the first since 1949, the definition of "counterrevolutionary" was sharply narrowed. A "reactionary" could not be "convicted of counterrevolutionary offenses" as long as he "commits no actions aimed at overthrowing" the government, according to the new ruling.

The accused must be brought to trial within five and a half months after arrest and not left in detention indefinitely. A defendant also would have the right to a lawyer.

COPING WITH SOCIAL PROBLEMS

Deng Xiaoping and his followers turned to "facts" as a source of truth. But the facts they set their minds on bespoke daunting problems facing China as a developing country. Of these, none was more pressing than China's large population threatening to outrun its meager resources. In an article published on August 13, 1979, Deputy Premier Chen Muhua said that the cost of raising the 600 million children born since 1949 had absorbed 30% of the national income. "China had little to start with," she said, "and the proportion of money that can be devoted to education is limited."

She added, "The rapid growth of the population has brought a lot of difficulties to the national economy, the people's livelihood and employment, creating a roadblock for socialist construction. Fast population growth has hampered the Four Modernaizations and the raising of the people's living standards."

As a result of the country's limited resources and the vast number of children, schooling could only be made available to some, she said. Chen said that 6% of children were not able to go to primary school, 12% of primary school students did not go on to junior high school, over 50% of junior high graduates could not attend high school and only 5% of high school graduates went to universities.

China, Chen said, aimed to reach zero population growth between 1985 and 2000, it was reported on August 13.

In an article in the *People's Daily*, Chen wrote that couples who had more than two children would be penalized through taxation and other economic sanctions. A law providing such penalties would soon be enacted, she said.

Chen said that the government's goal was to cut the birthrate to five per 1,000 people by 1985. She said the rate had already been lowered to 12.05 per 1,000 in 1978 from 23.4 per 1,000 in 1971.

The population problem was reflected on the social scene. The poor were impatient. About 400 Chinese staged a sit-in in front of a government building in Beijing on August 8, demanding jobs and assistance from the government.

The protesters had come to Beijing from various provinces. While some demanded an end to political persecution, the main emphasis was on issues of personal welfare: jobs, housing and food.

The demonstrators said their troubles started with the Cultural Revolution of the late 1960s and the following years when the Gang of Four ruled China. They had lost their jobs then and suffered persecution. Although the Gang of Four had been discredited and the government had taken a new direction, the protesters said, they were still without work.

No violence was reported at the protest. The government made no official comment on the demonstration, and the demonstrators said they had not been allowed to explain their grievances to any government or Communist Party officials.

Protests were spurred on by growing instances of official corruption. The Communist Party launched a drive to remove corrupt officials and end excessive privileges for top officials, according to a report on August 22.

The campaign was disclosed by a report in mid-August in the *People's Daily*. Earlier, on July 31, the newspaper reported a speech by Hu Yaobang, the party secretary-general and propaganda chief, in which Hu said that regulations "for enforcing party discipline should be immediately drawn up."

Western analysts said that it appeared that the anticorruption drive would be carried out in a more orderly fashion than previous purges, in an attempt to show that the rule of law had been restored. The leaders of the newly formed party disciplinary commission were Chen Yun, who had directed the economic reconstruction following the civil war, and Deng Yingchao, the widow of Premier Zhou Enlai.

A Western diplomat quoted in the *Los Angeles Times* of August 22 said, "With those two in charge, I wouldn't think there would be any complaints about favoritism or abuses. They're considered completely scrupulous and together they have enough clout to go after just about anybody in the politburo."

Two top officials reportedly might be in jeopardy because of the anticorruption effort. One of these was Wang Dongxing, the bodyguard of the late Mao Zedong. Wall posters charged that Wang had built a $4.3-million villa for himself at public expense. The other was

Deputy Premier Chen Muhua, who reportedly, while on a visit to Rumania, had refused to allow some Chinese athletes who had become ill to fly back with her to China on her plane.

An article in the *People's Daily*, quoted in a *Washington Post* report datelined August 24, said that "some regulations provide for a degree of privilege for officials far beyond what is necessary, far beyond the people's standard of living, and not in keeping with the reality that our country is still very poor and backward."

The article continued, "Some of these regulations were copied from the Soviet Union and form a strict hierarchy divorced from the masses. Some still bear the marks of the supply system, with everything taken care of by the state. Some even retain the characteristics of feudalistic special privileges."

PRODEMOCRACY SENTIMENT ON THE RISE

Approximately 1,000 Chinese attended a rally in Beijing's Tiananmen Square on September 13, denouncing special privileges among Communist Party officials and urging more human rights and free elections. The gathering was sponsored by a group calling itself the Democratic Scientific and Socialist Study Association.

One of the speakers asserted that the principal problem in China "is the contradiction between the powerful privileged class and the workers. We have wiped out capitalists, landlords and rich peasants, but now we have a new rich class."

Another speaker said he had not been connected with the society but decided to address the rally after learning that its leaders had disappeared on September 12, apparently arrested. He declared that "human rights is not a capitalist term; it has no class nature." He assailed "bureaucrats" who enjoyed all the privileges of their class "while many people's stomachs are empty."

In previous dissident actions in Beijing on September 10, high school graduates staged a protest march to the city's government offices charging they had been refused admission to college after passing their entrance examinations.

On September 9, a group of 300 writers met in a park to discuss the state of official and underground literature.

Another demonstration of Chinese protesting their poor economic condition was held outside government offices on September 6. They attached a poster outside the building promising not to leave "until we are victorious."

The demonstrators, all of whom were unemployed and poor, were seeking redress for a variety of grievances, many of them dating to the Cultural Revolution of the 1960s.

On September 22, about 200 demonstrators gathered on the steps of city hall and laid down posters demanding that they be allowed to live in Beijing instead of the countryside, where they had been sent during the Cultural Revolution. The protesters said they had been given grievance forms to submit, but the appropriate officials had refused to meet with them.

In a demonstration two days earlier, about 150 persons had demanded the right to move back to Beijing from the countryside. Another demonstration on September 20, involved about 100 railway workers and their families. They complained that the "railway bureau is not implementing the government's policy" and called on the Central Committee to deal with the problem.

A wall poster, described in a *Washington Post* story datelined September 22, accused the government of restricting its redress of grievances stemming from the Cultural Revolution to the top strata of society. The poster, which had apparently been torn down by authorities but was still circulating in Beijing, asked, "Why is it that officials have been rehabilitated while workers, peasants, intellectuals, demobilized soldiers . . . who had been persecuted and sent back to their old homes in the countryside only have their cases reversed, but don't have their jobs returned to them or their food rations augmented?"

On October 10, more than 2,000 students and faculty members from People's University in Beijing demonstrated against the occupation of their campus by an army artillery unit. The protesters, shouting "Down with militarism," marched and staged a sit-in in front of the Communist Party headquarters in the capital demanding that the soldiers be withdrawn. Classes also were boycotted.

The army agreed on October 13 to withdraw the 1,000 soldiers and their dependents from the campus in stages. No date for the withdrawal was set.

At the same time, 40 wall posters appeared at Beijing University demanding an improvement in living conditions at the school. An open student association letter to the school administration charged that the presence of the troops was causing great inconvenience. The statement said that because of the soldiers' use of the university's facilities, the cafeteria lacked tables and chairs, access to the library was restricted and electricity was often turned off in the early evening, preventing students from studying.

The dispute stemmed from the Cultural Revolution in the 1960s, when the army was sent into campuses and factories to restore order. In 1978 the government had reopened Beijing University and directed the army to withdraw from there and from other institutions. The army, however, ignored the order and remained at the university and at other schools around Beijing, ostensibly because of a housing shortage in the city.

In another school protest, about 800 students and teachers of the Beijing Institute of Finance marched through the city on October 12, demanding the removal of a company that manufactured cigarettes at their school.

At first, the Chinese authorities responded to these protests in a conciliatory manner. The *People's Daily* reported on September 15 that the government had set up a special commission of 1,000 officials to look into the complaints of the petitioners, estimated to number as many as 20,000.

The newspaper said the officials would hear the petitioners' cases and then escort the petitioners back to their native areas, where local officials would resolve the problems. The government acknowledged that "in some areas and units, a few wrong and false cases have not yet been resolved" and "some petitioners have been retaliated against after returning to their native places." The paper continued, "Seventy to 80% of the petitioners have come to Beijing repeatedly."

Soon conciliation gave way to repression. On October 16, a Beijing court sentenced leading dissident Wei Jingsheng to 15 years in prison.

Arrested in March, Wei was convicted at his one-day trial of having given an unidentified foreigner military intelligence on China's war with Vietnam. He also was found guilty of having written articles for a magazine he edited, *Exploration*, that "agitated for the overthrow of the dictatorship of the proletariat," the Xinhua news agency reported.

Commenting on the severity of Wei's sentence, another *Exploration* editor said, "It looks like the bureaucrats are willing to sacrifice our billion people to keep themselves in power."

On October 17, the U.S. said it was "surprised and disappointed" at the "severity" of Wei's sentence. A State Department spokesman said U.S. Ambassador Leonard Woodcock had conveyed the Carter administration's concern to Chinese officials. The spokesman said Wei had the right to appeal and urged Beijing to moderate his jail term.

Beijing's High People's Court, on November 6, rejected Wei's appeal against his conviction and 15-year sentence.

More arrests and crackdowns were to follow. Four persons were arrested at the Democracy Wall on November 11 and another three were seized there on November 18 during the sale of the transcript of the October trial of dissident Wei Jingsheng. Reasons for the arrests were not clear, since Wei's trial was said to have officially not been made public.

Then, on December 6, Chinese authorities ordered the shutdown of Beijing Democracy Wall, the traditional site in the center of the city for affixing wall posters. The decision to close China's only established public forum for free expression followed government charges that a recent upsurge in using the wall for protesting messages was endangering the country's freedom and democracy.

Starting December 8, the government permitted the use of another wall in a remote park in Beijing. Its use, however, was restricted to six hours daily, except Mondays and afternoons on Tuesdays and Thursdays. The poster's author would be required to register his name, address and work unit.

One official, critical of the use of the Democracy Wall, said it had "become an important site for a small number of foreigners with ulterior motives who seek intelligence that jeopardizes the fundamental interests of the Chinese people."

2

OPENING TO THE WEST

DENG VISITS THE UNITED STATES

The new policy which the Chinese government adopted during the 3d plenum of the 11th Central Committee, in December 1978, called for increasing cultural and economic ties with the outside world. It was called the open-door policy—*kaifeng rhenze*. Its objective was not only to acquire scientific knowledge and technology essential to China's modernization, but also to stimulate China's stagnant economy by linking it to world economy.

In line with this new policy, Beijing stepped up its diplomatic activities with the West, particularly with the United States, with which it had normalized diplomatic relations on January 1, 1979. Deng Xiaoping dramatized the new phase of Sino-American relations by making a well-publicized visit to Washington.

Deng arrived in Washington on January 28, to start the first official call to the U.S. by a top Chinese communist leader. Deng's nine-day visit was aimed at solidifying diplomatic relations between the United States and China.

Deng held a series of talks with President Carter at the White House on January 29–30 and on January 31, both men signed agreements on cultural and scientific exchanges. The accords included:

• The establishment of U.S. consulates in Shanghai and Canton, and Chinese consulates in Houston and San Francisco, and provisions for reuniting families and protecting citizens if arrested.
• An overall science and technology pact, and a separate energy agreement providing for U.S. assistance in constructing a nuclear-particle accelerator in China.
• A space technology accord, enabling China to purchase services of the National Aeronautics and Space Administration (NASA) for launching a civilian communications satellite.
• A cultural agreement aimed at increasing contacts and exchanges in a wide variety of fields.
• A science agreement providing for the exchange of students.

In addition to these formal accords, Beijing also agreed, in principle, to permit American news organizations to set up bureaus in China.

Carter called the agreements "a new and irreversible course" in Chinese-American relations. While both nations "have agreed to consult regularly on matters of common global interest," Carter conceded that "the security concerns of the United States do not coincide completely, of course, with those of China, nor does China share our responsibilities."

Deng praised the agreements as "significant," but noted that "this is not the end but just a beginning." He added, "There are many more areas of bilateral cooperation and more channels waiting for us to develop."

Deng stressed what he called the Soviet menace to world peace in a speech on January 29, at a full-dress welcoming ceremony on the White House lawn before his first session with Carter. Without mentioning the Soviets by name, Deng warned Carter that the threat of war was increasing and that "our two countries are duty bound to work together" to maintain peace.

Before leaving for the U.S., Deng had depicted the Soviet Union in a *Time* magazine (Feb. 5 issue) interview as "a hot bed of war" and warned that Moscow's military strength "may surpass that of the United States in the near future." As a result, he advised the U.S. not to sign any agreement limiting weapons development.

The U.S. and China issued a joint press communique on February 1, on the Carter-Deng talks, which indirectly criticized the Soviet

Union. The criticism, however, was softened at Washington's insistence.

The Chinese had demanded the incorporation into the text of the word "hegemony," Beijing's term for Soviet expansionism. The U.S. had insisted on adding the word "domination," which would appear to cover aggression in general. As a result, the communique read that the U.S. and China "reaffirm they are opposed to efforts by any country or group of countries to establish hegemony or domination over others."

The document also took note of the accords signed by Carter and Deng.

The press communique had been issued at the request of the Chinese, who argued that it would be less formal or binding than an official joint statement.

Meeting with 85 U.S. senators on Capitol Hill on January 30, Deng spoke of possible Chinese military action against Taiwan and Vietnam.

China, he said, hoped to unite Taiwan with the mainland by peaceful means and would "fully respect the realities" of the island. But the deputy premier said he could not categorically rule out the use of force to regain Taiwan because it would restrict his government's options in proposed reunification talks with the Chinese Nationalists.

Deng also left open the possibility of China's use of force against Vietnam to settle a dispute stemming from Vietnam's invasion of Cambodia and Chinese-Vietnamese border tensions. One senator quoted him as having said that to safeguard China's borders, "we need to act appropriately; we cannot allow Vietnam to run wild everywhere." Vietnam, Deng said, was seeking "regional hegemony."

Outside the official world of presidential meetings and communiques, Deng's visit to Washington was considered by most observers to have been a diplomatic tour de force.

Moving affably through a series of meetings, luncheons and private discussions, Deng displayed a charm, wit and candor that gained immediate rapport with his American audiences.

Deng ended his nine-day trip to the U.S. with visits to Atlanta, Houston and Seattle on February 1–5. Deng's tour of these three industrial centers dramatized China's quest for U.S. technological aid in its drive toward modernization.

Deng stopped off in Tokyo on February 6–7 to confer with Japanese officials before returning to Beijing on February 8.

In a meeting with former Premier Takeo Fukuda on February 7,

Deng criticized the U.S. for lack of firmness in Iran and said that Washington's measures "in dealing with Cuba are no good."

Deng was quoted as having told Fukuda: "If chaos continues in Iran it will produce a chain reaction in Saudi Arabia. There is a sign that the chain reaction has reached India. India seems ready to recognize the fake regime in Cambodia, if asked to do so."

Deng also told Premier Masayoshi Ohira that Vietnam must be "punished" for its invasion of Cambodia and that Beijing would have to impose "sanctions."

Ohira later told parliament that he did not think Deng meant that China intended to use force against Vietnam.

THE TAIWAN ISSUE

As intimated by Deng during his Washington trip, the normalization of relations between China and the United States was overshadowed by two regional issues.

One was the Indochinese war. Following the invasion of Cambodia by Vietnam in December 1978, China amassed its troops along the Vietnamese border and, on February 17, 1979—shortly after Deng's return from his trip to the U.S.—launched an attack on Vietnam. Two hundred thousand to 300,000 Chinese troops participated in the invasion. The Chinese action drew condemnation from Moscow and Washington. The Vietnamese offered stiff resistance and Beijing decided to pull its troops out. By March 15 the Chinese withdrawal was completed less than a month after the military action had commenced.

The other issue was not resolved so quickly. It was the Taiwan problem. When establishing normal diplomatic relations with Beijing, the United States made it clear that it would continue to maintain its economic and cultural relations with "the people of Taiwan." This formula, which permitted Washington to deal with both Communist and Nationalist China, was not entirely satisfactory to either of these parties.

Recognition of the Chinese government meant rescinding recognition of the Nationalist regime on Taiwan. On the day this occurred (January 1, 1979) President Chiang Ching-kuo of Nationalist China called for his country's reconquest of China. "The responsibility of carrying out the historic task of recovering the mainland and delivering from Communist slavery and tyranny compatriots whose blood is the same as ours rests squarely on the shoulders of each of our 17 million people," Chiang said.

He rejected Beijing's offer on December 31, 1978 of a resumption of trade and other links with Taiwan. A government spokesman said that "under no circumstances will we enter into any kind of talks with the Chinese Communists."

In another peace overture to Taiwan, on January 4, China offered to permit Nationalist Chinese airliners to land at Beijing and Shanghai. A Taiwan official rejected the bid, saying "it is this government's policy not to negotiate, compromise, trade, or whatever with Communist China—not to mention flying our planes to the mainland."

Yet in another overture, on January 9, Deputy Premier Deng Xiaoping offered to allow Taiwan to retain its own government and armed forces in exchange for ceding sovereignty after it was unified with the Chinese mainland.

Deng broached the issue during a discussion in Beijing with four visiting U.S. senators.

A statement issued by the American delegation on its conversation with Deng said: "It was indicated that Taiwan would retain full autonomy with China for as long as the people of Taiwan would so desire, and in the future Taiwan authorities would possess the same powers they now enjoy."

As for the Chinese Nationalists' armed forces, "there would be no requirement that Taiwan disarm in order to achieve reunification," the statement continued.

The senators also said that Deng had "indicated that China would not use force to change the system and way of life on Taiwan," except under two circumstances: in the event of "an indefinite refusal by Taiwan to enter into negotiations" with Beijing on its future relations with China, and in case of "an attempt by the Soviet Union to interfere in Taiwanese affairs."

On January 11, Chinese Nationalist Premier Sun Yen-suan rejected Deng's proposals for reunification, asserting that his suggestion for negotiations was "merely another form of class struggle."

Speaking on nationwide television, Sun said Beijing was seeking "to induce us to surrender. Peace talks is one of the Chinese stages and also one of their ultimate approaches for communizing of all China." He said Deng's proposals were "lies and tricks" designed "to confuse the American people, to deceive the American Congress and American press and to weaken their support" for Taiwan.

With Taiwan unalterably opposed to reunification with the mainland on Beijing's terms, Beijing showed a keen interest in curbing the flow of U.S. arms to the Nationalist regime on the island.

In his announcement on December 15, 1978 that the U.S. and China would establish formal ties, President Carter had not specifically made public the fact that China had insisted on the ban as a condition to normalizing relations.

However, State Department spokesman Harvey Feldman, director of Taiwan affairs, told a news conference that during their secret negotiations on relations, China had insisted that the U.S. end its mutual defense treaty with Taiwan as soon as Washington established ties with Beijing. Refusing this demand, the U.S. said that it would adhere to the Taiwan pact's stipulation of giving a year's notice before terminating the accord.

The Chinese had "made clear that they had not agreed to our continuing to sell arms [to Taiwan] after normalization," Feldman said. Beijing, he pointed out, was "particularly concerned that we'd sell arms after the announcement of normalization and prior to termination of the treaty" with Taiwan.

The Chinese, Feldman continued, accepted the American proposal to sever the defense treaty with Taiwan on January 1, 1980 with "the understanding that the United States would not conclude" new agreements in 1979 for the sale of offensive weapons to the Chinese Nationalists.

The U.S., the State Department official noted, would continue to provide Taiwan with the $600–650 million worth of military equipment already bought or promised to Taiwan. These deliveries would continue in 1979 and the following years. The U.S. would sell defensive weapons to Taiwan starting in 1980. The afore-mentioned U.S. arms policy had been outlined by Secretary of State Cyrus Vance on December 17, 1978.

On January 15, administration officials assured U.S. businessmen that relations with China would not prevent the expansion of U.S. trade with Taiwan. At a State Department meeting, Cabinet officials asserted that increasing trade with China would not result in an end to trade with Taiwan.

Total U.S. trade with Taiwan was estimated at $7.3 billion during 1978. U.S.-Chinese trade for 1978 was estimated at $1.4 billion.

The businessmen who attended the State Department meeting belonged to either the National Council of United States-China Trade or to the U.S.A-ROC Economic Council. (ROC stood for Republic of China, Taiwan's official name.)

The main speakers were Treasury Secretary Michael Blumenthal and Commerce Secretary Juanita Kreps, but the businessmen also heard from Secretary of State Cyrus Vance and national security adviser Zbigniew Brzezinski.

The Cabinet officials said other countries that had broken with Taiwan in favor of Beijing had nevertheless increased their trade with Taiwan. Japan's trade with Taiwan more than doubled after Tokyo established ties with Beijing; Australia's trade with Taiwan more than tripled after Australia recognized China, and Canada's trade with Taiwan increased more than five times after Ottawa extended recognition to China, they said.

At a news conference in Washington on January 26, President Carter cautioned Congress that he would not approve any legislation it might send him "that would be contradictory or that would violate the agreements we have concluded with the People's Republic of China."

"I, myself, am committed to a strong and a prosperous and a free people on Taiwan," Carter said. "We intend to carry on our diplomatic relations with the People's Republic of China as the government of China, but we will have trade relationships, cultural relationships with the people on Taiwan."

The President said he thought the statements of Chinese leaders concerning the Taiwan issue had been "very constructive and have indicated a peaceful intent."

Carter referred to his legislative proposals on the issue, sent to Congress that day, as "a good foundation" for the proper U.S. relationship with Taiwan.

The proposals called for establishment of a private institute to handle relations with Taiwan on a nongovernmental basis.

Diplomats assigned to the institute would be separated from the U.S. Foreign Service, with reinstatement available as soon as they left the institute.

Carter's threat of a veto was made in the face of some powerful dissent regarding the administration's intended course.

Senator Frank Church (D, Idaho), chairman of the Senate Foreign Relations Committee, described the administration's Taiwan legislation on January 26, as "deficient."

The "most glaring" deficiency, he said, was the lack of "a statement of official U.S. policy concerning the future security of Taiwan."

It was "crucial," Church said, for the U.S. to "adopt a firm statement of policy, having the force of law, that U.S. recognition of China rests on the assumption that any resolution of the Taiwan question will be sought only by peaceful means."

Several resolutions to that effect had already been introduced in Congress. One of them, sponsored by Senators Edward M. Kennedy (D, Mass.) and Alan Cranston (D, Calif.), stated that the U.S. would consider an armed attack on Taiwan "a danger to the stability and peace of Asia."

The Carter administration addressed these congressional concerns for Taiwan's security and was able to secure cooperation from the

Nationalist regime in making changes consonant with the new U.S.-China policy.

On February 15, President Chiang Ching-kuo of Taiwan said that his government had agreed to create a new organization to continue ties between his country and the United States.

The organization, the Coordination Council for North American Affairs, would be the counterpart of the American Institute in Taiwan established by the U.S. The council would have an office in Washington and eight branches in other parts of the country.

President Chiang said his government had tried to lessen the damage caused by the U.S. recognition of the Beijing regime, but that Taiwan had agreed to the arrangement because "the long-lasting and inseparable close relations between the peoples of the two countries must be maintained continuously."

"Reality requires that we have to swallow the bitter pill and handle the current changed situation with all the fortitude at our command," he added.

The private institutes would handle trade, cultural and consular matters previously administered by the embassies of the two countries.

The Nationalist Chinese would continue to maintain, however, that they considered their relations with the U.S. to have the "quality of officiality," sources said.

Meanwhile, Congress deliberated on a new legislation, the U.S.-Taiwan relations bill, which would provide a legal basis for the quasi-official relationship Washington was to establish with the Chinese Nationalists.

The legislation stated that the U.S. agreed to conduct its relations with Taiwan through a private corporation, the American Institute in Taiwan. The Nationalist Chinese continued their relations with the U.S. through an unofficial Coordinating Council in North America.

The U.S.-Taiwan relations bill also stated that all trade, cultural and transportation links between the two countries would continue.

The bill also said the U.S. would take unspecified actions in the event of an attack on Taiwan, stronger language than President Carter had wanted. The bill further pledged continued arms sales to the Nationalists.

Even before the bill was voted on, Beijing lodged a protest on March 16. The protest was delivered to U.S. Ambassador Leonard Woodcock by Foreign Minister Huang Hua, Carter administration officials disclosed on March 25. Huang called the legislation setting up new arrangements between Washington and Taipei "unacceptable to the Chinese government."

The Chinese news agency Xinhua was especially critical of a clause in the U.S. legislation recognizing the existence of a separate government on Taiwan and barring Beijing from taking over property of Taiwan's former embassy in Washington.

The House passed the final version of the measure on March 28 by a 339–50 vote, and the Senate approved it on March 29 by an 85–4 vote.

The final compromise version of the bill tied the U.S. somewhat closer to Taiwan than the Carter administration had intended.

Nevertheless, President Carter signed the bill on April 6. The new legislation became known as the Taiwan Relations Act.

Deputy Premier Deng Xiaoping complained about the new American law at a Beijing meeting on April 16 with a delegation of U.S. senators, all members of the Foreign Relations Committee.

Deng said that the measure had come close to nullifying the normalization of relations reached by the U.S. and China in December 1978.

The leader of the delegation, Senator Frank Church (D, Idaho), later said in an interview that Deng "was very strong in saying this [legislation] is a violation" of the agreement establishing American-Chinese relations. Deng also indicated that any U.S. guarantee of Taiwan's military security could have "very serious" implications for Sino-American ties, Church said.

EXPANDING TRADE RELATIONS WITH THE UNITED STATES

The normalization of diplomatic relations paved the way for expanding U.S.-Chinese trade relations. On March 1, the date set for upgrading the liaison offices in Beijing and Washington to full embassy status, U.S. Treasury Secretary Michael Blumenthal was in Beijing concluding a draft agreement on property claims.

Resolution of the assets issue was seen as an essential step in the establishment of normal economic ties between the two countries. Blumenthal described the accord as "good and fair." U.S. officials argued that the settlement was desirable because it would prevent the issue from being the subject of protracted litigation.

Under this agreement, China would pay the U.S. about 41¢ on the dollar in settlement of $196.6 million in claims for U.S. property seized when the Communists gained control in 1949.

The accord called for China to pay U.S. claimants a total of about $80.5 million: the first $30 million on October 1 and the remainder in five yearly installments of $10 million each.

In paying the claims, China would use the $80 million it had in assets that had been frozen by the U.S. If, as was likely, China would not be able to recover all of those claims, it would have to use additional cash to settle the U.S. claims, the *Wall Street Journal* reported on March 2.

Blumenthal announced the agreement on his last day in Beijing before leaving for Shanghai. He had arrived in China on February 24. His talks with Chinese officials dealt chiefly with economic issues, although he did convey U.S. concern over China's invasion of Vietnam.

The agreement on assets would have to be approved by Congress. In addition to the agreement, China and the U.S. set up a joint economic committee to monitor commercial and financial relations between the two countries. The U.S. also invited the Bank of China to open an office in the U.S., a proposal to which the Chinese responded positively.

The two nations agreed to "proceed rapidly," Blumenthal said, on negotiations to reach a bilateral trade agreement. They agreed that the accord should include reciprocal tariff concessions, provision for physical facilities for businessmen in China, patent and copyright protections and rules for deciding trade disputes.

In a separate development, U.S. officials in Washington said on February 23 that American and Chinese cargo ships would start sailing between Seattle and Shanghai. It would be the first time since the Communists took power that the two countries would open ports to each other's ships.

The agreement was negotiated privately between the Lykes Brothers Steamship Company and the China Ocean Shipping Company. The governments of the two countries favored the step.

The agreement on assets was formally signed in Beijing on May 11 by U.S. Commerce Secretary Juanita Kreps and Chinese negotiators.

Secretary Kreps was in Beijing to conclude a commercial treaty and discuss related matters. She began her talks with Chinese officials on May 7, and an agreement establishing commercial relations between China and the United States for the first time since 1949 was initialed by Chinese Foreign Trade Minister Li Jiang and Secretary Kreps on May 14.

The pact would lower tariff restrictions on most Chinese exports to the U.S. by granting Beijing most-favored-nation trading status. An agreement on the amount of Chinese textile exports to the U.S., however, remained to be worked out. Vice-Foreign Trade Minister Chen Jie complained that the quotas demanded by the U.S. remained too low.

In 1978, the U.S. exported $824 million worth of goods to China and imported $324 million in Chinese goods.

While in China, Secretary Kreps announced, on May 13, that the United States and China had agreed, on May 8, on exchanges in scientific, technological and business affairs. Specifically:

- Both countries would cooperate in such scientific and technological areas as precision measurements and standards, building technology, analytical chemistry, materials research and applied mathematics.
- China and the U.S. would exchange scientific and technological reports, establish joint conferences and exchange experts in the scientific and technical managements field.
- Both countries' oceanographers and fishery scientists would trade information under a marine agreement.
- An agreement would provide for exchanges of trade exhibitions by American and Chinese businessmen.
- A meteorological accord would establish cooperation in atmospheric science and technology.

The new commercial agreement required approval by the U.S. Congress. Congressional approval was believed to be dependent upon the outcome of another set of negotiations, then in progress in Beijing, for the conclusion of a textile agreement under what was known as the Multi-Fiber Agreement, an arrangement signed in Geneva to limit the growth of textile imports from 18 developing nations.

After one month of negotiations, the Beijing talks between Chinese and American negotiators ended on May 25 in a stalemate. U.S. Special Trade Representative Robert S. Strauss arrived in Beijing on May 26. He met on May 30 with Deputy Premier Deng Xiaoping and held further discussions with other Chinese officials on May 31 in an effort to break the deadlock.

With these talks failing to break the impasse, the U.S. set quotas on Chinese cotton work gloves, cotton blouses, cotton shirts, cotton trousers and synthetic fiber sweaters. The imports were to be limited over the next 12 months to levels existing in the 12 months ended Feb. 28.

On May 31, Strauss said that the issue discussed was "part of a common problem we both seek to solve." He referred to China's need to earn foreign currency for import of foreign technology from the U.S. and other industrialized nations. Beijing sought to use revenues from its textile exports as a major source of foreign currency.

Despite failure to reach a textile pact, it was announced on May 25 that both sides achieved an agreement on resumption of direct mail service between the U.S. and China, broken off in 1949. Its implementation, however, would have to wait until the two parties concluded negotiations of an aviation agreement. Currently, mail between the U.S. and China was routed through Hong Kong and Japan.

The momentum of Sino-American rapprochement was maintained, in spite of the failure to conclude a textile agreement. On July 7, the U.S. and China formally signed the commercial agreement that had been initialed in May.

The agreement was signed in Beijing, with Foreign Trade Minister Li Jiang representing China and Ambassador Leonard Woodcock signing for the U.S.

The new tariffs set by the pact would lower the average impost on Chinese goods to 5.7% of their value from the current average of about 34%. Other provisions allowed U.S. companies to set up business offices in China and afforded patent, trademark and copyright protection.

The Commerce Department estimated that the agreement, if approved by Congress, could lead to a doubling in 1979 of the $1.1 billion in two-way trade registered in 1978. Annual two-way trade could reach $5 billion in five years, the department predicted.

The U.S. exported substantially more to China than it imported. The most significant U.S. exports were wheat, cotton and corn, although China had also bought some manufactured goods, such as oil drilling equipment. China, in return, exported textiles, tin, feathers, firecrackers and some other items.

The following day, July 8, the Chinese government announced a code covering foreign companies that invested in joint venture enterprises in China.

The law left some matters vague or unstated—including the level of corporate and individual tax rates—but it also provided certain guarantees and incentives designed to attract foreign investors. In particular, the code promised that foreign companies and their employees would be permitted to remit abroad after-tax earnings in foreign currencies. It also said that companies that brought "up-to-date technology by world standards" to China would get a full or partial exemption from taxes for the first two or three years they made a profit.

Although the code did not specify the maximum share of an enterprise that could be held by foreign investors, Chinese officials had indicated that in most cases foreign ownership would be limited to 49%, it was reported on July 9. However, 100% ownership would be permitted in some cases, and the law stipulated that the foreign share had to be at least 25%.

The code said that the chairman of each joint-venture company would be appointed by the Chinese, but that other high-level executives could be appointed by the foreign partner. Hiring and firing procedures would be "stipulated according to law in the agreement or contract concluded between the parties to the venture," the code said.

Other provisions of the joint-venture law were:

- Foreign partners who reinvested earnings in China would qualify for rebates of taxes already paid.
- The joint ventures could sell their products in China or abroad, using Chinese export corporations or their own facilities.
- Arbitration would be used to settle disputes.
- The ventures would be permitted to borrow funds directly from foreign banks.

The Xinhua news agency said that two new offices were being created to deal with joint-venture proposals. One, the Foreign Investment Control Commission, would decide whether to approve specific proposals; the other, the China International Trust Investment Co., would "coordinate the use of foreign investment and technology."

THE U.S. GRANTS CHINA MOST-FAVORED-NATION STATUS

The pace of Sino-American rapprochement was further quickened by U.S. Vice-President Walter Mondale's week-long visit to Beijing in August. Mondale arrived in Beijing on August 25 and held talks on the 27th and 28th with China's two top leaders: Deputy Premier Deng Xiaoping and Communist Party Chairman Hua Guofeng.

After their meetings on August 28, the three officials signed an expanded cultural exchange pact and a protocol under which the U.S. would help China develop hydroelectric power. Under the latter agreement, experts of the U.S. Army Corps of Engineers, the Tennessee Valley Authority, the Department of Energy and the Bureau of Reclamation would help China plan, design and supervise construction of 20 projected power-generating dams.

The cultural accord put into effect a generalized agreement signed by Deng and President Carter in Washington on January 31. This included the exchange of visits of English- and Chinese-language experts, staffs of Voice of America and Radio Beijing and books and documents of the Beijing Library and the Library of Congress.

In reporting on his two days of talks, Mondale told a news conference on August 28 that his meetings with Deng and Hua were "extremely productive and friendly" and helped move the normalization of relations between China and the U.S. into "concrete reality." The friendship between the two countries "is not directed against anyone" and the U.S. did not "anticipate a military relationship" with China, Mondale said.

In a televised speech from Beijing University on August 27, Mondale declared that a "strong and modernizing" China was in the interest of the U.S. "Despite the sometimes profound differences between our two systems, we are committed to joining you to advance our many parallel and bilateral interests," the vice-president said. He cautioned that "any nation which seeks to weaken or isolate you in world affairs assumes a stance counter to American interests," an apparent reference to the Soviet Union.

Mondale also disclosed that the U.S. was prepared to lend China $2 billion over a five-year period through Export-Import Bank credits. "If the pace of development warrants it, we are prepared to consider additional credit agreements," Mondale said.

At a later briefing with Western reporters, U.S. officials said that Mondale's promise of quick congressional action on the American-Chinese trade agreement signed in May and his warnings against isolation of China did not mean any "tilting" of U.S. policy toward China. "It remains the policy of the United States to seek improved relations with both China and the Soviet Union," the officials said.

But there were complicated political problems, domestic and foreign, that prevented speedy normalization of trade relations between China and the U.S. It was not until October 23 that President Jimmy Carter announced his decision to grant China most-favored-nation tariff status. When announcing the decision, Carter did not mention possible repercussions involving the Soviet Union, but officials told the *Washington Post* that the administration hoped that a parallel action to provide trade advantages for Moscow eventually could be taken.

Nevertheless, observers saw the Carter decision as a departure from the stated U.S. policy of "evenhanded" treatment of the two communist giants.

Congress was involved in the most-favored-nation decision because of the 1974 Jackson-Vanik Amendment. That amendment prohibited normal trade relations with a communist nation unless the President stipulated, and Congress agreed, that the country allow free emigration.

Because of the Jackson-Vanik Amendment, the U.S. had never fulfilled a 1973 promise to normalize trade relations with the Soviets by granting them most-favored-nation status and access to credit from the U.S. Import-Export Bank.

The Chinese had told U.S. officials that they allowed free emigration, a statement partially corroborated by U.S. officials in Hong Kong.

The U.S.S.R., while allowing more Jews to emigrate, had refused to provide written assurances of free emigration, claiming it was an internal matter.

Meanwhile, the textile question continued to poison U.S.-China trade relations. It was reported on September 27 that the U.S. had embargoed all shipments of men's and boys' cotton shirts from China because the May quota had been reached. The quota for sweaters woven from man-made fibers was also close to being reached, according to U.S. officials. The U.S. hoped that China would soon be willing to resume negotiations on a bilateral accord.

Then, on October 30, a week after Carter's announcement on most-favored-nation status for China, the U.S. imposed yet another set of quotas on textile imports from China. The new quotas, which were to go into effect on October 31 for a 12-month period, applied to woven cotton blouses for women, girls and infants and coats from man-made fibers for women, girls and infants. The Carter administration's decision to impose the quotas was reported to have been motivated by a desire to forestall any resentment in the U.S. Congress against the influx of Chinese apparel, and thus ease congressional approval of the recently proposed China trade agreement.

TRADE RELATIONS WITH EUROPE AND JAPAN

In 1979, China expanded its trade relations with Europe and Japan as well. To highlight major developments: Great Britain and China signed a £7-billion ($14-billion) economic cooperation agreement in Beijing on March 4.

The British committed themselves in this five-year agreement to supplying the Chinese with support credit of £2.5 billion ($5 billion). The line of credit would be handled through a special British governmental agency, the Export Credit Guarantee Department.

British Steel Corp., which had sold 350,000 tons of steel to China in the previous 12 months, agreed to a joint project of modernization of China's Shoudu steelworks.

Britain and China had also been negotiating contracts in such areas as coal mining, power station construction and aircraft sales, although no agreements in these areas were made final.

The signing of the agreement came at the end of a nine-day visit to China by Britain's industry secretary, Eric Varley, and a delegation of 10 British industrialists.

An agreement was signed on May 9 in Paris, permitting China to borrow $7 billion from a group of 18 French banks through 1985. It was believed to be the largest loan ever negotiated by China. The accord came within the framework of a trade agreement signed by France and China in December 1978.

The money to be obtained from the French banks would be used to finance Beijing's purchases of French industrial goods and services, possibly including two nuclear power stations. The credit line included inexpensive French government funds provided by the government-controlled Francaise Banque du Commerce Exterieur, with interest rates varying between 7.25% and 7.50%.

The bank's head, Francoise Giscard d'Estaing, said China was unlikely to make much immediate use of the new credit facility. He said this was because "it takes time" to build the needed accompanying facilities for major projects, such as an aluminum factory.

The French loans were part of China's current drive to arrange foreign borrowing. In recent months it had obtained several billion dollars in credit in Europe and Japan.

A little over a month later, China agreed on June 12, to revive a $1-billion contract with Nippon Steel Corp. of Japan for the construction of a steel complex near Shanghai. The contract, along with 21 others negotiated with Japanese companies in December 1978, had been suspended since February because of China's shortage of foreign currency.

The other Japanese firms with which China had renewed contracts included Hitachi Ltd., an electric and electronic products manufacturer, and Kanebo Ltd., a fibers producer. Several other Japanese companies had earlier received notices from China to renew their frozen contracts.

Under the new Nippon accord, China would pay for the plant equipment over a five-year period at an annual interest rate of 7.25%, rather than cash on delivery, as originally agreed, in December 1978.

Bonn joined the pack. West German officials announced that West Germany and China had signed an agreement on June 19 covering technical assistance and industrial raw materials, it was reported July 10.

Under the agreement, West Germany would assist China in developing its mineral resources and Chinese scientists would get training in West Germany.

West Germany, it was planned, would export industrial equipment and technology to China and receive raw materials in return. The West German Economics Ministry said that China was seen as serving as one of West Germany's major raw materials suppliers in the future. Among the materials China could export were manganese, coal, vanadium, tungsten and oil.

The accord was signed in Beijing, with Vice-Premier Fang Yi representing China, and Friedrich Bender, president of the Federal Bureau for Geological Science and Raw Materials, signing for West Germany.

This was soon followed by the conclusion of an agreement on July 18 in Beijing between China and the European Community granting China most-favored-nation trade status and setting limits on its textile exports to EC nations.

The pact cut EC tariffs on Chinese exports to an average value of 6.7%.

Fourteen categories of textile products were given export limits by the accord, and an overall limit of 40,000 metric tons was set for those categories. France did not initial the accord because it opposed the terms governing the amount of cotton cloth China would be allowed to export; France had pressed for a limit of 18,000 tons, but the pact appeared to open the way for an additional 2,000 metric tons of cloth exports.

Roy Denman of Britain, the head of the EC delegation to China, said that "the agreement takes very carefully into account the extreme difficulties experienced at this time by textile industries" of the EC countries.

HUA GUOFENG VISITS EUROPE

Against the backdrop of increasing economic relations with Europe, Hua Guofeng, premier and chairman of the Communist Party, went on a historic three-week, four-country tour of Europe in the fall of 1979 the first such trip made by a head of China.

Hua arrived in Paris on October 15 to a lavish welcome by French President Valery Giscard d'Estaing and Premier Raymond Barre. At his arrival, Hua noted the close ties between the key aims of Europe and Asia, and Europe's "pivotal role in international affairs." Hua said he was hoping to use the trip to attain a "better understanding of the realities of your advanced countries so as to inspire me in the modernization program I have in mind."

Hua's visit was the source of some concern to the Soviet Union. Moscow Radio said in a broadcast that the Chinese premier's trip caused "a perfectly understandable feeling of disquiet in Western public opinion because of Beijing's openly hostile attitude toward

questions of detente, disarmament and the maintenance of peace,"
it was reported on October 16.

The Chinese, on the other hand, warned the West against acqui-
escence to Soviet "agression." At a news conference on October 18,
Chinese Foreign Minister Huang Hua, who was accompanying Hua,
said that Vietnam's actions in Indochina were a "very key element
of the Soviet Union's global strategy," adding that if the "international community bows before a Vietnamese fait accompli in Cambodia, it would be an extremely dangerous precedent, not just for
peace in Indochina, but for peace throughout the world."

Hua held talks with Giscard on October 17, in which Cambodia
was discussed at length. That same day, the two leaders also signed
agreements providing for economic, cultural and technological cooperation up to the year 2000.

French officials said that Hua had started his European tour with
Paris because France was the first Western nation to open diplomatic
relations with China after the Communists gained power.

Hua's next stop was Bonn, West Germany. Hua arrived on October 21 and met with Chancellor Helmut Schmidt the following day
for private talks.

The West Germans, while welcoming the Chinese premier's visit,
were reportedly concerned about the possibility of China's antago-
nism towards the Soviet Union's intruding upon West Germany's
policy of detente with the Soviet bloc. Hua contributed to his West
German hosts' unease with remarks at a dinner on October 22. Hua
said, "Our two countries, though geographically far apart and with
different societies, do have a common task, namely to keep world
peace and to fight aggression and war. We are convinced that it is
absolutely possible to delay the outbreak of war and gain a longer
peace when all peace-loving countries and people join together with
effective means to demand a stop to aggression and hegemonism."

Schmidt spoke in less confrontational tones. He said at the dinner,
"We Germans, we Europeans together, are attempting to learn from
the experience of two world wars, which brought immeasurable suffering to our people. Therefore, the foreign policy of my country is
primarily, and before all other things, a policy of peace."

Hua also voiced Chinese support for the reunification of Germany. "It is abnormal," Hua said, "that Germany has been artificially divided into two parts. The Chinese people understand fully
how the German people feel in wishing to see their nation reunited
and we support those legitimate aspirations of the German people."

The East German official news agency responded on October 22
by criticizing Hua for supporting "the revanchist designs of German

imperialism against the German Democratic Republic [East Germany]."

On October 23, Hua paid a visit to the house in Trier that was the birthplace of Karl Marx, the founder of modern communism. This pilgrimage was combined with trips to major industrial plants around West Germany.

On October 24, officials for China and West Germany signed agreements designed to promote economic and cultural cooperation. Hua noted that the "strengthening of cooperation is not only in the interests of our two countries but also in the interest of world peace."

Leaving Germany on October 28, Hua flew to London, where he was warmly greeted by Prime Minister Margaret Thatcher. The British government was somewhat less concerned about possibly offending the Soviet Union than had been the French and the Germans, and Hua took advantage of this to reiterate China's worries about the Soviets. At a dinner in his honor at 10 Downing Street, the prime minister's official residence, Hua praised Thatcher for recognizing the Soviet threat.

"Just as Winston Churchill exposed the ambitions of the Nazis," Hua said, "Prime Minister Thatcher has unequivocally identified the source of the war danger and called for effective countermeasures." While Hua did not mention the Soviets by name, no one doubted that he was referring to them.

During his stay of about a week, Hua met with business leaders and saw some of the traditional tourist sights.

On November 1, Thatcher told Hua that Britain was prepared to sell China its Harrier jump-jet fighter plane and other defense equipment. The sales would be subject to Britain's consultation with its allies, and the question of what form payment would take remained to be resolved. China was reportedly interested in purchasing about 70–90 of the jet planes.

Also on that same day, Hua and Thatcher approved accords to expand cultural ties between their two countries and to institute regular air service. Thatcher asked Hua to try to curb the flow of Chinese illegally emigrating to Hong Kong, a British crown colony. Hua said he would try to deal with the situation, but he did not specify what he would do.

On a visit on October 31 to Highgate Cemetery to lay a wreath at Marx's grave, Hua was met unofficially by a contingent of British workers who complained about his frequent praise for Thatcher. One of the workers in the group, which was made up of members of the Public Employees' Union, commented: "We thought that since he has been talking to Mrs. Thatcher and boosting her image, it was about time he met a few genuine workers. Karl Marx would turn in his grave if he saw how Chairman Hua is talking to a woman who is keeping workers' wages down."

Hua left London on November 3 for Italy, the last stop on his European trip. He was greeted by Premier Francesco Cossiga on his arrival at the Rome airport, and then journeyed to Venice, where he visited the house of Marco Polo, the 13th-century traveler who opened communication between Venice and China.

During a meeting with President Sandro Pertini of Italy on November 5, Hua indicated his backing for the reported willingness of North Atlantic Treaty Organization nations to permit new nuclear missiles to be based on their soil before renewing arms limitation talks with the Soviet Union.

Hua left Italy to return to China on November 6. Before departing, he concluded three agreements designed to strengthen ties between the two countries. The accords provided for closer scientific, technical and cultural cooperation, more economic collaboration and the opening of consulates in Milan and Shanghai.

Hua met informally with Enrico Berlinguer, the leader of the Italian Communist Party, at a reception at the Chinese embassy and at a dinner given for Hua by Pertini. The meetings prompted press reports that the long-standing gulf between the Communist parties of China and Italy had been bridged. In France, which also had a strong communist party—but one that was more aligned with the Soviet Union than was the Italian party—Hua did not meet with Georges Marchais, the leader of the French Communist Party.

At the Rome airport, before leaving for home, Hua declared that his European trip had been "crowned with success." He thanked the leaders of the four nations he had visited—France, West Germany, Britain and Italy—for establishing "personal ties of friendship" with him.

"China," he said, "wants Europe to be strong and united. We have always maintained that a Western Europe that is jealous of its independence and security and highly advanced in science and technology is an important factor for peace and stability in the world."

3

RIDING AN ANTI-SOVIET WAVE

THE SOVIETS WEARY OF SINO-AMERICAN RAPPROCHEMENT

The Soviet Union entertained serious misgivings about the evolving Sino-American relationship. The Chinese were openly critical of the Russians and tried to enlist American support in resisting Russian expansionism—"hegemonism." For the United States, China, the most populous nation, situated next to the Soviet Union, held out the alluring prospect of holding down the bulk of Soviet forces along the Sino-Soviet border.

But the Carter administration had yet to develop an internal consensus on its policy toward China in the context of its global strategy. At a meeting with businessmen at the State Department on January 15, 1979, national security adviser Zbigniew Brzezinski and Secretary of State Cyrus Vance offered different interpretations of the effect of U.S. ties with China on U.S.-U.S.S.R. relations.

Vance assured his audience that the U.S. will "insure continuity of trade, cultural and other unofficial relations" with Taiwan. He said Washington-Beijing relations would promote "a stable system of independent nations in Asia," and "a stable equilibrium among the United States, Japan, China and the Soviet Union."

Vance declared that the U.S. "acted in a way that does not threaten any other nation," referring to the U.S.S.R. He said both China and the Soviet Union have "an important role to play in the search for global peace and stability."

"For this reason," Vance concluded, "we also look forward to the early conclusion of the SALT [Strategic Arms Limitation Talks] agreement with the Soviet Union and to improvement of our trade relations with the Soviets as well as the Chinese."

Brzezinski, who followed Vance, echoed the secretary of state's emphasis on multi-lateral cooperation with China and the Soviet Union. However, he expressed less certainty that Moscow would accept the U.S.' goal of multilateralism.

Brzezinski said that "a fundamental choice the Soviet Union faces is whether to become a responsible partner in the creation of a global system of genuinely independent states, or to exclude itself from global trends and derive its security exclusively from its military might and its domination of a few clients."

He declared that "whichever path the Soviet Union chooses, we will continue our efforts to shape a framework for global cooperation based not on domination but on respect for diversity."

On February 1, in an effort to assuage Soviet misgivings, Secretary of State Cyrus Vance assured Soviet Ambassador Anatoly F. Dobrynin that the United States' policy, as stated in the Carter-Deng joint communique, was not aimed at forging a Washington-Beijing alignment against Moscow. Moscow was not to be easily persuaded. On February 1, the Soviet press agency, Tass, called on the U.S. for "clarification" of its feelings about Deng's remarks. Some of his "incendiary statements," Tass contended, "were actually an attempt to undermine the positions of President Carter, who wants the conclusion of a new treaty with the Soviet Union on the limitation of strategic arms."

Tass asked for the Carter administration's explanation in view of Deng's "slanders against the policy of detente," his "condemnation of efforts" to restrict the arms race, his "calls to create 'a united front against the Soviet Union' " and the American-Chinese agreement to consult regularly on matters of common interest.

On February 4, the Soviet Communist Party newspaper, *Pravda*, criticized the U.S. for permitting Deputy Premier Deng to denounce the Soviet Union during his American tour.

The journal said the Carter administration was involved in "an innocent game" in attempting to disclaim the anti-Soviet tone of

Deng's comments. "The Soviet public cannot close its eyes to the fact" that Deng "was given a wide podium (in the U.S.) for slander of the U.S.S.R.," *Pravda* said.

The Soviet newspaper also was critical of the joint American-Chinese communique issued on February 1, which contained the word "hegemony." "It seems that anti-Sovietism is the basis of the 'common interests and similar views' " of the joint statement, *Pravda* said.

A further complication arose when China invaded Vietnam on February 17, 1979. On March 2, President Leonid Brezhnev of the Soviet Union, called China "the most serious threat to peace in the whole world." In a campaign speech before elections to the Supreme Soviet (parliament), Brezhnev warned of dire consequences for Beijing if Chinese troops were not withdrawn from Vietnam.

Brezhnev did not specify what the Soviet Union would do if Chinese troops were not withdrawn. He merely repeated Moscow's earlier promise to abide by the provisions of the Soviet-Vietnamese friendship treaty.

Brezhnev did not refer to Soviet charges that the U.S. had encouraged the Chinese attack on Vietnam. His speech took a milder tone toward the U.S. than in past months, according to observers.

The Soviet leader was optimistic that the strategic arms limitation talks with the U.S. would soon produce a treaty. He said the treaty "probably will be signed during my meeting with President Carter . . . in the near future."

He continued: "From our point of view, of course, the treaty could have been better in some respects. . . . But it is a reasonable compromise that takes into consideration the interests of both sides."

Brezhnev said the treaty would "create . . . a definite barrier to further stockpiling" of nuclear weapons. It would "continue curbing the arms race" and "undoubtedly have a beneficial effect on the international climate as a whole," he added.

Brezhnev added that a meeting with Carter to sign the treaty would give the U.S. and Soviet leaders a chance to discuss detente and other topics of importance to the two nations.

A month later, China informed the Soviet Union that it had decided not to extend its 1950 friendship treaty with Moscow when it expired in 1980.

The decision had been taken on April 2 by the Standing Committee of the National People's Congress (the legislature). The Xinhua news agency said "great changes had taken place in the international situation and the treaty had long ceased to exist, except in name, owing to the violations for which the Chinese side is not responsible."

On April 4, the Soviet Union denounced China's decision to permit the pact to lapse. Beijing's action, a Soviet government statement said, "was taken contrary to the will and interests of the Chinese people. . . . All responsibility for the termination of the treaty rests with the Chinese side."

At the same time, the Chinese government showed greater receptivity to strategic cooperation with the U.S. During his meeting with a group of U.S. senators on April 16, Deputy Premier Deng Xiaoping was asked by Senator Joseph R. Biden (D, Del.) whether Beijing would permit the U.S. to station intelligence monitoring equipment in China. Deng replied in the affirmative.

China, he said, would be willing to use American equipment on Chinese soil to monitor Soviet compliance with Moscow's proposed strategic arms limitation treaty with the U.S. The Chinese would share the gathered data with Washington but would not permit the U.S. to establish its own bases on Chinese territory.

AFGHAN FALLOUTS

Beijing used its new opening with Washington—an American card— to strengthen its hand in dealing with Moscow. As its relations with the U.S. grew closer and warmer, the Chinese government turned to Moscow with an offer to negotiate for the normalization of Sino-Soviet relations.

This offer, which was formally made on May 5 by China's deputy foreign minister to the Soviet ambassador to China, elicited a favorable response from Moscow. In a televised address on June 1, President Leonid Brezhnev of the Soviet Union, said that his government would give the Chinese offer "serious and positive consideration."

Then a jarring note was struck by a clash between Chinese and Soviet troops on the Kazakhstan-Xinjiang border on July 16, which left one Chinese dead and another wounded and taken prisoner. Beijing and Moscow reported the incident on July 24, but gave different versions of how it happened.

China said its Foreign Ministry delivered a protest note to the Soviet embassy on July 16, charging Soviet soldiers with ambushing a Chinese Communist Party official and a veterinarian who were inspecting sheep along the border. The party official, who was killed, and the veterinarian were taken back across the border by Soviet troops, the Chinese charged.

In reply, the Soviets said a four-man Chinese security team penetrated into Soviet territory, where it was intercepted by Soviet border guards. The Soviets said one man was killed and another captured, along with a quantity of documents.

According to reports, the incident took place in the area near the Chinese city of Tacheng.

Despite the clash, the Soviet Union agreed on July 25, to a Chinese proposal to reopen high-level talks on improving relations. A Chinese spokesman in Beijing said the talks would begin in September.

The Chinese negotiating team arrived in Moscow on September 23. The official talks opened on October 17, preceded by three weeks of preparatory consultations at the working level.

During the preparatory consultations, the two sides agreed on September 27 to alternate their meeting sites between Moscow and Beijing. That was the only agreement to come out of the talks so far, as the two sides remained far apart on the question of an agenda.

The Soviets wanted to restrict the scope of the talks to matters relating only to the two nations. China, however, wanted to deal with Vietnam's invasion of Cambodia. The formal session on October 17 failed to clear up the difference.

Meanwhile, a Chinese government official in Urumchi told the *New York Times* that the Soviet Union was encroaching on Chinese territory in Xinjiang province. In an interview datelined September 29, Abdulla Rahmin, deputy director of the Urumchi foreign affairs office, said Soviet border guards had moved border fences into Chinese territory in 20 areas along the 1,990-mile (3,250-kilometer) border between Xinjiang and the Soviet Union.

The Sino-Soviet talks, off to a faltering start, ran up against another obstacle when the Soviet Union airlifted thousands of its troops to Afghanistan in December, 1979. The Soviet invasion of Afghanistan was orchestrated with the coup of December 27 in which President Hafizullah Amin of Afghanistan was ousted.

Moscow said its troops had been invited in by the Afghan government to help it combat "provocation of external enemies." Many of the Soviet troops were deployed in the northern part of the country, where Moslem rebels had been engaged in fierce fighting with government forces in the past several months. The Soviet soldiers also were reported to have clashed with dissident Afghan army troops in Kabul and elsewhere.

An Afghan broadcast from Kabul said Amin was executed after a revolutionary court sentenced him to death for "crimes against the state." He was replaced by former Deputy Premier Babrak Karmal, who was installed with a new government on his return from exile in Eastern Europe.

The U.S. and other countries denounced Moscow's military intervention and President Carter warned of "serious consequences" unless the Soviet troops were withdrawn.

Carter's warning was contained in a message sent to the Soviet leader on the Washington-Moscow hot line, installed for emergency communications. Carter disclosed the sending of the message on December 29 and elaborated on it in a television interview on December 31.

The President denounced the reply he had received from Brezhnev, asserting that the Soviet leader was "not telling the facts accurately." Carter said Brezhnev's explanation that the Soviet Union had been invited to send troops into Afghanistan "was obviously false, because the person he claimed invited him in, President Amin, was murdered or assassinated after the Soviets pulled their coup. The leader that's presently been imposed upon the Afghan people was apparently either brought in by the Soviet Union or has not come into Afghanistan—he's not been seen since he was anointed to be the leader by the Soviets and their cohorts in Afghanistan."

As a result of the Soviet push into Afghanistan, "my opinion of the Russians has changed more drastically in the last week than even the previous two and a half years," the president said.

Carter added that it was "imperative that within the next few days that (world) leaders make it clear to the Soviets that they cannot take such actions as to violate world peace without severe political consequences."

On December 31, the U.S. State Department said it had received evidence that the coup had been plotted and conducted virtually without Afghan participation. A department spokesman said that the first announcement of the uprising had been made from "prerecorded tapes broadcast from transmitters inside the Soviet Union, purporting to be Radio Afghanistan."

At the time these broadcasts were being made, Kabul radio was carrying normal broadcasts, the spokesman said.

The U.S. had first reported the massing of Soviet troops on the Afghan border on December 21. It said that more than 30,000 soldiers had been placed on the alert there and that at least 1,500 combat soldiers had been sent to Afghanistan recently, raising the Soviet military presence in the country to more than 5,000 troops and military advisers.

A revised U.S. estimate of the Soviet buildup issued on December 26 said that an airlift in the previous 24 hours had raised the Soviet military total in Afghanistan "to a new threshold." Carter administration officials said that 6,000 men had been brought in and that 50,000 Soviet troops were now deployed along the Afghan frontier.

The State Department called "on the international community to condemn such blatant military interference in the internal affairs of an independent sovereign state."

On December 23, the Soviet Union had described U.S. charges of a buildup as "pure invention." Soviet policy remained one of non-interference in the internal affairs of Afghanistan and all other nations, *Pravda* said.

On December 30, the U.S. reaffirmed its military commitment to Pakistan in the face of the Islamabad government's uneasiness over the Soviet move into neighboring Afghanistan.

National security adviser Zbigniew Brzezinski said the U.S. would honor its 1959 defense treaty with Pakistan, which obligated it to take "appropriate action, including the use of armed force," in the event Pakistan became the victim of communist aggression.

President Carter had been in telephone contact with Pakistani President Muhammad Zia ul-Haq about the Afghan crisis. He weighed resumption of military supplies to Pakistan, which had been suspended since April in a dispute over Pakistan's nuclear development.

On December 31, India, long at odds with Pakistan, expressed concern to the U.S. about its plans to increase military aid to the Islamabad government. Indian officials summoned Ambassador Robert Goheen to discuss the matter.

A number of other nations denounced the Soviet move into Afghanistan.

Britain and West Germany voiced their displeasure on December 28. Prime Minister Margaret Thatcher of Great Britain sent a message to President Leonid Brezhnev the following day, saying she was "profoundly disturbed" by the Soviet intervention.

Foreign Minister Sadegh Ghotbzadeh of Iran denounced Moscow's intervention in a note handed to Ambassador Vladimir Vinogradov of the Soviet Union. The message called the move "a hostile action against Iran and all Moslems of the world." It called the coup another attempt by the "superpowers" to divide the world.

On December 29, Pakistan deplored what it called "external military intervention." A government statement denounced the Soviet move as "a serious violation of the United Nations Charter."

Similar complaints were sounded on December 30 by Turkey, the United Arab Emirates and New Zealand.

The Egyptian People's Assembly (parliament) on December 31 condemned "the Soviet attempt to impose a Marxist regime on the people of Afghanistan."

China on December 30 condemned the Soviet action in Afghanistan. It charged that "escalation of the Afghanistan intervention will only result in the spread of the flames of armed rebellion into a conflagration and Moscow will get its fingers burned." Beijing, calling the Soviet action "a threat to China's security," demanded the withdrawal of the Soviet forces.

Chinese Foreign Minister Huang Hua flew to Islamabad on January 18, 1980 to confer with President Muhammad Zia ul-Haq, Foreign Minister Agha Shahi and other Pakistani officials. Huang's visit originally had been scheduled as a courtesy call, but he said on his arrival that it took on "new significance" in light of the Afghan crisis.

Two days later, at a meeting with Afghan refugees at a camp near Peshawar, Huang said China would do everything to relieve their plight.

Huang left Islamabad on January 21, having assured the Pakistanis of China's assistance against any future threat from Soviet forces in Afghanistan. Meanwhile, on January 19, the Soviet Union launched a new airlift into Afghanistan, bringing in more troops to reinforce the estimated 85,000 already there. Heavy military transports landing at Kabul also were ferrying in new supplies of food and equipment. Many of the fresh troops were said to have come from Soviet garrisons in Eastern Europe.

Under these circumstances, Beijing decided not to pursue normalization talks with Moscow. A Foreign Ministry statement on January 19 said that future meetings had been called off because of the Soviet invasion of Afghanistan. The Soviet move, it said, "threatens world peace and China's security. It creates new obstacles for normalizing relations between the two countries."

UNITED STATES TO SELL MILITARY EQUIPMENT TO CHINA

The sudden change in the international environment following the Soviet invasion of Afghanistan augured well for closer American-Chinese relations. In May 1979, a group of U.S. military officers from the National Defense University in Washington, D.C. made a tour of Chinese military installations, including those near the Soviet border. However, the U.S. government placed a tight restraint on the sale of arms to Beijing.

As late as October 4, 1979, Secretary of State Cyrus Vance reaffirmed this policy. Vance's statement was in response to the publication by the *New York Times* of October 3 of a hitherto secret Defense Department study suggesting that the U.S. supply arms to

China to assist the West in any war with the Soviet Union. Vance said:

"Let me state flatly and categorically that it's [the article] nothing more than a story. We have no intention of changing our policy. We are not going to sell arms to the Chinese."

The study, titled "Consolidated Guidance No. 8: Asia During a Worldwide Conventional War," was a staff paper submitted in May to Defense Secretary Harold Brown by a member of his staff. Seeking to minimize its significance, one Defense Department official said, "The study is purely a think piece. We have other think pieces that express an opposite view."

Another department official said the study "in no way represents the policy of the Defense Department or the United States government."

The document suggested that, in view of China's "pivotal role" in world affairs, it would be to the U.S.' advantage "to encourage Chinese actions that would heighten Soviet security concerns." This could be done by providing China with arms, advanced technology and intelligence information, holding joint military exercises with China and enabling China to produce American weapons, the report said.

The study also recommended consideration of military aid to Beijing in the event of war between China and the Soviet Union. It said: "If the West remained neutral in a Sino-Soviet conflict, a substantial weakening of China could occur. This, in turn, could lead to significantly reduced Soviet defense requirements in Asia and concurrent strengthening opposite the North Atlantic Treaty Organization."

Under those conditions, the study concluded, it would be to NATO's advantage "to deter (or to help China to defend against) either large-scale, conventional or nuclear attacks by the Soviets."

The first intimation of change in the U.S. policy appeared when U.S. Defense Secretary Harold Brown held talks with Chinese military officials in Beijing on January 6–9. The Soviet invasion of Afghanistan was high on their agenda.

Reporting to newsmen on January 9, on his discussions, Brown said that he had "found a convergence of views between our two governments" on Afghanistan, the threat of Soviet expansion and the need to provide Pakistan with military aid to cope with a possible Soviet threat from Afghanistan. However, as of now, the U.S. and China were not planning any joint steps in the Afghan crisis, Brown said.

Although Brown reiterated the Carter administration's refusal to sell arms to China, progress had been made in his talks on providing Beijing with advanced technology with military potential, the defense secretary said. On January 8, Brown had announced that the U.S. would sell China a ground station for receiving information from the Landsat Earth Resources Satellite, which had possible military applications.

Brown also told his news conference that China had agreed to send a military delegation to the U.S. later in the year. The trip would be in exchange for Brown's trip, the first by a U.S. defense secretary to China since 1949. Brown said the Chinese also had expressed concern about the recent U.S. decision to sell arms to Nationalist China and the continued presence of American troops in South Korea.

On January 7, the Soviet Union had criticized Brown's visit, saying it was an American attempt "to exploit the anti-Soviet policy of Beijing to strengthen pressure on the Soviet Union and, by the same token, to improve the global position of the United States."

On January 24, the Carter administration announced that it was willing to sell military equipment to China for the first time. The sale of weapons, however, would be exempt. The move, announced by the Defense Department, was a major policy change linked to the Afghanistan crisis.

Defense Secretary Harold Brown had disclosed the American decision to Chinese officials during his visit to Beijing earlier in January. A Defense Department spokesman said Brown had informed the Chinese that the U.S. "was prepared to consider, on a case-by-case basis, the sale of certain carefully selected items of support equipment, suitable to military use, such as trucks, communications gear and certain types of early-warning radar."

The types of items to be sold to China could be expanded later to include more sophisticated equipment such as transport planes and battlefield computers, a Defense Department official said.

A new turn in Sino-American relations helped other matters along. Thus, on January 24:

- A memorandum of understanding was signed in Beijing to construct an earth station to enable China to receive data from an American satellite. The information would assist Chinese agriculture, forestry and mining. The signing ceremony climaxed the first meeting of the U.S.-Chinese Commission on Scientific and Technical Cooperation.
- The U.S. House of Representatives, by a vote of 294 to 88, and the Senate, by a vote of 74 to eight, approved most-favored-nation trade status for China. The action put into effect a bilateral trade agreement signed in July 1979.

BOYCOTT OF THE MOSCOW SUMMER OLYMPICS

With Russian troops embroiled in the Afghan war, Washington stepped up its attack on the Soviet policy. On January 20, President Carter proposed that the 1980 Summer Olympics be removed from the Soviet Union, postponed or canceled unless the U.S.S.R. withdrew its troops from Afghanistan within one month. Failing any of these changes, Carter called for an international boycott of the summer games.

The President's remarks were made on a television news program, "Meet the Press," and were contained in the text of a letter to Robert Kane, president of the U.S. Olympic Committee (USOC).

Carter said in his letter to Kane that he did not wish to "inject politics into the Olympics." However, he argued that the Kremlin attached "enormous political importance" to the summer games and "if the Olympics are not held in Moscow because of Soviet military aggression in Afghanistan, this powerful signal cannot be hidden from the Soviet people and will reverberate around the globe."

The President asked the USOC to cooperate with his proposals. He also urged the nations of the world to "eliminate future political competition" by joining to establish a permanent Summer Olympics site in Greece.

Kane reacted to Carter's suggestions with a promise to give them careful consideration at an upcoming meeting of the USOC's executive board. He said Carter had given the USOC "some flexibility" by going through the "proper channels."

In Dublin, Lord Killanin, president of the International Olympic Committee (IOC), reiterated his earlier stand that it would be "both legally and technically impossible" to move the Summer Olympics from Moscow. He said that Carter's tentative call for a U.S. boycott was a "hasty decision" that would be "disastrous" if it became a reality.

On January 21, Tass, the official Soviet news agency, compared Carter's tactics to the situation of the U.S. hostages held in Iran. "Athletes and the sports movement are assigned, in his present adventure, the role of some kind of hostages, even though Carter of late has repeatedly denounced the use of hostages for the attainment of political ends," the agency said.

British Prime Minister Margaret Thatcher, speaking before the House of Commons on January 17, had disclosed a decision by her cabinet to seek to move the Summer Olympics.

On January 22, the governments of Australia and New Zealand also sided with the U.S.' proposal to move the games.

Other U.S. allies, including Israel, Austria, Belgium and Japan had expressed reservations about sending their athletes to Moscow, but indicated that the decision rested solely with their national Olympic committees.

France, it was reported on January 21, was the only Western nation to categorically reject the notion of an Olympic boycott. However, the French were said to be studying Carter's proposal to move the games.

Other nations, including West Germany and the People's Republic of China, were reported to have taken a "wait-and-see" position concerning Carter's proposals.

A strong support for President Carter's call for the boycotting of the Moscow Olympics came from the Conference of Islamic States which met in Islamabad on January 27–29, 1980, and was attended by the foreign ministers of 36 Moslem nations.

All but six (Syria, South Yemen, Uganda, Upper Volta, Guinea-Bissau and Egypt)—in addition to Afghanistan—condemned the Soviet invasion of Afghanistan.

A resolution issued at the conclusion of the conference denounced "the Soviet military aggression against the Afghan people" and demanded "the immediate withdrawal" of all Soviet troops from Afghanistan.

At the same time, the organization suspended Afghanistan from the Islamic grouping and called on all Islamic nations "to withhold recognition from the illegal regime in Afghanistan and sever diplomatic relations with that government until the complete withdrawal of Soviet troops." Afghanistan boycotted the parley.

The resolution also urged the member states to boycott the Summer Olympics in Moscow unless the Soviets pulled their forces out of Afghanistan.

At home, Carter's Olympic boycott enjoyed broad-based support. On January 23, the Foreign Affairs Committee of the U.S. House of Representatives overwhelmingly approved a resolution in support of Carter's stand that the United States not take part in the Summer Olympics unless they were removed from Moscow.

The executive board of the U.S. Olympic Committee voted unanimously on January 26, to ask the International Olympic Committee to move, postpone or cancel the 1980 Summer Olympics because of the Soviet invasion of Afghanistan. The summer games were scheduled to begin in July in Moscow.

In the face of mounting pressure to cancel the Summer Olympics, the International Olympic Committee met in Lausanne, Switzerland on April 21–23. The key issue of the meeting was finding ways to circumvent a boycott of the 1980 Summer Olympics in Moscow.

On April 23, Lord Killanin disclosed that the organization had decided to allow teams the option of not using their national flags or anthems at Olympic ceremonies. The teams could march under the Olympic flag or any other emblem of their choice, he said.

Killanin also said there was no rule requiring the nations to take part in the opening or closing ceremonies.

He offered the aid of the IOC to national committees who wished to send athletes to Moscow but were under political and/or financial pressure from their governments.

The moves to jettison the trappings of nationalism at the games were viewed as attempts by the IOC to defuse the political issues surrounding the Moscow Olympics.

Killanin invited President Carter and Soviet President Leonid Brezhnev to meet with him at an undecided future date to discuss means of avoiding a boycott and "save the Olympic ideals."

The IOC's attempt to save the Olympics from politicization proved to be of no avail.

In Afghanistan, the Moslem rebellion against the Soviet troops and the Soviet-backed regime gained ground. More nations joined the boycott of the Summer Olympics: Iran, April 11; Norway, April 14; Gambia, April 22; and Canada, April 22. On April 24, the Chinese Olympic Committee set a May 24 deadline for Soviet troop withdrawal and declared a boycott if the troops were not withdrawn by that date.

On May 1, international workers day, ambassadors from more than a dozen countries boycotted Moscow's traditional parade as a show of protest against the Soviet invasion of Afghanistan.

Absent from the parade in Moscow's Red Square were the envoys from: Australia, Belgium, Canada, China, Denmark, Great Britain, Ireland, Italy, Japan, Luxembourg, the Netherlands, Norway, the U.S. and West Germany. But France, Iceland, Greece and Turkey were the NATO members who sent representatives to the parade.

Unlike 1979, the May Day parade had no military display. But one float contained a map of Afghanistan and an expression of solidarity with the "revolutionary people there."

On May 24, the Japanese Olympic Committee voted, 29–13, to join the boycott of the 1980 Summer Olympics. The decision came after a report that the government had threatened to revoke the passports of Japanese athletes unless they joined the boycott.

CHINA'S GLOBAL ROLE ENHANCED

Afghanistan was a boon to China's foreign policy. While China's arch-rival, the Soviet Union, was widely condemned for its Afghan intervention, the Chinese were able to improve their international standing and play a more active role in global politics.

On February 6 China attended the opening of the 1980 session of the Conference of the Committee on Disarmament (CCD) for the first time since the conference was created in 1962. Chinese Deputy Foreign Minister Zhang Wenjin used the session to deliver a sharp attack on the U.S.S.R.

Zhang charged that detente was a pretext for Soviet expansionism. He asserted that the Soviet Union and the U.S. were about equal in nuclear arsenals. The Soviets, he continued, had "obvious superiority" in conventional armed forces. The Soviet military intervention in Afghanistan, he declared, extended Moscow's "practice of military aggression and occupation to the Third World and Islamic countries."

Turning to specific problems of disarmament, Zhang said his country favored drafting arms control treaties with the CCD as a whole. Usually, draft treaties were drawn up by the U.S. and the U.S.S.R. in bilateral discussions and then presented to the CCD for debate.

Zhang added that it was up to the two superpowers to take the first step in reducing their nuclear arsenals. Only then could the rest of the world be expected to agree to arms reduction programs, he declared.

Two months later, in April, China joined the International Monetary Fund (IMF) and became one of the few Communist countries that were members of the Fund.

The formal vote by the IMF to admit China into its membership was taken on April 17, at which time China's quota with the IMF was set at $693 million, the equivalent of 550 million Special Drawing Rights (SDRS).

Although not specifically mentioned in the announcement following the vote, the entrance of China into the IMF implied the expulsion of Taiwan. Taiwan was known to have completed arrangements to settle its outstanding debt with the IMF, about $158 million.

China's entry into the IMF paved the way for its eventual membership in the World Bank, the IMF's sister institution. Robert S. McNamara, the head of the World Bank, had arrived in Beijing on April 11 for five days of consultations with Chinese officials.

"A TRIANGULAR AXIS"

With anti-Soviet moves afoot, the Chinese found themselves more closely aligned with Japan and the United States than before. Premier Hua Guofeng visited Japan from May 27–June 1, 1980. It was the first such trip by a Chinese head of government to Japan in the 2,000-year relationship between the two countries.

In his first round of political talks with Premier Masayoshi Ohira, on May 27, Hua said that he was convinced that North Korea would not exploit the political unrest in South Korea by launching an attack across the demilitarized zone. Ohira warned that the North would pose "a grave threat to peace in Asia" if it took advantage of the current turmoil in the south. Ohira urged Hua to use his country's influence to restrain North Korea from military action.

Both leaders also discussed Afghanistan, Iran and the growing importance of the Association of Southeast Asian Nations. On Afghanistan, Hua said the Soviet invasion was part of Moscow's global strategy. This required China, Japan and other nations to close ranks to "guard themselves against the Soviet threat," Hua was quoted as saying.

In discussions with the Japanese premier on May 28, Hua said China would support Japan's military buildup in accordance with Beijing's global anti-Soviet strategy.

Hua said China's first test launch, on May 18, of an intercontinental ballistic missile, committed Beijing to the development of strategic weapons to "break the nuclear stranglehold of the superpowers."

Hua went back to Tokyo the following month, this time to attend the July 9 memorial service for the late Prime Minister Masayoshi Ohira.

The occasion provided a meeting between Hua and President Jimmy Carter on July 10.

The President said after his talks with Hua that the growing Chinese-American friendship would "minimize the threat of the Soviet military buildup."

In a Japanese television interview shortly before his meeting with Hua, Carter said: "We should not combine our efforts against another nation. We should combine our efforts to maintain peace and freedom of each country to make its own decisions free of outside interference and certainly free of invasion."

The Soviet military buildup, Carter pointed out, had been "exemplified most vividly" by Moscow's intervention in Afghanistan and its "support of the Vietnamese invasion" of Cambodia.

In a briefing after the Carter-Hua discussions, a White House spokesman said the U.S. and China shared "similar perspectives and concerns" about the situation in Afghanistan and Cambodia.

Irritated by the Carter-Hua talks, on July 10, the Soviet Union asserted that the talks were aimed "at advancing the process of creating a U.S.-Japan-China tripartite alliance." Such a grouping, Moscow warned, "can seriously destabilize the situation in Asia."

Moscow's concern had previously been reflected in a statement made on July 8 by an East European diplomat in Tokyo. He was quoted as saying that "in meeting for the first time on Japanese soil, President Carter and Premier Hua will consolidate what the Soviet Union sees as a triangular axis from Washington to Beijing to Tokyo."

UNITED STATES TRADE PACT SIGNED

These developments provided the backdrop for the signing of major trade agreements, on September 17, in Washington, covering textile, trade, civil aviation, consular services and shipping. The accords completed the initial phase in the move to restore normal diplomatic relations between the two countries.

The pact was signed in White House ceremonies by President Carter and Deputy Premier Bo Yibo, who had started a visit to the U.S. on September 14 as head of a 21-member commercial and financial mission. Carter called the Sino-American ties a "new and vital force" for world peace.

Among the major points of the agreements were:

- For the first time since 1949, both countries would establish direct commercial airline service and mutual port access and cargo-sharing.

   The air service would connect New York and Beijing, with stopovers in San Francisco, Los Angeles, Honolulu, Tokyo (or another point in Japan) and Shanghai.

   Chinese-flag vessels would be given access to 55 specified U.S. ports on a 14-day notice, while American-flagged ships would be permitted to dock at 20 specified Chinese ports on a seven-day notice.
- China would be allowed to export six categories of textiles and apparel to the U.S.
- The number of U.S. consular offices would be increased to five from two, subject to Senate confirmation. The two current consular missions were in Shanghai and Canton; the three additional sites were yet to be chosen.

Executives of the American clothing industry were critical of that part of the agreement dealing with the export of Chinese textiles and apparel to the U.S., asserting it would be harmful to their business.

One executive, Stuart H. Green, vice-president of the Phillips-Van Heusen Corp. of New York, said, "It completely violates the president's white paper on bilateral trade accords, which promised to prevent surges in apparel imports and to assume a global approach."

Green, who also was chairman of the American Apparel Manufacturers Association, said the increased imports "will create tough, low-price competition in an industry which has already lost lots of jobs because of imports."

Another executive, Thomas N. Roboz, chairman of the Stanwood Corp. of Charlotte, N.C., said the industry was incensed over the Administration's failure to carry out its 1979 pledge to negotiate agreements along "current import levels."

Under the accord, the importation of Chinese cotton trousers would be increased by 65% in the next three years over the 1979 unilaterally controlled level. The total of the six major categories of imported apparel from China would be boosted about 40%.

4

THE TRIAL OF THE GANG OF FOUR

PRAGMATISTS IN CHARGE

Deng Xiaoping was able to re-orient post-Mao China's domestic and foreign policies generally along his pragmatic views. But the success of his policies depended on the people who would implement them. A realist steeped in the ways of Chinese society, long accustomed to the rule of man, not of law, Deng appreciated the importance of having men of proven competence and loyalty to him in strategic positions of the Communist Party and the state bureaucracy.

The coalition in which he shared power with Hua Guofeng served his purpose during the period of transition. It was bound to be short-lived. Participants in the succession struggle in post-Mao China played for a high stake, with the winner monopolizing power. By the spring of 1980, it became clear that the balance of power had shifted decisively in favor of Deng and his followers.

This was shown by the decisions taken during the Fifth Plenum of the 11th Communist Party Central Committee in February 1980; in particular, the removal from the politburo of four members known to be critical of Deng's policies (Wang Dongxing, Ji Dengkui, Wu De and Chen Xilian), and the promotion of Hu Yaobang and Zhao Ziyang to the politburo Standing Committee. Both Hu and Zhao had been handpicked by Deng for national leadership.

At this time, it was also reported that a sweeping reorganization of China's military command had been ordered. According to foreign and Chinese officials in Beijing, the replacement of "hundreds" of senior and middle-level officers was under way in a move to modernize China's five-million-man armed forces.

Six of the country's 11 regional military commanders were replaced. The shakeup was not attributed to political factors.

The shuffle resulted in a major promotion for Xu Shiyou, a member of the Communist Party politburo and former commander of the Guangzhou military region. He was relieved of his post so that he could be available for work in Beijing as assistant to Defense Minister Xu Xiangqian, observers noted.

On February 19, the official Chinese news agency reported the appointment of a new navy commander, Ye Fei, to replace Xiao Jingguang. Other reports cited the appointments of four new members to the Military Affairs Commission, which governed the armed forces.

Deng himself, who had held concurrently the positions of vice chairman of the Military Affairs Commission (MAC) and the Army Chief of Staff, gave up the latter position, according to an announcement from the Chinese Ministry of Foreign Affairs on February 25. Yang Dechi, 70, was appointed the new Army chief of staff. Yang had formerly been the commander of the Kunming military region bordering Vietnam.

Changes were made in the personnel of the state bureaucracy, also. The Standing Committee of the National People's Congress on April 16 appointed two new deputy premiers—Zhao Ziyang and Wan Li. Zhao had been purged during the Cultural Revolution and was considered one of the leading candidates to succeed Hua Guofeng as premier. Wan was a first party secretary in Anhui province.

At the conclusion of a week-long meeting the Standing Committee also accepted the resignations of General Chen Xilian and Ji Dengku as deputy premiers and former Beijing Mayor Wu De as a deputy chairman of the National People's Congress. All three had been ousted from the party's politburo in February.

Deputy Premier Deng Xiaoping announced on April 17 that "the day-to-day work" of government was now in the hands of Deputy Premier Zhao. Deng made the disclosure when asked by visiting Italian journalists whether Zhao would become premier.

ATTACK ON MAO'S CULT OF PERSONALITY

The new leadership, once securely installed, set to work removing the vestiges of Maoism. On March 15, the Communist party issued a new set of guidelines for its 38 million members.

Called "principles for internal party political life," the code barred a cult of personality, the celebration of government leaders' birthdays, the construction of museums for officials or the presentation of gifts to them.

The new rules forbade officials from "using their position and power to seek preferment for family or relatives with regard to such matters as enrollment in schools, transferring from one school to another, promotions, employment and travel abroad."

A new system also was introduced making it easier to transfer, retire or dismiss officials, who now virtually served for life, unless purged.

The issuance of the guidelines followed a recent speech by Deputy Premier Deng Xiaoping, who criticized many party members as "below standard." He said there was great need to "revive the party's fighting strength."

At first indirect, attack on Mao's personality cult became more direct. The Chinese Communist Party Central Committee issued a directive on August 11, calling for the removal of all but a few of the public portraits, slogans and poems of Mao Zedong because the practice was "lacking in political dignity."

The directive called for "less publicity to individuals" because "inappropriate commemoration" of Mao and other veteran revolutionaries caused "alienation of leaders and the masses" and "fosters the incorrect view that history is created by individuals."

Most of Mao's portraits and slogans on public buildings in the center of Beijing had been removed two weeks earlier. The portrait of Mao on the Tiananmen gate remained, however, indicating that Mao wouldn't be totally repudiated.

The directive also ordered a halt to the construction of commemorative halls, pavilions and monuments for other veteran revolutionaries.

A further indication of Chinese efforts to bring an end to the worship of individual leaders came on August 16 with a Chinese foreign ministry announcement that portraits of Joseph Stalin, Karl Marx, Friedrich Engels and V. I. Lenin would also be removed from Tiananmen Square.

On August 17, the Soviets responded to the removal of Mao's portraits in a commentary in the newspaper *Pravda*. The commentary said the decision was one made by "hypocrites" and did not mean that China was moving away from Mao's teachings. The commentary failed to mention the decision to remove portraits of Stalin, Marx, Engels, and Lenin.

The August 11 directive was seen as the latest step in the campaign to downgrade Mao's position.

Hu Yaobang, secretary-general of the Communist Party, was reported on July 8 to have told Yugoslav journalists that Mao's "errors have been the cause of great misfortunes for the party and the Chinese people."

In an interview with Yugoslav journalists on August 10, party Chairman Hua Guofeng, Mao's hand-picked successor, openly criticized him: "As chairman of the party, Comrade Mao Zedong, of course, bore responsibility" for the "grievous and serious mistakes" committed by the party during the decade of the Cultural Revolution from 1966–1976.

Hua went on to say that Mao was "a human being and not a god, and therefore fallible."

ZHAO ZIYANG REPLACES HUA GUOFENG AS PREMIER

By the time Hua went public with his criticism of the late Chairman Mao—his patron—he was on his way out. He performed his constitutional role, both as chairman of the Party and premier, during the annual meeting of the National People's Congress which opened on August 30, 1980.

He delivered the opening address, in which he disclosed that the government had decided to abandon its 10-year economic development plan (1976–85) because it had been found to be based on inaccurate information and far too ambitious. The program would be replaced by a new 10-year plan (1981–90) and a new five-year plan (1981–85).

China's economic planning, he said, had been impaired by the disruptions of the Cultural Revolution and "leftist deviations." These deviations, he noted, had led officials to disregard laws and set high targets that were impractical, preventing China from demonstrating the superiority of its socialist system.

U.S. Republican presidential candidate Ronald Reagan came in for sharp criticism from Hua for his China-policy stand. Hua warned that Beijing was opposed to anyone who supported a two-China policy or a policy of one China and one Taiwan.

Beijing, Hua insisted, was determined to unify China by getting back Taiwan. Reunification was inevitable, he said.

Hua assailed Soviet intervention in Afghanistan, prompting diplomats from several Eastern European countries to walk out. This was the first time in more than 15 years that China permitted foreign diplomats and journalists to attend a meeting of the Congress.

Hua's only reference to Mao Zedong was the brief use of a slogan that had been popularized by Deng Xiaoping—the essence of Mao's philosophy was "seeking the truth from facts."

On September 7, halfway through the congress, Hua submitted his resignation as premier, saying that his decision to resign was "in line" with the Communist Party's new policy of barring officials from holding both party and government posts simultaneously to prevent overconcentration of power.

In its closing meeting on September 10, the congress accepted Hua's resignation and named Hua's choice, Deputy Premier Zhao Ziyang as his successor.

An expert on agricultural affairs, Zhao had attained national prominence through his innovative work in the Sichuan province. He had been assigned the party first secretary of the province in 1976. While serving at that post, he had introduced the "responsibility system" which allowed each peasant family to manage its farm and to dispose of its produce at the free market after meeting its share of the state quota. It proved to be immensely popular. He had also successfully experimented with a new incentive system in factory management.

Confirmed by the National People's Congress (NPC) as the new premier on September 11, Zhao Ziyang pledged government reforms to "arouse the masses to greater enthusiasm" and said he would seek a wider role for workers in the operation of factories and other enterprises.

He reaffirmed the new economic guidelines set forth by Deputy Premier Deng Xiaoping, which were intended to make China a "modernized, highly democratic and civilized socialist state" by the year 2000.

Speaking at a banquet honoring visiting Prime Minister Robert Muldoon of New Zealand, Zhao said: "We should restructure the economic system step by step, combine regulation through planning with regulation by the market and run our economy by relying on economic leverage and legislation."

He called for a concentrated drive "to expand the decision-making powers of enterprises and the power of their workers and staff to participate in management."

Zhao's program was similar to the one he put in force as Communist Party chairman of Sichuan province. The program raised it from one of the poorest to one of the most prosperous areas in China.

The new policy was already in place, as explained by Finance Minister Wang Bingqian in his report to the NPC on August 30. The Chinese government, Wang announced, would launch a major program to revamp China's institutions and economic practices. The new policy was designed to promote economic growth by encouraging the profit motive.

The program would be aimed primarily at individual entrepreneurs such as carpenters and shopkeepers. On the basis of limited experiments in the previous two years, there would be an increased dispersal of economic authority by the central government to provinces, counties, communes and businesses.

Wang said banks would be operated independently and would be responsible for their own loans and cash flow. State-owned enterprises would turn over their profits to the state as before, but would pay taxes on their profits as well as regulatory and resources levies.

State-owned businesses and factories would immediately be charged interest for the use of money requested from the government for their operations. These companies, starting in 1981 on a trial basis, would also be required to pay the state a use tax on the fixed assets the government had previously provided.

Also beginning in 1981, investment in capital construction would have to be paid for in the form of interest on loans from banks, replacing interest-free financial assistance from the state.

Provinces would receive money from the government in direct proportion to how much money they collected from their enterprises. Two provinces—Fujian and Guangdong—had already been given responsibility for their own finances after turning over a fixed sum to the government, Wang said.

Wang said farmers and workers were being encouraged to form cooperatives, business partnerships and individual enterprises such as family stores. Business tax laws, he said, were being changed to reduce tax burdens on such enterprises and to "promote the development of the collective economy."

In another major change, five deputy chairmen of the Standing Committee of Congress, whose ages averaged 84, resigned as part of the campaign to lower the age of the country's leaders. They were replaced by five men who averaged 65.

Three new deputy premiers were appointed. They were Foreign Minister Huang Hua, 67, Zhang Aiping, 70, an army deputy chief of staff, and Yang Jingren, 62, a Chinese Moslem who headed the Nationalities Affairs Commission. Seven of the country's 18 deputy premiers resigned.

The chairman of the Standing Committee, Ye Jianying, declared that the retirement "of some leading personnel of the state is a major step forward in the reform of the system of state leadership. Those who volunteered to leave office, set a shining example" at a time when it was vital for China to end the practice of granting lifelong posts to leading officials. Ye, himself 81, remained as head of the Standing Committee.

The National People's Congress also adopted the following measures:

- Article 45 of the constitution was abolished. The article, proclaimed by the late party Chairman Mao Zedong, had established the "four freedoms to speak out freely, air views fully, hold great debates and write" wall posters criticizing government policy.
- A new marriage law was enacted raising the minimum age to 22 for men and 20 for women, a two-year increase, in an effort to curb population growth. Requirements for divorce were eased.
- Overseas Chinese were prohibited from holding both Chinese citizenship and citizenship of the country in which they resided.
- A 33% tax was levied on foreign companies participating in joint ventures with the Chinese government in China.
- China's first income tax law was instituted, but it would affect only foreigners in the country and about 21 Chinese artists and writers who earned high royalties.

The tax levy on foreign ventures and the income tax law had been outlined at the September 2 session by Peng Zhen, deputy chairman of the congress.

In addition to the 33% levy, any profits that foreign partners in joint ventures wanted to remit abroad would be taxed a further 10%. In a move to attract joint ventures, China would exempt the foreign firms from taxes for the first year of their operation and require that they pay half of the normal rate in their second and third years, an official of the State Planning Commission said.

Foreign diplomats in China would be exempt from paying income taxes. Nondiplomats who earned more than $520 a month would be taxed. The rate would start at 5% and increase to 45%.

THE GANG OF FOUR INDICTED

On October 29, 1980, less than two months after the closing of the National People's Congress, a bomb exploded inside the Beijing railway station, killing nine persons and injuring 81.

The only official government announcement of the bombing came from the Xinhua news agency, which said the blast had been caused by "an unknown person."

On November 3, a Chinese official said police believed the man responsible for the blast was blown up by his own bomb, but they had no clue to his identity. Police believed the man was carrying the bomb through the station in a bag when it exploded. They were not sure whether he meant to set it off at that moment or whether the explosion was accidental.

Then, on November 10, police in Beijing said they believed that the man who had set off the bomb in the city's railway station had reacted to the government's refusal to permit him to return to his home in the Chinese capital after being forcibly resettled in the countryside in 1970.

The man, identified as Wang Zhigang, 29, was said to have left a suicide note at his place of work in Shanxi province. He then took a train to Beijing and blew himself up at the railway station.

Interestingly enough, the Chinese authorities took pains to dissociate the incident from the forthcoming trial of the Gang of Four and six other defendants. It was an important trial, if only because the accused included the widow of Chairman Mao.

It was also a political show aimed at consciousness-raising of the masses about the excesses of the Cultural Revolution. If successful, it would permanently discredit the radical Maoist faction opposed to Deng's pragmatic reforms. The fact that the Chinese government took the trouble to deny any link between the bomb explosion and the forthcoming trial served to underscore the state of uneasiness as the critical event approached.

The trial had been scheduled to start in mid-October, but a government official announced a delay on November 1. The postponement came about because one of the Gang of Four, Jiang Qing, widow of Mao Zedong, had refused to confess during pretrial hearings and insisted that everything she had done during the Cultural Revolution was done at Mao's request.

Another member of the gang, Zhang Chunqiao, also had declined to admit his guilt, it was reported. The two other gang members were said to have been more cooperative. They were Yao Wenyuan and Wang Hongwen. Also facing trial were the five generals who were associates of the late Defense Minister Lin Biao and Chen Boda, Mao's former secretary.

Zhang was a former deputy chairman of the Communist Party, Yao was a party polemicist, and Wang served as a security guard in a Shanghai textile mill before Mao selected him as the third-ranking member of the party hierarchy.

Among the five generals to be tried were Huang Yungsheng and

Wu Faxian, who in 1971 served as commanders of the army and air force, respectively. The other three military men had been chief political officer of the navy, a deputy chief of staff of the army and the commander of the air force headquarters in Beijing.

Indictments against the 10 defendants had been given to 35 specially appointed judges on a tribunal whose formation had been announced on September 27.

According to the chief prosecutor, the charges included sedition and conspiracy to overthrow the government; persecution of party and state leaders; suppression of the masses; and plotting to murder Mao and foment a counterrevolutionary armed rebellion.

The trial commenced on November 20. Prior to its opening the details of the indictment had been released by Chinese authorities in four installments between November 15 and 18.

The first portion, made public by the Xinhua news agency, said the 10 defendants had persecuted large numbers of officials while in office, plotted to assassinate Communist Party Chairman Mao Zedong, attempted to overthrow the state and planned "an armed rebellion in Shanghai," once a stronghold of the radicals. The alleged crimes were among "48 specific offenses" committed by the 10 during the Cultural Revolution and up to Mao's death in 1976, the report said.

Xinhua said the indictment named six other figures in the case, all of them dead. They included Lin Biao, the late defense minister, and Kang Sheng, secret police chief, who had been rehabilitated posthumously in October.

The indictment alleged that Mao's widow, Jiang Qing, Kang and Chen Boda, Mao's former secretary, had "declined without authorization" to hold a public rally against one-time head of state Liu Shaoqi and his wife, in July 1967. Liu, who died in 1969, was rehabilitated posthumously in February.

Jiang also was charged with having "decided without authorization" to have 11 persons arrested, interrogated and tortured to "rig up false evidence" against former Defense Minister Lin, who reportedly died in a plane crash in 1971 after unsuccessfully trying to launch a coup against Mao.

Lin had triggered the campaign against Liu in August 1966 when he ordered Liu's wife to dictate a letter of false accusations against Liu, the indictment said.

In a letter to Jiang in July 1968, Kang had listed 88 of the 193 members of the party's Central Committee as "enemy agents, . . . elements having illicit relations with foreign countries or antiparty spies," the document added. Another portion of the indictment, made public on November 16, said the 10 defendants were responsible for "persecuting to death" 34,380 persons during the Cultural Revolution.

Among the victims were six mayors and deputy mayors of Beijing and Shanghai. They included Wu Han, a deputy mayor of Beijing, who had written a historical play that was regarded as an allegorical attack on Mao. An article written under Mao's supervision in 1965 criticizing Wu's play was regarded as the start of the upheaval later known as the Cultural Revolution.

In one of the worst incidents cited by the indictment, 16,322 persons were put to death in Inner Mongolia. They were said to be among 346,000 persons there framed and harassed in connection with a fictitious organization known as the Inner Mongolian People's Revolutionary Party.

The indictment asserted that the killings were carried out "under the instigation" of Kang Sheng and another police security official.

The third part of the indictment, aired November 17, said that Lin Biao, his wife, his son and five senior generals had plotted to assassinate Mao in 1971. Lin's son, Lin Liguo, a deputy director of operations of the air force, died in the 1971 plane crash along with his father and mother, after their plot was uncovered.

The indictment said the plotters had "planned to attack Mao's special train" on its way from Shanghai to Beijing.

The plan to kill Mao, the indictment said, had been drawn up in February 1971 when Lin Biao and his wife sent their son to Shanghai, "where he called together key members of the joint three—as they described their counterrevolutionary special detachment." The indictment did not explain why the plot failed.

The fourth and final part of the indictment, released on November 18, said three members of the Gang of Four had planned an armed uprising in Shanghai shortly after Mao's death in September 1976 in an attempt to seize power.

The three were Zhang Chunqiao, Yao Wenyuan and Wang Hongwen. Jiang Qing was not mentioned as part of the plot.

According to the indictment, the three had trained a 33,500-member militia in Shanghai because they did not control the regular army. They had started forming the militia in 1967 in order, in Zhang's words, "to use the gun to protect the revolution."

The three were arrested by surprise in October 1976. The indictment said other leaders of the militia then planned to launch the uprising by blocking the Shanghai airport and scuttling ships in the harbor. The document did not say why the rebellion failed to materialize.

JIANG QING DEFIANT AT THE TRIAL

As the trial proceeded, two members of the Gang of Four, Wang Hongwen and Yao Wenyuan, admitted on November 24, that they had attempted to prevent Deng Xiaoping from becoming deputy premier in 1974. They said they had tried to persuade Mao not to appoint Deng to the post by hinting that Deng and Premier Zhou Enlai were plotting against Mao.

Testifying for the first time at her trial, on November 26, Jiang denied that she had tried to stop Mao from naming Deng as deputy premier in 1974, as charged in the indictment. Jiang's denial was in response to the prosecution's query as to whether she had invited the three other Gang of Four members to her home to discuss blocking Deng's nomination.

Three of the 10 defendants had testified on November 25 that they had taken part in a plot by the late Defense Minister Lin Biao to assassinate Mao in 1971. Two of them—Huang Yungsheng, then army chief of staff, and Lin Zuopeng, former political commissar of the navy—said they had passed on information about Mao to Lin.

The third defendant, Jiang Tengjiao, then political commissar of the Nanjing military region, said he had been appointed head of the conspiratorial group by Lin's son, Lin Liguo, at a secret meeting. Lin Liguo was believed to have actually organized the plot.

Another of the 10 defendants, Wu Faxien, testified on November 23, that as deputy chief of the armed forces he had inflicted "unimaginable damage" on the air force by permitting Lin Liguo to be named deputy chief of operations of air force headquarters and to take full command. "This enabled Lin Liguo to gang up with followers and organize a 'joint fleet' to carry out a great deal of counterrevolutionary activity," a television broadcast of the trial proceedings said.

Wu said Liu Liguo's appointment "caused chaos in the air force. It made Lin Biao grow stronger, but in the process it nearly destroyed the air force as many of my colleagues were killed."

The 10th defendant at the trial was Qui Huizuo, a former deputy chief of staff.

Six others listed as defendants were dead. They were Lin Biao, his wife, Ye Qun, and their son, Lin Liguo; Zhou Yichi, an air force political officer; and Kang Sheng and Xie Fuzhi, public security chiefs.

On December 3, Jiang admitted that she had personally directed a special group formed to persecute Liu Shaoqi, former head of state, and his wife during the Cultural Revolution. Her confession was a reversal of statements she had made in previous trial hearings in which she pleaded innocent to all charges against her.

Jiang finally acknowledged her involvement in Lin's case after being confronted with a series of documents bearing her signature. According to the documents, Jiang led the special group ordered to investigate Liu in May 1967. The group "arrested many innocent people and extorted confessions by torture" in order to line up evidence against Liu, the prosecution charged.

One of the victims, Liu's cook, testified that he was arrested by the group in June 1967 and was told he would be released from prison if he provided evidence against Liu and his wife. He refused and remained in jail for six years and was tortured, he said.

Another witness, Zia Meng, chief administrator of the group headed by Jiang, said Jiang had criticized him for failing to find evidence that Liu's wife was an American spy.

Another of the 10 defendants, Chen Boda, had confessed on November 28, that he, too, had a role in the campaign to persecute Liu. He also confessed to complicity on two other counts related to charges that he persecuted party and state leaders. On December 18, Chen and defendant Wu Faxien both admitted all of the charges of "counterrevolutionary activity."

The trial proceedings were interrupted on December 12 as Jiang Qing repeatedly interrupted a witness, Liao Mosha, a former Beijing party official who had been jailed for eight years after Jiang branded him as an "enemy agent." Jiang was ordered to leave the courtroom.

On December 23, the court concluded hearing Jiang's case and the prosecutor delivered his summation the following day. In the December 23 hearings, Jiang was charged with contempt of court after she shouted at the judges and prosecutors that they were "fascists" and agents of the Taiwan government.

A statement issued by the prosecutor said Jiang was guilty of "conspiring to subvert the government and split the nation" to gain power for herself and her colleagues. She did so by ordering the arrest and imprisonment of innocent people and by torturing many of them to extract confessions, the prosecutor charged.

A series of witnesses appeared in court throughout the trial to back up the prosecution's charges.

At the December 23 session, the prosecution introduced written testimony by four witnesses charging that Jiang had falsely accused the minister of coal mining in December 1966 of being a counterrevolutionary. The minister died the following January after ceaseless interrogation and torture, according to the testimony, which was given by four former officials of the coal ministry.

On December 24, speaking on her own behalf because she was denied a defense lawyer, Jiang formally pleaded innocent. Among other things, she insisted that she had acted at Mao's behest in moving against Communist Party officials during the Cultural Revolution. She declared that her criticism of party officials did not constitute a crime "in the historical context of the period," since her actions had been approved by the party.

The prosecutor sought to undermine Jiang's argument that she had acted on behalf of Mao. Although Mao "was responsible [for the people's] plight during the Cultural Revolution," his merits outweighed his mistakes and "it is futile for Jiang Qing to cover up her counterrevolutionary crimes by using Chairman Mao's high prestige," the prosecutor concluded.

In her final defense statement, Jiang said: "All my basic actions were in line with the decision of the party's Central Committee headed by Chairman Mao. You can go and check materials still locked in my personal safe. If you can find anything that shows I violated policies of the former Central Committee headed by Mao, then I would be guilty of plotting."

The chief prosecutor demanded that she be sentenced to death. The prosecution also asked for severe punishment for another Gang of Four member, former Deputy Premier Zhang Chunqiao, who had remained silent throughout the trial. The eight other defendants had confessed to most or all of the charges and asked for leniency.

On hearing the prosecutor's call for her execution, Jiang shouted, "I am prepared to die." Her outburst prompted the judge to order her removal from the courtroom.

Anticipating the imposition of the death sentence after the prosecutor called for "severest punishment," Jiang had declared in her defense on December 27, "it is more glorious to have my head chopped off" than to yield to accusers. "I dare you people to sentence me to death in front of one million people in Tiananmen Square," she told the court.

JIANG SENTENCED TO DEATH

The trial of Jiang Qing and nine other defendants ended on December 29, 1980. On January 25, 1981, the special court convicted Jiang of committing crimes during the Cultural Revolution and gave her a two-year suspended death sentence. The sentence could be changed to life imprisonment if she showed signs of repentance. Otherwise the court could order her execution.

Zhang Chunqiao, another Gang of Four member, also received a death sentence with a two-year reprieve.

A life sentence was given to Wang Hongwen and a 20-year term to Yao Wenyuan, the two other Gang of Four members. Their terms started from the day they had been imprisoned in 1976.

The remaining six defendants were given sentences ranging from 16 to 18 years and were deprived of their political rights for five years. They were Huang Yungsheng, Wu Faxien, Chen Boda, Li Zuopeng, Qui Huizuo and Jiang Tengjiao. They had been in custody for more than nine years, which would count toward their sentences.

None of the sentences could be appealed.

After her sentence was pronounced Jiang was dragged from the courtroom shouting, "Down with the revisionists led by Deng Xiaoping." "It is right to rebel," and "Making revolution is no crime."

The January 25 decisions of the Beijing special court were affirmed on March 3 by China's chief judge, Jiang Hua, president of the Supreme People's Court.

On January 25, 1983, the Court commuted to life imprisonment a death sentence imposed on Jiang Qing and one of her co-defendants, Zhang Chungqiao.

ECLIPSE OF HUA GUOFENG

While the trial of the Gang of Four was in progress, Hua Guofeng, still the Communist Party chairman, came under attack in the Chinese press, along with the late Chairman Mao.

An article appearing on December 16 in the party journal *Red Flag* said that "quite a number of party leaders are not up to standard" and that the leadership must be improved "no matter what persons are involved."

Although the article did not mention Hua by name, it was signed "Special Commentator," which usually meant that it had been written or endorsed by an important party official.

On December 30, Hua was implicitly accused of "arresting and killing outstanding young people upholding Marxist truth" in an article in *Worker's Daily*, a Communist Party trade union newspaper.

Hua's troubles stemmed from his record as minister of public security from 1972 to 1977. At the time, Hua reportedly had played a role in suppressing a demonstration April 5, 1976 in honor of Zhou Enlai, then prime minister.

Deng Xiaoping, China's principal leader and the deputy chairman of the party, had been blamed for the riot and purged, as was Hu Yaobang, the party's current general secretary.

On December 22 the *People's Daily* carried a front-page article saying: "Mao made mistakes during his late years, especially in initiating and leading the Cultural Revolution. These mistakes brought grave misfortunes to the party and people."

The article, however, made a distinction between Mao's "mistakes in political work" and the "counterrevolutionary crimes" of his widow and other defendants on trial.

In launching the Cultural Revolution in 1966, Mao had sought to "prevent the party from degenerating and prevent the state from changing its political coloration," the commentary pointed out.

Mao was at fault in his basic assessment of the situation during that period, although he was well-intentioned, the *People's Daily* said.

"In view of the complicated mixture of crimes and mistakes during the Cultural Revolution," the article continued, it was important to make a distinction between the two because of their relation "to the basic interests of the party and the people."

It was not Mao "alone who made mistakes," the People's Daily noted. Some other party members "also made mistakes in varying degrees during the Cultural Revolution. But these mistakes differed basically in nature from the conspiracies conducted" by those currently on trial.

Hua was absent at the New Year's reception given by the Communist Party Central Committee, fueling speculation that he had been removed as the Party chairman.

It was announced on January 3 that Deng had assumed the key post of head of the Communist Party's military commission. Deng had taken the position, the *New York Times* reported on January 4, to assure his authority over army commanders who had been brought up on the revolutionary precepts of Mao and were disturbed that Hua had been removed from power without a vote of the Central Committee.

Hua made a brief reappearance on February 4, when he was mentioned in news broadcasts, after having been out of the public eye since late November 1980. The prolonged absence from view, combined with veiled criticism of Hua in the press, had led Western observers to conclude that he had been removed from power through the efforts of Deng Xiaoping, party deputy chairman.

The February 4 broadcasts dealt with a dinner Hua attended that day, in company with Vietnamese defector Hoang Van Hoan, former vice-chairman of Vietnam's National Assembly, to celebrate the Chinese New Year. The television broadcast also showed Hua at the dinner.

While Hua's reappearance cast into question the theory that he had been virtually ousted as party chairman, it did not totally discredit it. That Hua was shown dining with a defector from the Vietnamese leadership on New Year's Eve, rather than meeting with the party leadership and attending the celebration in the Great Hall of the People, was taken by observers as evidence of his separation from the party.

Chinese sources cited in the Western press said that Deng, by moving so sharply to remove Hua from power, had aroused resentment among many people in the party hierarchy. According to one theory offered to explain Hua's reappearance, it was intended to allay these resentments by giving the party chairman a graceful departure.

Hua Guofeng, Mao's handpicked successor, had been kept as a figurehead while the Communist Party he nominally headed staged a political trial of Mao's widow that brought her condemnation.

5

CONSOLIDATION OF POWER

THREAT OF INFLATION

Zhao Ziyang, who assumed the premiership in September 1980, faced the immediate problem of balancing China's national budget, which in 1979 had registered an $11 billion deficit. Minister of Finance Wang Bingqian, in his report to the National People's Congress on September 1, 1980, gave the following analysis:

In 1979, the government had spent more than was planned in a number of areas. Defense needs, in particular, had absorbed $14.47 billion—$1.32 billion more than was budgeted—and programs to create nine million urban jobs and raise wages for city workers had cost $4.87 billion—$1.62 billion over budget. By the end of 1980, China's foreign debt would come to some $3.4 billion.

The government, Wang said, was able to cover part of the deficit with $5 billion drawn from its reserves. The remainder of the money, he said, came from an "overdraft" on the People's Bank of China—in other words, the government borrowed the savings of private citizens from the bank.

The deficit would be cut to $5.2 billion in 1980, and $3.25 billion in 1981. For China to achieve the deficit reduction for 1980, government revenues would have to grow by $4.16 billion, or 6%. The increase, Wang said, would result from a 5.5% expansion in the gross value of industrial and agricultural output—a goal that he termed "ambitious, yet realizable." Also, 1980 expenditures would have to be cut $8.51 billion below the level for 1979.

In China's planned economy, the government's budget problem was directly linked to the performance of the national economy. On January 19, 1981, *Business Week* pointed out that the new Chinese model of economic development, shaped by Deng Xiaoping, was being threatened by an unexpected rate of inflation as high as 7% in 1980, and 10%–12% for consumer prices.

In their attempts to shift China's centrally planned economy to a more market-oriented one, China's new leaders had adopted policies calling for freeing prices on many consumer goods, allowing farm production teams and industrial enterprises more leeway in setting production targets and making investment decisions, providing pay and profit incentives and promoting competition.

Because of the pragmatic approach, *Business Week* said, light industry expanded rapidly in 1980, and retail sales reached a record $135 billion. In addition, construction of housing in China's cities boomed. As a result, China's gross national product in 1980 expanded 7% to $587 billion, over 1979's GNP.

The expansion of light industry was carried out at the expense of heavy industrial projects. Government subsidies for large industrial projects were made subject to taxes and projects of a size that would require many years to build were being reexamined or shelved.

The most notable example of this re-emphasis was the shelving of the $5 billion Baoshan Steel Works near Shanghai, which had been regarded as the centerpiece of China's industrial modernization drive. As a result, the United States Export-Import Bank announced on February 3 that it had canceled a $60 million loan commitment to China for work on the project.

By cutting back on large projects, China's rulers hoped to save capital construction outlays in 1981 by 40%. In 1980, outlays had soared to $33 billion.

To achieve a 40% drop in capital construction outlays and to gain control of other segments of the economy, China's leaders had created a variety of governmental commissions and agencies, run by Deng's supporters. These included such diverse agencies as the Energy Commission, State Economic Commission and Import-Export Commission.

The new commissions had created another bureaucratic level through which foreigners doing business in China had to pass, and additional expenses for government, which had run a budget deficit of $12 billion in 1980—$1 billion more than the 1979 government deficit.

To reduce the deficit, China's leaders had tried to increase exports. The policy met with some success in 1980, when the trade deficit narrowed to $700 million, from $1.7 billion in 1979. Parallel exchange rates were introduced at the end of 1980 to induce Chinese exporters to sell more goods abroad, but this was having the adverse effect of causing some Western bankers to think that the yuan was overvalued.

This weakened China's position with trade partners, especially the U.S. Two-way trade between the U.S. and China totaled $4.3 billion in 1980, compared with $2.3 billion in 1979 and $1.1 billion in 1978. Despite a major U.S.-China trade pact signed in September 1980, the deep slashes that China had made in its heavy industrial projects were expected to negatively affect the volume of trade between the two countries, which the National Council of U.S.-China Trade estimated would exceed $6 billion in 1981.

Deputy Premier Yao Yulin outlined the government's economic policy to deal with the situation in his speech before the Standing Committee of the National People's Congress on February 28. The government, he said, planned to balance the 1981 budget by reducing expenditures by $9.8 billion to $64.6 billion. The savings would be achieved by cutting capital construction from a previously planned figure of $36.4 billion to just under $20 billion, a 45% reduction.

The austerity program was in line with the government's new policy of attaining slow and practical economic results in contrast to the "quick results" sought under previous programs such as the Great Leap Forward, Yao said.

The government, he said, sought to "regulate the economy according to the pressures of supply and demand in the market, within the state plan." But he added: "Where necessary, administrative measures should be used to control market forces so as to avoid economic anarchy."

Yao announced large budget cuts in oil and coal production, and in defense and administrative costs. The goal, he pointed out, was to bring government spending in line with revenues.

Yao said there would be an expansion of the system by which farmers and factories would be permitted to produce what they wanted. He also called for the development of private businesses in cities. While public ownership would continue to predominate, it should not be exclusive, Yao said.

The Chinese government pursued a multifaceted policy to stabilize the nation's economy. On March 8, it announced a plan to sell up to $3.3 billion in treasury bonds in 1981. The bonds, which would carry a 4% rate of return and would be paid back in installments from 1987 to 1990, would be the first such bonds issued in China since the 1950s.

The government viewed the bonds as a means of eliminating excess liquidity. With inflation running considerably over the 4% level, the bonds were not a particularly good investment. The government planned to make purchase of them mandatory for selected state-owned factories, wealthy communes, army groups and local governments, the ministry of finance said. For individuals, purchase of the bonds would be voluntary.

Beijing applied for a large loan from the International Monetary Fund (IMF). Approval of a $550 million loan was announced by the IMF on March 2, 1981.

The credit could be drawn in several currencies over the next 12 months, the IMF said. The loan would carry interest charges of 4.375%–6.875% a year, and repayment was to take place three to five years after the credits were drawn.

The new credit, when drawn down, would bring China's total borrowing from the IMF to support its stabilization program to about $1.1 billion. China's subscription, or borrowing quota, with the IMF was 1.8 billion special drawing rights, which worked out to about $2.19 billion.

The IMF awarded credits to a country only when the 141-nation organization was satisfied that the country's economic policies were essentially sound. In announcing the new loan, the IMF noted that, after a period of rapid growth in 1977 and 1978, China had experienced difficulties, since "the large investment program and the priority given to heavy industry at the expense of other sectors prevented a balanced growth of the economy."

Consequently, the IMF said, China had been forced to readjust its policies, and it was this stabilization effort that the new loan was intended to support. The IMF said that the readjustment was designed to "reduce the investment ratio, slow down the growth of heavy industry, encourage the growth of light industry and agriculture, speed up the introduction of new technology, and initiate management reforms to decentralize decision-making and improve the efficiency of resource allocation." China's main objectives for 1981, the IMF said, were to curb inflationary pressures, redirect investment to foster rapid growth and hold the current account deficit at "a sustainable level."

The IMF also noted that Chinese authorities were "applying stricter control over administered prices and are supervising the price formulation of nonadministered prices."

EFFECTS ON FOREIGN TRADE AND INVESTMENT

In line with its retrenchment policy, in the latter part of January 1981, Beijing canceled about $1.5 billion in contracts with Japanese companies for steel and petrochemical plants, it was reported on February 4.

These setbacks caused warnings by Japanese officials that such contract cancellations could chill economic relations between the two countries. Saburo Okita headed a special delegation from Japan that went to Beijing and met with Vice-Premier Gu Mu to discuss the situation, it was reported on February 13. Okita also met with Communist Party Vice-Chairman Deng Xiaoping, who indicated that the projects might be revived if the terms were altered.

The three petrochemical projects involved were in Nanjing, Shengli and Beijing. Contracts for these facilities were canceled a week after China informed Japanese companies that it was not proceeding with a second phase of the giant Baoshan steel complex near Shanghai.

Some Japanese companies faced heavy losses, having already manufactured or supplied equipment connected with the projects. An official at one of the companies, quoted in the Asian *Wall Street Journal* of February 4, said, "We thought the Chinese might postpone the projects for a while, but we didn't dream that they would cancel them."

According to a report on February 17, Gu said that a major reason behind the cancellation of the contracts was that China realized its oil production and resulting revenues would be considerably less than had been projected earlier.

Okita was told by Deng that, "if no better way can be found for the time being, we [China] will assume appropriate economic responsibility" for compensating foreign companies that suffered losses because of the breaking of the contracts. Deng added, however, "We hope a better solution will be found through joint efforts such as using government loans or starting joint ventures so that the canceled projects may be continued."

Japan was not the only country affected by the cancellation of the projects. West Germany's Schloemann-Siemag AG stood to lose a $400 million contract to provide a cold-rolling steel mill, according to Japanese business sources cited in the *Wall Street Journal* article.

Similarly, U.S. companies involved with major mining and petrochemical projects in China had their contracts either canceled or indefinitely postponed. However, as noted on February 11 by Christopher Phillips, president of the National Council for U.S.-China Trade, the Chinese government fully paid for all services already performed as part of the contracts.

The cancellations stemmed from a review China was conducting of its ability to handle foreign investment. Phillips said that the Chinese had indicated that those companies that responded sympathetically to China's problems would "not be forgotten" when China was again able to undertake major investment projects.

The cancellations, Phillips said, covered virtually all "major" projects.

Later, in April, Beijing sent a delegation to Tokyo in an attempt to reactivate three of the four petrochemical plants to be built by Japan that had been canceled in January. For this, Japan was asked to provide $2 billion in long-term, low-interest loans. A report from Tokyo on April 20 said that Japan had turned down the Chinese request, pointing out that the size of the loans was too large and therefore impossible to provide.

Despite rejection of its request, China would go ahead with the three planned petrochemical factories, according to the Japanese. A fifth project canceled in January, a $390 million steel plant at Baoshan, would remain scrapped.

The Baoshan plant had fallen victim to poor planning, the shift to light industry, and an economic retrenchment program, according to the September 2 *Wall Street Journal.*

Conceived in 1977 as one of the most advanced steel works in the world, Baoshan was the centerpiece of China's modernization effort. It was to have been built in two stages, with completion of the first half due by the end of 1982. Later, however, the second stage had been scrapped altogether and the first postponed for several years.

Chinese planning had failed to consider two factors, according to the story: problems of delivering adequate ore supplies and electrical power, and overestimates of China's ability to produce coal to fire the plant and oil to pay for the costly project. Chinese critics of the undertaking reportedly were putting the total cost of the project at some $14 billion, once support facilities such as electrical plants, wharves, housing and roads were taken into consideration.

The Mitsubishi Corp. was to receive over $40 million in compensation for its outlays, with the remainder going to other Japanese contractors. Mitsubishi reportedly had been asking $80 million for its out-of-pocket expenses. A Chinese official, in announcing the settlement, said Mitsubishi would be given competitive priority in future contracts if the project were resumed.

A similar delay was encountered in oil exploration. Petroleum ministry officials told an American banker that bids for a South China Sea drilling project would not be sought until the first quarter of 1982.

Willard C. Butcher, chairman of the Chase Manhattan Bank, reported on June 27 that contract and tax problems had necessitated another delay in the project, which had already been delayed twice in 1980.

The project, whose contract was being sought after by 46 oil companies from 11 countries, involved exploratory drilling in the South China Sea.

The companies had done seismic studies of areas to be explored and had submitted them to the petroleum ministry for analysis.

The ministry had had difficulty negotiating arrangements for the determination of exploration and production costs. Also, a proposed tax on profits of 45% to 50% posed complications for U.S. tax laws.

Butcher said that he was disappointed by the delay, but added that "we applaud the more deliberate approach you have adopted, the prudent concern for reality."

Trade figures for the first half of 1981 showed imports outstripping exports. China's trade deficit for the first half of 1981 was 800 million yuan ($454.6 million), the Xinhua news agency reported on July 14. This amount was as large as the entire deficit for 1980.

China's foreign trade had increased in volume by 19% in the first half of 1981, to the equivalent of $17.33 billion. That increase was less than the 24% growth of all of 1980 and the 28% rise posted for 1979.

The news agency reported that the first-half deficit resulted from a 23% rise in imports, compared with a 15% increase in exports over the same period in 1980.

There was an increase in the export of rare metals. The China Metallurgical Import and Export Corp. reported on July 13 that contracts totaling over $290 million had been signed in the first half of 1981. The contracts, which provided for the sale of rare strategic metals, surpassed the value of rare metals contracts signed for the entire year in 1980.

The rare metals involved in the deals included tungsten, titanium, molybdenum, vanadium and germanium. These metals were important in the manufacture of aircraft, missiles, computer chips and in a variety of other industrial uses.

China's contracts were with the major industrialized countries of the West, with the U.S. the principal buyer in most areas.

According to Western sources, China had vast reserves of these strategic metals and was fast becoming a major source of supply. China was considered a more preferable source than some of the other major suppliers, such as the Soviet Union and South Africa.

On the other hand, China's imports of grain to meet domestic needs added strains on its balance of payment, raising concerns among its trade partners. Canada, for one, had exported to China a record

$866 million in 1980, up 45% from 1979. Grain sales were the single largest item, at $527 million.

By contrast, China's exports to Canada had declined in 1980 by C$13 million to C$154 million. The largest category of exports was in textiles and clothing, which accounted for two-thirds of the total sales.

The growing concern over foreign trade was apparently related to China's reluctance to incur foreign debts to finance its imports. For this reason, growth of Canadian exports of manufactured goods and consumer items to China had been stagnant.

However, an increase in sales of sulfur, potash and steel was seen as encouraging by some Canadian officials, who believed that there was a strong potential for more sales of these items. The growth of sales of these items was considered particularly important in view of the Chinese government's decision to curtail a number of its industrial modernization plans.

China had signed a four-year agreement with the U.S. in 1980 to buy at least six million to eight million metric tons of wheat and corn per year.

China's grain imports from the U.S. in 1980 were about 7.8 million metric tons, of which 6.1 million metric tons were wheat and 1.7 million metric tons were corn.

The U.S. deputy secretary of agriculture, Richard E. Lyng, said on July 13 that China was expected to continue its grain imports at current levels of the foreseeable future.

Lyng said that China's port and transportation facilities limited the amount of grain it could handle and distribute. Lyng's assessment came after U.S. grain experts visited China in June. China's sustainable level of imports was estimated at about 15 million metric tons of grain per year.

POLITICAL UNREST SPREADS

The trial of the Gang of Four signaled a repudiation of radical policies which were Maoist in inspiration. It therefore raised expectations of return to more relaxed normal life. These expectations were bound to be disappointed, if only because they were unrealistically high, far beyond the ability of the government to deliver. The situation was further compounded by the fact that the modernization programs called not only for re-orientation and re-education of Party and administrative cadres, but, often, their reshuffling and purging. The People's Liberation Army (PLA) was ordered to cut 400,000 men in 1980, with bigger cuts in manpower to follow in the ensuing years. Resistance developed in parts of the country.

In late January and February, 1981, the Chinese media reported widespread unrest in the country. The disturbances, including bombings, strikes and protest demonstrations, were said to have centered in Xinjiang, Shanxi and Yunnan provinces, Tibet and Shanghai.

The Communist Party's official newspaper said on January 31, "a pessimistic wave of sabotage, protests and despair have [sic] been sweeping the country." It warned that if the turmoil were not suppressed, "it is bound to ruin our hard-earned stability."

The party's theoretical journal, *Red Flag*, said on January 31: "In our society, there is still class struggle and factors of instability, so we must not let up on our vigilance."

A Shanghai newspaper had reported the previous week that followers of the Gang of Four were operating illegal cells and publications under cover of "democracy."

A report from Xinjiang said thousands of urban youths sent to work in the countryside had been agitating to return home. Their protests were said to have continued despite rejection of their demands.

A broadcast from the Jiangxi city of Nanchang on February 6 reminded Communist Party members that they were forbidden to support dissident activity. Any "divergent ideas" could be expressed within the party, the broadcast said.

A report of a party conference in the January 31 issue of a Shanxi newspaper quoted an official as saying: "A very few counterrevolutionaries and criminals are carrying out sabotage activities that seriously harm social order. A very few antiparty and antisocialist elements and people who desire to see the whole world in chaos stir up antisocialist trends of thought."

On February 18, *Red Flag* called for a crackdown against dissidents who it charged were advocating a second Cultural Revolution. Many of them, some of whom were followers of the Gang of Four, had distributed anticommunist and reactionary leaflets. Some of them had established illegal organizations and published illegal magazines alleging that a new "bureaucratic class" had been formed in China, according to *Red Flag*.

According to an article in *Beijing Review* on April 13, demonstrations had been carried out by young people who wanted to return from border regions where they had been sent to work by the government. It said the strikes by workers had been staged to protest low wages and small bonuses and that student unrest was provoked by the manner in which officials handled elections and by the serving of poor food in the universities.

Diplomatic sources in China said 20 to 30 demonstrations had occurred in the country in the fall of 1980.

Beijing Review said some of the outbreaks were justifiable and reasonable demands would be met. Unreasonable demands, the article added, would be handled through persuasion.

Unemployment resulting from a reduction of China's army also was causing unrest in some areas, according to a report from Beijing on April 1. China's unemployed were said to total 20 million.

The report, citing released government documents, said the military was being cut down to modernize it and to save money. One government agency, the ministry of civil affairs, acknowledged that "there are many accumulated problems in the resettlement of demobilized personnel."

The seriousness of the problem was further emphasized by the State Council (cabinet), which said: "The proper resettlement of retired military cadres and demobilized soldiers is a task affecting economic construction, national defense-building and stability and unity."

Against this backdrop of widespread unrest, the Chinese government took steps to increase its control of the army.

First, new army recruits would now be required to take a loyalty oath, swearing allegiance not only to the Communist Party and the government, but to the government's modernization policies as well, the Xinhua news agency announced on March 3.

The army's general headquarters staff and the general political department had issued the directive. Veteran soldiers were ordered to attend the new oath-taking ceremonies at some unspecified time in 1981.

The news agency said the new recruits would be required to observe the following four declarations of the new oath: support the Communist Party and the central government; obey party, government and army orders; study and work hard in military training, including "keeping military secrets," and "sacrifice everything, fight heroically and win victory for the cause of safeguarding the motherland and its program of modernization."

The new oath, supposedly the first to be issued since the Communists took power in 1949, was believed by some nonmilitary Chinese sources and diplomats in Beijing to have been drawn up to counter reported growing discontent in the army, as well as outright resistance to the present Chinese leadership's policies and directions.

Second, Deputy Premier Geng Biao was named China's first civilian defense minister on March 6, replacing ailing Marshal Xu Xiangqian, 79, who had given up his post as deputy premier in September 1980.

The naming of Geng and 11 other ministers was announced at the final session of a nine-day meeting of the Standing Committee of the National People's Congress, which had convened to review economic policy and confirm ministerial appointments.

Geng, considered a loyal follower of Communist Party Vice-Chairman Deng Xiaoping, was also secretary-general of the military commission of the party's Central Committee.

Third, the pragmatic leadership of the Chinese Communist Party toned down its criticism of the late Chairman Mao out of deference to the People's Liberation Army's devotion to Mao's memory. A detailed assessment of the role of the late Chairman Mao Zedung in China's history was published in a long article appearing April 11 in the *People's Daily* and other major newspapers throughout the country. In essence, it said that Mao's merits outweighed his mistakes.

The article, written by General Huang Kecheng, a high-ranking party official, was first published April 10 in the *Liberation Army Daily* and then reprinted in the other newspapers the following day.

"While Chairman Mao committed mistakes in his later years and some of his statements were incorrect or out-of-date, the essence of Mao's thought will continue to guide the party and the people in their march forward," wrote Huang, secretary of the Central Discipline Commission of the party's Central Committee. The commission dealt with complaints against party officials.

Mao's "two main errors" during his leadership, Huang wrote, were his policy of pursuing "socialist revolution and socialist construction" too far and too fast and of pushing the "class struggle in absolute terms."

The article specifically blamed Mao for having followed policies that led to "great disorders" during the Cultural Revolution, for having lost "contact with the day-to-day life of the masses," and for the excesses of the "antirightist campaign and the Great Leap Forward economic drive of the late 1950s.

While the entire Central Committee shared the blame for the above mistakes, as chairman of the committee, Mao "should be held responsible as its principal leader," the article said.

On the day Huang's article was published, April 10, Chinese security officers arrested political activists Xu Wenli, former editor of the defunct dissident magazine *April 5th Forum*, and his colleague, Yang Jing, on undisclosed charges. Their seizure spurred fears of an impending government campaign against the remaining few dissidents, underground publications and unofficial organizations that escaped the government's 1979 antidissident drive.

A few days earlier an article had appeared in *Red Flag*, threatening judicial action against "counterrevolutionaries" who conducted secret meetings to exchange their experiences and "conspire to spread chaos."

Xu's magazine had ceased publication in 1980 as a result of government pressure. Since then, he and a group of colleagues connected with the *April 5th Forum* had published private newsletters continuing their call for greater democracy and freedom.

In another move aimed at containing criticism of the government, on April 20 the *Liberation Army Daily* accused writer Bai Hua of attempting to smear the image of the nation, the Communist Party and the late Chairman Mao Zedong, in his screenplay for the controversial movie, "Bitter Love."

The army newspaper said that Bai's script was "saying that the new society is not as good as the old society, that the Communist Party is not as good as the [ousted] Nationalist Party, [and] that socialism is not as good as capitalism. . . ."

The film had been shown privately to select audiences at the start of the year but was suddenly withdrawn in February.

UNCOOPERATIVE NATURE

People were not the only problem Deng Xiaoping and company had to be concerned with. There was a severe drought in northern China in existence since 1980. According to a report on April 24, 1981, as many as nine provinces were in its grip. Western observers and international relief officials estimated that the disaster left more than 130 million people facing varying degrees of food shortages. But they stressed that there was no starvation and that the government's relief effort was under way and well-organized.

One of the hardest-hit areas was Hubei province, which also had been struck in the summer of 1980 by torrential rains and subsequent flooding of the Yangtze River.

Chinese officials had told a United Nations survey team that 550 people had died in the flooding and that about 41,000 had been injured. The floods had swept away whole villages, grain and vegetable crops and farm animals.

The Chinese government had applied for international relief the previous fall, for the first time in more than 30 years. At that time, Chinese officials were said to have deliberately underestimated the extent of the drought and flood. They reportedly had understated the effects of the disaster for fear of alarming donor nations, antagonizing other Third World disaster victims and harming international political stability. As a result, the Chinese limited their appeal for relief assistance to only the most hard-hit provinces containing about 21 million people.

The foreign aid received by China included emergency United Nations shipments of vitamins to supplement emergency grain rations. The EC and Japan had pledged powdered milk and other food supplies.

The U.N. survey team in March had estimated that China would need $700 million in food and other aid for disaster victims in Hebei and Hubei provinces alone. Despite China's pressing needs, it had pledged $1 million in relief efforts for African refugees at a conference in Geneva earlier in April.

The summer brought another natural disaster. Floods swept through China's Sichuan and Hubei provinces during July 1981, leaving 753 dead, 558 missing and 28,140 injured, it was reported July 25 by the Xinhua news agency. The official tally of casualty figures was much lower than previous estimates, which had soared as high as 4,000 dead.

In the worst flooding since 1949, 1.5 million persons were estimated to be homeless, and the damage to homes and crops was estimated at more than $1.14 billion.

After a three-day downpour in Sichuan beginning July 12, the Yangtze overflowed its banks and flooded nearly half a million acres (200,000 hectares) of farmland. The floodwaters then surged eastward through central China, the swollen Yangtze rising to its greatest height since 1905, in some places 60 feet (18.3 meters) above normal levels.

The unabated torrent reached the newly-opened Gezhouba Dam in Yichang at dawn on July 20, threatening China's largest water control project, still under construction, with inundation. The hydroelectric project, however, stood up to the 20-foot (six-meter) waves, with an estimated 200,000 workers reinforcing dikes downstream of the dam to protect the central plains of Hubei province. When completed, the $2-billion project was expected to slow the river's flow through Hubei and to produce 120% of the province's present power consumption.

The damage to China's rice and soybean crops was reported to be extensive.

The chief cause, according to the government, was indiscriminate tree-cutting that had denuded most of the watershed areas of the Yangtze River since the early 1950s.

In half the countries of central Sichuan, forests now accounted for less than 3% of the land. In Wusheng County, for instance, where flooding was particularly severe, forests had been reduced from nearly

25,000 acres (10,000 hectares) to fewer than 140 acres (5.6 hectares) over the previous 30 years.

On August 20, the Chinese government put the blame for the extensive flooding on Mao Zedong's agricultural policies.

Declaring grain to be the "key link" to China's development, Mao had encouraged the stripping of forested land and its conversion to grain production.

In an effort to reverse the effects of deforestation that had been going on in Sichuan—and throughout China—for decades, on October 1 Beijing ordered a gigantic tree-planting program. Vice-Premier Wan Li, announcing the program, said "afforestation is an urgent task." He said, "In many regions water sources are drying up and soil erosion has become a serious problem." Every Chinese citizen was thus being told to plant three to five trees a year and tend them as they grew or face punishment.

The government estimated damage from two consecutive summer floods along the Yangtze River at $1.5 billion. "The extent of the flooding and the losses sustained were unprecedented in New China," Wan said.

CONSOLIDATION BY PURGES

The new administration under Premier Zhao Ziyang tackled these and other daunting problems, apparently with some success. The year-end report Zhao presented to the National People's Congress on November 30, 1981, presented a picture of an economy improving at a steady pace. It was, Zhao said, far better than expected. A budget deficit that, by his reckoning, had reached about $10 billion in 1979 had been reduced to about $7 billion in 1980 and about $1.5 billion in the current year, he said. The harvest would be the second highest since the Communists came to power in 1949, and China could expect a 3% growth in gross industrial and agricultural output in 1981.

Foreign trade, Zhao said, would increase dramatically over 1980's total of $31 billion, and foreign companies were welcome to invest in joint ventures in mining and manufacturing.

On the negative side, Zhao said that retrenchment in heavy industry had resulted in a 5% drop in output, a much worse result than had been planned.

Zhao denied recent reports that the country's oil output was decreasing and that China might soon become a net importer. "I can assure you that this will not happen," he said. China would increase its coal production, however, to spare as much oil as possible for export.

Despite the generally optimistic assessment, Zhao said it would probably take another five years to achieve the government's ultimate goal of balanced growth, and in the meantime austerity measures would be maintained. A tight lid would have to be held on overall economic growth until that time, he said.

Meanwhile, China's modernization and economic development had spawned an assortment of corrupt practices and crimes previously unknown while the country remained puritanical under the Maoist ideology. Thus, for example:

China's "open door" had given rise to a booming smuggling industry in the provinces near Hong Kong. Official news releases quoted in a November 16 story said smuggling was "rampant" in Fujian, Zhejiang and Guangdong provinces. Over 800 foreign and Chinese boats had been seized for smuggling between March and September, the government said, and a national conference had been called in August to combat the problem.

The country's top leadership ordered a campaign against urban crime in the wake of a sharp upturn in violent crime, the *Los Angeles Times* reported on August 24. Beijing's mayor called on residents to "fight total war" on gangs that had made the capital unsafe at night.

Of particularly serious concern to the government was the spread of corruption in the officialdom, involving Party and administrative cadres at various levels.

On November 13, the *People's Daily* exposed a massive confidence game by a bogus chemical engineer, whose "research institute" actually employed no researchers and technicians and had no equipment. Instead, for four years, the "institute" had employed only the swindler, his friends and children of government officials who supported him. The Xinhua news agency called it the "most serious fraud" incident since 1949.

The government's anticorruption campaign was making public many stories of bribery and official misdeeds. The *People's Daily*, for instance, reported from one provincial city that "those in charge live like princes," according to a story in the October 8 *Los Angeles Times*. The same story said auditors in Guangdong province had uncovered nearly $14 million in bribes paid by over 2,000 different enterprises to get raw materials for production.

Bureaucratic obstructionism appeared to be a serious problem on both the local and national levels, according to the *Financial Times of London* of November 6. Many senior officials were stubbornly resisting economic policies that stressed individual initiative as a departure from the teachings of Mao Zedong.

Deng Xiaoping was contemplating a massive purge of the Communist Party with the twin objectives of getting rid of incompetence and corruption and consolidating his power. A word to the effect that some two to three million of the Party's 39 million members were expected to be purged at the Party's 1982 congress leaked to the Western press, as reported by the *Times* of London on October 19. The Party leadership, it was reported, would attempt to weed out those who had abused their power or who clung rigidly to Maoist attitudes.

Paramount leader Deng Xiaoping laid down his "organizational line" in a compendium of his views, dating from 1977 to the present, published on November 2.

In this publication, Deng strongly attacked the bureaucratism and corruption of party officials. Bureaucratism, he said, consisted of (among other things) "abusing one's power," "thinking in a rigid way, sticking to convention," "being dilatory, being irresponsible," "suppressing democracy, deceiving one's superiors."

Deng denounced the corruption and self-indulgence of some party officials, which, he said, were putting the party out of touch with ordinary people. He warned that uncooperative officials would be purged.

Deng took pains to insist that his authority derived from Mao. However, Deng cautioned, "We are facing conditions that Mao did not come across." Seizing opportunities for technological progress and encouraging foreign investment "can be regarded as upholding the great banner of Mao," he said.

The strength of Deng's attacks and his stress on the legitimacy of his authority suggested to many observers that he was engaged, once again, in heavy political infighting. The statements were carried in all three of China's leading publications, the *People's Daily*, *Red Flag* and the *Liberation Army Daily*.

Red Flag, the party journal, warned, on November 19, of removal of party officials who continued to obstruct Deng's policies, actively or passively. All party officials would be judged on their effectiveness in implementing Deng's policies, the editorial said.

A new wave of purge in the Party and the bureaucracy was presaged in a statement by Premier Zhao on December 1, pledging firm steps to slash China's "bloated, overlapping administrative structure." He also urged a renewed crackdown on corruption in the bureaucracy.

The next day, the *Red Flag* echoed Zhao's criticisms and opened a new attack on foreign concepts such as free speech, vowing "struggles on both fronts" in a harsh 30,000 word editorial. "Corrupt bourgeois ideology," it warned, "could spread like an infectious disease to harm the people's stability and unity of the whole society."

"It could even result in a catastrophe like the Cultural Revolution," the article said, referring to the political upheaval that had swept through Mao's China in the 1960s.

In what was interpreted as the first step in an announced shake-up of China's bureaucracy, over a dozen elderly deputy ministers had resigned at the request of the government, it was reported on January 19, 1982.

The resignations were hailed as exemplary patriotic acts by the official press.

The ostensible goal of reorganization was to streamline a government that Premier Zhao Ziyang had described as bloated and "bogged down in endless debates." One official at the recent National People's Congress had disclosed that China now had nearly 1,000 ministers and deputy ministers and another 5,000 senior department and bureau heads.

A second goal, in the eyes of many observers, was the removal of the remaining radicals who had risen to prominence during the Cultural Revolution of the 1960s.

While this shake-up was underway, Deng did not appear at public functions for several weeks. Vice-Premier Wan Li said, on February 6, that Deng had "withdrawn from the first line and is now in the second line" of decision-making.

Wan's remarks, coming after Deng's conspicuous absence from several government functions, had sparked numerous theories about Deng's future. The theories ranged from the possibility that Deng was setting an example to other elderly officials who were being urged to resign, to the widely held notion that he was simply consolidating his influence in his proteges who held top government posts, to enable Deng to take a powerful backseat role in long-range decisions.

Wan sought in his statement to eliminate at least one of the rumors about Deng's temporary withdrawal, stating that "his health is perfect."

On February 11, the foreign ministry hastened to quiet speculation about Deng's position, according to a Reuters report from Beijing.

A spokesman declared that Deng still held all of his government posts, remaining as chairman of both the Communist Party Military Commission and the Chinese People's Political Consultative Conference, as well as continuing in his post as party deputy chairman.

Deng Xiaoping reemerged into public view on February 18 at a nationally televised state luncheon held in honor of the exiled Cambodian leader, Prince Norodom Sihanouk.

The well-publicized re-emergence was apparently intended to quell widely circulated and divergent rumors about a change in the leader's status or his dominant place in the structure of China's political bureaucracy.

Deng was quoted as telling Sihanouk that he had been resting outside Beijing for several weeks, and that China was enjoying "unprecedented stability."

Referring to the current campaign to reduce and streamline China's aging government bureaucracy, Deng assured the former Cambodian leader that it was "going on very smoothly. The comrades in our party, including the older ones, hold identical views on this issue. I think the job can be finished much earlier than expected."

Deng was also quoted as having told Sihanouk: "We are determined to take it as a revolution . . . Of course, this is a revolution in administrative structure, not a revolution against anyone."

"A revolution in the administrative structure" shifted into main gear on March 8 as the Standing Committee of the National People's Congress put its seal of approval on the government's plan to effect sweeping changes in its organization.

Under the new and far-reaching plan, the 12 current ministries would be telescoped into six, the number of vice-premiers would be cut to two from 13, and the 98 state council organizations would be reduced to 52. The cutbacks, according to the Xinhua news agency, would reduce the ministerial staff to 32,000 from 49,000.

The restructuring would begin with the highest economic ministries, merging the foreign trade ministry, ministry of economic relations with foreign countries, state foreign investment commission and state administrative commission on import-export affairs into one body, to be headed by Vice-Premier Chen Muhua. The current group of nine agencies dealing with commerce, trade and energy would have their staffs reduced by a third.

Two women, including Mrs. Chen, were among the officials promoted to minister. Five former ministers were dismissed, and two were demoted.

In addition, the plan called for new age limits to be imposed, requiring officials of ministerial rank to retire at 65, and vice-ministers and department directors at 60. The age limits would be imposed "under normal conditions," a provision that would presumably allow exceptions to be made in the case of top officials already exceeding the new age limits.

Two prominent casualties of the streamlining plan were Gu Mu, a deputy prime minister who headed two trade commissions, and Wang Lei, the minister of commerce.

Additional provisions in the plan called for the creation of state councilors, to be equal in rank with vice-premiers, and a new standing committee of the state council, to consist of the premier, vice-premiers, state councilors and a secretary-general. Also, each ministry would limit the number of its deputy heads, at present totaling 20 or more in some ministries, to four.

In announcing the shake-up of the bureaucracy on March 2, Premier Zhao Ziyang said that its first priority was "economic reconstruction." Calling the task "arduous and large in scale," he maintained, nevertheless, that it should not interrupt work or cause a major disturbance.

"In carrying out this profound revolution," he told the parliament, "we mean to reform that part of the state administrative structure that is incompatible with the requirements of economic, cultural and political work. We are not making revolution against persons." The latter remark was seen as a reassurance that the present plan was not to be compared to the so-called Cultural Revolution of 1966–1976.

The crackdown gained momentum as it continued through the spring. Politics crept into it. Moving beyond its original goal of increasing administrative efficiency, the purge now included, among its intended victims, an incongruous mixture of the puritanical radicals of the Cultural Revolution vintage and sundry offenders of anticorruption decrees.

In a speech published on March 9, Premier Zhao Ziyang called for a purge of radical Gang of Four supporters from high bureaucratic posts. "People who built their careers as 'rebels' . . . and who are heavily influenced by factional ideology . . . as well as smash-and-grabbers . . . should definitely not be promoted, not a single one of them, and those who are already in leading posts must be resolutely ousted," he declared.

Shortly after the publication of Zhao's speech, the *People's Daily* published an article on March 15 which touched on the corrupting power of contact with the West through foreign trade, but then went on to blame the effects of that contact on corrupt members within the party itself. The commentary said China's open-door policy made it necessary for its party officials to resist "the influence of decadent capitalist ideology . . . and fawning mentality of seeking a foreign way of life." "The main danger," it continued, "comes from none other than the degenerates within the party."

On March 28, Xinhua reported that the editor-in-chief of *China*

Finance and Trade Journal had been charged with betraying state secrets to "a foreigner" and sentenced to five years in prison. The cited foreigner was reportedly a Japanese journalist to whom Li Guangyi had given information about the party Central Committee's June 1981 meeting, which had been devoted to the formulation of an official judgment on the late Chairman Mao Zedong. The severe sentencing, widely publicized, was regarded as a move toward more stringent government limitation of contact with outsiders.

The following day, the *People's Daily* reported that four municipal party officials who "rose to power through rebellion during the Cultural Revolution" had been dismissed for their former political activities and for opposition to Deng's economic and political policies. The paper described the treatment of the four, who had been fisheries bureau officials in the northern port city of Tianjin, as a "profound lesson" for the party at all levels. The same paper said, on April 10, that the government would soon begin executing corrupt officials, as provided for in the recently revised criminal code, which authorized the death penalty for "serious offenses" in smuggling, black-marketeering, bribery, currency speculation, drug-trafficking or the theft of cultural relics. The article stated that it was "necessary to kill one to warn a hundred."

Indeed, two officials of an electronics firm in the Shenzhen special economic zone near Hong Kong had been dismissed and could face criminal charges for their part in corrupt dealings with foreign exporters, according to an April 11 account in the *People's Daily*. The case allegedly involved smuggling, foreign currency speculation, tax evasion and forgery. The story emphasized the potential for corruption in the special zones, where foreign influences were a part of daily life.

Finally, the massive reorganization campaign reached the Communist Party Central Committee, according to Xinhua on May 16. The Committee's 30 departments were targeted for staff reductions of 17%. New party appointments listed by the *People's Daily* included a number of supporters of Deng Xiaoping and of Hu Yaobang, the party chairman.

The streamlining of the Central Committee, Xinhua announced, was proceeding "side by side" with that of the government ministries, and would replace 13% of the department heads with younger successors.

Only 13 department heads were named in the announcement. They included Hu Qili, formerly mayor of Tianjin and a protege of Hu Yaobang, as new director of the Committee's general office; Wang Zhen, a former deputy prime minister, as new director of the Committee's party school; and the agronomist Du Runsheng as head of the rural party research center for the Committee's secretariat, an important post in that it involved agricultural policy-making.

THE TWELFTH PARTY CONGRESS

The reorganization of the state bureaucracy and the Party had the effect of consolidating the power of Deng Xiaoping and his followers. It now remained for the Party congress to ratify it. The historic congress met in Beijing on September 1–11 and took major steps to shed the Communist Party of the ideological and political legacies of the late Chairman Mao Zedong. These were the highlights of the congress:

Deng Xiaoping, addressing the opening session of the congress on September 1, emphasized the need for socialist modernization to achieve China's economic goals.

Deng outlined a new party program that he said would "create a new situation in all fields of socialist modernization and bring prosperity to our party, our socialist cause, our country and all our nationalities."

Deng specified three principal tasks for China in the 1980s: modernization; the reunification of China, particularly the recovery of Taiwan from the Chinese Nationalists, and an independent foreign policy that would "combat hegemony and safeguard world peace."

China could accomplish these tasks, Deng maintained, through "economic construction."

Hu Yaobang, general secretary of the Communist Party, presented a 34,000-word report praising Deng's leadership and his pragmatic policies. The Party, he said, had "broken through the heavy chains of the protracted 'leftist' mistakes." Deng's influence had helped China eliminate the "fetters of dogmatism and the personality cult" that had deified the late Chairman Mao Zedong, Hu claimed.

Hu criticized the 11th Communist Party Congress, held in 1977, for failing to correct "the erroneous theories, policies and slogans" of Mao's Cultural Revolution.

Hu also reported on the party's economic goals. China would strive to quadruple its farm and industrial production to more than $1.7 trillion by the year 2000, improve standards of living, switch to light industry from heavy industry and continue the system of limited free enterprise.

China would achieve its goals, Hu stated, only if the functioning of the party took a "fundamental turn for the better" through a "thoroughgoing ideological education."

The party was to remold its membership over a three-year period, beginning in late 1983, Hu said, to purify its ideology and organization. The revitalization program to eradicate "pernicious influences" would require all 39.6 million party members to reregister.

A new constitution of the Party was adopted on September 6, which eliminated the vestiges of Maoism and encouraged aging party officials to retire.

The constitution aimed at preventing the rise of any individual to absolute power. It banned "all forms of personality cult," a reference to the near-deification of Mao. It affirmed that China's ideology was "the crystallized collective wisdom of the Communist Party, and not that of a single person."

The constitution departed dramatically from Maoist ideology on the issue of class struggle. It stated that "most of the contradictions in Chinese society don't have the nature of class struggle, and class struggle is no longer the principal contradiction.

"The principal contradiction in Chinese society is that between the people's growing material and cultural needs and the backward level of our social production."

The constitution abolished the posts of party chairman and vice-chairmen and provided for a general secretary to rule the secretariat. The secretariat handled day-to-day party affairs.

To encourage aging officials to retire, the constitution established a Central Advisory Commission to consist of members of 40 years' standing. The commission was to give advice "upon request" to the Central Committee.

The constitution also stipulated that the chairmen of the Central Advisory Commission and the Military Commission and the first secretary of the Central Commission for Discipline Inspection had to be members of the politburo's standing committee.

- A new Central Committee was elected on September 10, consisting of 210 members, of which more than half were new faces. Two-thirds of the members of the new committee were under 60 years of age.

Vice-Chairmen Deng Xiaoping and Hua Guofeng were reelected to the Central Committee.

The congress also elected a 172-member Central Advisory Commission. Deng Xiaoping and two lesser politburo members, Geng Biao, 73, and Xu Shiyou, 76, took seats on the commission.

No other top leaders joined Deng in the advisory role. Of those party members who stepped down from the Central Committee, more than 40 joined the advisory commission.

- The new Communist Party Central Committee, in its first meeting on September 12, dropped Hua Guofeng from the ruling politburo and its standing committee.

  The party had declared its intention of purging the remaining followers of the late Chairman Mao Zedong throughout its 12th congress.

- The Central Committee elected Hu Yaobang as Communist Party general secretary and reelected Deng as head of the party's military commission.

- The Central Committee elected a new politburo, which was expanded to 25 full members from 22.

  The new politburo had eight military members. The average age of the members was over 70.

- The Central Committee reelected the members of the former Standing Committee, with the exception of the ousted Hua Guofeng. Its six members were Premier Zhao Ziyang, 63; Ye Jianying, 85; Li Xiannian, 77; Deng Xiaoping, 78; Chen Yun, 77, and Hu Yaobang, 67.

  The average age of the standing committee, which made all major party decisions, was 74.5.

  Ye Jianying and Li Xiannian had both opposed the policies of Deng.

  The Central Committee also elected an 11-member secretariat.

- Chen Yun was reelected chairman of the party's discipline and inspection commission on September 13. The new constitution had given the commission wider powers to combat corruption.

Finally, the newly established Central Advisory Commission elected Deng as its leader. The vote was a formality, since Deng was the only eligible candidate.

Excerpts from the Chinese Communist Party Constitution

Following are excerpts from the new constitution adopted September 6 by the 12th national congress of the Communist Party of the People's Republic of China:

General Program

The Communist Party of China is the vanguard of the Chinese working class, the faithful representative of the interests of the people of all nationalities in China, and the force at the core leading China's cause of socialism. The party's ultimate goal is the creation of a communist social system.

The Communist Party of China takes Marxism-Leninism and Mao Zedong thought as its guide to action

Applying dialectical materialism and historical materialism, Marx and Engels analyzed the laws of development of capitalist society and founded the theory of scientific socialism. According to this theory, with the victory of the proletariat in its revolutionary struggle, the dictatorship of the bourgeoisie is inevitably replaced by the dictatorship of the proletariat, and capitalist society is inevitably transformed into socialist society in which the means of production are publicly owned, exploitation is abolished and the principle "from each according to his ability and to each according to his work" is applied—with tremendous growth of the productive forces and tremendous progress in the ideological, political and cultural fields, socialist society ultimately and inevitably advances into communist society in which the principle "from each according to his ability and to each according to his needs" is applied. Early in the 20th century, Lenin pointed out that capitalism had developed to the stage of imperialism, that the liberation struggle of the proletariat was bound to unite with that of the oppressed nations of the world, and that it was possible for socialist revolution to win victory first in countries that were the weak links of imperialist rule. The course of world history during the past half century and more, and especially the establishment and development of the socialist system in a number of countries, has borne out the correctness of the theory of scientific socialism.

After the elimination of the exploiting classes as such, most of the contradictions in Chinese society do not have the nature of class struggle, and class struggle is no longer the principal contradiction. However, owing to the domestic circumstances and foreign influences, class struggle will continue to exist within certain limits for a long time, and may even sharpen under certain conditions. The principal contradiction in Chinese society is that between the people's growing material and cultural needs and the backward level of our social production. The other contradictions should be resolved in the course of resolving this principal one. It is essential to strictly distinguish and correctly handle the two different types of contradictions—the contradictions between the enemy and ourselves and those among the people.

The general task of the Communist Party of China at the present stage is to unite the people of all nationalities in working hard and self-reliantly to achieve, step by step, the modernization of our industry, agriculture, national defense and science and technology and make China a culturally advanced and highly democratic socialist country.

The focus of the work of the Communist Party of China is to lead the people of all nationalities in accomplishing the socialist modernization of our economy. It is necessary vigorously to expand the productive forces and gradually perfect socialist relations of production, in keeping with the actual level of the productive forces and as required for their expansion. It is necessary to strive for the gradual improvement of the standards of material and cultural life of the urban and rural population, based on the growth of production and social wealth.

The Communist Party of China leads the people, as they work for a high level of material civilization, in building a high level of socialist spiritual civilization. Major efforts should be made to promote education, science and culture, imbue the party members and the masses of the people with communist ideology, combat and overcome decadent bourgeois ideas, remnant feudal ideas and other nonproletarian ideas, and encourage the Chinese people to have lofty ideals, moral integrity, education and a sense of discipline.

The development and improvement of the socialist system is a long historical process. Fundamentally speaking, the socialist system is incomparably superior to the capitalist system, having eliminated the contradictions inherent in the capitalist system, which the latter itself is incapable of overcoming. Socialism enables the people truly to become masters of the country, gradually to shed the old ideas and ways formed under the system of exploitation and private ownership of the means of production, and steadily to raise their communist consciousness and foster common ideals, common ethics and a common discipline in their own ranks. Socialism can give full scope to the initiative and creativeness of the people, develop the productive forces rapidly, proportionately and in a planned way, and meet the growing material and cultural needs of the members of society. The cause of socialism is advancing and is bound gradually to triumph throughout the world along paths that are suited to the specific conditions of each country and are chosen by its people of their own free will.

The Chinese communists, with comrade Mao Zedong as their chief representative, created Mao Zedong thought by integrating the universal principles of Marxism-Leninism with the concrete practice of the Chinese revolution. Mao Zedong thought is Marxism-Leninism applied and developed in China—it consists of a body of theoretical principles concerning the revolution and construction in China and a summary of experience therein, both of which have been proved correct by practice—it represents the crystallized, collective wisdom of the Communist Party of China.

The Communist Party of China led the people of all nationalities in waging their prolonged revolutionary struggle against imperialism, feudalism and bureaucrat-capitalism, winning victory in the newdemocratic revolution and establishing the People's Republic of China—a people's democratic dictatorship. After the founding of the People's Republic, it led them in smoothly carrying out socialist transformation, completing the transition from new democracy to socialism, establishing the socialist system, and developing socialism in its economic, political and cultural aspects.

The Communist Party of China leads the people in promoting socialist democracy, perfecting the socialist legal system, and consolidating the people's democratic dictatorship. Effective measures should be taken to protect the people's right to run the affairs of the state and of society, and to manage economic and cultural undertakings and to strike firmly at hostile elements who deliberately sabotage the socialist system, and those who seriously breach or jeopardize public security. Great efforts should be made to strengthen the people's liberation army and national defense so that the country is prepared at all times to resist and wipe out any invaders.

The Communist Party of China upholds and promotes relations of equality, unity and mutual assistance among all nationalities in the country, persists in the policy of regional autonomy of minority nationalities, aids the areas inhabited by minority nationalities in their economic and cultural development, and actively trains and promotes cadres from among the minority nationalities.

The Communist Party of China unites with all workers, peasants and intellectuals, and with all the democratic parties, non-party democrats and the patriotic forces of all the nationalities in China in further expanding and fortifying the broadest possible patriotic united front embracing all socialist working people and all patriots who support socialism or who support the reunification of the motherland. We should work together with the people throughout the country, including our compatriots in Taiwan, Xianggang (Hong Kong) and Aomen (Macao) and Chinese nationals residing abroad, to accomplish the great task of reunifying the motherland.

In international affairs, the Communist Party of China takes the following basic stand: it adheres to proletarian internationalism and firmly unites with the workers of all lands, with the oppressed nations and oppressed peoples and with all peace-loving and justice-upholding organizations and personages in the common struggle against imperialism, hegemonism and colonialism and for the defense of world peace and promotion of human progress. It stands for the development of state relations between China and other countries on the basis of the five principles of mutual respect for sovereignty and territorial integrity, mutual nonaggression, non-interference in each other's internal affairs, equality and mutual benefit, and peaceful coexistence. It develops relations with communist parties and working-class parties in other countries on the basis of Marxism and the principles of independence, complete equality, mutual respect and non-interference in each other's internal affairs.

In order to lead China's people of all nationalities in attaining the great goal of socialist modernization, the Communist Party of China must strengthen itself, carry forward its fine traditions, enhance its fighting capacity and resolutely achieve the following three essential requirements:

First, a high degree of ideological and political unity. The Communist Party of China makes the realization of communism its maximum program, to which all its members must devote their entire lives. At the present stage, the political basis for the solidarity and unity of the whole party consists in adherence to the socialist road, to the people's democratic dictatorship, to the leadership of the party, and to Marxism-Leninism and Mao Zedong thought and in the concentration of our efforts on socialist modernization. The party's ideological line is to proceed from reality in all things, to integrate theory with practice, to seek truth from facts, and to verify and develop the truth through practice. In accordance with this ideological line, the whole party must scientifically sum up historical experience, investigate and study actual conditions, solve new problems in domestic and international affairs, and oppose all erroneous deviations, whether "left" or right.

Second, whole-hearted service to the people. The party has no special interests of its own apart from the interests of the working class and the broadest masses of the people. The program and policies of the party are precisely the scientific expressions of the fundamental interests of the working class and the broadest masses of the people. Throughout the process of leading the masses in struggle to realize the ideal of communism, the party always shares weal and woe with the people, keeps in closest contact with them, and does not allow any member to become divorced from the masses or place himself above them. The party persists in educating the masses in communist ideas and follows the mass line in its work, doing everything for the masses, relying on them in every task, and turning its correct views into conscious action by the masses.

Third, adherence to democratic centralism. Within the party, democracy is given full play, a high degree of centralism is practiced on the basis of democracy and a sense of organization and discipline is strengthened, so as to ensure unity of action throughout its ranks and the prompt and effective implementation of its decisions. In its internal political life, the party conducts criticism and self-criticism in the correct way, waging ideological struggles over matters of principle, upholding truth and rectifying mistakes. Applying the principle that all members are equally subject to party discipline, the party duly criticizes or punishes those members who violate it and expels those who persist in opposing and harming the party.

Party leadership consists mainly in political, ideological and organizational leadership. The party must formulate and implement correct lines, principles and policies, do its organizational, propaganda and educational work well and make sure that all party members play their exemplary vanguard role in every sphere of work and every aspect of social life. The party must conduct its activities within the limits permitted by the constitution and the laws of the state. It must see to it that the legislative, judicial and administrative organs of the state and the economic, cultural and people's organizations work actively and with initiative, independently, responsibly and in harmony. The party must strengthen its leadership over the trade unions, the communist youth league, the women's federation and other mass organizations, and give full scope to their roles.

The party members are a minority in the whole population, and they must work in close co-operation with the masses of non-party people in the common effort to make our socialist motherland ever stronger and more prosperous, until the ultimate realization of communism.

Chapter 1
Membership

Article 1: Any Chinese worker, peasant, member of the armed forces, intellectual or any other revolutionary who has reached the age of eighteen and who accepts the party's program and constitution and is willing to join and work actively in one of the party organizations, carry out the party's decisions and pay membership dues regularly may apply for membership of the Communist Party of China.

Article 2: Members of the Communist Party of China are vanguard fighters of the Chinese working class imbued with communist consciousness.

Members of the Communist Party of China must serve the people whole-heartedly, dedicate their whole lives to the realization of communism, and be ready to make any personal sacrifices.

Members of the Communist Party of China are at all times ordinary members of the working people. Communist Party members must not seek personal gain or privileges, although they are allowed personal benefits and job functions and powers as provided for by the relevant regulations and policies. . . .

Chapter II
Organizational System of the Party

Article 10: The party is an integral body organized under its program and constitution, on the principle of democratic centralism. It practices a high degree of centralism on the basis of a high degree of democracy.

The basic principles of democratic centralism as practiced by the party are as follows:

(1) Individual party members are subordinate to the party organization, the minority is subordinate to the majority, the lower party organizations are subordinate to the higher party organizations, and all the constituent organizations and members of the party are subordinate to the national congress and the Central Committee of the party.

(2) The party's leading bodies of all levels are elected except for the representative organs dispatched by them and the leading party members' groups in non-party organizations.

(3) The highest leading body of the party is the national congress and the Central Committee elected by it. The leading bodies of local party organizations are the party congresses at their respective levels and the party committees elected by them. . . .

(5) Party committees at all levels function on the principle of combining collective leadership with individual responsibility based on division of labor. All major issues shall be decided upon by the party committees after democratic discussion.

(6) The party forbids all forms of personality cult. It is necessary to ensure that the activities of the party leaders be subject to supervision by the party and the people, while at the same time to uphold the prestige of all leaders who represent the interests of the party and the people.

Article 11: The election of delegates to party congresses and members of party committees at all levels should reflect the will of the voters. Elections shall be held by secret ballot. The lists of candidates shall be submitted to the party organizations and voters for full deliberation and discussion. There may be a preliminary election in order to draw up a list of candidates for the formal election. Or there may be no preliminary election, in which case the number of candidates shall be greater than that of the persons to be elected. The voters have the right to inquire into the candidates, demand a change or reject one in favor of another. No organization or individual shall in any way compel voters to elect or not to elect any candidate. . . .

Article 15: Only the Central Committee of the party has the power to make decisions on major policies of a nationwide character.

Lower party organizations must firmly implement the decisions of higher party organizations. If lower organizations consider that any decisions of higher organizations do not suit actual conditions in their localities or departments, they may request modification. If the higher organizations insist on their original decisions, the lower organizations must carry out such decisions and refrain from publicly voicing their differences, but have the right to report on the next higher party organization.

Newspapers and journals and other means of publicity run by party organizations at all levels must propagate the line, policies and decisions of the party.

Article 16: Party organizations must keep to the principle of subordination of the minority to the majority in discussing and making decisions on any matter. Serious consideration should be given to the differing views of a minority. In case of controversy over major issues in which supporters of the two opposing views are nearly equal in number, except in emergencies where action must be taken in accordance with the majority view, the decision should be put off to allow for further investigation, study and exchange of opinions followed by another discussion. If still no decision can be made, the controversy should be reported to the next higher party organization for ruling.

When, on behalf of the party organization, an individual party member is to express views on major issues beyond the scope of existing party decisions, the content must be referred to the party organization for prior discussion and decision, or referred to the next higher party organization for instructions. No party member, whatever his position, is allowed to make decisions on major issues on his own. In an emergency, when a decision by an individual is unavoidable, the matter must be reported to the party organization immediately afterwards. No leader is allowed to decide matters arbitrarily on his own or to place himself above the party organization. . . .

Chapter III
Central Organizations of the Party

Article 18: The national congress of the party is held once every five years and convened by the Central Committee. It may be convened before the due date if the Central Committee deems it necessary or if more than one-third of the organizations at the provincial level so request. Except under extraordinary circumstances, the congress may not be postponed.

The number of delegates to the national congress of the party and the procedure governing their election shall be determined by the Central Committee.

Article 19: The functions and powers of the national congress of the party are as follows:

(1) To hear and examine the reports of the Central Committee.

(2) To hear and examine the reports of the Central Advisory Commission and the Central Commission for Discipline Inspection;

(3) To discuss and decide on major questions concerning the party;

(4) To revise the constitution of the party;

(5) To elect the Central Committee, and

(6) To elect the Central Advisory Commission and the Central Commission for Discipline Inspection.

Article 20: The Central Committee of the party is elected for a term of five years. However, when the next national congress is convened before or after its due date, the term will be correspondingly shortened or extended. Members and alternate members of the Central Committee must have a party standing of five years or more. . . .

The Central Committee of the party meets in plenary session at least once a year, and such sessions are convened by its Political Bureau.

When the national congress is not in session, the Central Committee carries out its decisions, directs the entire work of the party and represents the Communist Party of China in its external relations.

Article 21: The Political Bureau, the standing committee of the Political Bureau, the Secretariat and the general secretary of the Central Committee of the party are elected by the Central Committee in plenary session. The general secretary of the Central Committee must be a member of the standing committee of the Political Bureau.

When the Central Committee is not in session, the Political Bureau and its standing committee exercise the functions and powers of the Central Committee.

The Secretariat attends to the day-to-day work of the Central Committee under the direction of the Political Bureau and its standing committee.

The general secretary of the Central Committee is responsible for convening the meetings of the Political Bureau and its standing committee and presides over the work of the Secretariat.

The members of the Military Commission of the Central Committee are decided on by the Central Committee. The chairman of the Military Commission must be a member of the standing committee of the Political Bureau.

The central leading bodies and leaders elected by each Central Committee shall, when the next national congress is in session, continue to preside over the party's day-to-day work until the new central leading bodies and leaders are elected by the next Central Committee.

Article 22: The party's Central Advisory Commission acts as political assistant and consultant to the Central Committee. Members of the Central Advisory Commission must have a party standing of forty years or more, have rendered considerable service to the party, have fairly rich experience in leadership and enjoy fairly high prestige inside and outside the party.

The Central Advisory Commission is elected for a term of the same duration as that of the Central Committee. It elects, at its plenary meeting, its standing committee and its chairman and vice-chairmen, and reports the results to the Central Committee for approval. The chairman of the Central Advisory Commission must be a member of the standing committee of the Political Bureau. Members of the Central Advisory Commission may attend plenary sessions of the Central Committee as non-voting participants. The vice-chairmen of the Central Advisory Commission may attend plenary meetings of the Political Bureau as non-voting participants and, when the Political Bureau deems it necessary, other members of the standing committee of the Central Advisory Commission may do the same.

Working under the leadership of the Central Committee of the party, the Central Advisory Commission puts forward recommendations on the formulation and implementation of the party's principles and policies and gives advice upon request, assists the Central Committee in investigating and handling certain important questions, propagates the party's major principles and policies inside and outside the party, and undertakes such other tasks as may be entrusted to it by the Central Committee.

Article 23: Party organizations in the Chinese People's Liberation Army carry on their work in accordance with the instructions of the

Central Committee. The general political department of the Chinese People's Liberation Army is the political-work organ of the Military Commission. It directs party and political work in the army. The organizational system and organs of the party in the armed forces will be prescribed by the military Commission.

Chapter IV
Local Organizations of the Party

. . . Article 25: The functions and powers of the local party congresses at all levels are as follows:

(1) To hear and examine the reports of the party committees at the corresponding levels;

(2) To hear and examine the reports of the commissions for discipline inspection at the corresponding levels;

(3) To discuss and decide on major issues in the given areas . . .

Chapter V
Primary Organizations of the Party

Article 30: Primary party organizations are formed in factories, shops, schools, offices, city neighborhoods, people's communes, cooperatives, farms, townships, towns, companies of the People's Liberation Army and other basic units, where there are three or more full party members . . .

Article 32: The primary party organizations are militant bastions of the party in the basic units of society. Their main tasks are:

(1) To propagate and carry out the party's line, principles and policies, the decisions of the Central Committee of the party and other higher party organizations, and their own decisions; to give full play to the exemplary vanguard role of party members, and to unite and organize the cadres and the rank and file inside and outside the party in fulfilling the tasks of their own units.

(2) To organize party members to conscientiously study Marxism-Leninism and Mao Zedong thought, study essential knowledge concerning the party, and the party's line, principles and policies, and acquire general, scientific and professional knowledge.

(3) To delegate and supervise party members, ensure their regular participation in the activities of the party organization, see that party members truly fulfill their duties and observe discipline, and protect their rights from encroachment.

(4) To maintain close ties with the masses, constantly seek their criticisms and opinions regarding party members and the party's work, value the knowledge and rationalization proposals of the masses and experts, safeguard the legitimate rights and interests of the masses, show concern for their material and cultural life and help them improve it, do effective ideological and political work among them, and enhance their political consciousness. They must correct, by proper methods, the erroneous ideas and unhealthy ways

and customs that may exist among the masses, and properly handle the contradictions in their midst. . . .

Chapter VI
Party Cadres

Article 34: Party cadres are the backbone of the party's cause and public servants of the people. The party selects its cadres according to the principle that they should possess both political integrity and professional competence, persists in the practice of appointing people on their merits and opposes favoritism. It calls for genuine efforts to make the ranks of the cadres more revolutionary, younger in average age, better educated and more professionally competent. . . .

The party should attach importance to the training and promotion of women cadres and cadres from among the minority nationalities. . . .

Article 37: Leading party cadres at all levels, whether elected through democratic procedure or appointed by a leading body, are not entitled to lifelong tenure, and they can be transferred from or relieved of their posts. . . .

Chapter VII
Party Discipline

Article 38: A Communist Party member must consciously act within the bounds of party discipline.

Party organizations shall criticize, educate or take disciplinary measures against members who violate party discipline, depending on the nature and seriousness of their mistakes and in the spirit of "learning from past mistakes to avoid future ones, and curing the sickness to save the patient."

Article 39: There are five measures of party discipline: warning, serious warning, removal from party posts and proposals for their removal from non-party posts to the organizations concerned, placing on probation within the party, and expulsion from the party. . . .

It is strictly forbidden, within the party, to take any measures against a member that contravene the party constitution or the laws of the state, or to retaliate against or frame up comrades. Any offending organization or individual must be dealt with according to party discipline or the laws of the state. . . .

6

THE TAIWAN ISSUE FLARES UP

REAGAN STRIKES UP FOR TAIWAN

The American conservatives who had developed a close sense of identification with Taiwan entertained profound reservations about the Carter policy to move ahead with the normalization of U.S. relations with China. For one thing, it was, in their view, too one-sided, being done largely on Beijing's terms. For another, they were not satisfied that the continuation of unofficial relationship with Taiwan would be an adequate substitute for a formal defense treaty in terms of safeguarding Taiwan's security and U.S. interests in the island.

Represented by Senator Barry Goldwater (R, Ariz.) they had challenged the constitutionality of abrogating the U.S. mutual defense pact with Taiwan (the Republic of China) by filing a suit in the U.S. District Court for the District of Columbia. They had won the first round of their legal battle when Judge Oliver Gasch found that Carter had violated the Constitution by unilateral abrogation of the defense treaty without the consent of Congress. Upon appeal, the ruling was reversed.

On November 30, 1979, by a four-to-one vote, the U.S. Court of

Appeals for the District of Columbia ruled Carter's action legal, stating that the president must have the power "to conduct our foreign policy in a rational and effective manner."

Judge George E. MacKinnon, although indicating that he concurred in part with the majority, dissented from the ruling. MacKinnon said Carter would need the approval of both houses of Congress to terminate the treaty on January 1, 1980.

The unsigned majority opinion said its decision did not mean the president's authority to end treaties was absolute. "History shows us that there are too many variables to lay down any hard-and-fast constitutional rules," the decision stated.

But the court noted the "novel and somewhat indefinite relationship" between the U.S. and Taiwan and said: "The subtleties involved in maintaining amorphous relationships are often the very stuff of diplomacy, a field in which the president, not Congress, has responsibility under our Constitution."

Not the ones to surrender after one setback, they injected the Taiwan issue into the 1980 presidential election campaign. Governor Ronald Reagan, the Republican candidate for president, advocated upgrading U.S. relations with Taiwan, making them official between governments, rather than an unofficial relationship between the U.S. and "the people of Taiwan." This turned into a long-distance diplomatic spat with China on August 16–26, 1980.

The question arose on August 16 at a news conference in Los Angeles as Reagan's running mate, George Bush, prepared to leave on a trip to China and Japan.

Reagan's call for the U.S. to re-establish an official government relationship with Taiwan was "not going to be the subject matter on the table," Bush assured reporters. "I know these people," he added. Bush had been head of the U.S. liaison office in Beijing for a year before normal diplomatic relations were established.

Under the Taiwan Relations Act of 1979, official government relations between the U.S. and Taiwan were ruled out. Diplomatic relations were handled by the American Institute, a private foundation financed by the U.S. government.

In proclaiming official U.S. diplomatic recognition of China on January 1, 1979, the U.S. agreed with Beijing that Taiwan, which called itself the Republic of China, was a province of China.

At the news conference on August 16, Reagan said he had been misunderstood as advocating full diplomatic relations with Taiwan.

As the conference continued, Reagan was asked if he no longer favored governmental relations with Taiwan.

He replied that from the very first he was "talking about an official government relationship." There were provisions of the Taiwan

Act for governmental relations, he said. "They just haven't been implemented."

"Would you advocate their implementation, establishing government-to-government relations?" he was asked.

"Yes, I think that liaison office is what I stress," he replied. "That could be official."

China's Communist Party newspaper, *People's Daily*, protested Reagan's remarks in a commentary on August 19. It was "sheer deception," the paper said, for Reagan to try to "convince people that the U.S. can establish 'official' relations with Taiwan while continuing friendly relations with the People's Republic of China."

Reagan's remarks constituted a "flagrant speech attempting to create two Chinas," the paper said.

Bush, in Tokyo for a meeting with Japanese Prime Minister Zenko Suzuki, denied, on August 19, that Reagan was advocating a "two-Chinas" policy.

Arriving in Beijing August 20, Bush assured Chinese reporters the Taiwan Act was the law, and that under it, there was "no give-ground, no set-the-clock-back, no two-Chinas policy."

"I hope you will accurately convey what I say on this matter," he told reporters for Chinese news agency Xinhua.

At a meeting with Chinese Foreign Minister Huang Hua in Beijing on August 21, Bush was told: "We hold that any remarks that have the effect of retrogressing from the current state of Sino-American relations would do harm to the continuing basis on which our relations are built and . . . to the interests of the Chinese and American people and the people of the whole world."

Bush reportedly assured Huang that Reagan would not renew official U.S. ties with Taiwan. The Republican Party platform called for "continuing to improve relations with the People's Republic of China," he said.

Despite Bush's assurances, the Chinese continued to protest Reagan's use of words and phrases such as the "Republic of China," and "that country" and "official" relations in connection with Taiwan, which by most of the world's nations had been relegated diplomatically to the status of a province of China.

Bush's explanation on August 22 was that Reagan used the phrases "out of habit." During the day, Bush met privately with Deputy Prime Minister Deng Xiaoping.

Back in the U. S., Reagan was reluctant to discuss the subject at a news conference in Dallas, but he conceded on August 22 he still favored "official government relations" with Taiwan.

Bush's mission to reassure China about Reagan's Taiwan policy was being "canceled out" by such statements, Xinhua said, on August 23.

Reagan's remarks were "absolutely not a slip of the tongue," it said, and he had "insulted one billion Chinese people."

If Reagan's "erroneous advocacy of two Chinas is put into practice, it will seriously harm" relations, it said. "It is better to state this point clearly and early."

Returning home, Bush joined Reagan at another news conference in Los Angeles on August 25, for release of their "definitive" policy statement on Taiwan and China.

If elected, Reagan said, he would abide by the Taiwan Relations Act and not try to change the status of the office of Taiwan.

That liaison office, although technically a private foundation, he went on, was so permeated with government influence that it was, in essence, an official office of the U.S. government.

"I would not pretend, as Carter does, that the relationship we now have with Taiwan, enacted by our Congress, is not official," he said. "I am satisfied that this act provides an official and adequate basis for safeguarding our relationship with Taiwan, and I pledge to enforce it."

Asked why he was changing positions from a former stance that the Taiwan office was unofficial and should, in fact, be upgraded into an official relationship, Reagan responded that if that was the case "then I misstated."

It was clear, he said, that he and the Beijing government "don't see eye to eye on Taiwan."

On August 26, U.S. Ambassador to China Leonard Woodcock warned that comments by Ronald Reagan had endangered diplomatic ties with the People's Republic of China.

Woodcock, holding a news conference in the Chinese capital, said: "To endanger the carefully crafted relationship between the P.R.C. and the U.S., which is progressing so well and to mutual benefit, is to run the risk of gravely weakening the American international position at a dangerous time."

Woodcock maintained that he was expressing his own opinion and was not acting on orders from the Carter administration.

He noted that both Republican and Democratic administrations had shaped current U.S. policy with regard to Taiwan and China. "I think it goes without saying that this triangular relationship is most delicate. . . . It is essential that we preserve both the fact and the appearance of unofficiality in the United States-Taiwan relation."

BEIJING WARY OF REAGAN POLICY

In view of Reagan's controversial stand on the China-Taiwan issue, the Chinese government responded to his election with a distinct lack of enthusiasm. The statement issued by the foreign ministry following the election stressed the importance of adhering strictly to the terms of the past U.S. agreements which recognized Beijing as the only legitimate government of China and Taiwan as a province of the country.

Aware of the uneasy feeling in Beijing about the incoming Reagan administration, two prominent U.S. Republicans visited China January 2–5 and Taiwan January 5–8. Anna Chennault, a member of the party's finance committee, and Senator Ted Stevens (R, Alaska) assistant majority leader in the new Republican-controlled Senate, insisted they were not visiting the two places as emissaries for the incoming administration of President-elect Ronald Reagan.

Chennault and Stevens also denied they were bearing messages or acting as mediators between China and Taiwan.

Chennault, a native of China, was the widow of Lieutenant General Claire Lee Chennault, who had commanded the World War II Flying Tigers, an American volunteer air group in China and Burma. She was a staunch supporter of Taiwan and reiterated her backing for its government on completion of her tour.

However, she was also quoted by the *Los Angeles Times* on January 5 as stating: "In politics and international affairs, you must keep an open mind and keep on learning and look at the world in reality. . . . My way of looking at the world in the '60s was different from the '50s, and in the '70s, it was different from the '60s, and now we are coming into the '80s. We have to reassess our positions, broaden our base, be humble enough to learn and have the courage to change our positions. . . . If you don't learn, you . . . look at the world in an unrealistic way."

Chennault and Stevens met with a number of Chinese leaders in Beijing and on January 4 they conferred with Deputy Premier Deng Xiaoping.

During their stay in Taipei, Chennault and Stevens met with President Chiang Ching-kuo and other Nationalist leaders.

Whatever effect this visit by two prominent American Republicans had on Beijing, it did not reduce Chinese sensitivity to arms sales to Taiwan by the United States or any of its allies. If anything, it was heightened. The country which drew Beijing's hypersensitive reaction at this point was the Netherlands, which on November 29, 1980, had approved a sale of two submarines to Taiwan following consultation with Washington. On January 19, the Chinese government informed the Netherlands envoy in Beijing that it was downgrading its diplomatic relations with The Hague in retaliation for the planned Dutch sale of two submarines to Taiwan. A foreign ministry note handed to Ambassador Jan Knepplehout called for his departure and his replacement by a charge d'affaires.

The note said the proposed sale, first approved by Holland on November 29, 1980, "seriously infringes on China's sovereignty . . . interferes with and hinders the cause of peaceful reunification of Taiwan . . ." and "does harm to peace and stability in the Asian-Pacific region."

Beijing's action followed weeks of protest to the Dutch government. China had first warned Knepplehout on January 2 of his possible expulsion if the deal with Taiwan was implemented.

On January 17, the Chinese press had accused the U.S. of being involved in the deal. Xinhua said the Dutch government had disclosed on December 4 that it had sought U.S. advice and was told by Washington that the Netherlands "would have to pay a certain political price for the sale," but that its ties with China would not suffer great damage.

Xinhua scoffed at the Dutch arguments that the sale was merely a transaction between private Dutch and Taiwanese companies. There was quite "a difference between submarines and butter or beef," the news agency said.

China and the Netherlands recalled their envoys from each other's countries on February 27 and March 2, respectively. The Chinese envoy had not been at her post in The Hague since she left it in October 1980, when the dispute over the Taiwan deal first surfaced.

China decided on recalling the envoys after Dutch Premier Andreas van Agt had given final approval to the submarine sale on February 20. The lower house of the Dutch parliament voted, on March 5, to uphold the premier's decision.

The Reagan administration came in for direct criticism from Beijing when, on May 12, White House counselor Edwin Meese told visiting newsmen from Taiwan that the United States remained committed to the 1979 Taiwan Relations Act. Washington, Meese told them, was bound to support the act, including its provisions permitting arms sales to Taiwan and allowing certain Taiwan officials into U.S. government offices.

On May 14, the Chinese news agency, Xinhua, attacked Meese's statement, saying: "Meese's remarks, which run counter to the basic principles laid down in the 1978 communique on the establishment of Sino-American relations, cannot but arouse concern among the Chinese people."

China regarded the Taiwan Relations Act as incompatible with the U.S.-China normalization accord and was especially concerned about arms sales to Taiwan.

On May 14, the U.S. State Department said Meese's remarks did not imply that the U.S. had an official relationship with Taiwan.

THE UNITED STATES TO SELL ARMS TO CHINA

The Reagan administration decided to bolster faltering American-Chinese relations by making major changes in U.S. policy with regard to arms sale and the transfer of technologies. The bearer of the "good tidings" was Secretary of State Alexander M. Haig, who arrived in Beijing on June 14 for a three-day visit.

In Haig's first meeting with Foreign Minister Huang Hua on June 14, both men were in agreement that the world's principal problem was "Soviet hegemonism," a senior aide to Haig told reporters.

In a banquet toast later that day, Huang said Beijing "attached importance to the strategic relationship between China and the United States" despite their differences "in policy and point of view."

Haig, in turn, said in his toast that "Chinese-American cooperation is all the more important when we confront serious threats to peace and tranquility."

At the conclusion of the visit, Haig announced on June 16 that the U.S. had decided to sell weapons to China. The decision had been made, the secretary said, to remove China from the munitions-control restrictions preventing any sale of lethal weapons to that country. All sales of military equipment to China would be made on a case-by-case basis, Haig said. But he pointed out that it was not certain that China would want to purchase what was offered or that the U.S. would find it "prudent" to sell the materiel most desired by China.

Haig said he had informed the Chinese officials in his discussion that President Reagan had made the policy decision to treat China "as a friendly nation with which the United States is not allied but with which it shares many interests."

As for the U.S. position on Taiwan, Haig said he had explained that the "unofficial relationship" between Washington and Taipei, in effect since diplomatic relations had been ended in 1979, "will be continued" and that "this was understood" by the Chinese officials with whom he had conferred.

Haig's visit, according to the secretary's announcement, produced the following agreements:

- Premier Zhao Ziyang had accepted an invitation from President Reagan to visit the U.S., probably in 1982.
- A Chinese delegation headed by Liu Huaqing, deputy chief of

state for the army, would visit the U.S. in August to work out the specifics.

- The U.S. would introduce legislation to amend U.S. laws that "lump China with the Soviet bloc." This applied especially to export-control procedures that would be eased to facilitate expanded trade. (The U.S. National Security Council had agreed, on June 4, on the measures to ease trade with China. The aim was "to treat China as a friendly, less-developed country and no longer as a member of the international communist conspiracy," one official said.)
- China would permit American tax experts to come to China to discuss problems raised by American oil company operations in China. The U.S. firms feared double taxation by Chinese and U.S. authorities in connection with their exploration activities in Chinese waters.
- The U.S. had lifted the ban on the export of IBM computers to China for use in a United Nations-sponsored census of China. The Defense Department had held up the shipment of the computers for fear they might be used for military purposes.
- The U.S. and China would establish a special joint commission on commerce and trade. It would supplement the committee on joint economic affairs already in existence.
- Consular agreements would be expanded. China would open new missions in New York, Chicago and Honolulu. It already had two in operation—in San Francisco and Houston. The U.S. would set up consulates in Chengdu, Shenyang and Wuhan in addition to the two at Canton and Shanghai.

In a farewell dinner given by Haig later on June 16, Foreign Minister Huang Hua said the secretary's visit "has helped to deepen our mutual understanding and yielded positive results."

President Reagan, asked about the prospective arms sales to China in his press conference on June 16, said that he himself considered it "a normal part of the process of improving our relations" with China, to "move them to the same status of many other countries, and not necessarily military allies of ours. . . ."

The Nationalist regime on Taiwan did not share the president's calm assessment. The Taipei foreign ministry assailed the U.S.-China arms agreement on June 17, saying "it is not in the interest of peace and stability of East Asia and the Pacific region." The accord, the ministry said, would be harmful "to both the United States and the other free nations in this region."

At the same time, the ministry praised President Reagan for having expressed support at his June 16 news conference for the Taiwan

Relations Act. Reagan said, "I have not changed my feeling about Taiwan." The act, the President noted, "provides for [U.S.] defense equipment being sold to Taiwan" and "I intend to live up" to it.

Following up on the agreement reached by Secretary of State Haig during his trip to Beijing, the Commerce Department announced, on July 9, that it planned to ease standards governing the export of high technology goods to China. The items covered included computers, microprocessors and machine tools. Officials said the items were more advanced than those that had been sold to the Soviet Union before such trade was restricted in response to the Soviet invasion of Afghanistan.

The items had possible military applications, and the decision to permit their sale to China required the approval of the Coordinating Committee, a group made up of members of the North Atlantic Treaty Organization.

BEIJING RENEWS UNITY BID TO TAIWAN

In the aftermath of normalization of American-Chinese relations, the Chinese government held out an olive branch to the Nationalist regime on Taiwan. Indeed, there were indications that the relations between the mainland and Taiwan were improving on a number of fronts.

One aspect of this was China's decision to let goods from the mainland be exported customs-free to Taiwan, it was reported on April 7. According to the General Administration of Customs in Beijing, "This new measure has been adopted to promote trade between foreign trade corporations on the mainland and industrial and business circles in Taiwan under existing conditions."

China and Taiwan, according to a news report on April 9, 1980, were encouraging U.S. companies to carry on business with both the mainland and the island community. Many U.S. companies used separate divisions to carry on commerce with China and Taiwan, but this was viewed as no longer necessary by some American businessmen. Robert Parker, president of the American Chamber of Commerce in Taiwan, said that U.S. companies and the State Department were being overly cautious with regard to doing business on both sides of the Formosa Strait.

"They're falling behind on this back in the home offices and in Washington," Parker said.

Another point of contact between Taiwan and China was revealed on April 9, when an official of the Chinese coastal province of Fujian said that China had helped rescue 1,000 Taiwanese fishermen in distress in 1979. The fishermen had been permitted to return to Taiwan, the official said.

The official noted that Taiwan had also provided assistance to some fishermen from the mainland.

There had been reports that fishermen from both sides had been involved in smuggling activities in which television sets and tape recorders from Taiwan were exchanged for traditional medicines from the mainland. Both governments had sought to avoid publicizing this commerce.

Following Secretary of State Haig's visit to Beijing, the paramount leader, Deng Xiaoping, renewed a call for political union to the Nationalists. The message was contained in a *Min Bao* newspaper article on August 25, which gave the text of an interview with Deng held on July 18. After stressing that the Communists had succeeded in unifying China where the Kuomintang had failed, Deng offered a significant change in the Chinese approach to the unity question.

"The Chinese Communist Party wants to persist in its leadership and to be good in exercising leadership," he said. But he was reported as saying—citing two past instances of cooperation between the Communists and the Kuomintang, the Chinese Nationalist Party, that the two parties "can cooperate for a third time. They can compete with each other. They can even lead together."

Since it began pressing for unification talks in 1979, Beijing had always maintained that while Taiwan could maintain its own army and economic system, the Taiwan leadership would have to accept Taiwan's status as a province of a Chinese nation led by the Communists.

The "joint leadership" idea was floated a second time in an early September commentary by the *Hong Kong News*, an English-language paper that often transmitted the Communist point of view.

The commentary, as quoted in a story datelined September 15, told readers, "It is also possible to have joint leadership." The paper continued, "This means Taiwan's Nationalist Chinese Party can not only cooperate, but can also jointly lead the country."

The commentary also offered an unprecedented threat of force in the event of Taiwan independence. Although Taiwan had denounced Beijing's previous unity gestures as "united front tricks," President Chiang Ching-Kuo was believed to remain as committed as the Communists to reuniting China, albeit under different leadership. It was felt in Beijing, according to Western diplomats, that prospects of stemming the Taiwan independence movement and reuniting China would be better while the ailing Taiwan president survived than under any possible successors.

A *Los Angeles Times* story of September 10 said that President Reagan was being urged by some of his advisers to visit both Taiwan and Beijing in 1982 in an effort to get unity talks off the ground.

Despite the interest aroused by the oblique overtures from Beijing on reunification, Taiwan's rejection of them was firm. In his opening speech of the current session of the Legislative Yuan on September 15, Premier Sun Yen-suan dismissed them as merely "a trick."

This, however, did not discourage Beijing from proceeding to a more formal official statement issued on September 30 under the signature of Marshal Ye Jianying, the chairman of the Standing Committee of the National People's Congress.

After extending "festive greetings" to all Chinese, "including the compatriots in Taiwan," Ye declared that "a relaxed atmosphere has set in across the Taiwan Straits."

"I would take this opportunity," he said, "to elaborate on the policy concerning the return of Taiwan to the motherland for the realization of peaceful reunification."

His statement then made the following nine proposals:

- Talks should begin "as soon as possible" on a reciprocal basis "to accomplish the great cause of national unification."
- Mutual arrangements should be made to facilitate exchange of mail, trade and tourism between Taiwan and the mainland.
- After unification, Taiwan could retain "a high degree of autonomy as a special administrative region," with the right to maintain its own armed forces; Ye pledged China would "not interfere with local affairs on Taiwan."
- Taiwan's "current socioeconomic system," including property rights and foreign investments, could be preserved.
- "People in authority" in Taiwan "may take up posts of leadership in national political bodies and participate in running the state."
- The central government would provide aid "when Taiwan's local finance is in difficulty."
- China would extend freedom of entry and exit and freedom from discrimination to any Taiwanese who wished to settle on the mainland.
- Taiwan businessmen would be encouraged to invest in the mainland, with a "guarantee" of their "legal rights, interests and profits."
- Beijing would welcome "proposals and suggestions" from "public figures of all circles" in Taiwan regarding reunification, which the statement called "the responsibility of all Chinese."

"Taiwan's return to the embrace of the motherland," Ye said, "is a great and glorious mission history has bequeathed to our generation."

The final passage appeared to reflect an increasing sense of urgency in Beijing over growing Taiwanese sentiment for permanent independence from the mainland—an idea once as abhorrent to the Kuomintang leaders as to the Communists:

"We hope that the Kuomintang authorities will stick to their one-China position and their opposition to 'two Chinas' and that they will . . . forget previous ill will and join hands with us," Ye urged, "so as to win glory for our ancestors, bring benefit to our posterity and write a new and glorious page in the history of the Chinese nation."

Despite the wide-ranging proposals, three significant conditions remained. Chinese Vice-Premier Bo Yibo had spelled them out in an interview September 28, two days before Ye's dramatic public appeal.

The first two were symbolic. Taiwan must, he said, abandon the name "Republic of China" and agree it was part of the People's Republic. Taiwan must also adopt the communist flag as its national flag.

Finally, Bo said, Taiwan must relinquish all responsibility for foreign affairs to the central government. Within this national framework, however, Taiwanese autonomy could be extensive. "We won't interfere in their way of life," he said.

Although Ye's proposals emphasized the carrot rather than the stick, there was nothing in his statement to indicate that the conditions spelled out by Bo did not still apply.

All previous feelers had been rejected, and the latest was immediately labeled "propaganda" by Taiwan. A September 30 *New York Times* story, however, said that the new proposals were unofficially being "studied" by Taiwan.

Beijing followed up with yet another overture—this time, an invitation from Hu Yaobang, the general secretary of the Communist Party, to President Chiang Ching-kuo and other nationalist leaders. Hu's invitation announcing October 10 as marking the "Double Tenth" national holiday, said that the Taiwanese leaders would be welcome to visit their "native places" on the mainland.

Hu told a Beijing rally there would be no conditions. "It would be good if they wanted to talk to us, but they are also warmly welcome if they do not want to talk," he said.

Hu warned outsiders, however, that "the question of Taiwan is entirely China's internal affair."

This move on the part of the mainland leadership fared no better than its previous overtures. President Chiang had told a Kuomintang meeting on October 7: "To talk peace with the Chinese Communists is to invite death. . . . We shall never negotiate with the Chinese Communists."

ARMS SALES TO TAIWAN

One of the key elements in U.S. policy toward China—one that turned out to be troublesome—had to do with arms sales to Taiwan, which Beijing objected to as intervention in China's internal affairs. At the time when the Reagan administration made a decision to proceed with arms sales to Beijing, it had a sale of new fighter planes to Taiwan under consideration.

Taiwan's air force flew American F-5E Tiger fighters and as early as 1978 had made overtures to the U.S. about buying more sophisticated replacements, such as a more advanced version of the F-5 known as the F-5G or the high-powered F-16. (The term FX was used to describe both fighters under consideration.)

Beijing registered its objection to this prospective arms sale in the strongest terms. Thus, in advance of Secretary of State Haig's Beijing trip, on June 10 the Chinese foreign ministry declared that China "would rather not buy any U.S. weapons, than agree to the U.S. continuous interference in China's internal affairs by selling weapons to Taiwan."

The ministry added: "Should the U.S., defying our repeated vigorous opposition, continue to sell weapons to Taiwan, we will be compelled to make a strong response."

A government commentary published on June 12 by the Xinhua news agency warned that U.S. attempts to "sell arms to China in exchange for China's consent to U.S. arms sales to Taiwan" were "doomed to failure."

Noting the constant U.S. reference "to China's strategic position and role," the commentary insisted, however, that "the crux of further strategic relations between the two countries remains that the United States stop developing all contacts with Taiwan that go beyond nongovernmental relations in keeping with the principles laid down in the [1978] China-U.S. joint communique on the establishment of diplomatic relations."

Indications that the Reagan administration was considering selling advanced fighters to Taiwan were of increasing concern to China. Senator John Glenn (D, Ohio) reported August 17 on talks with the Chinese leaders. Glenn said that they believed the U.S. had reneged on an understanding that arms sales to Taiwan were to be slashed or stopped after the normalization of U.S.-China relations in 1979.

The Chinese government brought up this question when former President Jimmy Carter and his wife Rosalyn paid a visit to Beijing in the latter part of August. After three days of meeting with Chinese leaders, Carter declared on August 27 that the U.S. had never agreed to limit the duration of its arms sales to Taiwan. Carter said, however, that he had promised in 1978 that the U.S. would sell only "defensive" weapons to Taiwan.

Carter commented on administration policy on several occasions. On August 28, Carter called Reagan's China policy "compatible" with his own and said that administration officials had assured him they intended to fulfill Carter's agreements. He added that arms sales to Taiwan "should not pose any threat whatsoever to the mainland."

The U.S. arms sale to Taiwan soon turned into the thorniest issue in American-Chinese relations. Chinese Foreign Minister Huang Hua visited Washington, D.C. for two days of talks with administration officials on October 28–29. Early accounts said the talks skirted the arms issue entirely, but later ones said it had been a key question.

A story in the November 10 *Los Angeles Times* said an alternative plan had arisen in the wake of Huang's visit, to extend Taiwan's contract for the F-5E while upgrading the plane's engines and electronics. One diplomat acknowledged that Beijing would never "accept" any arms sale to Taiwan but said, "This is something they might not object so loudly to."

The administration was near to approving the sale, according to a story in the same day's *New York Times*. Although the State Department insisted there had been "no decision even in principle," the *Times* quoted unidentified officials in the White House, the Defense Department and the State Department as saying planning for the sale was proceeding. The F-16 had been ruled out, the story said, and the improved F-5E Tiger was now in the running.

A November 11 article by the Xinhua news agency, datelined Washington and written in response to the recent press reports, restated China's uncompromising opposition to the sale. "How to handle this crucial issue is a litmus test of whether the U.S. government respects the sovereign rights of China," the article warned. China had long hinted that it would be forced to review its relationship with the U.S. if the arms sale went through.

The Chinese ambassador to the U.S. seemed to give credence to the idea of an enhanced F-5E as a possible solution. On November 16, Chai Zemin said Beijing objected "in principle" to a sale and warned that U.S.-China relations would "stagnate or even backtrack" in the event of a sale. But he also said for the first time that Beijing's reaction "will be determined by the circumstances, in light of the nature and amount of sales."

On November 25, however, China closed that door. "Sales of weapons, whatever type they might be, constitute . . . an intervention in China's internal affairs," said a Xinhua commentary. "The only possible way out is to abandon policies that violate China's sovereignty and interfere in her internal affairs," it said. The imminent U.S. decision suggested in November did not materialize.

A senior Chinese diplomat, quoted by the *New York Times* on December 27, said "We have put our message through to American officials." The gist of that message, he said, was that if the administration went ahead with the sale, "it doesn't leave us much room to maneuver. We won't have much choice except to retaliate strongly."

On December 28, the administration announced a large-scale sale of spare parts to Taiwan. Officials said the $97 million sale was unconnected with the FX issue and that China had not been notified in advance.

A State Department spokesman said: "We feel our position with the People's Republic of China has been consistent. We intend to continue defensive arms sales to Taiwan in a prudent manner."

On December 31, the *People's Daily* printed a tough response to the American sale. It said the U.S. had "failed to honor its commitment" to respect China's sovereignty and had "resorted to various prevarications" on the issue for three years. It called the issue a "severe test" of American intentions toward China.

The paper said: "We must state explicitly that, if the United States desires to preserve and develop its relations with China, it must seek, on the basis of genuine respect for China's sovereignty, a solution to the issue of selling arms to Taiwan. There is no other way."

The Reagan administration circumvented the Chinese objection with a decision, announced on January 11, 1982, not to sell the advanced fighter aircraft Taiwan had requested, but to let Taiwan continue coproducing the model that was the mainstay of its air force.

The State Department announcement said the FX had been ruled out on the grounds that "no military need for such aircraft exists"; Taiwan could meet its requirements by replacing "aging aircraft," it said. The statement reaffirmed President Reagan's "personal concern for the well-being of the people of Taiwan" and said continued production of the F-5E would fulfill a commitment to enable Taiwan "to maintain a sufficient self-defense capability."

There was immediate criticism from conservatives in Congress, who were generally strong supporters of Taiwan. Senator Jesse Helms (R, N.C.) said President Reagan had assured him "only last month" of his "total support" for Taiwan. "If we're going to play rhetorical games," Helms warned, "I will have to be more cautious in the future."

Other legislators criticized the administration for not consulting Congress. Senator John Glenn (D, Ohio) said that Secretary of State Alexander Haig had "guaranteed" that Congress would not be shut out of the decision and complained that that pledge had not been kept.

Congressman Stephen J. Solarz, chairman of the House Foreign Affairs Asian affairs subcommittee, however, praised what he called a "farsighted decision."

Administration officials told Congress that a quick decision was necessary because the Polish crisis required China to be part of a united front against the Soviet Union, according to the *Washington Post* on January 13.

Senator Charles Percy (R, Ill.), chairman of the Senate Foreign Relations Committee, had confidentially informed members of the committee on December 15, 1981 that they would be consulted, according to the story. Percy and Senate Majority Leader Howard H. Baker Jr. (R, Tenn.) were informed of the plan by cable while on overseas trips a few days before the announcement.

On January 12, the Taiwan foreign ministry said it took exception to the claim that Taiwan's defense needs could be met by replacement of existing aircraft. It said Beijing had not abandoned its intention of subjugating Taiwan by force.

Beijing, on its part, also took exception to the Reagan administration's decision to sell arms to Taiwan. Speaking through its official news agency, Xinhua, the Beijing government issued a "strong protest" on January 11, saying that "the current problems in Sino-American relations" resulted from "Washington's obstinate stand on arms sales to Taiwan," which the agency described as "one of China's provinces." The responses were made as Undersecretary of State John Holdridge opened talks in Beijing aimed at persuading China to accept the sale.

Chinese officials were particularly vexed that the administration's decision was presented as a fait accompli, according to a January 12 *New York Times* story. The Chinese were told of the decision by Holdridge the same day that the administration made its public announcement. White House officials said press accounts had forced a premature announcement of the sale.

China took no immediate action in response to the announcement, and, on January 13, Holdridge described his confidential talks with Chinese leaders as "useful and a success." The Chinese statement, however, said only that areas of "mutual concern" had been discussed.

With Beijing and Washington locked in disagreement over U.S. arms sales to Taiwan, there was no fanfare to mark the tenth anniversary of the Shanghai communique of 1972, issued at the end of former President Nixon's historic visit to China. President Reagan and Prime Minister Zhao Ziyang exchanged letters, both dated February 28. Otherwise, there was no public commemoration of any kind.

Beijing's strenuous opposition notwithstanding, the Reagan administration moved ahead with its decision to sell $60 million worth of military supplies and spare parts to Taiwan. The administration sent a letter of notification to both houses of Congress on April 15, as required by the law. Unless both houses rejected the request within 30 days, the sale would be approved. Formal notification had been delayed for several months in light of warnings from China about a possible deterioration in relations, but no substantial congressional opposition had arisen to date.

A State Department spokesman stressed that there were "no weapons of any kind involved" in the package. The contents, which had not been publicly disclosed, reportedly included replacement parts for the aging F-5E fighters that were produced in Taiwan under American license, as well as for their F-100 and F-104 fighters. The Defense Department stressed that the sale of equipment to the Taiwan government "will not affect the basic military balance in the region."

As expected, the Chinese government immediately lodged a "strong protest." But its response this time was milder than had been feared, coming after weeks of warnings from Chinese government officials and from press reports that the sale would occasion "a retrogression" in relations with Washington, sparking apprehensions that American-Chinese relations would be down-graded.

In the Chinese protest, received by the U.S. at the Chinese foreign ministry on April 14, Beijing acknowledged what it called Washington's "three-point explanation and assurance" of the Taiwan sale. The three points were as follows: The spare parts package had been promised to Taiwan before the U.S. and China began discussions on the matter last fall; the sale did not involve any weapons, only spare parts; and the U.S. wouldn't consider military transfers to Taiwan while Beijing and Washington "were continuing their bilateral discussions on a settlement of the question of arms sales."

The Chinese statement concluded: "If the U.S. government should continue to disregard China's sovereignty and go back on the above assurance given to the Chinese side, it must be held responsible for all the consequences arising therefrom."

THE UNITED STATES AGREES TO CUT ARMS SALES TO TAIWAN

In the wake of the arms sale to Taiwan, two Republican senators went to China, one to Beijing and the other to Taipei. The one who went to Beijing was Senate Majority Leader Howard Baker (R, Tenn.) His three-day trip in the first week of June coincided with a trip by Senator Barry Goldwater (R, Ariz.) to assure the Nationalist government of continuing U.S. support.

Baker met with reporters on June 1, following his talks with Communist Party Vice-Chairman Deng Xiaoping. Deng, Baker said, wanted the U.S. Congress to abrogate the Taiwan Relations Act which authorized the sale of weapons to Taiwan. Although stating that he doubted whether Congress would "abrogate or modify" the act "to a major extent," Baker noted that its language didn't "require" the arms sales. His statement implied that an agreement might be reached that didn't necessitate amending the act.

In replying to a question about the Taiwan Relations Act, Baker hastily corrected an apparent slip of the tongue concerning Taiwan's status, saying: "I think the Taiwan Relations Act spells out a reasonable relationship between our two countries and—no, no, not between our two countries—the people of Taiwan."

Upon his departure on June 2, Baker told reporters that the Chinese "took my hide off about Taiwan."

Saying that Deng was clearly "concerned for the future of the relationship" between China and the U.S., Baker added that the Chinese leader had invited Reagan to China.

Goldwater, who made a weeklong trip to Taipei ending on June 4, urged continued U.S. arms sales to Taiwan, rejecting Beijing's reunification proposals. Senator Goldwater's position on this issue was being backed by U.S. conservatives. Not surprisingly, the leaders of 28 conservative groups sent a letter to President Reagan on July 8, warning him that any reduction in U.S. arms sales to Taiwan would infuriate "millions of conservative voters."

Gary Jarmin, a member of the coalition and director of the American Council for a Free Asia, said in a news conference that any move toward cutting off military support for Taiwan would bring on "such a vicious backlash" against Reagan that it would "make his head spin."

The statement was endorsed by leaders of such groups as the National Conservative Action Committee, the Young Republicans and the Moral Majority.

It was made in response to a report that, shortly before his June 25 resignation, former Secretary of State Alexander M. Haig Jr. had recommended an eventual phaseout of all U.S. arms sales to Taiwan. That recommendation had been designed to alleviate the increasing tension with Beijing over the Taiwan issue.

The conservative leaders warned Reagan not to accept Haig's recommendation. They said that such a policy change would deal "an ultimate and humiliating blow to Taiwan."

The conservatives also called for a downgrading of U.S. relations with Beijing. China had threatened such a diplomatic breakdown if the Taiwan arms sale issue was not resolved. The conservative leaders stated, "In fact, such a downgrading would help to restore a more realistic and balanced China policy."

The conservatives were fighting a losing battle. By then, the bilateral discussions between China and the U.S., looking toward a resolution of the thorny issue, had made significant headway. In a *New York Times* story, datelined July 28, Senator Barry Goldwater (R, Ariz.) was reported as disclosing that the U.S. was awaiting Beijing's response to a U.S. plan to resolve the Taiwan arms issue by pledging to Beijing not to sell Taiwan any higher quantity or quality of arms than it currently was getting from the U.S.

The upshot of the plan, according to Goldwater, was that somewhere "down the road" Taiwan would need "better quality and more quantity but won't be able to get that from us."

In the report, Goldwater described the status of the plan as in "State Department language" that had not yet been finally approved by President Reagan.

The Sino-American agreement on arms sales to Taiwan was announced in a joint communique issued August 17, 1982. In this agreement, which was the result of ten months of negotiations, the U.S. promised a gradual reduction in arms sales to Taiwan in return for an affirmation by Beijing of its "fundamental policy of striving for a peaceful solution to the Taiwan question." The U.S. approved vague language calling for an eventual reduction in military support for Taiwan, but did not agree to a specific date to cut off all Taiwan arms sales, as Beijing had sought.

More specifically, the nine-point agreement included the following provisions:

- The U.S. reaffirmed its acceptance of Beijing as the "sole legal government of China," and reiterated that it had "no intention" of pursuing "a policy of 'two Chinas' or 'one China, one Taiwan.' "
- China declared its commitment to "striving for a peaceful reunification" of Taiwan with "the motherland."
- The U.S., saying it "understands and appreciates" China's com-

mitment to peaceful reunification, stated that it "does not seek to carry out a long-term policy of arms sales to Taiwan, that its arms sales to Taiwan will not exceed, either in qualitative or quantitative terms, the level of those supplied in recent years since the establishment of diplomatic relations between the United States and China, and that it intends to reduce gradually its sales of arms to Taiwan, leading over a period of time to a final resolution."

• In order to bring about "a final settlement of the question of U.S. arms sales to Taiwan," the two governments agreed to "make every effort to adopt measures and create conditions" conducive to such a settlement.

John H. Holdridge, assistant secretary of state for East Asian and Pacific affairs, in his testimony before the Senate Foreign Relations Committee, defended the communique. He emphasized the importance of the Chinese statement that a peaceful Taiwan settlement was "a fundamental policy." If that policy should change, Holdridge said, the U.S. "would, of course, reexamine" its position.

Holdridge also stressed that the communique did not "provide either a time frame for reductions of U.S. arms sales or for their termination."

"We will continue to make appropriate arms sales to Taiwan based on assessments of Taiwan's defense needs," he said.

On August 17, President Reagan released a statement calling the communique "a mutually satisfactory means of dealing with the historical question of U.S. arms sales to Taiwan," and saying it was "consistent with our obligations to the people of Taiwan."

The Taipei government reacted to the communique with a ritualistic denunciation questioning U.S. commitment to Taiwan under the Taiwan Relations Act and criticizing the U.S. for having "mistaken the fallacious peaceful intentions of the Chinese Communists as sincere."

Despite the tone of the official statement, officials in the Taiwan government were not surprised by the content of the communique.

James C. Y. Soong, a senior government official, admitted, "We aren't looking for a pro-Taiwan policy. We understand the constraints on the Reagan administration." But he said that if Taiwan lost its military support from the U.S., it would be "denied the right to self-defense."

Beijing used the occasion to reiterate its position calling for a complete phaseout of U.S. arms sales to Taiwan. The foreign ministry statement on August 17 said the present communique "only marks a beginning of the settlement of this issue." The Chinese government, it said, considered the "final resolution" referred to in the communique to mean a complete cutoff of U.S. arms sales to Taiwan. The wording "certainly implies that the U.S. arms sales must be completely terminated over a period of time," the ministry said.

An editorial published on August 18 in the *People's Daily*, condemned the Taiwan Relations Act because it implied that Taiwan was a political entity separate from mainland China.

Should "the policymakers in Washington" insist on handling relations between the U.S. and Taiwan on the basis of the Taiwan Relations Act, the editorial said, "Chinese-American relations, instead of being further developed, will certainly face yet another grave crisis."

On Capitol Hill, the August 17 agreement met with mixed reaction. Senator Barry Goldwater (R, Ariz.), one of Congress' leading supporters of Taiwan, condemned the communique as "a bad agreement" and said it was "full of double talk and false statements." Senator Gordon Humphrey (R, N.H.) said the agreement proved that the State Department was full of "weaklings, sissies and people with mush for brains."

Senator Henry M. Jackson (D, Wash.) supported the terms of the agreement, saying "There's only one China and it makes no sense to indulge in the fiction that there are two."

Senator S. I. Hayakawa (R, Calif.) praised the agreement in a different way. "The wonderful thing about language is its ability to mean whatever you want it to mean," he said. "There are enough ambiguities in the agreement so that no one should be seriously offended, no one should feel sold out."

7

SOCIALIST MODERNIZATION

A NEW (FOURTH) CONSTITUTION

The Fifth National People's Congress met in Beijing for a 15-day session on November 26, 1982. One of the major items on its agenda was the adoption of a new constitution, the fourth since the founding of the People's Republic in 1949.

As with previous constitutions, the adoption of a new constitution would signify the emergence of national consensus for a new direction—with power to back it. It would ratify the political changes that had already taken place and, at the same time, set forth in authoritative terms the outlines of new programs.

By the time this historic People's Congress met, Deng Xiaoping had firmly established himself as the paramount leader, which meant that he could now count on the loyal support of China's armed forces. He had also succeeded in placing two younger men of his choice, Hu Yaobang and Zhao Ziyang at the head, respectively, of the Communist Party and the state bureaucracy. The "second echelon" of the leadership was thus securely in place.

The new leadership in Beijing was embarked upon a novel experiment. It was to build a new kind of socialist state with a prosperous economy, or "socialism with Chinese characteristics." Their strategy was to incorporate selective features of capitalism—such as market-determined pricing and private entrepreneurship—into their centrally planned and managed economy. They sought pragmatic solutions to China's chronic problems, rejecting the Maoist approaches given to excessive politicization of economic issues. The new constitution reflected their beliefs.

The draft of the new constitution had been prepared by a special commission headed by Peng Zhen. It was ready for public deliberation in April, when it was published by the government. Both in form and content, the new constitution bore close resemblance to the republic's first charter of 1954. Compared with the previous constitutions, it was notable for the elimination of most, if not all, programs of the late Chairman Mao Zedong. Among the key features of the revised constitution are the following:

It restored the post of chief of state, or president, which had been abolished by Mao after its holder, Liu Shaoqi, was denounced and imprisoned in 1968. Mao, himself, assumed the powers of the office, and the 1975 constitution eliminated the position altogether.

China's armed forces, under the new constitution, would be led by the reinstated Central Military Council, to be headed by a person elected by parliament. Deng Xiaoping, who as chairman of the Communist Party's military affairs commission currently ran the armed forces, was considered a likely candidate for the post. Whether the party's military commission would be dissolved or subsumed under the new council was unclear.

Another proposed administrative change was that of a five-year term for the new president and vice-president, with a limit of two consecutive terms for both offices. This provision represented a radical alteration in policy, since Chinese officials had traditionally held their posts for life, quitting them only when purged or accused of crimes. The proposed limited tenures would apply also to the posts of chairman of the new military council, premier and deputy premier, chairman and deputy chairman of the National People's Congress Standing Committee, president of the Supreme Court and the nation's chief prosecutor. (The Standing Committee performed most of the legislative work for China's nominal parliament.)

The new charter would formally remove the right to strike in China, which had been included in the 1975 and 1978 constitutions.

One of Mao's most daring innovations, the people's communes, would also be drastically altered. The power of the communes, which had acted both as local governments and managers of huge collective farms, would be greatly reduced. The rural government would be returned to elected township officials, and the communes would remain only as economic units.

The constitution professed to allow power to reside in the National People's Congress and expanded the authority of its Standing Committee. However, effective power was expected to remain in the hands of the premier, vice-premiers, and state councilors, who made up China's new cabinet.

The charter also provided for an economic system divided into state-owned and collectively-owned sectors; established an auditing body to supervise government finances; restored a reference to the role of intellectuals in building socialism alongside workers and peasants; and eliminated the right to strike, which had been inserted in the 1975 charter by Mao.

On individual and human rights, the constitution promised freedom of religion, the inviolability of personal dignity and of the home, freedom of speech, and privacy of communication, except where breaches of national security were concerned. It guaranteed the rights of ethnic minorities and restored a provision making all citizens "equal before the law."

The charter stipulated that foreigners could invest in China and cooperate with Chinese economic organizations, and protected the "lawful rights and interests" of foreign economic organizations.

The basic principle of the nation's foreign policy, the constitution provided, was that of independence.

Peng Zhen made a formal presentation of the new constitution to the NPC on its opening day, November 26. In his speech, he referred to a provision of the draft constitution setting up special administrative regions. Peng said that Taiwan would be designated such a region when it was reunited with the mainland. He noted that the preamble to the constitution referred to Taiwan as "part of the sacred territory of the People's Republic of China."

Peng declared that while China remained unequivocal on the principle of its sovereignty over Taiwan, it was nevertheless "highly flexible as regards specific policies and measures" for reuniting Taiwan with the mainland.

Peng said that Taiwan, as a special administrative region with rules different from those in the rest of the country, would have a high degree of autonomy. He promised that "the current social and economic systems in Taiwan, its way of life and its economic and cultural relations with foreign countries will remain unchanged."

Peng's report also stressed the importance of the nation's modernization program; endorsed an independent foreign policy opposing "imperialism, hegemonism and colonialism"; and pledged that China would continue to expand economic, technical and cultural exchanges with other countries.

On December 6, the National People's Congress ratified the 138-article constitution by a vote of 3,037 to none, with three abstentions.

NEW FACES AT THE TOP

Along with the new constitution, the Chinese government planned personnel changes in its key cabinet posts, replacing elder statesmen with younger men. On November 19, 1982, prior to the convening of the Fifth National People's Congress, the Standing Committee of the NPC accepted the resignations of two key members of the cabinet: Defense Minister Geng Biao and Foreign Minister Huang Hua. Geng was replaced by Zhang Aiping, deputy secretary-general of the Communist Party Military Commission, and Huang by Wu Xueqian.

The Standing Committee made "some other appointments and removals," but gave no details of those changes.

The announcement of Huang's retirement came one day after his return from the Soviet Union, where he had led the Chinese delegation at the funeral of President Leonid I. Brezhnev. Huang had also held talks with Soviet Foreign Minister Andrei A. Gromyko on improving Sino-Soviet relations.

Huang, 69, who had been in ill health for some months, retained his position as a state councilor.

Geng had been named China's first civilian defense minister in March 1981. He had been a compromise candidate for the position and was reportedly unpopular with some sections of the military. Geng had been dropped from the politburo at the Communist Party congress in September. He had taken a seat on the Central Advisory Commission, newly created to encourage aging officials to retire. Geng was 73 years old.

The new ministers, Wu and Zhang, were both supporters of the pragmatic policies of Chinese leader Deng Xiaoping. Both had been purged during the Cultural Revolution of the late Chairman Mao Zedong.

Wu, 60, had been appointed deputy foreign minister in May, after a career in the Communist Youth League and in the international liaison department of the Communist Party. He was a protege of Hu Yaobang, party general secretary, who had formerly headed the youth league.

Zhang, 72, an army veteran, was a longtime ally of Deng. He had previously served as a deputy prime minister and as head of the Science and Technology Commission for National Defense.

This was followed in February of the following year by the resignation of Marshal Ye Jianying, 85, as head of the Standing Committee of the National People's Congress, a largely ceremonial post which, under the old constitution, doubled his role as head of state. One of the few surviving heroes of the revolution, Ye had been in failing health for some years and was unable to carry out his duties unassisted. He had reportedly resisted resigning for several years, despite a campaign by Deng to retire aging officials and professionalize the bureaucracy.

Further appointments were made during the June, 1983 session of the NPC, including the election of Li Xiannian as president. Li was officially reported to be 74 years old, but it was generally believed that his actual age was 78.

Li was a former finance minister and deputy premier and a member of the Communist Party's ruling politburo and its Standing Committee. He was a proponent of orthodox economic policies— heavy industry spurring rapid economic growth—that had been abandoned under Deng. Li's appointment was widely regarded as a compromise. Despite his opposition to the prevailing economic policies, he had the support of relatively conservative elements in the leadership, and his elevation to the presidency apparently satisfied the old guard in the Communist Party.

As president, Li would perform mostly ceremonial duties, such as receiving foreign visitors and presiding over affairs of state. He was also empowered to promulgate statutes, appoint or fire the premier and other state officials, proclaim martial law or a state of war, appoint envoys and ratify or abrogate treaties.

The decision to revive the presidency was widely seen to reflect the desire of China's leaders under Deng Xiaoping to establish a collective leadership in formal institutions. This was to replace the cult of personality that evolved during the rule of Mao.

In other appointments, Peng Zhen, 81, was elected chairman of the National People's Congress to succeed Ye Jianying, who retired in February. Deng Xiaoping was named chairman of the new Central Military Commission, a body created under the 1982 constitution to lead China's armed forces. Deng already led the Communist Party's Military Affairs Commission, and the two bodies would now be merged under his command.

On June 18, in his first official duty, Li reappointed Premier Zhao Ziyang to a new five-year term, as expected.

Two days later, the congress approved the appointment of two new vice-premiers, bringing the total to four. Former Foreign Min-

ister Huang Hua was one of three state councilors who were replaced by Zhao in a reshuffle of his cabinet, to which several new
ministers were also appointed. The new vice-premiers were Li Peng
and Tian Jiyun and the new state councilors were Wu Xueqian, the
minister of foreign affairs, Wang Bingquian, the minister of finance,
and Song Ping, who was also named minister of planning.

THE SIXTH FIVE-YEAR PLAN

1982 marked the second year of China's sixth five-year economic
plan (1981–1985). The plan represented a downward revision of the
ambitious economic goals adopted in 1978 under Hua Guofeng, which
had since been discarded as "leftist errors." After a period of setbacks, China's economy made a marked improvement, helped by a
bumper harvest and higher industrial production in 1982.

On November 4, 1982, in details of the economic improvement,
China Daily announced a total yield of spring rice and summer grain
crops of 121.55 million tons (110.26 million metric tons). This was an
increase of some eight million tons over the yield for the same period in 1981.

Total grain output for the year was expected to exceed the record
332.1 million tons (301.2 million metric tons) harvested in 1979.

Preliminary government figures announced on January 29, 1983,
said that in 1982 imports fell by 12% to $17 billion, while exports
rose 3.5% to $21.6 billion. The announcement on 1983 trade said
imports for that year would rise 40.6% to $23.9 billion and exports
were expected to rise to $22 billion.

The 1982 drop in imports contributed to a decrease of 4.4% in the
value of overall trade, to $38.6 billion from $40.4 billion in 1981. This
was the first drop in overall trade value since 1976.

The large trade surplus in 1982 strengthened China's balance of
payments position. In the 12 months ending September 1982, foreign exchange reserves rose to $9.23 billion.

On April 29, 1983, the Chinese government released a report on
China's economy for 1982, which included, for the first time, the
nation's gross national product figures. According to the report,
the 1982 GNP—the total value of goods and services—rose 9% over
the 1981 level to $495 billion.

There were some surprises in the report. Although China's economic readjustment program, introduced in 1979, had shifted the
focus of the economy to light, rather than heavy, industry, in 1982,
production of heavy industrial goods rose 9.9% to $125 billion,
whereas production of light industrial goods rose 5.7%, short of the

7% target. Investment in capital construction in state-owned units, which China had also hoped to curb, rose 25% to $28 billion.

The report identified several problem areas, including an excessive increase in capital investment, insufficient improvement in production and construction, and an imbalance between light and heavy industry resulting in the failure to meet the increased demand created by rises in consumer spending.

As a result of improved productivity in agriculture and industry, state revenues had also increased in 1982. (This rise in revenues was the first in five years.) State expenditures had increased as well. Finance Minister Wang Bingqian, in his report to the NPC on December 1, 1982, said that revenues for 1982 would total $55.9 billion—up from $55 billion in 1981—and government spending would reach $57.4 billion, leaving a budget deficit of $1.5 billion. The lagging state revenues were attributed by Wang to inefficiency—"chaotic management" and "inadequate" financial control and supervision—in the state-run enterprises.

The government's policy to address these economic realities and move the nation further along the path of modernization was spelled out in a master plan, named the Sixth Five-year Economic Plan, which Premier Zhao Ziyang unveiled before the National People's Congress on November 30, 1982. As before, the plan placed its emphasis on higher productivity, increased profitability, and "real growth," and not simply on increased agricultural and industrial output. China would make more use of foreign loans, investments and joint ventures, Zhao said, to modernize its industries and spur growth.

Rejecting earlier ambitious targets, the new five-year plan set a moderate limit to growth of 4% to 5% a year. This rate was slower than in the previous 28-year period, Zhao acknowledged, but necessary to insure that China did not overreach itself as it emerged from a period of "economic readjustment."

The new plan projected total government revenues of $300.7 billion for the five-year period. Expenditures were expected to total $308 billion, the premier said. This left a cumulative budget deficit of $7.3 billion.

Among the key elements of the plan were the following:

- Total investment in capital construction was set at $142 billion. Of this figure, nearly 40% was for the energy and transportation sectors and 39% was for plant renovation. Of the $27 billion designated for energy projects, $7.3 billion was to be invested in the oil industry.
- The gross value of industrial and agricultural output would rise to $435.5 billion in 1985, an increase of 21.7% over 1980. This rep-

resented an average annual rise of just over 4%. China excluded the service sector and government activities from its output figures.

- Exports were to reach $20.1 billion annually by 1985, a growth of 8.1% each year. Imports were expected to reach $22.6 billion, an annual growth of 9.2%. Total foreign trade would increase to $43.4 billion by 1985, or 51.8% more than in 1980.
- Grain output would reach 360 million tons (327 million metric tons) annually, compared with 320 million tons (290 million metric tons) in 1980.
- Coal production would rise to 700 million tons (635 million metric tons) annually, up 13% from the 1980 figure of 620 million tons (562 million metric tons).
- Steel production would reach 39 million tons (35 million metric tons) annually by 1985, an increase of 5.1% over 1980.
- Education, science, culture, sports and public health would receive $49 billion, or 16%—up from 11% in 1980—of total government expenditures.

LABOR CONTRACTS AND NEW TAXATION

The success of the new plan hinged on increased productivity of China's economy and its corollary, increased state revenues, with which to finance China's modernization. It required far-reaching reforms in the way the Chinese Communist system had operated. In the months following the publication of the sixth five-year plan, the Chinese government experimented with new methods of boosting production and efficiency at state-owned enterprises.

One of the new systems involved the use of labor contracts, allowing employment decisions to be based on workers' merits. This represented a radical departure from China's established labor system, commonly known as the "iron rice bowl." The late Chairman Mao Zedong had advocated guaranteeing a job to every worker, regardless of his or her skill—hence, a system of life-time employment with guaranteed wages.

The current Chinese leaders, who rejected the Maoist approach, saw the "iron rice bowl" as the cause of much of the laziness and carelessness among workers that stood in the way of China's economic development. Annual losses in one of every four state enterprises were attributed to inefficiency of workers, overemployment and mismanagement.

According to the official announcement on December 30, 1982, the labor contract system would be launched on a trial basis in Beijing.

Eventually, some 200,000 new jobs were to be filled through examinations. If accepted, workers would serve a probationary period and sign a contract agreeing to requirements set by the employer.

The labor contract system was modeled after those employed in south China's special export-processing zones. Foreign investors in the zones were permitted to test, regulate and fire employees of joint venture businesses. If the Beijing experiment was successful, it was reportedly to be considered for use throughout China.

The Capital Iron and Steel Co. in Beijing had already been experimenting with the merit system since 1979. The company had reassigned 8,000 inefficient workers to more lowly jobs and reported annual profit increases of 20% for each year the program had been in operation.

Another new method introduced at this stage, formally decreed June 1, 1983, had to do with collecting state taxes. As in the case of labor contracts, the new system was adopted after it had been tried in a pilot project with a small number of state-run enterprises.

During four years of experimentation with the system in 456 state enterprises, revenues to the state and to the firms involved had reportedly increased. However, problems had arisen because each enterprise was taxed individually. Under the new system, tax rates were assigned to fixed industrial categories.

Under the new system, industrial enterprises would no longer have to remit all their profits to the state, as had been done previously. Instead, most enterprises were to pay an annual income tax of 55% on profits. The remaining profits were to be split with the state. Smaller enterprises would be subject to a graduated tax on profits, and hotels, restaurants and catering companies would pay a 15% tax. The enterprises would use their share of the profits for reinvestment, to upgrade equipment or to pay fringe benefits to workers.

TOWARD FULLER INDIVIDUAL RESPONSIBILITY

The implementation of the five-year plan was carefully monitored from year to year, with readjustments made in its production targets when deemed necessary. On June 7, 1983, Yao Yilin, minister in charge of the State Planning Commission, presented a survey of China's economy to the National People's Congress. It showed that in 1982 the economy performed better than expected, with growth of 9%; however, excessive spending was outpacing state revenues, with the result that the national budget continued to show a deficit.

Moreover, because production and distribution costs had risen so much in the first months of 1983, less profit was being turned over to the state than in the comparable period during 1982. In the first quarter of 1983, heavy production had grown more than light production, despite efforts to readjust toward light industry.

Yao reported that investment in fixed assets in 1982 totaled $42.3 billion, $5.5 billion over the target. Excessive spending by local authorities and enterprises was blamed for inadequate funds to complete projects under the national plan. The economic plan for 1983 called for continuing readjustment, restructuring and consolidation with lower targets than those attained in 1982: industrial production, 4% growth, with efforts to reach 5%; heavy industry, 3.9% compared with 4.1% for light industry; investment in fixed assets, $34.7 billion, down 11.6% from the 1982 growth level and agricultural production to grow by 4%.

Premier Zhao Ziyang was more outspoken about the shortcomings of the Chinese economy when he addressed the opening session of the National People's Congress on June 6, 1983. Zhao charged that a proliferation of small development projects had drawn funds away from major national ones and that a growing sector of the economy was placing itself beyond the control of state planners. Zhao said the government would take measures to restrict the authority of enterprises and local communities to plan their own development projects. He added that attempts would be made to recover funds lost by the state treasury to enterprises and localities.

The premier condemned the "appalling waste" of human and material resources in ill-managed enterprises and said that "resolute measures" had to be taken to correct the situation. Factories that failed to reduce production costs, he warned, would be penalized with higher taxes, and those that continued to be mismanaged might be forced to close. Zhao reported that the combined losses of industrial enterprises in 1982 totaled $2.1 billion. Adding losses in grain and commercial transactions, the combined losses in the state-owned sector amounted to $5 billion, he said.

He cautioned that falling state revenues threatened the nation's economic goals and that wages and welfare had to rise at a slower pace than taxes and profits to the state.

In his presentation, Zhao also rebutted charges that the government's economic reforms eroded socialism by introducing taxes, interest rates, floating prices and other components of capitalism. Zhao said that the reforms were intended to improve socialism by making it more efficient. He said further reforms were being drawn up, including employment and wage policy changes and "market regulation" for planning production, allocating resources and setting prices.

China's experiments under the new government, with its selective features of capitalism, limited private enterprise and competition with individual managers making economic decisions guided by market trends, yielded encouraging results. In 1983, industrial production had risen 10.5% and agricultural production 9.5%, according to Premier Zhao's report to the NPC on May 15, 1984. In the first quarter of 1984, he reported, industrial output alone rose 12% over the same period in 1983.

Buoyed by this development, Beijing resolved to advance along the "capitalist road." New reform measures were adopted in 1984, Beijing's aim being in the words of Premier Zhao, to "bring into fuller play the initiatives of all enterprises and workers." China's main task, Zhao said, was to differentiate between well-run and poorly-run enterprises and between employees who worked more and those who worked less.

The new system, Zhao declared, would give managers increased powers to hire and fire workers, set prices within state guidelines, buy raw materials directly from suppliers, invest development funds and start joint ventures with other firms.

Workers should be paid according to how well they performed their jobs, Zhao said, and managers would be made responsible for the performances of their enterprises. Managers would be able to set wages and disregard a ceiling previously set on bonuses. An experimental program allowing enterprises to retain part of their profit after taxes would be extended to all state-run enterprises, Zhao said.

Also under the reforms, the commodity circulation system would be simplified, with an increase in the flow of goods between regions and between the towns and the countryside.

Zhao said the changes would first take effect in the construction industry, which had been plagued by cost overruns and delays. Henceforth, Zhao said, major projects would be open to bidding, and efforts would be made to reduce costs, improve quality and increase the return on investment in that industry.

Politically, the success of the reform was linked directly to eliminating the remaining traces of radical leftism introduced during the Cultural Revolution. An editorial in the *People's Daily*, on May 15, said "If we do not remove the obstacles to the effective management of socialism, if we do not overcome the effects of leftist thinking, we cannot advance."

FOREIGN INVESTMENT POLICY

In 1979, when the new open-door policy was inaugurated in line with the government's modernization policy, China established four special economic zones—Shenzhen, Zhuhai, Shantou and Xiamen Island—in an effort to upgrade the nation's industry by attracting foreign capital and technology. The zones offered beneficial tax rates and suspended restrictions in effect in other parts of the country. Five years later, in 1984, it was reported that 14 coastal cities would follow the policies currently in effect in the special economic zones. The cities included Canton, Shanghai and Tianjin.

On July 7, 1983, the Chinese government published—for the first time—foreign investment figures since 1979. Liu Shulong, an official at the ministry of foreign economic relations and trade, said that in that period, China had agreed to more than 10,000 joint ventures and other types of investment contracts with foreign companies. Between 1979 and the end of 1982, he said, China had received $12.6 billion in foreign funds, including about $2 billion in direct total foreign investment. The remainder had been in the form of loans from foreign government agencies, financial institutions and commercial banks.

By the end of 1982, China had repaid $5.1 billion of these loans and was scheduled to repay a further $2.4 billion over the next five years. On June 20, Beijing began paying about $487 million in loan repayments to the International Monetary Fund. The repayments on a loan made in 1981 were being made 10 months early.

Liu said foreign exchange reserves at the end of 1982 totaled $11.1 billion.

Liu added that in the future, China would increase its borrowing from foreign countries and establish more joint ventures with foreign companies to construct key projects, including hydropower and nuclear power plants, railroads, coal mines, steel mills and mineral development.

In March 1983, China announced disappointing foreign-equity investment figures for 1982. Feng Tienshun, another official from the ministry of foreign economic relations and trade, said that foreign-equity investment in 1982 had dropped sharply, totaling less than $50 million. Feng said that in 1982 the number of joint ventures formed fell to eight from 20 in each of the two preceding years. He blamed the decline on China's readjustment program, which shifted the emphasis to light industry from heavy industry, on investor wariness. Many foreign investors had been reluctant to participate in joint ventures in China because Beijing had yet to issue detailed rules governing a joint-venture law adopted in 1979. The rules were expected to be issued in October 1983.

China was also seeking to participate in joint ventures abroad, particularly in natural resource projects. Investments abroad were viewed as a means of securing stable supplies of raw materials and of acquiring advanced management experience and technologies. In April, China's leaders had been preparing to send delegations to various countries to explore investment possibilities. On June 13, the Nanjing Telecommunications Works agreed to invest $2 million in a U.S. technology concern, Santec Corp., marking China's first industrial overseas investment since 1949. Days later, China announced that Guangdong province was to invest in a forestry project in the Solomon Islands.

China was particularly interested in investing in iron mines abroad and had sent a delegation to Australia to seek out possible investments. China mined about 120 million tons of iron ore a year but still had to import between seven million and nine million tons of higher grade ore. More would be needed on completion of the giant Baoshan steel plant near Shanghai. On June 7, China began construction on the second phase of the steel complex, which had been the centerpiece of the nation's modernization effort. Work had been stopped on construction in 1981 because of a lack of funds.

One of the main concerns of foreign companies doing business in China had been the unsettled state of China's tax laws. The Chinese government addressed this concern by introducing a new tax law to the NPC on December 7, 1981. The draft law passed the Congress on December 13 and went into effect on January 1, 1982.

The government promised that the law would be structured in such a way that companies could offset their Chinese taxes against tax liabilities at home.

The law was progressive, tying the taxation rate to annual profits in five broad bands. In the words of one assembly official, "The general principle will be that the more profit you earn, the more tax you will have to pay." The minimum rate of 20% would be levied on annual profits of about $150,000 or less. With larger profits, the tax rate would rise five percentage-point increments, reaching a maximum of 40% on profits over approximately $590,000.

There would also be a local surtax of 10% on taxable income, which was defined as income earned after deductions for costs, expenses, and losses.

The details of the new law had been awaited eagerly by foreign concerns—particularly oil companies with an interest in exploring China's offshore reserves. Until now there had been no comprehensive law. Instead, individual commercial agreements had stipulated how profits would be divided between the company and the Chinese government.

The law was expected to benefit U.S. oil companies if the tax could be credited against their U.S. liabilities. The U.S. Internal Revenue Service was not expected to issue a definitive ruling on the question until 1982, however.

One unusual feature of the new law was that interest earned by foreign banks on loans to China at standard commercial rates would be taxable as income. This measure effectively penalized banks that did not loan at preferential rates.

In explaining the law, the Xinhua news agency said that a foreign oil company earning about $6 million a year could expect a combined tax burden of about 48.75%, while a concern earning under $300,000 a year might pay a tax of some 30%–32.5%.

"This would be lower than the tax burdens, not only in certain developed countries, but in many developing countries," the agency said.

Some specialists pointed out that the joint-venture law introduced in September 1980 offered an alternative. Under its terms, a foreign-Chinese joint venture would be taxed at a 33% rate, with an additional 10% withholding tax on profit repatriated to the foreign country. The higher corporate rate might induce some foreign companies to put their investments into joint ventures, in this view.

For the moment, many foreign businessmen were adopting a wait-and-see attitude, according to the December 9 *Financial Times* of London, until the specifics of the tax rates and surtax became clear.

The long-awaited new regulations governing joint ventures between foreign investors and Chinese companies were issued on September 26, 1983.

The regulations supplemented China's 1979 joint venture law. They covered only equity joint ventures, where partners created a legal entity to do business in China and each partner received a share of the earnings in proportion to its own investment.

Among the new rules was an exemption for certain imported raw materials from customs duties and industrial and commercial taxes. Also, joint-venture products urgently needed in China or that would otherwise be imported could be sold in the domestic market. Previously, investors were discouraged from marketing their products inside China, as joint ventures were primarily designed to generate foreign currency.

A third rule stipulated that disputes between Chinese firms and their foreign partners could be arbitrated in the country where the sued party was situated or in a third country if both sides agreed. Further, the board of directors of a joint venture—not government departments—was to be responsible for final planning decisions.

Efforts to update Chinese laws to accommodate foreign investors continued. On January 15, 1984, Beijing announced that it had begun a systematic review of all laws and regulations issued in the past 35 years. An official at the State Council's economic legislation research center said working groups had been formed in 31 ministries, commissions and bureaus to undertake the revision, and provincial governments were to follow suit. As a result of the revision, foreign companies and governments would have a better understanding of China's legal system, the official said. He added that trade and economic relations would be improved and foreign investors would be more likely to invest in China.

Yuan Baohua, deputy chairman of the state economic commission, said at a gathering of business executives in Davos, Switzerland, that China would sign 1,000 contracts in 1984, up from 700 in 1983. He said foreign capital and technology imports were "major policies for China's economic construction." China would need to increase borrowing, Yuan said, in order to finance the purchases, and would seek loans from the World Bank and Western bankers. He specified farming, energy, transportation, communications, textiles, pharmaceuticals and the production of construction machinery as areas in which Western companies could be of particular help to China.

Yuan said Beijing would encourage foreign companies to set up fully owned plants in China. Foreign companies would be allowed to sell more in the domestic market, and their income taxes would be reduced or eliminated, he said. (Effective February 1, China introduced rules exempting some joint ventures with foreign companies from paying taxes on several imported items.)

DIPLOMACY OF HIGH-TECH TRANSFER

While new technologies for China's industrial development materialized through normal business transactions, in most cases, the acquisition of advanced technologies with potential for military uses had to go through intergovernmental negotiations.

As early as 1978, the Chinese government had shown an interest in purchasing atomic reactors from France. An agreement was ready for signature when French President Giscard d'Estaing paid a visit to Beijing on October 15–22, 1980. Under the agreement, China was to buy two French-made 900-megaton atomic reactors, each costing about $950 million. The actual purchase, however, was postponed because of China's retrenchment program.

Two years later, in November, 1982, China and France reached another agreement, this time providing for joint research that would include the exchange of scientists between the two countries.

An official of the French Atomic Energy Agency said that it was the "first such agreement that we know of that China has ever signed."

A French foreign ministry spokesman said there was no "direct relationship" between the agreement and continuing efforts by France to sell nuclear reactors to China.

This agreement was followed by the conclusion of another Sino-French agreement on May 4, 1983, which provided for the purchase of four nuclear reactors. The sale was agreed to during a five-day visit to China by President Francois Mitterrand of France in talks with China's Premier Zhao Ziyang.

The agreement involved the sale of four 900,000-kilowatt reactors for two planned power stations, one near Canton in Guangdong province and the other in eastern China. The Guangdong station would be China's first commercial atomic power plant and would serve Hong Kong and much of southern China.

Meanwhile, the Chinese had developed their own nuclear reactor and put it into operation, the Xinhua news agency revealed on February 10, 1981. From the Chengdu date-line of the Chinese reports, it was assumed that the reactor was located in Sichuan province.

The facility was described as a "high-flux test and research atomic reactor" with a power capacity of 125,000 kilowatts. The reports said it had begun operation in December 1980 after two years of trials.

The plant was designed by the Southwest China Nuclear Reactor Engineering and Research Institute.

The news agency said, "China is now able to design, manufacture and build nuclear power stations independently." The Chinese reporters who described the plant said that all of the components of the reactor had been designed and built in China, and that almost all of the scientists and engineers who had worked on the project were young and had been trained in China since the Communists took control in 1949.

The opening of an indigenously-built nuclear reactor may have been a triumph for China's science and technology development, but it fell short of attaining China's technological independence. Not long afterwards, Chinese officials in Washington were discreetly exploring possibilities for nuclear cooperation with the Reagan administration, as revealed by Deputy Secretary of State Walter J. Stoessel Jr. in his speech before the National Council on U.S.-China Trade on June 1, 1982. Stoessel stated that the U.S. had been "conducting discussions with the Chinese on the possibility of an agreement for peaceful nuclear cooperation, which would enable us to compete commercially in the development of China's nuclear power program."

State Department officials reportedly confirmed the disclosure.

Officials cited by the *New York Times* said the first private discussions had begun in the fall of 1981 but had been impeded by China's adamant refusal to sign the nuclear non-proliferation treaty, which had been negotiated by the U.S., Great Britain and the Soviet Union and agreed to by many other countries since the mid-1960s.

In addition, the officials said, while China had agreed to use the exported U.S. technology only for power generation, it had not agreed to allow inspection of its facilities by the International Atomic Energy Agency.

Stoessel said President Reagan had adopted a policy of "substantial liberalization" in regard to the export of technology to China. It was expected that another round of talks between top officials of the two nations would be needed to resolve the remaining issues.

The question of nuclear cooperation came up for discussion during Foreign Minister Wu Xueqian's visit to Washington on October 10–13, 1983. Progress was reportedly made toward agreements on sales of U.S. high technology to China and on civilian nuclear cooperation. China's refusal to give assurance that sensitive technology would not be transferred to a third country remained a major obstacle to a high technology agreement.

The nuclear accord was finalized the week before President Ronald Reagan's visit to Beijing, April 26–May 1, 1984, after China agreed to seek U.S. consent before enriching or reprocessing fuel from U.S.-built reactors, or before storing materials that could be used for nuclear weapons.

Reagan witnessed the initialing of the long-awaited nuclear cooperation accord by lower-level officials. The accord established terms for curbing the proliferation of nuclear weapons-grade material and cleared the way for U.S. firms to participate in building Chinese nuclear reactors.

China was considering building between 10 and 12 nuclear reactors, the first of which was already under construction near Shanghai. Contracts to develop the nuclear industry in China were expected to be worth an estimated $20 billion over the next 20 years.

During a speech by Zhao at the signing ceremony, Reagan, who had appeared tired, reportedly dozed briefly.

A Sino-American nuclear cooperation accord was initialed during President Reagan's visit to Beijing. However, on June 21, following June 15 reports that China might be aiding Pakistan in its nuclear weapons program, the U.S. said that the accord probably would not be approved by Congress in 1984.

In announcing the likely delay, White House spokesman Larry Speakes said the administration remained "concerned about unsafeguarded nuclear activities in Pakistan."

White House officials said that Reagan would not send the agreement to Congress until he received stronger assurances from China that U.S. technology would not be used to help other countries produce nuclear weapons.

China had not signed the 1968 international nuclear nonproliferation treaty, claiming that it discriminated against developing countries. The accord initialed in April contained no guarantee by China concerning nonproliferation.

The only assurances China had provided on nonproliferation were in a toast made by Premier Zhao Ziyang in Washington in January and in virtually identical language adopted by the National People's Congress during its annual session in May. Recalling Zhao's assurances, a Chinese foreign ministry spokesman said on June 20, "We by no means favor nuclear proliferation nor do we engage in such proliferation, by helping other countries to develop nuclear weapons."

The spokesman confirmed that U.S. officials had sought further assurances on China's use of nuclear materials from the U.S., but said China would offer no further public statements.

Senator Alan Cranston (D, Calif.) on May 17 had criticized the Reagan administration's handling of the April agreement. He said, "The Reagan administration has not made a case to Congress and has kept secret from Congress the text of a major agreement with a communist foreign power for weeks after it was initialed."

Senator William Proxmire (D, Wis.) criticized the pact after he learned that it did not contain a provision for the application of International Atomic Energy Agency safeguards. He said on May 12 that the Reagan administration was "cavalier about verifying that China won't use the nuclear material we send to build nuclear weapons or to help other countries build nuclear weapons."

In briefings for legislators and congressional staff members, administration officials had termed the language of the agreement "unorthodox," acknowledging that it was an amalgam of the U.S. position stressing specifics and the Chinese position stressing generalities, the *New York Times* reported on June 21.

On June 20, the Chinese foreign ministry released a statement accusing the Reagan administration of deliberately holding up the agreement and of going back on its agreement to sell nuclear technology to China.

The nuclear cooperation agreement was formally signed on July 23, 1985, during the state visit to Washington by Chinese president Li Xiaunian.

The U.S. Senate approved the pact on November 21. However, in a surprise vote on December 9, the Senate approved, 59–28, a measure requiring the president to certify that nuclear technology sold to and bought from China was subject to International Atomic Energy Agency safeguards against the proliferation of nuclear weapons. But under pressure from the Reagan administration, on December 16, House–Senate conferees agreed to drop the proposal on restrictions, which was attached to a catchall spending bill, and which the House had not included when it voted, 307–112, to approve the nuclear cooperation pact on December 11. The vote by the conferees was 15–7.

The original version of the 30-year pact, signed in July, had come under criticism by U.S. lawmakers because of its failure to provide adequate safeguards against China's exporting nuclear technology to third countries. Senator Alan Cranston (D, Calif.) had drafted a number of conditions to be attached to the bill, and these were approved by the foreign affairs committees of both the House and Senate in separate votes on November 13. However, many opponents, including Senator John Glenn (D, Ohio), still argued that the restrictions were not stringent enough.

The restrictions provided for a 30-day waiting period between the time a U.S. corporation won a contract from China and the time an export license was issued for the nuclear technology involved. Compromise wording required that in that time the U.S. president certify to Congress that "reciprocal arrangements" with China were "effective in ensuring peaceful uses" of the nuclear technology concerned and that China had provided "additional information" proving it was not helping spread nuclear weapons.

Outside the field of nuclear cooperation, barriers to high-tech transfer were gradually removed. In 1981, the Reagan administration eased curbs on Chinese purchase of U.S. technology. During 1982, the U.S. sold $400 million worth of "dual-use" technology (usable for industrial and military purposes) to China, but was reluctant to grant export licenses for other sophisticated hardware. China had requested a $12 million ground satellite-tracking system, 23 earth stations for gathering geological data and $15 million worth of computers, all of which could be converted to military use.

China was pressing for the further removal of barriers to trade. U.S. companies selling high technology equipment in China had also urged the removal of restrictions, claiming that stringent regulations made U.S. firms less competitive in bidding for Chinese projects.

The U.S. government's policy to further liberalize trade regulations involving sensitive technology transfer to China was announced by U.S. Commerce Secretary Malcolm Baldrige on May 25, 1983, during his six-day visit to Beijing.

Baldrige, who arrived in China on May 21, led a U.S. delegation that participated in the first session of the Sino-American Joint Commission on Commerce and Trade on May 23–25.

Baldrige vowed that the U.S. would streamline existing regulations governing the export of sensitive high technology items and that the effects of liberalized export guidelines would be apparent in 60 days. He said that the items under consideration included some that were intended for industrial use but that could have military applications.

Following up on Baldrige's pledge, on June 22, the U.S. Commerce Department placed China in export-control category "V," a more lenient trade category than the special category "P" that had previously applied to China. Category "V" applied to nations considered friendly and nonallied.

The change, the Department announcement said, was "in keeping with a U.S. policy of support for China's modernization and of encouraging participation of U.S. firms" in that effort. However, restrictions would remain on "certain products and technologies which present a national security concern to the United States."

U.S. Defense Secretary Caspar Weinberger had reportedly opposed the shift in policy because some of the equipment that could now be sold to China had a potential military use.

U.S. officials estimated that, under the eased rules, an increase of $1 to $2 billion in bilateral trade could be expected over a period of years.

JAPAN'S FINANCIAL INPUT

Of all the foreign nations that were involved with China's modernization programs, none played a more crucial role than Japan. Japan was China's largest trade partner, the most important source for China of modern technology and loans.

Xinhua reported on July 22, 1983 that Japan had agreed to a new loan of $286.6 million. The loan would be used for various development projects, including the construction of a railway between Yanzhou and Shijiusuo in Shandong province. The news agency said Japan had lent China $959.9 million in low-interest loans since a five-year agreement in 1979. The loan agreement was due to expire late in 1983, by which time China would have received an estimated $1.5 billion. Negotiations had begun on a second round of loans, expected to total about $2 billion.

Separately, Japan had agreed to help China modernize outdated industrial plants, it was reported on June 16. At the fourth Sino-Japanese talks on bilateral economic cooperation, China put forward a list of 40 plants it wanted to modernize with Japan's help. In response, Japan proposed that China draw up renovation plans on a plant-by-plant basis and that China conclude technical cooperation agreements with Japanese firms, giving them priority when purchasing new equipment for the plants.

The close economic ties thus forged paved the way for political cooperation on regional problems such as the Korean question. Following the Rangoon incident, in which 16 South Korean officials were killed by a bomb explosion allegedly set off by North Korean agents, the Communist Party general secretary, Hu Yaobang, made a special trip to Tokyo.

Hu began his eight-day visit to Japan on November 23, 1983. A major issue on the agenda of the talks with Japanese leaders was stability on the Korean peninsula. Maintaining stability on the peninsula had been a primary aim of China's foreign policy. Beijing had recently been trying to encourage contacts between Washington and North Korea and had suggested that Washington and Beijing cooperate to achieve that end. China had also been pressing Japan to make overtures to North Korea. The October bombing in Burma that killed four South Korean cabinet members had been a major setback to China's efforts.

In talks with Japanese leaders on November 24, Hu said North Korean President Kim Il-sung had assured him that Pyongyang would not invade the South and did not have the power to do so. Hu and the Japanese officials agreed that intensification of tensions on the peninsula should be avoided.

Japanese Premier Yasuhiro Nakasone proposed establishing a "committee for 21st-century Japan-China friendship," and Hu accepted the proposal. Hu assured Nakasone that attempts to normalize ties between Beijing and Moscow would not be at the expense of China's friendship with Japan.

Hu commented on the succession to a new leadership in China on November 26. He said some observers believed that China would be devastated when its current leader, Deng Xiaoping, aged 79, died. However, Hu said, the succession would proceed smoothly under China's new system of changing leaders. He added that the Communist Party was now recruiting a new generation of leaders in their 30s, 40s and 50s.

In talks with Nakasone the same day, the subject of Japanese purchases of Chinese coal was raised. Nakasone made no firm commitment, saying that many countries were trying to sell coal to Japan.

On March 16 of the following year, Japan's cabinet approved the proposed sale to China of a pressure vessel to hold the reactor of China's first nuclear power plant, scheduled for completion in 1989.

Mitsubishi Heavy Industries Ltd. was competing with West German and French companies for the sale, which was worth about $4.3

million. Cabinet approval meant that Mitsubishi would be able to get an export license for the component if it won the contract.

Japan granted such licenses only after guarantees by the importing country that the nuclear equipment would be used only for peaceful purposes and that Japanese technicians would be allowed to visit the site to verify that the plant was being built there.

China had balked at the latter requirement, but on March 2 the two countries had agreed on a formula allowing "good-will visits" by Japan to the plant site at Qingshan, near Shanghai. The agreement, which came during talks on an overall nuclear power agreement, paved the way for Japanese cabinet approval.

Japanese officials admitted, though, that no agreement had been reached on how Japan would verify that the spent fuel from the plant would not be made into plutonium for the manufacture of atomic weapons.

The cabinet's decision had been made in time for Prime Minister Nakasone's visit to China, scheduled for March 23–26, 1984. Nakasone opened the visit on March 23 with an offer of $2.1 billion in low-interest loans over the next seven years for use in rail, port, communications and energy modernization projects. It was the largest foreign aid package Japan had ever given.

In what was seen as an unusual gesture of friendship toward Nakasone, Communist Party General Secretary Hu Yaobang held a luncheon on March 24 for the Japanese leader at his home rather than in a public hall. It was the first such event ever held for a visiting head of state at the home of a Chinese leader.

The next day, Nakasone met with China's paramount leader, Deng Xiaoping, who urged him to increase Japanese investment in China. Japan had reportedly been reluctant to put money into Chinese ventures, fearing China's political and economic instability. Deng was said to have assured Nakasone, however, that China was working on measures to safeguard foreign investments and compensate investors if projects were suspended.

On the question of Korean reunification, Chinese Premier Zhao Ziyang reaffirmed his government's support for North Korea's proposed peace talks involving the two nations and the United States, it was reported on March 25. He stressed that China would not take part in such talks. Nakasone backed South Korea's plan for talks between the Korean regimes only.

Chinese leaders did agree to a request made on behalf of South Korea by Nakasone that Koreans living in China be allowed to visit and receive relatives from South Korea.

FOREIGN OIL COMPANIES IN OFFSHORE DRILLING

China is richly endowed with coal and oil. However, the rapid industrialization elevated the nation's demand for energy resources so fast that a World Bank report in 1981 said that China could be forced to import oil by 1985, according to a United Press International dispatch published October 13. Declining crude output and rising internal demand were threatening China's oil exports, the report said. With effective use of coal and hydroelectric power, China might hope to maintain exports at about $4 billion a year; they were $4.7 billion in 1980. If conservation measures were not effective, China could become an importer by 1985 and face "impossible import levels" in 1990, the report said.

With onshore production declining, China was putting increasing efforts into offshore oil exploration. A "high-yield" find off Tianjin was announced on May 13, and a major oil find in the South China Sea was reported on September 3. The government announced on September 22 that it would be ready to call for bids by foreign companies to exploit its offshore reserves by early 1982.

Reports about China's oil strikes outside of China's northeastern oil-producing region had been circulating in the West since 1980. *Gas and Oil Journal* reported on November 26 of Chinese Petroleum Minister Song Zenming's telling an American Gas Association delegation that oil had been found south of Hainan Island in a well of 6,500 feet (1,970 meters) in 230 feet (70 meters) of water. He also was said to have told the delegation that wildcat wells on the Luichow peninsula north of Hainan had yielded 500 to 600 barrels of oil a day.

On August 24, Senator Henry M. Jackson (D, Wash.) had made a similar observation. Speaking at the end of a three-week visit to China, the senator said he believed the Chinese might have reserves of 100 billion barrels of oil, compared with a proven 30 billion barrels in the U.S. He suggested Beijing would help reduce American dependence on Arab producers by 1985.

Jackson did not indicate who told him about the discovery at Hainan, which he believed had been made in June or July. He described the output as "sweet" or low-sulfur crude oil. It was believed to be China's first offshore well.

The Chinese government invited a select group of 46 foreign companies to bid for development of the offshore oil deposits. Forty out of the 46 did so by the stipulated deadline, according to Xinhua on May 28, 1982.

Contracts would be negotiated in 1982, with exploration of the 150,000-square-kilometer (58,000-square-mile) area to begin in 1983. Atlantic Richfield Co. (ARCO) became the first U.S. company to gain permission to commence oil exploration and development projects in the South China Sea.

The pact, signed September 19, 1982, gave ARCO and its partner in the venture, Santa Fe Minerals Inc., the right to explore for oil in a 3,500 square mile (9,000 square kilometer) area south of Hainan Island. ARCO had an 80% interest in the concession and was to contribute four-fifths of the project costs in return for four-fifths of the foreign profits. Sante Fe Minerals, a drilling and construction concern, was to contribute the remaining one-fifth of the costs in return for a one-fifth share of the foreign profits.

The contract followed four years of negotiations between ARCO and the Chinese government. In 1979, ARCO had signed an agreement with China allowing the company, on an exclusive basis, to bid for exploration blocks south of Hainan Island. ARCO and Santa Fe Minerals had since undertaken seismological surveys in this location, at a cost of $20 million.

Paul Ravesies, president of ARCO International Oil and Gas Co., said on September 19 that ARCO was to begin full-scale exploration by April 1983. Ravesies did not expect the company to begin pumping any oil for at least five years.

On September 19, ARCO refused to reveal the details of the contract, which was to expire in 25 to 35 years' time. However, Ravesies reported that the company had agreed to train local workers and transfer technological expertise to China during the exploration. He described the agreement as a "production sharing contract."

Another 33 foreign oil companies had submitted drilling bids to the Chinese government in August. However, observers did not expect China to award any contracts based on these bids for another year.

The Chinese government had earlier stated that it expected offshore drilling to uncover some 10 to 20 billion tons (9 to 18 billion metric tons) of oil. Western estimates had placed the figure closer to four billion tons (3.6 billion metric tons).

China, reportedly, was eager to develop its offshore oil because onshore production was stagnant. Figures released in April, 1983 showed that just over 745 million barrels of crude oil were produced in 1982, according to a news story on May 11. That figure represented an increase from the 1981 level of only 0.9%. China had offered 58,000 square miles (150,000 square kilometers) for development.

On May 10, 1983, another contract, this time with a group of five

Western oil companies headed by British Petroleum Co., Ltd. (BP) was signed.

The deal was the first following an initial round of bidding by 33 foreign companies in 1982. Sixteen U.S. companies submitted bids in that round, but none were included in the contract, reportedly because they were holding out for better terms. ARCO had submitted a separate bid, and, in 1982, became the first U.S. company to win oil exploration rights.

The companies which were awarded the current contract were: BP and its four partners, one Australian and two Canadian companies and Petrobras International, the Brazilian state-owned oil company. BP held 45% of the venture.

The contract allowed the companies to explore five sites totaling more than 5,400 square miles (about 14,000 square kilometers) in the Yellow Sea and the South China Sea. Exploration operations were expected to begin in the last quarter of 1983, financed wholly by the five companies. China was entitled to handle up to 51% of the production.

This was followed by the signing of contracts on August 6, by two groups of foreign oil concerns headed by the Occidental Petroleum Corp. of Los Angeles. Each of the two groups won drilling rights to some 500 square miles (about 1,300 square kilometers) in the South China Sea. Occidental had a 50% interest in one group and 55% in the other. Its partners were firms from Britain, Spain, Australia, and France. China would be entitled to take 51% of any oil found but would not be required to pay any of the production costs.

DRIVE AGAINST ECONOMIC CRIMES AND "SPIRITUAL CORRUPTION"

The open-door policy, which exposed China's Communist society to Western influences and the capitalist way of doing business, apparently spawned a variety of corrupt practices. Of particular concern to the Chinese government were growing numbers of economic crimes. China's chief judge, Jiang Hua, reporting to the National People's Congress on December 8, 1982, announced that 26,000 people had been jailed in the first nine months of 1982 for economic crimes. The figure included 3,706 government officials charged with corruption. Jiang said 44,874 offenders had surrendered to gain lenient treatment after China introduced harsher penalties—including execution—for serious crimes.

Economic crimes included embezzlement, smuggling, tax evasion and bribery.

The previous week, Premier Zhao Ziyang had told the congress that a total of 136,024 cases of economic crimes had been reported through September. Zhao said, "Some of the cases were major and appalling, involving huge sums of ill-gotten money."

Zhao said that where senior officials in the Communist Party had been involved in crime, it was because they had been duped by criminals or had abused their rank to gain privileges.

China's crackdown on economic crime came in the wake of an open-door economic policy designed to increase foreign investment in China. Ideological hardliners claimed that the open-door policy allowed bourgeois ideas to infiltrate the nation and corrupt the Chinese people.

The Chinese Communist Party's central discipline commission had uncovered 192,000 cases of economic crimes committed by party officials and others during the last 16 months, it was reported on July 29, 1983.

The *Washington Post* cited a report published in *People's Daily* that said an anticorruption drive had found smuggling, bribery and foreign currency speculation to be widespread. The commission's investigators blamed foreign influences and "unhealthy tendencies" within the party.

Since the crackdown began, 30,000 offenders had been sentenced, 8,500 expelled from the party, and two party members executed.

In an editorial accompanying the report, *People's Daily* compared corrupt party members to "termites gnawing at the edifice of socialism." The editorial said official corruption was a negative aspect of China's open-door economic policy but defended that policy as being necessary for China's modernization program.

In addition to its crackdown on economic crimes, the government had taken measures to reduce contacts between Chinese citizens and foreigners living in the country. Guidelines issued to primary schools warned young children to be wary of foreigners, it was reported on July 31.

The government also began a campaign against what it called Western "pornography," which included rock music. In June, the People's Music Press issued a booklet titled "How to Distinguish Decadent Songs." The booklet, quoted in an October 27 news article, said decadent songs could be identified by their "unclear, loose, drunken pronunciation" and "quivering rhythms." It described jazz as being "against the normal psychological needs of man."

This campaign to purge China of Western influences merged with the Communist Party's plan, adopted by its Central Committee on October 12, 1983, to weed out extreme rightist and leftist elements.

The political purge campaign was outlined in a 13,000-word document made public after the close of the committee's two-day session. It called for three years of reeducation, reorganization and re-registration of party members, the largest purge since the 1966–76 Cultural Revolution. Three types of people were identified as targets:

- "Followers of the rebellion led by the liquidated Lin Biao [the late former defense minister, accused of plotting a coup against the late Mao Zedong] and the imprisoned Jiang Qing [widow of Mao]."
- "Those who are seriously factionalist in their ideas."
- "Those who gained party membership during the '10-year domestic turmoil' by means of beating, smashing and looting."

Press reports said the campaign was aimed primarily at this last group, the 17 million Maoist members of the 40 million-member party. They had joined during the Cultural Revolution, a virtual civil war, and were said to be seen by Deng Xiaoping, China's supreme leader, as a threat to his modernization policies. Deng had been purged twice in those years, and had long wanted to purge disruptive elements of the party both to advance his economic reforms, such as the encouragement of private enterprise, and to ensure their success once he relinquished power, the *Washington Post* reported October 10.

The document accused many party officials of "embezzling state funds, building houses for themselves with public money, extorting bribes for contracts and setting up their children in the best jobs." These special privileges would be lost upon ouster from the party. The purge, the *Washington Post* reported, would coincide with an anticorruption drive that had already touched thousands of officials.

The document vowed that more women and young people would be allowed into the party, to which only 4% of the population belonged, but said that no quotas had been set for the campaign. Diplomats estimated that anywhere from one million to three million Chinese could lose their party membership, the *New York Times* reported on October 11, but leaders avoided giving any figures. Officials also did not make clear how many of the 4.2 million members of the heavily Maoist armed forces would be hit by the purge, but the *London Times* reported on November 3 that military propaganda organs had been warned to produce literature that held to the party line.

The party stressed, however, that the campaign would not turn into the kind of bloody witch-hunt characteristic of the Cultural Revolution.

The first phase of the program called for reeducation of all party members. Deng's "selected works" and the works of Karl Marx, among other material, were required reading. As the next step, party units in offices and factories would decide who should and should not be allowed to rejoin the party. Those who passed all the necessary ideological tests would then reregister.

Deng Liqun, the Communist Party's propaganda chief, confirmed that the party's "rectification" drive, or bloodless purge, was closely linked to a crackdown on the so-called "spiritual pollution" of Western ideas and those who espoused them, the *New York Times* reported on November 4. These people were known as "liberals." The document referred to the "corrosive influence" of China's opening to the West. It called some party members anti-Marxists who "propagate bourgeois liberalism," the *Washington Post* reported on October 12.

At the time the program was adopted, the liberal purge was seen as slapping the wrists of the right before chopping off the hands of the left, the *Financial Times* reported on November 18, a mere prelude to the more important Maoist purge. But an analyst quoted in the *New York Times* on November 13 said he saw it differently, saying, "The leftists are anti-Deng, but they are still communists. In the long run, Western ideas and wealth are the real threat to the party."

Although most Chinese had little knowledge of Western culture, the *Asian Wall Street Journal* said on November 22, leaders were said to fear its effect on young people whose ideas about communism had soured during the Cultural Revolution. "Once you question the scientific precision of socialism," said a Western analyst quoted in the *Washington Post* of November 14, "you threaten to undermine the legitimacy of the whole regime. A little skepticism goes a long way in one of the world's most alienated societies."

The leader of official literary circles in China became one of the early victims of the purge, the *Financial Times* reported on November 18. Zhou Yang was forced into public self-criticism after writing a paper suggesting that the Marxist notion of worker alienation under capitalism could also apply to socialism. He was forced to recant his ideas in the press.

As part of the crackdown, two editors of the *People's Daily* were fired, Reuters reported on November 13. Students at Beijing University were chastised for their interest in the works of Jean-Paul Sartre, the French philosopher. A revue in Canton was closed when it was deemed that the female singers had shown too much thigh. Many books, films and plays were banned, and officials blamed the rebirth of many old superstitions on the collapse of socialist ideas.

An article in *Red Flag*, quoted in the *New York Times* on November 4, seemed to reveal a dilemma among many Chinese. It said "many comrades" were aware of the rising Western influence, but "dared not resist for fear that they may be accused of being 'left.' "

As a party member quoted in the *Miami Herald* of October 30 put it, "It is not so easy for us to figure out who they want."

The campaign against "bourgeois liberalism" failed to get off the ground. In November and December, 1983, the scope of the campaign had reportedly been limited to such a degree that it had become meaningless. Articles in the official press were said to have removed Western dress, music, art, literature, science and technology from the purview of the campaign. The press had also warned that the drive must not restrict foreign trade or cultural exchanges, the *Los Angeles Times* reported on January 12, 1984.

In December, 1983, Deng Liqun, the Communist Party's propaganda chief, ordered that the country's rural population be exempted from the campaign. The peasantry made up 80% of China's population.

The campaign was said to have gone beyond the boundaries originally set for it. Yu Qiuli, head of the PLA, had warned that the drive "must not be extended to everyday life and a clear line must be drawn between minor problems in thinking and a clearly bourgeois way of life."

Party newspapers had warned that the campaign would antagonize young people by seeking to alter their way of life and taking their attention away from work and school. Peasants who were engaged in family farming in accordance with the government's reforms were accused of "ideological contamination—putting money ahead of everything."

Economic production had reportedly fallen off during the campaign as workers were forced to spend time studying and to surrender books and other materials considered unsuitable. Foreign trade had also suffered, the *New York Times* reported, as Chinese officials shied away from Western contacts.

The drive had proved politically embarrassing to Premier Zhao Ziyang on his recent trip to Canada and the United States, as he was forced to explain the "anti-West" campaign.

Communist Party General Secretary Hu Yaobang stressed that in spite of the campaign's cessation, China wasn't shifting "back and forth," the *Asian Wall Street Journal* reported on January 9.

8

PURSUIT OF INDEPENDENCE

NATIONALISTIC FOREIGN POLICY

The "spiritual pollution," with its moralistic tone, was a Chinese way of describing the social problems common among developing countries while they were going through social changes—suspended, as it were, between the old and the new.

In the 1980s, China, under the pragmatic leadership of Deng Xiaoping, was forging ahead on its modernization programs. Pockets of modern economy sprang up in the special economic zones set up in the coastal regions. Farmers were producing more, using their own ingenuity, and the new system of responsibility enabled them to retain more of their produce for their private use. At the same time, the onset of general prosperity accentuated disparities in individual standards of living, and emerging differences in individual life-styles.

Only a few years earlier, during the Cultural Revolution, the nation had been mesmerized by the Maoist rhetoric of permanent revolution and resigned to the sacrifices it called for. Now, the Chinese people were shown a vision of happiness through increased material wealth. The rural cadres who used to run communes, relieved of some of their former responsibilities, were turning themselves into a new class of rural entrepreneurs. High party officials in key government positions could now demand bribes and kickbacks in return for the favors they did for foreign investors and domestic businessmen.

There inevitably developed a slackening of social discipline, a confusion of values, and a general malaise. The kind of emotional vacuum that had come to exist in China's national psyche, as it no longer was exposed to the steady ideological drumbeats, could not be filled by the pragmatists' matter-of-fact slogan, "learn from facts." Yet, the success of the pragmatic reforms required a unity of the nation, a sustained national purpose and, indeed, national pride.

The Chinese foreign policy in the 80s reflected this reality of China's internal situation.

During the 1960s and the 70s, China had adopted an ideological line which identified it with the Third World. Not only was this congruent with China's self-image as a developing country; it also served its foreign policy interest in being able to navigate the treacherous waters of international politics without being dominated by either of the two superpowers.

In the 80s, the independent foreign policy gained a new significance both as an expression of, and spur to, Chinese nationalism. Coinciding in time with the rise of the "second echelon" leadership, it helped that new leadership to consolidate its power by lending it an aura of legitimacy.

SOLIDARITY WITH THE THIRD WORLD AND OVERTURES TOWARD EASTERN EUROPE

The importance which the Chinese government attached to its independent foreign policy was underscored when Premier Zhao Ziyang went on a four-week trip to Africa, December 20, 1982–January 17, 1983. The trip was the first to Africa by a Chinese premier since Zhou Enlai toured the continent in 1963.

The trip was seen as an effort to cement relations with African nations and promote economic cooperation as part of a revived policy of cultivating Third World nations.

The week before Zhao's departure, a senior official said the premier would propose no major aid projects, but that China would focus on small and medium-sized projects such as providing medical aid teams and agricultural technicians.

An editorial in the *People's Daily* of December 20 described Zhao's trip as "a major event in the history of Sino-African relations," proclaiming, "China always holds that it is her sacred internationalist duty to resolutely support the African and Arab peoples in their struggle against imperialism, colonialism, hegemonism, South African racism and Israeli expansionism."

African diplomats viewed Zhao's tour as having four major goals:

- To overcome strained relations caused when China's foreign policy swung in favor of the U.S., Japan and Western Europe in the late 1970s. In 1978 China had cut its African foreign aid program because of the needs of its own modernization plans. It currently provided Africa with an estimated $100 million in aid annually.
- To gain support for an effort to win for the Cambodian resistance coalition, headed by Prince Norodom Sihanouk, the country's vacant seat at the nonaligned summit meeting in March 1983.
- To set the groundwork for expanded trade.
- To pursue a foreign policy revived by Foreign Minister Huang Hua during an earlier tour of Africa, depicting the U.S. and the U.S.S.R. as superpowers wanting to expand their domination of the Third World. That policy had been revived after a period of normalized relations between China and the U.S.

The Egyptian talks were expected to deal with the nonaligned movement and Chinese arms and technical assistance.

In addition to Egypt, Zhao was to visit Algeria, Morocco, Guinea, Zaire, the Congo, Zambia, Zimbabwe, Tanzania and Kenya.

During his stop in Zaire on January 3, Premier Zhao Ziyang canceled a $100 million debt owed by Zaire since 1973.

Zhao made the announcement in a meeting with Zaire's President Mobuto Sese Seko on the second day of a three-day visit to that country.

The previous day, January 2, Zhao said at a banquet hosted by Mobutu that developing countries should strengthen economic cooperation in order to better deal with the world economic crisis. He said that while certain unidentified nations had "let the burden of their economic crisis fall on the shoulders of others," China would "reinforce its solidarity and cooperation with countries of the Third World."

Zhao added that China would "take measures to oppose hegemonism for the maintenance of peace in the world and the establishment of fair and rational international economic relations."

Mobutu said in his speech that Chinese cooperation was the best in the world and that Zaire had to "do everything to consolidate our cooperation and solidarity with China."

Zhao left Zaire for the Congo on January 4, where he was greeted by President Denis Sassou-Nguesso in the nation's capital, Brazzaville. Zhao had already visited Egypt, Algeria, Morocco, Guinea, and Gabon.

In meetings with Kenyan President Daniel arap Moi, Zhao pledged to increase China's trade with the East African nation and agreed to provide aid to help build a sports complex in the capital, Nairobi. Nairobi was to be the site of the next All-Africa games.

In the next-to-last leg of his tour, Zhao spent five days in Tanzania, January 11–15. He inspected development projects funded by China both in mainland Tanzania and on the semiautonomous island of Zanzibar off the Tanzanian coast. Zhao also joined Tanzanian President Julius Nyerere in celebrating the 19th anniversary of a 1964 revolt by leftist African nationalists establishing a socialist government.

Zhao concluded his month-long African tour on January 17, departing from Kenya, the last stop on his 10-nation itinerary.

Zhao's African trip was followed, in May, 1983, by the Communist Party General Secretary Hu Yaobang's trip to Eastern Europe. Hu visited Rumania and Yugoslavia on May 4–15. Before leaving Beijing, he said the purpose of his trip was to "convey friendship, study experience, exchange views and enhance unity."

Rumania and Yugoslavia were the only Eastern European countries with which China maintained party-to-party relations.

In an apparent reference to Rumania's independence from Moscow, Hu said in the northern town of Brasov on May 9 that the nation's Communist Party was to be praised for defending Rumania's independence and taking into account its "national conditions." Similarly, in the Yugoslavian capital of Belgrade on May 10, Hu praised the nation's independent stand on nonalignment. Before leaving for Beijing, he said, on May 15, that the Chinese and Yugoslav Communist parties would continue to "think with our own heads, walk with our own feet, resolute in our respect for independence, equality and noninterference."

Qian Qichen, China's deputy foreign minister, who left Beijing with Hu, was to travel on to Hungary, Poland and East Germany.

A Chinese foreign trade official confirmed, on May 4, that a Chinese delegation had also visited Albania a month earlier. The delegation reportedly discussed the resumption of trade between the two countries. China had suspended trade and assistance to Albania in 1978, after the Albanian government had criticized Beijing's pragmatic reforms since the death of Chairman Mao Zedong.

The *Financial Times of London* said on May 10 that China had recently granted Yugoslavia a short-term loan of $120 million. The article also said that in March the two countries had signed a trade pact to increase two-way trade in 1984 to $1.2 billion, up from $50 million in 1982.

IRRITANTS IN SINO-AMERICAN RELATIONS

China's increased interest in Eastern Europe was widely viewed as an attempt to improve ties with the region at a time when relations with the U.S. were at a low point and normalization talks with the U.S.S.R. were making little progress.

Beijing's relations with the United States were being strained by Washington's attempt to curb China's textile exports to the U.S., continuing adherence by the Reagan administration to the Taiwan Relations Act and other minor—but unexpected—incidents.

China was the world's leading producer of textiles and ranked as the fourth largest supplier to the U.S., accounting for 10% of all U.S. textile imports. Chinese textile sales to the U.S. in the first 10 months of 1982 amounted to $750.5 million, a 32% increase over the same period in 1981.

The two sides had been negotiating a new agreement since August 1982, and talks were scheduled to continue in the second week of January 1983. The old agreement expired on the last day of 1982.

The U.S., late in 1982, had published a list of quotas to be imposed on January 15, 1983 if the two nations had not by then reached accord on proposed limits on Chinese exports of textiles and clothing to the U.S.

In the talks, held from January 6–13, 1983 the U.S. pressed China to restrict its increases in textile imports to an annual 1.5%–2%. China sought an annual export increase of 6%, arguing that in the first 11 months of 1982 its overall imports from the U.S. had amounted to $617.6 million more than its exports. Thus, the Chinese contended, they deserved a larger share of the U.S. textile market.

The U.S. countered that Chinese textile sales in the U.S. had grown considerably since 1980.

On January 13, the U.S. unilaterally set curbs on imports of Chinese textiles after the failure of a week of talks on limiting textile imports from China. In retaliation, China announced on January 19, that it was banning further purchases in 1983 of U.S. cotton, soybeans and chemical fibers.

The U.S. set quotas on more than 30 categories of Chinese textiles and clothing imports. The curbs were retroactive to the beginning of 1983 and held China's 1983 textile imports to their 1982 level.

The textile issue was compounded by the still simmering dispute over U.S. policy toward Taiwan. There was a belief that the dispute had been dealt with, on the whole, satisfactorily, by the 1982 Sino-American communique on the arms sale to Taiwan. That turned out to be wishful thinking. The ambiguous language used in the communique, which enabled the parties to reach an agreement, virtually ensured continuation of the dispute.

President Reagan proved the point when he gave an interview to *Human Events*, a U.S. weekly, which was published in February, 1983. In the interview, Reagan was quoted as having asserted that the U.S. "did not give an inch" when it signed the communique. He reiterated the U.S. stance that its commitment to gradually reduce arms sales to Taiwan was tied to progress by China in peacefully resolving its dispute with Taiwan. He added that the U.S. would continue to aid Taiwan in maintaining its military strength and would not improve its relations with Beijing at the expense of Taiwan.

The publication of the article provoked a charge from Beijing that the U.S. was going back on its word. The Chinese accusation, published through Xinhua on February 25, said Reagan's comments disregarded all nine points of the communique and that they amounted to a "serious retrogression" in the U.S. position. The agency accused Reagan of interfering in China's internal affairs by making statements on Taiwan.

On February 26, the State Department issued a denial of the Chinese charge, saying Reagan wanted a strong, stable relationship with China and that the U.S. had consistently pledged that it would abide by the terms of the communique.

While the two countries differed on important policy issues, their bilateral relations were further complicated by unforeseen developments. One had to do with the defection of Hu Na, China's top-ranking tennis star, during a tennis tournament in California in July 1982. Hu subsequently applied for political asylum in the United States. Her application was granted April 4, 1983.

The U.S. Immigration and Naturalization Service (INS) had delayed making a decision on her application for asylum for eight months, despite a favorable recommendation by the State Department. The INS reportedly feared that approval would create a precedent that would be used by some of the more than 1,000 other Chinese people in the U.S. who had applied for political asylum.

A U.S. Justice Department spokesman said on April 4, that the INS had granted Hu asylum under the Refugee Act of 1980 because she had established her case for a "well-grounded fear of persecution" if she returned to China. Hu had complained that Chinese officials had tried to coerce her into joining the Communist Party.

She said she did not want to join for fear that she might be victimized in a political purge in the future. Hu cited examples of what she described as local political instability to support her case.

China had argued that the authorities would not prosecute Hu if she returned home.

Following approval of Hu's application, a Chinese foreign ministry spokesman, Qi Huaiyuan, claimed on April 5 that the U.S. had "long premeditated and deliberately created" Hu's defection. Qi said Hu's request to remain in the U.S. had resulted from "coercion by a handful of Americans and the Chiang element of Taiwan working in collusion." (Hu had retained a Chinese-American lawyer with ties to the Taiwan government of President Chiang Ching-kuo.)

In a formal protest on April 6, China called the U.S. action "not only untenable from the legal point of view but also condemnable morally." China complained that, "in spite of its oft-repeated professed desire to develop friendly relations with China, the U.S. government has kept doing things that infringe on China's sovereignty, interfere in its internal affairs and hurt the feelings of the Chinese people."

On April 7, China canceled nine cultural exchange programs and said its athletes would not participate in 10 international sporting events to be held in the U.S. in 1983. Chinese officials said Beijing's decision, which applied only to events sponsored by the U.S. government and not to those privately organized, resulted from the U.S. government's "unfriendly action." The Xinhua news agency reported on April 7, that Communist Party Secretary Hu Yaobang had said the U.S. was luring Chinese athletes and students into defecting and that he had described such behavior as "hegemonistic." Until very recently, China had used the label "hegemonist" only in reference to the Soviet Union.

That same day, the U.S. embassy in Beijing said it regretted the "overreaction of the Chinese to the Hu Na case."

In a strong personal attack on President Reagan, *People's Daily* April 10 accused Reagan of having "seized away" Hu from her parents and of having "offered himself as her foreign father." The article referred to the handling of relations with China by U.S. policy makers as "stupid."

In an article datelined April 10, the *Washington Post* cited diplomats in Beijing who said the U.S. agreement to grant Hu political asylum represented a loss of face for China's top leader, Deng Xiaoping, who had personally appealed for Hu's return. Deng had promoted China's open-door policy, increasing contacts with the West, despite opposition from hardliners who charged that contacts with the U.S. compromised China's sovereignty and national dignity.

Another issue arose from an arcane legal suit filed in the U.S. District Court in Birmingham, Alabama, by nine Americans in a class action on behalf of 280 U.S. holders of Hukuang railways Sinking Fund Gold Loan bonds. The bonds had been issued in 1911 by the pre-revolutionary Chinese government under the Manchus. They had been in default since the 1930s.

In September, 1982, a U.S. district judge issued a ruling, saying that the Beijing government should pay the U.S. bond holders $41 million plus interest. The 1982 ruling enabled the defendants to take the final step of requesting the courts to seize Chinese property in the U.S.

The Chinese government lodged a protest with the Reagan Administration over the court's ruling. The protest, contained in a note handed to Secretary of State George Shultz on his trip to Beijing, on February 2–5, 1983 said China would "take measures accordingly" if its property were seized. The note claimed Beijing was "immune from the jurisdiction of any foreign court" and said the current government was not responsible for debts incurred by previous "reactionary" governments. It urged the State Department to "handle the case properly so that Sino-American relations and normal trade and economic exchanges may not be impaired."

However, the 1976 Foreign Service Immunities Act prevented the State Department from intervening in the case. The act prohibited the executive branch from entering into legal disputes such as that involving the Chinese rail bonds. The State Department in the past had informally advised Beijing that if China were to present its case to the Alabama court, its claim of sovereign immunity would undoubtedly be recognized.

SHULTZ GOES TO BEIJING

Improving relations with Beijing was the main objective for U.S. Secretary of State George Shultz when he went on a 12-day trip to East Asia, which included visits to Japan, China, South Korea and Hong Kong. He spent four days in Beijing, February 2–5, 1983 talking with Chinese leaders.

On his first two days in Beijing, February 2–3, Shultz held talks with Foreign Minister Wu Xuequian on a wide range of topics, including world economic problems and China's new independent foreign policy.

In private talks on February 2, Wu urged the U.S. to pressure Israel to find a peaceful solution to the Middle East crisis and to prevail on South Africa to grant independence to Namibia (South-

West Africa). Shultz responded that the U.S. was attempting to find equitable solutions in both those areas but that the problems were complicated.

Referring to a joint communique on Taiwan issued in August 1982, Wu said the communique "represented an important step toward removing . . . obstacles" in relations between the U.S. and China. However, he continued, "that does not mean our relations have since embarked on a smooth path."

Shultz had reportedly hoped to keep the issue of Taiwan in the background, as it had been a major source of contention between the two countries.

Wu further told Shultz that while China opposed hegemonism, it was willing to "maintain and develop normal relations with all countries." Wu said China wanted peace so that the nation could concentrate on its economic development.

In a public toast on the evening of February 2, Wu said China attached "importance to its relations with the U.S." but added that "further solid efforts are no doubt necessary in order to remove the obstacles and dispel the dark clouds." Shultz responded by stressing the importance of Sino-American relations "in confronting the economic and strategic challenges that threaten the well-being of us all."

On February 4, the third day of his stay in Beijing, Shultz met with China's defense minister, Zhang Aiping, and the two men reached an agreement to take steps to revive high-level military contacts between their two countries and to begin exchanges in military education, medicine and logistics. Sino-American military cooperation had largely been suspended after President Ronald Reagan took office in 1981.

The same day, Shultz met with Premier Zhao Ziyang, who expressed China's fears that the U.S. would not live up to the terms of the August 1982 communique on Taiwan. Shultz reassured Zhao that President Reagan was committed to the communique, in which the U.S. pledged to phase out weapons sales to Taiwan and Beijing promised to reunite Taiwan peacefully with mainland China.

Zhao accepted an invitation from President Reagan to visit the U.S. at an unspecified date and extended an invitation to Reagan to visit China. Later, at a news conference, Zhao told reporters that he hoped to visit the U.S., even though "the obstacles in our relations cannot be removed." He said Taiwan remained the main obstacle to improved ties.

Zhao and Reagan had met briefly in Cancun, Mexico at an economic summit in 1981.

In talks with Finance Minister Wang Bingqian on February 4, Shultz discussed means of accelerating the sale of advanced technology to

China. Shultz also raised the possibility of resuming textile talks that failed in January over the question of limiting textile imports from China into the U.S.

Shultz also met that day with Prince Norodom Sihanouk, former Cambodian head of state and president of the exile Cambodian coalition government. Sihanouk reportedly expressed the hope that all friendly nations would provide the coalition with arms and training but did not explicitly ask the U.S. for weapons.

Shultz concluded his round of talks on February 5 with a meeting with China's supreme leader, Deng Xiaoping. Afterward, he gave a news conference in which he said his visit had taken the edge off tensions arising in Sino-American relations in the past two years.

Shultz reiterated the U.S. intention of living up to the Taiwan communique and touched on the matter of Chinese tennis player Hu Na, who had defected to the U.S. in 1982.

Shultz said that with increasing exchanges between the two countries, "incidents" such as that involving Hu were likely.

Later, at a farewell banquet, Shultz summed up his visit by saying, "We depart having set the stage for renewed advances built on a stronger foundation of confidence and mutual trust." He said his discussions made "important progress in renewing and enriching the dialogue" between the U.S. and China, and had left him "more convinced of the real opportunities for enhanced cooperation."

On February 6, Xinhua offered a less optimistic view of Shultz's visit just hours after Shultz had left Beijing for South Korea.

Citing official sources, the news agency said the talks had been helpful "to some extent" in reviewing U.S. and Chinese positions on international and bilateral affairs. However, the agency continued, until the issue of U.S. arms sales to Taiwan was resolved, any hope of building up trust was "out of the question and bilateral relations cannot possibly develop on a sound basis."

Chinese officials had accused the U.S. of bad faith in observing the terms of the 1982 communique on Taiwan, the news agency said. It cited certain Chinese leaders who said U.S. officials had misinterpreted the communique by linking the phaseout of U.S. arms sales with Beijing's progress toward peaceful reunification of Taiwan with the mainland. Beijing claimed no such prerequisites were acceptable and furthermore that they violated China's sovereignty, the news agency stated.

Chinese officials also reportedly protested to Shultz over the opening of a new Taiwan liaison office in Boston; the attendance of the U.S. assistant on national security affairs, William P. Clark, at a Taiwan national day reception in Washington in October 1982; and the U.S. interpretation of the Taiwan communique provision regarding future arms sales to Taiwan. The news agency said China had complained that actual U.S. arms sales far exceeded the maximum annual figures published by Washington.

According to the news agency, Chinese officials told Shultz that the 1979 Taiwan Relations Act governing U.S. relations with Taiwan and mandating the sale of defensive weapons should be annulled because it was "a serious stumbling block in the way of Sino-American relations."

The agency also cited foreign news stories that said the U.S. wanted to renew its dialogue with China "to exercise some kind of check on the forthcoming Sino-Soviet consultation."

On a more positive front, the news agency said that the U.S. and China maintained close positions on the issues of Soviet troops in Afghanistan and Soviet-backed Vietnamese forces in Cambodia. The agency said also that the U.S. and China were close on arms control. This was the first public statement by China that the two nations were in agreement on arms control.

Summing up, the news agency said Chinese officials had told Shultz that "actual deeds rather than empty words and promises are essential if relations are to be developed and mutual trust and confidence established."

MOSCOW MOVES CLOSER TO BEIJING

The Soviet Union saw, in the downturn in U.S. relations with China, an opportunity to improve its relations with Beijing. Soviet President Leonid I. Brezhnev issued an appeal on March 24, 1982 to end more than two decades of public hostility between China and the Soviet Union.

Brezhnev's remarks, made in Tashkent, were the latest in a series of Soviet overtures that some analysts said were designed to take advantage of growing tensions between Washington and Beijing over Taiwan.

In his speech, Brezhnev said that the U.S.S.R. was "ready at any moment" to resume border talks with China and to "come to terms, without any preconditions, on measures acceptable to both sides to improve . . . economic, scientific, cultural as well as political relations."

Brezhnev stressed that the U.S.S.R. recognized Beijing's claim to Taiwan. "We have never supported and don't support—not in any form—the so-called 'two-China concept,' " he said.

Despite the presence of the thousands of Soviet troops along the Sino-Soviet border, the Soviet president denied that the U.S.S.R.

posed a military threat to China. "We haven't had and don't have any territorial claims on [China]," he insisted.

In contrast to past criticisms of China's internal economic development, Brezhnev emphasized that "We have never denied and do not deny now the existence of a socialist system in China, even though Beijing's association with the policy of imperialists around the world contradicts, of course, the interests of socialism."

Following up on Brezhnev's Tashkent speech, the Soviet Union initiated steps toward normalization of its relations with China. In October, Deputy Foreign Minister Leonid F. Ilyichev went to Beijing to negotiate on resumption of bilateral talks. Prior to his departure, in what Western analysts saw as a concerted move, Brezhnev spoke on September 26, stressing the importance of improving Soviet relations with China.

"As regards Asia," Brezhnev said in a nationally televised speech to Communist Party leaders in the Soviet Azerbaijan capital of Baku, "we would deem it very important to achieve a normalization, a gradual improvement of relations between the U.S.S.R. and the People's Republic of China on a basis that I could describe as that of common sense, mutual respect and mutual advantage."

In his speech, Brezhnev affirmed the Soviet commitment to detente. "We do not hold that detente can and must be" limited to any single area of the world, he said. Although detente "for a number of historical reasons had struck deeper roots" in Europe than in other areas, Brezhnev contended, "there exist possibilities" for detente in Asia that should be explored. However, he warned that detente "in no case must be put at the mercy of the narrow-minded egotistic politicians in the camp of imperialism."

Cool, at first, to Soviet overtures, Beijing sounded more forthcoming after Ilyichev spent two weeks talking mainly with Chinese Vice-Foreign Minister Qian Qichen in complete secrecy. Chinese Communist Party General Secretary Hu Yaobang announced on October 17 that China and the Soviet Union had agreed to resume formal negotiations in an effort to normalize strained relations.

Sino-Soviet relations should "embark upon the road of healthy development," Hu told reporters traveling with French Communist Party leader Georges Marchais. Marchais' pro-Soviet party was also establishing closer ties with China.

Hu went on to criticize Soviet foreign policy. "We have pointed out time and again that the Soviet leaders have been pursuing a hegemonist policy for a considerably long period," he declared. "We are against it." China had called for the withdrawal of Soviet troops from the Sino-Soviet border, Mongolia and Afghanistan and an end to Soviet support for the Vietnamese occupation of Cambodia.

On October 20, Moscow television broadcast an announcement of the resumption of talks with China. The report criticized Hu's attack on Soviet foreign policy.

The bilateral talks between China and the Soviet Union were to be held alternately in Moscow and Beijing. The next round of meetings took place in Moscow in March 1983.

Soviet Deputy Foreign Minister Leonid Ilyichev hosted the Chinese delegation, led by Vice-Foreign Minister Qian Qichen. The Soviet Communist Party newspaper *Pravda* described the two officials as "special representatives" of their governments, a distinction that appeared to indicate increased commitment to the talks, according to Western diplomats.

The same day, China made public a plan calling for a phased withdrawal of Vietnamese troops from Cambodia and an end to Soviet military support of Vietnamese forces. The plan urged a "joint commitment" by other nations in the region to Cambodian independence and neutrality and "genuinely free elections" under United Nations supervision.

On March 7, *the People's Daily* criticized the Soviet refusal to discuss its military position in Afghanistan, Southeast Asia and Mongolia. "The problems involving third countries all stem from direct use of Soviet military force or Soviet support for another nation's use of military force or the deployment of Soviet troops in another country," the *People's Daily* said. "They constitute a grave threat to China and the peace and stability of Asia."

"If the Soviet Union really is sincere about improving relations with China," the editorial continued, "it should not offer excuses or stall, but should take a number of practical steps to eliminate the obstacles in the way of normalization."

The talks ended on March 22, producing an agreement on increasing educational and cultural exchanges, but no agreement on political and strategic issues.

Vice-Foreign Minister Qian Qichen, who headed the Chinese delegation to Moscow, said the talks had been "beneficial" but added that "differences still exist" between the two nations. No substantive progress had been made in the political arena, Qian confirmed.

Under the new agreement on cultural exchange, China and the Soviet Union agreed, in principle, to exchange 10 students from each country for the fall semester. The exchanges would be the first in 19 years, according to Western analysts. The two sides also decided to increase athletic and cultural exchanges. Chinese gymnasts were scheduled to visit Moscow, and a Soviet soccer team was to visit Beijing. A Chinese opera singer was to perform in Moscow.

On March 10, while the high-level talks were in progress, Soviet and Chinese trade delegations signed an accord to boost the volume of trade between the two nations by nearly 150% in 1983. The U.S.S.R. planned to export lumber and steel in return for imports of Chinese textiles and food. The Sino-Soviet trade accord came in the wake of a U.S. curb on Chinese textile exports.

In the third round of talks, which were held in Beijing, on October 6–21, strategic questions were taken up. The Chinese foreign ministry spokesman, Qi Huaiyuan, confirmed October 5 reports that Chinese Vice-Foreign Minister Qian planned to raise China's concern about the deployment of Soviet SS-20 missiles along the Sino-Soviet border. Qi noted, however, that the Chinese stance reflected a long-standing demand for Soviet missile and troop reductions along the border. China would also continue to demand the withdrawal of Soviet troops from Afghanistan and an end to Soviet support for Vietnam's occupation of Cambodia, Qi said.

The Soviet Union was represented in the talks by Deputy Foreign Minister Leonid F. Ilyichev. The Qian-Ilyichev talks reportedly produced no progress on strategic and political questions. But they were able to conclude an agreement to double trade between the two nations, to a total of $1.63 billion annually from an estimated $815 million. In addition, the ministers agreed to increase the number of exchange students on each side to 100 from 10 and modernize an old Soviet-built factory in northern China. Agreement was also reached on expanding cultural and sports exchanges, but no details were disclosed.

A formal trade agreement, which provided for an increase of trade between the two countries by about 50% in 1984 ($1.2 billion), was signed in Beijing on February 10, 1984.

The talks between Qian and Ilyichev followed a visit to Beijing on September 8–16 by Soviet Deputy Foreign Minister Mikhail Kapitsa. Kapitsa, who headed the Asian affairs section of the Soviet foreign ministry, was the most senior Soviet official to visit China since the 1960s, according to Western diplomats. During his stay as a guest of Qian, Kapitsa met with Chinese Foreign Minister Wu Xueqian.

Several hours after Kapitsa's departure on September 16, the Chinese foreign ministry issued its strongest statement thus far on the Soviet downing of a South Korean commercial airliner on September 1. The Chinese statement called on the U.S.S.R. to compensate the families of the passengers killed in the attack. "This incident," the Chinese statement said, "concerns how to safeguard the established norms ensuring the safety of international civil aviation in the future and the compensation for bereaved families."

In a separate development, China and the Soviet Union had opened two border crossings in Central Asia on July 1, that had been closed since the 1960s. The opening for trading purposes of a mountain pass at Trurugart and another at Korgas was seen as a largely symbolic gesture toward improving relations between the two countries.

The lack of progress in Sino-Soviet talks toward narrowing the gap on important strategic and political questions prompted Moscow to accuse China on January 14, 1984, of deliberately impeding progress toward better relations by reviving territorial disputes. On January 23, China denied that it had any territorial claims on the Soviet Union.

The Soviet charge came in a commentary published in the Soviet magazine *New Times* and carried by the news agency Tass. The commentary accused China of accelerating the circulation of academic books and journals containing maps and articles that laid claim to border territory in the Soviet Far East and Siberia.

China had long claimed that the Soviet Union occupied 580,000 square miles (1,500,000 square kilometers) of territory gained under unequal treaties imposed on weak Manchu emperors in the 19th century. In recent years, China had dropped the territorial issue as a precondition for improved Sino-Soviet ties and agreed to recognize Soviet sovereignty over the border land. However, China insisted that its history books record that the land was ceded under unfair treaties.

The Soviet commentary maintained that Beijing was generating anti-Soviet hostility among the Chinese people by charging that the disputed territory had been seized illegally. It further said that China continued to accuse the Soviet Union of "hegemonism and expansionism." The commentary claimed that China was "keeping the border issue 'in reserve' as a ready-made, 'sure' expedient for retarding the process of normalization."

China's denial was contained in a commentary in the official magazine *World Affairs*. The commentary said that *New Times* had deliberately linked China's historical accounts of the seizure of Chinese land with current efforts to improve ties "by way of launching wanton slanderous attacks on China's principled stand on these matters."

The commentary added that China favored peaceful negotiations based on the "unequal" treaties to end the border issue. It pointed out that Beijing had repeatedly denied any claim on the Soviet Union and no longer demanded the return of the disputed land. The commentary said that China sincerely hoped for improved ties with the Soviet Union and would "make continuous efforts" toward that end.

The Chinese commentary omitted any reference to a previous demand that the Soviet Union pull out of other disputed territory— islands in the Ussuri and Amur border rivers and land in Soviet central Asia—before any final settlement of the border dispute could be reached. The commentary also omitted a previous demand that the Soviet Union admit that it had gained Chinese land under unfair treaties.

The Soviet Union made public its position on Sino-Soviet relations on March 1, in the first policy statement by Communist Party General Secretary Konstantin U. Chernenko since he had assumed the post on February 13.

Chernenko made a cautious approach to improving relations with China, while seeming to rule out Beijing's demands for the withdrawal of Soviet troops from China's northern border and from Afghanistan and for an end to Soviet military support for Vietnam's occupation of Cambodia. "The normalization of relations with the People's Republic of China could, of course, contribute to the growth of socialism in international affairs," Chernenko said. "We are consistent proponents of this normalization. Political consultations show, however, that there remain differences on a number of questions of principle. In particular, we cannot make any agreements to the prejudice of interests of third countries."

This Soviet line apparently irked the Chinese. Xinhua reported Chernenko's call for improved relations but criticized him for rejecting the conditions China had set for normalization.

"Eluding China's proposal for removing barriers to normalization of relations between the two countries," the news agency said, "Chernenko went so far as to say that the Soviet Union 'cannot make any agreements to the prejudice of the interests of third countries.' "

The criticism of Chernenko's speech came a day after Chinese Vice-Premier Wan Li confirmed that Soviet First Deputy Premier Ivan Arkhipov would visit China to discuss trade issues. The level of diplomatic contact between the two nations had been rising, culminating in Wan's trip to Moscow for the funeral of Soviet President Andropov. Diplomatic observers noted that Wan had been the highest-ranking Chinese official to visit the U.S.S.R. in 20 years and that Arkhipov would be the highest Soviet official in China in 15 years.

WASHINGTON REMOVES IRRITANTS

In the summer of 1983, with Sino-Soviet rapprochement seemingly proceeding on course, the U.S. government was under considerable pressure to improve its relations with China. But it was stymied by internal political considerations. Not the least of these was the continuing lobbying by American friends of Taiwan for arms sale to the Nationalists. On July 15, as Washington was getting ready to accommodate Beijing, the Pentagon announced that it planned to sell $530 million worth of arms to Taiwan, thus adding another irritant to Sino-American relations.

The sale would include spare parts for aircraft, surface-to-air and sea-launched missiles and conversion kits for M-4 tanks. The package was the largest single sale of its kind under the administration of President Ronald Reagan. Earlier in the year, the U.S. had agreed to sell Taiwan F-104 jet fighters worth $30 million.

In a joint communique with China in August 1982, the U.S. had agreed to gradually reduce arms sales to Taiwan from the 1979 total of $600 million. However, the U.S. had projected sales for 1983 of $800 million, dropping to $780 million in 1984. The administration argued that those figures represented a reduction from the 1979 level after allowing the adjustment for inflation. China rejected the inflation indexing explanation and charged the U.S. with violating the terms of the 1982 communique.

China lodged a protest with the U.S. State Department on July 22. In it, China's ambassador in Washington, D.C., Zhang Wenjin, scored the U.S. for not discussing the sale beforehand with Beijing item by item. He charged that the sale involved three kinds of antiaircraft missiles more advanced than those Taiwan already possessed. Zhang said, "The U.S. contention that the provision of the new types of missiles in Taiwan will not raise Taiwan's antiaircraft capabilities is untenable."

Zhang added that the U.S. should "strictly keep the amount of its arms sales to Taiwan below the level of those supplied in recent years and markedly reduce such sales year by year and withdraw all plans for selling to Taiwan any weapons which qualitatively exceed those already possessed by Taiwan."

While the Taiwan arms sale issue caused strains, the U.S. government set in motion a series of moves designed to improve its ties with China.

First, on August 18, the U.S. State Department intervened to set aside an earlier ruling by a federal judge in Birmingham, Alabama, which found China in default on the Hukuang Railway bonds issued in 1911. The Chinese government filed papers in U.S. district court in Birmingham on August 12, asking that the case be dismissed. Secretary of State George Shultz added an affidavit to the request in which he said the judgment should be set aside in the interest of U.S. foreign policy. Shultz said that when he met with Chinese leader Deng Xiaoping earlier in the year, Deng had expressed his concern over the ruling. Deng had said the judgment would be a "major irritant in bilateral relations," Shultz wrote. Accepting Shultz's recommendation on February 27, 1984, Federal District Judge U. W. Clemon set aside his earlier judgment, saying that his action was in the public interest and in the interest of fairness.

Second, on August 19, China and the U.S. signed a five-year agreement on Chinese textile exports to the U.S. The agreement ended a trade dispute that had lasted almost 12 months.

Under the agreement, Chinese textile exports to the U.S. were permitted to grow at an average rate of 3.5% over the next five years. Beijing had been demanding a growth rate of between 6% and 7%. The U.S. had originally offered around 1%. (In 1982 South Korea, Taiwan and Hong Kong had accepted growth rates of less than 1%.)

U.S. textile manufacturers criticized the new accord, charging that the permitted growth rate was unreasonable. In July, observers from the U.S. textile manufacturing sector had walked out of negotiations held in Geneva between the U.S. and China. They charged that the U.S. negotiating stance was too soft. No details of the agreement had been released at that time.

U.S. textile manufacturers were disturbed by the rapid growth of Chinese textile sales to the U.S. Such sales rose to $834 million in 1982 from just $69 million in 1979.

The textile dispute had had repercussions for U.S. farmers. The previous pact between the U.S. and China expired in December 1982, but several rounds of talks begun in August 1982 had failed to come up with new terms. In January 1983 the U.S. had unilaterally set import quotas on Chinese textiles and China had retaliated by banning imports of some U.S. farm goods. U.S. farm sales to China had dropped dramatically in the first six months of 1983.

In a separate development on August 22, the International Trade Commission (ITC), a U.S. government trade panel, voted that penalty duties should be assessed against print cloth imports from China. The panel determined that U.S. textile companies had suffered economic injury as a result of Chinese dumping of the polyester-cotton cloth, to which dyes could be applied.

In July the U.S. Commerce Department had determined that China had been dumping the polyester-cotton cloth in the U.S. at prices that were 22.4% below its fair market value. The department recommended that corresponding duties of 22.4% should be imposed.

Then, in September, Defense Secretary Casper W. Weinberger went on a trip to Beijing in an effort to increase military cooperation between the two countries.

During his trip, from September 25–29, Weinberger stressed the need for strategic cooperation and pressed for an exchange of military missions. However, China reiterated its determination to remain independent and not to become attached to any power bloc.

In talks with Defense Minister Zhang Aiping on September 26,

Weinberger warned of the dangers of the Soviet military buildup around the world and said the U.S. was willing to grant China access to U.S. weapons, particularly defensive ones. Weinberger told Zhang that 32 advanced technology items would be made available to China and a further 11 would be made available if China gave its assurance that the technology would not be passed to a third country. Weinberger also explained to Chinese leaders the new U.S. regulations under which China could buy dual-purpose (civilian and military) technology and weapons. In June the U.S. had upgraded China's export rating to allow the sale of more sophisticated high technology equipment.

Premier Zhao Ziyang issued a statement on September 27 that apparently turned aside the U.S. effort to promote greater military cooperation. The premier said that "if we have the need and the ability to buy military equipment from the U.S., I would not exclude such a possibility." However, he added that although China needed to modernize its defenses and would not be able to do so solely through its own resources, "it would be inconceivable for us to rely on imports of defense equipment."

Weinberger told reporters on September 28 that progress made on his visit could "mature . . . into actual transfers of weapons systems, if that is what the Chinese want." He said air defense and antitank weapons had been among the items discussed.

Weinberger also announced that Zhao would visit the U.S. in January 1984 and that President Reagan would travel to China in April 1984. Before leaving on September 29, he announced that U.S. and Chinese military officials would exchange visits in 1984 to study each other's training, logistics and other military skills.

ZHAO AND REAGAN EXCHANGE VISITS

On December 6, the Chinese government confirmed an exchange of visits between Premier Zhao Ziyang and President Reagan, despite its dissatisfaction with U.S. replies to China's protests over recent expressions of support for Taiwan by members of the U.S. Congress.

The Senate Foreign Relations Committee had adopted a resolution on November 15 declaring that Taiwan's future should be settled peacefully "in a manner acceptable to the people in Taiwan." The resolution was sponsored by Senator Claiborne Pell (D, R.I.). Further, Congress passed an appropriations bill on November 18 authorizing funds for the International Monetary Fund and other international lending institutions. The bill included an amendment stating that Taiwan should remain a full member of the Asian Development Bank regardless of whether Beijing was admitted. Both the Senate committee resolution and the amendment referred to Taiwan by its official name of the Republic of China.

Hu Yaobang, the leader of the Chinese Communist Party, warned on November 26 that Reagan's planned visit to China in April 1984 might be jeopardized if Reagan did not satisfactorily respond to a formal protest by Beijing regarding the November 15 resolution. Hu said the resolution constituted "interference in China's domestic affairs."

Larry Speakes, the White House spokesman, said on November 28 that both the amendment and the resolution represented "the views of members of Congress, who voted for them on specific issues." He confirmed that the administration's policy was that the People's Republic of China was "the sole legitimate government of China." Speakes said Reagan would sign the appropriations bill, but that his signing would in no way reflect support for the amendment. Reagan signed the bill on November 30.

Reagan told a group of schoolchildren on December 2 that the U.S. would not "retreat from our alliance and our friendship with the Chinese on Taiwan" while building its relationship with Beijing. Reagan said, "We are not going to throw aside one friend in order to make another." An article in China's *People's Daily* on December 6 called Reagan's remarks "very puzzling."

Premier Zhao Ziyang paid his visit to the U.S. in January 1984. The highlight of the visit was the signing, on January 12, of a new accord on industrial cooperation and a renewal of a pact on science and technology.

One accord continued a commission to encourage the exchange of information on science and technology. The other called for promotion of trade between the countries and laid the groundwork for more agreements in specific areas, such as offshore oil development.

Progress also was reported during Zhao's visit toward a nuclear power accord between the U.S. and China, one that could be ready for signing by President Reagan in Beijing in April, if current planning continued unchanged.

Zhao delivered a firm pledge against the spread of nuclear weaponry. "We do not advocate or encourage nuclear proliferation," he said in a White House dinner toast on January 10. "We do not engage in nuclear proliferation ourselves, nor do we help other countries develop nuclear weapons."

He repeated the pledge in a meeting, the next day, with a large group of congressional leaders on Capitol Hill.

Zhao also had a separate meeting on January 11 with Senate Republican Leader Howard H. Baker Jr. (Tenn.) and Senate Democratic Leader Robert C. Byrd (W. Va.).

Zhao met privately with President Reagan on January 10, a meeting later opened to admit a number of cabinet members. The China group went to the State Department for a lunch and talks with Secretary of State George P. Shultz. Treasury Secretary Donald T. Regan visited the delegation later in the day and that evening the visitors attended a state dinner in Zhao's honor at the White House.

The differences between the two countries over the Taiwan issue were expressed, but privately instead of publicly.

At their private meeting, Reagan was reported to have stressed to the Chinese "that we take seriously our commitment to our friends," speaking in reference to Taiwan. Zhao was said to have made "a strong presentation" on Taiwan. His point was that Beijing was "uncomfortable" with a whole range of issues dealing with Taiwan, including the Taiwan Relations Act passed by Congress in 1979.

But friendship and trade were the paramount public issues during Zhao's visit to Washington.

Reagan, in signing the accords on January 12, said Zhao's trip "has solidified the good will between us." He described U.S.-China relations as "a business deal that . . . is based on mutual benefit."

At the welcoming ceremony on January 10, Zhao spoke of the "ups and downs" of U.S.-China relations, but, he said, "considerable progress" had been made on the whole.

On trade, he urged the congressional leaders, on January 11, to change the U.S. law that banned communist Third World countries from being granted most favorable trade and economic aid conditions from the U.S.

For its part, Zhao told the National Council for U.S.-China Trade in a luncheon speech on January 11, "China has opened its door, and will never close it again." What was needed now, he said, was "massive capital and advanced technology."

It was now President Ronald Reagan's turn to reciprocate the Chinese premier's visit. While making preparations for the President's forthcoming trip, scheduled for April 26–May 1, U.S. Treasury Secretary Donald T. Regan and Wang Bingqian, China's minister of finance, initialed a tax treaty, on March 21, that would avoid double taxation of U.S. companies and citizens working in China.

The treaty would guarantee American businesses U.S. tax credit for taxes paid in China and would reduce Chinese withholding taxes on U.S. firms operating in China. Regan said the treaty was similar to those the U.S. had concluded with other countries with centrally planned economies, such as Hungary and Poland.

President Reagan and Chinese Premier Zhao Ziyang were expected to sign the treaty during Reagan's April visit to China.

Talks were continuing on a bilateral investment agreement that, like the tax treaty, was expected to improve the investment climate in China for U.S. firms. The agreement would protect U.S. firms against nationalization by the communist government.

President Reagan arrived in Beijing April 26 to an unprecedented 21-gun salute in Tiananmen Square at the Great Hall of the People.

That evening, at a banquet in his honor hosted by President Li Xiannian, Reagan spoke on the need for "mutual respect and benefit" between the two countries.

Reagan's first major speech was reserved, however, for April 27, the President's first full day in China. In comments delivered at the Great Hall of the People, Reagan extolled the virtues of capitalism, criticized the Soviet Union, and expressed his belief in the benefits of faith in God. He also formally announced the conclusion of a bilateral agreement on nuclear cooperation.

In praise of the free enterprise system, Reagan told his audience of business executives, scientists and diplomats that the societies that had made the "most spectacular progress" were ones in which "people have been allowed to create, compete and build, where they have been permitted to think for themselves, make economic decisions and benefit from their own risks." Reagan said, "Nothing could be more basic . . . than economic reward for legitimate risk and honest toil."

Reagan welcomed changes made by China's supreme leader, Deng Xiaoping, including economic incentives and attracting foreign investment to fund China's program of economic modernization.

On the subject of the Soviet Union, Reagan used harsh language in alluding to the Soviet threat to China's borders, the occupation of Afghanistan, the "crushing" of Cambodia, and the downing of a South Korean airliner by the U.S.S.R. in 1983.

Although Reagan said the U.S. and China had to acknowledge the "fundamental differences in ideology and institutions between our two societies," he stressed that "I have not come to China to hold forth on what divides, but to build on what binds us." Reagan said the U.S. wanted greater cooperation in trade, space exploration, U.S. investment in China and the sharing of advanced technology.

Chinese television broadcast Reagan's speech later in the day, but censored remarks critical of the Soviet Union and praising religion and freedom in the U.S.

Also, on April 27, Reagan met with Premier Zhao Ziyang, who criticized the U.S. President's policies in Central America, the Middle

East, Taiwan and Europe. Reagan met with Deng Xiaoping on April 28 and turned down a request from the Chinese leader that the U.S. urge Taiwan to move toward reunification with mainland China.

Later, Reagan said in a television interview that the issue of reunification was "a problem of the Chinese people on both sides of the strait to work out for themselves." Reagan said, "We do not believe that we should involve ourselves in this internal affair."

Deng told Reagan that he was "reasonably satisfied" with the flow of U.S. technology into China but that he would like it to be speeded up. The meeting with Deng concluded Reagan's official talks in Beijing.

For the second consecutive day, on April 28, President Reagan's remarks were censored before being broadcast on television.

In an interview with a Chinese television network, Reagan had alluded to Soviet troops along the Chinese border when he said the U.S. had "no troops massed on your border." He described Americans as "people of peace." These comments were deleted when the interview was broadcast.

U.S. officials had said before the trip that one of its chief goals was to impress upon China an understanding of U.S. actions against Soviet aggression throughout the world.

Also deleted was Reagan's comment that "economic growth and human progress make their greatest strides when people are secure and free to think, speak, worship, choose their own way and reach for the stars." And the Chinese omitted a plea for China to trust in communication and commerce rather than confrontation and conflict in Chinese-American relations.

An official at the Chinese foreign ministry explained that China did not want to allow the leader of one country to attack another country publicly while in China. The official, Qi Huaiyuan, said it was "inappropriate for the Chinese media to publicize the comments by President Reagan on a third country."

Chief White House spokesman Larry Speakes issued a public protest on the censorship on April 28. Speakes said the U.S. regretted the omission of statements that "would have given the Chinese people a better understanding of our country and its people."

Beijing and Moscow had been involved in talks aimed at normalizing relations between their two countries, and a Soviet deputy premier was due to visit China in May. Tass charged on April 28, that Reagan's China trip was being used for "crude attacks on the Soviet Union and other socialist countries." Tass said Reagan was "shamelessly distorting the policy of the Soviet Union." The Soviets criticized Reagan for attempting to improve U.S. ties with China in order to confront the Soviet Union. Tass also referred to Reagan's opportunism in professing amity with China after backing Taiwan for most of his political career.

Reagan followed his official talks in Beijing with a sightseeing tour, visiting the Great Wall. That evening, President and Mrs. Reagan gave a turkey dinner for their Chinese hosts at the Great Wall Hotel. The theme of cooperation between the two countries was again a major topic of conversation.

The President flew to Xian on April 29 and visited the more than 2,000-year-old tomb of China's first emperor, Qin Shi Huang. The tomb, discovered in 1974, contained 8,000 life-size terra-cotta figures of soldiers and horses.

Back in Beijing on April 30, President Reagan formalized three agreements on scientific and cultural exchanges, economic cooperation and the development of nuclear power.

Reagan signed the tax measure, which had been initialed in March by Treasury Secretary Donald T. Regan. The accord limited the taxes Peking was permitted to impose on corporate income, providing guarantees against double taxation for U.S. companies operating in China.

The tax and nuclear accords still required the approval of the U.S. Senate.

Reagan repeated some of his censored remarks in an address to students at Fudan University in Shanghai April 30.

Asked earlier that day, during a tour of the Foxboro Corp. electronics manufacturing plant, why he insisted on preaching to the Chinese about democracy, Reagan had replied, "That's my thing." (The Foxboro plant was China's first industrial joint venture with a U.S. firm.)

Reagan spoke to the students of political, religious and personal freedoms in the U.S. and indirectly criticized the U.S.S.R. He said the U.S. looked forward to the possibility of "cooperating [with China] in the development of space" and emphasized medical research in space and satellite communications.

China had launched its first permanently orbiting communications satellite on April 8, according to the Xinhua news agency. The geosynchronous satellite was later boosted into a position over the Moluccan Sea near Indonesia and began experiments on telephone communications and radio and television transmissions. [A geosynchronous satellite was set in a fixed position relative to the Earth.] China's satellite was believed to have no reconnaisance capacity.

Referring to how his early experiences helped him in later life, Reagan told the students, "You'd be surprised how much being a good actor pays off."

9

RECOVERY OF HONG KONG

CHINA CHALLENGES UNEQUAL TREATIES

The Territory of Hong Kong consists of Hong Kong Island and Stonecutters Island off the southeast coast of the People's Republic of China; the Kowloon Peninsula on the mainland; and the New Territories, partly located on the mainland.

Hong Kong came under Chinese suzerainty between 221 B.C. and 214 B.C. Great Britain occupied Hong Kong Island in 1839, and China ceded the island to Britain under the 1842 Treaty of Nanking that ended the 1839–1842 Opium War.

Under the 1860 Treaty of Beijing, the Kowloon Peninsula and Stonecutters Island were ceded to Britain in perpetuity.

In 1898, the New Territories were leased to Britain for 99 years under the terms of the Beijing Convention, which expires July 1, 1997. The New Territories made up about 90% of Hong Kong territory.

Since the Communist takeover in China in 1949, the government in Beijing had insisted that the "unequal" treaties giving Britain control over Hong Kong were invalid. Beijing pressed its claim to sovereignty over the whole territory.

THATCHER VISITS CHINA: FOCUS ON HONG KONG

Doubts about the long-term future of Hong Kong, and, in particular, the intentions of China toward the British-ruled enclave, had contributed to a decline in stock market prices and other economic activity, according to press reports in the latter part of July and early August. The Hang Seng stock index had dropped 166 points, nearly 13%, from July 15 to August 3, according to a *Wall Street Journal* report on August 4, 1982.

Contributing to the uncertainty was the fact that Chinese Communist Party Vice-Chairman Deng Xiaoping had asked a group of prominent Hong Kong Chinese to Beijing to discuss Hong Kong's future, the *Economist* reported on July 31. Also, Britain's 99-year lease on the New Territories—which accounted for the greater part of Hong Kong's land mass—was due to run out on July 1, 1997. While this was still 15 years in the future, it was a factor that had to be taken into account for anyone signing a long-term mortgage or engaging in other long-term business activities. A report in the *Asian Wall Street Journal* on July 23 indicated that the uncertainty regarding the colony's future status was a reason behind governmental inaction on plans to construct a new airport.

While the reports agreed that China aimed to reestablish its sovereignty over Hong Kong, it also appeared that China was willing to tolerate considerable autonomy for the area, presumably including retention of Hong Kong's flourishing capitalistic business system. In part, this was understood to reflect self-interest: China derived 30%–40% of its annual foreign-exchange earnings from Hong Kong, and the colony's financial services and international contacts were also helpful to the communist state.

British Prime Minister Margaret Thatcher was scheduled to visit Hong Kong in September. While it was not expected that an agreement would be reached on Hong Kong's future on that trip, there was some hope that Britain and China would take some joint action to study the issue, according to the July 23, 1982 report in the *Asian Wall Street Journal*.

The Hong Kong government announced July 29 that it would buy back a block of land in the New Territories from a consortium, Mightycity Co., controlled by China's chief trading company in Hong Kong. The accord gave Mightycity a continued role in the development of the land, and in fact, required the consortium to spend the money from the sale on the construction of a housing project on a portion of the land involved.

The real estate market in Hong Kong had undergone a depression from the time the land was originally purchased by Mightycity. Some observers viewed the government's purchase of the land as essentially a bailout operation for the consortium, contrary to the government's usual laissez-faire philosophy. This view was denied by the government, but an unnamed diplomat quoted by the *Asian Wall Street Journal* on July 30 commented, "Hong Kong wants China to have favorable economic experiences and a more direct investment in the [Hong Kong] economy. It's another hook Hong Kong has into China."

Prime Minister Margaret Thatcher visited Japan, China and Hong Kong in the second half of September, meeting government leaders and discussing trade and other issues.

She arrived in Beijing on September 22, 1982, the first visit to China paid by a British prime minister in office.

In her meetings with Premier Zhao Ziyang and other Chinese officials, Thatcher discussed Afghanistan, the Soviet Union and economic relations between China and Britain. But most press attention focused on another topic of the discussions: Hong Kong.

Zhao, speaking to reporters on September 23, said that "of course China must regain sovereignty" over the colony. But, Zhao added, China would "certainly take a series of measures to guarantee Hong Kong's prosperity and stability."

The joint statement, announced on September 24, after Thatcher had talked with Deng Xiaoping, said that the two leaders had held "far-reaching talks in a friendly atmosphere on the future of Hong Kong." The positions of both sides had been made clear, the statement said, and it had been agreed to hold talks "through diplomatic channels following the visit, with the common aim of maintaining the stability and prosperity of Hong Kong."

On September 24, Thatcher emphasized that "the whole thing must now be speeded up and discussed much more intensely and in much greater detail than it has been before."

While Zhao had made it clear that China believed it should regain sovereignty over Hong Kong, on September 27, Thatcher insisted that the treaties granting the land to Britain should be respected. "If a country will not stand by one treaty, it will not stand by another," she said, noting that their abrogation would be "very serious indeed."

The Thatcher comments evoked a rebuff from China on September 30. A Chinese foreign ministry statement said that "Hong Kong is part of Chinese territory. The treaties concerning the Hong Kong area between the British government and the government of the Manchu dynasty of China were unequal treaties that have never been accepted by the Chinese people. The consistent position of the government of the People's Republic of China has been that China is not bound by these unequal treaties and that the whole Hong Kong area will be recovered when conditions are ripe."

While the two sides had staked out negotiating positions that differed considerably, some observers said that there was room for compromise. The British position that its sovereignty over part of Hong Kong was legally sound was conditioned, the observers said, by the perception that the eventual return of the New Territories might leave the remainder of the colony economically unviable. And the Chinese desire to regain sovereignty did not necessarily mean that China desired the colony to abandon its flourishing free-enterprise economic system, which earned China about 40% of its foreign exchange.

Thatcher arrived in Hong Kong on September 26 for a three-day visit to the colony. She told reporters, the next day, that Britain had "a moral responsibility" to Hong Kong, and that it took that responsibility "very, very seriously."

The British prime minister said that she believed China and Britain could "reconcile their differences" over Hong Kong, and noted that both countries had stressed the preservation of Hong Kong's prosperity.

Nevertheless, the lack of a concrete agreement caused worries to grow in the colony, and the Hong Kong stock exchange slipped 8% on September 27. "If you are not worried, you are either a liar or a fool," said Ronald Li, the chairman of the Far East Stock Exchange. "Nobody in his right mind will start a major project in Hong Kong until the dust settles," Li continued.

Thatcher declined to give details of her discussions with the Chinese leaders and also discounted the significance of the stock market drop. Fluctuations were to be expected in sensitive places like Hong Kong, she said.

CHINA ADAMANT ON SOVEREIGNTY

In the months following Thatcher's visit, Hong Kong's financial market fell sharply and many Hong Kong Chinese took their money from the colony. This added urgency for China and Britain to reach a negotiated agreement on the future status of Hong Kong. China proposed, in December 1982, to run Hong Kong as a special administrative zone, allowing it to maintain its own social, economic and legal system. This, however, did not mean, as China's foreign ministry indicated July 13, 1983, that China would change its constitution to allow the colony to have a status separate from that of the mainland.

The Sino-British negotiations on the retrocession of Hong Kong were to go through many rounds of talks held in Beijing. In 1983, the negotiators from both sides held talks July 25–26, August 2–3, September 22–23, October 19–20, November 14–15 and December 7–8.

China had agreed that negotiations with Britain should remain confidential. However, since talks resumed in July 1983, Beijing issued several official statements and press reports relating to Chinese plans for Hong Kong and denouncing the British position. Britain was generally believed to be seeking a continued administrative role in the colony after its leases for the New Territories expired in 1997. China insisted on complete control of Hong Kong at that date, rejecting Britain's argument that continued British administrative control was necessary for the future prosperity of Hong Kong. Beijing repeatedly said it would ensure Hong Kong's future as a major financial center after 1997, claiming that the colony's prosperity was not due to Britain but to the diligence of the population and the support of the Chinese mainland. (Of the total population of five million in Hong Kong, 98% were of Chinese origin.)

China hardened its position through public pronouncements, especially after the third round of talks in September. Hu Yaobang, China's Communist Party general secretary, told reporters on August 6 that Beijing intended to recover sovereignty over Hong Kong on July 1, 1997, the day after Britain's leases on the New Territories expired.

The *People's Daily* stated on October 6 that China would unilaterally announce its policy toward Hong Kong if Britain "stubbornly sticks to its wrong stand." The editorial continued: "China, as a sovereign state, will recover its sovereignty over Hong Kong and the administration of it is not for discussion." On October 3, Xinhua had charged British officials with making "inappropriate remarks" regarding the talks. Xinhua's criticism was apparently directed at Prime Minister Margaret Thatcher and Richard Luce, the junior minister of staff at the Foreign Office in charge of Hong Kong. On September 23, Thatcher had said that Hong Kong would have gained its independence years before, as Singapore had, if not for the treaties leasing the colony to Britain. Luce said, on September 28, that China's public statements on the situation were "unhelpful." Luce had also maintained that China's efforts to place an early deadline on negotiations "could be counterproductive."

China condemned Thatcher's comment on September 25 on Hong Kong's independence, charging that the comparison with other British colonies was improper because Hong Kong was part of Chinese territory ceded through unequal treaties.

The uncertainty over Hong Kong's future, particularly following the latest round of talks, caused the Hong Kong dollar to plunge and stock prices to tumble. Panic-buying of consumer goods had also begun. The colony's currency was selling at 9.55 to the U.S. dollar on September 24, a record low, and down 9.2% from the day before. The value of the currency had fallen 32% since early January.

Hong Kong's financial secretary, Sir John Bremridge, had said on September 16 that the colony's uncertain political future was hindering the recovery from the 1982 world recession. However, he added that strong export growth in the first half of the year would contribute to an expansion in Gross Domestic Product in 1983 of an inflation-adjusted 5.5%–6%, to HK$180 billion (US$22.44 billion). In February, Bremridge had predicted a growth of 4%. Had it not been for the recent lack of investment confidence, Bremridge said, Hong Kong could have expected growth at a double-digit rate.

The talks on the future of Hong Kong continued into 1984, with the negotiators meeting each month for two days. The tempo of the negotiations picked up following the visit of British Foreign Secretary Sir Geoffrey Howe to Beijing in the latter part of April.

On January 16, China presented its most comprehensive plan to date on the future of Hong Kong. The plan was detailed in an interview with Ji Pengfei, the state councilor with responsibility for Hong Kong, that was published by the China News Service. Ji confirmed that the colony's social, legal and economic systems would remain the same for 50 years after Britain's lease expired in 1997. He said Hong Kong would be a special administrative zone run by officials selected from the present resident population of the colony. Key officials would be named after consultation with, or election by, the people of Hong Kong and would be appointed by Beijing. Hong Kong would run its own affairs, except for defense and foreign policy, which would be controlled by Beijing, Ji said.

After the February talks, Richard Luce, the British minister of state at the Foreign Office in charge of Hong Kong affairs, indicated that the two sides were approaching an agreement. He said on February 28, that the talks were focusing on detailed matters and were "proceeding steadily." Luce commented, "There is a convergence of interests among the parties." He also said that any settlement had to be acceptable to the people of Hong Kong.

Disturbed by the prospect of a settlement, on March 14 Hong Kong's Legislative Council voted unanimously in favor of a resolution demanding a voice in negotiations between Great Britain and China over the future of the colony.

The Legislative Council did not ask for a direct role in the negotiations but passed a resolution demanding the right to debate any proposals on the colony's future before a final accord was approved by London and Beijing. The council also wanted to be informed of the progress of the talks. China was said to oppose a role for the Legislative Council, regarding the future of Hong Kong as a bilateral issue between Beijing and London.

After the 11th round of talks, Sir Geoffrey Howe made a trip to Beijing April 15–18, where he held talks with Chinese leaders. Howe met with Wu Xueqian, the Chinese foreign minister, on April 16. That evening, Howe said he was "heartened" by the progress made on the Hong Kong talks since the visit of Prime Minister Margaret Thatcher to Beijing in 1982. Howe said, "The excellent relations which exist between Britain and China encourage me in the view that we can reach an agreement under which Hong Kong's stability and prosperity can be maintained." However, Howe had made clear before his China trip that his visit was aimed at reviewing the progress made by the negotiators and that much remained to be resolved.

Howe met with Deng Xiaoping on April 18. After the meeting, the Xinhua news agency announced that "important matters" had been agreed upon. Howe flew to Hong Kong the same day, where he made the April 20 announcement that it would "not be realistic" to expect any other solution than Britain's withdrawal from an administrative role in 1997. Howe said the talks between China and Britain had been focusing on "other ways of securing the assurances necessary for the continuity of Hong Kong's stability, prosperity and way of life." He said Britain was seeking an agreement that would assure Hong Kong "a high degree of autonomy under Chinese sovereignty." Howe denied the "idea of a sellout."

This deepened the concern of the Hong Kong residents. In June, three members of the Executive and Legislative council journeyed to Beijing to present their views to Deng Xiaoping. They had a meeting with the paramount leader, during which they were told bluntly that the councils had no role in deciding how China would reincorporate the colony in 1997.

Deng said China had "already decided our stand on policy" on the issue. Further, he rejected the notion presented by one of the visitors that the councilors represented the views of the people of Hong Kong.

Deng's reportedly harsh tone in his meeting with the delegation raised a storm in Hong Kong over whether China understood the concerns of the Hong Kong people relating to the return to Chinese rule in 1997.

Members of the Executive and Legislative councils had been lobbying in London to insist on a continued British administrative role in Hong Kong after 1997.

For its part, Britain took steps to prepare Hong Kong for self-government, looking toward Hong Kong's change of status in 1997. On July 18, Hong Kong's governor, Sir Edward Youde, issued a Green Paper outlining plans for political reforms in Hong Kong.

The changes reduced the power of the governor and aimed at a more representative government. The Green Paper made no mention of the return to Chinese sovereignty in 1997.

Under the plan, indirect elections would be held to elect 24 officials to the Legislative Council by 1988. The Legislative Council would elect eight members to the Executive Council by 1991. Currently, the governor was responsible for the appointment of members of the councils.

The plan ruled out direct elections of council members.

Foreign Secretary Howe said on July 18 that "the need for stability at a crucial time in Hong Kong history dictates the gradual approach" adopted in the Green Paper. Howe also ruled out a referendum among Hong Kong residents on the future of the colony. He maintained that a referendum would have "very real drawbacks" and that "factional divisions or disturbances" should not be provoked.

On July 19, China commented that it had "no obligation" to honor the proposal.

Then, on August 1, Britain announced that it had reached an accord with China on the future of Hong Kong. Sir Geoffrey Howe made the announcement in Hong Kong after holding talks with Chinese leaders in Beijing on a visit July 27–31. Chinese officials had reported at the conclusion of the talks that a breakthrough had been achieved. On July 31, Deng Xiaoping said, "Now we can . . . say that Prime Minister Margaret Thatcher will bring an end to British colonial rule."

As recently as July 19, British officials had been quoted in the British press as saying that "intractable problems" remained to be resolved in the negotiations on Hong Kong's future. Britain was reported to want a detailed agreement on the return to Chinese sovereignty, while China was said to want a more general accord.

In announcing the accord, Howe said a draft agreement would be signed in September outlining the terms under which Britain would turn Hong Kong over to China when Britain's leases on most of the colony expired in 1997. The preliminary agreement would be debated in the British Parliament and, if accepted, finalized by the end of 1984.

China had set a September deadline for an agreement, threatening to unilaterally announce its own plans for Hong Kong if the deadline were not met.

Detailing some of the terms of the accord, Howe said it provided for "the preservation of all the rights and freedoms which the people of Hong Kong now enjoy." He affirmed that the colony's educational and legal and judicial systems would be maintained in the 50 years after 1997.

Howe said the accord insured the convertibility of the Hong Kong dollar to other currencies; the freedom to move capital in and out of Hong Kong; pension rights; freedom to participate in international organizations and trade agreements; and the right to own property, trade freely and travel.

Howe said that the people of Hong Kong would be allowed time to consider the agreement. After it came into force, a Chinese-British liaison group would be created to oversee the transition to Chinese rule until the year 2000.

The formation of the liaison group had reportedly been an issue of contention in the negotiations. Addressing fears in Hong Kong that the establishment of the group would allow China to interfere in the administration of Hong Kong before 1997, Howe gave assurances that the group would have no supervisory or administrative role. China's foreign ministry, in a statement carried by the Xinhua news agency on August 2, confirmed Howe's assurances.

Several "matters of substance, including land, civil aviation and nationality" were still under discussion, Howe said. (Chinese law did not permit dual nationality. Some two million Hong Kong residents held Hong Kong–British passports.)

Howe praised China's plans to incorporate Hong Kong as a special administrative region, calling the "one country, two systems" concept "farsighted" and asserting that it held "enormous potential for the future of Hong Kong."

Following Howe's statement, on August 2, Hong Kong's two leading banks cut their prime lending rates by two percentage points to 15%. Heavy stock trading sent the Hang Seng Index, the Hong Kong market's main indicator, up 8%—the largest jump in two and a half years. The index improved 66.95 points on the day, closing at 893.69.

Prior to the announcement, the stock market had been in a steady decline since late April, when Howe announced that Britain would not retain an administrative role in the colony after 1997.

On August 2, Taiwan criticized the agreement, comparing it to pledges made by China to Tibet when it installed a communist government there in 1953.

AGREEMENT INITIALED

On September 26, 1984, Britain and China initialed a draft agreement on the future of Hong Kong after it reverted to Chinese rule on July 1, 1997. The joint declaration contained assurances that Hong Kong would retain considerable autonomy as a Chinese special administrative zone when Britain's leases over most of the territory expired.

The agreement was signed at the Great Hall of the People in Beijing by Richard Evans, the British ambassador to China, and Chinese Deputy Foreign Minister Zhou Nan.

Under the joint declaration, Hong Kong was to become a special administrative region of China and would retain "a high degree of autonomy except in foreign and defense affairs." As promised earlier, Hong Kong would be allowed to maintain unchanged its capitalist system and life style for 50 years after 1997. The declaration said: "Rights and freedoms, including those of the person, of speech, of the press, of assembly, of association, of travel, of movement, of correspondence, of strike, of choice of occupation, of academic research and of religious belief will be ensured by law."

Hong Kong would have its own executive, legislative and independent judicial powers, and would maintain its present laws virtually unchanged. However, a potential loophole existed for China to change Hong Kong laws: The agreement said the territory's laws would remain valid except for those that contravened the basic law that China would enact, codifying the policies set out in the draft agreement. China's National People's Congress probably would not enact the proposed basic law until after the agreement was ratified, and could include qualifiers overriding Hong Kong law.

Local inhabitants would make up the government and legislature of Hong Kong, the accord stated. The chief executive would be selected by consultation or election and would be appointed by Beijing. Principal officials would be nominated by the chief executive and appointed by Beijing, also. Procedures for elections and consultations were not spelled out in the accord.

Hong Kong's status as a free port, separate customs territory and international financial center were assured, and its foreign exchange, securities, gold and futures markets were protected. The Hong Kong dollar was to remain freely convertible, and the territory would be permitted to develop economic relations with other countries, under the name Hong Kong, China. Beijing would not levy taxes on Hong Kong.

The territory would issue its own travel documents and maintain responsibility for public order. China would station troops on Hong Kong, but the declaration stated that they should not interfere in Hong Kong's internal affairs.

As a special administrative zone, Hong Kong would be permitted to display its own flag and emblem alongside those of China, and the English language could be used in the government and the courts. After 1997, foreign warships would have to obtain permission from Beijing to visit Hong Kong, and countries not recognized by Beijing would not be allowed to have official offices in the territory. Provision was made for Great Britain to maintain a consulate general in Hong Kong.

Civil aviation, along with land and nationality, had been among the last of the issues to be resolved by Great Britain and China. Under the agreement, Hong Kong retained the right to assign air routes to and from the territory that did not stop in mainland China.

An annex referring to land leases stipulated that revenues from the leasing of land before 1997 would be shared by the current and future governments of Hong Kong. Land leases would be offered until 2047, 50 years after the joint declaration came into effect, and existing leases would generally be renewed, if desired.

Separate memoranda issued by Great Britain and China referred to the nationality of Hong Kong residents. After 1997, all ethnic Chinese would be considered Chinese nationals, and the approximately three million British Dependent Territory citizens would lose their United Kingdom citizenship but would receive a new status entitling them to travel on British passports.

Another annex to the joint declaration provided for the creation of a joint Sino-British liaison group to oversee the transfer of power.

Zhou Nan, China's chief negotiator in the talks that led to the agreement, said on September 27: "There are explicit provisions which state what kind of freedom the people of Hong Kong will have and what kind of authority the government of the special administrative region will have." He added, "Those who might seek to change the policies will find their efforts futile."

However, Zhou said it was "too soon" to say precisely how Hong Kong would be governed after 1997.

TAIWAN CONDEMNS ACCORD

On September 26, Premier Yu Kuo-hua of Taiwan urged resistance to communist rule over Hong Kong.

Yu said, "We urge the Chinese residents of Hong Kong and Kowloon more vigorously to pursue their struggle against communism for freedom." He continued, "We will assist and support this struggle using various methods and via different channels."

In a message to the Chinese people of Hong Kong, Yu suggested that they take part in local elections to increase their strength. This, he said, would enable them to "deal with Chinese communist ambitions for control, and thereby to help protect and secure freedom and democracy." Yu encouraged Hong Kong Chinese to settle in Taiwan, promising them one-year multiple entry visas, and the right to deposit and withdraw funds from Taiwan's offshore bank and to arrange to have their children educated in Taiwan.

A spokesman for the foreign ministry of Taiwan denounced the Sino-British pact on Hong Kong as an "invalid" act by a "rebellious" government in Beijing. The spokesman charged that the agreement "fails to honor Hong Kong residents' longing for continued economic prosperity and a democratic political system."

ACCORD FORMALIZED

The agreement was signed in Beijing by Chinese Premier Zhao Ziyang and British Prime Minister Margaret Thatcher, who arrived in the Chinese capital on December 18, 1984.

Hong Kong's Legislative Council had endorsed the draft treaty on October 18, the British Parliament ratified it after debates in the House of Commons on December 5–6 and in the House of Lords on December 10, and China's nominal parliament, the National People's Congress, was to ratify it sometime before July 1985.

After the signing ceremony, Zhao commented: "We have accomplished a task of historical significance." Thatcher responded by referring to the pact as "a landmark in the life of the territory, in the course of Anglo-Chinese relations and in the history of international diplomacy."

Thatcher praised the concept of "one country–two systems" embodied in the agreement. She also said the agreement had brought China and Great Britain closer together and "increased our mutual understanding, respect and trust." (The same day, the prime minister announced that Queen Elizabeth II had accepted an invitation to visit China, probably in the second half of 1986.)

Hu Yaobang, the general secretary of the Chinese Communist Party, told Thatcher that she had brought about "a red-letter day, an occasion of great joy" to the Chinese people.

Both Hu and Zhao gave credit to Deng Xiaoping for the element of the agreement that induced Britain to accept it: the retention of Hong Kong's capitalist system for 50 years after the accord would go into effect. Deng told Thatcher that China would need Hong Kong's thriving economy until the middle of the 21st century to help its own economic modernization process.

The exchange of the instruments of ratification—the last formal step in the treaty-making procedure—took place on May 17, 1985, in a brief ceremony in Beijing.

Meanwhile, the 10 members of the Sino-British Joint Liaison Group that was to oversee the transfer of Hong Kong to China were named on May 21. The group's first meeting was scheduled for July.

Membership of the group had long been disputed, with China objecting to the inclusion of Hong Kong's trade and industry secretary, Eric Ho, a Hong Kong Chinese. Beijing, which did not consider Hong Kong to have an independent stance, maintained that Ho, who held a British Dependent Territories subject passport, was a Chinese citizen. The dispute was settled when Britain agreed to give Ho full British citizenship. Britain had wanted Ho on the committee because of his expertise related to the issue of Hong Kong's membership in the General Agreement on Tariffs and Trade and other international trade agreements.

REACTION OF RESIDENTS

In the meantime, on November 29, 1984, the government of Hong Kong published a White Paper which reported that most of the colony's inhabitants found the agreement between China and Great Britain "acceptable."

Following the initialing of the draft treaty by Britain and China in late September, residents of Hong Kong had sent letters to the government's Special Assessment Office, giving their opinion of the accord for publication in the White Paper.

Despite the general acceptance of the treaty, the paper cited a number of reservations expressed in the letters, particularly about the acceptance overseas of Hong Kong travel documents after 1997.

A report by a British team monitoring the objectivity of the Assessment Office's survey criticized the office for not guaranteeing the confidentiality of the names of those submitting opinions until several weeks after the survey began. The monitoring team said that those residents who accepted the agreement "do so chiefly because they regard reunification as inevitable and are relieved that the terms of the draft agreement are as good as they are."

In a statement on November 28, the unofficial members of Hong Kong's executive and legislative councils had urged that residents of the colony be given a say in drafting the new basic law to be prepared by China, incorporating Hong Kong into its territory. They also demanded that Hong Kong representatives be allowed to sit in on the Anglo-Chinese liaison group that was to oversee the transfer of power.

The council members listed several concerns regarding the treaty, including human rights, the stationing of Chinese troops in Hong Kong and the status of British Dependent Territory citizens after 1997.

Excerpts from the Joint Declaration on Hong Kong Initialed by Great Britain and China

Following are excerpts from the agreement on Hong Kong that was initialed Sept. 26, 1984 by Britain and China, as made public by the British Foreign Office:

Joint Declaration

The government of the United Kingdom of Great Britain and Northern Ireland and the government of the People's Republic of China have reviewed with satisfaction the friendly relations existing between the two governments and peoples in recent years and agreed that a proper negotiated settlement of the question of Hong Kong, which is left over from the past, is conducive to the maintenance of the prosperity and stability of Hong Kong and to the further strengthening and development of the relations between the two countries on a new basis. To this end, they have, after talks between the delegations of the two governments, agreed to declare as follows:

[1]

The government of the People's Republic of China declares that to recover the Hong Kong area (including Hong Kong Island, Kowloon and the New Territories, hereinafter referred to as Hong Kong) is the common aspiration of the entire Chinese people and that it has decided to resume the exercise of sovereignty over Hong Kong with effect from 1 July 1997.

[2]

The government of the United Kingdom declares that it will restore Hong Kong to the People's Republic of China with effect from 1 July 1997.

[3]

The government of the People's Republic of China declares that the basic policies of the People's Republic of China regarding Hong Kong are as follows:

(1) Upholding national unity and territorial integrity and taking account of the history of Hong Kong and its realities, the People's

Republic of China has decided to establish, in accordance with the provisions of Article 31 of the Constitution of the People's Republic of China, a Hong Kong Special Administrative Region upon resuming the exercise of sovereignty over Hong Kong.

(2) The Hong Kong Special Administrative Region will be directly under the authority of the central people's government of the People's Republic of China. The Hong Kong Special Administrative Region will enjoy a high degree of autonomy except in foreign and defense affairs, which are the responsibilities of the central people's government.

(3) The Hong Kong Special Administrative Region will be vested with executive, legislative and independent judicial power, including that of final adjudication. The laws currently in force in Hong Kong will remain basically unchanged.

(4) The government of the Hong Kong Special Administrative Region will be composed of local inhabitants. The chief executive will be appointed by the central people's government on the basis of the results of elections or consultations to be held locally.

Principal officials will be nominated by the chief executive of the Hong Kong Special Administrative Region for appointment by the central people's government. Chinese and foreign nationals previously working in the public and police services in the government departments of Hong Kong may remain in employment. British and other foreign nationals may also be employed to serve as advisers or hold certain public posts in government departments of the Hong Kong Special Administrative Region.

(5) The current social and economic systems in Hong Kong will remain unchanged, and so will the life style. Rights and freedoms, including those of the person, of speech, of the press, of assembly, of association, of travel, of movement, of correspondence, of strike, of choice of occupation, of academic research and of religious belief will be insured by law in the Hong Kong Special Administrative Region. Private property, ownership of enterprises, legitimate right of inheritance and foreign investment will be protected by law.

(6) The Hong Kong Special Administrative Region will retain the status of a free port and a separate customs territory.

(7) The Hong Kong Special Administrative Region will retain the status of an international financial center, and its markets for foreign exchange, gold, securities and futures will continue. There will be free flow of capital. The Hong Kong dollar will continue to circulate and remain freely convertible.

(8) The Hong Kong Special Administrative Region will have independent finances. The central people's government will not levy taxes on the Hong Kong Special Administrative Region.

(9) The Hong Kong Special Administrative Region may establish mutually beneficial economic relations with the United Kingdom and other countries, whose economic interests in Hong Kong will be given due regard.

(10) Using the name of "Hong Kong, China," the Hong Kong Special Administrative Region may on its own maintain and develop economic and cultural relations and conclude relevant agreements with states, regions and relevant international organizations. The government of the Hong Kong Special Administrative Region may on its own issue travel documents for entry into and exit from Hong Kong.

(11) The maintenance of public order in the Hong Kong Special Administrative Region will be the responsibility of the government of the Hong Kong Special Administrative Region.

[4]

The government of the United Kingdom and the government of the People's Republic of China declare that, during the transition period between the date of entry into force of this joint declaration and 30 June 1997, the government of the United Kingdom will be responsible for the administration of Hong Kong with the object of maintaining and preserving its economic prosperity and social stability; and that the government of the People's Republic of China will give its cooperation in this connection.

[8]

This joint declaration is subject to ratification and shall enter into force on the date of the exchange of instruments of ratification, which shall take place in Beijing before 30 June 1985. This joint declaration and its annexes shall be equally binding.

Annex I
China's Basic Policies

Upon the resumption of the exercise of sovereignty over Hong Kong on 1 July 1997, the (Chinese) National People's Congress shall enact and promulgate a basic law of the Hong Kong Special Administrative Region stipulating that after the establishment of the Hong Kong Special Administrative Region, the socialist system and socialist policies shall not be practiced in the Hong Kong Special Administrative Region and that Hong Kong's previous capitalist system and life style shall remain unchanged for 50 years.

The government and legislature of the Hong Kong Special Administrative Region shall be composed of local inhabitants. The chief executive shall be selected by election or through consultations held locally and be appointed by the central people's government. Principal officials (equivalent to secretaries) shall be nominated by the chief executive of the Hong Kong Special Administrative Region and appointed by the central people's government. The legislature of the Hong Kong Special Administrative Region shall be constituted by elections. The executive authorities shall abide by the law and be accountable to the legislature.

In addition to Chinese, English may also be used in organs of government and in the courts in the Hong Kong Special Administrative Region.

Apart from displaying the national flag and national emblem of the People's Republic of China, the Hong Kong Special Administrative Region may use a regional flag and emblem of its own.

The Hong Kong Special Administrative Region shall be a separate customs territory. It may participate in relevant international organizations and international trade agreements (including preferential trade agreements) such as the General Agreement on Tariffs and Trade and arrangements regarding international trade in textiles. Export quotas, tariff preferences and other similar arrangements obtained by the Hong Kong Special Administrative Region shall be enjoyed exclusively by the Hong Kong Special Administrative Region.

The Hong Kong Special Administrative Region shall retain the status of an international financial center. The monetary and financial systems previously practiced in Hong Kong, including the systems of regulation and supervision of deposit-taking institutions and financial markets, shall be maintained.

The Hong Kong Special Administrative Region government may decide its monetary and financial policies on its own. It shall safeguard the free operation of financial business and the free flow of capital within, into and out of the Hong Kong Special Administrative Region. No exchange control policy shall be applied in the Hong Kong Special Administrative Region. Markets for foreign exchange, gold, securities and futures shall continue.

The Hong Kong dollar, as the local legal tender, shall continue to circulate and remain freely convertible. The authority to issue Hong Kong currency shall be vested in the Hong Kong Special Administrative Region government.

The Exchange Fund shall be managed and controlled by the Hong Kong Special Administrative Region government, primarily for regulating the exchange value of the Hong Kong dollar.

The Hong Kong Special Administrative Region shall maintain Hong Kong's previous systems of shipping management and shipping regulation.

The Hong Kong Special Administrative Region shall maintain the status of Hong Kong as a center of international and regional aviation.

The Hong Kong Special Administrative Region shall maintain the educational system previously practiced in Hong Kong. Institutions of all kinds, including those run by religious and community organizations, may retain their autonomy. Students shall enjoy freedom of choice of education and freedom to pursue their education outside the Hong Kong Special Administrative Region.

Subject to the principle that foreign affairs are the responsibility of the central people's government, representatives of the Hong Kong Special Administrative Region government may participate, as members of delegations of the government of the People's Republic of China, in negotiations at the diplomatic level directly affecting the Hong Kong Special Administrative Region conducted by the central people's government. The Hong Kong Special Administrative Region may on its own, using the name "Hong Kong, China," maintain and develop relations and conclude and implement agreements with states, regions and relevant international organizations in the appropriate fields, including the economic, trade, financial and monetary, shipping, communications, touristic, cultural and sporting fields.

The application to the Hong Kong Special Administrative Region of international agreements to which the People's Republic of China is or becomes a party shall be decided by the central people's government, in accordance with the circumstances and needs of the Hong Kong Special Administrative Region, and after seeking the views of the Hong Kong Special Administrative Region government.

Foreign consular and other official or semiofficial missions may be established in the Hong Kong Special Administrative Region with the approval of the central people's government. Consular and other official missions established in Hong Kong by states which have established formal diplomatic relations with the People's Republic of China may be maintained.

The United Kingdom may establish a consulate general in the Hong Kong Special Administrative Region.

The maintenance of public order in the Hong Kong Special Administrative Region shall be the responsibility of the Hong Kong Special Administrative Region government. Military forces sent by the central people's government to be stationed in the Hong Kong Special Administrative Region for the purpose of defense shall not interfere in the internal affairs of the Hong Kong Special Administrative Region. Expenditure for these military forces shall be borne by the central people's government.

Religious organizations and believers may maintain their relations with religious organizations and believers everywhere, and schools, hospitals and welfare institutions run by religious organizations in the Hong Kong Special Administrative Region and those in other parts of the People's Republic of China shall be based on the principles of nonsubordination, noninterference and mutual respect.

Entry into the Hong Kong Special Administrative Region of persons from other parts of China shall continue to be regulated in accordance with the present practice.

Annex II
Joint Liaison Group

In order to meet the requirements for liaison, consultation and the exchange of information, the two governments have agreed to set up a Joint Liaison Group.

The functions of the Joint Liaison Group shall be:

(a) To conduct consultations on the implementation of the joint declaration.

(b) To discuss matters relating to the smooth transfer of government in 1997.

(c) To exchange information and conduct consultations on such subjects as may be agreed by the two sides.

Matters on which there is disagreement in the Joint Liaison Group will be referred to the two governments for solution through consultations.

Matters for consideration during the first half of the period between the establishment of the Joint Liaison Group and 1 July 1997 shall include:

(a) Action to be taken by the two governments to enable the Hong Kong Special Administrative Region to maintain its economic relations as a separate customs territory, and in particular to insure the maintenance of Hong Kong's participation in the General Agreement on Tariffs and Trade, the Multifiber Agreement and other international agreements; and

(b) Action to be taken by the two governments to insure the continued application of international rights and obligations affecting Hong Kong.

The two governments have agreed that in the second half of the period between the establishment of the Joint Liaison Group and 1 July 1997, there will be need for closer cooperation, which will therefore be intensified during that period. Matters for consideration during this second period shall include:

(a) Procedures to be adopted for the smooth transition in 1997.

(b) Action to assist the Hong Kong Special Administrative Region to maintain and develop economic and cultural relations and conclude agreements on these matters with states, regions and relative international organizations.

Annex III
Land Leases

All leases of land granted or decided upon before the entry into force of the joint declaration and those granted thereafter and which extend beyond 30 June 1997 and all rights in relation to such leases shall continue to be recognized and protected under the law of the Hong Kong Special Administrative Region.

All leases of land granted by the British Hong Kong government not containing a right of renewal that expire before 30 June 1997, except short-term tenancies and leases for special purposes, may be extended if the lessee so wishes for a period expiring not later than 30 June 2047, without payment of an additional premium.

From the entry into force of the joint declaration until 30 June 1997, new leases of land may be granted by the British Hong Kong government for terms expiring not later than 30 June 2047. Such leases shall be granted at a premium and nominal rental until 30 June 1997, after which date they shall not require payment of an additional premium but an annual rent equivalent to 3 percent of the rateable value of the property at that date, adjusted in step with changes in the rateable value thereafter, shall be charged.

A Land Commission shall be established in Hong Kong immediately upon the entry into force of the joint declaration.

United Kingdom Memorandum

All persons who on 30 June 1997 are, by virtue of a connection with Hong Kong, British Dependent Territories citizens (BDTC's) under the law in force in the United Kingdom will cease to be BDTC's with effect from 1 July 1997 but will be eligible to retain an appropriate status which, without conferring the right of abode in the United Kingdom, will entitle them to continue to use passports issued by the government of the United Kingdom. This status will be acquired by such persons only if they hold or are included in such a British passport issued before 1 July 1997, except that eligible persons born on or after 1 January 1997, but before 1 July 1997, may obtain or be included in such a passport up to 31 December 1997.

Chinese Memorandum

Under the Nationality Law of the People's Republic of China, all Hong Kong Chinese compatriots, whether they are holders of the "British Dependent Territories citizens' passport" or not, are Chinese nationals.

Taking account of the historical background of Hong Kong and its realities, the competent authorities of the government of the People's Republic of China will, with effect from 1 July 1997, permit Chinese nationals in Hong Kong who were previously called "British Dependent Territories citizens" to use travel documents issued by the government of the United Kingdom for the purpose of traveling to other states and regions.

The above Chinese nationals will not be entitled to British consular protection in the Hong Kong Special Administrative Region and other parts of the People's Republic of China on account of their holding the above-mentioned British travel documents.

10

THE GREENING OF CHINA

CHINA CELEBRATES 35TH ANNIVERSARY

October 1, 1984, marked the 35th anniversary of the establishment of the People's Republic of China. The Chinese government celebrated the occasion with a parade displaying its military weapons and renewed its call to Taiwan for peaceful reunification.

The military review in Beijing was the first since 1959 and marked the first time China had displayed its modern missiles. The parade included tanks, self-propeled howitzers, css-4 intercontinental ballistic missiles and China's new submarine-launched css-nx-4 ballistic missiles.

Military observers noted that the weapons—Chinese-made—were of good quality but that most were outdated. Some were said to be modeled on Israeli, Soviet, Brazilian and Canadian prototypes.

Marchers in the civilian section of the parade carried busts of four deceased leaders: Chairman Mao Zedong, Premier Zhou Enlai, President Liu Shaoqi and Marshal Zhu De, the founder of the People's Liberation Army. The floats signified the theme of progress and prosperity under the pragmatic rule of China's preeminent leader, Deng Xiaoping, 80. The displays on the floats included a 20-foot-high chicken, a huge refrigerator full of food and bottles of beer, and a stereo system, washing machine and color television.

Banners bore slogans such as "Time is money, efficiency is life."

Deng, along with Premier Zhao Ziyang, Communist Party General Secretary Hu Yaobang, Deng Yingchao, Zhou's widow, and deposed Cambodian leader Prince Norodom Sihanouk watched the parade from the balcony of Tiananmen (the Gate of Heavenly Peace).

After inspecting 6,000 troops wearing the army's new uniform, Deng made a speech in which he called for a strengthening of the national defense "in the seriously deteriorating international situation." He said members of the military "must be alert at all times, constantly improve their military and political qualities and strive to gain knowledge and ability for modern warfare."

Citing reunification with Taiwan and socialist modernization as China's other priorities besides defense, Deng predicted that "an irresistible trend, the peaceful reunification of our motherland, will sooner or later come true." He said China had "placed socialist modernization above everything else in our work. Our primary job at present," he continued, "is to reform systematically whatever is impeding our progress in existing economic structures."

LIBERAL ECONOMIC REFORMS

The Chinese government, at this juncture, was poised to intensify its drive to revitalize Chinese economy through further integration of capitalist market forces into its state planning. The Communist Party Central Committee was scheduled to meet in Beijing. On October 12, Deng Xiaoping was reported to have said that the "significance of the forthcoming session will go down in history."

As predicted, the Central Committee announced on October 20 its decision to introduce a series of far-reaching reforms in the structure of Chinese Communist economy, to be introduced gradually over the next five years.

In a communique, the committee said the plan "inevitably calls for the reform of every aspect of the entire economic structure." A major area of focus was the state-controlled price system, which the communique said was "irrational" and "has to be reformed." Reform of the price system was considered "the key to reform of the entire economic system," the communique said.

Under the new measures, central planning would be limited. The state would retain control over important sectors of the economy such as banking, energy, steel and mining, but in other areas market forces would be introduced. Factory managers operating under guidelines would have more say in running state enterprises and would be allowed to find their own markets, plan production and set wages and prices. Subsidies on consumer goods would be phased out and competition encouraged.

China's more than one million industrial enterprises would become "independent and responsible for [their] own profit and loss," according to the communique. Government departments for the most part would relinquish control over the management and operation of these enterprises. Some prices would be allowed to float freely and price controls on many items would no longer be set by the state but would be adjusted to more accurately reflect supply and demand.

The communique stressed, however, that the elimination of subsidies "will never bring about a general and spiraling price rise." Workers' wages would rise as subsidies were removed, and, as prices of commodities such as coal became higher, industries would have to reduce costs by cutting consumption, and communique said. Economic levers for regulation such as taxation and interest rates would be used.

China's leaders also pledged to expand foreign trade, promote younger technical experts, retire older managers and tie wage increases to increases in productivity.

The communique noted that "the profound changes that have taken place in the 35 years since the founding of the People's Republic are an initial demonstration of the superiority of the socialist system." However, the statement continued, "this superiority, it must be pointed out, has not been brought into full play."

The communique listed failures of the current system, including government domination of economic enterprises, central planning that was too rigid and too extensive, a pricing system that did not take into account production costs, bureaucratic rivalries and a lack of incentives for workers. The new measures, it was hoped, would "help break the blockade and monopoly hampering the growth of production, lay bare the defects of enterprises quickly and stimulate enterprises to improve technology, operation and management."

The communique referred to the changes as "the inevitable trend of history and the wish of the people." It noted that "Socialism does not mean pauperism, for it aims at the elimination of poverty." Maoist egalitarianism, the document admitted, was a "serious obstacle" to economic growth. It said, "General prosperity cannot and will never mean absolute egalitarianism or that all members of society become better off simultaneously or at the same speed." The principles of more pay for more work and wage differentials according to skills were advocated.

Along with the intensification of its drive for economic liberalization, the Chinese government was also going to pursue collateral reforms in its domestic and foreign policies.

Deng Xiaoping reaffirmed his open-door policy in a speech before the Communist Party's Central Advisory Committee on October 22, 1984 (published January 1, 1985). He was said to have described the policy of opening to the West as the only way to end the backwardness China had brought upon itself through hundreds of years of isolation.

Deng said the open-door policy of encouraging foreign investment, introducing more modern ways and other changes was the only way to overcome "poverty, backwardness and ignorance" caused by China's previous isolation. The policy would continue "for a long time to come," Deng said, claiming that it was essential to China's goal of quadrupling its gross national product to $1,000 billion by the year 2000. He said reaching that goal would give China "much greater influence internationally."

Assuring those who feared that China would become a capitalist country, thereby negating a lifetime of dedication to communism by many "old comrades," Deng said that the basic means of production would remain in state hands and that there would be no "new bourgeoisie."

Consistent with Deng's open-door policy, on January 2, 1985, State Councilor Gu Mu announced that China planned to open up four industrialized areas that would offer tax and trade benefits to foreign companies.

China already had established four special economic zones and opened up 14 coastal cities to foreign investment. The four new areas to be liberalized were the Pearl River delta, the Yangtze River delta, the Liaodong Peninsula and the Shandong Peninsula. All four were industrial and trade centers.

Stock issues made an appearance in Shanghai. Thousands of people lined up to participate in Shanghai's first stock issue, it was reported on January 18.

After running advertisements on local television, the collectively owned Yanzhong Industrial Corp. sold out the entire offering of 100,000 shares in less than eight hours.

Most shares were reserved for collective and state-owned institutions. Individuals wanting to invest formed a mile-long line hours before the offering opened.

The shares were valued at 50 yuan (US$17.85). They could only be resold to Yanzhong or to the Bank of China, and at par. They netted 13% interest annually—more than twice the bank interest rate.

The offering was permitted under a 1984 law allowing companies to raise capital for investment by selling shares. A few other offerings had been publicized elsewhere since the law went into effect, but none had been received so enthusiastically.

Yanzhong manufactured photocopying and duplicating machines, among other products.

Writers were promised new creative freedom. The delegates to the 12,500-member Chinese Writers Association, a state-run union that paid and managed writers, adopted a new constitution on January 5 endorsing the freedom to write about all aspects of life. The previous constitution had recommended that writers focus on issues serving the interests of peasants, workers and soldiers.

The new charter said writers "should develop a great variety of new themes, styles, forms and genres and start a free competition so as to raise the ideological and artistic levels of literary creation." They should "emancipate their minds and be bold to break new ground," the charter said.

However, it retained the requirement that writers remain faithful to the Communist Party and be guided by Marxism-Leninism.

But, more importantly, China's army—which was the largest in the world—had been persuaded to cut its size. This was made public by the army chief of general staff, Yang Dezhi, in an interview published on January 2. According to Yang, the 4.2 million man People's Liberation Army would be reduced in the interest of saving money and assisting the nation's economic modernization. The cut would free an undisclosed number of personnel to work on economic projects.

Under the late Chairman Mao Zedong, the army had developed its own schools, farms, factories, hospitals, newspapers and transportation system and came to control much of the civilian administration.

However, under Deng, the army had already been ordered to shift some of its defense industries to the production of consumer goods. Yang said that in 1984, the army took part in 1,100 state and local projects and opened some of its facilities, such as ports and airports, to civilian use.

On proposed cuts in military spending, Deng had said in his Central Advisory Committee speech (October 22, 1984) that by the year 2000—when the nation was stronger and 5% of the gross national product allocated for the military could bring the budget up to $50 billion—it might be possible to buy "a few more atomic bombs, missiles and equipment."

In a New Year's Day speech published on January 2, 1985 Premier Zhao Ziyang referred to wide-ranging economic reforms. Zhao said the nation's rigid wage scale system for government employees was outdated and would soon be changed. At the same time, he promised that more luxury goods such as washing machines and television sets would be available in 1985. *Red Flag*, on January 2, stressed that consumerism was not incompatible with socialism.

Also on January 2, comments made by Zhao on December 31, 1984 on the economic reforms, were published by the Xinhua news agency. Zhao was quoted as saying that pay raises were scheduled for some state employees, including those in education, science and technology, health and culture. He said subsidies to cities for food, clothing and housing would be cut, and denied that a recently announced plan to eliminate the state's monopoly on the purchase and sale of major farm products would cause price increases. The move would extend the role of the market under state guidance, Zhao said.

As much as half of China's budget was estimated by some economists to be spent on subsidies.

While moving ahead with the reforms aimed at structural changes in the Communist system, the leaders of the Chinese government strained to assure the nation—and themselves—of their continuing fidelity to Communism. The gist of their messages was that the adoption of capitalistic features would not make China less communistic, but more so.

Communist Party leader Hu Yaobang said in a January 19 speech made public the next day that the party had "wasted 20 years" since coming to power because of "leftist radical nonsense."

Hu said the goal of modernization had been jeopardized by the political convulsions—apparently a reference to the Cultural Revolution of Chairman Mao Zedong between 1966 and 1976.

Hu said, "After the establishment of the new China, counting from 1949, we hoped that we could use the next 100 years, that is, by 2049, to catch up economically with the most developed capitalist countries. But of these hundred years, 36 have now passed, and there are not many of these in which we could say we have done a good job."

Hu continued, "From now on we cannot afford to mess things up, we can never again undertake such radical leftist nonsense as 'Take class struggle as the key link' and 'Better to have socialist weeds than capitalist seedlings.' " Those slogans were coined by Mao during the years of the Great Leap Forward of 1958–59 and the Cultural Revolution.

Speaking in a more positive vein, on March 7, Deng Xiaoping affirmed that communism remained the nation's "ultimate goal," despite the program of economic reforms permitting private enterprise and foreign investment.

Deng said China would "hold firmly" to its new economic program but that the purpose of the reforms was to enhance socialism and not to revive capitalism.

Deng urged the nation's press to imbue the people with what he called "lofty ideals, communist ethics, culture and a sense of discipline, so they would not become captives of capitalist ideas."

In an earlier assurance that capitalism was not China's goal, Premier Zhao Ziyang had said on February 12 that "private business is the capitalist component of our socialist economy." He said private businesses would be allowed to flourish but that they would never control the nation's economy.

The reforms were in progress in the rural areas as well. By the middle of 1985, China had completed its dismantling of the main pillar of the Maoist system, China's rural communes.

The communes had been formed by combining small villages during Mao's Great Leap Forward in the 1950s, an economic experiment aimed at increasing agricultural and industrial output. The program of dismantling them had begun in October 1983.

Citing a report by the official Xinhua news agency, the *Journal of Commerce*, on June 6, said the nation's 56,000 communes had been replaced by 92,000 townships in which economic and administrative functions were separated. The communes' production brigades had been replaced by 820,000 elected villagers' committees.

The Chinese government defined townships as communities with at least 3,000 residents, of whom 40% or less were engaged in farming.

OLD-TIMERS EASED OUT

Simultaneously with the institution of new reforms, personnel changes were being made, in which old-time revolutionaries—often in their 70s and 80s—were eased out to make room for younger people. In line with this policy, three deputy foreign ministers were replaced, it was reported on September 7, 1984.

Zhou Nan, Zhu Qichen and Liu Shuqing replaced Han Xu, Gong Dafei and Wen Yezhan. Zhou had headed the Chinese negotiating team that recently finalized an accord with Great Britain on the future of Hong Kong.

The September 7 report cited Hu Yaobang, who said a major reshuffling of ministers and provincial leaders was being prepared.

In a further development, two ministers in key science and economic positions were replaced on September 20. Fang Yi, 68, a member of the ruling Politburo, was replaced as minister in charge of the state science and technology commission by Song Jian, 52, a former deputy minister of astronautics. Zhang Jingfu, 70, was replaced as minister in charge of the state economic commission by Lu Dong, 69, a deputy minister of the commission.

Deng Xiaoping lent his personal support to this campaign of rejuvenation in an October 22 speech made public at the end of December. He urged that "old comrades" accept their replacement by younger people, a policy that was also being carried out within the Communist Party. Throughout 1984 China's leaders had continued a drive to purge older, hard-line leftists and replace them with younger, better-educated officials. In some of those developments:

- In accord with a rectification campaign announced in October 1983, the Communist Party had launched a reexamination of all 40 million party members for the purpose of expelling some 40,000 leftist members, it was reported on November 26. Prison terms were stipulated for those sympathetic to the ultra-left.
- A Communist Party directive of November 20 said more intellectuals, particularly middle-aged and young people, should be admitted to the party.
- The *People's Daily* of November 13 praised the first election by secret ballot for the powerful position of provincial party secretary. Introduced in Shaanxi province, the new system aimed at electing better-educated, more able officials.
- On November 2, China formally ended 35 years of class war, removing the label of "class enemy" from "landlords, rich peasants, counterrevolutionaries and bad elements." The public security ministry said 20 million people had been "remolded" since the Communists took power in 1949. The "class enemy" designation had been removed from the last 79,504 people accused of belonging to the four categories in that class, the ministry said.

On December 22, 40 top officers of the People's Liberation Army were retired. Most of the officers were over age 60 and were at corps level or above, (equivalent to the rank of three-star general and above in the U.S.). The retirements marked a major advance in the effort to replace veterans who were resistant to the pragmatic policies of Deng Xiaoping.

THE "THIRD ECHELON" PICKED

As part of his program to replace China's aging leadership, Deng Xiaoping ordered the selection of young officials to be groomed as candidates for ministerial and provincial posts. One thousand such officials had been chosen, according to the party newspaper *People's Daily*, April 28, 1985.

The new leaders would make up the "third echelon" of leadership. The "first echelon" referred to the revolutionary generation, many of whom were now deceased, and the "second echelon" to those who had risen to leadership since 1949. The "third echelon" would carry the nation into the twenty-first century, according to Deng.

On April 9, Communist Party General Secretary Hu Yaobang had said that 70% of the leaders in party and State Council departments and in provincial, municipal and regional governments would be replaced in 1985. He added that 900,000 officials had retired during the drive to purge aging and unqualified leaders. Two million of the nation's 22 million party officials would have stepped down by the end of 1986, he said, and 15% of the party's 210 Central Committee members would be replaced by new appointees under the age of 60.

Along with the selection of a new leadership with a far-sighted goal, on May 28 the Chinese government decreed educational reforms that would raise the general level of education for the Chinese people.

A Communist Party Central Committee document outlined the changes, which moved the system away from the egalitarian policies introduced under the late Chairman Mao Zedong. Key elements of the new system were as follows:

- There would be nine years of compulsory education for students in major cities and coastal areas by 1990, extending to rural areas and small towns and cities by 1995. Currently, 95% of all Chinese children had six years of primary school education, but only two-thirds had an additional three years of secondary school education. The new policy conformed to the economic policy of giving priority to economic growth in coastal areas and large cities.
- Government grants and subsidies would gradually be reduced and replaced by scholarships awarded on merit. Some students would finance their own college educations, while others would pay a nominal fee and a portion of their personal expenses.
- Colleges and universities would be granted greater control of their budgets and more flexibility in developing curricula and hiring and promoting administrators.
- Local authorities would have responsibility for basic education.
- Enrollment in vocational training in secondary schools would increase to 50% of all students—who numbered 50 million—from the current 32%.

- Teacher training would be improved. Also under the new program, universities and colleges would be encouraged to arrange academic exchanges with other countries.

In a separate development, on May 29 the government announced that more than eight million high school and college students would be required to perform military training beginning later in 1985. The students would form a reserve officer corps. The more marked a step toward the nation's goal of achieving a more educated leadership in a streamlined army. (On April 19, Hu Yaobang had announced that the army would be cut by one million, or almost one-fourth, by the end of 1986.)

GENERATIONAL CHANGE IN FULL SWING

The administrative purge moved into a higher gear in the latter part of 1985. The Standing Committee of the National People's Congress, China's nominal parliament, announced on June 8, the dismissal of nine government ministers who were being replaced by officials with an average age "below 55."

Six ministers were forced into retirement, and two were shifted to other, unspecified positions. The education minister, He Dong-chang, was to take a lesser position in a new state education commission that would replace the ministry of education.

Reflecting the new importance being given to education, Deputy Premier Li Peng was named to head the commission. Li, 54, who was widely considered to be a possible successor to 65-year-old Premier Zhao Ziyang, was a Soviet-trained engineer who had helped oversee China's recent economic reforms.

In the shuffle, new ministers were appointed to the ministries of aeronautics, railways, radio and television, and the coal, electronics, ordnance and petroleum industries. The minister of the state science, technology and industry commission for national defense, which did research for the military, was also replaced.

The youngest new appointee was Li Tieying, 48, who became the new minister of the electronics industry. At age 54, Zou Jiahua was the oldest of the appointees. He would head the ordnance industry ministry.

All the new ministers were reported to be university graduates "or the equivalent." The ministries they were to head were mostly economic-related, reflecting the emphasis China's leaders placed on the nation's economic overhaul program.

Additional appointments of younger officials to head five ministries replacing older men past the new retirement age of 65 were announced on September 6.

Among those replaced were the heads of the police and state security: Ruan Chongwu, a 55-year-old deputy mayor of Shanghai, replaced Liu Fuzhi as public security minister, and Jia Chunwang, 47, was named minister of state security, replacing Ling Yun.

Three deputy ministers were promoted to head ministries. They were Qi Yuanjing, 56, who was named minister of the metallurgical industry; Zhao Dongwan, 59, who moved from the machine-building ministry to become minister of labor and personnel; and Zhu Xun, 54, who was named to head the ministry of geology and mineral resources.

In other appointments, Rui Xingwen, recently ousted as minister of urban and rural construction and environmental protection, on June 22 was reported to have been named Communist Party secretary in the key port of Shanghai; and Jiang Zemin, ousted a week earlier as minister of the electronics industry, was named deputy secretary and also mayor of Shanghai. The central government had been critical of the outgoing administrators because of Shanghai's sluggish response to Deng's reforms.

The enforced generational change Deng had initiated in 1983 along with his open-door policy and economic reforms had resulted in the replacement of more than a million civil servants, military officers and managers of business enterprises. The process culminated in one of the largest political shake-ups ever announced by the Communist Party Central Committee on September 16.

Ten of the 24 members of the politburo and 64 of the more than 340 Central Committee members retired. The changes were announced at a session of the Central Committee, the body that formally appointed the politburo, after five days of secret meetings. (The politburo reportedly had been superseded as the nation's policy-setting body by the Central Committee's secretariat and the State Council's inner cabinet, comprising the premier, four vice-premiers and 10 state councilors.)

The resignations of the Central Committee members were submitted in a joint letter that said, "We regard it as our bounden duty to the party and the cause of communism to implement this strategic decision. . . . De facto life-long tenure in leading posts will be abolished and a system of constant renewal of members of the leading organs will be established."

Most of the retirees were age 70 and over. The most senior official to be ousted from the politburo was Marshal Ye Jianying, 88, a former military commander and one of the six members of the politburo's standing committee.

Ye was believed to have had reservations about Deng's economic policies.

Marshals Xu Xiangqian, 84, and Nie Rongzhen, 86, two other revolutionary veterans, were retired from the politburo, reportedly unwillingly. Also stepping down were: Li Desheng, 69, until recently the commander of the Shenyang military region, who was said to be opposed to some of Deng's policies; Deng Yingchao, 81, the widow of Premier Zhou Enlai, and Ulanfu, 81, the nation's vice-president since 1983. The remaining four to retire were all veteran generals: Wang Zhen, 77; Song Renqiong, 76; Wei Guoqing, 72, a former army political commissar, and Zhang Tingfa, 68, until recently the air force commander.

Two cabinet members were among those retired from the Central Committee. They were Defense Minister Zhang Aiping, 75, and Culture Minister Zhu Muzhi, 69. Also removed were the navy commander, Liu Huaqing, 69, former Foreign Minister Huang Hua, 72, and Wang Dongxing, 69, the former head of the late Chairman Mao Zedong's bodyguard.

Surprisingly, former party Chairman and Premier Hua Guofeng, 64, who came to power after Mao's death, retained his position on the Central Committee in the September 16 shuffle.

Hua had been dismissed as chairman in 1980 and as premier in 1981, and in 1982 he was dismissed from the politburo and its standing committee. Since then, China's leaders had criticized the economic policies he implemented while in power.

Other opponents or critics of Deng's policies retained their posts. Among these were Chen Yun, 80, a senior economist, and China's president, Li Xiannian, reported to be either 76 or 80. Chen and Li retained their positions in the standing committee. Hu Qiaomu, 73, the politburo's ideologist, and secretariat member Deng Liqun, 71, the party's propaganda chief, also were untouched by the shake-up.

In other changes, 36 or 37 of the 162 members of the Central Advisory Committee retired, and the Central Discipline Inspection Commission lost 30 of its 129 members.

Following closely on the heels of these shake-ups, the Communist Party held a special conference on September 18–23, 1985 at which new members were elected to the Central Committee and other bodies. The last special conference had been held in 1955 to discuss high-level expulsions from the party. Upon being formed, the new party Central Committee in a one-day meeting on September 24 elected new members of the politburo and the secretariat.

Five new members were named to the politburo and Deputy Premier Yao Yilin, 68, an alternate (nonvoting) member, was promoted to full membership. Ten politburo members had retired a week earlier, and the new body consisted of 20 members compared with the previous 24, with two alternate members.

The newcomers included two whom observers considered probable future leaders in China. They were Hu Qili, 56, the permanent secretary of the secretariat, whose inclusion in the politburo had been widely predicted and who had been tagged as a successor to Communist Party Secretary General Hu Yaobang, 69, and Deputy Premier Li Peng, 57, who observers said could be expected to take over from Premier Zhao Ziyang, 66, when Zhao stepped down. Both new appointees had risen rapidly in recent years, as proteges of Deng. Li was the foster son on the late Premier Zhou Enlai.

The other three politburo appointees were Deputy Premier Tian Jiyun, 56, Foreign Minister Wu Xueqian, 64, and Qiao Shi, 61, the former party organization director and an alternate member of the secretariat.

Yao, Li and Tian had been instrumental in implementing Deng's pragmatic policies.

There were no new appointments to the politburo's inner circle, the standing committee, which now numbered five with the retirement of Marshal Ye Jianying. The failure to replace Ye and the naming of only six replacements to the politburo were seen by some observers as an indication that there had been dissension over proposed appointments.

Li, Qiao and Tian were also among five persons named as members of an enlarged secretariat, the body that handled China's day-to-day affairs and whose power had grown under Deng. Also named were Wang Zhaoguo, 44, and Hao Jianxiu, 50. The resignation of three secretariat members was announced at the same time, bringing total membership to 11. Hao was the only woman among the new appointees named on September 24.

In other appointments that day, Li Desheng, ousted days earlier from the politburo, was named to the Central Advisory Commission, headed by Deng and made up of elderly party members.

Twenty-nine new full members and 35 alternates were named to the Central Committee September 22, and 27 alternate members were given full membership. The average age of the 64 new members—three of whom were women—was slightly above 50, and 76% of them were college educated.

Twenty-two recently appointed governors or provincial party secretaries joined the Central Committee, as did 14 newly appointed government ministers. Among those who joined the committee were the new air force chief, Wang Hai, and Ye Xuanping, Marshal Ye's son. The younger Ye recently had been named governor of Guangdong province in the wake of an import scandal there. Also promoted was Deputy Foreign Minister Qian Qichen, China's representative in talks with Moscow on normalizing relations.

The same day, 56 new members joined the Central Advisory Commission, and 31 appointees joined the Central Discipline Inspection Commission, which policed the behavior of party members.

DISSENTING VOICE

The economic reforms implemented in 1984 had led to an overheated economy, with high inflation and overspending, and the government had applied brakes to halt the growth.

Growth in industrial output in the first half of 1985 was 23.1%, according to figures released by the state statistical bureau on July 30. This compared with 14.6% in the same period a year earlier and was far above the 8% targeted. Capital investment construction grew in the first half by 43.5%; growth of 1.1% for the entire year had been planned.

In the same 1985 period, the government recorded a budget surplus of $4.03 billion, even though a $1 billion deficit had been projected.

A key element of the reform program was the lifting of price controls on a number of industrial and agricultural products. The move led to price increases of between 30% and 50%, and the government had moved quickly to punish profiteers. When the reforms began, many government officials were said to have started their own businesses and to have speculated in scarce commodities and manipulated prices.

Beijing city authorities announced steep increases in the price of nonstaple foodstuffs, effective May 10, 1985. The announcement prompted shoppers to stock up on items such as meat, fish and chicken in the days leading up to the increases.

The prices of 1,800 nonstaple items rose an average of 50%, the largest price hikes since the Communists took power in 1949. To help meet the higher costs, Beijing's 9.5 million residents were promised a monthly per capita grant of 7.50 yuan (US$2.62) each.

Similar price hikes had already been implemented in 22 other cities. The increases were part of the government's efforts to introduce market mechanisms into the economy.

In a speech before the National People's Congress March 27, 1985, Premier Zhao Ziyang conceded that there were problems with China's economic reform programs.

He contended that some problems were inevitable in a program of change that was so extensive, aiming as it did to reform all levels of the economic system. Other problems, however, had arisen "because of the failure to give adequate consideration beforehand or to exercise strict supervision later, from which we should draw a lesson," Zhao admitted.

Such an admission of misjudgment on the part of China's leaders was rare.

The premier announced that bureaucratic controls only recently eased would be tightened to prevent the economic reform program from being undermined by corruption among local officials and by indiscriminate wage, credit and price rises. Zhao accused both individuals and organizations of having used new powers to control prices, wages and investment to "justify their pursuit of their own units' interests at the expense of those of the state and the people."

Among the new measures, Zhao said, would be the setting of tighter controls on the sales of luxury consumer items. The premier advocated "severe punishments" for anyone artificially raising prices and profiteering, and he spoke out against excessive bonuses and taking of bribes.

Zhao noted that a "conspicuous problem" was a lack of control over the currency, which was partly responsible for the rise in prices. He indicated that China's banks were largely to blame. Zhao said the People's Bank of China, the nation's central bank, would be strengthened and the amount of credit and cash in circulation tightened.

Bank loans had risen almost 30% when the banks were granted increased lending authority in 1984, Zhao said, and half of that increase occurred in December of that year.

Zhao's public criticism of bank officials had been preceded by the sacking of the nation's highest banking officials. The Chinese government appointed Foreign Trade Minister Chen Muhua to succeed Lu Peijian as president of the People's Bank of China, it was reported March 22. The move came after Jin Deqin resigned as president and vice-chairman of the Bank of China, the nation's foreign exchange bank. His resignation was reported on March 16, but Chinese officials said privately that Jin had been dismissed in February after being criticized in a secret Communist Party document.

Chen was succeeded by Vice-Foreign Trade Minister Zheng Tuobin, and Jin was replaced by Zhao Bingde. Lu was named auditor general of the auditing administration. He replaced Yu Ming-tao, who was removed after it was disclosed on March 13 that China had lost some $1.2 billion in 1984 because of accounting "irregularities." These included excessive operation costs, concealed profits, faked losses, goods issued to employees and tax evasion.

The reshuffling in the three top economic posts was part of an attempt by the government to deal with a recent rash of economic crimes by state and party officials. The corruption threatened to undermine an economic reform program introduced in 1984.

But it fell short of uprooting economic crimes. By far the most spectacular instance of economic crime came to light July 31, 1985, when the government revealed details of a financial scandal involving officials of the island of Hainan who had resold at enormous profits luxury goods imported duty free. It was said to be the biggest profiteering scandal since China began its open-door policy in 1979.

Hainan was a duty-free port in Guangdong province.

The Xinhua news agency reported that Hainan officials took advantage of the nation's open-door policies to embezzle some $1.5 billion. The scheme involved encouraging the creation of private companies to import consumer goods and resell them at two or three times their original price. Loans were issued by local banks to finance the purchases.

According to subsequent revelations, Chinese navy planes were used to illegally transport the consumer goods from Hainan to Sichuan province for resale. It was illegal to take these products out of Hainan.

Among the goods imported in the racket were 2.9 million television sets, 122,000 motorcycles and 89,000 motor vehicles.

Three leading Hainan officials were reported to have been dismissed and 143 criminal cases were under investigation. Among those dismissed was Lei Yu, the Communist Party deputy secretary in Hainan and head of its government.

The economic and social problems incidental to China's socialist modernization programs gave pause to more conservative-minded Chinese leadership than Deng. On September 23, Chen Yun, a member of the politburo's standing committee, criticized the reformist approach in a speech to the party conference.

In an unusual public challenge, Chen, an orthodox Marxist, criticized Deng's line on agriculture, the new emphasis on market forces, and the movement away from ideological indoctrination. However, he said he endorsed the succession of younger leaders.

Chen warned that the move away from agriculture could cause social disorder. He argued that central planning should be the economy's base, not market regulation that he said meant "blindly allowing supply and demand to determine production." He reminded the delegates: "We are a communist country. Our goal is to build socialism."

Calling it an error to downgrade party departments responsible for ideology and propaganda, he said the move had led to speculation and corruption in pursuit of personal gain by people who had "turned their backs on serving the people." He urged the new appointees to the Central Committee to adhere to the Marxist principle of "democratic centralism."

In his own speech the same day, Deng defended his policies and said they would not change. However, he agreed that leading party cadres should study Marxist theory more, and that the importation of "undesirable goods" should be prevented and "the pernicious influence of capitalism" halted.

11

Exit Hu Yaobang

THE OPEN-DOOR POLICY IN FULL SWING

The open-door policy, which encouraged foreign companies to trade with and invest in China, had produced the desired effect of stimulating China's economic growth. But success created its own problems. There was a basic contradiction between China's commitment to socialism and its newly found faith in the capitalist market economy. The economy took off when the state got off the backs of individual farmers and workers and set them to work on their own, awakening in them the joy of making money. The growing prosperity made a mockery of the communist system.

Deng Xiaoping and his fellow reformers tended to make light of the problem. If they saw the contradiction, it was to them a contradiction like any other—a challenge to overcome. The key lay in retaining control of political power. So long as they could dominate China's political processes, they were not daunted by the spectre of "bourgeois liberalism." Capitalist sins—such as they were—could be rendered harmless by enforced cultivation of socialist virtues.

Thus, in 1985, as the nation was gearing up for the seventh five-year plan (1986–1990), China opened its doors still wider, with its high-ranking officials actively involved in economic diplomacy.

In April, Hu Yaobang, the general secretary of the Communist Party, went on a five-day trip to Australia, one of the principal suppliers of wheat and iron ore. He arrived in Perth, Australia on April 13. In an unusual welcoming display, Australian Prime Minister Bob Hawke flew to Perth to greet the Chinese leader, whom he accompanied throughout the tour.

The visit, which was viewed in part as a public relations effort to strengthen Hu's image at home, was reported to be very successful. Hu reportedly impressed Australians with his expansive style, leading one Australian adviser to describe him as "strong, outgoing and colorful." After Hu's departure, Prime Minister Hawke began referring to him as "my dear friend, Hu Yaobang."

After departing Australia, Hu was scheduled to visit New Zealand, Western Samoa, Fiji and Papua, New Guinea.

Official talks in Australia were dominated by discussion of trade relations, which were important and considered to be improving. In one of the trip's highlights on April 14, Hu and Hawke visited the remote mining town of Parraburdoo in western Australia. At Channar, the site of a proposed joint venture between China and the Hamersley Iron unit of Rio Tinto-Zinc Corp., Hawke handed Hu a piece of iron ore and joked, "The first export of Channar ore to China, no royalties, no taxes." In response, Hu said, "For us this is a piece of treasure."

On April 16, the two leaders issued a joint communique stating that the prospects for cooperation in iron and steel projects were "very good."

Two months later, it was Premier Zhao Ziyang's turn to make a trip to Western Europe, visiting Britain, West Germany and the Netherlands from June 2 to 19. China had downgraded diplomatic relations with the Netherlands in 1981, after The Hague had agreed to sell Taiwan two submarines. The rift had been healed in December 1983, when the Dutch government prohibited further sale of submarines to Taiwan and subscribed to "one China" policy.

The trip had as its main purpose the forging of economic ties with the nations of Western Europe. Zhao's traveling party consisted of Deputy Foreign Minister Wu Xueqian and three deputy ministers from the state planning commission, the state economic commission and the ministry of foreign economic relations and trade.

Zhao arrived in London on June 2. After two hours of talks the next day, Zhao and British Prime Minister Margaret Thatcher signed an agreement on the peaceful use of nuclear energy. The agreement, which covered goods, services and technology, reportedly provided a framework in which British companies could promote exports to China. It prohibited the transfer of nuclear technology to a third country.

Zhao and Thatcher also signed an economic cooperation agreement for 1986 to 1990 that would replace an existing pact signed in 1979.

On June 4, Zhao met with the heads of several British banking and industrial organizations and invited them to invest in China and help with its economic restructuring program. He said the recent pact that provided for the return of Hong Kong to mainland China in 1997 had opened new prospects for Sino-British cooperation in trade and other fields.

In a meeting with British Trade and Industry Secretary Norman Tebbit that day, Zhao said China sought more concessions from British companies bidding for a nuclear power plant in Guangdong province. The British government had offered to provide as much as £350 million of export credits, at a 9.85% rate of interest, to British firms that won contracts to provide China with turbines and generators. The credits would be repaid over 15 years, beginning six years after completion of the plant. Britain's General Electric Co. PLC was the main contractor expected to provide that equipment.

Zhao lunched with Queen Elizabeth II at Buckingham Palace on June 6 and spoke on China's foreign policy at the Royal Institute of International Affairs. In his speech, Zhao pledged that China would not ally itself with either the U.S. or the Soviet Union, but would seek better relations with both of them. He urged both to cease their "dangerous arms race." Zhao asserted that China would "forever stand together with the Third World."

Zhao's speech was perceived to be unusually warm in its comments on relations with Britain.

On June 8, the Chinese delegation left for Bonn where, on June 10, Wu and West German Foreign Minister Hans-Dietrich Genscher renewed an economic cooperation agreement through 1995. In addition, China and Kraftwerk Union AG, a German nuclear plant contractor, signed a memorandum of understanding on the possible sale to Beijing of two water pressure nuclear power plants to be built in Sunan, west of Shanghai. Negotiations on the sale had begun in 1979. Kraftwerk was a subsidiary of the electronics company Siemens AG.

Bonn and Beijing also signed a double taxation treaty aimed at inducing West German companies to form joint ventures in China.

Zhao left West Germany on June 16 to spend four days in the Netherlands. On June 19, in Eindhoven, he signed an agreement in principle with the Dutch electronics group N. V. Philips, to establish a joint venture in Nanjing, in Jiangsu province, for the production and sale of color television tubes and deflection coils.

Zhao's trip to Britain was preceded by a special British trade mission to Beijing in February and March of that year, led by Britain's Lord Young, minister without portfolio.

- On March 7, British Oxygen Co. signed a letter of intent to buy a 50% share in the Wu Sung chemical company, the first such investment in China by a foreign firm.
- Cable and Wireless PLC signed an agreement on March 7 with the Guangdong posts and telecommunications administrative bureau to provide China's Pearl River delta with telephone service. On March 4, the company had signed memoranda with the ministry of posts and telecommunications for two feasibility studies; one would give Cable and Wireless a major role in improving telephone service in the Yangtze Delta, and the other would establish a telecommunications technology center in Beijing.
- On March 4, Aveling Barford International finalized a $65.4 million (£61 million) deal to produce 600 dump trucks over a seven-year period.
- Also on March 4, Rolls-Royce Ltd. signed a protocol for a £15 million order from the China National Aerotechnology Import and Export Corp. for three gas turbine electricity-generating sets for an oil field development in northwest China. The conclusion of the deal was reported on April 15.

In separate deals:

- On April 17, Airbus Industrie won an order to supply the Chinese Civil Aviation Administration with three A-310 Series 200 wide-bodied airliners worth $150 million, with an option on two more. Airbus Industrie was a consortium of British, West German, French and Spanish interests. BAe had a 20% stake in the company.
- A spokesman for Rupert Murdoch, the Australian-born publisher, announced on May 1 that Murdoch's News Corp. would build a US$40 million international hotel and news media center in Beijing.

China Aviation Supplies Corp. and British Aerospace PLC (BAe) were reported on June 1 to have signed a definitive $150 million contract committing China to buy 10 BAe 146 jet airliners.

The contract followed a memorandum of understanding signed in April.

The 86-seat, so-called "whispering jet" was manufactured jointly by BAe, the U.S. firm of Avco Lycoming and Sweden's Saab-Scania AB, but was approximately 50% British.

The U.S. pursued its economic interests in China in a more complex diplomatic environment, however. On January 11, 1985, Reagan administration officials said that the U.S. had reached a preliminary understanding on providing Beijing with naval weapons, the Washington Post reported on January 12. The officials' disclosure came the day before U.S. General John W. Vessey Jr., chairman of the Joint Chiefs of Staff, was due to begin three days of talks with Chinese military and government officials in Beijing.

U.S. officials denied throughout Vessey's stay in China that the general was discussing arms sales or the transfer of military technology. They said his visit was aimed at getting to know Chinese military leaders and understanding China's military position.

The *Washington Post* article cited unidentified U.S. officials as saying that the preliminary agreement, involving the sale of modern antisubmarine warfare equipment to China, was reached during a December 1984 visit to the U.S. by a Chinese naval delegation. The equipment included submarine detection devices, sonar and gas turbine engines.

The officials also said China had agreed to a call by three U.S. destroyers to the port of Shanghai in April 1985. It would be the first such port call since the Communist takeover in 1949.

One official cited in a *New York Times* article datelined January 12, said the weapons to be sold to China were defensive in nature and were used primarily by surface ships in antisubmarine warfare. In addition to naval sales, the official said, the U.S. Army had discussed selling antitank defenses to the Chinese, and the U.S. Air Force had had similar talks on air defense. China had turned down some weapons offered by the U.S., the official said.

The U.S. Congress cleared the way for the first government-to-government military sales to China, when it failed to act by an October 30 deadline on a Chinese request for $6 billion worth of ammunition plant blueprints and designs. This failure to act meant that the sale would automatically proceed. The Defense Department reportedly could offer as much as $98 billion worth of military technology and equipment to China.

Against this backdrop of improving business climate, Vice-President George Bush visited China on October 13–18 on what he described as a mission aimed at showing U.S. support for China's economic reforms and demonstrating the "progressive relationship" that had developed between the two countries.

During his visit, he announced that the U.S. and its industrial allies had agreed to speed the export of some high-technology items to China.

In Beijing, Bush met with many of the nation's top officials, including: Deng Xiaoping; Hu Yaobang, the general secretary of the Communist Party; Premier Zhao Ziyang; and President Li Xiannian.

Bush chose to focus on the opportunities for U.S. investment in China, although he pointed out that Beijing needed to improve the investment climate. The U.S. and China had been negotiating an investment treaty since 1983 that would guarantee foreign investors the same treatment in China as Chinese investors.

Just before leaving Beijing for Chengdu in Sichuan province on October 16, Bush announced that the U.S. and its allies in Cocom (the Coordinating Committee for Multilateral Export Controls)—a 15-nation organization that oversaw exports of sensitive Western technology to communist countries—had decided to ease restrictions limiting sales to China of high-technology items with potential military applications. He announced the easing of licensing restrictions on 27 categories of equipment—about half the total. Computers and medical equipment were among the categories affected.

INCREASING TRADE DEFICIT

As a result of Beijing's increasing trade with the West, imports skyrocketed in 1985, leading to a trade deficit in the first half of $3.2 billion, rising to $7.8 billion in the first seven months. According to figures from China's statistical bureau reported on September 25, imports in the first half rose 70% to $14.4 billion, whereas exports rose only 1.3% to $11.3 billion. Total trade for the period was $25.7 billion, up 29% from the same period in 1984. The bureau said the nation faced a trade deficit of $18 billion in 1985 that would "seriously affect" foreign reserves.

More complete trade figures for 1985 became available the following year, 1986, between January and March. But these figures were confusing.

Four different Chinese agencies produced separate trade figures which were often contradictory. China generally used trade figures released by the ministry of foreign information and trade (Mofert) in its trade discussions, but figures released by the customs administration bureau were considered in the West to be more accurate. The bureau's figures included, for example, imports of parts for re-export.

According to Mofert figures reported on January 23, China's trade deficit in 1985 was $7.61 billion, the largest deficit ever. Imports rose 31.8% to $33.41 billion, and exports rose only 5.7% to $25.8 billion. Trade volume increased to $59.21 billion—a record, Mofert said.

Trade with Japan, reported to be China's largest trading partner, rose 30.2% to $16.5 billion, with China registering a deficit of $4.37 billion, up from $2 billion in 1984. Japan exported $10.47 billion worth of goods to China and imported $6.1 billion worth of Chinese goods, according to Mofert.

The ministry reported that in 1985, trade with the U.S. increased by 7.6% to $6.4 billion and that China had a deficit of $2.04 billion in its trade with the U.S., up from $1.5 billion in 1984. The U.S. disputed those figures, stating that they did not include Chinese goods exported to the U.S. via Hong Kong. Unofficial figures from the U.S. Department of Commerce released by the U.S. embassy in Beijing showed total Sino-American trade in 1985 of a record $8.1 billion, up 26% from the year before. The figures, reported on February 26, showed that the U.S. had a deficit with China of $369 million, down slightly from the $377 million deficit the U.S. recorded in 1984.

China's deficit with the European Community rose 24.5% to $3 billion, Mofert said. West Germany increased its trade with China by 27.9%, Great Britain by 20.1%, France by 36.2% and Italy by 25.7%. China said it had a deficit on trade with West Germany of $1.6 billion on total trade of $2.84 billion, a deficit of $530 million with Britain on $1.43 billion of trade, of $330 million with France on trade totaling $790 million, and of $290 million with Italy on $830 million of trade.

Trade with the Soviet Union rose 61%, with China recording a surplus of $1.9 million, according to Mofert.

Contradicting these figures, the customs administration bureau reported in January that China's trade deficit was a record $13.7 billion in 1985, almost double the figure released by Mofert, according to a news story on February 6. The bureau said total trade was $66.7 billion, with imports at $40.2 billion and exports at $26.5 billion. Sino-American trade was placed at $7.2 billion, with China recording a $2.7 billion deficit with the U.S.

A third set of figures was released by the state statistical bureau March 2. The bureau said China's trade deficit in 1985 was $14.9 billion, with exports rising 4.7% and imports 54.2%. A bureau spokesman, asked about the discrepancy in the three sets of figures released to date, said the authorities were "cross-checking our statistics."

The fourth set of statistics would be released by the People's Bank of China.

In other figures released by the statistical bureau on March 2, retail prices in 1985 rose 8.8%, the highest recorded rise since the 1950s; industrial production rose 18% to $273.7 billion, well above the target of 8%; agricultural output rose 13% to $140.9 billion; real (inflation-adjusted) income in urban areas rose 10.8%; and oil production was up 8.9%, at 912.5 million barrels of crude.

Foreign investment in China increased sharply in 1985, to $4.6 billion, it was reported on January 30.

However, the foreign trade ministry conceded that the increased investment had not brought the advanced technology that had been desired, and few ventures were in key sectors such as transportation, communications and energy.

China reported that more than 1,300 equity, 1,500 contractual and 46 entirely foreign-owned joint ventures were agreed upon in 1985, for a total of $5.85 billion—up 120.7% over the previous year. The majority of foreign investments, 80%, came from Hong Kong. U.S. investment was estimated at between $1.4 billion and $1.8 billion.

To spur foreign investment, China, as of February 1, implemented eased joint venture curbs that extended to 50 years from 30 the maximum duration of most ventures with foreign companies. In addition, restrictions on the repatriation of joint-venture profits by foreign companies were eased. The move aimed to curb criticism that China's tight control on joint-venture foreign exchange was discouraging investment.

A VISION OF PRIVATIZED ECONOMY: THE SEVENTH FIVE-YEAR PLAN

Determination to proceed with socialist modernization—or "socialism with Chinese characteristics"—was clearly indicated in the seventh five-year plan (1986–1990), to which the National People's Congress gave its formal approval on April 12, 1986.

The plan, which had been approved by the Communist Party Central Committee in September 1985, called for the transfer of administrative power to local governments from central authorities and the gradual removal of all levels of government from business and industry, except for "a few special government departments and industries." Manufacturers, wholesalers and retailers would have "full authority for their own management and full responsibility for their own profits and losses."

Under the plan, the state would gradually reduce the gap between controlled and free-market prices, and while some major items would continue at prices set by the state, price controls on consumer goods would gradually be allowed to fluctuate with demand. A social security system would be introduced as subsidies and guarantees to workers were removed.

Domestic airlines, and post and telecommunications departments would be allowed to set rates sufficient to enable them to make profits, 90% of which they would be permitted to retain. Port facilities and railways would be decentralized, and the state would contract for their services if it required them.

The plan provided for local governments to take over the management of education, currently controlled by the central government.

At the request of deputies attending the congress, the final version of the economic plan contained sections on agriculture and intellectuals. The added section on farming referred to agriculture as "the foundation of our national economy" and urged stepped-up rural reforms. The section on intellectuals said they should help people "work heart and soul" for modernization.

In presenting the plan to the National People's Congress at its opening session on March 24, Premier Zhao Ziyang said that China remained committed to reforms instituted under Deng Xiaoping which aimed at liberalizing and decentralizing the economy.

Zhao said the program to implement a "socialist economic structure with Chinese characteristics" had already succeeded in replacing a "petrified economic structure" with "a vigorous new one appropriate to the planned development of a commodity economy based on public ownership."

However, he admitted that some mistakes had been made and that it "takes time to understand economic laws." Zhao said the key areas of telecommunications, transport and energy had been neglected and needed particular attention. The shortage of foreign exchange, he conceded, would "remain a prominent economic problem for a long time to come," and production, technology and labor productivity would "remain at a relatively low level" for some time.

Referring to excessive consumption and investment and to nonessential expenditure that had threatened the reforms, Zhao said capital investment, consumption and credit would be restricted through 1987.

The premier warned that China's poor export performance would have to improve to prevent foreign exchange considerations from limiting growth.

Through 1990, Zhao said, China aimed to achieve 44% growth in gross national product and a 40% increase in trade volume, with corresponding expansion in the use of foreign capital and technology. In February China had said that from 1986 to 1990 it would double the amount of foreign capital it took in under the previous five-year plan, to more than $20 billion.

Industrial production would rise by 7.5% annually compared with 18% in 1985 and with an average of 12% over the 1981–85 period. Output of goods and services would increase 7.5% annually—lower than the average 10% annual growth achieved under the previous five-year plan.

Agricultural output would grow by 4% annually compared with 8.1% from 1981–85, Zhao said. The low target apparently reflected an expected drop in grain production. According to figures released on December 30, 1985, grain production fell 7% in 1985, to 380 million metric tons, down from the record 407 million metric tons in 1984. This was the first such drop in several years.

The decrease was due in part to workers leaving rural areas to take higher-paying jobs under the new economic reform program. It prompted plans, reported on January 17, for incentives for farmers to grow more grain. Farmers would be allowed to put more grain on the market at negotiated prices and reduce the amount they were obliged to sell to the state, leaving more to be sold at higher prices on the open market. Preferential loans were to be offered for production expenses.

Zhao said foreign trade would reach $83 billion in 1990, an increase of 40% from 1985. Exports would grow 47% to $38 billion and imports 35% to $45 billion. The trade deficit in 1990 would therefore be $7 billion.

Zhao said that by 1990, a framework for a new economic structure would be in place. Businesses would be wholly responsible for their profit and loss, and for energy and raw material prices, while rents would be determined by market forces.

In budgetary terms, China was much better positioned to embark upon the new five-year plan that it had been in 1980. 1985 produced a budget surplus of $840 million compared with a deficit of $937 million in 1984, according to Finance Minister Wang Bingqian's report to the NPC on March 26. Wang attributed the surplus to the nation's liberalization measures. He reported government revenues of $55.62 billion in 1985—an increase of almost 25% from the year before—and expenditures of $54.78 billion. For the current year, Wang projected revenues and expenditures balanced at $71 billion.

Spending for various sectors in 1986 was set as follows: capital construction, $19 billion; agriculture, $4 billion, up 16% from 1985; education, health and science, $12 billion, up 12.6%; and the military, $6 billion, or less than 10% of the budget—down from 12% the year before.

Wang said China would need to borrow $1.7 billion in 1986, up from $780 million in 1985. (Foreign bankers said that that estimate was underestimated.) Payment on principal and interest on outstanding loans would be $1.28 billion.

Wang said a wide range of new taxes might be introduced in the future.

The Central Committee of the Communist Party followed up the new five-year plan with the publication on September 28 a code of conduct for its Party members—a set of guidelines they should follow in carrying out the open-door policy of Deng Xiaoping.

The guidelines, adopted in the sixth plenary session of the 12th Central Committee, were contained in a "Resolution on Guiding Principles for Building Socialist Society with an Advanced Culture and Ideology." Some observers read the resolution as an attempt on the part of the Chinese Communist leadership to consolidate Deng's reforms and provide them with an ideological framework, to replace Maoist ideology.

Declaring that its objective was the construction of a "socialist spiritual civilization," the resolution affirmed that the economic modernization program to increase living standards through foreign contacts was "a basic, unalterable policy."

While backing the reforms, the resolution at the same time warned against the growing official corruption and economic crime associated with modernization. It cautioned the Chinese people not to "blindly worship bourgeois philosophies and social doctrines," stressing that "socialist morality rejects both the idea and the practice of pursuing personal interests at the expense of others; putting money above all else; abusing power for personal gain; cheating; and extortion."

The resolution attacked "bourgeois liberalization," which meant "negating the socialist system in favor of capitalism." However, it affirmed that while China was still in the early stages of socialism, it must allow some individuals to become prosperous before prosperity could be achieved for all.

The document reiterated that the "iron rice bowl" policy of equal pay regardless of effort had to be dismantled. "China will on no account regard egalitarianism as an ethical principle in our society," the resolution said. China had announced on September 2 that, effective October 1, guaranteed lifetime employment for urban workers under the "iron rice bowl" system would be phased out, and that all new workers in the nation's state-owned enterprises would be hired under labor contracts assuring work for a fixed period. The new rules did not affect demobilized servicemen or those already on the payrolls of state enterprises.

The resolution backed Deng's calls for political reforms to promote democracy, although there was no agreement on what kind of changes should take place. Political reform, which was to be tackled in 1987, had been the subject of much debate in recent months. Proposals had been put forth suggesting, among other changes, the separation of party and government and a redistribution of political power.

In a speech delivered on July 31 and published in the People's Daily on August 15, Deputy Premier Wan Li said that there should be a "democratization" of the nation's over-centralized decision-making process. Wan complained that China's decision-makers currently lacked systems for consulting, appraising, supervising and feedback.

In urging greater freedom of expression, the resolution repeated a slogan introduced by the late Chairman Mao Zedong in 1956, saying it was necessary to "let a hundred flowers bloom, let a hundred schools of thought contend." Mao's Hundred Flowers movement had encouraged intellectuals to speak out, but when many had responded by criticizing the Communist Party, they had been purged in a 1957 campaign against the right of free expression; consequently, many intellectuals were said to be dubious about the new Hundred Flowers campaign.

POLITICAL UNREST SURFACES

Amid celebrations of success, and brave and confident talks of continuing success in the future, there lurked hints of trouble and of the embattled leadership's contemplating retirement.

Prior to the formal publication of the seventh five-year plan, the Communist Party leadership had decreed, on November 24, 1985, another wave of purges aimed at ridding the Party of corrupt officials and Maoist hardliners at the village and township level. Some 20 million Party members were to be scrutinized.

Deng himself absented himself from public view for about three months in the first part of 1986. When he reappeared on March 25 to welcome visiting Danish Premier Poul Schuler, he was quoted as having said, "The question I'm now considering is when I am going to retire." Deng was then 81 years old.

A similar suggestion was made by Hu Yaobang, 71, the general secretary of the Communist Party. Speaking before the Royal Institute of International Affairs in London on June 11, 1986—during his Western European tour—Hu said that, in 1987, he and Premier Zhao Ziyang, 66, would probably disengage themselves from leadership, in order to give greater responsibility to younger officials.

However, he assured the audience that China's economic reforms had struck "deep roots," and would easily survive into the next generation. He stated that China had not been "led astray" into following Western-style capitalism, and said its reforms would "only help to perfect China's socialist system."

By then, there were growing indications that China was headed for a new surge of political instability. Student demonstrators made an oblique attack on Hu by staging demonstrations on September 18–November 20, 1985, against Japan. Beijing had publicized Hu's close association with Japanese Prime Minister Yasuhiro Nakasone.

A thousand students, some of them carrying banners referring to the 1931 Japanese invasion of Manchuria, staged a protest on September 18 in Beijing. After that incident, the authorities warned students against taking part in further demonstrations.

However, on October 10, a small number of students were reported to have staged an anti-Japanese protest in Xian the previous week. In a further demonstration, on November 20, several hundred students in Beijing held a vigil in Tienanmen Square to protest what they described as Japan's "economic aggression," reflecting concern over China's new open-door policies.

Meetings between student leaders and Communist Party officials followed, in part with the aim of forestalling protests on December 9. This was the 50th anniversary of one of China's best-known student protests, the 1935 Beijing rally against Japan by young political activists. The anniversary passed without incident.

Anti-Japanese sentiment had gained visibility after Japanese Premier Yasuhiro Nakasone visited, on August 15, the Yasukuni shrine in Japan commemorating the nation's war dead—the first such visit by a Japanese premier since World War II. The Chinese government assailed Nakasone for his action, and he later canceled another scheduled visit to the shrine.

Japan's increasing commercial presence in China had been another source of tensions. On December 3, Deng Xiaoping issued a warning that Japan's rising trade surplus with China threatened economic contacts and trade between the two nations.

The following year, 1986, several hundred people who had been exiled to the countryside during the Cultural Revolution (1966–1976) staged a sit-in at the Beijing municipal government and Communist Party building on April 22–29, demanding to be allowed to return to the capital.

The former Red Guard members and their families—many of whom had lived in Shanxi province since 1968—were reported to have arrived in the capital to press their case after individual pleas failed to produce results. Their number dwindled from the hundreds to about 70 by the end of the protest.

An estimated 20,000 of the 400,000 people sent to Shanxi province—one of the nation's poorest—were said to remain there.

Authorities barred foreign reporters from the city hall area on April 27 and urged the protesters not to talk to foreigners. The demonstration was not reported in Chinese newspapers until after it ended.

According to the *People's Daily* of April 30, Mayor Chen Xitong and Beijing's party secretary, Li Ximing, had met with the demonstrators on April 29 and had told them that they were disturbing the public order and ordered them to return to their jobs. The newspaper said it remained "the glorious obligation and responsibility of youth in the capital to support the countryside and frontier areas and vitalize the undeveloped interior."

However, it was reported on May 9 that the authorities had sent circulars to work units in Beijing, inviting applications to return to the capital on behalf of three categories of those who had been sent to the countryside: those who were single, those who had married other Beijing residents, and those who had married spouses who remained in Beijing.

Student discontent manifested itself in a xenophobic incident on May 24, involving African students. For five hours, some 400 Chinese students at Tianjin University besieged a group of Africans at a party celebrating African Liberation Day.

Bottles and rocks were thrown in the melee, which developed from complaints by Chinese students about the noise at the party.

The affair led to a week of unrest at the university, and at the nearby Nankai University. A group of 18 African and Asian students who had been staying at a hotel since the incident fled to Beijing on May 31, after being warned by university officials of a planned attack by Chinese students.

Some 200 African students marched through Beijing on June 6 to protest what they described as racial discrimination. In a rare press conference on June 7, Chinese officials denied that racism was the motive for the violence.

Beijing showed its nervousness when, on July 23, it expelled the Beijing bureau chief of the *New York Times*, John F. Burns, 41.

Burns had been detained on July 17 on suspicion of "entering an area forbidden to foreigners, gathering intelligence information and espionage," according to Beijing officials. He was expelled for "activities incompatible with his status as a journalist."

The charges related to a motorcycle trip Burns had taken through the Chinese countryside, accompanied by a U.S. lawyer and a Chinese national. From June 29 to July 5, the three had traveled the 1,000 miles (1,600 km) from Taiyuan in Shaanxi province, southwest of Beijing, to Zhenba in Shaanxi province, near the border of Sichuan province. The three had been following the route taken by the journalist Edgar Snow in 1936, when he went to find the Communist armies at their headquarters in Yenan in northern Shaanxi.

Burns and his companions had been detained on July 5 on the Sichuan border by officials of the public security bureau. They were stopped for traveling by road without authorization and entering an area of Shaanxi province that had been closed to foreigners. After writing self-critical explanations for infringing on travel regulations, the three were returned to Beijing on July 7.

Burns was at Beijing airport with his wife and two children when he was again detained on July 17. The family had been waiting for a flight to Hong Kong, where they were going on vacation.

The other American who had accompanied Burns on the motorcycle trip had already left the country on business. He was Edward McNally, who was on leave from the U.S. Justice Department to teach law at Beijing University.

Burns was held incommunicado until July 21, when British and U.S. officials, as well as his family, were permitted to visit him.

The executive director of the *New York Times*, A. M. Rosenthal, and the paper's foreign editor, Warren Hoge, also visited Burns on July 21. They had come to China to help secure his release.

On expelling Burns, Beijing authorities said he was guilty of an "act of spying and intelligence-gathering which will not be tolerated by a sovereign state." Beijing specifically charged that Burns had entered forbidden military areas, and confiscated photographs he had taken during his trip.

No charges were ever filed against Burns and he was never formally arrested.

Confronted with the growing restiveness of the population, China's leaders first showed an attitude of tolerance, urging intellectuals to speak out and proclaiming that democratization must be a part of the nation's modernization process; but, at the same time, warning against unauthorized protests.

As the year drew to a close, demonstrations became more frequent. In November, students in Hunan province staged demonstrations, demanding more democracy. The provincial authorities met some of the demands by allowing student participation in local government.

In Hefei, the capital of Anhui province, students demonstrated peacefully on December 5 and 9 demanding democracy. They were also seeking better living conditions on campuses and changes in the way candidates for the local People's Congress were selected.

On December 12, students on two campuses in the city began an illegal poster campaign to press their demands. A similar campaign was reported in Beijing and in the central city of Wuhan, in Hubei province, where protesters marched on December 9.

The protests spread to at least three other cities without any apparent interference by the authorities. In Kunming, the capital of Yunnan province, several thousand students marched on December

17 shouting, "Long live democracy." Demonstrations took place in the Shenzhen special economic zone on December 14–15 to protest proposed tuition increases, which, reportedly, were later retracted.

The unrest spread to Shanghai on December 20, when as many as 35,000 students marched through the streets in the largest such rally since 1976.

Apparently, a factor in the protests was the refusal of authorities at Jiaotong University to approve greater students' rights.

Students had begun gathering in the People's Square and at government offices on the night of December 19. They presented Mayor Jiang Zemin with four demands: reinstatement of their right to put up posters and hold large open debates; freedom of the press—by which they meant press coverage of their demonstrations; guarantees for the safety of student protesters; and a statement from the mayor that the protests were legal. The mayor reportedly agreed to the latter two demands.

Police were said to have broken up sit-ins at the congress building and city hall in the early hours of December 20, but protests resumed later in the day. Police barricaded People's Square and took video pictures of the demonstrators.

That day, the official Xinhua news agency acknowledged the demonstrations for the first time, in an interview with a leading official of the state education commission. The unidentified official said citizens had a constitutional right to protest, and was quoted as saying, "One of the important planks of the restructuring of the political system is to expand socialist democracy."

Again, on December 21, tens of thousands of protesters massed in Shanghai's downtown area, with factory and other workers joining in support of the students. As many as 50,000 people were reported to have flocked to People's Square throughout the day. As on the previous day, there were some reports of students being beaten and hundreds arrested—but these were unconfirmed. A city spokesman denied any arrests or beatings, although a China news agency report said that there had been seven arrests on the evening of December 21 outside city hall.

Meanwhile, the Xinhua news agency issued an article that evening quoting city officials, who accused the students of "illegal actions" that "will affect social stability and unity." It claimed that protesters had broken into the municipal government offices the day before and had beaten 31 police officers.

In the first official newspaper reports on the Shanghai protests, local papers on December 22 attributed the unrest to students who did not have "an adequate understanding of our reform." One article spoke of "a handful of people with ulterior motives who put up posters with reactionary content."

Within hours of the December 22 ban on further demonstrations without a permit, the thousands of protesters in People's Square dispersed, and students who had threatened a boycott began returning to class. The police order promised that violators would be "severely punished."

Foreign observers noted that, despite the scale of the protests, they were poorly organized and led, and there was no agreement on how much democracy should be introduced.

The protest was joined on December 23 by Beijing students. Some 1,000 students from Qinghua University marched through the capital on December 23, and protests also took place for the first time in Nanjing, continuing through December 27. In Shanghai, students from Tongji University defied a ban on further demonstrations in that city, and students in Yianjin joined the protests December 24.

On December 23, *People's Daily* warned against "extreme action" by students. The warnings were intensified on December 25, with the *People's Daily* comparing the protests to the 1966–1976 Cultural Revolution and stating that they could lead to anarchy.

On December 26, officials in Shanghai and Beijing announced that five days' notice was required for demonstrations—effectively banning protests—and four sites in Beijing were placed out of bounds to protesters.

A second protest was held in Beijing on December 29 in defiance of the new law, by students from the Beijing Normal University. The local Communist newspaper, the *Beijing Daily*, that day continued its criticisms, quoting from the criminal code to warn protesters of possible jail sentences.

Students at Beijing Normal University were prevented by police from staging a second day of protests on December 30—the first day for weeks that no demonstrations were reported in any Chinese city.

Meanwhile, as the protests waned, wall posters, criticizing the government in Beijing, continued to appear in the capital.

On January 1, 1987, more than 2,000 students rallied in Tiananmen Square—recently declared off limits to protestors—and continued their marches and rallies around the capital well into the morning of January 2. They carried banners supporting China's supreme leader, Deng Xiaoping, and his "four modernizations" program and condemning "conservatives and reactionaries." This was a reference to those who opposed the economic reforms introduced by Deng.

A number of arrests were made after the demonstrators began to move toward the city hall on the afternoon of January 1. The detainees were reportedly freed after students marched on the home of the president of Beijing University, demanding their release.

Campuses in the capital were generally quiet, but at Beijing University illegal wall posters appeared on January 2 urging China's top leaders to take a public stand on the protests. To date, only officials who were widely regarded as having resisted Deng's reforms had spoken out publicly in condemnation of the protests.

Meanwhile, on January 1, the *People's Daily* attacked what it called a trend toward "bourgeois liberalism," and accused a handful of people of debilitating China by denying the leadership role of the Communist Party. The Xinhua news agency criticized the U.S. Voice of America broadcast service, charging it with encouraging dissent.

On January 5, students at Beijing University burned copies of the *People's Daily* and the *Beijing Daily*. The previous day, posters had appeared at the campus urging students to burn copies of the local paper—whose criticism of the students had been the most bitter—for distorting events in recent reports. The posters also urged Deng to respond to the demands for democracy and expressed support for his economic policies.

On January 5, the *Beijing Daily* accused the students of practicing "anarchism."

HU YAOBANG REMOVED

The spreading of student demonstrations caught Hu Yaobang in a political bind. Observers suggested that students had probably taken Hu's backing of change as a sign of tacit support for their protests within the party hierarchy. (Hu was the party's senior specialist in youth affairs and propaganda.)

Conservatives in the party were said to have criticized Hu for his lenient attitude toward the student demonstrators and "bourgeois liberalization," and for his tendency to make off-the-cuff remarks. Despite Hu's participation in the Long March of 1934–1935, some military leaders reportedly believed he did not have the credentials to head the party's Central Military Commission. That position was now held by Deng, who was widely expected to relinquish it at a special party congress scheduled for October.

But, most importantly for Hu, his inability to bring student demonstrations under control cost him the support of his patron, Deng Xiaoping. Indicative of Deng's disenchantment with the Party's general secretary and his policy—according to the *Washington Post* in its January 8 edition—was his calling for the ouster of leading members of the Communist Party who had advocated Western-style democracy. (The *Post* had cited the January 7 edition of the pro-communist Hong Kong newspaper *Wen Wei Po*, which had direct connections with Beijing.)

Further, Reuters, the British news agency, citing a letter apparently written by Deng on December 29, 1986, reported that Deng had secretly ordered a tougher line against demonstrators after the protests spread to Beijing.

The new hard line against student demonstrators appeared in an editorial in *People's Daily* on January 6 which repeated the charge of "bourgeois liberalism," used to disparage the democratic values of the West. It said there had been a failure in the party's "ideological work," with the result that conditions had been created for "bourgeois liberal thoughts to grow and spread. This is a grave lesson." The editorial accused unidentified officials of having "turned a blind eye" to efforts by some to lead China toward capitalism.

Underscoring the importance of the editorial, it was read on nationwide television that evening.

The warnings against bourgeois liberalism spread to workers and intellectuals on January 7 and 9.

The *Workers Daily*, in a front-page editorial on January 7, called for measures against those who attempted to sabotage factory production by spreading "bourgeois" ideas to workers.

A number of workers had attended demonstrations in Shanghai in December 1986. However, while they had expressed sympathy for the students, they were reported to be more concerned with countering price increases than with promoting democracy.

Guangming Daily, the leading newspaper for intellectuals, on January 9 contained a front-page commentary quoting extensively from a 1984 speech by Deng in which he attacked those who advocated "bourgeois liberalization." It charged that there were a few party members who "think they are special and who have not adhered to the four basic principles." Those principles, laid down by Deng in 1979, were: the permanence of the people's dictatorship; the unequivocal rule of the Communist Party; adherence to socialism; and the dominance of Marxism and the thought of Mao Zedong.

The criticism of intellectuals was seen to be in keeping with the reported decision by Deng to back away from a campaign, in effect since the spring of 1986—to encourage discussion of political, economic and cultural ideas.

Deng further distanced himself from his protege by dismissing Hu's close associates from key positions. On January 11, it was reported that the Communist Party's propaganda chief, Zhu Houze, had been temporarily suspended. Zhu was closely affiliated with General Secretary Hu and politburo member Hu Qili.

The same day, the firing of the propaganda department's information director, Zhong Peizhang, was reported by *Wen Wei Po*. Zhong was reported to have been replaced by Wang Furu, the deputy information director.

Deng made his first public comments about the student protests on January 13, calling them "a very big mistake," but at the same time indicating his intent to go ahead with his reform program.

Deng made his comments in a meeting with Noboru Takeshita, during which he told Takeshita that the demonstrations had not influenced China's open-door policy to the West.

Deng singled out three intellectuals for criticism: Fang Lizhi, Liu Binyan and Wang Ruowang. Deng said that Fang, Wang and Liu should have known better than to become involved in the student movement because they were party members.

Two of the three intellectuals criticized by Deng were censured by the Communist Party on January 12 and 14, respectively.

Fang Lizhi, 50, a leading astrophysicist, was dismissed on January 12 as vice-president of the University of Science and Technology in Hefei. The student unrest had begun in Hefei, where the protesters had won concessions from the authorities on the election of representatives to the local legislative body. Fang was accused of slandering the socialist system and defaming the party leadership. He had also come under criticism recently for proposing a complete "Westernization" of China, for rejecting the Communist Party leadership and for stirring up the student protests.

The student demonstrators had frequently hailed Fang for defending academic and intellectual freedom and for advocating broader rights.

The university's president, Guan Weiyan, was dismissed along with Fang for failing to keep his subordinate in check and for being "responsible for the nationwide bad influence" caused by the unrest at the university.

Wang Ruowang, a prominent Shanghai writer and Marxist theorist who had been a critic of corruption in the party and government, was expelled from the Communist Party on January 14. Wang was accused of a number of "major mistakes," including his description of socialism in China as "feudal or semifeudal in essence." The Xinhua news agency referred to him as a "founder of bourgeois liberalization."

Further, there were reports the same day that Liu Binyan, 60, an internationally known author and reporter for the *People's Daily*, had also been ousted from the party. He, too, had vigorously opposed official corruption. General Secretary Hu was reported to have served as Liu's protector.

The ouster of the intellectuals was accompanied by increasingly harsh editorials in the official press demanding greater party discipline and warning against bourgeois liberalism and "spiritual pollution." The official press accused unidentified party leaders and government officials of ideological laxity.

In the meantime, the rumors about Hu's trouble spread after he failed to appear in public after December 29, 1986. Party spokesmen recently had cited illness as a reason for his absence from public view, but had done nothing to dispel rumors that he was in disfavor. Speculation that Hu had fallen into disfavor was fueled when, on January 14, the national television network announced that the Communist Party had convened an extraordinary meeting of high-level officials.

At a special meeting of the enlarged politburo—consisting of politburo members and other influential Communist Party members outside that body—Hu Yaobang submitted his resignation. The Party communique of January 16 said that Hu resigned as the general secretary of the Central Committee of the Communist Party after admitting to his major mistakes.

According to the January 16 communique, Hu was accused of unspecified "mistakes on major issues of political principle." He delivered a self-criticism at the meeting, the communique said, in which he admitted violating "the party's principle of collective leadership during his tenure." The enlarged politburo then unanimously agreed to Hu's request to approve his resignation, the communique said.

Hu retained his position on the politburo, its five-member Standing Committee and the party's Central Committee.

The communique also announced the appointment of Zhao Ziyang as the acting general secretary of the Communist Party. The same communique declared that China would continue Deng's economic reforms and its policy of opening up to the West.

Nonetheless, Hu's ouster was seen by some observers as delivering a major blow to reformists who backed economic changes, and marking a shift toward the view of conservatives who believed Deng's reforms had moved too fast. In addition, the prospect for planned political reforms appeared clouded.

Hu's forced ouster was also widely viewed as damaging to the party's efforts to present itself as stable after the chaos of the Cultural Revolution of 1967–76. Observers saw Hu's removal as a blow to Deng's plans for an orderly succession.

12

RETREAT FROM REFORMS

A BALANCING ACT

Hu Yaobang's ouster as general secretary of the Communist Party signaled a change of policy. But the nature of the change could not easily be determined.

Deng Xiaoping, the central figure of China's ruling circles, March 8, 1987 said economic and political reform would continue. "China will not change its policies," he said, and the country would continue trying to lower the average age of leadership.

In the weeks following the January backlash, Western analysts had puzzled over whether Deng now opposed the reform agenda that he had done much to foster. A group of six party documents issued in January 1987 painted him as an unflinching enemy of the disorder that traditionalists said the reforms had visited upon China.

According to the documents, Deng had spoken out against bourgeois liberalization in September 1986, and they confirmed that he had said bloodshed might be needed to stop the December student demonstrations.

The documents quoted praise by Deng for the "cool head" shown by Poland's communist leaders with their 1981 declaration of martial law. And the documents said he had asserted: "We cannot adopt Western ways, because if we do, it will mean chaos."

On January 18, two days after Hu's resignation, the *People's Daily* questioned freedom of expression. It quoted an official of the Academy of Social Sciences, who cautioned that in the exchange of ideas, "Letting one hundred schools contend must be carried out under Marxist guidance."

This was a reference to the Hundred Flowers movement, revived by the Chinese leadership in 1986 to encourage a looser rein on art and ideas.

The same paper gave front page prominence, on January 20, to arguments for less economic freedom made by members of the Standing Committee of the National People's Congress. Newspapers also urged a return to earlier days of "struggle and thrift" and otherwise countered Deng's belief that consumerism would bring prosperity.

This was followed by an official Communist Party announcement on February 3 that it had fired Zhu Houze who would be replaced by Wang Renzhi, known as a Marxist hard-liner.

The deposed Zhu, 56, was considered an ally of former General Secretary Hu Yaobang and, with him, had encouraged freer artistic and intellectual expression.

After Hu, the former propaganda chief was the highest ranking among the recent string of purge victims. Three intellectuals denounced by Deng Xiaoping had also been disciplined, with Liu Binyan of the People's Daily, on January 23, becoming the last to lose his party membership. A journalist of international standing, his probes into official corruption had made Liu a hero to many among his wide readership in China.

However, the top leaders of China gave no public indication of changing its foreign or domestic policy. On January 20, Deng had stood by his foreign investment policy. "If there are any shortcomings in implementing our open policy, the main one is that China needs further opening," he told the visiting prime minister of Zimbabwe, Robert Mugabe. But he appeared to concede that his economic reforms had been overambitious. "Our goals now are realistic and practical," Deng said.

Deng affirmed his commitment to the open-door policy when he spoke privately with U.S. Secretary of State George P. Shultz on March 3. The 82-year-old Deng was reported to have told Shultz that "political difficulties" had forced him to slow his push toward modernization, but that he had not given up the campaign.

Zhao Ziyang, the newly-appointed acting general secretary of the Communist Party, was much more explicit on China's continuing with its modernization programs.

Speaking on the occasion of the Chinese New Year, Zhao told his listeners that "comprehensive reform, the opening to the outside world, invigorating the domestic economy, as well as the policy of respecting knowledge and trained personnel will not be changed."

The "current work of opposing bourgeois liberalization" would target only party members, Zhao said, and the drive would be largely confined to "the political ideological field." The campaign would not reach into rural areas, and only a "very limited number of party members" would be disciplined, the premier added. Approximately 44 million people belonged to the party, out of a population of over a billion.

No "practices of 'leftist' mistakes will be repeated or will be permitted," Zhao declared. This was an apparent reference to the Cultural Revolution (1966–1976), during which a series of purges had brought chaos to the country.

Zhao also raised the issue of "political structural reform," a policy Hu had championed. Zhao said there would be reforms in county elections, including "nominating more candidates for election than required for each post."

Zhao returned to the same theme when he addressed the National People's Congress on March 25. In his speech, he spoke out for economic reform and openness to foreign investment, but he acknowledged worries in the party that such changes could feed social instability.

"We must take note of the fact that some people favoring [economic] reform and the open policy are not sober-minded enough, and the others who stress adherence [to Marxism] are not mentally emancipated enough," Zhao said.

Zhao assailed the "pernicious influence" of "bourgeois liberalization," the term critics of reform used to refer to the spread of Western political and cultural beliefs. Zhao said that until recently the country's leadership had been "weak and lax" and that bourgeois liberalization had been "quite widespread."

Zhao said the trend had been "curbed," but that "immense efforts" were still needed to defeat it. He forecast a long struggle, and listed the battle as one of the "major tasks" facing the country in 1987.

But Zhao warned that it could never be "permissible to stifle democracy on the pretext of opposing bourgeois liberalization." As used among China's leaders, "democracy" meant the free expression of policy ideas by all ranks of officials.

In defending economic change, Zhao urged critics to acknowledge "the obvious achievements of our reforms." Without offering details or a timetable, he said the country must go ahead with such key economic reforms as a relaxation of the nation's "very irrational" system of fixed prices and the loosening of party control over factories.

Both reforms had been reported to be in trouble. Proposed legislation to curb the authority of party officials over factory managers had been shelved days before the congress convened.

CONSERVATIVE BACKLASH

While Hu Yaobang's resignation followed on the heels of the student unrest, it was reported that deep-seated differences between Hu and hard-line conservative members of the party over policy lay at the root of his dismissal. Hu had been a staunch advocate of political and economic reform. He was in favor of freeing the economy from rigid state control and of more flexible, Western-style management, and had spoken out in favor of permitting free discussion and criticism of party policy. He had publicly attacked the late Chairman Mao Zedong and backed political changes that would have curbed the role of Communist Party cadres in government and industry.

The conservative hardliners seized the opportunity to roll back "bourgeois liberalism." Thus, on January 22, the Chinese government created a bureau to exercise "supervision and control" of the press and book publishing. It would operate under the State Council, a body headed by Premier Zhao.

Officials of this bureau said May 15 that the new government body would press the campaign against "bourgeois liberalism"—the spread of political and cultural ideas imported from the West.

News accounts agreed that the authorities had found few cultural figures willing to take part in the new drive for cultural orthodoxy. But officials had closed at least four newspapers, and an April 7 news account said they had also forced 39 sensational magazines to suspend operations. The magazines, all published in Guangxi province, had a combined audience of millions.

The authorities also stepped up their surveillance of foreign journalists.

Even though Zhao Ziyang had earlier declared that the campaign against unorthodox beliefs would be confined to discipline of party members on the CCP Central Committee, on February 7 ordered the national circulation of posters urging citizens to join the fight against so-called bourgeois liberalism, a "struggle without end" that would be waged "without magnanimity."

The military, neglected during the reformers' ascendancy, signaled its readiness to join the campaign on February 14, when the general political department of the People's Liberation Army declared that "officers, soldiers and staff should take part" in the "serious struggle against bourgeois liberalization."

News accounts agreed that most citizens were ignoring the orthodoxy campaign and living their lives undisturbed. But official praise for the late Mao Zedong was revived, with broadcasts of his speeches at some universities, and the press and university students found themselves under tighter control while some economic changes prized by the reformers were diluted or delayed.

According to press reports on February 6, the authorities had arrested 19 supposed ringleaders of the democracy protests. Universities had been instructed to stress communist ideology in student classes, and regulations for screening out politically unreliable college applicants were reported on May 4. College adminstrators would be called on to pay less attention to entrance tests and more to applicants' display of the so-called five loves—among them "love for the Communist Party."

Many party officials now neglected communist ideology themselves, the *Far Eastern Economic Review* said in its July 30 issue. It cited the failure of more than 60 of a group of 129 cadres to pass an examination in basic Marxism-Leninism.

During the Cultural Revolution, millions of students had been sent to the countryside for forced labor. This practice was discontinued in the latter part of the 1970s as the authorities had decided that students should be allowed more time for study instead. It was revived by the government's decision announced by Vice-Premier Li Peng on March 28, making more than one million students spend their summer vacation doing compulsory rural labor, according to a July 5 report.

At the same time, the Communist Party Central Discipline Inspection Commission tightened the Party discipline, putting Party officials on notice July 3 that they would be subject to expulsion from the Party for accepting a bribe. The Party focused new attention on problems of privilege and abuse of power on the part of its officers.

A spate of bribery cases had been brought to light about this time with 185 members arrested and expelled for corruption during the first five months of 1987. Instead of being secret, the proceedings had been held in civil court.

The conservative reaction was noted in economic policies as well. On March 10, agriculture Minister He Kang said authorities would encourage peasants to grow more grain by allowing them to sell more of the crop on the free market. The state purchase figure for grain would drop to 10% of output from the current 14%, He said.

Western analysts agreed that China faced a grain shortage that stemmed not only from persistent poor weather, but also from the determination of peasants to grow crops that were more profitable under the country's economic reforms.

Figures in the Chinese Communist Party who were dubious about reform had long argued that the authorities would invite "chaos" if they allowed grain production to be neglected. "Peasants are no longer interested in growing grain," the traditionalist Chen Yun had warned in September 1985. He continued: "They are not even interested in raising pigs and vegetables, because in their opinion there can be no prosperity without engaging in industry."

Annual grain production had stood at 305 million tons, at the start of the reforms. By 1984, it had reached a record 407 million tons, but had dropped to 380 million tons in 1985, rising only to 390 million tons in 1986. Authorities were now said to doubt whether the country could reach its 1987 target of 400 million tons.

Another retrogressive move involved stock and bond issues. On April 7, the State Council (cabinet) announced new rules which restricted the issuing of stocks and bonds by state and collective enterprises. The regulations came in response to complaints about inflation, and marked one of several efforts to curb the economic changes introduced by government reformers.

The new rules barred state enterprises from issuing stock but allowed them to issue bonds, while collective enterprises would be able to issue stock but not bonds. Neither type of enterprise would be allowed to issue more stock or bonds than were allowed for in annual state plans, and all bond issues had to be for "key construction projects" outlined in state economic plans.

IMPACT OF CHANGE ON SINO-JAPANESE RELATIONS

Hu Yaobang's ouster as the leader of the Communist Party removed a friend of the West, and of Japan, from China's ruling circles. There was a surge of anti-Japanese feeling following his resignation in January, attributable to Hu's widely publicized close relationship with Japanese Prime Minister Yasuhiro Nakasone.

Older Chinese leaders who had objected to Hu's domestic reforms also still vividly remembered China's struggle against Japanese invaders, a conflict that had not ended until the occupation of Japan by the U.S. in 1945. One reason for Hu's downfall was believed to be his supposed practice of having made overtures to Japan without consulting his party colleagues.

Wartime bitterness had been fanned by Japan's lifting in January of a long-standing cap on its defense spending. Many Chinese leaders now warned of a return of Japanese "militarism."

Anti-Japanese sentiment was further provoked by a Japanese high court's February 26 decision that a disputed dormitory located in Kyoto, Japan did not belong to China but instead to Taiwan and its Nationalist Chinese regime. In addition, the ruling had referred to Taiwan as "the Republic of China" and said the country could be a party in Japanese civil cases.

On May 6, Beijing threatened to take action against Japan over a range of issues. Among the issues cited was Japan's chronic trade surplus with China. The May 6 announcement said Japan had "talked much but done little" to lessen the imbalance. The surplus had dwindled during 1986, but only to $4 billion. China now threatened to take "active measures" to attack the problem.

It had been reported on April 29 that Japan had by far the largest share of China's import market. In 1986, the report said, Japan had exported $12.4 billion worth of goods to China, an amount equivalent to 28.9% of Chinese imports for that year. Hong Kong had come second, with a 13.1% share based on exports of $5.6 billion. The U.S. was third, with a share of 10.9% and exports of $4.7 billion.

Two days later, on May 8, the Chinese government accused a Japanese reporter of illegally obtaining "national intelligence" and ordered him to leave the country within 10 days. The journalist, Shuitsu Henmi of the Kyodo news agency, was the third foreign reporter to be expelled from China in 11 months and the fourth in three years.

Henmi's supposed transgressions were not spelled out until May 12, when the official Chinese press quoted charges that he had paid monthly bribes of $135 in order to obtain secret documents.

The accusations singled out a paper prepared for the Central Committee of the Chinese Communist Party, one that had commented on the party's current struggle between reformers and traditionalists. Henmi was one of three foreign reporters who had written articles about the document. The three journalists agreed that a Chinese official had deliberately leaked the paper to them.

Henmi denied all charges made against him, and on May 12, Japan expressed its "deep regret" over the Chinese action.

The issue of Japanese military buildup exercised the Chinese. Beijing warned Japan against "militarist thinking" many times, including in discussions held on May 29–June 3 with General Yuko Kurihara, director of the Japanese Defense Agency. Kurihara's Beijing visit was the first trip to China by a Japanese defense minister since the departure of Japanese invaders from that country in 1945.

After Kurihara's visit, Deng Xiaoping was quoted on June 4 as saying that Japan's planned increase in military spending would please those Japanese who wanted their country to become a military power once again.

The Deng remark had prompted a senior official of the Japanese foreign ministry to say that the Chinese leader was "out of touch." The comment, publicized in newspaper accounts that quoted the official anonymously, caused China to lodge a formal protest.

The Japanese government tried to smooth its relations with China by sending a delegation of cabinet ministers to Beijing. The delegation made a visit to the Chinese capital on June 27–28.

Deng Xiaoping told the visitors on June 28 that their country was to blame for the troubles. The 82-year-old leader suggested that he had been painted as an "old muddlehead" by the Japanese.

The tattered relationship between Beijing and Tokyo was patched up a year later by a new loan agreement which Japanese Prime Minister Noboru Takeshita announced on August 25, 1988, at the start of his six-day visit to China. Under the new agreement Japan would provide China with a loan package worth about 800 billion yen (US $6 billion), to be spread out over the years 1990 through 1995.

FALLOUTS ON AMERICAN-CHINESE RELATIONS

Unlike Sino-Japanese relations, U.S. relations with China did not immediately register the impact of China's domestic change. Strains developed here as well, in combination with other developments.

U.S. Secretary of State George P. Shultz visited China on March 1–5. The trip came shortly after Hu's resignation and as the Reagan administration struggled with the Iran arms scandal.

Shultz conferred with the top Chinese leadership on March 2–3. He spent a total of almost seven hours on March 2 with Foreign Minister Wu Xueqian, Defense Minister Zhang Aiping, President Li Xiannian, Premier Zhao Ziyang and Deputy Premier Li Peng. The U.S. had asked that Shultz be allowed to meet with several of China's vice-premiers, but his hour-long talk with the Soviet-trained Li Peng—considered an enemy of the reformers—was the only such visit the Chinese scheduled.

On March 3, Shultz spent almost an hour talking privately with Deng. After his meeting with the Chinese leaders, Shultz made a statement that same day that Chinese leaders had assured him China would continue its openness to Western investment and its experiments with economic liberalization. There would be no "return to the restrictions and repressions of the not-too-distant past," Shultz said he had been told.

"It makes sense," Shultz added, asserting that the economic "reforms have worked and the people are better off." He suggested that China was "irrevocably" committed to modernization, although he stressed that this would be "a Chinese form of modernization."

However, some analysts suggested that the Chinese actually disagreed about the economic policy but wanted to show Shultz a common front.

Among the matters taken up in the talks was a recent apparent warming of relations between China and the Soviet Union, as well as the continuing occupation of Afghanistan by the Soviets and of Cambodia by Vietnam, a Soviet ally. Shultz also raised the issue of the recent expulsions from China of two U.S. reporters.

Problems of bilateral trade required a high-level discussion. Trade between China and the United States reached about $8 billion a year. China did not count exports reaching the U.S. through Hong Kong, but the U.S. did—causing each country to claim that it suffered a balance of payments deficit relative to the other. According to U.S. figures, China had exported $5.241 billion in goods to the U.S. during 1986 and had imported only $3.105 billion in U.S. goods.

In addition, China's alleged role as a major arms supplier to Iran figured as a new issue. Here, Shultz was handicapped in pressing China to heed the U.S. call for an end to weapons sales to Iran by the Reagan administration's Iran arms scandal. China said it was not selling weapons to that country, but U.S. officials believed that China was selling Iran billions of dollars of arms each year and had become that country's top weapons supplier. On March 3, Shultz said that in their talks the Chinese had questioned whether the U.S. could credibly ask others not to sell weapons to Iran after secretly doing so itself.

China's arms sales to Iran continued to plague U.S. relations with China, especially in June, 1987, after U.S. warships started escorting American-flagged Kuwaiti tankers. China was suspected of selling—among other weapons—Silkworm anti-ship missiles which were being set up near the Strait of Hormuz.

On June 6, White House national security advisor Frank Carlucci said in Rome that China had, thus far, supplied Iran with 20 of the coastal defense missiles, and would ultimately deliver twice that many. The Silkworms—also known as HY-2s—were in the "process of becoming operational" but had not yet been deployed for combat, he added.

On June 7, White House Chief of Staff Howard Baker, in Venice, warned that full deployment of the missiles by Iran would be interpreted as a "hostile act" that could bring U.S. retaliation.

The *Washington Post* reported that the Reagan administration was debating whether or not to launch a preemptive strike against the missile sites. In June 5 closed testimony before the Senate Armed Services Committee, Admiral William J. Crowe Jr., chairman of the Joint Chiefs of Staff, reportedly said he was opposed to such a strike. He expressed doubts that Teheran would use the Silkworms to attack American flag vessels and thereby risk a direct conflict with the U.S.

On June 10, a Chinese foreign ministry spokesman insisted that Beijing maintained "strict neutrality" in the Iran–Iraq war and was not selling weapons to Teheran. In the past, Chinese officials had claimed that whatever Chinese arms were reaching Iran had come from third parties acting independently—particularly North Korea. But Western, Arab and Asian diplomats said China was deliberately using North Korea as a conduit for the arms sales to provide an element of deniability.

China was believed to have signed agreements with Iran for the sale of a wide range of weapons, including Chinese-made versions of Soviet MiG warplanes, tanks, artillery and various missile systems. A Kuwaiti newspaper reported that China had also agreed to build factories in Iran for producing ammunition, rockets and tank spare parts.

According to some press accounts, China was being paid in oil from Iran in a barter arrangement. An Asian diplomat, cited in the *New York Times*, said China had become Iran's largest arms supplier, primarily for strategic, not economic, reasons. In this view, Beijing was building up Iran as an independent counterweight to the U.S.S.R. and its presence in neighboring Afghanistan. Finally, on October 22, the Reagan administration announced that it was curbing plans to export certain high-technology American products to China in retaliation for China's alleged sale of Silkworm missiles to Iran. The decision came after Beijing refused to acknowledge it was selling arms to Teheran, and after Iranian missiles thought to be Silkworms struck a U.S.-owned tanker, a U.S.-flagged tanker and a Kuwaiti oil terminal.

It was reportedly the first time the U.S. had acted against a third country for selling arms to Iran. It was also said to be the first time the U.S. had imposed new curbs on China since the two nations began improving ties in the early 1970s.

The decision came after a series of U.S. warnings and Chinese denials on the Silkworm issue. The final straw reportedly came when Beijing's denials continued even after the State Department called in

Chinese officials and showed them U.S. satellite photographs of the missiles leaving China and arriving on the same ship at the Iranian port of Bandar Abbas.

On October 23, Xinhua said, "It is not reasonable at all for the United States to halt the review of relaxing controls of high-tech exports to China under the pretext of mounting tensions in the Gulf."

By then, relations between Beijing and Washington had already been strained by the ongoing Tibetan uprisings, considered the most serious since the Chinese troops suppressed an armed independence movement in 1959.

China had historically claimed sovereignty over the region, and had effectively controlled Tibet since Chinese troops moved into the area in 1950. After harsh policies during the 1960s and early 1970s, Beijing had moderated its stance toward Tibet and attempted to improve living conditions in the region, which was among China's most impoverished.

Part of the government's plan, however, had been a widely resented resettlement program for Chinese that had resulted in the six million Tibetans now being outnumbered by 7.5 million Chinese in the area. The more moderate Chinese policy had been championed by Hu Yaobang, the former Communist Party chief.

In September, 1988, the Dalai Lama, Tibet's spiritual leader, came to the U.S. for a 10-day visit which ended on September 29. He spoke out for Tibet's independence. While the Dalai Lama was still in the U.S. a small group of Buddhist monks in Lhasa staged a demonstration on September 27 that ended in the arrest of at least 27 lamas.

The Buddhist monks, who were carrying the outlawed Tibetan flag, marched outside the Jokhang temple, chanting "Tibet wants independence." Scuffles broke out when police moved in to arrest the marchers. Chinese officials reported that 27 policemen had been injured. Foreign eyewitnesses claimed that the monks were beaten with shovels as they were taken into custody.

On September 28 the Chinese government complained that the U.S. was partly to blame for the unrest, because it had allowed the Dalai Lama to speak out for Tibetan independence during his recent U.S. visit.

Hundreds of Tibetans battled Chinese police in the central city of Lhasa on October 1. Chinese officials said six policemen had died in the clash, but Tibetans and foreign tourists who witnessed the violence said 10 policemen and at least nine demonstrators, including three Buddhist monks, had been killed.

The demonstration began when a small group of Buddhist monks, or lamas, marched in Lhasa outside the Jokhang temple, Tibet's most sacred Buddhist site. The march turned violent when Chinese police arrested between 25 and 50 lamas, and a crowd of hundreds of Tibetans began hurling stones at police. The rioters then attacked and burned a police station and several police cars in an effort to free demonstrators who had been arrested.

Chinese officials claimed that some protesters used police weapons to shoot at police. Foreign tourists at the scene said that after the police station had been set ablaze, police officers fired in the air to disperse the crowd and then fired at the demonstrators.

On October 6, Western doctors in Lhasa said that at least eight Tibetans had been shot to death in the incident.

On October 6, heavily armed Chinese police arrested 60 Buddhist monks who had marched to Lhasa to demand the release of lamas arrested in the earlier protests. Eyewitness accounts of Western news correspondents said that the police had beaten the monks, who were chanting the Dalai Lama's name before they were arrested.

On October 6, the Reagan administration announced support for China's attempts to curb the rioting in Tibet, but the U.S. Senate the same day voted, 98–0, to condemn the crackdown by Chinese security forces.

The Senate measure was attached as an amendment to a State Department authorization bill. The measure urged President Reagan to meet with the Dalai Lama, and also mandated certification by the president that progress had been made on human rights in Tibet before the U.S. approved any new weapons or technology sales to China.

The State Department strongly criticized the Senate measure and affirmed its position that Tibet was part of China. That stance apparently reflected the administration's fear of damaging Chinese relations and its recognition that Beijing had sought to improve its policies in Tibet.

The Tibetan rebellion continued into the next year. On February 11, 1988, a Washington-based human rights group, Asia Watch, released a report denouncing China for the systematic repression of Tibetan rights.

The 74-page report, which was based in part on interviews with residents of Tibet both before and after the violent demonstrations in 1987, documented a number of human rights violations carried out by the Chinese authorities against Tibetans.

The abuses included the systematic and arbitrary arrest of those who advocated Tibetan independence, the commonplace use of torture and the practice of inducing abortions without the consent or knowledge of the mother in order to enforce family planning laws.

A spokesman for the Chinese embassy in the U.S. claimed the

rights-abuse report contained inaccuracies and was based on some "questionable" sources.

THIRTEENTH PARTY CONGRESS

Against the backdrop of deepening domestic crisis—compounded by China's external problems—the Chinese Communist Party held its national congress on October 25–November 1, 1987. The congress—the Party's first since 1982—heralded the rise to power of a new generation of Chinese leaders and seemed to reaffirm the course of economic reform that had been adopted by Deng Xiaoping.

Deng, 83, resigned most of his key party posts at the end of the congress. He turned over the reins of leadership to his protege, Premier Zhao Ziyang, who was elected CCP general secretary.

Along with Zhao, 68, dozens of younger leaders were elected to the Central Committee, pushing into retirement many of the hardline party veterans who had opposed Deng's moves toward economic liberalization.

On November 1, Deng became China's first Communist leader to voluntarily resign his top party leadership positions. He stepped down from the Central Committee, thus removing himself from the ruling politburo and its dominant Standing Committee. The five-member Standing Committee was the inner circle of the Communist Party.

Deng was reelected to the powerful Central Military Commission on November 2, at a meeting of the newly elected Central Committee.

Deng was expected to retain ultimate authority within the party, according to Chinese officials. But his resignations from the other top party posts set the stage for Zhao to assume control of the CCP. On November 2, Zhao was elected party general secretary.

Zhao was also named first vice chairman of the Central Military Commission, a post second in command only to Deng. The military commission, which controlled the Chinese armed forces, was considered a key to power within the CCP, according to Western observers.

The formal confirmation of Zhao to the top party post made him in effect the party's leader, although it appeared Deng would continue to strongly influence the course of party policy. Zhao said, "I will often ask Mr. Deng's advice so that I will be able to do things better."

Deng's withdrawal from active party leadership and Zhao's ascension to power were seen by Western observers as a sign that Deng had marshaled sufficient support to resume his economic reforms.

Deng's agenda of reforms had been thrown into doubt during recent debates within the party.

Zhao, in a two-and-a-half-hour opening speech to the congress on October 25, called for far-reaching changes in the nation's economy. He advocated allowing the free market, rather than the state, to control supply and demand.

"We should gradually establish a system under which the state sets the prices of a few vital commodities and labor services while leaving the rest to be regulated by the market," Zhao said. He declared support for private enterprise, which he said "promotes production, stimulates the market, provides employment opportunities and helps in many ways to meet people's needs."

Zhao also pledged to further open the nation's economy to foreign investment. "Closing one's country to external contact results only in increasing backwardness," he declared.

Party conservatives had criticized such reforms as being capitalistic.

Zhao's report also harshly criticized government bureaucracy and advocated the creation of a civil service system based on examinations, which would reduce party control over the administration of government.

The 1,936 delegates at the party congress unanimously approved Zhao's report on November 1.

On November 1, the party congress chose a 175-member Central Committee that included more than 60 new members. Many of the new members were advocates of the economic reforms called for by Deng and Zhao. Ninety-six members of the previous committee, chosen in 1982, were not reelected.

Many of the conservative leaders who had dominated the party for more than 50 years were removed from power. Chen Yun, 82, who had been one of the main critics of Deng's economic policies, retired from the Central Committee along with President Li Xiannian, 82, and Peng Zhen, the 85-year-old chairman of China's legislature. Peng was a member of the outgoing politburo, and Li and Chen were members of the politburo's Standing Committee.

Other notables dropped from the Central Committee were: Deng Liqun, 73, a member of the Central Committee's secretariat and a persistent critic of Deng's political reforms; Defense Minister Zhang Aiping; Yang Dezhi, 77, the former chief of the armed forces; Yu Qiuli, 73, chief political commissar of the People's Liberation Army; and Hu Qiaomu, 75, the Communist Party's leading ideologue. Yang, Yu and Hu were members of the outgoing politburo.

The average age of the members of the new Central Committee dropped to 55 from the previous average of 59.

Also on November 1, the constitution was amended to permit Deng to retain leadership of the Central Military Commission even though he was no longer a member of the Central Committee or politburo. Other amendments gave the politburo firm control over the secretariat and eliminated references to people's communes.

The Central Committee, in its first meeting, November 2, elected a ruling politburo consisting of 17 full members and one nonvoting alternate.

The new politburo included 11 members reelected from the previous body and seven new members.

The members reelected were: Zhao; Hu Yaobang, who remained on the politburo although he was removed from the standing committee; Vice-Premiers Li Peng, Wan Li, Tian Jiyun, Qiao Shi and Yao Yilin; Hu Qili; Yang Shangkun; Foreign Affairs Minister Wu Xueqian; and Beijing military commander Qin Jiwei.

The new members were: Li Ruihuan, mayor of Tianjin; Jiang Zemin, the mayor of Shanghai; Li Ximing, the Beijing party secretary; Yang Rudai, the Sichuan province party chief; State Councilor Song Ping; Li Tieying, 51, minister in charge of the commission for restructuring the economy and minister of the electronics industry, and Ding Guangen, the alternate member.

In other votes on November 2, Chen Yun was named chairman of the Central Advisory Commission, replacing Deng Xiaoping, and Qiao Shi was named head of the party's Discipline Inspection Commission.

The Central Committee also elected a five-man Standing Committee on November 2 that included four new members: Hu Qili, and Vice Premiers Li Peng, Qiao Shi, and Yao Yilin. Zhao was the only member remaining from the previous Standing Committee.

Of these new faces, Li Peng's rise to prominence showed a shifting of balance in the Chinese government. Zhao indicated that he wanted to resign as premier after assuming the top Party post on November 2. Li was named acting premier by the Standing Committee of the National People's Congress on November 24 and officially confirmed as premier at a meeting of the full National People's Congress in the following spring (March 25–April 11).

Li Peng, 59, was born in Sichuan province. He was the adopted son of former Premier Zhou Enlai. Li joined the Communist Party in 1945 and studied in the Soviet Union from 1948–54. He was elected to the Central Committee in 1982 and rose to the Politburo in 1985.

He was considered by Western diplomats to be a more cautious advocate of economic reform than either Zhao or Deng Xiaoping.

In a speech on November 24, following his appointment, Li declared that the economy should be "further stabilized," and announced that he would adhere to communist principles while carrying out any reforms.

Li declared, "A lot of things are waiting to be done, and the tasks facing us are not easy. We should tackle them in a bold, prudent and earnest way."

Along with the changes in the political leadership, on November 27 Deng Xiaoping replaced China's top three military staff officers. The change of command appeared to be in keeping with his policy to replace aging veterans with younger, more reform-minded leaders.

The army chief of staff, Yang Dezhi, 77, was succeeded by Chi Haotian, 61, who had been political commissar of the Jinan Military Region. Yu Qiuli, director of the general political department (the army's No. 2 staff post), was succeeded by Yang Baibing, 66, former political commissar of the Beijing Military Region. Hong Xuezhi, director of the general logistics department, was succeeded by his deputy, Zhao Nanqi, 52.

Hong retained his seat on the party's Central Military Commission, but Yang Dezhi and Yu were dismissed from the commission.

DISTRESS SIGNALS ON ECONOMIC FRONT

Following the 13th Party Congress, the new Chinese leadership set to work on the chronic problems of their overheated economy, which was threatening to get out of control. According to a report released by China's state statistical bureau on February 23, 1988, the nation's gross national product increased 9.4% in 1987 to 1.09 trillion yuan (US $292.9 billion). Retail prices rose 9.1% during the year, but wages increased at a significantly slower pace. Average real wages for urban workers increased only 1.7%, while agricultural wages rose 5.3%.

The statistical bureau also reported that 21% of the nation's urban households had suffered a declining standard of living during 1987, and 10% of such households were below the poverty line of 450 yuan (US$120) in annual income.

The statistics also showed another problem area: population control. In the late 1970s, the government had introduced a policy of one child per couple. Parents who gave birth to more than one child faced economic penalties.

But this policy apparently had not achieved its declared objective. More than 22 million babies were born in China during 1987, up about one million from 1986, the government's family planning director announced on February 15. China's total population increased to 1.07 billion during the year.

The natural population growth rate—the birth rate minus the death rate—reached 14.08 per thousand in 1987, according to Liang Jimin, director of the general office of the State Family Planning Commission.

Experts had said the nation would have to limit its natural growth rate to 10 per thousand if it were to meet its goal of limiting the total population to 1.2 billion by the year 2000, news reports said.

"We are faced with an acute population situation and our tasks are arduous," Liang declared. He said local officials would be punished if they did not strictly enforce population control measures.

China's foreign trade showed a healthy growth in 1987. The official figures conflicted with one another, however. The ministry of foreign economic relations and trade announced, on January 22, that the nation had recorded an overall surplus of US$1.9 billion on trade of US$67.3 billion during 1987, reversing a three-year string of deficits.

According to the trade ministry, exports had increased 28.1% in 1987, to US$34.6 billion, while imports had declined 1.1% over the same period to US$32.7 billion.

The state statistical bureau reported an overall trade deficit of US$3.5 billion in 1987, while the general administration of customs had reported a deficit of US$3.94 billion for the year, according to an Associated Press report on January 19.

According to the customs administration, exports had jumped 29% in 1987, to US$39.92 billion. Imports had increased 2.2% over the same period, to US$43.86 billion. Overall trade had increased 14% during the year, the administration asserted.

In his speech before the National People's Congress March 25, 1988, Premier Li Peng declared that the "outstanding problem" currently facing the country was high inflation. "An excessive rise in commodity prices," the acting premier said, "has . . . retarded improvement of the people's living standard and has even lowered the living standard of some urban residents."

To combat the problem of inflation, on January 19, the state council, China's cabinet, reimposed price controls on most basic raw materials and services. The move suspended a two-year-old program under which the government had attempted to reduce the role of central planning within the economy in favor of letting the marketplace set prices.

Price controls were reimposed on oil, gas, electricity, steel, timber, coal, rubber and other raw materials, as well as on shipping, railway and air transportation, a United Press International report said.

The state council declared that the controls were put back into effect in an effort to restrain "wildly" rising prices that were causing "market chaos."

The 1988 national budget presented to the National People's Congress in the spring of 1988 showed Beijing's preoccupation with stabilizing economic growth. The rate of expansion of China's gross national product was set at 7.5% in 1988, down from the 1987 growth rate of 9.4%. The budget would include a 9% increase in revenues over the previous year, to US $68.7 billion. Expenditures were expected to rise at the same rate, to US$70.85 billion, leaving a deficit of US$2.15 billion, about the same as 1987.

The largest increase under the new budget was for the state subsidies to consumers, which were set to jump 22%, to US$9.64 billion. Combined with the financial aid given to state enterprises, the total for subsidies amounted to US$20.7 billion, or about 29% of all expenditures, up two percentage points from 1987.

Foreign borrowing by the government was set to increase 18.4%, to about US$3.3 billion. (In 1987, actual foreign loans taken by the government had amounted to 70.5% of the amount budgeted for that year.) The government also planned to issue US$2.42 billion in bonds to help raise funds, Wang announced.

Spending on agriculture under the new budget would jump 14.5%, in part to stimulate the production of grain and pork, which had been rationed in several cities since the end of 1987.

A LOSING BATTLE

Zhao Ziyang and his liberal-minded reform faction struggled to maintain the momentum of their movement in the face of mounting opposition. In a major policy statement published on January 23, 1988, General Secretary Zhao announced plans to further open the nation's economy to foreign business.

The key to Zhao's plan was an expansion of export industries in China's coastal provinces aimed at attracting foreign investment and boosting trade.

"We should be able to attract sizable foreign investment, since our coastal areas boast the advantages of low-paid laborers with high expertise, good transport facilities and infrastructure, and scientific and technological development capability," the general secretary said.

About 20% of the nation's total population of 1.07 billion people lived in the coastal regions, which were already considerably more developed than China's poorer interior provinces.

Zhao's plan to encourage growth along the coast represented a fundamental change from the policies of the late Chinese leader Mao Zedong, who had advocated greater development of the interior regions of the country, Western analysts said.

Zhao acknowledged the disparity between the two areas of China, but maintained that "it is impossible to promote economic development in different parts of the country at the same high speed."

As part of his plan, Zhao called for a greater role for foreign experts in the expansion of Chinese businesses. "Their involvement in enterprise management will help shake off the fetters of the old Chinese system and make enterprises profitable," Zhao observed.

On March 20, the Xinhua news agency published another major policy statement by Zhao Ziyang, this one, a speech he had made before the 175-member Communist Party Central Committee which met in Beijing on March 15–19.

In this speech, which was compared to Soviet leader Mikhail S. Gorbachev's campaign for *glasnost*, Zhao declared, "We must speak the truth to the whole people about major incidents concerning social stability, explain policies and enlist people's support and cooperation through extensive dialogues."

The general secretary proposed the establishment of local consultation boards that would give ordinary citizens a voice in the development of national policy. He said the government "should solicit the opinions of the people from all walks of life" before deciding on major reforms. Such a system of citizen participation, Zhao said, would act as a "mechanism of checks and balances" on the government and the party.

Zhao also urged measures to increase foreign trade and investment in the country and continued to promote his plan to stimulate industrial development in China's coastal provinces.

Western analysts said a number of high-ranking party officials, including acting Premier Li Peng, were resisting Zhao's calls for far-reaching change and favored a more conservative approach to reform.

Under Zhao's prodding, on April 12, the National People's Congress passed two amendments to the nation's constitution legitimizing reforms instituted by the Communist Party leadership.

The first amendment provided legal sanction for private enterprise. It read: "The state permits the private sector of the economy to exist and develop within the limits prescribed by law. The private sector is a complement to the socialist public economy."

In 1987, according to the Xinhua news agency, more than 13.5 million private businesses in China employed 21.5 million people and accounted for 12.8% of the country's total retail sales.

The second amendment permitted individuals and groups, both

foreign and domestic, to transfer land use rights—a practice that ran counter to the communist principle that all land should be controlled by the state. The constitution was amended to read: "The right to use of land may be transferred according to law."

In its final session, on April 13, the congress passed legislation giving factory managers greater control over their industries. Previously, most factories had been controlled by committees of Communist Party bureaucrats.

Under the new law, local managers would be granted freedom to respond to changes in market demand, to negotiate with foreign concerns and to hire and fire workers. Factories that failed would no longer be rescued from bankruptcy by the state; instead, their managers would be held criminally responsible.

The law was considered by Western observers to be among the most important legal changes adopted in support of the economic reform movement.

These developments gave the appearance that the reformist wing of the Chinese Communist Party was winning the battle. Apparently encouraged by such a trend, Fang Lizhi, China's most prominent dissident, on May 4 made his first political address since his ouster from the Communist Party in January 1987. Speaking to an audience of about 500 students at Beijing University, Fang called for "more democracy in China," and urged the Communist Party to "recognize the concept of human rights above all."

On May 15, the Chinese government removed price controls on certain basic foodstuffs in Beijing and Shanghai as part of its effort to wean the nation from an economy dominated by central planning in favor of one governed by free market forces.

Prices in state stores in those and other cities increased between 30% and 60% as the government ended its subsidies for eggs, pork, vegetables and sugar.

Subsidies had been used by the government for years to keep food prices in China artificially low. The gradual removal of such price controls in recent months had sparked unprecedented inflation in China—especially in urban areas.

At the beginning of May, residents of Beijing and Shanghai had begun receiving a stipend of 10 yuan (US$2.70) a month to help offset the rise in prices.

In the summer of 1988, China's inflation rate had reached its highest level in nearly 40 years, according to figures released July 19 by the state statistical bureau.

The bureau reported that retail prices in June were up 19% from the same month in 1987—the largest increase since the Communists had taken power in 1949. Some Western economists, though, believed the true inflation rate could be as much as twice the reported level.

The 19% figure represented inflation calculated by the Western method, in which prices were measured on a given date and then compared on the same date one year later. The Chinese, on the other hand, figured the inflation rate by averaging price increases over the course of a given period.

Using the Chinese method, consumer prices were 13% higher during the first six months of 1988 than they were in the first six months of 1987. Food prices were up about 17%, and clothing prices were up 10%, the government reported.

The gross national product rose 11% during the first half of the year, and industrial output rose 17%. The unemployment rate was reported to be 2%.

The figure on unemployment was deceptive. On June 13, the *People's Daily* reported that as many as 30 million workers in China's urban labor force of 130 million had no real jobs and spent their working hours playing cards or watching television.

Such overstaffing cost the state about 60 billion yuan (US$16.2 billion) a year in wages and benefits, which was equal to half the amount of revenues generated by state-owned industries, one government official was quoted as saying.

Overstaffing also bred inefficiency and was turning China into a nation of idlers, the newspaper report said.

Convinced that the solution to this chronic problem of economic inefficiency was more, not less, utilization of market economy, the Chinese Communist Party leadership approved a five-year plan aimed at reforming the country's system of wages and prices, the Xinhua news agency reported on August 18. The changes heralded "an all-around deepening of China's reforms," the news agency said.

The five-year plan was approved during a meeting of the party politburo on August 15–17 in the coastal town of Beidaihe. The meeting was chaired by party leader Zhao Ziyang.

Under the new program, the state would continue to set prices for a few basic commodities, but would remove or liberalize price controls over most other goods, the news agency reported. Other changes would make state-run companies fully responsible for their profits and losses.

Separately, on July 25, the Chinese government had removed price controls for cigarettes and liquor. The government-mandated controls had kept prices artificially low, news reports said. The removal of the controls was widely expected to lead to substantial price increases.

The evident determination on the part of the liberal wing of the

Communist Party leadership to proceed with its programs for China's economic modernization appears to have aroused greater anxiety among the conservatives. During a national conference of state security officials held in Beijing on July 5–6, 1988, Premier Li Peng and Public Security Minister Wang Fang warned that the country faced the possibility of "upheaval" and "turmoil," as economic and political reforms continued to alter the structure of Chinese society, Xinhua news agency reported.

On July 5, Li noted that the government's economic reforms had already caused some "shocks" among the people, and he asserted that further "social upheavals" would be unavoidable, the official news agency reported.

"Organs of public security should be fully prepared to deal with any kind of trouble-making, riots, sabotage and serious crimes," the news agency quoted the premier as saying.

On July 6, Wang, China's top police official, echoed Li, declaring that the country faced "possible turmoil" in the near future as reforms continued. Wang revealed that there had been a "sharp increase" in crimes such as prostitution, gambling and use of illegal drugs. He said that "riots . . . involving antirevolutionary activities" were "on the rise," and claimed that "sabotage instigated from abroad" had also increased, the news agency reported.

Minor civil disturbances had flared in June as students at Beijing University demonstrated following the death of a classmate and peasants in Fangshan, about 50 miles (80 km) from the capital, who clashed with police while protesting against industrial pollution.

The conservatives found their ally in the rising inflation and spreading social unrest. The party politburo convened a meeting of the "central work conference" in Beijing on September 15–21.

The conference, attended by 217 of the country's top party government and military leaders, decided to recommend to the Central Committee of the party that the planned price reform be postponed for at least two years.

Key party leaders had come to believe that the recent surge in prices had been triggered by the loosening of central control over the economy, it was reported.

A number of the leaders also feared that the reduced role of the party and the government in managing the economy was leading to a parallel loss of influence in other areas of national life.

A week later, this recommendation was approved by the Communist Party Central Committee which met in Beijing on September 26–30. The meeting was attended by 162 (out of 175) members of the Central Committee along with several hundred other senior party officials.

Speaking at a closed meeting on September 26, according to a Xinhua news release on October 27, Party General Secretary Zhao Ziyang said:

"To us, it may appear to be late in the day to, only now, realize the full extent of the problem and take action to settle it," Zhao said. "However, it is still not too late to solve this problem, and even more serious problems will follow if we continue to hesitate to do so."

Zhao said that China would have to push inflation "conspicuously lower" in 1989 than it was in the current year. "This is the touchstone by which to test the party's and government's ability . . . to be in command of the situation," he declared.

Inflation in China was reported to be running at an annual rate of more than 20%, with some cities recording rates of as high as 50%. The target for 1989 would be to keep inflation below an annual rate of 10%, Zhao said.

"If the rate goes above the two digit figure, economic and social stability will be affected," he said.

In his speech, Zhao introduced a number of anti-inflationary measures. He announced that China would reduce its investments in fixed assets, particularly construction projects, by about 20%, or $13.5 billion, in 1989. The *China Daily* reported on October 27, that more than 100 building projects, with a total value of $242 million—including seven joint Chinese-foreign hotel ventures worth $54.5 million—had recently been canceled or delayed.

Prices on many consumer goods were to be frozen, reversing decisions earlier in the year to allow prices to be set by the free market.

Loans to local governments and industries would be cut, Zhao said, to slow the overheated growth of the economy, which was fueling inflation.

Zhao also argued for the central government to reassert stronger control over regional and local authorities.

"It is correct for central authorities to divert some power to lower levels, but the power that belongs to the central authorities must be centralized rather than weakened," he said.

The committee's decision to curb the reform program was considered by Western observers to be a severe setback for the general secretary of the CCP, Zhao Ziyang, who was the party's most outspoken advocate of swift economic change.

The move also reflected the increased influence of Premier Li Peng among the upper echelons of the CCP, analysts said. Li had long favored a more conservative approach to reform than Zhao.

Following the meeting in Beijing, Li announced that, for at least the next two years, the government would concentrate on reducing inflation and regaining control of the economy rather than embarking on further reforms.

"We have before us quite a few difficulties and problems, the prominent one being the evident inflation in our economic lives with excessive increases in prices," Li declared. "It is essential to control total social demand and curb inflation."

13

THE TRAGEDY AT TIANANMEN SQUARE

SINO-SOVIET RAPPROCHEMENT

Since November 1982, China and the Soviet Union had been holding talks aimed at normalizing their bi-lateral relations. The talks were held twice a year—in the spring and the fall—alternately at Moscow and Beijing, each round lasting for about two weeks. These talks, while making no progress on disputed political and military issues, produced agreements that expanded cultural and economic relations between the two countries.

The volume of two-way trade between the two countries amount to about 370 million in 1980, down from $500 million in 1979. It increased to $800 million in 1983, rising to $1.2 billion in 1984.

In an effort to clear the obstacles that barred speedy conclusion of the talks, First Deputy Premier Ivan V. Arkhipov of the Soviet Union, visited China on December 21–29, 1984. The trip yielded what China called "the most substantial agreements since relations between our two countries were strained in the 1960s."

At the start of the visit, on December 21, Arkhipov called for Sino-Soviet relations to enter "the orbit of friendship and good-neighborliness." Arkhipov also appeared to praise China's recent free-market reforms, saying the country had "a magnificent plan for the future."

Chinese Premier Zhao Ziyang, meeting Arkhipov on December 23, told him that China "cherishes very much the traditional friendship" between the two countries.

Zhao said that although "really major obstacles" blocked better relations between China and the Soviet Union, these differences need not affect "bilateral relations." Chinese officials often used this phrase to refer to trade and other matters outside the political sphere.

The "obstacles" Zhao mentioned included such long-standing sources of Chinese complaints as the deployment of Soviet troops along China's border, the Soviet invasion of Afghanistan and Soviet backing for Vietnam's invasion of Cambodia.

On December 28, China announced the signing of four agreements with the Soviet Union. One increased by 22% the amount of trade the two countries had agreed to in an accord concluded a month before. The new ceiling was set at $1.8 billion.

Under an accord for economic and technical cooperation, the Soviet Union agreed to help modernize several dozen of the factories and other projects it had built in China during the 1950s. A third pact, for scientific cooperation, allowed for exchanges of "groups, scholars and experts." A fourth provided for a committee to monitor cooperation in the three areas.

Returning Deputy Premier Arkhipov's visit to China, Chinese Deputy Premier Yao Yilin traveled to Moscow in the early part of July, 1985 on an eight-day visit. He was the first member of the Chinese Communist Party politburo to visit the Soviet Union in more than two decades.

While in Moscow on July 10, Yao signed a $14 billion trade pact for 1986–1990, and an agreement on economic and technological cooperation. Signing the agreements on behalf of the Soviet Union was first Deputy Premier Ivan Arkhipov.

Under the trade pact, China and the Soviet Union agreed to almost double their bilateral trade during the life of the agreement, which provided for China to supply the Soviet Union with consumer goods, agricultural commodities and some raw materials. The Soviet Union would provide China with machinery, machine tool equipment, chemicals, cars and building materials.

Under the economic cooperation pact, the Soviet Union would build seven new plants in China and help modernize industrial installations in the energy, metal processing, machine building, coal, chemicals and transport sectors.

Deputy Premier Arkhipov went to Beijing again in the spring of 1986, this time leading a special delegation to Sino-Soviet talks on trade and technology which were held March 16–21. Arkhipov conferred with Vice-Premier Li Peng. The talks resulted in an agreement to increase Soviet technological assistance to China as well as to increase trade between the two countries.

On April 14, following these talks, Soviet Foreign Minister Eduard A. Shevardnadze proposed a summit meeting between China and the Soviet Union. The proposal was offered during the eighth round of regular Sino-Soviet talks for normalization, which was being held in Moscow with Vice-Foreign Minister Qian Qichen representing China.

The Chinese foreign ministry rejected the proposal as "unrealistic." Ma Yuzhen, a spokesman for the Chinese foreign ministry, disclosed that Shevardnadze had suggested "upgrading the level of political dialogue and holding meetings between the leaders of the two countries."

Ma explained that the "key to the normalization of relations between the two countries lies in the removal of the [three] obstacles" frequently cited by Beijing: Soviet support for the Vietnamese occupation of Cambodia, the large-scale presence of Soviet troops on the Chinese border; and Soviet intervention in Afghanistan.

Soviet leader Mikhail S. Gorbachev renewed a bid to normalize relations with China in his speech on July 28, 1986, at the Soviet Pacific port of Vladivostok. Speaking to Soviet officials, he addressed two of the three obstacles to improved ties, cited by Beijing, and invited China to cooperate on space exploration and in strengthening trade.

"The Soviet Union is prepared—at any time and at any level—to discuss with China questions of additional measures for creating an atmosphere of good neighborliness," he asserted.

On the Afghanistan issue, Gorbachev announced a plan to withdraw six regiments from that country.

Addressing the second obstacle, Gorbachev announced that the U.S.S.R. and Mongolia—a landlocked country in north-central Asia, located between China and the Soviet Union—were examining "a question of withdrawing a substantial part of Soviet troops from Mongolia."

According to various Western estimates, there were about 450,000 Soviet troops on the Chinese border, with as many as 60,000 of them stationed in Mongolia.

In another border matter, Gorbachev spoke of the dispute over the Amur River, a waterway that formed a 120-mile (200-km) boundary between China and the U.S.S.R. Moscow traditionally claimed ownership of the Amur; however, Gorbachev appeared to accept

Beijing's view that the border "could pass along the main ship channel" of the river.

The Soviet leader did not address China's concern over the Cambodian situation. Instead, he only expressed a wish for peace between Beijing and the Soviet-backed government of Vietnam.

Gorbachev indicated that his China bid was part of an overall diplomatic initiative to improve relations between the U.S.S.R. and the nations of Asia and the Pacific. He cited the Soviet drive to draw closer to Japan as an example of Moscow's sincerity.

"The Soviet Union is also an Asian and Pacific country," he said. "It realizes the complex problems of this vast region."

Gorbachev offered a five-point plan for regional cooperation. The plan called for:

- An Asia/Pacific conference on confidence- and security-building measures, similar to the 1975 Helsinki Conference.
- A "radical reduction" of conventional forces in the region.
- Finding means to block the proliferation of nuclear arms in the region. Gorbachev pledged that the Soviet Union would not increase its arsenal of SS-20 missiles targeted on the Far East.
- Talks on seeking solutions to political conflicts in the region.
- Talks on the reduction of naval activity in the Pacific. He stated that if the U.S. were to "give up" its bases in the Philippines, the U.S.S.R. "would not leave this step unanswered."

U.S. analysts regarded the last statement as an oblique suggestion that Moscow might reduce its military presence at Cam Ranh Bay, in Vietnam, in return for U.S. concessions in the Philippines. Cam Ranh Bay, a major U.S. naval and air base during the Vietnam War, was believed to be the largest Soviet naval post outside the U.S.S.R. Hanoi had turned the base over to the Soviets in 1979, following the Chinese invasion of northern Vietnam.

Gorbachev's Vladivostok speech also touched on other areas of Soviet-American relations. He said he had received President Reagan's response to the latest Soviet arms proposals, which was being given careful study. Gorbachev also said that he favored another summit with Reagan, but only if the meeting would improve "the international situation and . . . speed the course of talks on the reduction of armaments."

The speech by General Secretary Gorbachev was carried on the front page of the *People's Daily* on July 29.

On that same day, China's foreign ministry said only that it was "studying" the speech.

A Chinese news agency radio commentary, monitored in Hong Kong, said that Moscow's planned withdrawal of some troops from Afghanistan would "not [substantially] affect the Soviet military presence" in that country. The commentary welcomed Gorbachev's statements on Afghanistan and Mongolia solely because the moves appeared to show a relaxation of Moscow's "long-term rigid attitude."

The news agency criticized Gorbachev's failure to address the Vietnam-Cambodia issue. It noted that Truong Chinh, Vietnam's new Communist Party leader, was in Moscow when Gorbachev made his speech.

It was reported that Victor P. Karpov, the Soviet Union's top arms control official, was in Beijing on July 26–29. The visit was believed to be directly related to General Secretary Gorbachev's China initiative. A joint Sino-Soviet communique, issued July 29, stated that the discussion had covered "preventing the arms race in space and other disarmament questions."

Beijing moved a step toward the summitry when, on September 2, Deng Xiaoping offered to meet Gorbachev if the Soviet Union was willing to move toward persuading Vietnam to remove its troops from Cambodia. Deng made his offer in an interview which was broadcast, on September 7, 1986, on the CBS television program "60 Minutes."

The Chinese leader said the withdrawal of Vietnamese troops would remove the main obstacle in Sino-Soviet relations. "Once this problem is resolved, I will be ready to meet Gorbachev," he said. Deng described such a meeting as "of much significance to the . . . normalization of Sino-Soviet state relations."

His offer was reportedly the first the Chinese leader had made to meet with Gorbachev.

Deng asserted that the Soviet Union was still undecided on its China policy, citing a recent conciliatory speech by Gorbachev which was followed soon after by a speech of a different tone by a Soviet foreign ministry official.

In the fall of that year, China received two heads of Eastern European states: General Wojciech Jaruzelski of Poland, who visited Beijing on September 28–30, and Erich Honecker of East Germany, who made a state visit on October 21–26.

The visits had the tacit blessing of the Soviet Union. China had taken the position that any normalization of party ties with Eastern Europe would have to be outside the sphere of Sino-Soviet relations.

Moscow's allies (with the exception of Rumania) had suspended party ties with China during the Sino-Soviet ideological rift in the 1960s.

Of the two visits, Honecker's was believed to have had a greater impact on restoring China's ties with Eastern European countries at the level of parties.

The Chinese treated Honecker's arrival with all the ceremony due an official visit by a head of state.

The East German leader was personally welcomed to Beijing by President Li on October 21, and held discussions with Li and party leader Hu the same day. (Honecker and Hu had first met at a communist youth gathering in Rumania in 1953).

The highlight of Honecker's trip was a lengthy meeting on October 23, with Deng Xiaoping. Deng had apparently not conferred with Jaruzelski during the Polish leader's visit.

At the close of the parley, Deng hugged Honecker and told him that party ties between China and East Germany "were never really broken."

Deng explained that the Chinese Communist Party had formulated "some new views on China's external and domestic policies, and on building its relations with other [Communist] countries.

Before he left, Honecker signed a 15-year agreement on Sino-East German economic and scientific cooperation.

Although there was no official announcement on the restoration of Sino-East German party ties, Western observers contended that Honecker's trip had effectively accomplished that.

The Soviet Union kept pressing for a summit meeting throughout 1987. The request was repeated by General Secretary Mikhail Gorbachev in an interview with a Chinese news magazine, *Liaowang*, which was published simultaneously in China and the Soviet Union on January 10, 1988. The interview was believed to be the first between a Soviet leader and Chinese journalists in nearly 30 years.

The Soviet news media gave the interview wide coverage. China's press omitted any mention of the summit proposal, but did quote Gorbachev on a variety of issues of interest to both sides.

In the interview, Gorbachev asserted that a summit would be a "logical development" that could lead to "mutually acceptable solutions."

The general secretary insisted that improved Sino-Soviet relations need not alarm the U.S. any more than improved Soviet-American relations need alarm China. "One cannot today build one's long-term policy at another's expense," he said. "It is necessary to look for a balance of interests, not against someone, but together with all."

Gorbachev said that he was willing to meet with Deng Xiaoping, China's semiretired paramount leader, at any site acceptable to Beijing.

Gorbachev's January initiative fared no better than his previous overtures. However, the Soviet Union tried to meet China's conditions. Its efforts bore fruit when the Vietnamese government formally announced in Hanoi on May 26, that it would withdraw 50,000 of its soldiers from Cambodia by the end of 1988. The exit was set to begin in June.

An earlier withdrawal, in late 1987, had reduced the number of Vietnamese troops in the country to 125,000 from 140,000, Western intelligence sources said. Hanoi had pledged in February, 1988, that all of its troops would be out of Cambodia by the end of 1990.

In addition to the withdrawal, Vietnam also announced that its remaining troops in Cambodia would be placed under the command of the Cambodian government and would be pulled back another nine miles (14.5 km) from the border between Cambodia and Thailand. Coming after a similar repositioning in 1987, the latest pullback would move Vietnamese troops at least 18 miles (29 km) away from the Thai border.

Later, the Chinese government, which bitterly opposed the Vietnamese presence in Cambodia, dismissed Hanoi's withdrawal announcement as nothing more than "deceptive talk," and called for the immediate withdrawal of all Vietnamese troops, it was reported on May 31.

Chinese and Soviet officials met in Beijing from August 28-September 1 for a series of talks on the Cambodian conflict. No concrete agreements were announced at the conclusion of the talks, but both sides hailed the conference as a positive development.

The Soviets were represented at the meetings by Deputy Foreign Minister Igor Rogachev. The head of the Chinese delegation was Deputy Foreign Minister Tian Zengpei.

Following the talks, Jin Guihua, a spokesman for China's foreign ministry, declared on September 1, "Obstacles still remain in Sino-Soviet relations, and normalization . . . has yet to be materialized." But Jin described the talks as "beneficial" and said they "promoted the mutual understanding of the two sides."

The next day, Rogachev echoed the Chinese line. He said that the conference had managed "to widen the sphere of understanding" between the Soviets and the Chinese.

The main sticking point between the sides apparently was the timetable for the withdrawal of Vietnamese troops from Cambodia.

The *Washington Post* cited some sources who said the Chinese were pushing for a nine-month withdrawal, to be completed in mid-1989.

Vietnam had declared in July that it would complete its withdrawal by the end of 1989 or beginning of 1990, but the announcement had been met with skepticism by the Chinese government.

China was pushing the Soviet Union to use its influence over Vietnam to speed up the troop exit. The Soviets argued that their influence was limited.

The Sino-Soviet rapprochement gained momentum, as Soviet and Chinese officials announced in Moscow on December 2 that Soviet President Mikhail S. Gorbachev and Chinese leader Deng Xiaoping would hold a summit meeting sometime in the first half of 1989.

The announcement came after a meeting between Gorbachev and Chinese Foreign Minister Qian Qichen.

The summit, expected to be held in Beijing, would be the first between leaders of the two communist superpowers since 1959.

According to the official Soviet news agency Tass, Qian told Gorbachev that the Soviet Union and China needed to "establish relations of a new type."

CHINA NOT TO COPY SOVIET CHANGES (PERESTROIKA)

China and the Soviet Union decided to normalize their relations at a time when their domestic policies were headed in opposite directions—China retreating from, and the Soviet Union moving full force toward, democratic reforms. The Chinese Communist Party leadership was far from unanimous on the new course it had adopted. Tension was evident at the meeting of the annual legislative session of the National People's Congress, which met in Beijing on March 20–April 4, 1988.

In stark contrast to the previous year's session, which had been characterized by unprecedented openness, the 1989 assembly was somber and guarded, with much emphasis placed on reasserting tighter central control over politics and economics.

Western analysts said the nation's economic woes and the uncertainty surrounding an emerging power struggle between Communist Party General Secretary Zhao Ziyang and Premier Li Peng had bred an atmosphere of extreme caution within China's top policy-making organs.

The congress, attended by 2,768 delegates, opened on March 20 with a two-hour keynote speech by Li reviewing the state of the nation. The speech focused largely on China's economy.

The premier told the delegates that both the government and the people "should be mentally prepared for a few years of austerity." The remark appeared to herald a continuation of the policy of economic retrenchment adopted by the Chinese Communist Party leadership in September 1988.

Inflation in 1988 had soared "beyond the endurance of the masses
. . . and the actual living standards of a considerable number of
urban residents dropped," Li reported. "This aroused concern and
great anxiety among the public and affected social stability and people's confidence in reform."

Li declared that China's leaders shared the blame for allowing inflation to spiral out of control. The leadership had been "too optimistic in our assessment of the economic situation in 1987" and "too
impatient for quick results," he said.

Li's admission was considered by Western observers to be a thinly
veiled criticism of party leader Zhao, who was the chief proponent
of economic liberalization.

Among other proposals, Li said industrial growth, consumer demand, price reform, investment loans and large-scale construction
projects should all be scaled back in an effort to stem inflation.

The only areas that would escape cuts would be education and
agriculture. Li said funding for education would be increased 15%
in 1989 to $10.05 billion, and agricultural spending would rise 12%
to $4.68 billion.

Li vowed that China would "never return to the old economic
order characterized by overcentralized, excessive and rigid control."
But he added, "Nor shall we adopt private ownership, negating the
socialist system."

The legislators, who reportedly were silent through much of the
premier's speech, erupted in applause when Li warned Western nations against supporting pro-independence demonstrations in Tibet.

"Any foreign force's support for such separatist activities, under
whatever pretext, constitutes an outrageous interference in China's
internal affairs and absolutely will not be tolerated," Li declared.

He specifically urged the U.S. to "refrain from interfering in China's internal affairs in any way and on any question, lest the existing
friendly relations between the two countries be impaired."

The latter comment appeared to be in response to a recent U.S.
Senate resolution condemning China's use of force in Tibet and an
earlier controversy involving a prominent dissident who had been
barred from meeting with President Bush during his visit to Beijing
in February.

On March 21, following Li's speech, Vice-Premier Yao Yilin and
Finance Minister Wang Bingqian unveiled the government's economic plans and budget for 1989.

Yao, head of the state planning commission, announced the imposition of a number of austerity measures that had been proposed
by Li.

He told the People's Congress that the government would sharply reduce capital spending and cancel or delay virtually all new construction projects until at least the end of July.

Other provisions included: restricting investment loans to privately and collectively owned businesses to reduce growth; closing down companies that produced poor quality goods or used excessive amounts of energy or raw materials; and establishing a new income tax system to "gradually narrow the wide gap" between the nation's rich and poor.

The 1989 state budget, which included a deficit for the third year in a row, was presented to the congress by Finance Minister Wang.

Revenues were expected to increase by about 10% over the previous year, to $76.75 billion, Wang said. Expenditures were expected to rise at nearly the same rate, to $78.74 billion. The resulting deficit would be $1.99 billion, down from $2.16 billion in 1988, the finance minister reported.

The largest expenditures in the proposed budget were government subsidies for state industries and consumers. Payments to industry were to total $14 billion in 1989, up 17% from the previous year. Subsidies for consumers were expected to reach $11 billion, an increase of 29% from 1988.

In an attempt to offset the effects of inflation in urban areas, where prices had been rising considerably faster than in the country as a whole, the government was planning to raise the wages of city workers, Wang said.

He also announced that a new 10% surcharge would be levied on the after-tax profits of private and collective enterprises.

China's fledgling human rights movement was set back March 29, when a senior government official at the congress dismissed an appeal for the release of all political prisoners in the country.

Wang Hanbin, vice-chairman of the Standing Committee of the National People's Congress, said the parliament "is not considering giving, nor does it think it necessary to offer, special pardons to prisoners on this occasion."

The same day, a group of seven human rights activists from Hong Kong reported that Chinese authorities had confiscated petitions signed by more than 24,000 people worldwide calling for the release of Chinese political prisoners. The petitions had been seized upon the group's arrival in China one day earlier, the activists said.

On its final day, April 4, the congress passed numerous pieces of legislation, including a new law that would allow citizens to sue the government.

Both Chinese officials and Western observers said passage of the so-called administrative litigation law marked an important step forward in the development of China's legal system.

Under the new law, citizens would have the right to sue government organizations or agencies to contest arbitrary jailings or fines as well as the infringement of certain individual rights. Previously, Chinese citizens had been restricted from challenging government actions.

Separately, a law extending special economic privileges to the southern city of Shenzhen attracted one of the largest totals of "no" votes and abstentions ever seen in the congress. The measure was opposed by 274 delegates, and another 805 delegates abstained. The law was still approved by a considerable margin, with 1,609 votes in favor.

The tenor of the National People's' Congress betrayed the uneasy feeling in Beijing about China's own reforms toward socialist modernization, and still more about what was going on in the Soviet Union under Gorbachev-led *perestroika*.

Premier Li asserted on April 3, that China had no plans to implement the type of extraordinary political changes, such as multicandidate elections, that were currently being carried out in the Soviet Union.

"China cannot mechanically copy the measures or policies adopted in the Soviet Union," the premier said. "Each country should proceed according to its own conditions."

Li's remarks came during a two-hour televised press conference near the end of the People's Congress.

The premier repeatedly stressed that China favored democracy, but at a considerably slower pace than had been embraced in the U.S.S.R.

"If the democratic process is carried out in haste, or excessively, then it will certainly affect our stability and unity," Li said.

China's official media had largely ignored the recent parliamentary elections in the Soviet Union, in which scores of Communist Party regulars had been voted out of office.

PRODEMOCRACY PROTESTS ERUPT

Sporadic—and even sustained—uprisings were endemic to Chinese politics under Communist rule. The Tibetan unrest, which surfaced in September 1987, was in its eighteenth month when the NPC convened in March 1989.

Major General Zhang Shaosong, political commissar of the Chinese army contingent in Tibet, was quoted by the Xinhau news agency as saying there had been 21 outbreaks of violence in the disputed region, resulting in "more than 600 casualties," during that period.

A violent confrontation between Chinese students and Africans studying at Hehai University in the eastern city of Nanjing triggered a storm of anti-African protests in the city on December 24–31, 1988.

The unrest apparently stemmed from an incident on December 24, in which fighting broke out between Chinese and African students attending a school dance. Each side accused the other of provoking the violence.

The unrest spread to Beijing and Wuhan on January 3, 1989, as Chinese students there staged anti-African protests. Approximately 2,000 students boycotted classes at the Beijing Languages Institute to demand the arrest of an African accused of assaulting a Chinese woman. In Wuhan, Chinese students threw stones at a university dormitory housing students from Africa and Asia.

But such protests had been on a small scale, localized for the most part; they did not pose a serious political threat to the Communist rule in China. On the other hand, a series of prodemocracy protests that erupted in Beijing on April 15, 1989, after the death of Hu Yaobang, took on the characteristics of mass uprisings. By April 27, they had swelled into one of the largest demonstrations against the government since the Communists had seized power in 1949. What distinguished the latest rallies from other recent demonstrations was not only their size but the fact that the student protesters were supported and joined by tens of thousands of workers.

The outburst of discontent was sparked by Hu's death April 15. Since being forced to resign as Communist Party general secretary in January 1987 for failing to crack down on student unrest, Hu had become something of a hero to Chinese intellectuals and liberal reformers.

Within hours of his death, hundreds of students at Beijing University, the country's leading educational institution, began hanging illegal posters across the campus mourning Hu and criticizing other prominent party figures, including China's paramount leader, Deng Xiaoping. Many of the posters implied that the wrong leader had died.

The poster protests, which also occurred at Qinghua and People's universities in the capital, continued on April 16.

The first demonstrations broke out April 16, as more than 1,000 students in the city of Shanghai marched and sang national songs in honor of Hu. Like the posters, the demonstrations were illegal.

Similar marches were staged April 17 in Shanghai and Beijing, where 500 students marched into Tiananmen Square, in the heart of the city, to lay wreaths in Hu's honor. The Beijing marchers also chanted slogans such as, "Long live democracy. Long live freedom."

On April 18, about 1,500 students marched in Shanghai, while in

Beijing some 2,000 students staged a predawn demonstration in Tiananmen Square to mourn Hu and call for more democracy and the "collective resignation" of China's leaders.

The protest in the capital swelled during the day, with as many as 10,000 students and apparently sympathetic onlookers gathering in the central square.

In the early morning hours of April 19, several thousand students marched from the square to the nearby Zhongnanhai compound, which housed the offices and residences of many party and government officials. The students tangled briefly with security guards before staging a sit-in outside the compound's walls.

Among the protesters' demands was to present their grievances to Premier Li Peng. The sit-in participants chanted, "Come out, come out, Li Peng."

Police later moved in to disperse the demonstrators.

Between 20,000 and 40,000 students and supporters returned to Tiananmen Square later that day for renewed protests. A smaller group of several thousand students marched to the Zhongnanhai compound to demand an audience with the party leadership.

The students again were dispersed by police, in the early morning hours of April 20. Several arrests and instances of beatings by police were reported. Demonstrations staged midday April 20 in the capital's central square attracted only about 10,000 students, in part because of heavy rain.

China's official media issued warnings April 20 that the students would be met with force if their protests continued.

A statement read on the national evening news program said that "future demonstrators will be dealt with severely according to the law" and new protests would "absolutely not be allowed."

A television commentator criticized the students for advocating "a China dominated by chaos."

According to Western observers, the warning marked the first time the protests had been mentioned on the news.

In defiance of the government's warning, more than 100,000 students and supporters filled Tiananmen Square on April 21–22 for a huge pro-democracy rally timed to coincide with the official Communist Party memorial service for Hu.

For the first time, students from outside Beijing and large numbers of workers joined the protests. In addition, thousands of Beijing citizens cheered the marchers as they moved through the city to the central square.

The demonstrators called for numerous political reforms, including freedom of the press, speech, and assembly increased funding for education, and publication of the income and assets of top party leaders. They also demanded the formal rehabilitation of Hu's reputation.

At the official memorial service, held April 22 in the Great Hall of the People, which bordered Tiananmen Square, Communist Party leader Zhao Ziyang praised Hu as a "brave" leader who had performed "immortal deeds." No mention was made of Hu's ouster from the top party post in 1987.

The first outbreaks of violence stemming from the protests occurred overnight on April 22–23 in the provincial capital cities of Xian and Changsha, the Xinhua news agency reported.

The agency said a group of "lawbreakers" in Xian went on a rampage after watching a televised broadcast of Hu's memorial service. The rioters attacked the city's government complex, burning 20 buildings and 10 vehicles. About 130 policemen were injured and 18 people were arrested, the news agency said.

In Changsha, a crowd of youths vandalized and robbed 24 shops and attacked a number of policemen, news reports said. About 100 rioters were arrested.

Tens of thousands of university students in Beijing April 24 began an indefinite boycott of classes.

Western news reports said that the boycott was honored by a majority of students at institutions throughout the capital. In addition, professors and other faculty members at some schools were openly supporting the students.

At Beijing University, which had become a hotbed of discontent since Hu's death, students appeared to have taken control of the campus, foreign observers said. About 90% of the 14,000 students at the school were boycotting classes, it was reported.

Similar percentages of students were reported to have joined the boycott at the Qinghua and People's universities.

On April 24, the government banned publication of the *World Economic Herald* after it printed articles criticizing the government and supporting the students' demands for reform.

The weekly newspaper, based in Shanghai, had a circulation of about 300,000.

The paper's editor, Qin Benli, was dismissed April 26 "on account of his serious violations of discipline," the government announced.

In a stern message read on national television and broadcast over loudspeakers at university campuses in Beijing, the government April 25 warned against continued protests.

"The whole nation must understand clearly that if we do not resolutely stop this unrest, our state will have no calm days," the warning said. "This is a grave political struggle facing the whole party and the people."

The government asserted that the unrest was the work of "a handful of people with ulterior motives" who were seeking to "poison people's minds, create national turmoil and sabotage the nation's political stability."

The warning was excerpted from an editorial published the following day, April 26, in the *People's Daily*.

Also April 16, the government outlawed three organizing committees formed by students in Beijing.

In the largest rally since the start of the unrest, between 100,000 and 150,000 demonstrators, cheered on by as many as half a million workers and other onlookers, marched through Beijing April 27 for more than 12 hours.

About half the marchers were from organized student groups, and the others were students or workers who participated on their own, the *New York Times* reported.

The size of the demonstration overwhelmed the thousands of police and army troops who had been called into the city to keep order.

On a number of occasions, crowds of thousands of workers formed human blockades to prevent troops from stopping the marchers.

In an apparent effort to rally worker support, the student leaders expanded their list of demands to include more populist issues, such as relief from inflation and an end to official corruption.

The government appeared caught off guard by the outpouring of support for the marchers. No mention of the protest was made on the official television news program that evening.

China's State Council, or national cabinet, April 27 said it would open a dialogue with protest leaders "at any time" after the students returned to their universities and adopted "a calm and reasonable attitude."

In a conciliatory gesture toward the students, the politburo member in charge of propaganda and the press, Hu Qili, on April 27, authorized nine major Chinese newspapers to give increased coverage to the student protests.

Hu told the papers' editors that they could report "the actual state of affairs" but would still be held accountable for their coverage.

Greater freedom of the press had been one of the students' key demands.

Chinese government officials met April 29 with a group of hand-picked student leaders to hear their demands, but the meeting was later dismissed by many students as inadequate.

Forty-five students from 16 universities met in Beijing with Yuan Mu, a spokesman for the State Council, He Dongchang, a vice-minister on the state education commission, and other officials.

Much of the three-hour meeting was broadcast later the same day on nationwide state-run television.

A number of students complained that the meeting did not constitute a real dialogue with the government because the student representatives had been chosen by the government. They also asserted that the meeting did not address many of their primary demands, including greater freedom of the press, speech and assembly.

A group of 60 university students rode bicycles into Beijing on May 2 to present a list of demands to leading organs of the Chinese government.

The petitions were delivered to the State Council, the National People's Congress and the Communist Party Central Committee.

The students gave the government 24 hours to approve the demands or face renewed demonstrations.

Chief among the demands was a call for new dialogue between the students and the government. The students also demanded that they be allowed to choose their own representatives, that the government send officials of the rank of deputy premier or politburo member to the talks, and that the dialogue be open to the public and broadcast uncensored on national television.

The government May 3 formally rejected the student petitions.

The following day, on the 70th anniversary of the founding of the May Fourth movement of 1919, 100,000 Chinese students and workers staged a march in Beijing.

The students also received support from several hundred Chinese journalists who staged a demonstration of solidarity outside the headquarters of the Xinhua news agency in the center of the capital.

The journalists called for press law reforms and the reinstatement of Qin Benli, who had been fired one week earlier as editor of the progressive *World Economic Herald*. The demonstration by the newsmen was considered highly unusual in China.

Smaller rallies were staged the same day in a number of other Chinese cities. A protest march in Shanghai attracted as many as 20,000 people. Between 8,000 and 10,000 demonstrators marched in the northeastern city of Changchun, and 2,000 people staged a protest in the port city of Dalian.

The Communist Party staged its own parades in the capital and other cities to commemorate the May 4 Movement, but the official events were dwarfed by the student protests.

Students at Beijing University, the nation's largest educational institution, voted May 6 to continue their two-week-old boycott of classes. The vote came after students at a number of other universities in the capital had begun returning to classes May 5. At the height of the boycott, more than 70,000 university students in Beijing had stayed away from class.

Chinese journalists May 9 presented the government with a petition signed by more than 1,000 reporters and editors calling for greater freedom of the press. The journalists asserted that they had been barred from reporting "comprehensively and objectively" on the recent protests. Among the signatories were employees of some of the nation's top media outlets, including the national television network, the Xinhau news agency and the *People's Daily*.

GORBACHEV VISITS CHINA

Soviet leader Mikhail Gorbachev visited China on May 15–18 for a summit meeting with Chinese leaders. He was the first head of the Soviet Communist Party to set foot on Chinese soil in 40 years, since Nikita Khrushchev's 1959 visit. Coinciding, as it did, with the rapidly rising pro-democracy ferment in Beijing and throughout China, Gorbachev's historic trip was destined to be eclipsed by Chinese student-led demonstrations.

For Gorbachev, the China visit was the culmination of a seven-year push by the Kremlin (four years with him as CP general secretary) to normalize relations. It also marked a triumph in his Asia diplomatic initiative.

The Gorbachev entourage included his wife, Raisa, Soviet Foreign Minister Eduard A. Shevardnadze and Aleksandr N. Yakovlev, the Soviet CP secretary in charge of foreign relations.

At first, it appeared that the pro-democracy demonstrations would provide merely a colorful backdrop to the Sino-Soviet rapprochement.

While the protests had an independent impetus, they became inextricably linked to the Gorbachev visit. Gorbachev was widely admired by the dissident students for initiating the Soviet policies of *glasnost* (openness) and "democratization."

Also, Beijing was filled with foreign journalists there to cover the summit. That gave the protesters an international media stage. The state-controlled Chinese press had initially given only scant coverage to the unrest.

When the Soviet entourage arrived in China, on May 15, some 150,000 demonstrators were camped in Beijing's Tiananmen Square, across from the Great Hall of the People, the headquarters of the Chinese regime. The authorities made no effort to remove them.

The protesters included about 1,000 students who had begun a hunger strike on May 13. The hunger strikers, who were reported to include the protest leaders, demanded, among other things, a televised meeting with China's leaders to discuss political reforms. The students also wished to meet with Gorbachev.

Some workers and intellectuals were among those in Tiananmen Square, continuing a trend of growing support by nonstudents for the aims of the pro-democracy movement.

The official welcoming ceremony for Gorbachev was to have been held in Tiananmen Square. Due to the protest vigil, the ceremony had to be held at Beijing's airport. Chinese President Yang Shangkun and Foreign Minister Qian Qichen greeted the Soviet leader.

When the visitors arrived at the Great Hall, they were ushered into the building through a little-used courtyard at the rear, thus avoiding contact with the demonstrators.

The bitter Sino-Soviet rift came to a formal end on May 16, when General Secretary Gorbachev met with Deng Xiaoping. Gorbachev also held separate discussions with Premier Li and Zhao Ziyang, the head of the Chinese Communist Party.

"We can publicly announce the normalization of relations between our two countries," Deng declared at the close of his meeting with Gorbachev. "We want to put the past behind us and chart a new course for the future."

On May 16 Soviet foreign ministry spokesman Gennadi I. Gerasimov told reporters that Gorbachev had discussed a variety of issues with the Chinese leaders and concluded that there was a large measure of "ideological agreement" between the Communist parties of the two countries.

Gerasimov said that there had been no substantial agreement on Cambodia, and that Gorbachev had proposed a "radical military detente" along the Sino-Soviet border, and had restated the Kremlin's determination to remove some Soviet troops from Mongolia.

According to Chinese officials, Gorbachev and Zhao agreed that economic liberalization did not violate Marxist-Leninist principles. But the Chinese party leader was said to have told Gorbachev that China could carry out economic reforms without "structural political reform."

Gorbachev and Zhao were said to have discussed China's pro-democracy protests. On May 16, the number of protesters in Tiananmen Square swelled to an estimated 250,000 people who called for the removal of China's leadership. Gorbachev was reported to have told Zhao that he (Gorbachev) had little sympathy for "hotheads" who demanded that change be accomplished overnight.

Later that day, Zhao sent a message to the students promising that the regime would take "concrete measures to enhance democracy and law, oppose corruption, build an honest and clean government and expand openness." Zhao also vowed that none of the protesters would be punished so long as they ended the unrest.

The summit was completely overshadowed on May 17, when over one million Chinese gathered in Beijing's central square to call for democratic reforms and demand that Deng and the rest of the nation's leadership step down.

In addition to students, the Beijing protest featured large numbers of workers, intellectuals, teachers and schoolchildren. Even some soldiers and low-ranking party officials from outlying districts participated. Beijing came to a virtual standstill during the demonstration.

It was believed to be the largest single outpouring of support for democratic change in China since the Communists came to power in 1949. (Some foreign journalists dubbed the pro-democracy movement the "Second Cultural Revolution," after the student-led anticonservative movement of the 1960s.)

The protests were not limited to Beijing; demonstrations were reported in at least 20 other Chinese cities on May 17.

As of May 17, some 3,000 students were fasting in Beijing. The health of some of those who had begun the hunger strike on May 13 was reported to be deteriorating and some were hospitalized. (At least part of the widening public support for the demonstrations was prompted by growing concern over the plight of the hunger strikers, news reports said.)

Premier Li and party chief Zhao visited some hunger strikers at a Beijing hospital. The visit was fully televised in China, even though some of the students expressed strong criticisms of the party.

The Chinese press had increased its coverage of the unrest. In contrast, the official Soviet media focused on Gorbachev and barely mentioned the protests.

Gorbachev, no longer the center of attention for most of the international media, said at a May 17 press conference at the Great Hall that he had received a letter from Chinese students praising Soviet political reforms.

"I value their position," he said with apparent caution. "These processes are painful, but they are necessary."

Gorbachev told the journalists that in his experience, negotiation was preferable to confrontation when dealing with internal disorders. He continued: "I would like to express the hope and the wish that in the course of this dialogue, solutions will be found that take into account the present situation and that would be considered appropriate by the Chinese people and the Chinese party."

The unrest forced Chinese officials to juggle Gorbachev's itinerary to avoid his coming in contact with protesters. For example, he and Raisa were to have attended a performance of the Beijing Opera (located off Tiananmen Square) on the evening of May 17, but that visit was canceled.

Gorbachev and his wife were able to visit the Great Wall of China, about an hour's drive from Beijing. He later addressed prominent Chinese intellectuals at the Great Hall.

In the speech, he outlined a plan to remove 120,000 troops (12 divisions), 11 air force regiments and 16 warships from the Soviet Far East military command.

On May 17, Soviet and Chinese officials agreed to increase economic and cultural cooperation.

General Secretary Gorbachev spent most of May 18 in the Chinese southern port city of Shanghai before returning to the Soviet Union. He was carefully shielded from the thousands of people demonstrating in the city that day.

Shanghai was China's economic capital, and a highlight of Gorbachev's visit was a tour of the Minhang Special Economic Zone, one of several duty-free areas created in China to attract foreign investment. The Soviets were contemplating setting up similar areas.

Before departing China, the Soviet leader hailed the summit as a "watershed event" of "epoch-making significance."

A joint communique was issued on May 18 saying that the two countries had agreed to "develop their relationship" on the basis of "mutual respect for sovereignty and territorial integrity, nonaggression, noninterference in the internal affairs of each other, equality and mutual advantage, and peaceful coexistence."

Other provisions stated that:

- Normalization was "not directed against third countries and does not infringe upon the interests of third countries." The statement appeared to be directed at possible U.S. concerns that China might draw away from Washington while moving closer to Moscow.
- Both sides, while disagreeing on what form a new Cambodian regime should take, agreed that Vietnamese forces should be fully withdrawn from that country and that military aid to the Cambodian factions should be halted. Both sides also agreed to "respect the results of general elections conducted by the Cambodian people under international control."
- Sino-Soviet border disputes were to be settled "fairly and rationally" through negotiations under international law. Both sides pledged to "take measures to reduce armed forces in the area" of the border.
- Neither side could claim "hegemony in any form in the Asian-Pacific region or in other parts of the world."

BEIJING UNDER MARTIAL LAW

During Gorbachev's stay in China, the student-led demonstrations, centered in Tiananmen Square in downtown Beijing, had swelled to unprecedented proportions.

Premier Li Peng and party leader Zhao Ziyang visited Tiananmen Square on May 18 to speak with the protesters. Despite the visit, the Beijing vigil showed no indication of abating.

Li and Zhao were reported to have told the student leaders that the party was willing to meet with them in a televised forum if the protests and hunger strikes were ended.

Zhao was said to have told the students: "You have good intentions. You want our country to become better. The problems you have raised will eventually be resolved. But things are complicated, and there must be a process to resolve these problems."

The events in the capital, and in dozens of other cities across China, were played out against a backdrop of uncertainty over the outcome of an apparent power struggle within the Communist Party between those leaders advocating a hard-line response toward the unrest, including Deng and Li, and a more moderate faction, led by the party's general secretary, Zhao Ziyang.

Li and other politburo hard-liners calling for a crackdown apparently won out over Zhao, who had advocated giving in to some of the protesters' demands. The hard-liners were likely supported by paramount leader Deng, who was not a member of the politburo but wielded ultimate control over the army.

Li announced the imposition of martial law in the capital in a speech broadcast on national television shortly after midnight on May 20.

"We must adopt firm and resolute measures to end the turmoil swiftly," the premier said. "If we fail to put an end to such chaos immediately and let it go unchecked, it will very likely lead to a situation which none of us wants to see."

In a separate announcement, President Yang said, "Units of the People's Liberation Army will enter Beijing to restore order."

The troops sent to the capital were reported to be from the 27th Army, based in Hebei province. Western news groups May 20 quoted unidentified Chinese sources who said that the commander of China's 38th Army, based in the city of Baoding, had refused an order to move against the protesters.

Li's decision to send the army into Beijing appeared to backfire May 20, as more than one million Chinese citizens poured into the streets of the capital to support the protesters.

Students, workers and ordinary citizens set up roadblocks and barricades along key thoroughfares into the city to prevent troops from reaching Tiananmen Square, where the main group of some 200,000 protesters, including 3,000 hunger strikers, was encamped.

Military convoys heading into the city found their paths blocked by buses, trucks, taxicabs and cars parked in the middle of the road, or by crowds of people who surrounded the army vehicles and implored the soldiers to turn back.

In some instances, citizens lay down in the roadway to prevent the military convoys from passing.

Outside observers said the acts of civil disobedience were reminiscent of the "people power" uprising that had ousted Philippine President Ferdinand E. Marcos in 1986.

Scattered clashes between troops and protesters were reported at several spots around the capital, but for the most part the confrontations were peaceful.

One of the most common slogans chanted by demonstrators facing the troops was, "The People's Army loves the people and the people love the People's Army."

The protesters appeared to enjoy at least the tacit support of many of the army soldiers, Western news reports said.

By the end of the day of May 20, army units were reported stalled on more than half a dozen main roads leading into the city.

At the same time, the capital's vast central square had been all but completely taken over by the student protesters and their supporters.

Scores of students sporting red armbands took up the job of directing traffic through the city, as the local police force was nowhere to be seen.

City residents by the thousands provided free food and other supplies to the demonstrators.

The 3,000 hunger strikers, who had been elevated to hero status among the demonstrators, ended their nine-day fast on May 21, reportedly to regain their strength for the expected confrontation with the military.

Rumors abounded among the protesters on May 21 that the army was planning a nighttime assault on Tiananmen Square to crush the uprising. The rumors brought hundreds of thousands of ordinary citizens into the city center to block the anticipated military action.

In at least two instances, groups of students and citizens on the outskirts of the capital stopped army tanks from advancing toward the city center, but the army made no concerted attempt to move in force against the protesters.

At dawn on May 22, the students and their citizen supporters broke into cheers with the realization that the army was not coming.

The huge protests in Beijing spawned similar prodemocracy rallies during the week in more than 20 cities across China.

The largest protests outside the capital were reported in Shanghai, where as many as 500,000 people took to the streets on May 23–24 in a show of support for the Beijing uprising.

Elsewhere, more than 300,000 protesters marched on May 20 in the northern city of Xian, and rallies of at least 100,000 protesters were reported on May 22 in Shenzen and on May 23 in Canton.

Chinese students and nationals staged sympathy rallies on May 21 in major cities around the world, including London, Paris, Tokyo and Washington, D.C., to protest the declaration of martial law in Beijing.

A huge pro-democracy protest was reported the same day in Hong Kong, which is slated to revert to Chinese rule in 1997.

More than 500,000 people marched through the territory's central business district, expressing support for the Beijing demonstrators and calling for the resignation of Premier Li.

The unrest in China triggered an 11% drop in the Hong Kong stock market May 22, the largest one-day fall experienced by the market since the October 1987 worldwide stock market crash.

In what was considered a major setback to Premier Li, a group of seven retired senior military leaders May 22 denounced the imposition of martial law in a letter sent to the *People's Daily*.

Although the letter was not published in the newspaper, copies of it were widely circulated in Beijing.

"In view of the extremely serious situation, we as veteran soldiers demand that the People's Liberation Army not confront the population, nor quell the people," the letter said. "The army must absolutely not shoot the people. In order to prevent the situation from worsening, the army must not enter the city of Beijing."

Among the principal signatories were former Defense Minister Zhang Aiping, former army staff chief Yang Dezhi, former navy commander Ye Fei and a former commandant of the Academy of Military Sciences, Song Shilun.

The retired military men were joined in signing the letter by more than 100 other officers, some of whom were on active duty, Western reports said.

The internal struggle for the leadership of the Communist Party began on May 23–25 to overshadow the ongoing demonstrations in Tiananmen Square.

Western observers said numerous reports in the Chinese media on May 23 appeared to carry thinly veiled criticism of Li, suggesting that Zhao was winning out in the power struggle.

One report, by the Xinhua news agency, grossly exaggerated the number of protesters involved in an antigovernment demonstration that day in the central square. The report said that nearly one million people participated, while Western sources said that the actual figure was closer to 100,000.

In addition, in what was considered by outsiders to be an unusual admission by a state-run news agency, the report noted that the "overwhelming majority of the slogans" chanted by the demonstrators were directed against Li.

The official Beijing radio network the same day also quoted demonstrators calling for Li's ouster.

On the following day, May 24, Zhao was mentioned by name and referred to as the party's general secretary in official newscasts for the first time since the imposition of martial law.

However, the consensus among Western analysts shifted May 25, as new reports suggested that Li, with Deng's backing, was emerging as the victor in the power struggle.

The state-run radio network and newspapers in the capital carried a message to Chinese troops from the army's general staff headquarters calling on soldiers to obey the martial law decree.

The army message, considerably harsher in tone than other recent government bulletins, said the unrest was the work of a "small group of people" bent on creating "chaos" in the country. The message accused the student demonstrators of being "counterrevolutionaries," which in China was equivalent to calling them traitors.

The release of the army bulletin was widely seen by outside observers as a sign that Li had won both the backing of the military and control of the media.

On May 20 (the evening of May 19 in the U.S.), in the wake of the declaration of martial law in Beijing, Chinese authorities ordered foreign television networks to cease broadcasting from the capital.

Viewers in the U.S. were able to watch live footage of Chinese officials entering production control rooms set up in Beijing by CBS and the Cable News Network and ordering them to stop transmitting.

The news blackout was lifted by the Chinese government on May 23 (Beijing time) without explanation, but was reinstated one day later, on May 24.

HARD-LINERS GAIN IN POWER STRUGGLE

The murky political situation in Beijing cleared up somewhat toward the end of May. Unconfirmed reports during the final week of May said that Communist Party General Secretary Zhao Ziyang, the party's most outspoken champion of economic and political liberalization, had been stripped of his power and placed under house arrest.

Among Zhao's political allies also reported to be in trouble were his top aide, Bao Tong, the party's propaganda chief, Hu Qili, and Vice-Premier Tian Jiyun.

Twenty-two members of China's Central Advisory Commission, which was made up of elderly party veterans, appeared on national television on May 26 to signal their support for Deng. The group released a statement denouncing "the conspiracy of the very, very small number of people who want to create chaos."

On May 26, Deng called more army units to the outskirts of Beijing, raising the number of troops surrounding the capital to 200,000.

The number of protesters encamped in the city's central square dwindled the same day to about 20,000. Most of those remaining were students. Thousands of Chinese workers, who had helped swell the ranks of protesters in earlier demonstrations, reportedly had been threatened with retaliation by their employers if they continued to support the protests.

On May 28, student leaders called protest rallies in Beijing, Shanghai and a number of other Chinese cities, and sympathy marches were staged the same day in Hong Kong, Taiwan, Australia and the U.S.

Only about 30,000 people, nearly all of them students, participated in the Beijing rally, but more than 100,000 students and workers marched in Shanghai.

Estimates of the number of people who participated in the Hong Kong rally ranged from 300,000 to as many as one million.

As a sign that he was firmly in control of the government, Premier Li was shown on Chinese television on May 25 meeting in Beijing with three newly arrived foreign ambassadors.

It was the first public appearance by a top Chinese leader since martial law had been declared in the capital five days earlier.

"The Chinese government is stable and capable of fulfilling its responsibilities and of properly dealing with the current problems," Li told the assembled envoys.

He said military units massed on the outskirts of Beijing would not enter the capital until the city's residents understood the army's purpose. He added that "anyone with common sense" could see that the army could enter Beijing if it wanted to.

Li also said, in an apparent snub to Zhao, that "the chief architect of China's reform and opening to the outside world is Comrade Deng Xiaoping and no one else."

A Chinese foreign ministry spokesman the same day asserted that

Zhao was still the party's general secretary, but Western journalists told of widespread reports that Zhao had lost all power.

The uncertainty surrounding the general secretary's fate increased on May 26, as Western reports said that documents condemning Zhao were circulating within the upper echelons of the Communist Party.

According to unidentified Chinese sources, the documents charged Zhao with a number of offenses, including fostering the recent unrest in an attempt to gain political power and revealing state secrets by disclosing to Soviet leader Mikhail S. Gorbachev that the party had voted to refer all important policy decisions to Deng.

Wan Li, chairman of the National People's Congress, China's nominal parliament, signaled his support for Premier Li on May 27.

In remarks reported by the official Xinhua news agency, Wan said the antigovernment demonstrations had been spurred on by a "small number of people" engaged in political conspiracy—an apparent reference to Zhao and his allies.

Wan was considered by outside observers to be a moderate. He had cut short a visit to the U.S. several days earlier to return to China to help resolve the leadership crisis.

Upon his return on May 25, Wan had been hospitalized in Shanghai for treatment of an unidentified medical problem, Chinese officials reported. Western diplomats said they believed Wan had been held under house arrest in Shanghai until he agreed to back the premier.

On May 30, Chinese authorities revealed that they had arrested 11 members of a motorcycle club that had played a prominent role in the recent demonstrations in the capital.

The bikers, who had served as messengers and scouts for the student protesters in Tiananmen Square, were charged with spreading rumors, threatening police and stealing gasoline.

The arrests were the first reported since the outbreak of the protests in mid-April.

Police also detained three workers on May 30, all of whom were members of a newly formed, unauthorized union. The three were released the following day.

THE MASSACRE

On May 29–30, a group of 20 Chinese art students erected a 33-foot-tall (10-meter) statue in Tiananmen Square, based on the Statue of Liberty in New York harbor.

The students' statue, made of styrofoam and plaster of paris, depicted a woman in a long robe holding aloft a torch with both hands. The students christened the structure the "Goddess of Democracy."

A crowd of nearly 100,000 students and workers flocked to the square to watch the construction of the statue and to cheer on the art students.

A Chinese television commentator May 30 denounced the statue as "an insult to our national dignity."

Chinese authorities June 1 imposed a number of new restrictions on foreign journalists in Beijing, banning press coverage, photographs and videotapes of any demonstrations in the city or of army troops enforcing martial law.

The following day, June 2, a front-page article in the *People's Daily* reported that army troops had taken up positions at "10 key points" in and around the capital.

The student protest movement, which had been flagging in recent days after weeks of nearly nonstop demonstrations, received a shot in the arm during the evening of June 2, when more than 100,000 people turned out in Tiananmen Square for a rally led by pop singer Hou Dejian, who began a hunger strike in support of the students.

The rally brought thousands of students and civilians into the streets of downtown Beijing.

Shortly after midnight on June 3, somewhere between 2,000 and 10,000 unarmed soldiers began a march down a central thoroughfare in the capital, headed toward Tiananmen Square.

The move appeared to be an attempt by the government to clear the vast 100-acre (40-hectare) square of protesters without using force.

The soldiers advanced to within several hundred yards (meters) of the square but then found their path blocked by tens of thousands of jeering students and workers.

In the face of the civilian resistance, the army troops, who seemed disorganized, fell out of rank and retreated. Many of the troops appeared to be peasants from outlying rural regions, Western observers said. They were taunted by demonstrators and stripped of their backpacks, canteens and uniforms as they withdrew. A number of soldiers reportedly were reduced to tears by the crowd.

The confrontation with the unarmed troops seemed to revive the pro-democracy movement. Hundreds of thousands of people in the capital poured into the streets during the morning of June 3 to show their support for the protesters.

The wild celebration by citizens was short-lived, however, as new clashes broke out at midday between demonstrators and army soldiers and police.

The first violence was reported shortly after 2:00 p.m. Beijing time

(3:00 a.m. eastern standard time). Police and troops fired tear gas and beat dozens of protesters with truncheons and electric cattle prods in a confrontation near the Zhongnanhai compound, which housed the offices and residences of much of the Chinese leadership.

Less than two hours later, soldiers and workers hurled stones and bricks at each other in a clash outside the Great Hall of the People, located off Tiananmen Square.

Scores of people were reported injured in the two incidents.

Tension escalated in the city throughout the evening amid increasing signs that the government was planning a major move against the protesters.

The evening television news warned that "armed police and troops have the right to use all means to dispose of troublemakers who act willfully to defy the law."

Another special bulletin broadcast on national television ordered citizens in Beijing to "stay at home to protect your lives."

According to Western press accounts, which were sketchy and sometimes contradictory, the all-out military assault against the protesters began at about midnight on June 4.

Dozens of tanks and armored personnel carriers and thousands of combat troops armed with automatic rifles and machine guns moved toward the central square from several points around the city.

Civilians once again moved to block the army units from reaching the square but, unlike on previous occasions, the troops did not back down. The confrontations, most of which took place within a 10-block radius of the square, quickly turned bloody as soldiers first fired warning shots in the air above the demonstrators' heads and then began firing directly into crowds.

Students and workers fought back with sticks, rocks, pipes and firebombs.

The first group of soldiers reached Tiananmen Square between 12:30 a.m. and 1:00 a.m. and sprayed the area with gunfire, sending students and their supporters scurrying for cover.

Each time the firing died down, though, the students regrouped in the square.

Violent clashes in the square and throughout the surrounding area were reported over the next several hours.

Western observers described numerous instances throughout the night in which troops fired indiscriminately or pointblank at groups of unarmed citizens.

Countless other unconfirmed reports by Chinese witnesses claimed that soldiers had bayoneted, shot or beaten to death hundreds of protesters and bystanders, including elderly civilians, women and children, during the unrest.

Several dozen army and police vehicles were destroyed by protesters during the night, and an unknown number of soldiers were killed.

On at least two occasions, soldiers who allegedly had shot unarmed civilians were set upon by protesters and hanged. A number of other lynchings of soldiers or crew members trapped in disabled tanks, trucks or troop carriers were reported.

At about 4:00 a.m., the government announced over loudspeakers in the square that "a counterrevolutionary rebellion" had erupted and ordered all citizens to leave the area. After the announcement, the large streetlights illuminating the square were turned off.

Forty minutes later, the lights came back on and the student protesters remaining in the square voted to leave. They were in the process of withdrawing when a large force of soldiers and armored vehicles broke into the square at about 5:00 a.m.

Tanks and troop carriers roared through the square, razing the makeshift student encampment and leveling the defiant "Goddess of Democracy" statue that had been erected by protesters less than one week earlier.

Some reports said scores of students left in the square were machine-gunned to death or crushed by tanks as they attempted to flee the army. Other reports of the incident, however, said that the students were allowed to leave the square unharmed, although some allegedly were shot as they fled through streets surrounding the central plaza.

At 7:40 a.m., the government announced that "the rebellion has been suppressed and the soldiers are now in charge" of the square.

Despite the announcement, intermittent confrontations continued throughout the capital for much of the day.

Large military convoys of tanks and trucks cruised up and down the main boulevards of central Beijing during the day, periodically shooting bursts of machine gun fire into the air.

On several occasions, crowds of thousands of protesters confronted army troops with taunts and jeers at various spots around the capital. According to Western news reports, the troops periodically opened fire on the crowds, killing dozens more protesters. The crowds would disperse temporarily, but later regroup and come back to harass the soldiers.

Sporadic clashes between soldiers and civilians continued on June 5–8.

According to Western reports, dozens of civilians were shot to death June 5, but the number of confrontations dwindled over the next several days and there were few additional reports of civilian casualties.

In an isolated incident that was widely portrayed by the Western media as a symbol of the entire upheaval in the capital, a single unarmed civilian was shown June 5 by foreign television cameras standing on Beijing's main boulevard, Changan Avenue (Avenue of Eternal Peace), and raising his hand to stop a column of army tanks for several minutes before he was hustled away by friends.

Following the crackdown, normal city life in Beijing all but ground to a halt.

The main thoroughfares were clogged with gutted army vehicles and remnants of student barricades. Public transportation, the principal means used by residents to get around the city, ceased to run.

Fewer than half the workers in the capital were reported to be showing up at their jobs, Western sources said.

Banks, schools and most stores remained closed for days after the violence, and postal service was suspended in the city.

Stores that remained open were besieged by residents seeking to stock up on food and other supplies in anticipation of expected shortages.

While the clashes between soldiers and civilians were dying down, the unrest in the capital assumed a new dimension on June 5, as Western observers said Chinese army units throughout the city were taking up what appeared to be defensive positions against possible attack by other military forces.

There were widespread reports during the day that rival army units believed to be loyal to various Chinese leaders were headed toward the capital from outlying regions, raising the specter of an outright civil war in China.

Foreign observers cited Chinese sources who said fighting had broken out on June 5 between army units on a road west of Beijing and on June 5–6 between rival forces at the Nanyuan military airfield south of the city.

Although the reports could not be confirmed, Western diplomats said there was reason to believe that the clashes involved China's 27th and 38th armies, each of which numbered about 45,000 troops.

The two units were among as many as 10 armies currently deployed in and around the capital. It was not precisely clear with which Chinese leader each army was associated, but the consensus among Western military analysts was that the 27th Army was the key unit involved in the Beijing crackdown and was in control of the center of the capital.

The 27th Army, said to be commanded by a nephew of hard-line President Yang, had been brought into the capital several weeks earlier, after the 38th Army reportedly refused an order to enforce the government's martial law decree.

In the wake of the crackdown, the 38th Army was reported to have taken up positions in confrontation with the 27th Army at several points across the capital. Western reports said troops of the 38th Army entering Beijing were greeted with cheers by city residents, who hailed them as liberators.

Extensive troop movements were reported all over the city during subsequent days, but Western observers said they were unsure to which army units the various troops belonged and what significance, if any, the movements held.

Protests by students and workers angered by the government's military crackdown in Beijing erupted on June 4–8 in numerous cities across China.

Major demonstrations were reported in Shanghai, Nanjing, Tianjin, Shenyang, Changchun, Chengdu, Wuhan, Xian, Canton, Urumqi, Changsha and Hunan.

Protesters in Shanghai, China's most populous city, brought traffic to a standstill and forced the suspension of all public transportation by placing barricades across most major thoroughfares in the city.

At least six people were reported killed in the city on June 6 when a train ran over a group of students and workers who had lain on the railroad tracks in a protest gesture aimed at halting local rail service. Enraged bystanders later stopped the train and set it on fire.

The state-run media made scant mention of the military assault against the protesters for more than two days after the crackdown.

The first official word on the unrest came during the evening of June 6, when a spokesman for China's State Council (cabinet) reported that 300 people, only 23 of whom were students, had been killed in the crackdown and 7,000 others—5,000 soldiers and 2,000 civilians—had been injured.

A later report by a Chinese military spokesman, however, denied that anyone had been killed in the square during the disorder.

Several days after the crackdown, the official television news programs began to show videotapes of the unrest, but the only scenes shown were of students attacking soldiers or setting fire to military vehicles. No mention was made of the shooting of unarmed civilians by the army troops.

Government sound trucks cruised through the city on June 8 broadcasting messages in support of the military crackdown. "There was no big killing," said one such message.

The question of who was in control of the Chinese government continued to baffle foreign observers throughout the crisis.

Western analysts believed that the fact that the military was finally ordered to crush the protests indicated that the hard-liners in the leadership, including Deng, Li and Yang, were in power.

However, the nation's top leaders disappeared from public view for days at a time during the unrest, and no official word on their whereabouts was available to the outside world.

To add to the information vacuum, no copies of the party's official *People's Daily* newspaper appeared for several days, and television news reports initially made no mention of the government or China's top leaders, devoting their entire broadcasts to foreign news or minor feature stories.

In the absence of any sign of the nation's leadership, rumors circulated widely among Beijing residents that leading government figures had become incapacitated.

One of the most prevalent rumors in the capital was that paramount leader Deng lay dead or dying in a hospital from prostate cancer.

An official television news program on June 6 dismissed the rumor as "a sheer fabrication" but made no mention of Deng's whereabouts.

The 84-year-old leader had not been seen in public since his May 16 summit meeting with Soviet leader Mikhail S. Gorbachev.

In another development, a broadcast on June 7 on official Beijing radio, hinted that Qiao Shi, a relatively unknown member of the powerful Standing Committee of the Communist Party politburo, had emerged as a possible successor to party chief Zhao, who was generally believed to have been stripped of all power.

Some of the speculation surrounding the Chinese leadership was quelled on June 8, when Premier Li reappeared on national television.

Li was shown praising a group of army soldiers in the Great Hall of the People, apparently for their efforts in support of the crackdown.

"Comrades, thanks for your hard work," Li said. "We hope you will continue with our fine efforts to safeguard security in the capital."

The premier did not display any outward sign that he had been wounded in an alleged assassination attempt.

Other announcements broadcast the same day by the government reinforced the feeling among Western analysts that the hard-liners were gaining secure control of the government.

The Communist Party's Disciplinary Inspection Commission, headed by Qiao, declared that the prodemocracy protesters were "a counterrevolutionary threat" and called upon all Chinese to turn in those people suspected of antigovernment activity.

INTERNATIONAL REACTION

The bloody military crackdown, which came two weeks after the government had imposed martial law in Beijing, provoked a wave of antigovernment sentiment in the capital and numerous other Chinese cities, and was harshly condemned by nations around the world.

Although casualty figures were difficult to verify, the Western press estimated that at least several hundred and possibly as many as 5,000 people were killed in the nighttime assault and its aftermath, and that as many as 10,000 others were injured. The casualties included both protesters and soldiers, as well as civilian bystanders caught up in the disorder.

Official Chinese accounts of the incident, presented variously by military and government spokesmen, were contradictory. The official statements listed death tolls ranging from zero to 300, with most of the casualties reported to be soldiers.

U.S. President Bush announced on June 5, a package of sanctions against the Chinese government in response to the crackdown in Beijing. But in his message that day and in other statements, the president stressed that he did not want to break off the relationship with China that the U.S. had cultivated since 1972.

Bush, who had served as the head of the U.S. Liaison Mission in China from 1974 to 1975, stated at a White House news conference on June 5 that he "deplored" the use of force against the prodemocracy protesters and urged the Chinese government to resume the restraint previously shown in its dealings with the demonstrators.

The president emphasized, however, that the situation in China required a "reasoned, careful action" and not "an emotional response," because of the uncertainty surrounding China's political leadership.

The primary sanctions announced by Bush were the suspension of sales of military equipment to China and of all government-to-government trade. He also suspended visits between U.S. and Chinese military leaders, offered medical assistance to the injured through the Red Cross and said that requests by Chinese students in the U.S. to extend their visits would be treated sympathetically.

The State Department June 6 encouraged Americans in Beijing to leave China. On the following day, June 7, the U.S. and other countries ordered the evacuation of the dependents of foreign service personnel after Chinese army troops raked the Jianguomenwai diplomatic complex in eastern Beijing with machine gun fire.

A number of foreign governments provided chartered air flights to aid the departure of their nationals. Many Americans returning to the U.S. were critical of the lack of coordinated efforts by the U.S. embassy in Beijing to help American citizens get out of the country.

In a prime time television press conference on June 8, Bush largely restated the themes from his message announcing the sanctions, but said that the U.S. could not have normal relations with China until the government in Beijing agreed to "recognize the validity" of the pro-democracy movement.

Bush disclosed at the news conference that he had tried to call the Chinese leaders on the telephone earlier that day, but "the line was busy."

The president had come under pressure from numerous members of Congress, including Senator Jesse Helms (R, N.C.) and Representative Stephen J. Solarz (D, N.Y.), to adopt a tough stance toward the Chinese government.

On June 8, Chinese Foreign Minister Qian Qichen criticized the U.S. sanctions and assailed American embassy officials in Beijing for providing refuge for a leading Chinese dissident, Fang Lizhi.

The Japanese government, after several days of low-key response, said on June 7 that the shooting of unarmed civilians by Chinese troops "could not be tolerated."

Japan, which was China's largest provider of foreign aid, had initially called the violence "regrettable."

Tokyo's reluctance over the years to criticize the Chinese government was said to stem from Japan's mindfulness of its invasion and occupation of China in the 1930s and 1940s and the atrocities committed there by Japanese troops.

Elsewhere in Asia, 150,000 people—nearly half the population—in the Portuguese colony of Macao staged a protest on June 4 against the Chinese government.

Ten thousand people rallied the same day in Taiwan's capital, Taipei. Prior to the shootings, students had formed a human chain across Taiwan in support of the Chinese demonstrators.

Thailand's foreign minister, Siddhi Savetsila, voiced concern June 6 that the upheaval in China could delay a settlement of the war in Cambodia.

On June 5, Australian Prime Minister Bob Hawke canceled a planned trip to China that had been scheduled for later in the year.

The European democracies joined in the condemnation of the violence in Beijing.

On June 6, Great Britain followed the U.S. lead and announced a ban, largely symbolic, on arms sales to China. Britain's position was complicated by its agreement to turn Hong Kong over to Chinese sovereignty in the year 1997.

On June 6, France announced a "freeze" in diplomatic relations with China.

The unrest in China reverberated most loudly in the British colony of Hong Kong, which is scheduled to revert to Chinese rule in 1997.

Hundreds of thousands of people turned out for demonstrations on June 4–6 against the Beijing crackdown.

A general strike was staged June 7 in the territory, but additional mass marches planned for the same day were canceled after an early morning rally erupted into a riot.

On June 5, the Hong Kong stock market plunged 581.77 points, or 22%, to 2093.61, as traders reacted to the events in China. The latest drop followed a similar fall in late May after martial law was imposed in Beijing.

On June 6, British Prime Minister Margaret Thatcher said that Great Britain would stand by its agreement to cede Hong Kong to China in 1997. She added that she would "see what can be done" in the ensuing eight years to reinforce the legal and constitutional rights of the territory's residents prior to the Chinese takeover.

In the first official Soviet response to China's military crackdown, the U.S.S.R.'s Congress of People's Deputies June 6 released a statement expressing cautious support for the Chinese government.

"The events happening in China are an internal affair of the country," the statement said. "Any attempts at pressure from the outside would be inappropriate."

The statement was criticized by a number of the more radical members of the congress, who asserted that Moscow should have strongly condemned the use of military force against unarmed citizens.

On June 5, among other communist countries, Cuba and Vietnam declared their unqualified support for the Chinese government's actions.

Hungarian leader Karoly Grosz, on the other hand, harshly denounced the Chinese crackdown on June 7 in a statement released by the official Hungarian news agency.

14

DENG RETIRES OFFICIALLY

CRACKDOWN ON PRODEMOCRACY MOVEMENT

The police sprang into action following the tragic night of June 4 when the Chinese government used elements of the People's Liberation Army in a bloody crackdown to drive prodemocracy students out of Tiananmen Square.

On June 9–15, Chinese authorities began arresting hundreds of prodemocracy activists in Beijing and elsewhere less than one week after the army had violently suppressed a student-led protest movement in the capital.

At the same time, the Chinese regime launched a sweeping propaganda campaign aimed at discrediting widespread reports that several thousand protesters had been killed during the army assault.

The nationwide crackdown coincided with the reappearance of China's paramount leader, Deng Xiaoping, who had not been seen in public since his May 16 summit meeting in Beijing with Soviet President Mikhail S. Gorbachev. During his absence, the 84-year-old Deng had repeatedly been rumored to have died.

On June 9, Deng and nine other top officials were shown on state-run television meeting with senior army commanders in the capital.

Outside observers said the broadcast was the clearest indication in a month that hard-liners were in control of the country.

Standing near Deng at the meeting were Premier Li Peng, President Yang Shangkun and Wan Li, the head of the National People's Congress, China's nominal parliament. Other figures at the gathering included Vice-President Wang Zhen, Deputy Premier Yao Yilin, Qiao Shi, the party's security chief, and Bo Yibo, the deputy chairman of the Central Advisory Commission. A pair of retired party veterans—former President Li Xiannian and Peng Zhen, the former head of the People's Congress—were also in attendance.

Conspicuously absent was Zhao Ziyang, the general secretary of the Communist Party, who was widely believed to have been stripped of his power.

Deng praised the army commanders at the meeting for their recent suppression of the protests in the capital, and he harshly denounced the pro-democracy activists and their supporters.

"A very small number of people started to cause chaos which later developed into a counterrevolutionary rebellion," Deng said. "Their aim was to overthrow the Communist Party and the socialist system."

He declared that the protests would not affect the course of the nation. "Our basic direction, our basic strategy and policy will not change," Deng said.

The paramount leader also called for a moment of silence to mourn the "heroes" who died in the military action, an apparent reference to soldiers and policemen killed during the disorder.

The government June 9 announced that an undisclosed number of "thugs" and "hooligans" had been arrested for suspected involvement in the prodemocracy demonstrations.

Chinese television news programs during the day repeatedly showed pictures of unidentified young men being brought in to police stations for questioning.

It was the first report of large-scale arrests since the protest movement had begun in mid-April. (On May 30, the government had said that 14 people had been detained in connection with the unrest.)

State-run news broadcasts said on June 10 that more than 400 people had been arrested in Beijing on various charges related to the protests, including beating soldiers, stealing ammunition from the military, burning army trucks and spreading rumors.

Among those detained was Guo Haifeng, one of the leaders of an independent student group that had helped organize the protests.

Additional arrests were reported the same day in the provincial cities of Chengdu, Xian, Shenyang, Nanjing and Changsha.

In a development that caused concern among foreign journalists covering the unrest in Beijing, the official Chinese media reported, on June 11, the arrest of a man who had been shown on ABC News June 5, harshly denouncing the military crackdown in the capital.

The unidentified man had told ABC News that army tanks had crushed protesters to death during the crackdown and that 20,000 people had been killed in the unrest. After his capture, he was shown on state television retracting his story.

On June 12, Chinese authorities ordered the abolition of all independent student and worker organizations, and announced that police had been authorized to shoot rioters on sight.

A "wanted" list of 21 student leaders was broadcast on June 13 on the official evening news program. The students were accused of organizing a "counterrevolutionary rebellion," a crime punishable in China by death.

Two of the student leaders, Zhou Fengsuo and Xiong Yan, were arrested on June 14, Chinese television reports said. A third leader, Xiong Wei, surrendered on June 15 to authorities.

According to Western estimates, a total of at least 1,000 people around the country had been arrested as of June 15 in connection with the disorders.

Three young workers in Shanghai were sentenced to death on June 15, for helping set fire to a train during a protest the previous week.

The sentences marked the first imposition of capital punishment against protesters seized during the recent unrest.

The three condemned men—Xu Guoming, Bian Hanwu and Yan Xuerong—had been charged with destroying public property in connection with an incident June 6 in which students and workers had set fire to a train that had run over a group of protesters lying on the railroad tracks, killing six of them.

No one had perished in the train fire, but several firefighters reportedly were beaten up and nine railroad cars were destroyed.

Earlier, a crowd of between 40,000 and 100,000 people had marched on June 9 in Shanghai to protest the military crackdown in Beijing.

By June 21, the total number of people arrested and detained numbered at least 1,500. The three workers in Shanghai who had been convicted of setting fire to a train were executed on June 21. The executions were carried out immediately after an appeals court declined to overturn the death sentences imposed on the workers.

Although details of the executions were not reported by the government, it was believed that the three men—Xu Guoming, Bian Hanwu and Yan Xuerong—were killed in the usual Chinese way, with a single bullet to the back of the head. (The death penalty was common in China, with hundreds of convicted criminals said to be executed each year.)

On June 21, Western governments, many of which had urged

clemency for the three, reacted to the executions with new expressions of outrage against China.

Coinciding with the executions, six other people in Shanghai were convicted on June 21, of participating in the same protest as the three workers. They reportedly were to be sentenced within a week.

In the city of Jinan, capital of Shandong province, 45 people were convicted the same day of "endangering public order," the official Beijing radio station reported.

Seventeen of the 45 were sentenced to death and another nine received death sentences commuted to two years' hard labor. The remaining 19 were given prison sentences of varying lengths.

Earlier, eight workers in Beijing had been sentenced to death on June 17, for participating in "riots" in which six buses and military vehicles were burned and a number of soldiers injured.

To date, the only people to be sentenced in the crackdown were workers; none of the student activists arrested had been publicly tried.

British Prime Minister Margaret Thatcher said she was "utterly appalled" by the death sentences. French Foreign Minister Roland Dumas declared, "What is happening in China is atrocious." The West German government said it was shocked by the "tragic hardening" of China's policies toward the protesters.

The reaction in the U.S. from the Bush administration was more subdued. Secretary of State James A. Baker III said, "We deeply regret the fact that these executions have gone forward." President Bush, who one day earlier had imposed new sanctions against China, declined to comment on the matter.

U.S. congressional leaders, however, were outspoken in their condemnation of the escalating crackdown. Senate Majority Leader George J. Mitchell (D, Maine) called the executions "barbarous" and urged the president to take "further steps" against the Chinese regime.

POLITICS OF REPRESSION

The mass arrest of dissidents was accompanied by a concerted effort by the government's propaganda organs to portray the Beijing crackdown as a heroic action by the army to save the country from turmoil.

Chinese television broadcasts during the week focused on the casualties incurred by the military and police in the suppression of the protests. Reports that hundreds of unarmed civilians had been massacred by army troops—reports that were well documented by

Western journalists and Chinese witnesses—were dismissed by the state-run media as nothing more than "rumors" spread by foreigners.

The Chinese broadcasts featured visits by government leaders to local hospitals where injured army troops were recovering, and interviews with angry citizens blaming the prodemocracy protesters for the disorder.

People purporting to be witnesses to the military action were repeatedly shown praising the army troops for their restraint.

The propaganda department of the Beijing branch of the Communist Party on June 14 released the government's first detailed version of the crackdown.

The report said that protesters in the capital, supported by "overseas reactionary political forces," staged an unprovoked attack on June 3–4 on military convoys moving through Beijing, killing nearly 100 soldiers and policemen and wounding thousands of others. Some 180 army vehicles were destroyed in the attack, the official account said.

The account claimed that the troops at first held their fire but were then compelled to shoot at the protesters in the face of extraordinary provocations. About 100 civilians were killed and 1,000 wounded in the turmoil, the report said.

China and the U.S. meanwhile became involved in a diplomatic confrontation over the fate of a prominent dissident being sheltered in the American embassy in Beijing. The dispute erupted on June 9, after the Chinese government accused the dissident, Fang Lizhi, of being a traitor who had incited the recent unrest in the capital.

Fang and his wife, Li Shuxian, had been in hiding in the American embassy since June 5. U.S. officials had refused to turn the couple over to Chinese authorities.

U.S. Secretary of State James A. Baker III met on June 10 in Washington, D.C. with China's ambassador to the U.S., Han Xu, in an attempt to settle the stand-off. Talks between the two officials ended, however, with the issue unresolved.

The Chinese government raised the stakes in the matter on June 11, when it issued a warrant for the arrest of Fang and Li. According to the Xinhua news agency the couple was accused of "committing crimes of counterrevolutionary propaganda and instigation" during the unrest.

Although Fang had avoided active participation in the student-led pro-democracy movement—reportedly for fear that the government would use his participation as a pretext to crush the protests—he was depicted in the Chinese media as the main instigator of the recent disorders.

Following the announcement of the arrest warrant, on June 12 Baker again met with Han in an effort to find an acceptable solution to the dispute.

On June 13, U.S. officials said they had proposed that Fang be allowed to leave the American embassy in China to go to a third country, but the offer had yet to be formally accepted or rejected by the Chinese government.

The long arm of oppression did not spare foreign correspondents. On June 10, Beijing expelled Peter Newport, a journalist for the Independent Television News in Great Britain, after he videotaped a student demonstration in Shanghai.

Newport was the first foreign correspondent to be forced to leave the country for covering the unrest.

Several days later, on June 14, two American reporters stationed in Beijing were also ordered expelled.

The Chinese government accused the two—Alan W. Pessin of the Voice of America and John E. Pomfret of the Associated Press—of violating martial law restrictions on press coverage of the disorder.

Then, on June 16, two British television correspondents who had been operating in Chengdu were expelled.

The two journalists, Vernon Mann and John Elphinstone of the Independent Television News, were accused of violating the terms of their tourist visas.

On June 19, an American free-lance reporter, Joseph F. Kahn, was ordered out of the country for conducting illegal interviews.

The crackdown of prodemocracy activists produced wide-spread international repercussions including defection by Chinese diplomats stationed abroad.

Two diplomats stationed at the Chinese consulate in San Francisco announced on June 11 that they were seeking political asylum in the U.S.

The two, identified as Zhang Liman, an acting consul for overseas affairs, and Zhou Liming, a vice consul for cultural affairs, made the announcement at a rally staged in front of San Francisco's city hall to protest the recent crackdown in Beijing.

The pair said they had decided to defect after the Chinese government began a propaganda campaign to deny that a large-scale massacre of civilians had ever taken place.

As many as 13 Chinese diplomats stationed in the U.S., Canada, Great Britain, Australia and Japan had sought political asylum in their host countries in the wake of the recent crackdown in Beijing, it was reported on June 17.

On June 20, the Bush administration announced that it was suspending all high-level contacts between U.S. and Chinese government officials to protest China's recent crackdown against prodemocracy activists.

In addition, the administration said it would urge international financial institutions "to postpone consideration" of Chinese loan applications.

The sanctions were the first imposed by the U.S. since the June 5 announcement of the suspension of arms sales to China.

A State Department spokesman said China currently had requests pending for $957.4 million in loans from the World Bank, and $336.4 million from the Asian Development Bank.

The World Bank had already postponed consideration of $450 million in loans pending a review of the situation in China.

In a related development, on June 20, Japan announced that it would review plans to implement a five-year, $5.59 billion economic aid program for China scheduled to begin in April 1990.

Amid the domestic and international protests against China's latest crackdown of prodemocracy forces, China's paramount leader stood by his decision seemingly unruffled. In a key speech published in the West on June 16, Deng reportedly said that the Communist Party leadership had been forced to crush the pro-democracy movement to prevent its own downfall.

Deng made the speech on June 9 before a group of senior army commanders in Beijing. A text of the address was published by the *China Daily News*, a Chinese-language newspaper in New York City.

Referring to the student-led protesters, Deng was reported to have said: "If we had not suppressed them, they would have brought about our collapse."

He told the assembled military leaders, "I myself, and all of you commanding officers present, would have been shoved under the guillotine."

"Whoever wins the battle for state power gets to occupy the throne," Deng was quoted as saying. "That is the way it was in the past, and that is the way it still is, in China as well as abroad."

Western sources said it was impossible to determine if the text was authentic.

ZHAO ZIYANG REPLACED

The suppression of the pro-democracy movement signified repudiation of Zhao Ziyang's liberal line. When this occurred, it was a foregone conclusion that he would be ousted from the position of general secretary of the Communist Party.

On June 16, China's chief government spokesman strongly hinted that Communist Party General Secretary Zhao Ziyang, who had not been seen in public for nearly a month, had been stripped of his power and would soon be replaced.

The spokesman, Yuan Mu, made the assertion in an interview with NBC News.

When asked whether Zhao had been officially ousted from the party's top leadership position, Yuan said, "It is true that certain individuals in the top Chinese leadership are guilty of supporting the counterrevolutionaries, of supporting turmoil . . . Their questions will be dealt with soon and will be made public."

Also during the interview, Yuan denied Western news reports that hundreds, perhaps thousands, of unarmed demonstrators had been killed by army troops in the military assault on the capital.

"Modern technology can . . . distort the truth of the matter," the spokesman declared.

He repeated the Chinese government's version of events, saying that only 300 people, most of them soldiers, had died in the unrest.

The widely anticipated event took place on June 24, at the end of a two-day secret meeting of the Communist Party's Central Committee.

Zhao, who had been an outspoken proponent of economic and political liberalization, was replaced by Jiang Zemin, the party chief of Shanghai. Jiang, 62, had reportedly gained favor among China's top leaders for his tough crackdown on pro-democracy protests that spread to Shanghai from Beijing.

In a communique released by the Central Committee at the close of its two-day session, Zhao was blamed for fostering a "counterrevolutionary rebellion," the term used by the party to describe the recent unrest.

"At the critical juncture involving the destiny of the party and the state, Comrade Zhao Ziyang made the mistake of supporting the turmoil and the splitting of the party, and he had unshirkable responsibilities for the development of the turmoil," the statement said.

Zhao, 69, became the party's second general secretary to be deposed in less than two and a half years.

He was stripped of all his party leadership posts, including his place on the 17-member politburo, on the 175-member Central Committee and on the powerful Central Military Commission, but apparently was permitted to retain his party membership.

The communique noted that Zhao had done "something beneficial for the reform, the opening of China to the outside world and the economic work" while he was general secretary, but said he had "obviously erred" by not adhering to party guidelines.

"The nature and consequences of his mistake are very serious," the statement said, adding that party leaders planned "to look further into his case."

Zhao had not been seen in public since May 19, when he had visited student demonstrators in Beijing's Tiananmen Square on the eve of the declaration of martial law in the capital, and no word was available on his whereabouts.

The communique also included a passage apparently aimed at reassuring outsiders that China's economic and foreign policies would remain unchanged in the wake of the unrest.

"The policy of reform and opening to the outside world, as the road to lead the country to strength and prosperity, must be implemented as usual in a steadfast manner," the statement said. "The country must not return to the old, closed-door path."

In addition to Zhao, the party dismissed Hu Qili, its propaganda chief, from the politburo's five-member Standing Committee. Like Zhao, Hu had been accused of supporting many of the demands of the student protesters. Hu apparently retained his posts on the full politburo and the Central Committee.

Replacing Zhao and Hu on the Standing Committee were Jiang and two other officials: Li Ruihuan, the mayor of Tianjin, and Song Ping, a conservative economic planner and party veteran.

The changes increased the membership on the Standing Committee, the party's top policy-making body, to six from five. The other members were Premier Li and Vice-Premiers Yao Yilin and Qiao Shi. All three were considered hard-line conservatives.

Also removed from leadership positions were two members of the Central Committee's secretariat who reportedly had sympathized with the pro-democracy movement. The two, Rui Xingwen and Yan Mingfu, were replaced by Li Ruihuan and Ding Guangen.

Jiang Zemin, the new party chief, was considered a relative unknown by Western analysts.

Born in 1926 in central Jiangsu province, he joined the Communist Party in 1946 and worked at an automobile factory in Moscow in the mid-1950s.

In 1982, Jiang became head of the electronics industry ministry and was elected to the Central Committee. He was appointed mayor of Shanghai in 1985 and joined the politburo in 1987. In April 1988, he was elevated to the post of party leader of Shanghai, China's most populous city.

PURGES AND PERSECUTIONS

On June 25, on the heels of the leadership shuffle, the Communist Party publicly called for the purge of officials at all levels who had supported the student-led pro-democracy movement.

"Those party members who deviated from the correct political stand and violated party discipline during the turmoil and the counterrevolutionary rebellion should be strictly punished," a party announcement said.

The announcement, broadcast on national television, was based on orders adopted by the party's Discipline Inspection Commission.

Thousands of government workers and low-level party officials had marched in support of the students during the unrest in Beijing, many of them parading behind banners that had openly displayed their work units or party departments.

In addition to the removal of unfaithful party members, the Discipline Commission's order called for the overhaul of party organizations "that had resisted the decisions made by the party's Central Committee or were controlled or manipulated by bad people" during the protests.

The politburo of the Chinese Communist Party, at the end of a closed meeting in Beijing on July 27–28, announced a seven-point package of reforms aimed at combating corruption among government officials and senior party members.

Among the most significant of the reforms was a measure that would bar the children and spouses of senior officials from "engaging in commercial activities" as of Sept. 1.

A related measure would abolish Kanghua Development Corp., which had been closely associated with Deng Pufang, the eldest son of China's paramount leader, Deng Xiaoping.

Other reforms included eliminating the "special supply" of gourmet foods available to top officials. Party leaders henceforth would receive "the same ration and pay the same price [for food] as ordinary citizens." The import of luxury sedans would be halted, and officials would be required to use Chinese cars in place of the currently favored Mercedes-Benz limousines. In addition, officials would be prohibited from using public funds for entertainment purposes, and new limitations would be placed on foreign junkets by members of the leadership.

Meanwhile, the government continued its crackdown on prodemocracy activists.

Two men convicted of arson during antigovernment demonstrations in June in Chengdu, the capital of Sichuan province, were put to death on July 8.

Chinese authorities, on July 13, sentenced Xiao Bin, a 42-year-old worker, to 10 years in prison for "rumor-mongering." Xiao had been arrested after denouncing the army crackdown in Beijing during an interview shown on U.S. television by ABC News.

Yang Wei, a prominent Chinese dissident, was arrested July 18 in Shanghai for conducting "demagogical propaganda for counterrevolutionary ends," the Xinhau news agency reported. Yang had been released from prison in January after serving a two-year sentence for participating in student-led demonstrations in late 1986 and early 1987.

A Chinese court in Beijing, on July 26, sentenced two men to die for crimes committed during the antigovernment unrest in May and June. The two were accused of disguising themselves as security guards and beating and robbing peasants during the disorder. Two other men also received death sentences the same day for an unrelated murder conviction.

Two men convicted of stealing weapons and ammunition from the military and killing a pregnant woman during the prodemocracy unrest were put to death July 30 in the central city of Wuhan. The executions raised to 31 the official number of people put to death since the start of the crackdown.

A Beijing schoolteacher was sentenced on August 11 to life in prison and two accomplices were given lesser jail terms for throwing paint at a huge portrait of Mao Zedong in Beijing's Tiananmen Square on May 23. The three, who had been turned over to the police by student demonstrators immediately after defacing the portrait, were found guilty of "counterrevolutionary destruction and counterrevolutionary incitement."

A 25-year-old student was sentenced on August 26 to nine years in prison for taking part in a Voice of America radio interview on June 6. The student, Zhang Weiping, was convicted of "counterrevolutionary incitement" and spreading "counterrevolutionary propaganda" for telling the VOA of unrest in the eastern city of Hangzhou. Zhang became the first student publicly sentenced in connection with the recent unrest.

INTERNATIONAL REPERCUSSIONS

The international community reacted to Beijing's crackdown on its opposition ranging from verbal condemnation to a mild form of sanction.

On June 27, the European Community announced a series of

sanctions against China to protest the "brutal repression" of prodemocracy activists.

The measures, the harshest yet imposed by the 12 Western European nations, were adopted during a two-day meeting in Madrid. They were similar to sanctions already announced by the U.S.

Under the EC sanctions, arms sales and military cooperation projects with China would be suspended and high-level contacts between Chinese and Western European officials would be prohibited.

The EC also called on the Chinese government "to halt executions and put a stop to repressive actions against those who legitimately demand their democratic rights."

On June 26, the World Bank announced that it was indefinitely suspending consideration of $780.2 million in loans to China that had been pending before the bank's board of directors.

On July 14, the U.S. Senate voted to impose new sanctions on China for its crackdown on prodemocracy activists.

The latest restrictions, which were similar to measures adopted on June 29 by the House of Representatives, suspended a federally funded private investment program in China, and banned the sale to China of police equipment and civilian nuclear materials.

The sanction legislation, approved by a vote of 81 to 10, was attached to the State Department's annual authorization bill.

In a related development, Amnesty International, the London-based human rights organization, on August 30 released a report accusing China of ordering the secret executions of dissidents seized during the unrest in June.

The report cited a directive, known as Document No. 3, that Amnesty said had been issued in early June by the Central Committee of the Chinese Communist Party. The directive had called on authorities to execute those "counterrevolutionaries" who engaged in "the most serious crimes," the rights group said. According to Amnesty, the Central Committee had also declared that "the number of executed and imprisoned people is not to be published," but that certain death sentences would be disclosed "in order to make examples."

Amnesty estimated that at least 1,000 people, most of them civilians, were killed in Beijing and another 300 died in the southern city of Chengdu when Chinese military troops moved in force on June 3–9 against the prodemocracy demonstrators.

"Some were shot in the back among crowds of people running away from troops firing at them," the Amnesty report said. "Some were crushed to death by military vehicles. Those killed included children and old people."

On August 31, a United Nations panel passed a resolution criticizing the Chinese government for its June crackdown on a student-led prodemocracy movement in Beijing and other major cities.

The measure was approved by a vote of 15 to 9 by the U.N. Subcommission on Prevention of Discrimination and Protection of Minorities. The subcommission was an arm of the U.N. Human Rights Commission.

The resolution said the panel was "concerned about the events which took place recently in China and about their consequences in the field of human rights."

Passage of the resolution marked the first time that China had been formally cited by the U.N. for its suppression of the democracy movement and the first time a permanent member of the U.N.'s Security Council had ever been censured by another U.N. group for human rights abuses.

Other provisions of the resolution included a call for clemency for those "deprived of their liberty" in the disorder and a request that U.N. Secretary-General Javier Perez de Cuellar provide the full rights commission with further information provided by China and "other reliable sources" on the crackdown.

CHINA DEFIANT

Outwardly, at least, the Chinese government affected indifference to the rising chorus of criticism abroad of its domestic policy since the Tiananmen incident. Rather than accommodate the popular demand for liberal reform, the new leadership in Beijing moved to choke off the demand at its source. The measures taken in this regard included the following:

- On July 14 the government imposed a ban on the sale of all foreign newspapers and magazines in China. The publication of books deemed to incite opposition to the government was also prohibited.
- On July 21, China's State Education Commission announced that it was reducing the size of the country's incoming college freshman class to 610,000 from 640,000 in September. The incoming class at Beijing University, the nation's largest college and a hotbed of unrest during the prodemocracy movement, was cut to 800 from a planned 1,900.
- On August 12, the Chinese government announced that college graduates would be required to work in rural villages or factories for one to two years before they would be allowed to continue their studies at the post-graduate level.

- On August 14, Chinese sources disclosed that the incoming freshman class at Beijing University would be required to complete one year of military training before beginning regular academic studies.

  The move came less than a month after Chinese authorities had announced that the size of the university's freshman class was to be reduced to 800 from nearly 2,000.

  Outside observers said the two official actions appeared aimed at discouraging political activism at the school, which had been at the center of the prodemocracy movement that arose in China during the spring.

- On September 2, Chinese education officials said they planned to limit the number of graduate students who would be permitted to study in the West.

The limits apparently were aimed at diminishing the extent of Western influence in the country, foreign analysts said. Chinese leaders had asserted that an overexposure on the part of students to Western ideas had been one of the major factors behind the recent turmoil.

In announcing the new policy, Vice-Minister of Education He Dongchang declared, "Opening to the outside world does not necessarily mean seeking knowledge from only a few Western countries."

Some 40,000 Chinese students had studied abroad in 1988, including about 27,000 in the U.S.

Earlier, the *Washington Post* had reported in a story datelined September 1 that China had imposed a ban on government subsidies to students studying in the U.S.

Along with these steps, on September 4, the Chinese government announced that Culture Minister Wang Meng and several other leading officials had been dismissed. Western news reports the same day quoted unidentified Chinese sources as saying that Liang Xiang, the governor of Hainan province and an ally of ousted party leader Zhao Ziyang, had also been removed from power.

The official government announcement of Wang's dismissal came at the end of a meeting in Beijing of the Standing Committee of the National People's Congress, China's nominal parliament.

No reason was given for the move, but foreign observers said they believed it signaled an attempt by the government to clamp down on artistic freedom in the wake of the recent disorder in the capital.

The appointment of Wang, a popular novelist, to the post in 1986, had been hailed by Chinese officials at the time as a sign of the government's newly liberalized policy on the arts.

Wang was replaced with He Jinzhi, a poet who had previously held a top position in the Communist Party's propaganda department.

On October 1, China celebrated the 40th anniversary of Communist Party rule with a day of parades and fireworks in Beijing's Tiananmen Square.

The festivities, staged amid extremely tight security, were reported to be more subdued than the last big celebration, in 1984, which had marked the party's 35th anniversary in power.

Only invited guests and performers were permitted anywhere near the capital's 100-acre (40-hectare) central square. The general public was barred from attending the celebration, apparently out of fear that dissidents might disrupt the event to protest the Chinese army's bloody suppression in June of a prodemocracy protest movement that had been based in the square.

Deng Xiaoping, and other senior officials, watched the celebration from a viewing stand on a balcony above the square. The balcony, known as Tiananmen Rostrum, was the site on which Mao Zedong had proclaimed the founding of the People's Republic of China on October 1, 1949.

Referring to the student-led protests earlier in the year, Deng told a North Korean official seated with him on the viewing stand, "What happened in Beijing not long ago was bad. But in the final analysis it is beneficial to us, because it made us more sober-minded." The comment was widely reported in the Chinese media.

Nearly all Western diplomats in China boycotted the anniversary ceremonies because they were held in Tiananmen Square, and even East-bloc countries sent relatively low-level envoys as representatives.

The top Soviet official in attendance was the deputy chairman of the Soviet-Chinese Friendship Society. Among the smattering of other foreign dignitaries were members of the politburos of North Korea, East Germany and Czechoslovakia, an official of Cuba's Communist Party, a member of Pakistan's National Assembly, Cambodian opposition leader Prince Norodom Sihanouk and cabinet ministers from Ecuador and Mongolia.

The only American on the reviewing stand was former Secretary of State Alexander M. Haig Jr., who was in China on an unofficial visit.

In the square itself, tens of thousands of young people specially chosen for the occasion danced in celebration of the party's anniversary beneath a 65-foot (20-m) banner that said, "Warmly hail the victory of suppressing the turmoil and the counterrevolutionary rebellion."

A new statue, depicting a soldier, a worker, a peasant and an intellectual, was unveiled on the site where student demonstrators had erected the defiant "Goddess of Democracy" statue at the height of the protests.

At night, a three-hour fireworks extravaganza was staged in the square.

The October 1 celebration was preceded by a news conference of newly installed Communist Party leader, Jiang Zemin, on September 26—his first since coming to power—which was staged in Beijing's Great Hall of the People.

The party leader used the briefing, which was broadcast live on national television, to deny that the army's suppression of the student-led democracy movement on June 3–4 had been a "tragedy."

Accompanying Jiang at the news conference were the other five members of the politburo's Standing Committee, which was the top policy-making body of the Communist Party. The five were: Premier Li Peng; Qiao Shi, the party's security chief; Vice-Premier Yao Yilin; Song Ping, who was head of the party's organization department; and Tianjin Mayor Li Ruihuan.

In response to an Italian reporter who asked whether "the Tiananmen tragedy" could have been avoided, Jiang said, "We do not believe that there was any tragedy in Tiananmen Square. What actually happened was a counterrevolutionary rebellion aimed at opposing the leadership of the Communist Party and overthrowing the socialist system."

Jiang was asked of the fate of Zhao Ziyang, his ousted predecessor, but he would only say that Zhao remained under investigation and was leading "quite a comfortable life."

The party chief also brushed aside a question from a French journalist inquiring about an unidentified female student who, the journalist said, had been arrested during the unrest in June and sent to a prison farm, where she allegedly had been raped three times in one week by local peasants. Jiang cast doubt on the report, saying, "I have heard stories that are like fairy tales from the Arabian Nights and that is regrettable."

On September 29, Jiang delivered a nationally televised speech recounting party policy in the aftermath of the turmoil earlier in the year.

The speech reportedly reflected the views not only of Jiang but of the rest of the senior party leadership as well.

In a sign that the party planned to continue its crackdown on dissent, Jiang declared, "Hostile forces, international as well as internal, are still engaged in activities of sabotage and subversion against us." He said that the authorities would "isolate and attack the handful of hostile elements" that had instigated the recent unrest.

Discussing the economy, the party chief reaffirmed that China planned to pursue a policy of economic retrenchment for at least the next three years. The move away from liberalization of the economy had begun a year earlier.

Jiang said that, within China, "two completely different views exist on the issue of reform and opening." The correct view, he said, favored steady modernization within the guidelines of socialism. The other view advocated "total Westernization" and would bring China "into the orbit of the capitalist system of the West," Jiang said.

Outside observers noted that the address was filled with Marxist-Leninist phrases that had been largely out of fashion in China during the last decade. For example, Jiang asserted that China was involved in "a serious class struggle" and warned against those who would support "bourgeois liberalization."

DENG RESIGNS LAST OFFICIAL POSITION

Deng Xiaoping was less sure of the wisdom of the harsh measures taken against prodemocracy activists at Tiananmen Square than his public pronouncements suggested. A Chinese-American physicist who had met him on September 16 told U.S. President Bush that the Chinese leader had acknowledged that "mistakes" were made by the government during the suppression of a prodemocracy movement in June.

The physicist, T. D. Lee, quoted Deng as having said, "We really have made mistakes. We must not shirk our responsibility, and we cannot blame the demonstrators."

On October 31, Deng met with former U.S. President Richard M. Nixon, who was visiting China on October 28–November 2. In a sign of the continued tension between the U.S. and China, Deng blamed Washington for fomenting the recent unrest.

"Frankly speaking, the United States was involved too deeply in the turmoil and counterrevolutionary rebellion that occurred in Beijing not long ago," Deng said. He added that he hoped for a warming of relations between the two countries in the near future, but he said that "it is up to the U.S. to take the initiative."

Nixon asserted after his meeting with the Chinese leader that the current impasse was "the most serious situation" in Sino-American relations since 1972.

The former U.S. president issued his harshest critique of the June crackdown in remarks on November 1 at a banquet hosted by Chinese President Yang Shangkun.

"The fact is that many in the United States, including many friends of China, believe the crackdown was excessive and unjustified," Nixon told the Chinese audience. "The events of April through June damaged the respect and confidence which most Americans previously had for the leaders of China."

Shortly after Nixon's meeting with Deng, the announcement was made in Beijing on November 9, that the paramount leader had stepped down as chairman of the Central Military Commission. The office had been his last formal position in the Communist Party leadership.

Deng's resignation was disclosed on November 9, at the end of a four-day meeting in Beijing of the party's Central Committee.

"After careful consideration, I wish to resign from my present post while I am still healthy," Deng said in his letter of resignation. "This will be conducive to the cause of the party, state and army."

The Military Affairs Commission, which controlled the nation's armed forces, was widely considered the key to power in China. Deng had been only the third leader to hold the chairmanship in 40 years of Communist rule. The other two had been Mao Zedong and Hua Guofeng.

The Central Committee voted to install the party's general secretary, Jiang Zemin, as the new chairman of the commission. China's president, Yang Shangkun, was named first vice-chairman, replacing deposed party chief Zhao Ziyang. Yang's younger brother, Yang Baibing, was chosen to be the commission's secretary general.

Western analysts believed that, despite his lack of any formal position, Deng would continue to wield considerable influence within the party for the near future.

Excerpts from Chinese Leader Deng Xiaoping's June 9 Speech

Following are excerpts from a speech delivered June 9 in Beijing by China's paramount leader, Deng Xiaoping, to senior military commanders, as translated by the Xinhau news agency and published in the West on June 30. The speech was considered the principal document outlining the Communist Party's response to the unrest and bloodshed in Beijing, and party leaders admonished Chinese citizens to study it:

You comrades have been working hard.

First of all, I'd like to express my heartfelt condolences to the comrades in the People's Liberation Army, the armed police and police who died in the struggle—and my sincere sympathy and solicitude to the comrades in the army, the armed police and police who were wounded in the struggle, and I want to extend my sincere regards to all the army, armed police and police personnel who participated in the struggle.

I suggest that all of us stand and pay a silent tribute to the martyrs.

I'd like to take this opportunity to say a few words. This storm was bound to happen sooner or later. As determined by the international and domestic climate, it was bound to happen and was independent of man's will. It was just a matter of time and scale. It has turned out in our favor, for we still have a large group of veterans who have experienced many storms and have a thorough understanding of things. They were on the side of taking resolute action to counter the turmoil. Although some comrades may not understand this now, they will understand eventually and will support the decision of the Central Committee.

The April 26 editorial of the *People's Daily* classified the problem as turmoil. The word was appropriate, but some people objected to the word and tried to amend it. But what has happened shows that this verdict was right. It was also inevitable that the turmoil would develop into a counterrevolutionary rebellion.

We still have a group of senior comrades who are alive, we still have the army, and we also have a group of core cadres who took part in the revolution at various times. That is why it was relatively easy for us to handle the present matter. The main difficulty in handling this matter lay in that we have never experienced such a situation before, in which a small minority of bad people mixed with so many young students and onlookers. We did not have a clear picture of the situation, and this prevented us from taking some actions that we should have taken earlier.

Rebellious Clique and the Dregs of Society

It would have been difficult for us to understand the nature of the matter had we not had the support of so many senior comrades. Some comrades didn't understand this point. They thought it was simply a matter of how to treat the masses. Actually, what we faced was not just some ordinary people who were misguided, but also a rebellious clique and a large quantity of the dregs of society. The key point is that they wanted to overthrow our state and the party. Failing to understand this means failing to understand the nature of the matter. I believe that after serious work we can win the support of the great majority of comrades within the party.

The nature of the matter became clear soon after it erupted. They had two main slogans: to overthrow the Communist Party and topple the socialist system. Their goal was to establish a bourgeois republic entirely dependent on the West. Of course we accept people's demands for combating corruption. We are even ready to listen to some persons with ulterior motives when they raise the slogan about fighting corruption. However, such slogans were just a front. Their real aim was to overthrow the Communist Party and topple the socialist system.

During the course of quelling the rebellion, many comrades of ours were wounded or even sacrificed their lives. Some of their weapons were also taken from them by the rioters. Why? Because bad people mingled with the good, which made it difficult for us to take the firm measures that were necessary.

Army are the Brothers of the People

Handling this matter amounted to a severe political test for our army, and what happened shows that our People's Liberation Army passed muster. If tanks were used to roll over people, this would have created a confusion between right and wrong among the people nationwide. That is why I have to thank the PLA officers and men for using this approach to handle the rebellion.

The PLA losses were great, but this enabled us to win the support of the people and made those who can't tell right from wrong change their viewpoint. They can see what kind of people the PLA are, whether there was bloodshed at Tiananmen [Square], and who were those that shed blood.

Once this question is made clear, we can take the initiative. Although it is very saddening that so many comrades were sacrificed, if the event is analyzed objectively, people cannot but recognize that the PLA are the sons and brothers of the people. This will also help people to understand the measures we used in the course of the struggle. In the future, whenever the PLA faces problems and takes measures, it will gain the support of the people. By the way, I would say that in the future, we must make sure that our weapons are not taken away from us.

In a word, this was a test, and we passed. Even though there are not so many veteran comrades in the army and the soldiers are mostly little more than 18, 19 or 20 years of age, they are still true soldiers of the people. Facing danger, they did not forget the people, the teachings of the party and the interests of the country. They kept a resolute stand in the face of death. They fully deserve the saying that they met death and sacrificed themselves with generosity and without fear. . . .

At the same time, we should never forget how cruel our enemies are. For them we should not have an iota of forgiveness.

Failure of Political Education

The outbreak of the rebellion is worth thinking about. It prompts us to calmly think about the past and consider the future. Perhaps this bad thing will enable us to go ahead with reform and the open-door policy at a more steady, better, even a faster pace. Also it will enable us to more speedily correct our mistakes and better develop our strong points. I cannot elaborate on this today. I just want to raise the subject here.

The first question is: Are the line, goals and policies laid down by the third plenum of the 11th Central Committee, including our "three-step" development strategy, correct? Is it the case that because this riot took place there is some question about the correctness of the line, goals and policies we laid down? Are our goals "leftist"? Should we continue to use them for our struggle in the future? These significant questions should be given clear and definite answers.

We have already accomplished our first goal of doubling the gross national product. We plan to use 12 years to attain our second goal of doubling the GNP. In the 50 years after that, we hope to reach the level of a moderately developed country. A 2% annual growth rate is sufficient. This is our strategic goal. . . .

So, in answering the first question, I should say that our strategic goal cannot be regarded as a failure. It will be an unbeatable achievement for a country with 1.5 billion people like ours to reach the level of a moderately developed nation after 61 years. . . .

The second question is this: Is the general conclusion of the 13th party congress of "one center, two basic points" correct? Are the two basic points—upholding the four cardinal principles and persisting in the open policy and reforms—wrong?

In recent days I have pondered these two points. No, we haven't been wrong. There's nothing wrong with the four cardinal principles. If there is anything amiss, it's that these principles haven't been thoroughly implemented—they haven't been used as the basic concept to educate the people, educate the students and educate all the cadres and party members.

The crux of the current incident was basically the confrontation between the four cardinal principles and bourgeois liberalization. It isn't that we have not talked about such things as the four cardinal principles, worked on political concepts, and opposed bourgeois liberalization and spiritual pollution. What we haven't done is maintain continuity in these talks—there has been no action and sometimes even hardly any talk.

The fault does not lie in the four cardinal principles themselves, but in wavering in upholding these principles, and in the very poor work done to persist in political work and education. . . .

I once told foreigners that our worst omission of the past 10 years was in education. What I meant was political education, and this doesn't apply to schools and students alone, but to the masses as a whole. . . .

Is there anything wrong to the basic concept of reforms and openness? No. Without reforms and openness how could we have what we have today? There has been a fairly satisfactory rise in the standard of living, and it may be said that we have moved one stage further. The positive results of 10 years of reforms must be properly assessed even though there have emerged such problems as inflation. Naturally, in reform and adopting the open policy, we run the risk of importing evil influences from the West, and we have never underestimated such influences. . . .

Persist in Our Basic Policy

Looking back, it appears that there were obvious inadequacies— there hasn't been proper coordination. Being reminded of these inadequacies will help us formulate future policies. Further, we must persist in the coordination between a planned economy and a market economy. There cannot be any change.

In the course of implementing this policy we can place more emphasis on planning in the adjustment period. At other times there can be a little more market adjustment so as to allow more flexibility. The future policy should still be a marriage between the planned and market economies.

What is important is that we should never change China back into a closed country. Such a policy would be most detrimental. . . . We should never go back to the old days of trampling the economy to death. . . .

In brief, this is what we have achieved in the past decade: Generally, our basic proposals, ranging from a developing strategy to policies, including reforms and openness, are correct. If there is any inadequacy, then I should say our reforms and openness have not proceeded adequately enough. The problems we face in implementing reforms are far greater than those we encounter in opening our country. In political reforms we can affirm one point: We have to insist on implementing the system of the National People's Congress and not the American system of the separation of three powers. The U.S. berates us for suppressing students. But when they handled domestic student unrest and turmoil, didn't they send out police and troops, arrest people and shed blood? They were suppressing students and the people, but we are putting down counterrevolutionary rebellion. What qualifications do they have to criticize us? . . .

What do we do from now on? I would say that we should continue, persist in implementing our planned basic line, direction and policy. Except where there is a need to alter a word or phrase here and there, there should be no change in the basic line or basic policy. . . .

We must conscientiously sum up our experiences, persevere in what is right, correct what is wrong, and do a bit more where we lag behind. In short, we should sum up the experiences of the present and look forward to the future.

That's all I have to say on this occasion.

INDEX